CONTRIBUTORS

ROBERT SOMERLOTT's articles have appeared in *American Heritage* and *The Atlantic,* among other publications, and he is the author of ten books. He is a regular contributor to the travel section of the *Mexico City News* and has lived in Mexico for more than 20 years. He is the editorial consultant for this guidebook.

ROBERT CUMMINGS, a resident of Mexico for over five years, has written numerous travel articles as well as a novella, and is currently working on a novel.

LARRY RUSSELL, a resident of Mexico City since 1973, has written many articles on travel and music. His work has been published in such magazines as *Geografía Universal* and *Caminos del Aire.* He has also collaborated with his wife on documentary films in and about Mexico City.

SUSAN WAGNER, the travel editor of *Modern Bride* magazine for ten years, has contributed to *Travel & Leisure* magazine, written a guidebook to Acapulco, and is a member of the Society of American Travel Writers. She attended graduate school in Mexico and returns there frequently.

CELIA WAKEFIELD, the author and photographer of *High Cities of the Andes,* has lived in Mexico for over 15 years. Her articles have been published in *The Christian Science Monitor, Saturday Review,* and *Punch.*

THE PENGUIN TRAVEL GUIDES

AUSTRALIA

CANADA

THE CARIBBEAN

ENGLAND & WALES

FRANCE

GERMANY

GREECE

HAWAII

IRELAND

ITALY

MEXICO

NEW YORK CITY

PORTUGAL

SPAIN

THE
PENGUIN
GUIDE
TO
MEXICO
1990

ALAN TUCKER
General Editor

PENGUIN BOOKS

PENGUIN BOOKS

Published by the Penguin Group
Viking Penguin, a division of Penguin Books USA Inc.,
40 West 23rd Street, New York, New York 10010, U.S.A.
Penguin Books Ltd, 27 Wrights Lane,
London W8 5TZ, England
Penguin Books Australia Ltd, Ringwood,
Victoria, Australia
Penguin Books Canada Ltd, 2801 John Street,
Markham, Ontario, Canada L3R 1B4
Penguin Books (N.Z.) Ltd, 182-190 Wairau Road,
Auckland 10, New Zealand

Penguin Books Ltd, Registered Offices:
Harmondsworth, Middlesex, England

First published in Penguin Books 1990

1   3   5   7   9   10   8   6   4   2

Copyright © Viking Penguin,
a division of Penguin Books USA Inc., 1990
All rights reserved

ISBN 0 14 019.913 6
ISSN 1043-4577

Printed in the United States of America

Set in ITC Garamond Light
Designed by Beth Tondreau Design
Maps by Mark Stein Studios
Illustrations by Bill Russell
Copyedited by Mitchell Nauffts

THIS GUIDEBOOK

The Penguin Travel Guides are designed for people who are experienced travellers in search of exceptional information that will help them sharpen and deepen their enjoyment of the trips they take.

Where, for example, are the interesting, isolated, fun, charming, or romantic places within your budget to stay? The hotels and resorts described by our writers (each of whom is an experienced travel writer who either lives in or regularly tours the city or region of Mexico he or she covers) are some of the special places, in all price ranges except for the lowest—not the run-of-the-mill, heavily marketed places on every travel agent's CRT display and in advertised airline and travel-agency packages. We indicate the approximate price level of each accommodation in our description of it (no indication means it is moderate), and at the end of every chapter we supply contact information so that you can get precise, up-to-the-minute rates and make reservations.

The Penguin Guide to Mexico 1990 highlights the more rewarding parts of the country so that you can quickly and efficiently home in on a good itinerary.

Of course, the guides do far more than just help you choose a hotel and plan your trip. *The Penguin Guide to Mexico 1990* is designed for use *in* Mexico. Our Penguin Mexico writers tell you what you really need to know, as well as what you can't find out so easily on your own. They identify and describe the truly out-of-the-ordinary restaurants, shops and crafts, activities, sights, and villages, and tell you the best way to "do" your destination.

Our writers are highly selective. They bring out the significance of the places they cover, capturing the personality and underlying cultural and historical resonances of a city or region—making clear its special appeal. For exhaustive detailed coverage of cultural attractions, we suggest that you also use a supplementary reference-type guidebook, such as the Michelin Green Guide (in Spanish) or the Insight Guide, along with the Penguin Guide.

The Penguin Guide to Mexico 1990 is full of reliable and timely information, revised each year. We would like to know if you think we've left out some very special place.

Alan Tucker
General Editor
Penguin Travel Guides

40 West 23rd Street
New York, New York 10010
or
27 Wrights Lane
London W8 5TZ

CONTENTS

MAPS

THE
PENGUIN
GUIDE
TO
MEXICO
1990

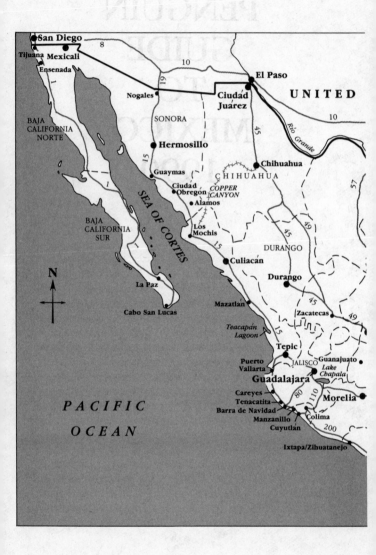

Mexico

| 0 | miles | 250 |
| 0 | kilometers | 400 |

Fort Worth • Dallas

STATES

35

Houston

San Antonio

35

Laredo

Rio Grande

85

Monterrey

57

180

Ciudad Victoria

Tula

San Luis Potosí

QUERETARO

180

Tuxpan

130

15

Mexico City

Tlaxcala

Veracruz

Campeche Bay

Toluca

150

Puebla

Fortín de las Flores

Cuernavaca

GUERRERO

190

OAXACA

180

Villahermosa

95

Oaxaca

ISTMO DE TEHUANTEPEC

San Cristóbal de las Casas

186

CAMPECHE

Acapulco

200

190

CHIAPAS

Tikal

BELIZE

Puerto Escondido

Huatulco
Puerto Angel

200

GUATEMALA

Guatemala City

HONDURAS

GULF OF MEXICO

YUCATAN

Merida

180

Isla Mujeres

Cancún

Isla Cozumel

QUINTANA ROO

OVERVIEW

By Robert Somerlott

Robert Somerlott's articles have appeared in American Heritage *and* The Atlantic, *among other publications, and he is the author of ten books. A regular contributor to the travel section of the* Mexico City News, *he has lived in Mexico for more than 20 years.*

For many visitors the most surprising discovery about Mexico is its foreignness. Travellers from the United States who thought they were just going next door are particularly astonished. Even if they have read books on Mexico, seen films set there, and studied photos of the country, they are seldom prepared for the reality that greets them. Europe, even for first-time visitors, seems familiar by comparison. In fact, you have to go to countries such as India and Thailand to find everyday scenes as exotic as those you'll encounter in Mexico.

The surprise often springs from the vivid colors and odd contrasts that abound in Mexico. You climb into an ordinary taxi in Mexico City, for example, and suddenly notice that the driver has transformed his dashboard into a shrine. The Virgin of Guadalupe, the country's patroness saint, lit by twinkling bulbs, presides over a bed of plastic flowers. When the taxi stops for an ordinary traffic light, an extraordinary quartet of fire eaters leaps into the street to entertain. Or you get on a modern, unusually handsome subway, only to discover as you change lines that the station is built around an Aztec temple complete with sacrificial altar. More remarkable still, it is not a "set" or reconstruction; the temple was once, centuries ago, just that, and the tens of thousands who pass it daily take this incongruity for granted. Or, driving on a new highway in the middle of nowhere, you suddenly overtake a procession of people walking on the shoulder of the road. Their dark, earthy faces are framed by straw hats and handwoven shawls, and they carry banners and religious icons. Oddly, this procession does not seem to end. You drive on, mile after mile, passing a multitude of men and women, many carrying babies. They are joyous, exalted; they sing, chant, and laugh as they trudge through the dust and heat and rain. You have come upon a religious pilgrimage to one of Mexico's several great shrines, where the pilgrims are counted in the hundreds of thousands and walk for days, sleeping at night in the open. You suddenly realize that the deep and powerful impulse that draws millions of Mexicans across fields, through marshes, and over mountains is far older than the religion whose banners they bear. While today the destination may be a church instead of a sacred well, the force that sets this human river in motion is unchanged and, as ever, awe-inspiring.

The sounds in Mexico are often as unfamiliar as the sights. In the middle of the night in an isolated hill town all the bells of all the churches suddenly begin to clang and peal at once. No, it is not a harbinger of revolution, or even an alarm. More than likely, a festival has just started, or a local *fútbol* team has won an important match, or a dignitary has arrived on an official visit. But what does it matter, really? Bells are made for ringing, and Mexico is a land of thousands of bells speaking to each other. In the same town, the shouts of vendors selling strawberries or crab or fresh asparagus mix with the melody of the scissors grinder and the off-key brass of a ragtag band as it marches down a street for no discernible reason.

Mexico, it quickly becomes clear, is not a European country. It is not even really what is today called a "Western country." Instead, it is a unique blending of cultures based on a civilization that built great and beautiful cities when northern Europe was a wilderness peopled by barbarians.

Mexicans, a traveller soon discovers, express themselves publicly, in rites, rituals, rallies, and fairs. Every town and every parish has its own saint to honor, its own anniversaries to commemorate, its own special reasons for flying banners. Octavio Paz once asked the mayor of a poor village how the town's income was spent. "Mostly on fiestas, señor," was the reply. "We are a small village but we have two patron saints."

The richness of life in Mexico is evident in its streets and plazas, in a gathering together, in a sense of community, that has nothing to do with conforming. Families are close, and clan ties are binding, even when disrupted by hardship and migration. But beyond the family, outside the home, lies another life, a necessary world of public ritual, where people stand close as fireworks shriek and explode in the night. "Viva México!" they shout—but the cheers are not for the government; Mexicans distrust all government. No, the cheers are for the land, for the people, for their families and way of life.

Mexicans are quite different from their neighbors to the north and south for reasons that are both historical (as you will see throughout this book) and racial. The first human inhabitants of the Americas were nomadic hunters from Asia who followed the herds they depended on over a broad isthmus that has long since been submerged under the shallow Bering Sea. We know little about these first "Americans," migrating as they did tens of thousands of years ago, but the evidence indicates that included in these various migratory waves of prehistoric peoples were many racial types. Later and larger migrations were mostly Oriental (Mongoloid) types, and they played the largest part in determining the physical traits of their descendants.

From the time of the last great migration (which ended around 9000 B.C.) until the arrival of the Spanish in the 16th century, there was no meaningful contact between the Old World and the New. The Americas, supporting a very small population relative to the rest of the world, developed independently and in isolation.

Civilization here rose in conjunction with the development of corn (maize), which became the food staple of much of the Americas (as it remains today). The Maya called its kernels the "sunbeams of God." Other Mesoamerican people displayed equal reverence toward this life-sustaining plant. (The picture of a lone man hoeing his mountainside patch of corn is a profound symbol of Mexico.)

Some three thousand years ago a mighty civilization suddenly rose and flourished on an unlikely piece of real estate, the swamps of coastal Tabasco just west of the Yucatán Peninsula. These people are today known as the **Olmecs**, but their early history remains unclear. We do know that the Olmecs invented the first form of writing used in the Americas, a numerical system that was later adopted and vastly expanded by the Maya, and that they also became accomplished at jade carving and developed methods of transporting huge boulders great distances.

Some two thousand years ago there was a stirring of collective activity throughout Mesoamerica. It was then that **Teotihuacán**, America's first true city, rose and flourished in the Valley of Mexico some 30 miles northeast of the modern capital. Its builders, who erected such imposing monuments as the Pyramid of the Sun and the Street of the Dead, were probably descendants of primitive villagers native to the area. Their name for themselves remains a mystery, but today they are called "Teotihuacanos." Within a century these vigorous people had come to dominate a huge region, sending trading parties out in all directions, some as far as present-day Guatemala. (In addition, trade goods, if not the traders themselves, found their way north up the great rivers of what is now the Southwestern United States.)

Over the next several centuries various civilizations rose and flowered: Teotihuacán and Xochicalco in the central highlands, the Zapotec centers in Oaxaca, and, most resplendent of all, the Classic-era cities of the **Maya** southeast. The latter were the first people in the world to develop the concept of a zero in mathematics, and their use of numbers and a calendar based on astronomical observation was far superior to the cumbersome systems in use in Europe at the time.

The Classic era, as it is called, a period of widespread culture and knowledge in Mesoamerica, started drawing to a close about A.D. 600, and three centuries later had ended completely. The great cities and ceremonial centers were abandoned; no one knows exactly why— although there are theories. A great plague or plagues has been suggested as one possible cause; a series of crop failures—leading to a rejection of traditional religion—is another. Other experts believe that the maintenance of so many priests and temples simply became too much, that these great civilizations were destroyed by nothing more than excessive taxation. At the same time, barbarian peoples from the north were roaming the land, yet their presence, according to the experts, seems not to have been the primary cause for the abandonment of one city after another, starting in the north and progressing to the south and east. In any case, by the end of the Classic era several qualities that would remain constants in the Mexican character were already evident: a devotion to ritual, a belief in the importance of pilgrimage, a fondness for bold color combined with a talent for handling it, and a love of exuberant music and dance.

In the tenth century the country suffered the invasion of a warrior people called the Toltecs, who bequeathed it an infusion of much-needed vitality as well as a variety of new styles of art. Today, the ancient ruins at **Tula** and **Chichén Itzá** are their greatest surviving monuments.

The Toltec conquest, however, proved only to be the prelude to the rise of the **Aztecs**, a fierce imperialistic society with a particularly bloodthirsty religion. After more than two centuries of Aztec rule, the stage was set for the arrival of Cortés in 1519.

The saga of the Conquest has been told and retold. Still, one important fact is often neglected: The conquistadors were defeated and put to flight by the Aztecs. Their eventual victory became possible only after they allied themselves with an army of natives, the Tlaxcalans. **Tenochtitlán**, the magnificent Aztec capital (over which Mexico City was built), was surrendered to Cortés on August 21, 1521.

Following the victory of the conquistadors, it was left over the next two decades to the missionaries of the church to subdue and secure the rest of the country. Employing tactics and rhetoric perfected during the long, grim decades of the Inquisition, the missionaries set about their task—one they were oddly suited for, believing as they did that Satan was a living presence, an insidious enemy who lurked invisibly at the shoulder of every would-be convert whispering foulness into his ear. Native books, art, buildings, and customs were seen as being steeped not just in sin but in even more dangerous magic. In the end, there was not only fanaticism but fear behind their destruction of some of the most glorious art ever created.

(Among the Mayan and Aztec materials destroyed were documents, so-called codices, painted or written on strips of pounded bark or parchment. Only three Mayan codices are known to have survived; all are in European museums. Other codices that remain in Mexico are post-Conquest copies of the originals.)

For almost three centuries Spain held sway over her New World colony, imposing on it her religion, art, and institutions—and still Mexico is only superficially Spanish. It is a curious fact, and one that is implicitly acknowledged on October 12, Columbus Day: In Mexico, it is not so much Columbus who is honored as it is the people of Mexico themselves, the unique Mexican race, or *raza,* and so the day is known here as the Día de la Raza. It is an entirely appropriate holiday, for today's Mexicans are mostly *mestizos,* a mixture of both Indian and Spanish. Of course, the proportion of the mix is impossible to determine and varies from region to region. Then, too, there are the purely Mayan or Zapotec or those of some other native group, as well as the purely Spanish, or *criollo.* (There are other, smaller European admixtures as well—French, Irish, and German, most notably. The African influence is relatively small. Slaves from the Indies sometimes reached the Gulf Coast, and a few were imported, but the Spaniards were afraid of black slavery in New Spain, being nervous about rebellions. Chinese were brought into the north as railroad builders; Lebanese entered the southeast first as peddlers, then storekeepers.)

During the centuries of colonial rule New Spain (as Mexico was called) was an intellectually somnolent land. Education was reserved for the privileged few, and what little was offered to the poor suffered a terrible blow when the Jesuits, the best and most selfless teachers, were expelled by the Spanish Crown in the 18th century. At the same time, Spain was careful not to permit the growth of an indigenous governing class. Mexico paid heavily for this after she gained her sovereignty in 1821: Her leaders had no experience in government, and little understanding of compromise and practicality.

The 19th century was a time of violence, hardship, and loss for Mexico. The United States invaded Mexico in 1846 and walked away with half its territory two years later. The French marched in 16 years later and, with the help of Mexican conservatives, put the puppet emperor Maximilian on a spurious (and wobbly) throne. Throughout the period, church and state battled without mercy. At one point the Pope blandly declared Mexico's constitution null and void. In another period, the 1920s, there was a strike by the clergy, the priests and nuns locking up the churches and departing. Parishioners shot the locks off church doors and conducted their own services, which brought the clergy rushing back, only to be expelled again—this time against their will. The subject remains a touchy one.

The modern Mexican state emerged from a bloody, brutal revolution that raged from 1910 into the 1920s, a struggle that was comparable in its ferocity to the U.S. Civil War.

The Mexico of today is the product of this long and tragic tumult. The sculpted bronze figures you see in public squares across the land are almost always of men who fought for a losing cause: Cuauhtémoc, the last Aztec ruler, tortured and slain; Hidalgo, Aldama, Allende, and Jiménez, martyrs in the struggle for independence at the start of the 19th century, executed and beheaded; José María Morelos, who continued the fight for independence, executed in 1815; Vicente Guerrero, staunch defender of the rights of the people, first against Spain, then against the rich and powerful of his own country, treacherously executed in 1831; Francisco Madero, the first president of modern Mexico and a great liberal reformer, murdered with his vice president in a Mexico City alley in 1910; Emiliano Zapata, land reformer and hero of the peasants, shot in cold blood in 1919; President Alvaro Obregón, defender, and eventual victim, of constitutional government, assassinated three weeks after his reelection in 1928. Their ideas and causes ultimately may have triumphed, but they themselves came to tragic ends, most of them believing their cause was lost. They are Mexico's true heroes, and there is a certain melancholy appropriateness to this in a nation too often beset by turmoil and trouble.

There is a saying here that goes, "Once the dust of Mexico has settled on your heart, you will find peace in no other land." Certainly, the traveller who discovers Mexico for the first time is likely to return again and again. One trip is not enough to comprehend it, of course; maybe even a lifetime is not sufficient, for its character is like a Mayan temple, built up layer upon layer, the newest façade hiding but not destroying the earlier ones. Nor do the centuries quietly vanish when their time is up; in Mexico, they linger on, the past mixing with the present, complicating judgments and making predictions all but impossible.

Most visitors come initially for the glorious beaches or the magnificent pre-Columbian ruins. We hope that after experiencing the pleasures of those you will prolong your stay or return to see the less publicized attractions we have chosen, such as the romantic streets and alleys of Guanajuato or the Indian color and serenity of Pátzcuaro.

Mexico is also a bargain. Prices do change and exchange rates fluctuate, so it is more of a bargain some years and in some seasons than others. Still, all things considered, a Mexican vacation is one of the best travel buys in the world. When this book labels something as "expensive," it is usually speaking of an amount that would be considered moderate in New York or Paris, and cheap in Tokyo.

Another reason to go to Mexico is the Mexican people themselves. Mexicans, in general, like foreigners, especially their northern neighbors on the continent. They are also full of a lively curiosity, and are tolerant and accepting of different kinds of behavior and tastes. Finally, they are generally kind and courteous.

Often, it's true, Mexican politicians and intellectuals sound as xenophobic as any in the world. The media here ring with screams about imperialism, arrogance, and exploitation. From a Mexican viewpoint, however, there is often good reason for this screaming. Mexico, after all, has suffered grievously at the hands of foreigners. The United States has stormed onto its soil not once but several times, and claimed a large part of it as its own. The French have also invaded, and the British, although less involved, are not innocent. Alas, Spain's conduct was simply unspeakable. And yet, despite this discouraging record, ordinary Mexicans like their foreign neighbors. No wonder the feeling is usually mutual.

If a visitor makes the least attempt at uttering a few Spanish words, however badly, Mexicans will go to extraordinary lengths to understand and be of help. A few gestures may inspire a whole pantomime. There is no snobbery here, no sense that those who do not speak the native tongue are considered little more than savages.

Almost everyone strives to be helpful. A car is mired on a country road, and suddenly half a dozen men appear from nowhere to push it out. When their efforts fail, someone fetches a team of oxen. Strangers will guide you, be infinitely patient in repeating directions, and sometimes even walk you to your destination. (This can lead to a sort of courtesy disaster, which happens when an informant doesn't really know the way but won't be so rude as to disappoint you. Truth must not interfere with politeness.)

Mexicans are often surprisingly familiar with the United States and Canada, at least on a second- or third-hand basis. After all, a chief export of the country is its own sons and daughters for labor abroad. Is there anyone, even in the remotest village, who doesn't have at least one cousin who has crossed two or more borders to find work? Or, so it seems at times, an uncle living in Los Angeles?

Because these temporary laborers and new immigrants are often exploited, the guilty American conscience expects hostility in return from Mexicans. Mexican fatalism usually prevents this: What happened was the fault of the system, the government, or just bad luck. Nothing personal, and all in all it wasn't so bad. *Así es la vida*—such is life! Why nourish bad feelings? This kind of fatalism moves like a tide through Mexican life, softening its hard edges and making bad times and economic failures bearable. Resignation may be an enemy of progress, but it is also a balm for the wear and tear of daily living.

There is one facet of the national character you probably won't understand, and it may ultimately annoy you, so be prepared. The Mexican concept of schedules and punctuality is a pre-Columbian mystery. At times it seems incredible that the ancestors of these people calculated the world's most accurate calendar. What is two o'clock? Well, it's two until it's three o'clock, clearly. Also, it's two when it's no longer one o'clock. Novelist Carlos Fuentes writes of an old man who wove palm hats as he walked from village to village. Thus, a certain village became two hats away, another one three. Each to his own clock, and you cannot expect a person to keep "English time," which is what the exact time is called.

All the jokes and stories about *mañana* are understatements. In part, the answer that your train/letter/money order will be there *mañana* is simple courtesy, a desire not to disappoint. In part, it is optimism. But it also stems from a belief that you will not take such a word as "tomorrow" literally. *Mañana* is a dream, a hope, a kindness—as well as a way of getting rid of an aggressive, impatient person.

In the end, you must simply relax and adopt this Mexican virtue of fatalism.

This book, intended as an introduction to a large and varied country, is *selective* rather than complete. Only the best, the most interesting places have been chosen. There is no point in muddying its contents with destinations few people would willingly choose. It also omits places—including a few of Mexico's larger cities—that are simply pass-through points en route to somewhere else. **Monterrey**, for example, Mexico's northeastern metropolis, has some attractive neighborhoods and an admirably renovated downtown section, but it remains a place for business, not for leisure or discovery. Many other large and prosperous cities are omitted for the same reason, among them Torreón, Durango, Ciudad Victoria, and León.

A different type of omission is neatly summed up by the famous remark of Dr. Johnson: "Worth seeing? Yes, but not worth going to see." Some places, even though attractive, are too remote or difficult to reach to be considered here. The once-flourishing mining towns of **Real de Catorce** and **Alamos** are examples. They are interesting if you happen to be in the neighborhood but for most people not worth a special and awkward trip. Many archaeological zones also fall into this category. Dedicated ruins buffs will easily find them in more specialized reference publications.

Two colonial silver cities, **San Luis Potosí** and **Zacatecas**, have attractions that are also not gone into detail here because they, too, do not quite justify the trip. If you find yourself in their neighborhood, however, do not neglect those handsome towns.

On the other hand, the **Copper Canyon** (and its train), also remote from usual destinations, is special. Its breathtaking natural beauty and the opportunity for adventure it affords justify a trip to Mexico's dusty northwest corner, and so we discuss this experience in detail.

Our exploration of Mexico begins, however, with the capital, **Mexico City**, the country's hub and crossroads. The world's largest city is full of both annoyances and charm. Its traffic is manic, its pace distinctly un-Mexican. Traditional Mexican courtesy is put to the extreme test here. Individuals in the D. F. (Distrito Federal, as Mexico City is officially known) are usually as kind and courteous as people in the provinces, even though as city dwellers they must be wary. But courtesy is not a usual trait of crowds, of mobs at the subway, of people rushing desperately to board the bus to get home.

For all its problems, there is much to admire and enjoy in the capital. The great *Zócalo* is a masterly achievement in urban design, with its cathedral, its fine government palaces, and, hidden just around a corner, the great Templo Mayor of the Aztecs. The National Museum of Anthropology is the country's finest "archaeological zone," and ranks among the great museums of the world. The pyramids at **Teotihuacán** are marvels of ancient achievement. Finally, the city itself is a museum of people and life, filled with quaint neighborhoods, odd little shops, and unexpected vistas.

Mexico City is also the jumping-off point for a number

of short trips, and four are outlined here: flower-filled **Cuernavaca**; serious **Puebla**, with its huge pyramid at **Cholula**; picturesque **Taxco**, town of noted silversmiths; and a northward loop including three points of interest, the National Museum of Viceregal Art at **Tepotzotlán**, the ruins of ancient **Tula**, and the 16th-century monastery at **Ixmiquilpán**, with its strange Indian murals.

That is as much as most travellers will be able to explore from the Federal District. Those with more time may also want to visit **Tlaxcala**, with its fanciful architecture.

Travellers often talk about discovering "the real Mexico," and while every part of the country is equally real, the sort of place they usually have in mind turns out to be in the historic **Bajío**, the Mexican heartland located more or less north of the capital. Although the Bajío lacks Mexico's two greatest attractions for foreign visitors—beaches and ancient archaeological ruins—it is indeed "the real Mexico," as well as the best place to discover what the country as a whole is doing and thinking. The Bajío comprises only an eighth of Mexico's land but produces most of its food. It is also here, in the mining towns of **Guanajuato**, **Querétaro**, **San Miguel de Allende**, and **Morelia**, that you'll see the finest colonial architecture and get the strongest sense of Mexico's colonial heritage, and so we discuss them extensively.

The valley that encircles **Guadalajara** blends into the Bajío without any sharp geographical separation, but Mexico's second city lies far enough west in relation to the capital to have developed its own ways and style. This area, the **Western Highlands**, probably had the worst of it during the Conquest, and the barbarity of the conquistadors seemed to reach special depths of sadism here (although it is difficult to rate historical suffering). Fortunately, the city of Guadalajara and the surrounding Jalisco region were spared from later foreign incursions. The invasion route taken by the armies of the United States was located far to the east, and the struggles with the French were north and south of Mexico City. Guadalajara also largely avoided the depredations of bandits in military uniforms during the years of revolutionary turmoil.

This comparatively benign history shows in its architecture, its style, and its people. Here is a friendly and vital city, one where sightseers will want to linger but not remain too long: its charms are many, but not infinite. Still, the Guadalajara area has the largest English-speaking expatriate colony in the world. Besides the one in the city itself, a second expatriate community has taken up residence in the small towns along the shore of **Lake Chapala**. An ideal climate is a powerful attraction, it seems.

Mexico's other celebrated lake, **Pátzcuaro**, is southeast of here, situated among rugged mountains rather than in a fertile valley. With the change in terrain there also comes a change in the people—from the cowboys (real or rhinestone) of Guadalajara to the sober Tarascans of Michoacán. Writer and intellectual Andrés Henestrosa has said, "Mexican songs are Indian inside, European outside—Spanish melody and Indian melancholy." Nowhere does that seem more true than in Pátzcuaro. But if the people are sober, their great market is a riot of color. Ultimately, Pátzcuaro seems outside of time, an Indian Brigadoon that no passing fancy affects too deeply.

The mountainous route between Pátzcuaro and Mexico City, via Morelia, is scenic country well worth exploring if you have a car, but not otherwise. You'll want to be able to stop, get out, look around, and breathe deeply—a luxury that buses simply don't offer. The towns themselves are not especially attractive, but the trip is lovely.

Far to the southeast lies **Oaxaca**, just as Indian as Pátzcuaro, but utterly different in temperament. Whereas the Tarascan people seem reserved, and as cool as their mountain lake, the Zapotec folk of Oaxaca are outgoing, lively, warm, and curious. In forested Pátzcuaro you are aware of shadows; the Valley of Oaxaca, on the other hand, is flooded with sunshine. Centuries ago two ancient cultures, the Zapotecs and later the Mixtecs, flourished in the valleys that converge at the city of Oaxaca. Today, the ruins of their many ceremonial centers, the greatest being **Monte Albán** and **Mitla**, stand as a reminder of that former glory. Two thousand years ago at Monte Albán the Zapotecs began to reshape a mountaintop, creating in the process ancient Mexico's only necropolis, a true city of the dead. Later, the Mixtecs added to Monte Albán's vast honeycomb of tombs, and created for their dead some of the most exquisite jewelry ever fashioned, treasures now displayed in the city of Oaxaca. But the charm of Oaxaca is by no means confined to archaeology. Today's city offers fascinating architecture, colorful craft markets, and the pageant of daily life around its welcoming plaza.

The **Gulf Coast** region is the least visited of the regions discussed here, but also the most varied. **Veracruz** is a burst of marimba music, a city full of gaiety and celebration. (Of course, it has its workaday side; not far from the plaza where the action is stands a Woolworth's.) Some of the more sober descendants of old, respectable families (Spanish, of course) lock their doors at *Carnaval* time and insert earplugs, but that staid face is not the one that Veracruz—either the city or the state—usually shows the public.

To the north of Veracruz, two archaeological sites deserve special attention: **Zempoala** and magnificent **El Tajín**, the latter considered by many to be a rival of some of the Mayan sites for beauty and mystery.

Our exploration of the Gulf Coast north of Veracruz ends at sleepy **Tuxpan**, a town with no particular beauty— and certainly little in the way of excitement. What it does have is character and a graceful, unhurried river. Farther north lies the modern port of Tampico, which we do not cover. Its attractions are exclusively for sportsmen, especially sportfishermen, although it does have good hotels and restaurants due to its status as a prosperous center for the petroleum industry.

To the south of Veracruz are the slightly dubious attractions of **Lake Catemaco**, not one of the more attractive destinations in this book. Fortunately, the big lake, nestled among volcanoes, makes up for the somewhat grubby town. At any rate, Catemaco is the start of a beautiful drive or bus ride east to **Villahermosa**, the gateway to the Mayan world, and a handsome city with a remarkable outdoor archaeological museum of Olmec materials.

Ancient Mesoamerican culture reached its zenith in the jungles of the **Yucatán** at such magnificent ceremonial centers as **Chichén Itzá**, **Uxmal**, and others. Oddly enough, the Maya seem to have done best where the soil was poorest and the climate most inhospitable. **Palenque**, down in the northern part of the state of Chiapas, while perhaps the most elegant Mayan ruin, is on the edge of a jungle so impenetrable that no one knows what other ruined cities might be concealed there.

Today, the Maya, fighting to keep their ancient traditions alive, are found not only near the great centers their ancestors erected but also in the highland fastness of **San Cristóbal de las Casas**, capital of the state of Chiapas, where the surrounding hamlets remain virtually untouched by the modern world.

They are also found in **Guatemala**, a separate country and one with very different traditions at certain levels of society. Ancient legend has it that a Mayan miracle took place here at **Tikal**, the largest, tallest, and in some ways most impressive of the Mayan cities. And while today the Maya struggle to come to terms with modern divisions that are artificial and political—and over which they had no control—Tikal remains a magnificent reminder of the continuity of Mayan culture, and a natural complement to exploring Uxmal, Palenque, and Chichén Itzá.

Mexico's beach and saltwater resorts are by far the country's most popular attractions with visitors, their names synonymous with pleasure and sometimes glamour. **Cancún, Cozumel, Acapulco, Ixtapa/Zihuatanejo,** and **Puerto Vallarta** are just the major ones, but we cover quite a few more that are modest in size—**Manzanillo, Mazatlán, Isla Mujeres**—and even some that are small and/or little known, **Careyes** and **Huatulco**, for example.

Of course, sand and sea are international, and so are the vacationers who flock to find both in Mexico, including Mexicans themselves. Yet each resort has its own special identity and flavor. Cancún, for example, has a close Mayan neighbor in **Tulum**, one of the last outposts of Mayan greatness, and a surprising bonus for vacationers. In fact, none of the great resorts we cover is merely a "hotel culture" (though Cancún comes close). Cozumel has a strong island character all its own, and Acapulco is one of Mexico's largest and most vibrant cities. In all of them you'll find more than clear water, warm sands, and palm trees: They also share the warmth of Mexico.

Baja California is a very special place and the subject of many books in its own right (see the Bibliography for two of them). While we don't cover Baja the way we do, say, the Colonial Heartland, we describe it briefly as a possible route to the **Los Cabos** resorts—which are discussed in detail.

In the discussions of various regions in this book there is much mention of **crafts and shopping**. But because we cover the subject piecemeal throughout the book, perhaps a broader look here will be of value.

In many countries travellers find shopping to be incidental. They may well pick up some souvenirs or buy a destination's famed specialties—jades in the Orient or perfumes in Paris, for example.

Mexico, as in so many things, is different. Shopping in the craft markets, or at least browsing, is one of the decided pleasures of visiting Mexico. (The same is true in Guatemala, where crafts are not far behind Tikal as an attraction.) But the Mexican scene is often so rich that visitors find it confusing. What to look for?

First, those things you *cannot* buy. It is illegal to purchase and take pre-Columbian art and artifacts out of the country. Not surprisingly, Mexican authorities take a very serious view of the matter; it is an offense that can lead to imprisonment and heavy fines.

Then why, you might ask, are all these vendors jumping out of the bushes at archaeological sites and offering me carvings? Why aren't they arrested? The answer, of course, is simply that they are offering nothing but fakes. If you find an object attractive and reasonably priced, buy it as contemporary art—but don't think of it as old. Reproductions of ancient works, especially ceramics and clay sculptures, are created in studios under government license. Shops everywhere offer them, especially in the resort centers. Often, they are lovely, striking, and unusual. Enjoy them for what they are—not what someone *says* they are and you won't be disappointed.

Mexico expresses its character in its handicrafts, which are often beautiful and quite fragile. Nowadays the best is quickly shipped all over the country and soon appears on shelves in Mexico City and Acapulco. On the other hand, if you want to search for the best at the *source,* here are some tips:

- *Silver.* Mexico City, Taxco, Guadalajara, and Oaxaca.
- *Tinware.* San Miguel de Allende.
- *Blankets and rugs.* Tlaxcala, Oaxaca, San Miguel de Allende, and Pátzcuaro.
- *Clothing.* Morelia, Pátzcuaro, Mérida, Guadalajara, San Miguel de Allende, and Mexico City.
- *Ceramics.* Oaxaca, Pátzcuaro, Tonalá, Puebla, and Mexico City.
- *Hand-blown glass.* Guadalajara.
- *Lacquerware.* Pátzcuaro, Morelia, and Uruapan.
- *Copperware.* Mexico City, Guadalajara, San Miguel de Allende, and Santa María del Cobre (near Pátzcuaro).
- *Brass.* Mexico City and San Miguel de Allende.

- *Woodcarving.* Paracho (Michoacán) and Pátzcuaro.
- *Gold filigree.* Mérida.

Every region of Mexico has its special character and unique attractions, as you will see in this book. Every traveller will find places that become personal favorites— be they ruins, dazzling beaches, tile-encrusted palaces, or fragrant plazas.

Yet there is something more in Mexico, an elusive quality, that makes the whole more than the sum of its parts. Writer Charles Flandrau, after sojourning through the country early in this century, understood this, and no one since has expressed it quite so well: "The most notable sight in Mexico is simply Mexico."

USEFUL FACTS

When to Go

Mexico is a fine year-round destination, but the various seasons have different attractions. Winter—December through March—is ideal because of the generally cool, dry weather. It's an especially good time to visit the Gulf Coast and Yucatán, which can get unbearably hot and humid at other times of the year. On the other hand, it's also the peak tourist season, when demand for all services is greatest. Discounts vanish, many prices rise sharply despite controls, and major beach resorts get crowded. Archaeological zones are also heavily visited at this time of year.

April and May are usually uncrowded, but spring is also the hottest, driest time of year in many places. The highland regions grow dusty, and the land turns brown.

Summer, the second most popular season for visitors, boasts rains that are usually brief but often torrential. Mornings and early afternoons tend to be clear and lovely. Summer, even on the coasts, is not as warm as spring.

Fall has temperate weather, with the rains continuing until the end of September. October and November are appealing, uncrowded months.

Mexico City closes down during Holy Week as millions of its inhabitants rush for the beaches. Avoid the resorts at that time. The capital, on the other hand, is an attractive alternative then, even though some businesses will be closed. Throughout the country all forms of transportation are packed at Easter.

Entry Documents

U.S. and Canadian citizens need only proof of citizenship and a tourist card, though naturalized citizens need a valid passport, as do Europeans. Tourist cards are issued at Mexican consulates, border crossings, major airports, and by some travel agencies. It will save confusion if you get the card before you actually get to an airport or are about to cross the border. The card, for which there is no charge, is stamped on entry. Keep it; it must be turned in when you leave the country. The length of permissible stay listed on the card is determined by the official issuing it. The time can be extended, not to exceed 180 days, at tourism offices throughout the country.

Entering with a car requires a permit, a document that must be surrendered upon departure. If you arrive with a car you must leave with the same car. The Mexican authorities are strict and very serious about this. All valid driving licenses are accepted in Mexico.

U.S. or Canadian auto insurance is not in force once you cross the border, but Mexican coverage, which is rather expensive, is available at ports of entry. *You must on no account drive in Mexico without proper Mexican insurance.* Uninsured drivers go to jail if involved in an accident.

Arrival at Major Gateways by Air

The major carriers providing direct service to Mexico are Mexicana, Aeroméxico, Continental, American, Delta, and Pan Am. With few exceptions international travellers will have to make connections in the United States, however. (Iberia, which offers direct Montreal–Mexico City service, and Canadian International Airlines, which has a direct Toronto–Puerto Vallarta flight on Saturdays only, are among the exceptions.)

Mexicana offers direct service to Mexico City and Guadalajara (with connections from the capital to every major city in the country) from a number of U.S. cities, including New York, Philadelphia, Miami, Chicago, Dallas-Ft. Worth, Denver, Seattle, San Francisco, and Los Angeles. Aeroméxico offers direct service to Mexico City and many of the major resorts from New York, Miami, Houston, Tucson, and Los Angeles. Continental flies direct from

New York and Newark to Mexico City and Guadalajara as well as most of the major resorts, including Acapulco, Cancún, Cozumel, Ixtapa/Zihuatanejo, Los Cabos, and Puerto Vallarta. American, which routes its Mexico service through Dallas-Ft. Worth, offers flights to Mexico City, Guadalajara, Acapulco, Cancún, Cozumel, and Puerto Vallarta. For further information contact your travel agent or any of the airlines mentioned above.

Taxis with regulated rates are available at the capital's airport. There is metro (subway) service from the airport, but it is confusing for passengers with little Spanish arriving in Mexico for the first time.

Some hotels in outlying cities will arrange to have a driver meet passengers at the customs exit gate at the Mexico City airport and transport them directly, thus letting them avoid a stopover in the capital.

Around Mexico by Air

The capital is the air hub of the country, and air service anywhere is often via Mexico City. There is good service from the D.F. to all larger resorts. For the other regions described in this book the airport gateways are: Morelia, León, and San Luis Potosí for the Bajío region; Guadalajara for the Western Highlands and beach resorts; Veracruz and Villahermosa for the Gulf; Villahermosa, Mérida, and Tuxtla Gutiérrez for the Mayan region; and Chihuahua for the Copper Canyon. Flights leave daily from Mexico City for Guatemala City.

Around Mexico by Train

Service is limited and tends to be slow. As in most affairs, everything is linked to the capital. There is good but not rapid service from the D.F. to Veracruz, Guadalajara, Querétaro, San Miguel de Allende, and Nuevo Laredo. While the trains are constantly being upgraded, they are not really a practical option for touring the country in general. If you are not travelling overnight, get a ticket that is first-class special (*primera especial*). This will guarantee you a comfortable seat.

Around Mexico by Bus

The bus is the donkey of motor vehicles in Mexico, able to get to the most remote backwater. The best service will be on a bus that runs first class (*primera clase*); ask for direct service (*directo*) to avoid too many stops and detours. Nevertheless, be prepared for the toilet to be out of order, and dress for the air conditioning to be likewise, or else working overtime. Bottled drinks are generally available, but on a long trip you should carry some sort of snack; some bus station restaurants are less than appetizing.

Second-class (*segunda clase*) buses are often identical to first-class vehicles except for the number of stops they make (although some are older and a bit more rickety). A second-class bus may stop anywhere along the road to load or unload things, including passengers, bundles of newspapers, chickens, goats, or a hundred pieces of hand-made pottery on the way to market. They may also be jammed to the roof: Try to grab a window seat if you can. Finally, don't get too discouraged; travelling like this can be fun and colorful. Or it may prove simply fast and uneventful.

Around Mexico by Car

If you're taking your own vehicle, you'll face the frustration of trying to find the unleaded gas called *extra* that most foreign cars use. Look for a **silver pump**, and, wherever you stay, ask ahead. Regular Mexican leaded Nova will do in a pinch, without poisoning your engine, until you can find the higher octane. Expect coughs and sputters from the lower-octane mix, however.

Getting to the more interesting parts of Mexico can be a long and expensive proposition. Combining means of transportation is probably your best bet: flying in, renting a car and driving to a particular destination, turning it in and taking a train, plane, or bus to the next spot, etcetera. Rental cars from companies whose name you'll recognize are widely available, though they will be more expensive than in North America. If you want an automatic transmission, you must ask; they aren't standard issue.

Except within a large city do *not* drive at night. The reasons are legion.

Local Time

Mexico is never on Daylight Saving Time. Most of the country is on Central Standard Time (Winnipeg, Chicago, Dallas), with the exception of the far west—Sonora, Sinaloa, Nayarit—and southern Baja California, which are on Mountain Standard Time (Calgary, Denver). Northern Baja California is on Pacific Time and is the sole exception to the Daylight Saving rule: It always keeps the same time as Los Angeles.

Currency

The monetary unit is the peso, indicated by a dollar sign and sometimes the abbreviation M.N. (*moneda nacional*). The exchange rate fluctuates in relation to the U.S. and Canadian dollars. Denominations of bills are 1,000; 5,000; 10,000; 20,000; and 50,000. The coins that matter are 100; 200; 500; 1,000; and 5,000. Smaller coins of no real value are much in circulation to weigh down purses and wear out pockets.

Travellers checks and foreign currency should be exchanged at banks or private exchange offices (*casas de cambio*) for the best rate. Most banks exchange only during early business hours. Airport exchange offices also give good rates.

Major credit cards are accepted in most larger establishments, except gasoline stations. You will see the familiar logos posted on doors or windows. If you don't, ask before trying to charge.

Electric Current

Electricity in Mexico is supplied at 110 volts, alternating current, the same as in the United States and Canada. The same type and sizes of sockets and plugs are also standard in all three countries.

Telephoning

The international code number for dialing directly to Mexico is 52. Long-distance calls within Mexico are cheap, but international calls are expensive because of taxes. These taxes do not apply to international calls made collect. A collect call to the United States or Canada is about a third of what a prepaid call costs. It is easiest to make calls through hotel switchboards, but all towns have *larga distancia* telephone offices where prepaid calls can be put through.

Business Hours

There is no simple answer to this mystery. The day seems to start soon after 9:00 A.M., but it can be an hour later. Most of the country pauses for a two-hour break at 1:00 or 2:00 P.M. This means that business is generally resumed between 3:00 and 4:00 P.M. Some offices will close at 5:00 P.M., which is a modern—and foreign—custom. Many establishments in Mexico City ignore the siesta, others keep it faithfully, and so far most attempts to change the old custom in the interest of efficiency have failed. Closing hour for most stores is commonly 7:00 or 8:00 P.M.

Museums and other public institutions that stay open on Sunday usually close on Monday. Archaeological zones are open seven days a week.

Holidays

Official holidays, when most businesses and all offices are closed, are: Jan. 1, New Year's Day; Feb. 5, Constitution Day; March 21, the birthday of Juárez; May 1, Labor Day; Sept. 16, Independence Day (but the celebration starts the night before); Nov. 20, Anniversary of the Revolution; and Dec. 25, Christmas.

Not official but close to it are: Holy Week (with work slowly grinding to a halt as the week progresses, and stopping completely on Thursday); May 5, Anniversary of the Battle of Puebla (*Cinco de Mayo*); Sept. 1, the presidential state-of-the-union report (*el informe*)—banks close; Nov. 2, Day of the Dead; and Dec. 12, Feast of Guadalupe, patroness saint of Mexico.

Also important are: May 10, Mother's Day; and Oct. 12, Columbus Day, called *Día de la Raza* in Mexico.

Every town has its patron saint, and takes a day to a week to celebrate his feast. Other religious holidays include: Jan. 6, Three Kings Day, the traditional day of Christmas gift giving (but losing ground to Santa Claus now); Jan. 17, St. Anthony's Day, the traditional day for the blessing of animals; Feb. 2, Candelaria, a rite of spring and the day candles and seeds are blessed; *Carnaval* (Mardi Gras), which is movable, with the best parties in Veracruz, Mazatlán, Mérida, and Guadalajara; late May or early June, Corpus Christi Day, with fairs and rites throughout the country; and Dec. 16–23, the long Christmas prelude, which is celebrated with processions, parties, much singing, and nativity plays.

Safety

Beware of pickpockets, especially at public celebrations and on public transportation. The metro in Mexico City is a favorite hunting ground for dips and cutpurses; museum entrances are another haunt. Public streets in general are comparatively free of violence, but normal precautions should be taken. Smaller cities are usually so safe that the only danger is in becoming careless. Theft of valuables from automobiles is common, however, so be careful where you park and leave nothing tempting in plain sight. Cameras and the like should be locked in the trunk.

Taxes

The onerous one is the I.V.A., called "Eva," a 15 percent sales tax on almost everything. By law it is supposed to be included in marked prices and quoted rates, but it often isn't. Ask if something is without tax, *sin* I.V.A. (*sin* "*Eevah*"), or if the tax is included, *con* I.V.A. (*con* "*Eevah*").

Health

High altitudes can play strange tricks on your system. Avoid too much exertion, overeating, and heavy drinking while your body is adapting to the change in its oxygen supply. Alcohol seems to work more swiftly and potently in the highland areas, and can sneak up on you if your usual habitat is located at sea level or thereabouts.

In most places tap water is not purified. The old admonition "Don't drink the water" always seems hardest to remember when you have a toothbrush or an iced drink in your hand. Potable water is provided, in jugs or bottles, by all decent hotels and restaurants. So is pure ice.

The bulk of medical opinion is against taking any medicine in advance as a preventive for diarrhea. Rest and moderation are the best cure in almost every case.

Dressing for Comfort

Tennis shoes, running shoes, or the like are strongly recommended. In all highland areas and even on the Gulf Coast a sweater or jacket is needed many nights. In winter a windbreaker should be added in Mexico City and at similar altitudes. Informality in dress is the norm, but some restaurants in the capital as well as elsewhere have dress codes: coat and tie for men, cocktail dress or the like for women. Mexico City is the only truly dressy place in the country, and even there casual wear usually prevails, except in business.

It is no longer necessary for women to cover their heads before entering churches. One dress taboo remains, however: shorts are not acceptable except in a beach or sports situation.

Rainwear will be needed in the late spring, all summer, and most of the fall.

—*Robert Somerlott*

BIBLIOGRAPHY

MARIANO AZUELA, *The Underdogs* (1916). A sweaty, gritty novel of the revolutionary upheavals between 1911 and 1920, and a book that changed the course of Mexican literature.

JOSEPH ARMSTRONG BAIRD, JR., *The Churches of Mexico*. A knowing survey of the major architectural achievements of New Spain.

SYBILLE BEDFORD, *Sudden View.* A needle-eyed lady's travel memoir of Mexico, originally published in 1954.

IGNACIO BERNAL, *Mexico Before Cortés: Art, History, and Legend.* A capsule version by the former director of Mexico's famed National Museum of Anthropology.

EMMET REID BLAKE, *Birds of Mexico*. The abundant avian life of Mexico presented by a distinguished ornithologist.

ANITA BRENNER AND G. R. LEIGHTON, *The Wind that Shook Mexico*. A long-repressed nation violently enters the modern world. Memorable photographs illuminate the text.

FRANCES CALDERÓN DE LA BARCA, *Life in Mexico* (1843). The Scottish-Bostonian wife of Spain's first ambassador to the newborn Mexican Republic penned a series of shrewd, gossipy, and witty letters. Delightful, and in some ways oddly contemporary.

JORGE CASTANEDA AND ROBERT A. PASTOR, *Limits to Friendship: The United States and Mexico.* Two informed viewpoints—often in disagreement, always thought provoking.

DANE CHANDOS, *House in the Sun*. The author's glasses were sweetly rose-colored even in the 1950s, but this fictionalized view of a vanished Mexican village remains charming.

MICHAEL D. COE, *The Maya*. A reliable introduction to the ancient Maya by a reputable scholar.

MAURICE COLLIS, *Cortés and Móctezuma*. Thoughtful speculation about the history of the Conquest, and insights into its two major figures.

MIGUEL COVARRUBIAS, *Indian Art of Mexico and Central America* (1952). The appreciative views of an artist-scholar. Some theories are now outdated, but the main points remain valid, and the author's illustrations are unsurpassed in the field.

————, *Mexico South: The Isthmus of Tehuantepec* (1946). A colorful visit to a corner of Mexico as it was yesterday and almost is today. Illustrations by an outstanding artist.

NIGEL DAVIES, *The Ancient Kingdoms of Mexico*. An excellent introductory survey of all the pre-Columbian archaeological periods except the Mayan.

————, *The Aztecs*. A political history of the last pre-Spanish conquerors of Mexico.

————, *The Toltecs*. An account of pre-Aztec conquest and culture.

BERNARD DE VOTO, *The Year of Decision* (1961). The parts of the book dealing with the Mexican War provide a brief but incisive treatment of this tragedy.

BERNAL DÍAZ DEL CASTILLO, *The Discovery and Conquest of Mexico*. Also published as the *Bernal Díaz Chronicle*. An exciting eyewitness account by one of Cortés's soldiers who lived that astonishing adventure. Essential; the book is basic in everything ever written about the era.

HARRIET DOERR, *Stones for Ibarra*. A penetrating novel of life and death in an isolated mining village.

ERNEST EDWARDS, *A Field Guide to Mexican Birds*. For on-the-spot identification. Where and how to watch, and what to look for.

ANDRE EMMERICH, *Art Before Columbus*. The best and most concise introduction, one that untangles a complex field.

————, *Sweat of the Sun and Tears of the Moon*. The use and veneration of precious metals in pre-Columbian art.

CARLOS ESPEJEL, *Mexican Folk Crafts*. A wide-ranging survey that is short on text but lavish in photographic illustrations by F. Catala Roca.

CHARLES M. FLANDRAU, *Viva Mexico* (1908). These traveller's tales sometimes cross the line into fiction, but always to the reader's enlightenment.

CARLOS FUENTES, *The Death of Artemio Cruz* (1962). A powerful and complex novel of the betrayal of revolutionary ideals by politicians and businessmen. Fuentes, a novelist, essayist, and diplomat, is the strongest voice currently speaking for Mexico.

————, *The Good Conscience* (1959). An intelligent and observant boy grows up in the provincial city of Guanajuato.

————, *The Old Gringo* (1984). The celebrated American author and social critic Ambrose Bierce vanished into the Mexican revolution. This is a fictional speculation about his last days, replete with pointed observations about Mexico, gringos, and life in general.

THOMAS GAGE, *A New Survey of the West Indies*. First published in 1648. Gage was the first English observer to report on New Spain, and he found little to his liking, establishing a British tradition.

CHARLES GALLENKAMP, *The Maya*. Ancient Mayan life and art, with a postscript about the Maya in modern times.

CATHERINE GAVIN, *The Cactus and the Crown*. Maximilian and his wife Carlota are given kinder treatment than they probably deserve in this readable fictionalized account.

GRAHAM GREENE, *The Power and the Glory*. After half a century, this novel of the suppression of the church in Mexico still crackles with suspense. At the same time, it has been denounced by many Mexicans, who charge that it, as well as Greene's lesser work, *The Other Mexico*, were subsidized by foreign oil companies wishing to destabilize Mexico.

BERTITA HARDING, *Phantom Crown*. A biographical work about Maximilian and Carlota.

MARIAN HARVEY, *Mexico's Crafts and Craftspeople*. Where and how Mexican popular arts are fashioned and who makes them. Many photographic illustrations by Ken Harvey.

————, *Crafts of Mexico*. A survey, appreciation, and explanation.

MCKINLEY HELM, *Man of Fire*. Mexican muralist José Clemente Orozco is presented in full color in this critical biography.

JOYCE KELLY, *The Complete Visitor's Guide to Mesoamerican Ruins*. A sensible and extensive work designed for the archaeology buff doing serious travelling and looking.

DIANA KENNEDY, *The Cuisines of Mexico*. Of the many books on Mexican cookery this is the most popular with foreigners and the most representative of the country's varied regions.

JOSEPH WOOD KRUTCH, *The Forgotten Peninsula*. A keen and wise observer examines Baja California.

DIEGO DE LANDA, *Yucatán: Before and After the Conquest*. Friar Diego's eyewitness work, written in the mid-1500s, is basic to all Maya studies.

D. H. LAWRENCE, *The Plumed Serpent* (1926). Lawrence redesigned Mexican mythology to fit his own views, but the atmosphere of Lake Chapala and the Mexican characters he evokes make the story rewarding.

————, *Mornings in Mexico* (1927). Lawrence wrote most of these observations and ruminations in Oaxaca, whose serene atmosphere lends the book a touch of peace uncharacteristic of the author's work.

A. STARKER LEOPOLD, *Wildlife of Mexico* (1959). Much of this work, written for hunters, has been rendered passé by game laws and extinction. Yet the information that abounds in its illustrated pages is still informative.

OSCAR LEWIS, *The Children of Sanchéz* (1961). A profound and moving portrayal of slum life in Mexico City. This true account by an anthropologist caused a sensation in Mexico when first published. Now a classic.

————, *Five Families* (1959). A cross-section of Mexican life in readable form.

————, *Pedro Martínez* (1964). The harsh life of Mexico's farms and villages.

MALCOLM LOWRY, *Under the Volcano* (1947). A cult classic for a generation, this disturbing novel of foreigners in Cuernavaca has moved into the mainstream of literature.

SALVADOR MADARIAGA, *Heart of Jade* (1944). This novel, tinged with mysticism and crammed with adventure, gallops across the Mexican landscape during the Conquest.

————, *Hernán Cortés*. A biography of the conqueror.

J. PATRICK MCHENRY, *A Short History of Mexico*. A concise, handy review, from pre-Conquest to 1960, unusually sympathetic to the church.

TOM MILLER AND CAROL HOFFMAN, *The Baja Book III: Map Guide to Today's Baja California*. The best overall practical guidebook for someone planning to drive the length of Baja California.

Minutiae Mexicana is a series of pocket-sized booklets in English usually available at tourist centers in Mexico and sometimes in the United States. They deal in summary form with everything Mexican from bird lore to witchcraft. Many titles, all carefully prepared.

SYLVANUS G. MORLEY, *The Ancient Maya* (revised by George W. Brainard) (1956). A distinguished Mayanist explores the field for beginners.

WRIGHT MORRIS, *Love Among the Cannibals* (1957). A witty novel about what happens to some jaded Los Angeles show-business types when they move down to the Acapulco of the 1950s to find themselves.

HENRY B. PARKES, *A History of Mexico*. A balanced, straightforward work that has become almost standard for English-language readers in this field.

OCTAVIO PAZ, *The Labyrinth of Solitude* (1962). Sharp, sometimes startling insights into Mexican life and character by a great contemporary writer and philosopher. A Mexican monument.

The *Popul Vuh,* or sacred writings of the Quiché Maya. History, legend, and theology are interwoven. Also known as the *Book of the Tiger Priests,* or the *Book of the Counsel.*

WILLIAM H. PRESCOTT, *History of the Conquest of Mexico*. This masterpiece, first published in 1843, has some faulty and doubtful judgments, yet remains the unsurpassed epic of the Spanish Conquest.

JOHN REED, *Insurgent Mexico* (1914). What a "red" *gringo* firebrand saw, or wanted to see, in the Mexican revolution.

ALAN RIDING, *Distant Neighbors*. A U.S. journalist turns a penetrating eye on the Mexico of yesterday and today.

JUAN RULFO, *Pedro Páramo* (1955). The living and the dead mingle elusively in this fictional masterwork of Mexican literature.

EDWARD SIMMEN, ED., *Gringos in Mexico*. Fifteen U.S. authors, including such unlikely companions as William

Cullen Bryant, Edna Ferber, and Jack Kerouac, rub elbows in this short-story collection.

LESLEY BYRD SIMPSON, *Many Mexicos*. Lively and sometimes trenchant essays on Mexican history, from Cortés through the 1960s. Indispensable.

BRADLEY SMITH, *Mexico: A History in Art*. The story of the country from earliest times as revealed by artists both known and unknown. Fine reproductions make this a lovely way to study history.

REX SMITH, ED., *Biography of the Bulls*. Everything a beginning aficionado needs to know about bullfighting. The concentration is on Spain, but the information also applies to Mexico.

ROBERT SOMERLOTT, *Death of the Fifth Sun*. This fictional autobiography of Malinche, Cortés's mistress and guide, gives a different view of the Aztec world.

JACQUES SOUSTELLE, *Arts of Ancient Mexico*. A short but solid survey lavishly illustrated with black-and-white photographs.

———, *Daily Life of the Aztecs*. A less-than-vivid treatment is saved by accurate, telling details.

JOHN STEINBECK, *The Pearl*. A timeless story about a Baja California fisherman and his covetous neighbors. The village life is sharply revealed.

JOHN STEINBECK AND EDWARD RICKETTS, *The Sea of Cortés*. A leisurely but interesting journey along the coast of Baja California.

MARIA STEN, *The Mexican Codices and Their Extraordinary History*. Fascinating stories and explanations of the "painted books" of the pre-Hispanic epoch. An introduction to ancient American writing.

JOHN L. STEPHENS, *Incidents of Travel in Yucatán*. Stephens and draftsman Frederick Catherwood were explorers in the Maya region. Their work, published in 1843, was dismissed as Marco Millions exaggerations. Time has made fools of the critics.

FRANK TANNENBAUM, *Mexico: The Struggle for Peace and Bread*. The outstanding foreign work about Mexico's continuing revolution.

FRANCES TOOR, *A Treasury of Mexican Folkways*. As packed as a piñata with sayings, customs, songs, superstitions, and other lore, this is the foremost work in its field.

MANUEL TOUSSAINT, *Colonial Art in Mexico* (1949). This pioneering work is the cornerstone of Mexican art history. Architecture, painting, sculpture, and a glance at popular arts.

B. TRAVEN, *The Bridge in the Jungle* (1938). An ironic parable of cultural collisions in the form of a novel.

——, *The Rebellion of the Hanged* (1952). The author wrote six novels of revolt set in Mexico's jungles. This, the fifth, is the most powerful.

JOHN KENNETH TURNER, *Barbarous Mexico*. Early in this century, the author, a muckraking journalist, penetrated slave camps in southern Mexico and exposed the horrors of the Porfirio Díaz dictatorship, causing a furor in the United States. The book remains sensational and gripping.

GEORGE C. VAILLANT, *The Aztecs of Mexico* (1941). An early work in this field, the book remains the most complete and the one most interesting to the general reader.

VICTOR W. VON HAGEN, *The Aztec, Man and Tribe*. A popular historical survey with informative illustrations.

JACK WILLIAMS, *The Magnificent Peninsula: The Only Absolutely Essential Guide to Mexico's Baja California*. Well, maybe not the *only* guide (see the Miller-Hoffman book), but it is practical; with photographs.

ERIC WOLF, *Sons of the Shaking Earth*. The land, people, history, and culture of Mexico and Guatemala.

BERTRAM D. WOLFE, *The Fabulous Life of Diego Rivera*. This biography of the tempestuous genius fully lives up to its title. Crammed with wine, women, and outrage.

AGUSTIN YANEZ, *The Edge of the Storm* (1947). A living, breathing, but fictional creation of a Mexican village. Mexico's first major psychological novel.

—*Robert Somerlott*

MEXICO CITY

By Larry Russell

A resident of Mexico City since 1973, Larry Russell has written numerous articles on travel and music for such Mexican publications as Geografía Universal *and* Caminos del Aire. *He has also, in collaboration with his wife, produced documentary films in and about Mexico City.*

Like wagon-wheel spokes to a hub—an immense hub—all major highways in the Republic of Mexico lead to its capital, Mexico City. Officially known as the Distrito Federal (D.F), the most populous city on the planet is situated in the Valley of Mexico (also called the Valley of Anáhuac) on a site that was chosen in the 14th century by the Aztecs for what would soon become Tenochtitlán, their storied capital. Today the D.F. sprawls over a flat, sun-baked plateau that rises some 2,240 meters (7,350 feet) above sea level and covers nearly 1,000 square kilometers (580 square miles). It is surrounded by three forested mountain chains, which dramatically set the stage for Popocatépetl and Iztaccíhuatl, the two perpetually snow-capped volcanoes that tower over the valley. On a clear day, the panoramic views from the city are breathtaking.

With the climatic effects of its semi-tropical latitude offset by its altitude, Mexico City has a temperate and invigorating climate that can be divided into two seasons: a dry season, which stretches from November to April, and a wet season, which lasts from May to October. (The peak of the dry season, when there are few cleansing

rains, may be the least comfortable time of year here.)
Temperatures average 16° C (60° F) over the course of the
year, and seldom rise above an average of 24° C (75° F) in
the hottest months (June and July) or fall below an
average of 7° C (45° F) during the coolest months (December and January). Nights are always cool, and there's a
marked temperature contrast between sunny and shady
places, as well as between the heat of midday and the
chill of early morning and evening.

According to the latest census figures, fully a quarter of
Mexico's population of 80 million people lives in the D.F.
Whereas the 1930 census counted only a million inhabitants in the entire metropolitan area, and there were less
than five million in 1960, the net growth rate of the
capital's population today is 1,000 residents *daily*. Projections for a decade from now run as high as 26 million
inhabitants.

As a result of this teeming population, the D.F. pulsates
with a vibrant energy that makes it a compelling place to
visit. In countless ways it epitomizes the best of Mexico—
except in the quality of its air. Though Mexico City is
notorious for its pollution, all signs seem to indicate that
this health-threatening problem may be ameliorated. The
seriousness of the situation has inspired determined—if
somewhat belated—action on the part of the people in
power, and the D.F. is where most of the nation's powerful live.

In fact, many of the country's persistent problems are
being addressed with a renewed vigor by a breed of
younger, involved politicians led by 40-year-old Harvard-
educated Carlos Salinas de Gortari, who began his six-
year term (Mexico's president is limited to a single term)
as President of the Republic in December 1988. Under
the Mexican constitution, which grants the President of
the Republic wide-ranging powers to accomplish his
goals, new legislation has been enacted to stem the ecological harm and deterioration in the quality of life that
unchecked pollution has brought to the Valley of Mexico.

For all its people, however, when it comes to crime in
the streets Mexico City is safer than New York, Hong
Kong, São Paulo, or Rome. In fact, according to government statistics, Mexico City has fewer per capita crimes
of violence than any other city in the world with a
population exceeding a million people. Moreover, visitors enjoy a privileged status here, and not only because
Mexicans have a long tradition of hospitality to strangers.

Lately, with the slump in oil prices and the general economy in trouble, tourism has represented one of the few reliable sources of foreign currency and non-polluting employment.

A visit to Mexico City today is like stepping into an enormous melting pot of history and cultures. The blending of these cultures, sadly, was usually forced, and involved much bloodshed. Perhaps the plaque at the Plaza of the Three Cultures in Tlatelolco says it best: "On the 13th of August, 1521, defended by the heroic Cuauhtemoc, Tlatelolco fell under the power of Hernan Cortez. It was neither a triumph nor a defeat, but the painful birth of the mixed race that is the Mexico of today."

One of the legacies of this painful past is the inherent sense of fatalism that seems to lurk within the souls of most Mexicans. In the D.F., this fatalism is nowhere more evident than in the wild and often reckless style of driving that prevails among its residents. (Public-transportation drivers, oddly enough, are usually the worst offenders.) The local saying here is that if you can drive—and survive—in Mexico City you can drive anywhere.

To those who have spent time here, it is not just macho boasting. In fact, as a visitor quickly learns, if you scratch a typical Mexico City native you'll find a soulful anarchist. Little wonder, then, that the city itself seems to mirror this side of the Mexican character, from the colorful, bustling street markets (*tianguis*), where the distinctive sound of the penny whistle signals the arrival of the itinerant knife-sharpener, to busy street corners where groups of traditionally attired Indians perform their native dances. Elsewhere, shabbily dressed street musicians congregate in residential neighborhoods to perform on their dented saxophones, beat-up clarinets, and toy-sized drums while a skinny kid collects the coins that residents rain down on them from their windows; balloon vendors with their fabulous bunches of *globos* defy gravity by staying earth-bound; barrel organists in funky khaki uniforms grind away in front of *cantinas;* bell-clangers lead the garbage trucks on their daily routes as if they were drum majors leading a parade; and Indian women, squatting on the sidewalk, sell handmade tortillas at twice the price of the government-controlled *tortillerias* ("The sweat from the palm of the hands is the secret ingredient," say the connoisseurs).

The almost palpable energy in the air is enhanced by

telling contrasts on every street and around every corner: sleek limousines parked cheek to jowl with unimpressed burros; chic boutiques selling international designer originals as barefoot Indian women hawk handicrafts made the night before on the sidewalk out front; a gourmet dining in an elegant French or Japanese restaurant while, down the street, a gourmand munches on tacos served from a portable grill.

And yet, despite these contrasts, Mexico City is no longer just a great Third World capital. Today it is a cosmopolitan *world* capital, one that need not take a back seat to any of the great metropolises in the quality of its architecture; the diversity of its museums, art galleries, public parks, and zoos; the variety and exuberance of its cultural presentations; the range of its hotels, restaurants, and shopping; and the availability of its public transportation. And, among the great cities of the world, it stands far above the others in one respect: the warmth of its hospitality.

MAJOR INTEREST

Museums
National Museum of Anthropology

Templo Mayor Museum
Rufino Tamayo Museum

Sights
The historic *Zócalo* area
Palacio de Bellas Artes
Central Paseo de la Reforma
The Floating Gardens of Xochimilco
The ruins of Teotihuacán

Neighborhoods
The Zona Rosa for shopping and café life
Polanco for dining and shopping
El Pedregal for spectacular homes
Coyoacán and San Angel

Parks
Chapultepec
Alameda

Ancient Mexico City

"Mexico City has almost always been the largest city in the world," according to Fernando Benitez, octogenarian

Mexican historian and author. "At the height of the Roman empire's glory, Teotihuacán, as Mexico City was then known, was acknowledged to have been more populated and much more splendid than Rome. It was the capital of an empire that stretched from what is today the northern border of Texas beyond the southern boundaries of the country we know as Guatemala."

In the early 14th century the Aztecs, an Indian tribe of mysterious origins from the north, arrived in what they called the Valley of Anáhuac and proceeded to build their capital of Tenochtitlán on an island in the middle of a vast mountain lake, near the site of the once-great city of Teotihuacán. Over the next two centuries they continually expanded Tenochtitlán with landfills, drainage programs, and cleverly constructed causeways. Today the center of that main island lies under the area known as the *Zócalo,* the large public plaza in the heart of Mexico City.

In 1519, when the Spanish, led by Hernán Cortés, invaded Tenochtitlán, they found a city possibly larger and more spectacular than any existing in Europe at the time. Reliable estimates put the population in excess of 300,000, many of whom lived on islands connected to the main island by an intricate series of canals. Eventually, however, the victorious Spanish, in the name of the King of Spain and the Catholic Church, systematically destroyed virtually every visible aspect of Aztec civilization and over the ruins of their great temples and the emperor's palace built their own Cathedral and a palace for Cortés. In fact, most of the foundations of the 16th-century structures here were built with the sturdy building stones taken from toppled Aztec temples. (Only in recent years, with the construction of the underground metro system, have some startling remains of Tenochtitlán been uncovered. See the Templo Mayor section below.)

From the first, the city—which the Spanish named Mexico (after the Aztecs' name for themselves, Mexicas, pronounced "Mesheekas")—functioned as the capital of New Spain. Nevertheless, the city grew slowly in its formative years, and only regained the population levels of Tenochtitlán early in our own century. Physically, however, Mexico City spread ever wider as the great lake, Texcoco, was drained, filled, and built over.

As it turned out, it was not a very practical site for heavy construction, and the old buildings almost immediately began to settle into the soft underbelly of the ancient lake bed—a process that has been continuing for centuries now. Frequent pumping of underground water and periodic flooding since the 16th century have also contributed to the city's "settling"—by some estimates over 23 feet during the last century alone. Experts claim the situation has been stabilized by the use of modern engineering techniques and the installation of an ingenious drainage system that has permanently eliminated flooding. Still, while the new avant-garde skyscrapers that are constantly going up seem to be in fine shape, you'll see many old colonial-era churches and buildings tilting at odd angles, especially throughout the historic downtown area.

The frequent earthquake activity in this region also has done its share of damage to the foundations of many slowly sinking structures. Although hundreds of newer buildings were devastated by the 1985 quake, the skyscrapers weathered the shocks thanks to their high-tech "floating" foundations. Most of the colonial structures were unscathed as well; some even lean less than they did before the quake.

Mexico City Orientation

It may be difficult for the first-time visitor to form a mental image of the city, what with its rambling vastness seemingly devoid of a sensible street plan, with many of its major thoroughfares crisscrossing diagonally, and with cul-de-sacs punctuating every neighborhood. Once you get your bearings, however, it is surprisingly easy to find your way around the areas of interest.

The two main arteries in Mexico City are the 27-km (16-mile) -long Avenida Insurgentes (in-sur-HEN-tays), one of the longest urban thoroughfares in the world, which basically runs north to south; and the 15-km (9-mile) -long Paseo de la Reforma, the 12-lane tree-lined Champs-Elysées of the Americas, which starts out by running parallel to Insurgentes in the northeast, curves and intersects the latter just north of the Zona Rosa, cuts through Chapultepec Park—the city's great public space and the site of the National Museum of Anthropology and other great cultural institutions—and finally turns southwest, where it eventually becomes Federal Highway 15 and continues on to Toluca. The Zócalo, the Zona Rosa, and Chapultepec Park are all within a 10- to 20-minute walk of the intersection of Reforma and Insurgentes, and it's here where you'll find most of the best hotels, restaurants, major foreign embassies, and other visitor attractions clustered. (The Reforma intersection is also where Insurgentes Norte becomes Insurgentes Sur.)

The *Zócalo* more or less serves as the eastern boundary of the area of most interest to visitors, and Chapultepec Park does the same to the west. The northernmost point of interest in the central urban area is the Basilica of Our Lady of Guadalupe (*Basílica de Nuestra Señora de Guadalupe*), which is reached by following Paseo de la Reforma to its beginning at the Tlaltelolco traffic circle (about 6 km/3½ miles from the intersection of Reforma and Insurgentes) and continuing north on Calzada de Guadalupe for two blocks. (The ancient ruins of Teotihuacán lie farther out past Guadalupe.)

Avenida Insurgentes Sur leads to all the major attractions in the southern part of the city, including the Siqueiros Cultural Polyforum; the Plaza México (the bullfight ring); the residential neighborhoods of Coyoacán and San Angel; the avant-garde architecture of the elegant residences in El Pedregal; the archaeological sites of Copilco and Cuicuilco; University City, with its famous murals; Reino Aventura (Mexico's Disneyland); and the floating gardens of Xochimilco. The latter, 25 km (15 miles) south of the intersection of Reforma and Insurgentes, is the southernmost boundary of the area of most interest.

The *Zócalo* is the heart of the old city. Besides the many historical sites, including the Cathedral and the excavations of the central Aztec temple complex, the surrounding area is home to the financial district. Colonial in feel and appearance, the narrow cobblestone streets are jammed with all types of shops. It is a bit seedy, perhaps, but picturesque nevertheless, and always churning with vitality. The *Zócalo* itself is off limits to vehicular traffic, and there are pedestrian malls scattered throughout the area, making it ideal for strolling and window-shopping. One of the ancient streets leading west from the *Zócalo* is Calle Madero. Only a few blocks long, it changes its name as it crosses Avenida Lázaro Cárdenas and becomes Avenida Juárez. At this point the preponderance of 17th-century colonial architecture merges with a dash of the Art Nouveau and other more contemporary styles. The elegant Bellas Artes (Palace of Fine Arts) is on the right, and to the left, towering above the hustle and bustle, is the Latin American Tower (*Torre Latinoamericano*), a modern 44-story skyscraper with an observation deck on the 42nd floor.

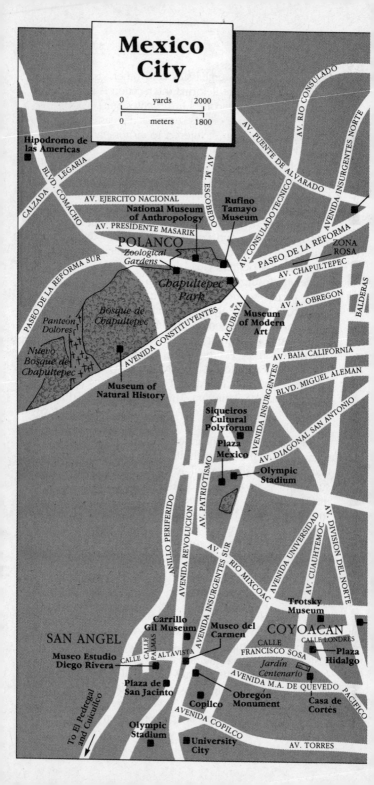

Mexico
City

| 0 | yards | 2000 |
| 0 | meters | 1800 |

Hipodromo de
las Americas

BLVD. LEGARIA

CALZADA COMACHO

AV. RIO CONSULADO

AV. PUENTE DE ALVARADO

AV. M. ESCOBEDO

AVENIDA INSURGENTES NORTE

AV. EJERCITO NACIONAL

National Museum
of Anthropology

Rufino
Tamayo
Museum

AV. PRESIDENTE MASARIK

AV. CONSULADO TECNICO

POLANCO

PASEO DE LA REFORMA

ZONA
ROSA

Zoological
Gardens

AV. CHAPULTEPEC

PASEO DE LA REFORMA SUR

Chapultepec
Park

AV. A. OBREGON

Bosque de
Chapultepec

TACUBAYA

Museum
of Modern
Art

BALDERAS

Panteon
Dolores

AVENIDA CONSTITUYENTES

AV. BAJA CALIFORNIA

Nuevo
Bosque de
Chapultepec

AVENIDA INSURGENTES

BLVD. MIGUEL ALEMAN

Museum of
Natural History

Siqueiros
Cultural
Polyforum

AV. DIAGONAL SAN ANTONIO

Plaza
Mexico

AV. DIAGONAL SAN ANTONIO

ANILLO PERIFERIDO

AV. PATRIOTISMO

Olympic
Stadium

AVENIDA REVOLUCION

AV. INSURGENTES SUR

RIO MIXCOAC

AVENIDA UNIVERSIDAD

AV. CUAUHTEMOC

AV. DIVISION DEL NORTE

Trotsky
Museum

Carrillo
Gil Museum

Museo del
Carmen

COYOACAN

SAN ANGEL

CALLE PALMAS

ALTAVISTA

CALLE
FRANCISCO SOSA

CALLE LONDRES

Plaza
Hidalgo

Museo Estudio
Diego Rivera

CALLE

Jardín
Centenario

Plaza de
San Jacinto

Obregón
Monument

AVENIDA M.A. DE QUEVEDO

Casa de
Cortes

PACIFICO

Copilco

AVENIDA COPILCO

To El Pedregal
and Cuicuilco

Olympic
Stadium

University
City

AV. TORRES

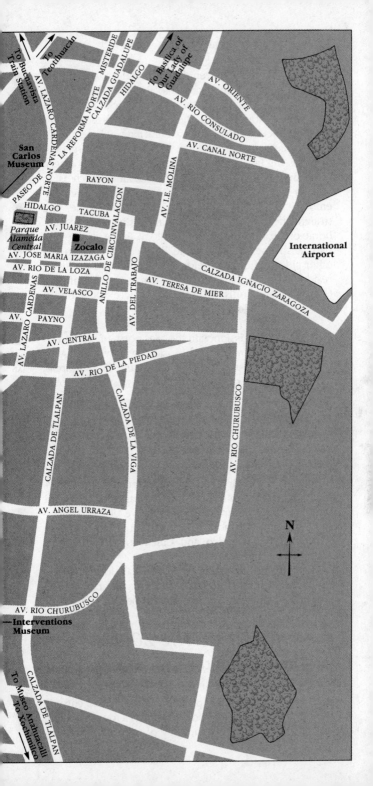

Continuing west on Avenida Juárez you'll pass beautiful Alameda Park and then come to Paseo de la Reforma. Avenida Juárez continues for another block and ends at the massive Monument to the Revolution in the Plaza of the Republic, but if you follow Reforma southwest you'll soon come to its intersection with Avenida Insurgentes. After passing Insurgentes, Reforma becomes the northern boundary of the Zona Rosa (Pink Zone), which is to Mexico City what Mayfair is to London. The American embassy is on the right at the next traffic circle, and straight ahead will be the beginning of Chapultepec Park, home of the Museum of Anthropology. To the north of the park is the newly fashionable Polanco district. On the other side of the park, Reforma leads into the exclusive residential district known as Las Lomas de Chapultepec (*lomas* means "hills" in Spanish), where you'll find a number of excellent restaurants.

We start our discussion with the area north of the *Zócalo* and then move toward the historic downtown area. After discussing the historic *Zócalo* and Alameda Park areas, we follow Paseo de la Reforma southwest to the Zona Rosa and then Chapultepec Park (and, to its north, the Polanco district).

After that we discuss the attractions along Insurgentes Sur—the Siqueiros Cultural Polyforum, then the Plaza México bullfight ring and the Coyoacán and San Angel districts—each a neighborhood in its own right, and interesting for their archaeological and historical sites, their many small museums, and the variety of crafts for sale. Finally, a bit farther south still, we discuss University City, with its famous O'Gorman mural, the archaeological sites of Copilco and Cuicuilco, and the canal district of Xochimilco.

The great pre-Aztec site of Teotihuacán, located northeast of the central city, is discussed in a separate section after the coverage for Mexico City proper.

NORTH OF THE ZOCALO
The Plaza of the Three Cultures

Site of the ancient city of Tlatelolco, 2½ km (1½ miles) north of the *Zócalo,* the plaza is, physically and chronologically, a good starting point for a day's tour that might include the Basilica of Our Lady of Guadalupe, 2½ km

(1½ miles) farther north of the plaza, and end back in and around the *Zócalo* itself.

The Plaza of the Three Cultures (which was inaugurated as such in 1964) is located at the northern end of Paseo de la Reforma (called Reforma Norte at this point). Examples of pre-Hispanic, colonial, and modern architecture are represented here by, respectively, Aztec ruins, the Church of Saint James Tlatelolco, and the sleek marble skyscraper housing the Foreign Ministry.

Tlatelolco, as the area was called in pre-Hispanic times and is still known today, was once an island in what was an immense, swampy lake, and was already inhabited when the Aztecs arrived in 1325. In fact, it was the most important commercial and market center in the Valley of Anáhuac, and the Aztecs, albeit begrudgingly, were its best customers. (It wasn't until 1473 that its Chichimec inhabitants, as the Aztecs called them, were forcefully annexed into the Aztec empire.) By the time the Spanish arrived in 1519, much of the lake between Tlatelolco and Tenochtitlán had been filled and built over, and it was here that Cortés and his troops came to marvel at the size and order of the native market. (It was also here that the last Aztec emperor, Cuauhtémoc, made his final stand against the Spanish.)

Today you can see part of what was once a pre-Hispanic ceremonial center as well as the remains of a palace, the walls of which were built of basalt and *tezontle,* the reddish-colored volcanic stone that is so characteristic of the native architecture of the period. There are, in addition, two smaller Aztec structures, one of them a square *tzompantli,* or "wall of skulls," near which thousands of human skulls were discovered, each with holes bored through the temples, presumably the result of having been displayed side by side on poles mounted around the sides of the building.

The **Church of Saint James Tlatelolco,** with a plain façade typical of the fortress-like churches of the early 17th century, was built in 1609 out of materials taken from an old Aztec pyramid. On the pendentives of the cross vault inside there's an interesting Indian carving of the four evangelists. The church, along with the Colegio de la Santa Cruz, which was founded in 1535 by Franciscan missionaries to teach the sons of the Aztec nobility Spanish, Latin, and Christianity, became a center for the study of native culture; it was here, in fact, that Fray Bernardino de Sahagún wrote his famous work on the history, beliefs, and religions of pre-Hispanic Mexico, *A History of Ancient Mexico (Historia General de las cosas de New España)*.

You can get to the Plaza of the Three Cultures on the metro (the number 3 line, "Tlatelolco" station stop). Or you can take the Indios Verdes bus north anywhere along Avenida Insurgentes and get off at the "Monumento a la Raza" stop, then walk two blocks east. By car, take Reforma Norte to the third traffic circle north of Alameda Park (which is where Reforma Norte ends).

The Basilica of Our Lady of Guadalupe

The Basilica of Guadalupe, located north of the Plaza of Three Cultures on Calzada de Guadalupe, the continuation of Reforma, is considered to be the holiest Christian shrine in all of Mexico, and it was here that Pope John Paul II appeared before hundreds of thousands of devout Catholics on his 1979 visit to the country. (It was also here, in the original church, that the Treaty of Guadalupe-Hidalgo, ending the Mexican War, was signed in 1848; under the terms of the pact, Mexico ceded all or parts of New Mexico, Colorado, Utah, Arizona, Nevada, and California to the United States—reducing her territory by over 50 percent while, at the same time, enlarging that of her northern neighbor by over 25 percent.)

According to legend, Juan Diego, one of the few Aztecs to convert to the Christian faith, was on his way to Mass one cold December morning in 1531, crossing the hill known as Tepeyac, when a vision of the Virgin Mary appeared before him and requested that a church in her honor be built on the spot. When the shaken Diego related this miraculous encounter to the bishop, Juan de Zumarraga, the skeptical bishop asked Diego to show him proof. Three days later the Virgin appeared again, instructing Diego to gather roses, which she then caused to bloom in the frozen ground before him and take them to the bishop. Shocked at finding roses blooming in winter, Diego bundled them under his cloak and hurried before Zumarraga, where he let the roses tumble to his feet. To the astonishment of both men, stamped upon the peasant Diego's cloak was an image of the Virgin. Needing no further proof, the bishop ordered the church built.

The miracle surrounding the construction of the church

was especially significant, in retrospect, for it marked the turning point in the Spanish missionaries' attempts to convert their new subjects to Catholicism. And, as it happened, the apparition occurred on the exact spot where the Aztecs' temple to Tonantzin, their earth goddess, had stood before it was destroyed by the Spanish.

The original church was completed in 1533 and subsequently enlarged several times to accommodate the thousands of pilgrims who came in a never-ending stream to worship at the site of the miracle. By 1970, however, the shrine had shrunk so far into the area's spongy subsoil, and had tilted so perilously as a result, that it was declared a safety hazard and closed to the public. In 1976 an ultra-modern basilica designed by the great Mexican architect Pedro Ramírez Vázquez (whose achievements include the National Museum of Anthropology in Chapultepec Park) was consecrated. (The original structure was eventually shored up and is again open to the public as a museum of religious artifacts.)

The interior of the new basilica is stark and massive. When its huge doors are opened, as many as 40,000 worshippers can participate in the Mass, including those jammed into its immense outside plaza. The shrine boasts no paintings, no statues, no cupolas, and just one relic: the miraculous cloak. (No satisfactory explanation has ever been given as to why the cloak itself has not long since deteriorated.) An underpass near the altar allows visitors to view the revered image without disrupting services; moving walkways prevent anyone from lingering too long.

Outside, the plaza is a constantly changing stage for a steady stream of humanity—worshippers, priests, vendors selling religious paraphernalia, and tourists. Many pilgrims cover the last mile or so of their journey on their knees—which often end up bruised and bloodied—as an act of penance. In addition, the annual anniversary of the second apparition, December 12, which draws tens of thousands of worshippers to the shrine, is a national holiday.

At the end of the plaza and to the right is a winding walkway that leads up the hill to a few tiny chapels. One of the more charming is the exuberant, Baroque-style **Capilla del Pocito**, inside of which is a well said to have first bubbled up during one of Juan Diego's apparitions. Built in the 18th century, the chapel is actually two chapels, the larger one distinguished by its blue-and-white tiled domes and its paintings of the Virgin by Miguel Cabrera.

At the top of the hill is the **Capilla de las Rosas**, a chapel built to commemorate the place where Diego gathered his miraculous roses. The chapel's interior boasts a mural by Fernando Leal that depicts the legend of the miracle.

From the basilica, you can take a taxi south to the historic Plaza de Santo Domingo, which is a five-minute walk north of the *Zócalo,* or, for music, to Garibaldi Square (which is at its best in the evening), a little to the northwest of the Plaza de Santo Domingo. (Teotihuacán, northeast of the basilica, is covered in a separate section at the end of the main Mexico City section.) First, though, Garibaldi Square.

Plaza Garibaldi

This large public square, surrounded by *cantinas,* restaurants, nightclubs, and food stalls, is the musical heart of the capital and a must to visit—at least briefly. It is located on Avenida Lázaro Cárdenas a couple of blocks south of the San Martín intersection heading toward the *Zócalo* on Reforma. You'll know you're getting close when you see dozens of mariachis gathered on the street, all of them ready to offer their musical services for a fee. (For better or worse, it's hard to tell the different mariachi bands apart: each player wears black silver-studded skin-tight pants and a short brocaded jacket along with his embroidered wide-brimmed sombrero. On cool evenings they add a serape to the costume, each with its own unique woven design and color scheme. Up close, however, there is a touch of seediness to the mariachis—as there is to the neighborhood in general. Also, watch out for pickpockets.)

In the plaza itself, the cacophonous sounds of trumpets, violins, guitars, and vocalists fill the air. Dozens of bands, playing different tunes in different keys simultaneously, compete with one another for the attention of would-be customers, and it is quite natural for local businessmen, relaxing after office hours with friends and a few tequilas, to hire a band to accompany them while they sing along.

Mariachis are always eager to provide some soulful music announcing one's desire, be it there on the spot or, better yet, under the balcony of the object of one's affection, wherever she may reside. Once a fee is agreed upon (and it is generally not inexpensive) the entire group will pile into a taxi, with the guitarron (a large, pregnant-looking guitar that fills the role of the bass) usually propped on the roof and held by an arm extended from an open window. Then, resembling nothing so much as the Keystone Kops, the mariachis will follow your car to the agreed-upon destination. (No matter the hour, neighbors never complain. While the sound of three trumpets, three guitars, two violins, and a choir of voices under your window is bound to get your attention, in Mexico it's exceedingly bad form to protest having your slumber interrupted. In fact, a ban on midnight serenades was imposed by a mayor of the D.F. some 30 years ago. His successor lifted the ban, as his first official act in office, to overwhelming public acclaim.)

Of course, an hour later they'll be back on the plaza ready for more good-natured competing with the other mariachis assembled there. In fact, even at the height of the tourist season there are usually a dozen musicians for every visitor, so it is a buyers' market. Don't hesitate to bargain during negotiations; it's expected.

Of the four nightclubs around the plaza, **Tenampa** is the most authentic and least exploitative. The energy level inside this huge and sleazy one-room establishment is always high, and three circulating quartets offer serenades. Fortunately, the service is swift and bouncers are placed strategically inside and out to discourage undesirables, so don't worry about giving it a try.

That same intensity of energy prevails throughout the rows of taco, *torta,* and tamale stands jammed together on each side of a narrow paved corridor north of the plaza. Delicate digestive tracts will best be served, however, by limiting the experience to looking and savoring the smells.

Diagonally across the avenue from the plaza is the famous old **Teatro Blanquita**, where top Mexican entertainment is presented nightly. Singers and musical groups, who normally would command fees five times what they earn at the Blanquita, keep in touch with the grass-roots segment of their public by appearing here between engagements at the more expensive nightclubs in the D. F. and provinces. The government-controlled admission charge makes a night at the Blanquita one of the capital's great bargains. (Many people choose to attend the 7:30 P.M. performance at the Teatro and then visit the plaza afterward.)

The Plaza de Santo Domingo
to the Zócalo

Legend has it that the Plaza de Santo Domingo was the spot where, in 1325, the Aztecs saw an eagle perched on a nopal cactus with a snake in its beak. According to Aztec prophecy, just such a sight—the central image on the modern Mexican flag—was supposed to mark the place where these nomadic warrior people were to settle down and build a great city. And so Tenochtitlán was born.

Located southeast of Garibaldi Square between Avenidas República de Brasil, Belizario Domínguez, and República de Cuba, this beautiful old colonial square is steeped in history. In fact, most of the materials used in the construction of its old buildings were thought to have been taken from the remains of the Emperor Cuauhtémoc's two palaces, which stood in the middle of what is now the plaza until the Spanish under Cortés demolished them in 1521. It was, in addition, the site of the first Dominican monastery in the Americas, built in 1539. And today, in the fountain in the center of the square, there is an attractive statue of Doña Josefa Ortíz de Domínguez, better known as La Corregidora, the most famous heroine in Mexican history (see the Querétaro section of the Colonial Mexico chapter for a more complete description of her role in the Mexican struggle for independence).

The square itself is bounded on the north by the Church of Santo Domingo, on the east by the Casa Chata (the former courthouse of the Inquisition) and the Casa Aduana (Customs House), on the south by a number of colonial-era homes, and on the west by the famous arcade known as **Los Portales de los Evangelistas**, where public scribes set up their tiny portable desks and chairs and, for a fee, pound out anything from legal forms and students' theses to love letters on their ancient typewriters, thereby carrying on a centuries-old tradition. (Seventeenth-century missionaries were the first scribes here, and hoped by offering their services to win the confidence—if not the conversion—of the local populace.) Flanking them on the sidewalk are half a dozen antique printing presses churning out posters, business cards, wedding invitations, and what not, all offering same-day service at very reasonable prices.

The Baroque-style Church of Santo Domingo was originally a Dominican convent, built between 1716 and 1736.

The nearby Customs House boasts *Patricians and Patricides,* a mural by David Alfaro Siqueiros that's well worth a look.

Walk one block east on Avenida González Obregón (a continuation of República de Cuba) until you come to Avenida República de Argentina, then turn north. At number 28, on the left side of the street, is the impressive **Ministry of Public Education** building.

Following the Mexican Revolution, poet-philosopher José Vasconcelos, the newly appointed Minister of Public Education, was directly responsible for commissioning a number of native-born artists and encouraging them to make their creative statements on the walls of government buildings in order to promote the development of Mexican cultural values and pride. In the process, a powerful Mexican artistic tradition was born.

To his later credit, Vasconcelos turned over most of the wall space at the Ministry of Public Education to a young artist by the name of Diego Rivera, who himself was just back from years of study in Paris, and who proceeded to paint some of his most important early works here. The results are striking. All the murals in the ministry—with the exception of one or two each by Montenegro, Charlot, O'Gorman, Mérida, de la Cueva, and Amero—are by Rivera, and, taken as a whole, create an epic visual poem of Mexican life, from pre-Hispanic times to the future— or, at least, Rivera's vision of the future. The emphasis of the 235 separate panels is, as would become the artist's trademark, on social struggle, and together they reveal an extraordinarily talented young artist who had not yet succumbed to the bitterness and cynicism that would color his later work.

As you leave the Ministry of Public Education turn right and head back to Avenida González Obregón, and then left (east) at the corner, where its name changes to San Ildefonso. Closed to traffic, the street is part of the old university area and is dominated by the block-long 18th-century former Jesuit seminary that once housed the **National Preparatory School**. Now part of the National University, it is still known by its earlier name.

To enter this beautiful building go south on Calle Carmen for one block, then take a right on Calle Justo Sierra and look for number 16 in the middle of the block. Restored in 1982, the ancient *tezontle* façade frames an elegant entrance that leads to the cradle of the modern Mexican mural (*muralismo*) movement: Minister Vascon-

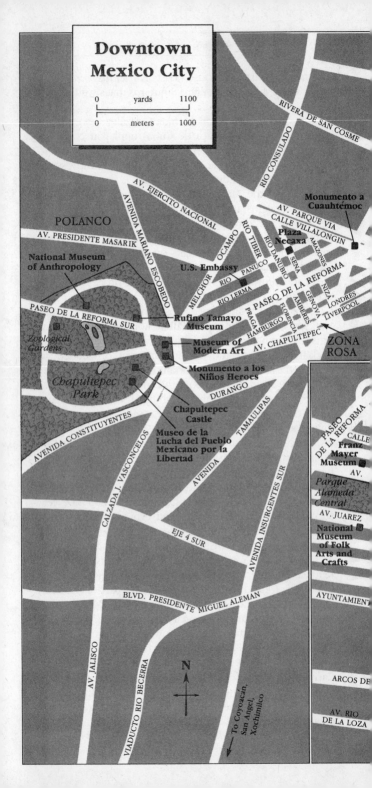

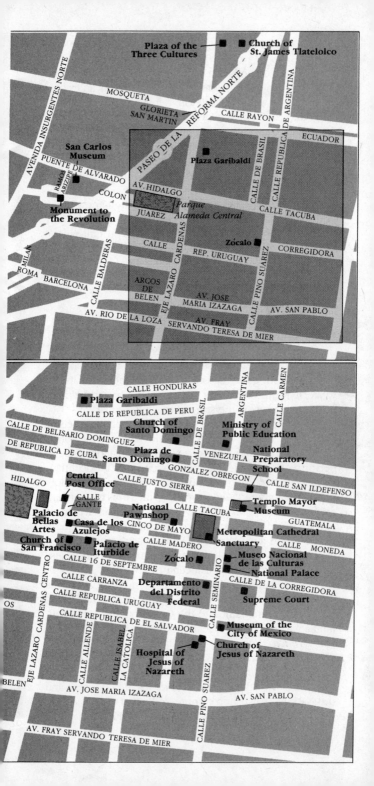

Top map:

Plaza of the Three Cultures

Church of St. James Tlatelolco

AVENIDA INSURGENTES NORTE

MOSQUETA

GLORIETA SAN MARTIN

PASEO DE LA REFORMA NORTE

CALLE RAYON

REPUBLICA DE ARGENTINA

ECUADOR

San Carlos Museum

PUENTE DE ALVARADO

RAMOS ARIZPE

COLON

Monument to the Revolution

JUAREZ

AV. HIDALGO

Plaza Garibaldi

Parque Alameda Central

CALLE DE BRASIL

CALLE REPUBLICA DE ARGENTINA

CALLE TACUBA

Zócalo

CORREGIDORA

MILAN

ROMA

BARCELONA

CALLE BALDERAS

CALLE

REP. URUGUAY

CALLE PINO SUAREZ

ARCOS DE BELEN

EJE LAZARO CARDENAS

AV. JOSE MARIA IZAZAGA

AV. SAN PABLO

AV. RIO DE LA LOZA

AV. FRAY SERVANDO TERESA DE MIER

Bottom map:

CALLE HONDURAS

Plaza Garibaldi

CALLE DE REPUBLICA DE PERU

CALLE DE BELISARIO DOMINGUEZ

Church of Santo Domingo

ARGENTINA

CALLE CARMEN

Ministry of Public Education

DE REPUBLICA DE CUBA

Plaza de Santo Domingo

CALLE DE BRASIL

VENEZUELA

National Preparatory School

HIDALGO

Central Post Office

CALLE JUSTO SIERRA

GONZALEZ OBREGON

CALLE SAN ILDEFONSO

CALLE GANTE

National Pawnshop

CALLE TACUBA

Templo Mayor Museum

Palacio de Bellas Artes

Casa de los Azulejos

CINCO DE MAYO

GUATEMALA

Metropolitan Cathedral

Church of San Francisco

Palacio de Iturbide

CALLE MADERO

Sanctuary

CALLE MONEDA

Zócalo

Museo Nacional de las Culturas

CALLE 16 DE SEPTIEMBRE

CALLE SEMINARIO

National Palace

CALLE CARRANZA

CALLE DE LA CORREGIDORA

CALLE REPUBLICA URUGUAY

Departamento del Distrito Federal

Supreme Court

EJE LAZARO CARDENAS CENTRO

CALLE REPUBLICA DE EL SALVADOR

CALLE ALLENDE

CALLE ISABEL LA CATOLICA

Museum of the City of Mexico

OS

Hospital of Jesus of Nazareth

Church of Jesus of Nazareth

BELEN

AV. JOSE MARIA IZAZAGA

CALLE PINO SUAREZ

AV. SAN PABLO

AV. FRAY SERVANDO TERESA DE MIER

celos's initial commission was given to Ramón Alva de la Canal, who, in 1921, painted the first true Mexican fresco on one of its walls. In addition, between 1923 and 1926 the great José Clemente Orozco painted some of his best early murals here. But the building's most notable work was created over the stage in the auditorium by Rivera. Painted in 1921 and titled *La Creacion,* the work, Rivera's first mural, is hardly recognizable as his by those acquainted only with his later murals, in which he developed his distinctive style of caricaturing well-known historical figures as either villains, victims, or heroes.

When you're ready to leave, turn west on Calle Justo Sierra and take the next left on Calle Seminario. A short walk south is the *Zócalo.*

EL ZOCALO

Although no longer the geographical center of Mexico City (the growth of the D.F. has been steadily to the west and south), the *Zócalo* site was and still is the capital's heart—and for good reason. Perhaps nowhere else in the Western Hemisphere has so much history and drama been enacted as on the stage of this huge square.

On the spot where the great Metropolitan Cathedral now dominates the *Zócalo,* majestic Aztec temples once stood, upon the high altars of which human sacrifices were performed wholesale. After the surrender of Tenochtitlán, Cortés ordered the pyramids razed and the Aztec idols broken into chunks. On a portion of the ruins he then had the foundation for a cathedral laid. The huge plaza in front of the Cathedral—today the second largest public square in the world after Moscow's Red Square—was modeled after Madrid's central plaza, and has remained more or less the same for four and a half centuries.

As it has been throughout its existence, the *Zócalo* is Mexico City's political and religious center. It is surrounded by, in addition to the Cathedral, the Metropolitan Sanctuary (*Sagrario Metropolitano*); the National Palace (*Palacio Nacional*); the Supreme Court (*Suprema Corte de Justicia*); the city government offices (*Departmento del Distrito Federal,* or DDF); the entrance to the Merchants' Arcade (*Los Portales de los Mercadores*); and the National Pawnshop (*Monte de Piedad*). The fascinating Templo Mayor and its adjoining museum, the site of recently uncovered Aztec ruins, are located a block north and east of the *Zócalo* behind the Cathedral.

While *Plaza de la Constitución* is the square's official name, everyone simply calls it the "*Zócalo*." (*Zócalo* is the Spanish word for a pedestal. In 1843 the government commissioned a monument to Mexico's independence here, and a *zócalo* was subsequently constructed in the middle of the great square. For various reasons, however, the project never materialized, and the pedestal was finally removed in the waning years of the 19th century—but by then the nickname had stuck. Today, every main square in every provincial Mexican town is also called the "*zócalo*," in imitation of the capital's grand public space.) Unemployed tradesmen congregate daily along three sides of the Cathedral looking for work. Each displays a hand-lettered sign stating his specialty. There are usually also a few groups of strolling native performers or costumed families dancing in circles, playing wooden flutes, and shaking their ankle castanets while the youngest member of the troupe passes the hat—except that it's more likely to be a feathered receptacle.

Every evening at 6:00 you can watch the presidential guards march out of the National Palace and ceremoniously lower the national flag from its gigantic flagpole in the center of the square. An especially fine vantage point for viewing the passing scene is the seventh-story rooftop restaurant of the **Hotel Majestic**, the entrance of which is located at the corner of Madero and the square.

The Cathedral

Tilting this way and that after centuries of settling into the soft subsoil of the *Zócalo,* the Baroque-style Cathedral—the largest ecclesiastical structure in Latin America—symbolizes as much as any single building in Mexico the brutal suppression of native culture by Cortés and his conquistadors. In fact, the building of the original structure, which was begun in 1525, was carried out by Aztec survivors of the Conquest under Spanish supervision, with many of the original foundation stones being blocks of *tezontle*—the reddish volcanic rock known to the Indians as the "stone of blood"—that had been salvaged from their ruined temples. (It wasn't mere coincidence that the site chosen for the Cathedral lay directly on top of leveled foundations of the demolished temple bases.)

Political strife and fire halted construction of the Cathedral often over the years, and it wasn't until 1813 that it was finally completed. As a result, generations of architects and artisans contributed to the final product. And yet, despite the combination of Baroque, Doric, Ionian, Corinthian, Renaissance, and Neoclassic elements, the exterior of the Cathedral is a remarkably harmonious synthesis of these different styles and impulses. In addition (and as was so often the case with many early colonial-era structures), the indigenous artisans' contributions here resulted in a style—a sort of "Indian Baroque"—that was, and remains, unique to Mexico. Today, it is most brilliantly evident in the the smaller chapel attached to the Cathedral, the **Metropolitan Sanctuary**, a Churrigueresque creation of the Spanish architect Lorenzo Rodriguez that was built between 1749 and 1758.

The interior of the Cathedral, on the other hand, is so dark and gloomy that it actually comes as a relief to visit the basement crypts, which are interesting for the 16th-century Gothic ribbing around their vaults (they weren't completed until 1623). This is where you'll find the remains of most of the archbishops of Mexico City, including those of Juan de Zumarraga, the first prelate of New Spain (and the man responsible for ordering the first shrine built in Guadalupe's honor).

The Cathedral and its adjoining chapel are illuminated at night on national holidays, creating truly startling shadow-and-light effects. On these occasions, the Mexican flag flies from its façade and, despite the ostensible separation of church and state—priests and nuns, for example, are prohibited by law from appearing in public in their religious attire—the ardently nationalistic church-goers of the D.F. join in the noisy celebration. The Cathedral itself, like all religious buildings in Mexico, is owned by the government.

The Templo Mayor and the Templo Mayor Museum

The Templo Mayor, or Great Temple, once the ceremonial heart of the Aztec capital of Tenochtitlán, is located directly north and east of the Cathedral. It was here that the Aztecs erected a 150-foot-high pyramid in honor of Huitzilopochtli, their bloodthirsty god of war, at the summit of which countless human sacrifices were offered up.

Prisoners-of-war were the usual victims, but if a military campaign failed to produce a sufficient number, slaves would then be purchased from Aztec slave-owners to fill the priests' quotas. Convinced that the sun would not rise and the world would end if the menacing god's appetite was not satisfied, their scribes recorded sacrificial statistics that, even by today's jaded standards, were mind-boggling. In fact, Bernal Díaz recorded a conversation between Móctezuma II and Cortés on the latter's first visit to Tenochtitlán (at which point the Spaniards were still being treated as honored guests) in which the Aztec emperor boasted that on one occasion they had had to feed Huitzilopochtli 20,000 human hearts before they managed to appease him.

Little wonder then that the Spanish, despite their own deviousness and greed, had no trouble recruiting other Indian tribes as their allies. With this native help, Tenochtitlán, the chief stronghold of the Aztec empire, was forced to surrender in 1521, and the victorious Spanish quickly went to work razing the magnificent architectural accomplishments of their Aztec enemies, including the Templo Mayor. (The temple proper actually consisted of two smaller temples set on a gigantic pyramidal base; the second temple was dedicated to Tlaloc, the god of rain. Both temples are believed to have been taller than the bell tower of the present-day Cathedral next door.)

Over the following centuries the rubble from the ruined Aztec city sank deeper and deeper into the subsoil under and around the *Zócalo*. Then, on August 13, 1790, 269 years to the day after the final defeat of the Aztec empire, a construction crew working on a restoration project at the Cathedral unearthed the famous **Aztec calendar stone**, a 24-ton marvel of pre-Hispanic astronomy that is now proudly displayed at the National Museum of Anthropology in Chapultepec Park.

In 1900, and again in 1913, other Aztec artifacts were unearthed in other excavations. But this door to the Aztec past wasn't completely opened until February 1978, when workmen from the city's light and power company, digging just six feet below ground level, uncovered the massive stone disk—10 feet in diameter and weighing eight tons—of Coyolxauqui, the Aztec moon goddess.

With this discovery, experts were forced to agree that, contrary to the long-held belief that the Templo Mayor was buried forever under the nearby Cathedral, the actual site of the central temple complex had indeed been

found. The light and power company's project was immediately halted and excited archaeologists took over. After
five years of careful excavation work all four sides of the
Templo Mayor were exposed; several other temples were
also uncovered, along with thousands of statues and relics, some in a remarkable state of preservation—though
many of the artifacts (some of them 600 years old) had to
be given immediate "first aid" to prevent them from
crumbling into dust upon contact with the air.

The quantity and quality of the finds unearthed at the
Templo Mayor site far surpass anything previously found
from this period of Mesoamerican history, and new discoveries are still being made almost daily. The whole site
will probably never be explored completely, however;
the massive Cathedral itself is adjacent to what archaeologists speculate could be some of the most impressive
discoveries, but the Cathedral site, though promising, is,
and will remain, off limits. The uncovered ruins of the
Templo Mayor are located at Calle Seminario 8, an outdoor museum complex that is far more extensive than
any archaeologist had originally dared to dream. Look, in
particular, in the stage 2 area, for the *piedra de sacrificios*
(sacrificial stone); the nearby chac-mool, to date the oldest piece discovered at the site, reclines calmly with its
receptacle for human hearts held snugly against its belly.
Also included within the uncovered ruins area is a recently constructed scale model of the original ceremonial
center, complete with a network of canals.

Adjacent to the eastern boundary of the excavated area
is the **Templo Mayor Museum**, which opened in October
1987. Objects of all sizes and every description are displayed here, including life-sized ceramic figures that are
known as the Eagle Warriors; giant stone serpent heads;
obsidian knives (which were used by Aztec priests to
remove the still-beating hearts from their sacrificial victims); sacrificial altars; and, the pièce de résistance, the
stone disk of the moon goddess Coyolxauqui, the discovery of which is responsible for this extraordinary exhibition. (There's also a wooden club on display about the
length of a standard-sized baseball bat, with a doughnut
of black obsidian blades ringing its thicker end. A strong
man swinging this weapon, according to one Spanish
scribe, could decapitate a horse.)

The museum is open daily with the exception of Monday; English-language tours can be arranged in advance.

Tel: 542-1717 between 9:00 A.M. and 10:00 P.M. to make reservations.

Also on the Zócalo

One block south and another block east of the Templo Mayor site, at Calle Moneda 13, the **National Museum of the Cultures** now occupies an 18th-century structure that originally housed the National Mint and then, much later, became the home of the National Museum of Anthropology. When the latter moved to its present location in Chapultepec Park in 1964, the National Museum of the Cultures was established in its place. Its building painstakingly restored to its former colonial glory, the museum boasts a variety of ethnographic displays from all over the world, including traditional ceramics, artwork, crafts, costumes, and tools. A Rufino Tamayo fresco graces the entrance to the museum.

The dominant structure on the *Zócalo,* however, is the **National Palace**, the elegant façade of which, handsomely set off by the wrought-iron railings of its many balconies, is made of gray sandstone and rose-colored *tezontle* and stretches nearly the length of the eastern side of the huge plaza. In addition to being a magnificent architectural creation, the Palace is the official residence of the executive power of the government, and the President of the Republic makes his most important pronouncements from its center balcony.

The first structure to occupy the site was the palace of Móctezuma II, who reputedly had an elaborate aviary installed as the centerpiece of a huge garden that took up the entire inner courtyard. After the Conquest, Cortés had Móctezuma's palace destroyed and, as reward for a job well done, was given the deed to the land by the King of Spain. He then had a new palace built from the rubble of the old, which, upon its completion, became the seat as well as the symbol of the Spanish Crown's power in New Spain.

Cortés himself lived in, as well as governed from, the Palace. In 1529, upon his return from a journey to what is now Honduras, his friends staged a bullfight in the patio (which more or less coincided with the dimensions and location of Móctezuma's splendid patio)—the first bullfight to be held in the Americas. In 1562, years after Cortés had sold the deed back to the Crown, the Palace became the official residence of the viceroys who ruled New Spain—a function it served until 1810, when Mexico declared its independence from Spain. After independence was finally achieved in 1821—and with the exception of Agustín de Iturbide and Maximilian's brief reigns as emperor—the Palace became the official residence of the Presidents of the Republic until 1884, when Porfirio Díaz moved the official residence to Chapultepec Castle. Although a number of renovations have altered the interior of the Palace considerably over the years, and a third story was added in 1927, it continues to serve as the working headquarters of the executive branch; the Chamber of Deputies is located on the second floor, along with the office of the president.

Access to the main patio is through the Palace's massive entrance, high above which hangs the famous church bell struck by Father Miguel Hidalgo in his hometown of Dolores to proclaim Mexico's independence in 1810. The patio itself is surrounded by ornate arches; to the left is an elegant staircase that leads up and past the memorable Diego Rivera mural depicting his vision of the class struggle. Rivera often linked contemporary events with incidents and episodes from different eras in Mexican history. Easily recognizable in this particular work are such leading figures of 20th-century capitalism as J. P. Morgan, John D. Rockefeller, and Cornelius Vanderbilt—all menacingly portrayed. Not surprisingly, given Rivera's political inclinations, the heroically drawn figure of Karl Marx stands out among the "villainous" capitalists. The mural on the northern wall of the patio, also by Rivera, depicts Mexico's history from pre-Hispanic days through the Revolution.

Of the two museums inside the Palace, the one of most interest is the Museo Recinto de Benito Juárez, which is located on the first floor and contains memorabilia belonging to the great man, who died on the premises in 1872 while serving his second term as president. Included in the exhibits is the correspondence between Juárez and Abraham Lincoln, with whom he is often compared; the entrance is through the door on the northern side of the Palace.

At the southern perimeter of the *Zócalo,* opposite the Cathedral, are the offices of the city government, the **Departmento del Distrito Federal**, including the office of the mayor of the D.F. Built in 1532, the structure was originally a town hall, and served over the years as a grain exchange, a city jail, and the national mint. Part of the building was destroyed in a civil uprising in 1692 and rebuilt between 1720 and 1724. The third and top floors were added much later. The indigenously flavored Churrigueresque façade features a number of ornately carved coats of arms and a watchtower at each corner.

The **Merchants' Arcade**, located on the west side of the *Zócalo*, still boasts its old pillars, but no longer has the stalls where merchants once sold their wares. Built in 1524, it was constructed after local merchants petitioned the newly established colonial government to erect a portico over the broad sidewalk as protection against the morning sun and bad weather. During its first two centuries of existence (before the activity was moved to its present location in the arcade of the Plaza de Santo Domingo), public scribes would set up their portable shops here.

Today the cramped, narrow stalls of the past have been replaced by cramped, narrow shops selling jewelry—perhaps the most visible vestige of a guild system, where a neighborhood consisting of several blocks confines itself to selling one particular product—that has operated in Mexico City since, according to Bernal Díaz, the days when it was known as Tenochtitlán.

Most of the commercial establishments in and around the *Zócalo* offer a ten percent discount off the listed price if you pay in cash rather than with a credit card. You should also be aware that, in general, prices are much lower here than elsewhere in the city.

Located on the northwest corner of the *Zócalo*, between Calles Cinco de Mayo and Tacuba, is the imposing **National Pawnshop**, built on the site of the former Aztec palace of Axayactl, where the conquistadors were first housed as guests by Móctezuma II. (It was on the roof of this former palace—nothing remains of it—that Móctezuma was stoned to death by his angry subjects as he was attempting to calm the furor over his acquiescence to the Spaniards.) Today the National Pawnshop (all pawn shops in Mexico are government owned) offers myriad unredeemed goods for sale. Chandeliers, antique books, office machinery, dentist chairs, art works, antique jewelry—just about every imaginable item is available in this huge colonial building that during business hours always seems to be teeming with humanity. In addition, every so often public auctions—at which, supposedly, great bargains are available—are held here to clear out the merchandise. (Although they're advertised as "once-a-month" events, it is not uncommon for "once-a-month" to become "once every few months," according to aficionados.)

South of the Zócalo

The seat of the judicial power in Mexico, the **Supreme Court** is located at the corner of Avenida Pino Suárez and Calle de la Corregidora on the southeastern corner of the *Zócalo*. During the viceroyalty period (1535–1821) the site was occupied by the Mercado del Volador, an open-air market to which fresh fruits and vegetables were brought from Xochimilco's floating gardens, 25 km (15 miles) to the south, along the Acequia Real (Royal Canal). The Supreme Court building itself, with its somber Baroque façade, was built in 1929 and completely remodeled in 1940.

Inside there are three murals by José Clemente Orozco, and one by his American contemporary George Biddle. Orozco was commissioned in the early 1940s to paint a series of murals in the building, but his third, *Injustice,* a powerful presentation executed in vivid colors on the landing of the second floor, was considered highly inappropriate by his sponsors, and the rest of the proposed series was unceremoniously cancelled. The Biddle mural is located at the entrance to the library.

On the stretch of Corregidora between the National Palace and the Supreme Court you can see a reconstruction of a segment of the old Acequia Real.

Three blocks south of the *Zócalo* at the corner of Avenida Pino Suárez and Calle República del Salvador is one of the area's more interesting landmarks, the **Museum of the City of Mexico**. Built in 1526 as a residence for Cortés's cousin, this mansion was remodeled in the 18th century for the Count and Countess of Santiago de Calimaya, and carried their name until it became a museum early in the 20th century.

The building alone is worth a visit. Built of deep red volcanic stone, its façade includes stone carvings of gargoyles in the form of cannons that surround the imbedded royal family crest. The cornerstone, salvaged from an Aztec ruin, is a sculpted plumed serpent's head that peers menacingly at the passing scene. (Legend has it that Cortés placed the stone here with his own hands.)

The museum's displays cover the history of the city from earliest pre-Hispanic times to our own day, although the emphasis begins with the founding of Tenochtitlán. Especially interesting are the models of the ancient Aztec capital, with people going about their work, shopping in the markets, or simply watching as Aztec nobles are carried by in ornate chairs. Depicted in another model is the colonial capital of New Spain, with miniature versions of many still-extant buildings, including the one housing the museum.

Diagonally across the street from the museum is the fortress-like **Church of Jesus of Nazareth**, with its entrance on Calle República del Salvador. The church's early Baroque-style façade is topped by a tile-faced cupola, and there's a plaque on the outside wall of the apse commemorating the first meeting between Hernán Cortés and Móctezuma II—an encounter that took place here, according to legend, on November 8, 1519, when it was still the site of an Aztec temple.

Inside is a superb (but unfinished) mural by Orozco depicting the Conquest, and another by him, entitled *Apocalipsis,* that covers the walls and ceiling behind the dome. (Work on the former was interrupted by Orozco's death in 1949.) The remains of Cortés are also, allegedly, interred here, in a tomb identified only by a small bronze plaque on a wall of the tallest altar.

Adjacent to the church is the **Hospital of Jesus of Nazareth**, which was founded by Cortés in 1524 and completed in 1535. Believed to be the first hospital established in the Americas, it is worth visiting if only to see its inner courtyard. Permission to enter this serene 16th-century patio will graciously be granted at the admittance desk; walk straight into the hospital and take your first left.

One block south on Avenida Pino Suárez is the Pino Suárez metro station, where there's a huge Aztec temple that was uncovered during construction on the metro in 1968. The temple, which dates from the 14th century, has been preserved as an integral part of the concourse. There is also an entrance here to a subterranean pedestrian walkway that leads back to the *Zócalo*. Expect lots of activity in this tunnel at all times—everything from wall-to-wall art exhibitions and sidewalk entrepreneurs to droves of people simply going about their business.

WEST OF THE ZOCALO

The **Palacio de Iturbide**, located at Francisco Madero 17, three blocks west of the *Zócalo,* is the most elegant structure in the neighborhood, its architecture a curious fusion of indigenous Baroque with an Italian flavor. The façade is constructed out of *tezontle* and gray sandstone, and the massive, beautifully carved doors open onto an equally striking courtyard. Designed by Francisco Guerrero y Torres and completed in 1780, it was for many years the residence of a Spanish marquis and later a count. Then, in 1821, it became the "palace" of its most famous occupant, Agustín de Iturbide, who won control of the government after Spain finally granted Mexico its independence that same year. No stranger to megalomania, the victorious Iturbide had himself crowned emperor, and from his palace ruled the country for ten months, during which time he managed to alienate most of his "subjects." He then took a six-year "sabbatical" in Spain, and upon his return was surprised to find that the provisional government had condemned him in absentia to death by firing squad.

The palace became, in the decades that followed, a hotel, an office building, and a shopping plaza. In 1965 the interior was restored and became the administrative offices of a branch of the Banco Nacional de México. A permanent exhibition of colonial religious art is open to the public during regular bank hours.

The **Casa de Los Azulejos**, or House of Tiles, at Calle Madero 4, across the street from the Church of San Francisco, was built in 1596 as a palace for the Count of Orizaba. Legend has it that one of the later counts had a son who did not measure up to his father's standards. One day the father reproached his son for his lack of ambition and ended by telling him, "Son, you will never have a house of tile." Stung by his father's criticism, the boy went on to marry a wealthy woman and then tiled the palace from top to bottom with glazed blue-and-white Puebla *azulejos*—to match the sky, as he later told the curious.

In 1904 two brothers from the United States, Walter and Frank Sanborn, opened the first soda fountain in Mexico a few doors away. The enterprising brothers soon installed a piano and hired a pianist who specialized in Viennese waltzes, and Mexico City's elite responded to the novelty. Ladies who rarely entered commercial establishments stepped out of elegant horse-drawn carriages to refresh themselves at **Sanborn's** with those amazing concoctions called ice-cream sodas. Walter, who held a degree in pharmacy, next set up a prescription counter so arranged that customers had to pass the tempting beverages and piles of sandwiches (then unfamiliar to Mexicans) in order to reach it.

By the end of the First World War the Sanborns had taken over the Casa de los Azulejos and spread an enormous amber-colored glass roof over its patio. What had been a popular drugstore soon became the most popular restaurant in the city. In time the Sanborns added a perfume department, silver shop, and fur department to cater to their ritzy clientele.

Nowadays a property of Walgreen Pharmacies, the Casa de los Azulejos is a comfortable place to relax after a morning of exploring the *Zócalo* area. The coffee is good, and there's even a 1925 Orozco mural winding up the wall of the stairwell.

Diagonally across the street from Sanborn's on the corner of Madero and Lázaro Cárdenas is the 44-story **Latin American Tower**, at 181 meters (594 feet) Mexico's third-tallest skyscraper (the PEMEX building and Hotel de México, both in the capital, now rank one and two, respectively). The enclosed observation deck on the 42nd floor affords panoramic views of the entire Valley of Mexico (on a clear day), and the Muralto, on the floor below it, is an adequate restaurant. The Tower's innovative "floating" foundation has withstood numerous earthquakes while preventing the building from sinking into the soft subsoil underlying much of the city.

Before you cross the avenue and begin to explore the Alameda Park area there's another cluster of buildings two blocks north on Lázaro Cárdenas that's worth a look. The elegant mansion at the corner of Lázaro Cárdenas and Calle Tacuba is home to the D.F.'s **Central Post Office**. Designed by the Italian architect Adamo Boari, whose masterpiece, the Palacio de Bellas Artes, is directly across the street, it was built between 1902 and 1907 and opened a year later. As post offices go, you'd be hard-pressed to find a more elaborate one. Particularly noteworthy are the sumptuous details of the building's exterior and the carved woodwork and bronze handrails of the main stairwell inside. There are stamp and coin museums upstairs.

The beautiful Neoclassical building next door is the former Palace of Mining, a creation of the multi-talented Spanish emigré Manuel Tolsá. Begun in 1797, it took 16 years to complete, and served as a school for mining engineers until 1945. In addition to its stately façade, the palace boasts a splendid patio and an exquisitely carved staircase. There's also a good 19th-century mural here by the Spanish artist Rafael Ximeno y Planes. In 1983, after the building had housed a variety of other tenants, the **National Museum of Art** was installed here. Although there are over 1,000 works of art on display at the museum, there are few outstanding ones. It is, however, the only museum in the capital that exhibits works of art from every period of Mexico's history, from the pre-Hispanic era to the present (the emphasis is on the 19th century).

In the Plaza Manuel Tolsá, the public square separating the two wings of the former palace, you'll find what is undoubtedly its namesake's most famous sculpture, the 29-ton, 15½-foot-tall "El Caballito." This massive statue depicting the despised King Charles IV (1788–1808) astride his horse—what many consider to be the finest equestrian statue in the world—was cast in 1803 and placed in the *Zócalo* opposite the Cathedral while Tolsá was creating the latter's magnificent Neoclassical dome. The odyssey of the "Little Horse" didn't begin in earnest, however, until after independence was achieved in 1821. Then, in order to protect it from the anti-Spanish sentiments of the people, Tolsá himself had it encased in a wooden globe and moved to the relative safety of a courtyard on the old university campus a few blocks away. There it sat until 1852 (the wooden globe was removed in 1824), when it was painstakingly moved—15 days to travel a little over a mile—to the intersection of Paseo de la Reforma and Calle Bucareli. It arrived at its present—and, one would hope, final—destination in 1978, and today is one of the capital's more popular attractions.

THE ALAMEDA PARK AREA
The Palacio de Bellas Artes

Located at the corner of Juárez and Lázaro Cárdenas, this huge, opulent building designed by Adame Boari is a Mexico City landmark as well as the nation's foremost cultural center. Eclectic in design—the building itself is a fusion of Neoclassical and Art Nouveau elements—the Bellas Artes (bay-yas ART-ease) is noted for its excellent acoustics and is home to both the world-famous Ballet

Folklórico (see the following section) and the National Symphony Orchestra.

Construction of the building, which was begun in 1904, was halted by the Revolution, and its plans were subsequently modified a number of times before its completion in 1934 (hence the mixture of styles). Today, the ground floor boasts a number of spacious galleries that are used for temporary exhibitions, while the second floor has a permanent gallery featuring the works of 19th- and 20th-century Mexican masters. (The Bellas Artes has also served as the headquarters of the National Institute of Fine Arts since 1946.) But it is the murals on the third and fourth floors that make the Bellas Artes such a fascinating and worthwhile stop. Here you'll find the most extensive display of Mexican *muralismo* anywhere in the world, with works by Rufino Tamayo, Juan O'Gorman, José Clemente Orozco, David Alfaro Siqueiros, Jorge Camarena, and Diego Rivera lined up one after the other. On the second floor you can also see a reworked version of Rivera's *Man at the Crossroads* (1934), the original of which was commissioned for New York City's Rockefeller Center but was painted over after Rivera's sponsors got a look at its graphic political message (they objected, among other things, to John D. Rockefeller being depicted as a devilish capitalist).

Unfortunately, it has been estimated that the Palacio de Belles Artes has sunk over 15 feet into the soft subsoil since it was opened in 1934, and it continues to sink at the rate of about three and a half inches a year, despite a number of innovative engineering schemes that have been tried to halt its downward progress.

Lovers of dance—which includes most Mexicans—will tell you that the richness and diversity of Mexican culture is nowhere more apparent than in their favorite art form. While most regional folk dances have remained unchanged since the 14th century, the Spanish influence, as exemplified by flamenco and the Dance of the Moors and the Christians, has also figured prominently in this rich tradition. Perhaps the best way to experience the full spectrum of dance in Mexico is to see a performance by the **Ballet Folklórico de México**, which takes the stage three times a week at the Bellas Artes. Authentic costumes, superb dancers, outstanding choreography, and masterfully performed traditional music all combine to make this an unforgettable experience. In addition, the Bellas Artes' 22-ton Tiffany curtain is displayed prior to each performance, its stained glass portraying the snow-capped volcanoes of Popocatépetl and Iztaccíhuatl at dawn and dusk—effects achieved with special lighting.

Performances are held Wednesdays at 9:00 P.M. and Sundays at 9:30 A.M. and again at 9:00 P.M. Reservations should be made in advance through your hotel or a travel agency. You'll get the best views from seats on the first (lowest) balcony.

Alameda Park

Bordered by Avenida Hidalgo on the north, Avenida Juárez on the south, and the Bellas Artes on the east, the park is a pleasant four-block stretch of greenery in the midst of the perennially clogged streets of the capital. Filled with ornate fountains, Neoclassical marble sculptures, wrought-iron benches, ice cream and balloon vendors, and towering poplar trees (the park's name is derived from *alamos,* the Spanish word for poplar), it's a good place to relax after a busy morning of sightseeing.

Dating back to 1596, it is also the capital's oldest public park. The western section, known as the Plaza del Quemadero (Square of the Burning Stake), was where heretics were burned during the Inquisition. Later, in the 19th century, the park became *the* fashionable place for Sunday promenades (see Diego Rivera's mural *Dream of a Sunday Afternoon in the Alameda* in the nearby Museo de la Alameda). Since the Revolution Alameda has been a people's park, however. Families and couples, mostly working class, congregate for picnics under the poplars, enjoying the free weekly concerts of classical, jazz, rock, folk, and martial music.

During the Christmas season, and especially in the days before the Day of the Three Kings (January 6), the normally lively park becomes even livelier, as dozens of Santa Clauses line up next to their plush crimson chairs and wait to pose with you for a small fee. Each Santa brings his own photographer with a shoe box camera, and traditionally there is always one Santa on stilts.

The **National Museum of Folk Arts and Crafts**, which is housed in a 16th-century structure that was once the Church of Corpus Christi, is located on Avenida Juárez directly across from the park's Juárez Monument. One side of the ground floor is devoted to a museum displaying traditional arts and crafts from different regions of the country, while the rest of the building's two floors are filled with copies of the museum collection at prices comparable to what you can expect to pay in the villages of their origin. Among the items for sale are woven sweaters and ponchos, hand-carved masks, onyx chess sets, bark paintings, and a variety of ceramics. The silver jewelry here is less expensive than it is in Taxco, where it comes from, and the wooden toys from the state of Michoacán are especially charming. Also of interest is the ceramic "tree of life," a traditional wedding gift fashioned in the shape of a candelabra and characterized by intricate decorative motifs featuring angels with trumpets, assorted biblical characters, and flowers. The best come from Metepec.

If you follow Avenida Juárez three and a half blocks to the west you'll come to **FONART**, a branch of the immense government-run operation that sells native arts and crafts at just about wholesale. Here you'll find handicrafts in precious, semi-precious, and garden-variety materials such as silver, onyx, glass, shell, leather, clay, wood, wax, papier-mâché, and even sugar. The government coordinates the manufacture, distribution, and sale of these goods, and also regulates their prices. The rural artisans are, in effect, subsidized—which is an absolute necessity if these craft traditions are to survive with future generations.

The new home of the recently restored Diego Rivera masterpiece *A Dream of a Sunday Afternoon in the Alameda* is the **Museo de la Alameda**, located just north of FONART on the corner of Calle Balderas and Colón. When it was first unveiled in 1948 the mural created an uproar because of a placard carried by one of its figures that stated *Dios No Existe* ("God Does Not Exist"), a quotation from a lecture given by the Mexican philosopher Ignacio Ramírez. As a result of the outcry, the mural was covered and remained so until 1956, when Rivera finally consented to paint over the objectionable words, substituting in their place the phrase "*Conferencia de la Academia de Letran de 1836*"—a reference to the lecture in which the controversial words had been pronounced.

The mural's original home was in the lobby of the nearby Hotel del Prado, but the hotel was all but destroyed in the 1985 earthquakes. Jolted and bruised, the mural nevertheless survived. It was subsequently restored and then moved to its present location, where you can also see an exhibit of some of Rivera's lesser works.

The **Franz Mayer Museum**, which is housed in the 16th-century Hospital of San Juan de Dios, Avenida Hidalgo 45, one block north and another block east of the Museo de la Alameda, boasts an extraordinary collection of mostly applied antique art. Mayer, a German-born financier who lived most of his life in Mexico as a Mexican citizen, bequeathed this collection of 16th- and 17th-century antiques to his adopted country upon his death in 1976, and today it stands as the best museum in the country devoted to the field.

The museum's library is also noteworthy, and comprises mostly collectors' items, including 770 different editions of *Don Quixote* as well as many books whose binding, typography, and illustrations are more valuable than their text. There are also numerous reference works on the particular applied arts that Mayer collected—furniture, carpets, goldwork, silverwork, timepieces, glass, crystal, and lamps, among others—as well as books on painting, engraving, and sculpture.

CENTRAL PASEO DE LA REFORMA

One long block west of the Franz Mayer Museum you again come to Mexico City's great thoroughfare, the Paseo de la Reforma. Originally called the Paseo del Emperador in honor of Maximilian, who during the course of his brief and ill-fated reign ordered a grand boulevard built along the lines of the Champs-Elysées, Reforma was completed in 1865 and renamed in 1877 in honor of the great reforms in government and civil rights initiated by Benito Juárez. Once exclusively residential, today it has become *the* chic address for everything from elegant hotels and foreign embassies to the sleek new office towers of national and multinational corporations.

It's also at this point that Reforma, as it proceeds on its stately way to Chapultepec Park and the southwestern environs of the D.F., becomes a veritable open-air museum of monumental statuary. The three principal monuments here are located at *glorietas,* or traffic circles, spaced about a half mile apart and serving as the hubs of major intersections. The first of these, as you look down Reforma to your left, features the Monument to Christopher Columbus, which was created by the French sculptor Charles Cordier and donated to the city by Don Antonio Escandon in 1877. The second *glorieta,* at the intersection of Reforma and Avenida Insurgentes, features the Monument to Cuauhtémoc, the last Aztec emperor, who is portrayed complete with plumed robe, feathered headdress, and spear in hand. The monument itself was designed by Francisco Jiminez and completed in 1887 by Ramon Agra (the figure of Cuauhtémoc was sculpted by Miguel Norena). The final *glorieta* before Chapultepec Park is dominated by Mexico's most celebrated monument, the Monument to Independence, better known as "The Angel." This startlingly beautiful landmark is a 150-foot column surrounded by sculpted figures and surmounted by a golden-winged angel. Begun in 1901 under the direction of Antonio Rivas Mercado and completed in time for the centennial of the Republic in 1910, the monument has become the most recognized symbol of the city.

Before heading down Reforma, there's a museum and another monument worth making a short detour to see. Located at Avenida Puente de Alvarado 50, the continuation of Avenida Hidalgo west of Reforma, five blocks west of the Franz Mayer Museum, the **San Carlos Museum** is housed in a beautiful Neoclassical structure that was designed by Manuel Tolsá in 1806 as an aristocrat's residence. The building itself is noteworthy for its unusual two-story oval patio and elegant stairway, and the museum's permanent collection of European art includes minor works by El Greco, Rubens, Bosch, and Van Dyke.

If you walk two blocks south of the museum on Calle Ramos Arizpe you'll come to the square known as the Plaza de la República and, in the middle of it, the nation's largest monument, the **Monument to the Revolution**. Originally this massive arch was designed to be the ceremonial entrance to a lavish legislative palace in which President-for-life Porfirio Díaz was to hold court. By the time the arch was completed, however, the Revolution had begun and Díaz had fled into exile. Today, the monument is the final resting place for many of the men who were responsible for ending the Díaz dictatorship: buried in crypts under the monument's immense pillars are, among others, Francisco "Pancho" Villa; President Francisco Madero, who succeeded Díaz only to be assassinated two years later; President Venustiano Carranza, himself a victim of modern Mexico's bloody birth; and President Lázaro Cárdenas, the man responsible for nationalizing the oil industry and implementing agrarian reform on a large scale.

The **National Museum of the Revolution**, located in the basement of the monument, is only recommended for history buffs.

The Zona Rosa

"Zona Rosa" (Pink Zone) is the unofficial name for a triangle of twenty-nine blocks southwest of the Alameda Park area, off Paseo de la Reforma on the way to Chapultepec Park. Bordered also by Avenida Insurgentes, Avenida Chapultepec, and Calle Florencia, the Zona Rosa was an exclusive residential district from the late 19th century through the 1950s. Today it's home to some of the nation's best art galleries, boutiques, antique shops, bookstores, hotels, restaurants, discotheques, bars (including gay bars), and nightclubs. Not surprisingly, just about every type of item imaginable is for sale somewhere within its borders, including clothing and jewelry of the highest quality (with prices to match). It is also the location of an old-fashioned type of market, the **Mercado Insurgentes**, which has over 200 stalls selling a variety of native handicrafts, silverwork, leather goods, onyx, and earthenware. Situated at the corner of Calle Florencia, between Calle Londres and Calle Liverpool, the market is accessible from both those streets as well. For the truly dedicated shopper, the **Plaza del Angel**, a shopping mall located between Calles Londres and Hamburgo, features a flea market in its patio where antiques prevail every Saturday.

In the years after the Second World War a smattering of small cafés began to infiltrate this neighborhood of luxurious two-story residences. Writers and artists such as Octavio Paz, Carlos Fuentes, and Rufino Tamayo soon were spending leisurely afternoons and evenings in these cafés enjoying each other's conversation and company. (One of the regulars from the old days, writer Luis Guillermo Piazza, is given credit for coining the name Zona Rosa. In Mexico, areas designated for legalized prostitution are called "Zonas Rojas," or red zones. Because some of the first cabarets to open in the area in the early 1950s offered entertainment bordering on the risqué, Piazza came up with the name "Zona Rosa." The rest is history.) The Zona's first hotel, the Presidente, opened soon after on the corner of Calles Hamburgo and Amberes, and visitors to the neighborhood discovered that its quaint cafés served excellent food. One by one, residents sold their homes and fled the Zona for the peace and quiet of the suburbs, and a variety of commercial establishments moved in to take their place.

The buildings throughout the Zona Rosa still reflect the turn-of-the-century taste for the Art Nouveau, a style known in Mexico as "Porfiriato" (after Porfirio Díaz, who was president during the period in which the neighborhood came into its own). These elegant survivors of modern urban planning are appreciated today as nostalgic reminders of the neighborhood's former genteel character. In addition, most of the Zona's side streets are now off limits to vehicular traffic, creating lovely pedestrian malls lined with welcoming cafés. (Umbrella-shaded tables prevail to such an extent that it is sometimes difficult to determine where one café ends and another begins.) During lunchtime the eateries and bars are crowded with tourists and local businessmen, who eventually give way to the evening crowd. But the Zona hardly ever sleeps. As the last revelers are wandering home in the early morning light, local businessmen are returning to the neighborhood for their breakfast *juntas* (meetings).

CHAPULTEPEC PARK

Spread over 67 square kilometers (40 square miles) just west of the Zona Rosa, Chapultepec Park, in Spanish Bosque (Forest) de Chapultepec, is the oldest public park in the Americas, as well as one of the largest in the world. Once on an island in a swampy lake of dozens of islands, the park's ancient ahuehuete trees were already a hundred years old by the time the Aztecs made their way to the Valley of Mexico. In the century that followed, Aztec emperors used the virgin forest as a hunting and recreation ground, only to give way to the victorious Spanish viceroys, who constructed vacation homes throughout the forest during the three centuries of the colonial era.

Today Chapultepec Park is a people's park, a place where tens of thousands of Mexico City residents come daily to decompress from the hustle and bustle of the world's largest metropolis. The great branches of the ahuehuetes meet high above wandering pathways to form lush green arcades; elsewhere, grassy stretches of open space attract sunbathers and picnickers alike (although 'in many areas of the park the grass has taken a beating). Signs prohibiting this and that are nowhere to be seen; the residents of the capital have a magnificent public space to live up to, and they do so with respect and appreciation.

The park itself is divided into three sections. The easternmost section is home to the National Museum of Anthropology; the Museum of Modern Art; the Rufino Tamayo Museum; the zoo (where the first pandas outside of China to be conceived naturally and in captivity were born); two artificial lakes, Lago Menor (where boats can be rented) and Lago Mayor (where the National Ballet performs *Swan Lake* every spring); and Chapultepec Castle, perched on its steep hill like something out of a children's fairy tale. The newer, middle section of the park has an amusement complex dominated by a gigantic roller coaster, two additional museums, and the splendid Restaurante del Lago. The hilly, mostly undeveloped third, or southwestern, section of the park, west of Dolores Cemetery, is crisscrossed by bridle and foot paths that meander through great clumps of ferns, and is a favorite with the equestrian crowd. (Public stables here rent out horses by the hour.) The pastoral clearings in this section of the park host frequent *fiestas de cumpleanos,* or birthday parties, which are easily identified by the vividly colored balloons strung between trees to mark the boundaries of the party. Less crowded than the other two sections of the park, it is also home to the **Atlantis Dolphinarium**, where superbly trained dolphins and sea lions delight the relatively few spectators who find their way here.

The Rufino Tamayo Museum

The best way to see Chapultepec Park is to start early in the day with a visit to this museum, which houses the personal collection of this great 20th-century Mexican painter. To get there, follow Paseo de la Reforma south and west. After crossing Mariano Escobedo, look to your right; on the corner will be a large signboard with the latest information on the museum's temporary exhibitions. Take a right on Calzada Mahatma Gandhi and walk the less than half a mile to the strikingly modern structure that houses the museum. The Sculptors' Patio at the front entrance is graced by a large Henry Moore. Inside, the first thing to catch your eye will be a major Picasso—part of the museum's permanent collection. While the Tamayo Room is limited to some of the master's lesser efforts, the other seven galleries are filled with splendid works by his contemporaries, both foreign and Mexican, and frequently host traveling exhibitions.

To continue your exploration of the park, walk back to Reforma, which runs in a straight line through the northeastern corner of the park, and take your pick from a steady flow of public transportation vehicles heading west. All buses and *peseros*—the light green collective taxis, which are actually safer than the buses—will stop in front of the National Museum of Anthropology, the next stop after the first traffic light.

The National Museum of Anthropology

This is one of the great museums of the world, and is reason enough in itself to visit Mexico City. At the very least it deserves the better part of a full day of your time.

Designed by Pedro Ramírez Vázquez, this deceptively simple rectangular structure is generally considered to be the greatest achievement of modern Mexican architecture, and certainly is one of the most harmonious settings ever conceived for the exhibition of antiquities. The exterior of the second floor, for example, is dominated by a window lattice that is characteristic of traditional Mayan ornamentation. And, of course, no truly "Mexican" building would be complete without a patio. In the case of Vázquez' design, the patio is surrounded by almost two dozen exhibition halls and is dominated by a huge inverse "umbrella." Resting on a single reinforced-concrete column decorated with reliefs, and stabilized by special steel stays, this massive concrete cover is designed to catch rainwater and then channel it into the reed-filled pond at its base.

Standing permanent sentry duty on a marble plinth at the entrance to the museum is Tlaloc, the Aztec god of rain. By all accounts the largest single-piece sculpture (it weighs 165 tons) created in the Americas before the arrival of Columbus, this particular Tlaloc was uncovered in a riverbed near the town of Coatlichán, 48 km (29 miles) north of the capital, and dates back to the heyday of Teotihuacán, sometime between A.D. 400 and 600. Transported to its present site with great logistical difficulty (it made the trip on a specially constructed tractor trailer that was escorted by the Mexican army), Tlaloc was greeted by thousands as he finally rumbled through the downtown area on the afternoon of April 16, 1964. Then, almost a month before the rainy season usually begins, the skies opened up and a tremendous downpour drenched the astonished onlookers—a downpour, as it turned out, that lasted three days.

The exhibition rooms inside are laid out in such a way that you can visit them in any order you choose, but to appreciate fully the treasures of this great museum you should probably start with the Orientation Room, dead ahead as you walk through the reception hall, where a 15-minute overview of Mesoamerica's ancient cultures are offered along with guided tours in English, Spanish, German, and French at half-hour intervals. Although the latter cover just a small portion of all there is to see, they do provide a valuable introduction to the pre-Columbian history of the region as well as the museum itself.

(All signs in the Museum of Anthropology are in Spanish only, so you'll want to visit the well-stocked bookstore, on the left as you enter the reception hall, which has an excellent selection of illustrated guidebooks in English.)

To the right of the Orientation Room is a Rufino Tamayo mural depicting the eternal struggle between good and evil. (Other Mexican painters whose works are exhibited in the museum include José Chavez Morado, Matías Goeritz, Carlos Mérida, and Pablo O'Higgins.) Near the Tamayo mural are the temporary exhibition halls, where recent discoveries from ongoing excavations are displayed. These new additions to the museum's collection arrive on a regular basis; one site near the *Zócalo,* for example, has recently produced a series of important pre-Hispanic relics. The rest of the ground floor is divided into collections classified by either region or culture. These include rooms devoted to Teotihuacán, Tula, the Aztec, Oaxaca, the Gulf Coast, and the Maya. What is probably the most popular piece in the museum is on display in the Mexica Room: the famous **Aztec calendar stone** (which is reproduced in miniature and sold in almost every souvenir shop in Mexico). This 24-ton basalt disk was unearthed during a restoration project on the Metropolitan Cathedral back in 1790, and then for years was left propped against one of the Cathedral's walls. More recently, experts have concluded that it is not so much a calendar as a vision of the Aztec cosmos, and was probably carved in the early years of the 16th century. Other well-known pieces in the museum's collection include **El Luchador**, an Olmec wrestler, and a huge Olmec head from the late pre-Classic period (about 200 B.C.). The famous Aztec obsidian monkey, one of the 140 priceless artifacts stolen during the Christmas Eve robbery of 1985, was recently recovered.

Outside the Maya room, in a lovely garden, a temple on the right contains three striking murals depicting Mayan warriors engaged in battle. These are reproductions of the originals, which were discovered in the jungles of southernmost Mexico, at a site known as Bonampak, in 1947. Painted sometime around A.D. 200, the murals pretty much discredit the theory that the Maya were dedicated pacifists. In fact, as depicted here, the Mayan warriors are definitely the aggressors in the violent struggle.

The second floor is devoted to ethnology exhibits illustrating the lifestyles of Indian groups in Mexico today, and is arranged so that its rooms relate as closely as possible to those below. Exhibits on this floor include maps, photographs, examples of arts and crafts, religious objects, farm and fishing implements, everyday wear, native costumes and ceremonial dress, and a number of life-sized replicas of traditional shelters created by Indian craftsmen.

The Museum of Anthropology has a passable restaurant and cafeteria, and is closed on Mondays. The best time to visit is on a weekday (other than Monday) to avoid the large weekend crowds.

Directly south of the museum and across Reforma is the entrance to the main body of the park. Immediately to the right is a children's zoo; the large man-made lake to the left can be cruised in a rented rowboat (ducks and swans cruise among the boats). At the southwestern corner of the lake is the Casa del Lago, a colonial-era home-cum-theater that presents concerts, plays, poetry readings, films, and round-table discussions on a variety of topics; admission to all of these events is free. In addition, daily workshops in painting, music, dance, drama, and arts and crafts, also free, are conducted on the large patio in front of the theater's entrance. The chess and checker boards set into stone tables and scattered about under the ancient lichen-covered ahuehuete trees are yet another popular draw.

Nearby is the entrance to the **Chapultepec Park Zoo,**

which first opened in 1923. The credit for creating the first public zoo in history goes to the Emperor Móctezuma II, who caged six jaguars sent to him as tribute and installed them on this very site at the beginning of the 16th century. Later, he moved the large aviary from his palace in the center of Tenochtitlán here in order to keep the jaguars company and then began to add other species to his collection. Eventually he allowed his favored subjects to visit the compound, and so the concept of a public zoo was born.

Today the zoo's most celebrated inmates are the pandas. A gift from the Chinese government, this pair arrived about a decade ago. Fame is fickle, however. The newest crowd favorite seems to be the four kangaroos that were recently donated by the Australian government.

Just outside the entrance to the zoo is a depot from which a miniature train departs for its leisurely trip around the entire first section of the park. Tickets are sold at the depot itself, and a complete round trip lasts about 45 minutes.

On the western side of the zoo is the **Jardín Botánico**, the origins of which also date back to the reign of Móctezuma II, who is supposed to have puttered around an herb garden on this site. West of the gardens is a small, recently inaugurated park that has one requisite for admission: You must be at least 50 years old. Inside its fenced-off confines are comfortable benches, beautiful tropical flora, and an ever-present choir of songbirds.

Toward the south from this small park-within-a-park is a pathway known as the Calzada de los Poetas (Poets' Walk), which is lined with statues of some of Mexico's greatest writers and poets. At the end of the walk, to the east, is the Móctezuma Ahuehuete Tree, the largest tree in a park filled with large trees, with a circumference of almost 50 feet. Besides being a natural wonder, the tree is an inspiration to all the health-conscious joggers who jam the path that winds by it every morning. The grassy knoll nearby serves as a workout area for fledgling matadors, who cape imaginary bulls under the tutelage of their trainers as the sun rises to warm the always chilly morning air.

Continuing in a southerly direction, you'll come to the Nezahualcoyotl (nez-a-wahl-COY-o-tal) Monument on Avenida Heroico Colegio Militar, the favored route for the capital's hordes of joggers. Nezahualcoyotl, the 15th-century poet-king of Texcoco and ally of the Mexicas of nearby Tenochtitlán, is the man most often given credit for supervising the planting of the area's ahuehuete trees, almost 700 years ago. You can see the remains of an ancient aqueduct nearby (another civic improvement reputedly instigated by Nezahualcoyotl), on the other side of which you face a choice of entering a tunnel and waiting your turn for the elevator to Chapultepec Castle or getting there by following the winding pathway to the top.

Chapultepec Castle and the National Museum of History

The hill of Chapultepec has been the site of one kind of fortress or another since the days when the Toltecs occupied the valley, almost 1,000 years ago. In 1521 an anonymous Spanish chronicler wrote: "The Emperor Moctezuma gazes every sundown at his canalled capital surrounded by lakes... from his fortress high on the hill. Here he is borne in his jewel-encrusted litter after dinner to smoke tobacco treated with amber and to feast his eyes on the great temples of the pagan gods in the city plaza, washed with the colors of sunset." By the end of the 18th century a combination fort, granary, and summer residence for the Spanish viceroys had been built on the site. That structure was converted into a military college in 1840, almost twenty years after Mexico won her independence from Spain, and in 1847, with U.S. troops threatening to overrun the college, six cadets—soon to be known to posterity as the Niños Heroes (Boy Heroes)—provided the young Mexican republic with its newest martyrs by leaping from the precipice wrapped in Mexican flags rather than surrender to the invading troops.

The Neoclassical design of the present-day castle dates back to France's short-lived (1864–1867) domination of Mexico. Austrian Archduke Maximilian and his wife Carlota, sent to rule Mexico by Napoléon III, almost immediately took up permanent residence in the castle, rather than in the National Palace, after Carlota was attacked by bedbugs on her first night in the Palace. Maximilian then ordered a complete remodeling of the castle, with results that today can be seen in the design of its gardens, winding stairways, and intimate patios.

After Maximilian was overthrown and executed, the

new president, Benito Juárez, reestablished the presidential residence in the National Palace. However, his successor, President-for-life Porfirio Diáz, moved the presidential residence back to the castle, where it remained until the populist Lázaro Cárdenas ascended to the presidency in 1934. Cárdenas viewed living in a castle as "undemocratic," and had the presidential residence moved to an abandoned hacienda nearby, Los Pinos, where it remains to this day. At the same time, Cárdenas ordered the castle converted to its present function: home to the **National Museum of History**. Today the museum boasts a collection of historical memorabilia dating back to the days of the Conquest—blood-stained uniforms, swords, and the like—along with a number of outstanding examples of Mexican *muralismo,* including Orozco's *Benito Juárez and the Reform,* David Alfaro Siqueiros's *The Revolution,* Jorge Camarena's *The Constitution,* and Juan O'Gorman's *Themes of the Revolution.*

Upstairs are exhibits featuring period furniture and clothing, clocks, coins, and jewelry, but perhaps the most interesting pieces are the two horseless carriages here—one an ostentatious coach designed especially for the ill-fated Maximilian, and the other a stark black coach favored by Benito Juárez (in fact, the coach was the actual seat of the provisional government for a short period following Maximilian's demise).

Before leaving the museum be sure to take a stroll around the outside patio for a look at the opulent French-style furnishings left behind by Maximilian and Carlota. The panoramic views of the city are worth the climb up.

Located just below the castle is the **Museo de la Lucha del Pueblo Mexicano por la Libertad** (Museum of the Struggle of the Mexican People for Liberty), also known as the Museo del Caracol, after its snail-like shape. You enter this glass-walled structure tucked into the hillside from the top, and then walk down a winding ramp past a variety of three-dimensional models depicting historical events, as well as other materials from Mexico's revolutionary past. At the bottom of the hill, you can rest on one of the chairs in the small circular garden known as the Audiorama while listening to recorded classical music.

Turning north and heading in the direction of Paseo de la Reforma, you'll soon see the unmistakable silhouette of the glass-faced **Museum of Modern Art**. The building itself is actually two low buildings connected by a short corridor and surrounded by a fenced-off sculpture garden.

The well-lit interior of the museum is dominated by a white marble staircase and an elegant glass dome. One section of the museum is devoted to contemporary arts of the past few decades, including photography, engraving, and sculpture. The other section is devoted to 19th- and 20th-century Mexican art, and includes works by Rivera, his wife Frida Kahlo, his mentor, José Maria Velasco, as well as contemporaries such as Orozco, Siqueiros, and Tamayo.

There are other structures in the first section, primarily performing-arts venues, but these will not be of as much interest to most visitors as the second section of the park.

The newer sections of the park, although not far, are difficult to get to on foot. Your best bet is to walk to Paseo de la Reforma and then take any bus marked "Reforma" heading west. The last stop before the bus leaves the park will be "Plaza Petroleos," where the Fountain of Oil stands as a monument to President Cárdenas's nationalization of the oil industry in 1938. If you'd like to do more exploring in the park, get off here and follow the long paved path to the **Natural History Museum**. After the exquisite architecture of the museums in the older section of the park, this series of ten drab-appearing domes will come as a bit of a letdown. Inside, however, a modern design and effective lighting have enhanced the displays of dinosaur skeletons, as well as exhibits on the creation of the universe, the evolution of aquatic and terrestrial life, and the flora and fauna of Mexico.

Just outside the front entrance to the museum is another miniature railroad depot. Although the tracks crisscross the middle section of the park, you'll soon discover that everything of interest in this section is easily accessible on foot. To the east, on the other side of a small artificial lake, for example, is the entrance to the amusement park, with its huge *montano ruso* (roller coaster). To the north is the **Restaurante del Lago**, which serves good international-style cuisine in a spacious glass-walled dining room that affords panoramic views of the lake from every table. The Lerma Fountain, with an underwater mosaic by Diego Rivera, is just outside the entrance to the restaurant in the middle of the traffic circle.

The paved paths to the west and south of the restaurant will lead you to sights of interest having to do with that most precious of commodities in this often parched land, water. The Fountain of Nezahualcoyotl and the Fountain of the Gods are long stone walls carved with bas-relief murals of Aztec gods and symbols submerged by cascading water. To the south of these fountains, the Cárcamo, or municipal waterworks, has a rare Rivera sculpture dedicated to Tlaloc, the Aztec god of rain.

Still further south, Avenida Constituyentes is filled with a constant stream of taxis, both private and collective. If you'd like to visit the third, and least developed, section of the park, take a taxi about a half mile west to the entrance to the Panteon (cemetery) Dolores. From there, follow the road due north and you'll soon find yourself in the heart of this urban oasis. The path to the left leads to the Dolphinarium, the one to the right to the stables and equestrian areas. If, on the other hand, you've had enough park exploring for the day and want to head back into town, cross Constituyentes and hail a taxi heading eastward; it's only a five-minute ride to the Zona Rosa.

Polanco

The *colonia* (neighborhood) of Polanco stretches along the northern perimeter of the first section of Chapultepec Park (the section that includes the National Museum of Anthropology and the Rufino Tamayo Museum), and extends as far as Avenida Ejército Nacional to the north, Avenida Mariano Escobedo to the east, and the Periférico Norte to the west.

Soon after the Conquest, mulberry trees were imported from Spain and planted on what became the Hacienda de los Morales, the first silkworm farm in the Americas. Most of the area remained relatively undeveloped until about 40 years ago, when a new generation of wealthy Mexicans began to carve up the empty fields for their mansions and estates. Many of the homes were built in the classic Art Nouveau "sand-castle" style, with carved stone trimmings proliferating around windows and façades. As was the case throughout the D.F., preparations for the 1968 Summer Olympic Games led to urban expansion and changed the character of the four main east-west avenues in the neighborhood—Campos Eliseos, General Masaryk, Horacio, and Homero—considerably.

Although it is still an exclusive residential district, the graciously opulent homes and colonial-style mansions (which tend to be clustered on the over 30 tree-lined streets running north to south across the avenues) here today have been joined by sleek, modern high-rise office buildings and condominiums; fashionable hotels and restaurants; the capital's largest department stores; a number of the most chic boutiques in the country; a variety of nightclubs; and, of all things, an authentic Jewish shopping district where the choicest fruits, vegetables, and kosher products are available (though at slightly higher prices than you'll find elsewhere in the city). The Chapultepec Sports Club, which is well known for its elegant tennis facilities, is located in Polanco's northwest corner, and is open to the public. The National Conservatory of Music is a few blocks away on Avenida General Masaryk.

On Avenida Campos Eliseos, near the back entrance of the Stouffer Presidente Chapultepec, the **Cultural Center for Contemporary Art** houses rotating exhibitions of 20th-century painting in its lower two floors. The upper two floors contain the **Cultural Center for Pre-Hispanic Art**—over 400 art objects dating from 1000 B.C. to A.D. 1521—and the **Cultural Center for Photographic Art**, whose permanent collection spans the entire history of photography and features works by Henri Cartier Bresson, Man Ray, Edward Weston, and other greats.

Hipodromo de las Americas

The Art Deco-style Hipodromo, Mexico City's only thoroughbred racetrack, was built in 1943 after the Second World War shut down U.S. tracks, and was a hit right from the start. The track, which is located just north and west of Chapultepec Park, is unique in that it operates year-round (with the exception of Easter Week and the last two weeks of the year), and the caliber of the thoroughbreds is on a par with all but the best tracks in the United States. Favorites win 35 percent of the time.

If you're going to spend an afternoon here, you might consider a table at one of the track's many restaurants. At the elegant Derby Club 2,000 pesos will get you a table with a glassed-in bird's-eye view of the finish line. Another possibility is the equally elegant Jockey Club (men must wear ties). The real bargain here, though, are the plush sky boxes, which go for 10,000 pesos and have room for up to 16 people; food and drink service is available, and each box has a color TV for monitoring the action. And, as in all the restaurant areas, there are betting windows just a few feet away.

You can make reservations for any of these alternatives by phoning 5-57-4700; an English-speaking agent will handle your request. There are 11 races a day on Tuesdays, Thursdays, and Sundays, and 12 each on Fridays and Saturdays; the track is closed on Mondays and Wednesdays. Post time during the week is 3:00 P.M., and a half hour earlier on weekends.

A steady stream of collective taxis leave from the metro's Tacuba station, or pass westward along Paseo de la Reforma marked either "Hipodromo," "Legaria," "San Isidro," or "Defensa Nacional." Any of these will drop you near the main entrance. If you're driving, take Periférico Norte and exit on Calzada Legaria. Turn left at the stop light; straight ahead is the massive Hipodromo parking lot.

THE SOUTH

There are a number of things to see and do along Insurgentes south of its intersection with Reforma. Down past the Siqueiros Cultural Polyforum and the Plaza México bullfight arena are two interesting neighborhoods to either side of the Monument to Alvaro Obregón: Coyoacán to the east and San Angel to the west. Both neighborhoods, besides being good for walking around, have small museums, historical sites, cafés, and markets.

Farther south on Insurgentes is University City, with its interesting art and architecture, and the archaeological sites of Copilco and Cuicuilco.

Finally, beyond University City to the southeast—but still accessible by metro—is the floating garden district of Xochimilco.

The 51-story Hotel de México, 5 km (3 miles) south of the intersection of Insurgentes and Reforma, is a monstrous structure that is still under construction after 24 years. Until the nearby PEMEX tower went up 15 years ago, the hotel was the tallest eyesore in the hemisphere. (The local nickname for it is *El Elefante Blanco*.) Nevertheless, the top floor, which has been functioning as a revolving restaurant for the last 18 years, affords great views of the city on a clear day. There is, in addition, a restaurant and nightclub on the ground floor.

In 1965 Manuel Suárez, the instigator of the Hotel de México project, commissioned David Alfaro Siqueiros to create the world's largest mural on a plot of land next to his as-yet-unoccupied hotel. Strange bedfellows, this pair.

Suarez was a self-made millionaire who had ridden with Pancho Villa during the Revolution; introduced the cement industy to Mexico; built the first highway from the capital to Acapulco, where he subsequently made a fortune from his real-estate holdings; and fathered 23 children. Siqueiros had been an officer in the Spanish Civil War and had then allegedly led a mob in an abortive attempt to assassinate Leon Trotsky in 1940. After spending a few years as a political prisoner in a Mexican jail for his outspoken criticism of the government he received a presidential pardon in 1964, and then agreed to take Suárez' commission with the understanding that he would have complete artistic freedom to paint what he liked.

After six years of labor, the **Siqueiros Cultural Polyforum** was inaugurated in 1971. Each of its twelve sides is covered with massive human figures painted in harsh, bright colors. (The designs are all Siqueiros's; the execution was carried out by some two dozen of his students.) Inside, the mural entitled *The March of Humanity on Earth Toward the Cosmos* is said to be the largest in the world (Siqueiros painted this one himself). The oval-shaped stage is, in actuality, a huge turntable on which more than 1,000 people can stand, inspecting Siqueiros's creation around and above them, as the platform slowly revolves 360 degrees (a full circle takes 15 minutes).

Downstairs is a multi-use theater, the outer corridor of which serves as a sort of museum for the display of native arts and crafts, while, on the level below, there are handicrafts shops and a number of art galleries.

Traditionally, one of the few public events to start on time in Mexico is the weekly presentation of the bullfights at the **Plaza México**, located a bit south of the Polyforum on Insurgentes Sur. Promptly at 4:30 P.M. every Sunday, a lone horseman in Medieval costume prances his steed across the ring and follows the ancient custom of requesting permission of the authorities to conduct a "running of the bulls."

The Plaza México has been the principal bullring in the capital since 1946. The best matadors in the country appear here from November through May, during the dry season; the rainy season, on the other hand, is the time for *novilleros* to fight younger, smaller bulls, and the spectators take their chances with the weather as well as the caliber of the artistry.

A good way to attend the bullfights, especially on Sundays, when it's always difficult to get a taxi in the D.F., is on a tour conducted by an English-speaking guide. The standard Sunday tour includes a morning performance at Bellas Artes by the Ballet Folklórico, followed by a gondola ride in Xochimilco's canals, lunch, and then the bullfights in the afternoon. All travel agencies and most hotels can make arrangements for you. The fee will include transportation and a reserved seat on the shady side of the ring, which will keep you out of harm's way from beer showers generated by disgruntled fans, most of whom seem to prefer the sunny side.

The Coyoacán Area

The Monument to Alvaro Obregón is a little over 3 km (2 miles) south of the Plaza México on Insurgentes Sur. To the right as you head south is the San Angel area; to the left, or east, is the Coyoacán area. First, Coyoacán.

From the monument, go east on Avenida Miguel Angel de Quevedo to Avenida Universidad, the first major intersection. Turn left and then take the next right onto Calle Francisco Sosa. The tiny 18th-century Baroque-style church on the corner, the Capilla de San Antonio, looks completely out of place among the modern structures lining both sides of the street. But then the scenery begins to change: as the narrow cobblestoned street heads toward Coyoacán Center, the architectural creations of the 20th century give way to moss-stained stone walls overhung by bougainvillaea that hide low-slung colonial mansions from prying eyes. Over the entrances to most of these mansions you'll find the centuries-old coats-of-arms of their former aristocratic residents. Coyoacán has always attracted the elite of Mexican society.

The settlement of Coyoacán can be traced back to the ninth century, when the Toltecs moved into the area. They were followed, in turn, by Chichimecs in the 12th century and Aztecs in the 14th (the Aztecs built their vacation homes here). Later, Cortés established Coyoacán as the provisional capital of New Spain while the ruined Tenochtitlán was being rebuilt as the Mexico City of the Zócalo area. Today it is a mellow, unspoiled oasis filled with colonial buildings and peaceful gardens. At times, it seems as if there could be an ocean between the serenity here and the intensity of the urban sprawl surrounding it.

Cramped Calle Francisco Sosa suddenly opens up onto the large and attractive **Coyoacán Center**, which consists of the Jardín Centenario and the Plaza Hidalgo. On its eastern perimeter stands the **Casa de Cortés**, built in 1522, and from which Cortés governed the colony until the National Palace was completed. His personal coat-of-arms can still be seen on the façade. The Casa de Cortés is now a municipal office building, and the surrounding area is dotted with sidewalk cafés. The 16th-century Church of San Juan Bautista overlooks the plaza, its plain, fortress-like exterior providing no indication of just how lavish and ornate the interior is.

From the Plaza Hidalgo walk north along either Aguaya or Centenario and then turn right on Calle Londres. The **Frida Kahlo Museum**, at Londres 127, is located in the house where the eminent painter was born and later lived with her husband, Diego Rivera. The house became a popular gathering place for artists, writers, poets, and intellectuals in the 1930s and 1940s, and among its more illustrious guests at one time or another were Leon Trotsky and D. H. Lawrence. Neither its lively history nor its bright blue exterior or cheery garden prepare the visitor for the ethereal and sometimes macabre self-portraits by Kahlo displayed within, however. Kahlo, who was afflicted by polio as a young girl and later was involved in a serious trolley-car accident, lived much of her life in pain—a fact that is clearly reflected in her art. A number of Rivera's drawings and mementoes of their life together are also on exhibit, as well as some Mayan and Toltec sculptures and ceramics in a hut in the garden.

Two blocks north and three blocks east of the Kahlo museum, at Calle Viena 45, is **Trotsky's house**, where the great revolutionary lived in exile and was eventually murdered by an assassin in the employ of his archrival, Joseph Stalin. Here, first impressions do tell the whole story, with the house resembling nothing so much as a fortress. The high bare walls are broken only by an equally tall and stark steel door; even the doorbell is hard to find. Keep ringing. Once inside the compound, you feel surrounded by a melancholy gloom that hangs heavily over the weed-choked garden with its small moss-covered monument to Trotsky (his ashes are interred within).

The rooms inside have been left much as they were at the time of the assassination. Dozens of large bullet holes—courtesy of a prior attempt on his life allegedly led by the painter David Alfaro Siqueiros—pockmark the walls of Trotsky's bedroom. Three months later, on August 20, 1940, Jaime Ramón Mercader del Río, an agent of Stalin's posing as the boyfriend of Trotsky's secretary, appeared at the door with a request that Trotsky read a paper of his. Granted admission to Trotsky's study, he then proceeded to smash the founder of the Red Army across the skull with the blunt end of an alpine ice pick he had concealed under his coat. Trotsky's shattered eyeglasses still lie on his desk where they fell.

To get to the **Museum of Foreign Interventions**, head south on Calle Morelos for three blocks, turn left (east) on Xicoténcatl, and continue in the same direction across Division del Norte until you come to the museum, which is housed in the former Convent of Churubusco on the corner of Calle de Agosto. The Franciscans were responsible for building the original structure on this site in the years immediately following the Conquest, which then became the base for their missionary activities in China, Japan, and the Philippines. It was renovated in 1768, and 79 years later became the scene of the so-called Battle of Churubusco, where badly outnumbered Mexican troops were overwhelmed by the U.S. army as it closed in on Mexico City.

Today the museum boasts eight exhibition rooms filled with the memorabilia of Mexico's anti-colonialist wars, including captured weapons, blood-stained uniforms, documents, photographs, drawings, and a tattered 1847 version of the Stars and Stripes captured by the Mexicans. In addition, one of the rooms has a 19th-century carriage that belonged to General (later President) Santa Anna, who led the attack on the Alamo, as well as Pancho Villa's bullet-riddled 1921 Buick, the car in which he was riding on the day he was gunned down in 1923. There is also a lovely garden inside the walls of the former convent with a monument to the fallen defenders of the Battle of Churubusco.

Back on Division del Norte, there are usually plenty of cruising taxis. To complete your tour of the Coyoacán area, flag one heading south and have it drop you off in front of the Museo Anahuacalli, the towering pyramid-shaped structure on Calle Museo, just off Division del Norte, about 2 km (1¼ miles) south of the Museum of Foreign Interventions. (This is a bit off the beaten path, so it's best to have your taxi wait for you as you explore the museum.)

Taking its name from the Aztec word for the Valley of Mexico, the **Museo Anahuacalli** was designed by Diego Rivera and built out of *tezontle,* the favorite building material of the Aztecs. Much of its ornamentation is derivative of Toltec and Mayan designs, and the overall effect is at once impressive and appropriate. Inside, the museum is filled with well-preserved artifacts, many dating back to the pre-Classic period, from Rivera's own collection. For the most part, these artifacts fall into three broad categories coinciding with the three most important cultures to arise from the Valley of Mexico: Teotihuacán, Toltec, and Aztec.

The largest room in the museum, on the second floor, served as Rivera's studio toward the end of his life, and is preserved just as it was at the time of his death. On one long wall there is even an unfinished mural with the likenesses of Stalin and Mao Tse-Tung charcoaled in. The museum is not without its controversy, however. Serious rumors persist about an anonymous craftsman who churned out excellent replicas of ancient Mesoamerican artifacts for the actress Dolores del Rio, a close friend of Rivera's, and who was later introduced to the great muralist himself. Nevertheless, the museum is well worth a visit, if only because of Rivera's achievement as the architect of the building.

The San Angel Area

This beautiful neighborhood just west of the Monument to Alvaro Obregón was known in pre-colonial days by the Indian name Tenanitla, meaning "at the foot of the stone wall"—an allusion to the vast lava field to the south now known as El Pedregal. Later, Spanish aristocrats built their gracious walled mansions here, and the area experienced its glory days in the 17th and 18th centuries. After Mexico gained its independence in 1821, San Angel continued to be popular, especially with well-known writers and artists, who spent their leisure time in country residences here. Today, despite having been engulfed by the rapidly expanding D.F., San Angel retains its small-town charm and character.

After a taxi, the easiest way to get from Coyoacán Center to San Angel is to take the number 56 or 116A bus, both of which make the trip via Avenida Hidalgo in about 15 minutes and stop right in front of the former Carmelite convent, now the **Museo del Carmen**, and its adjacent church. Located on the east side of Avenida Revolución, just north and east of the Plaza de San Jacinto (the plaza is the site of the Bazaar Sábado; see below), the structure, which was built in 1615, is a fine example of the ecclesiastical architecture of the period. On the other side of the main entrance is a beautiful garden that's graced by a lovely tile fountain and a number of ancient fig trees planted by the convent's founding friars and nuns.

The real attractions here, however, are the frescoes in various stages of disintegration. In a number of instances the topmost layer of paint has faded to reveal a totally different mural below it and yet a third below that, with probably a century elapsed between the first application of paint and the last. In addition, the crypt in the basement houses the mummified remains of several priests and nuns (the mummification occurred as the result of a sudden volcanic eruption some 200 years ago that took its victims by surprise). The adjoining church also has some excellent 18th-century religious paintings by the Spaniard Cristóbal de Villalpando.

A few blocks north of the Museo del Carmen, on the same (east) side of Avenida Revolución, is the building housing the **Carrillo Gil Museum**, with its outstanding permanent collection of modern Mexican art, including works by Rivera, Orozco, O'Gorman, and Siquieros. The museum also mounts frequent exhibits of other artists' work, foreign as well as Mexican.

From the museum, head back south on Avenida Revolución to the Museo del Carmen and then a bit to the southwest to the Plaza de San Jacinto. Mounted on a wall on the western side of the plaza is a plaque that reads: "In memory of the Irish soldiers of the heroic Battalion of Saint Patrick, martyrs who gave their lives for the cause of Mexico during the unjust North American invasion of 1847." The San Patricio Battalion was made up of deserters, most of them Irish-Catholic immigrants, from General Winfield Scott's army. Brutalized by the harsh treatment dispensed by their officers and lured by Mexican promises of citizenship and free land, these U.S. soldiers switched sides and fought against their former comrades-in-arms at the Battle of Churubusco. Eventually, however, superior discipline and firepower resulted in victory for Scott's troops, and the 71 members of the San Patricio Battalion were summarily tried and hanged in the plaza.

The **Bazaar Sábado**, in the northwest corner of the plaza, is an artisans' cooperative set up on two floors of a former 18th-century mansion, where you'll find almost 200 small shops arranged around an oval-shaped patio open to the outside and offering every kind of hand-crafted item imaginable. In fact, many of the artisans are themselves immigrants from Europe and the United States, and have been drawn to Mexico by the richness of its folkloric heritage. The bazaar is open from 10:00 A.M. to 8:00 P.M. every Saturday, and visitors can partake of an excellent afternoon buffet in the patio featuring traditional Mexican cuisine for non-Mexican palates (i.e., not too spicy). A marimba band in the native costumes of Chiapas adds just the right touch to this lively scene.

Outside the entrance to the bazaar you'll encounter Indian women squatting on the sidewalk selling their handicrafts at about half the cost of what you would pay inside. They expect—and look forward to—haggling over price; the prices inside, on the other hand, are fixed.

You will recognize the **Museo Estudio Diego Rivera** by its bright colors. Located at the corner of Calle Altavista and Calle Palmas (Altavista runs west from Revolución just one long block north of the Plaza de San Jacinto/Plaza del Carmen area), Rivera's studio-on-stilts was designed by architect-muralist Juan O'Gorman and opened as a museum in 1986 on the hundredth anniversary of Rivera's birth. This rather bizarre structure, which actually consists of two studios—the blue one was used by Rivera, the crimson one by his wife, Frida Kahlo—connected by a boldly modern concrete bridge, sticks out like the proverbial sore thumb in this neighborhood of discreet colonial mansions, and has been the cause of more than a few arguments. The continually changing exhibitions of the master's works on the ground floor, on the other hand, are almost always greeted with enthusiasm.

Diagonally across the street from the Rivera museum is the landmark 17th-century hacienda that, for years, has been one of the capital's most elegant restaurants, the **San Angel Inn**. It was perhaps inevitable that, with its colorful history (the San Angel served as headquarters for General Antonio López de Santa Anna during Mexico's war with the United States, and was used for the same purpose by Emiliano Zapata and Pancho Villa 64 years later) and outstanding architectural elements, the inn would become a stop for tour buses. The caliber of the food and service has dropped considerably. Still, a stroll through its grounds will give you a little taste of what hacienda life must have been like for the privileged few who enjoyed it during the long centuries of Mexico's colonial domination.

There is a taxi stand nearby; the valet at the inn will be happy to call one for you. Taxis also cruise on Avenida Revolución.

The pre-Classic archaeological site of **Copilco** is located about 1 km (½ mile) south of the Insurgentes Sur turnoff for the Plaza de San Jacinto, just north of University City. At only ten feet below a layer of ancient lava, excavations here in 1917 uncovered several tombs, pottery, clay figurines, and stone implements that date back as far as 1500 B.C. Today, three tunnels created by the original excavations have been converted into a museum, and several of the tombs are displayed in the same position and condition in which they were found, complete with the ceramic, stone, and bone objects that were found with them.

The site is open Tuesday through Sunday. The number 3 metro line will get you there from the *Zócalo* area in 15 minutes, while even the fastest taxi will take three times that. If you decide you simply have to drive yourself, take the "Copilco" exit off Avenida Insurgentes Sur (about 2km/1 mile south of the Monument to Alvaro Obregón) and turn left onto Avenida Copilco. Turn left again almost immediately and follow the signs. The entrance to the site is at Calle Victoria 54.

University City

A sea of molten lava from the eruptions of Ajusco and Xitle ("Little Smoking Mountain") almost 2,000 years ago marked the end of the ancient Cuicuilco culture. Today, this same lava field is the setting for one of the largest universities in the world.

Located about 15 km (8 miles) south of the *Zócalo* on Avenida Insurgentes Sur, the Universidad Nacional Autonoma de Mexico (more commonly known as UNAM) is also by succession the oldest university in the Americas, having first opened its doors to students on January 25, 1553. Over the next four centuries the university saw its facilities become scattered throughout the ever-expanding city, and it wasn't until 1950 that construction of a vast complex to consolidate its many activities and physical plant was begun.

The university now boasts more than 80 buildings and 300,000 students (medicine is the most popular field of study), in addition to its wealth of cultural facilities. The main reason most people visit the campus, however, is to enjoy the many spectacular murals here by some of Mexico's greatest 20th-century artists. With so much color and form commanding one's attention, it is perhaps the **Central Library mural** that catches the eye above all the others. Painted by the versatile Juan O'Gorman, it is a startingly dramatic depiction of Mexico's past, present, and future executed in a variety of materials, including stone, colored cement, tile, and blown glass. At first glance, the building itself appears to be windowless, but closer inspection reveals that its many windows discreetly serve as an integral part of the overall design.

Other outstanding examples of *muralismo* on the campus of the university include David Alfaro Siqueiros's three-dimensional *People for the University and the University for the People,* which incorporates a wall of the building known as the Rectory to make its statement; Jésus Chavez Morado's two murals in the auditorium of the university's science tower; and Francisco Eppens's huge mural entitled *Life and Death* on the façade of the School of Medicine building.

To the west of the campus across Avenida Insurgentes Sur is Mexico City's **Olympic Stadium**, the principal venue for the 1968 Summer Games. Here, as elsewhere in the capital, art serves a dual function: the stadium was designed to resemble a volcano, and is adorned with striking reliefs created by Diego Rivera.

To get to University City, take the number 3 metro line to the "Universidad" stop (the last stop). By bus, walk to Insurgentes Sur and take either the 17, 17A, or 17B bus; from Coyoacán Center take the number 19A bus west on Calle Centenario. A university-run bus will swing by the city bus stop and pick up passengers interested in making a circuit of the campus, with stops at all the major buildings.

To the west and south of the stadium, extending over an area bounded by Avenida Universidad, Boulevard de la Luz, the Periférico, and Calle Zacatepetl, you'll find the exclusive residential neighborhood of **El Pedregal** ("the field of stone"), where some of the finest examples of contemporary Mexican architecture hide behind an encircling wall. While the ancient lava field itself spreads to the east and south under University City and Coyoacán, it is here in El Pedregal where it is most noticeable. Formed almost 2,000 years ago when nearby Xitle erupted with tremendous force and devastating consequences, the result was a stark and almost surrealistic moonscape. About 40 years ago, the architect Luis Barragan began to encourage wealthy clients to purchase land here and then built them innovative yet elegant residences that adapted to the irregular and dramatic terrain of the area rather than requiring that it be leveled. Other architects began to follow Barragan's lead, and in time the neighborhood became one of the most desirable addresses in the city. Today the overall effect is stunning, and El Pedregal can hold its own with the world's most exclusive neighborhoods.

The best way to see El Pedregal is by taxi. If you're going to take your own car, head south on Insurgentes Sur to Avenida Universidad (the "Salida" exit), just before the stadium. Follow Universidad until you come to Paseo del Pedregal, then take a left. Courteous guards at the entrance to this walled-in community will screen visitors briefly—usually no more than a glance into the car—and then wave you in. A leisurely tour of the neighborhood will take about 15 minutes.

The earliest evidence of advanced civilization in the Valley of Mexico was uncovered at the archaeological site of **Cuicuilco**, just southeast of El Pedregal, during the construction of dormitories to house the athletes slated to participate in the 1968 Olympic Games. To everyone's surprise, under the almost 10 feet of lava that had engulfed much of the surrounding area as a result of the eruption of Xitle construction workers discovered a circular pyramid that, when it was finally uncovered, proved to be almost 18 meters (60 feet) high and 125 meters (41 feet) in diameter. Further excavation and study revealed evidence of irrigation canals at the site and established the pyramid as having been built around 500 B.C., predating Teotihuacán (see below) by some 300 years. The artifacts found here also indicated that the inhabitants of Cuicuilco had combined farming with subsistence activities such as hunting and fishing, and had abandoned the site in the first century B.C., just prior to the volcanic eruptions. Everything else about these early inhabitants of the valley remains shrouded by the mists of time. There is a small museum at the site with samples of the pottery uncovered here, as well as a map detailing all the pre-Classic sites that have been discovered in Mexico to date.

Cuicuilco can be reached by following Insurgentes Sur south (follow the "Cuernavaca" signs) to the "Villa Olim-pica" exit. Make a U-turn back on to Insurgentes and head north; the pyramid will be on the right.

XOCHIMILCO

The perfect way to experience both grass-roots Mexico and the feeling of ancient Mexico, when the Aztecs' capital city was spread out over dozens of islands, large and small, and connected by a network of canals, is to treat yourself to a Sunday afternoon gondola ride in Xochi-milco (so-che-MEEL-ko).

Ironically, in the centuries before the Conquest, Xochi-milco (the Aztec word for "fields of flowers") was just an ordinary village on the shores of a lake. Then someone came up with the idea of *chinampas,* or nursery beds, to increase the acreage under cultivation of this already fertile area. In the decades that followed, raftlike plots of cultivated earth were created on frameworks made of sticks and clay and then set afloat in the shallows of the lake while remaining attached to the shore by cables. Eventually the root systems of the cultivated plants would grow through the framework, anchoring the plot to the lake bottom, and so, over the centuries, the "floating islands" of Xochimilco were formed.

Today only five canals from the once-great Aztec city remain—all of them in Xochimilco—and the traffic on them is so heavy (especially on weekends) that at times they resemble nothing so much as bumper-car rides. But don't let that discourage you. Even though the waters are as murky as those in Venice, there are no unpleasant aromas emanating from them. Instead, the soft afternoon breezes—which are scrubbed free of the capital's notori-ous smog by prevailing winds—carry the aromas of freshly rolled tortillas, tacos, and a dozen other delicacies sold by pleasant Indian women out of their crude flat-bottomed canoes. Elsewhere, gondolas filled with ma-riachi or marimba bands glide by, auditioning for a chance to serenade you—for a small fee—as you glide along Xochimilco's waterways.

A standard-sized gondola, which has room for eight, will cost the same regardless of the number of people in your party. Each *remero* (the licensed gondolier, of which there are over 300 in Xochimilco) will provide a cooler filled with beer and soft drinks (you have to supply your own wine or Champagne). At the conclusion of the ride you pay the *remero* for his time as well as the beverages consumed—and, of course, you should tip him. (Tipping in Mexico differs somewhat from the norm in the United States and Canada. Taxi drivers, for example, expect no tip. If you're unsure of the proper etiquette in a given situation, just ask.) If you so choose, you can also rub shoulders with the locals on one of the larger gondolas, which hold about 50 people. An hour's cruise on one of these will cost approximately 400 pesos, and it's not at all a tourist trap; on weekends, nine out of ten of the larger gondolas will be filled with Mexican families out for a picnic or lovers sharing a bottle of wine. For those who would rather cruise the canals in relative solitude, the gondolas at Xochimilco are for hire every day of the week, at all hours. Still, it is well worth investigating a Sunday tour, which are offered by all the major travel agencies and many of the city's hotels. These tours usually include a morning performance of the Ballet Folklórico at Bellas Artes; a few hours in Xochimilco, with lunch and a gondola ride included; and either an afternoon bullfight at the Plaza México or a tour of the murals at University City.

Xochimilco has more than its gondola rides to recommend it, however. The public market here is always bustling with activity, and the fruits, vegetables, and flowers for sale are probably the freshest and cheapest in all of Mexico. In fact, most of the produce and flowers for sale in the hundreds of markets throughout the capital are grown right here, as they have been since colonial times, when they were transported by boat along the canals and eventually the Acequia Real, or Royal Canal, to the *Zócalo* area. In the first half of the nineteenth century, small steamships travelled between Xochimilco and towns as far away as Texcoco, 50 km (30 miles) north of Mexico City. (You can still view a portion of the Acequia Real at the southeastern corner of the *Zócalo,* between the National Palace and the Supreme Court; see the *Zócalo* section above.)

In addition, the town's own *zócalo* is one of the most charming in the entire country, its delicate *huexote* trees providing a lovely contrast to the more conventional species planted throughout the square. The 16th-century Church of San Bernardino, with its fortress-like appearance and an elaborate altar canopy inside, is well worth a visit, as is the Xochimilco School of Fine Arts, in the Barrio de la Concha at Avenida Constitución 600, with its murals by Manuel Tolsá (*Apotheosis*) and Acevedo Navarro (*Romantic Muses*). If you have a car, a ride of a few minutes will take you to the village of Santa Cruz Acalpixan and the **Xochimilco Museum of Archaeology**, which is located on Avenida Tenochtitlán and built into the side of an ancient pyramid.

Los Manantiales, an immense restaurant—it has seating for 1,000 diners—with an outrageously ugly exterior is located a few minutes' walk from the gondola docks over a short bridge, and serves surprisingly good international-style food even though it caters to tourists—which simply means that the hygenic standards here are superior to those maintained at the many food stands and smaller restaurants scattered around town. In general, however, the food in Xochimilco is highly regarded by the locals.

Although it's 25 km (15 miles) south of downtown Mexico City, Xochimilco is easily accessible on the metro system. Take the number 2 line to the recently inaugurated "Xochimilco" stop, the southernmost station on the line. Outside the station, *peseros* will be lined up and ready to take you to your destination. Take one marked "Embarcadero" and you'll be at the gondola docks in ten minutes. A regular taxi from the downtown area, on the other hand, will cost about 20,000 pesos one way.

THE PYRAMIDS OF TEOTIHUACAN

If you were limited to visiting only one archaeological site in all of Mexico, Teotihuacán (tay-oh-tee-whah-KHAN) would not be a bad choice. Teotihuacán, about 50 km (30 miles) northeast of downtown Mexico City, was once the religious and commercial center of a great highland civilization (also known to us as Teotihuacán) that predated the Toltecs by a thousand years and the Aztec empire by some fifteen hundred years. In fact, the Classic period of Mesoamerican civilization in Mexico's central highlands was dominated by Teotihuacán, whose influence was felt as far away as Oaxaca, the Yucatán (the Classic Maya civilization there was roughly its contemporary), highland Guatemala, and, to the northwest, Zacatecas. And yet, even as late as the early years of our own century all of this was still unknown, and Teotihuacán was considered merely a local culture roughly contemporaneous with the Aztecs.

Today the evidence seems to indicate that Teotihuacán

developed from villages that made their initial appearance in the Valley of Mexico sometime around the middle of the first millennium B.C. and gradually grew in size and sophistication. By 200 B.C. a small township had been established on the site, and for the next 800 years Teotihuacán flourished, reaching an estimated population of 200,000 by A.D. 600. Then, for reasons still unknown, the city was abandoned during the eighth century. For years the most popular theory concerning the demise of Teotihuacán held that it had fallen to marauding northern tribes, but a more recent theory maintains that its demise was probably the result of what today would be called poor resource management, or, more simply, Teotihuacán's having outgrown its available resources.

All the generally accepted names in the immediate area, including "Teotihuacán"—in the Nahuatl language, "the Place Where Men Became Gods"—were coined by the Aztecs when they discovered the ruined city more than five centuries after it was abandoned. By then, most of the ceremonial structures—which are believed to have originally been brightly painted—had been buried under a thick layer of dirt and debris. The Aztecs believed that these mounds of earth lining the main avenue at the site were actually the tombs of the deceased giants responsible for building the city in the first place, and named this central axis the Street of the Dead.

To date only an estimated one-tenth of this ancient city has been uncovered—a remarkably low percentage when you consider that several hundred murals, over 2,000 residential complexes, 80 temples, and over 700 workshops have already been uncovered. (There are several "archaeological" Teotihuacáns, numbered I to IV, with the last beginning around A.D. 650 and lasting less than a hundred years.)

As was the case elsewhere in Mesoamerica, the pyramids of Teotihuacán originally were built as platforms for ceremonial temples. However, no tombs have yet been linked to these structures—which distinguishes Teotihuacán from such sites as Palenque and Monte Albán. In fact, Teotihuacán is unique, as far as ancient Mesoamerican ceremonial sites go, in that the murals and sculpture uncovered to date do not contain the slightest hint of thematic violence. Instead, the religious symbolism of the artwork found at Teotihuacán revolves around the stars, the rain god Tlaloc, and the benign plumed serpent-god Quetzalcóatl.

A good starting point for your visit to Teotihuacán is the Unidad Cultural, a small complex at the southernmost entrance to the site (near the Temple of Quetzalcóatl and the Citadel) that contains shops, rest rooms, a second-floor restaurant with views of the site, and a good museum offering concise overviews of what is to follow. Lunch should also be considered before you begin, because restaurants at the site are few and scattered. **La Piramide**, located on the second floor of the Unidad Cultural, offers adequate, moderately priced Mexican and international-style cuisine. If you're looking for better fare, with prices to match, the best can be found at the nearby **Villa Arqueológica**, one of a chain of fine Club Med–operated hotels at archaeological sites. In addition to its fine food, the Villa Arqueológica boasts an excellent library with books in several languages, tennis courts, and a swimming pool. (The other advantage of the place, should you decide to stay here, is that you can start your exploration of Teotihuacán early in the morning, before the tour buses from the capital arrive. See the Accommodations section for Mexico City below.)

A few minutes' walk from the hotel is **Piramide Charlie's**, a branch of the popular Carlos 'n' Charlie's chain. For a more romantic setting try **La Gruta**, a restaurant built inside a massive natural cave. To get there, walk to the Pyramid of the Sun, turn east and walk through Parking Lot D to the access road, and then turn left. Both the food (Mexican geared to northern tastes) and music, which is enhanced by the cave's great acoustics, contribute to the charm of the place.

The most typically Mexican restaurant in the area is called **El Gran Teocalli**, and is located about 1 km (½ mile) from the Unidad Cultural in the village of San Juan Teotihuacán. Chicken enchiladas are the specialty here, and they live up to their reputation. The marimba music in the background is also good.

With lunch out of the way, begin your tour at the **Unidad Cultural museum**. In the vestibule stands a full-sized copy of the colossal statue of Chalchiuhtlicue, the goddess of rivers and lakes, the original of which, now on display in the National Museum of Anthropology, was unearthed near the Pyramid of the Moon. While you're here, look especially for the ornately decorated stone death-mask inlaid with jade, garnets, and other gemstones—one of the finest examples of Mesoamerican art ever uncovered.

Outside the entrance to the museum is the beginning

of the **Street of the Dead**, the broad avenue, a kind of Via Sacra, that serves as the axis around which the site was planned. The reasons behind its almost exact north-south orientation (it's actually aligned 15°30′ east of true north) are still being debated, though it's generally agreed they had to do with astronomical alignments.

Directly opposite the Unidad Cultural is the **Citadel**, one of the most interesting architectural groupings at Teotihuacán. This immense quadrangular complex is bounded by four platforms (three of which have two stories) surmounted by smaller temples. The entrance to the complex is via a broad staircase, which leads inside to a sunken patio. Usually, in Mesoamerican cultures, already existing structures were covered over and built upon rather than demolished. In the case of the Citadel, excavation revealed that it had been built on top of an older (circa A.D. 200), much more impressive structure, the **Temple of Quetzalcóatl**, now partially revealed at the rear of the complex. To reach the latter, walk across the patio to the squat temple platform with a staircase. On the far side of the platform you'll come upon the façade of this masterpiece of the Classic period, with its sculpted heads of the dragon-like Quetzalcóatl and the even more stylized figure of the rain god Tlaloc. The huge courtyard within is adorned with other well-crafted sculptures as well.

From the Citadel, proceed up the Street of the Dead to the massive **Pyramid of the Sun**, which, together with the Pyramid of the Moon, dominates the entire site. Believed to have been constructed during the first century B.C., the pyramid stands on a base only 3 meters (10 feet) shorter on each side than the Pyramid of Cheops but is less than half as tall. Nevertheless, it is the largest structure in the New World to survive from antiquity (the great pyramid in Cholula being larger but in ruins).

The pyramid itself consists of five superimposed platforms and is ascended by a double staircase that merges to form a single staircase two-thirds of the way up. Although the climb to the summit is a strenuous one, the view once you get there is breathtaking—if you have any breath left. Spread out below with a geometric exactness that is startling is all that remains of this more than 2,000-year-old city. Unfortunately, the mammoth gold statue that used to stand at the summit of the pyramid (it may have been placed there by the Aztecs) was ordered removed by Juan de Zumarraga, the first archbishop of Mexico City.

The next major attraction to the north is, aesthetically speaking, the most striking at Teotihuacán: the **Plaza of the Pyramid of the Moon**. An imposing patio surrounded by a variety of even more imposing platforms, the plaza is a worthy lead-up to the **Pyramid of the Moon**, located at the end of the Street of the Dead. Consisting of four sloping levels, and situated on a rise (which makes it appear as if it's the same height as the larger Pyramid of the Sun), the Pyramid of the Moon is the most harmoniously designed structure in this ancient city. Archaeologists have managed to reconstruct the façade and massive staircase of the pyramid, which was built around the same time as the Pyramid of the Sun, so that at least an impression of its original splendor is present.

On the west side of the plaza is the **Palace of the Quetzal Butterfly** (*Palacio del Quetzalpapálotl*), the only roofed structure to have been uncovered so far at an archaeological site in Mexico. First discovered in 1962 and subsequently restored, the rooms of the building are arranged around a patio whose elaborately carved pillars feature the stylized representations of birds and owls, as well as the butterflies that lend the palace its name.

Two other half-buried structures in the plaza area are also worth a look. The Palace of the Jaguars, due north of the Palace of the Quetzal Butterfly, has a portico on which you can still see some well-preserved murals depicting jaguars in plumed headdresses blowing into plumed conch shells. And, as you exit this courtyard, a modern tunnel to the right leads you to the Palace of the Plumed Snails, which dates from the 2nd or 3rd century and is distinguished by its bas-reliefs of feathered seashells with mouthpiece-like devices (presumed to be instruments) and red and green parrots ejecting streams of blue liquid from their beaks (the overall effect is best viewed from the southeast exit to the Street of the Dead).

The last stop at Teotihuacán is reached by taking a right at the Pyramid of the Sun, walking through Parking Lot 2, and then following the road to the ruins of the residential quarter of **Tepantitla**, about 1 km (½ mile) from the Street of the Dead. Along the way you will pass a room adorned with a mural of elegantly dressed priests in headdresses, and then come to an enclosure, the walls of what was once an atrium-like structure. Here you'll find the remains of the most famous mural of the Teotihuacán III period (350–650): *The Paradise of Tlaloc,* which de-

picts human figures sunbathing and chasing butterflies—
the Teotihuacáns' vision of a state of grace.

There is a sound-and-light show at the site (in English)
every day of the week except Monday. Traditional Indian
music, mostly wooden flutes and percussion, provides
haunting accompaniment to the impressive lighting displays of the temples and pyramids and the narration of
ancient myths. The shows start at 7:00 P.M., so bring
something warm to wear; the early evenings at this altitude are almost always chilly.

GETTING TO TEOTIHUACAN

You'll need an early start to enjoy this day away from the
hustle and bustle of the city in a leisurely way. Teotihuacán
is about a 100 km (60 mi) round trip, but unquestionably a
must. If your desire is just to visit the site, use the buses that
leave the D.F. at frequent intervals from the terminal across
the street from the "Indios Verdes" metro station, line 3.
The buses are marked "Piramides-Teotihuacán." The last
bus back to the capital leaves at 6:00 P.M. from the main
entrance to site, next to the Unidad Cultural. There is also
regular bus service to Teotihuacán from the Terminal de
Autobuses Norte, which can be reached via the number 17
or 17B bus, or on line 5 of the metro.

If, on the other hand, you wish to attend the sound-
and-light show (nightly except Mondays), head to the
Monument to the Revolution for the special 6:00 P.M. bus;
Tel: 535-6345 for reservations and return schedules.

All major travel agencies and most hotels offer tours to
Teotihuacán, with prices varying depending on the itinerary involved. You might also consider renting a taxi for the
day. If your visit is during the dry season (November
through May), the 7:00 P.M. sound-and-light spectacular is
well worth attending, and the optimum itinerary would
mean a 9:00 A.M. departure from and a 9:00 P.M. return to
your hotel, for a fare of about 100,000 pesos. You can also
stay overnight at the site at the Villa Arqueológica (see
Accommodations below).

If you are driving, head north on Avenida Insurgentes
and follow the signs to Highway 85D. At the 15-km (9-
mile) mark, take the toll rather than the free road toward
Pachuca. At the 25-km (15-mile) mark, bear right for
Teotihuacán after paying your toll. Follow the signs to
Highway 132. At the 34-km (20½-mile) mark you can
turn off and follow the signs to **Tepexpán**, less than a
mile away, where a small museum (open 10:00 A.M. daily;

closed Mondays) houses the fossil remains of mammoths unearthed nearby.

These remains have been dated at about 8,000 B.C. The most amazing display, however, is the remains of what is reputed to be the oldest human being ever discovered on the continent, unearthed from under a layer of saltpeter that corresponds to a period of drought that occurred some 10,000 years ago.

From Tepexpán return to Highway 132 and continue another 4 km (2½ miles) for the next side trip. Exit to the right and follow the road to the towering fortress-like walls of the monastery and church of **San Agustín Acolman**, now a museum (open daily from 10:00 A.M.; closed Fridays).

Among the first communities founded by the Augustinians in the New World, the monastery and adjoining church were begun in 1539 and completed in 1560.

The church is a stylized mixture of the Gothic and Baroque. At the end of the vast nave and around the cloister are unsigned murals depicting a group of monks, probably the dignitaries of the order. The murals themselves are believed to have been painted toward the end of the 16th century. The main altarpiece, Baroque in design, has paintings dating from the 17th and 18th centuries, while the side altarpieces are typical of the Churrigueresque style.

The second floor has two arcades made interesting by paintings from the 19th century, a library with a collection of theological works, and an exhibition room displaying pre-Hispanic artifacts uncovered during 20th-century excavations.

To the right of the church entrance, level with the first floor of the monastery, is a small open-air chapel with a picturesque arch framing its entrance. Inside is a well-executed fragment of a mural portraying Saint Catherine. The monastery itself, with its series of cramped cells, gives you a feeling for the austere life led by the monks.

After San Agustín Acolman it's back to the highway for the final 13 km (8 mi) to Teotihuacán.

GETTING AROUND IN MEXICO CITY

Public Transportation

Mexico City has an outstanding public transportation system, and the sparkling metro is one of the capital's pride and joys. French-designed and built, the trains run on rubber wheels from one brightly lit station to the next; the entire network covers a distance of 150 km (90 mi), and is still expanding.

At the time of publication the fare was 100 pesos. It's best to buy tickets in blocks of five, to avoid long lines. The maps posted in every metro car are quite comprehensive, and a symbol-color system is employed so that it is not necessary to understand Spanish. To change lines, follow the signs that say "Correspondencia" and the name of the terminal station on the line you want and in the direction you are going. Avoid rush-hour trips (7:00 to 10:00 A.M. and 5:00 to 8:00 P.M.) if at all possible. During these hours, cars are segregated by sex, although a female may accompany her male companion on a "male only" car. Cumbersome luggage is also not permitted during rush hours. Smoking is prohibited at all times and classical music fills the air most of the time. Maps and general assistance are provided at information desks in all the major stations.

On Saturdays all lines operate between 6:00 A.M. and 1:30 A.M. On Sundays and holidays all lines operate between 7:00 A.M. and 12:30 A.M.. On weekdays all lines operate between 6:00 A.M. and 12:30 A.M.

Peseros
Peseros are collective taxis (usually Volkswagen Combis) painted pale green that run up and down the major avenues. They charge 350 pesos a person minimum, and extra on top of that if you travel beyond a certain point—usually 5 km (3 mi) from the spot where you were picked up. When the driver has room aboard he cruises slowly and holds up his fingers outside his open window to indicate the number of available seats, and you can get off at any point along the set route. *Peseros* are safer than buses because there is no standing room allowed, cramping the style of potential pickpockets. Say *"Baja, por favor"* when you wish to get off.

Buses
At your own risk. There is no maximum capacity, so they often resemble cattle cars. The fare is extremely reasonable, 100 pesos a ticket, but buses are a pickpocket's paradise. Still, they're an efficient way to travel if you know precisely where you and the bus are going (the drivers tend to be reckless, however). Buses only pick up

and discharge passengers at *parada* signs, and will stop only when the buzzer at the rear exit is pressed.

Taxis

Volkswagen Beetle taxis are the least expensive. Make sure the driver turns on the meter after you get in. If he doesn't, settle on the price in advance (many meters are allegedly "broken"). There is, by law, a current price list pasted to the rear side window that translates the meter reading.

While *sitio* taxis charge more, their drivers are also usually more knowledgeable about the city. (Private limousines, with commercial license plates and hooded meters, are found parked outside major hotels. They charge about three times the normal fare, but most of their drivers speak some English. They will also hire out by the hour.) In general, fares for private taxis are about a third of what their counterparts north of the border would charge. Nighttime prices are slightly higher, and drivers do not expect a tip. A *libre* sign in the window means the taxi is available. Strangely enough, a lighted front beam at night indicates the taxi is occupied, while no beam means it's available—but good luck distinguishing a "no-beam" as a taxi in the dark.

Any taxi is authorized to take passengers *to* the airport, although only those belonging to the airport concession are permitted to bring passengers into the city *from* the airport. In other words, don't be lured into jumping from your place in line to flag down an empty city taxi as you're waiting to get out of the airport.

Car Rental

Renting and driving a car in the capital is not recommended unless you are a veteran Mexico City driver and do not mind paying twice what the same car would cost to rent in the U. S. or Canada.

Consider only the major international agencies. Vehicles from private agencies are often unreliable mechanically, and the road service, in the event of a breakdown, is unpredictable.

The Mexican National Railway

Although it's not a fact well-known among tourists, Mexico has a fairly extensive passenger rail network. In fact, it's possible to traverse the country from coast to coast and north to south in comfort and safety, as well as with a minimal amount of aggravation.

Sixteen large cities and border towns are connected to Mexico City by direct rail service. (The Buenavista Station, located on Avenida Insurgentes a few blocks north of its intersection with Paseo de la Reforma, is the *only* station with connections to all sixteen destinations.) For those with limited finances and the luxury of time (punctuality has not yet been elevated to a virtue by the National Railway), it's a great way to travel.

On most long trips you'll have a choice of sleeping arrangements: a *couchette,* a *dormitorio,* or, the most expensive, a Pullman car. The former is a chair that reclines enough to allow you to sleep (in theory); a *dormitorio* is a cramped 6-bunk version of a Pullman; a Pullman, with two beds to a cabin, is well worth the added cost.

You can purchase tickets for any destination at any of the windows in the Buenavista Station, or from most travel agencies in town.

ACCOMMODATIONS
Most of the best hotels in the D.F. are centrally located within walking distance of each other, and range from elegant contemporary to intimate colonial in style. With one exception (the Fiesta Americana Aeropuerto), the ones recommended here can be found within an area bounded by the *Zócalo* to the east and Chapultepec Park to the west. Generally speaking, the more moderately priced accommodations will be found north of Paseo de la Reforma in the neighborhoods around the U.S. embassy. The "Big Four"—the María Isabel-Sheraton, the Camino Real, the Hotel Nikko México, and the Stouffer Presidente Chapultepec—are all located west of the U.S. embassy. Expensive by local standards but about 20 to 25 percent less than you would pay for comparable accommodations in New York, Toronto, or London, these four—each with many more rooms than most hotels in the Zona Rosa or near the U.S. embassy—have everything a seasoned traveler expects from a luxury hotel: excellent restaurants; first-rate fitness facilities; chic boutiques; interesting nightlife; and easy access to the major tourist attractions in the city.

The better hotels in the D.F. all have air conditioning, but it's usually not needed here except for a few days in early May just before the rainy season commences. The months of peak occupancy are December through March (especially Christmastime) for the luxury hotels, and July and August for the more moderately priced ones.

The country code for Mexico is 52; the area code for Mexico City is 5.

Chapultepec Park Area

The **Camino Real**—one of Mexican architect Ricardo Legoretta's masterpieces—is a stark low-slung structure that covers a city block facing the eastern perimeter of beautiful Chapultepec Park. Outside, the Camino Real is one of the best examples of "Mexican minimalism," a term coined by Legoretta himself when asked to describe his austere designs. Inside, the parquet floors in the huge lobby provide an ideal background for a mural by Rufino Tamayo and a Calder stabile in yellows, purples, and shocking pinks. The Camino Real's more than 700 rooms are spacious and comfortable, and each is equipped with a marble bath. In addition to its three first-rate restaurants—especially **Fouquet's**—its nightclub and bars, four swimming pools, rooftop tennis courts, and 24-hour coffee shop, the Camino Real is within walking distance of the outstanding museums in Chapultepec Park and only a ten-minute cab ride from the shops and cafés of the Zona Rosa or the newly fashionable Polanco district, making it an ideal site from which to explore and enjoy Mexico City. The hotel has a garage and in-house travel agent; telex and fax machines, valet service, and car rentals are also available.

Mariano Escobedo 700; Tel: 203-2121; to make reservations in the United States and Canada: (800) 228-3000.

The **María Isabel-Sheraton**, east of the park on Reforma and next door to the U.S. embassy, is conveniently located a few minutes' walk from the heart of the Zona Rosa. There are over 800 rooms in the hotel as well as several good restaurants, and the **Restaurant Veranda** offers spectacular views of the Monument to Independence, otherwise known as "The Angel," in addition to its offbeat evening entertainment (things like poetry readings). Other services and facilities include a rooftop pool, two tennis courts, an in-house travel agent, two bars, a nightclub, a garage, laundry and valet service, a fully equipped gym, a variety of shops, and telex and fax machines.

Paseo de la Reforma 325; Tel: 211-0001; to make reservations in the United States and Canada: (800) 325-3535.

The 38-floor Japanese-built and -operated **Hotel Nikko México**, next door to the Stouffer Presidente Chapultepec (see below), opened its doors in 1987. Like the other major luxury hotels in the D.F., it is a huge affair, with 750 spacious and tastefully decorated rooms, several bars and restaurants (featuring excellent Japanese, Mexican, and French cuisine), a nightclub and discotheque, an in-house travel agent, laundry and dry-cleaning services, a jogging track and fully equipped gym (complete with sauna), three tennis courts and a rooftop swimming pool, a heliport, and telex and fax machines. What separates the Nikko México from its competitors are its high-tech touches: doors are locked and unlocked with electronic card-keys and the telephones are connected to a central computer system that notes things like guests' dining preferences and their birthdays. In addition, the top floors of the hotel are reserved for those who desire the royal treatment, or a reasonable facsimile: private registration, an exclusive clublike lounge, and private secretarial services are among the extras. There are also two authentically decorated, and very costly, "Japanese" suites in this part of the hotel.

Campos Eliseos 204; Tel: 203-4020; to make reservations in the United States and Canada: (800) 645-5687.

Entering the large and modern **Presidente Chapultepec**, which was recently purchased by the Stouffer chain, is a unique experience. Guests are immediately confronted by a beautiful five-story lobby shaped like a pyramid and featuring a skylight ceiling and a luxurious garden. In addition to its 800 rooms there are five good restaurants here, with the best being **Maxim's**. The live music in the lobby's bar attracts a young singles crowd most nights, and there are a number of exclusive boutiques lining the mezzanine. Conveniently located overlooking Chapultepec Park, the Presidente also has a garage, an in-house travel agent, a nightclub, a swimming pool, and telex and fax machines.

Campos Eliseos 218; Tel: 250-7700; to make reservations in the United States and Canada: (800) 472-2427.

Zona Rosa

The **Aristos**, located in the heart of the Zona Rosa, has large and nicely decorated rooms; those on the upper floors have great views of Paseo de la Reforma. Other amenities here include restaurants, a bar, a nightclub, an in-house travel agent, laundry service, telex and fax machines, and a garage.

Paseo de la Reforma 276 (entrance on Calle Copenhague); Tel: 211-0112; to make reservations in the United States and Canada: (800) 223-0888.

The **Century Zona Rosa** has Roman-style marble baths in all of its rooms. Its bar, decorated in African-safari style, is a bit garish but fun. A swimming pool, restaurant, car-rental desk, garage, and telex and fax machines round out this likable establishment.

Liverpool 152; Tel: 584-7111.

A member of the Westin Hotel chain, the **Galería Plaza** has an international rather than Mexican atmosphere, its beautiful lobby with splashing fountain serving as the centerpiece. Facilities and services include a swimming pool, three restaurants, a lobby bar, a disco, a shopping arcade, an in-house travel agent, laundry service, telex and fax machines, and a garage.

Hamburgo 195; Tel: 211-0014; to make reservations in the United States and Canada: (800) 228-3000.

The **Krystal Zona Rosa** has recently been refurbished; as a result, its large and comfortable rooms are now elegantly decorated. Other facilities and services include a swimming pool, two restaurants, a bar, a nightclub, an in-house travel agent, laundry service, and telex and fax machines.

Liverpool 155; Tel: 211-0092.

The **Royal Zona Rosa** is a pleasant family-style hotel with comfortable rooms, a restaurant, a bar, an in-house travel agent, laundry service, a swimming pool, garage, and telex and fax machines.

Amberes 78; Tel: 525-4850.

Another pleasant, ultra-modern hotel, the **Plaza Florencia** has spacious (and soundproof, according to management) rooms, a restaurant, a nightclub and bar, a garage, and telex and fax machines.

Florencia 61; Tel: 533-6540.

Thirty years ago the **Calinda Geneve Quality Inn** was the D.F.'s most popular tourist accommodation. After slipping a bit in subsequent decades, it was purchased and refurbished by the Calinda Quality Inn chain a few years ago and today has regained much of the colonial charm of its heyday. Its rooms encompass a range of styles and décor (a pre-registration check of the room you have been given is advisable), and the "jungle bar," located at the back of the lobby in an area that resembles a giant greenhouse, is a D.F. landmark. The facilities and services here include a restaurant and bar; tobacco, beauty, and barber shops; an in-house travel agent; a car-rental desk; and laundry service.

Londres 130; Tel: 211-0071; to make reservations in the United States and Canada: (800) 228-5151.

For those who prefer cooking facilities in their rooms, the following establishments are recommended.

The **Marco Polo**, a sleek, modern structure with 60 beautifully designed rooms, provides cooking facilities for the preparation of breakfast as well as semi-private dining areas. The four penthouse rooms are well worth the extra cost. The Marco Polo also has a restaurant and bar, laundry service, a garage, and telex and fax machines.

Amberes 27; Tel: 511-1839.

In addition to the cooking facilities in its 48 compact but comfortable rooms, the **Internacional Havre** has a restaurant and bar, laundry service, and a telex machine.

Havre 21; Tel: 211-0082.

The **Suites Imperiales Niza** has 51 well-designed suites with kitchenettes, a garage, laundry service, and a telex machine.

Niza 73; Tel: 511-9540.

Around the U.S. Embassy

Comfortable, modestly priced accommodations are the rule across from the Zona Rosa north of Paseo de la Reforma in the vicinity of the U.S. embassy. Though of course this is a little bit farther away from the shops and great restaurants in the heart of the Zona Rosa, for most people the added savings will more than make up for the slight inconvenience.

The **Romano Diana** has adequate rooms and a restaurant decorated to look like a pirate ship. There's also a nightclub and bar, as well as a garage.

Río Lerma 237; Tel: 211-0109.

The **Bristol**, with pleasant rooms, is a good value for the money. Facilities and services include a rooftop pool, a bar in the lobby, a restaurant and garage, and laundry service.

Plaza Nécaxa 17 (at the corner of Río Panuco and Río Sena); Tel: 533-6060.

The **Hotel Del Angel** has comfortable if modest rooms, and offers good value for the price. Other facilities and services include a restaurant and bar, an in-house travel agent, a garage, and laundry service.

Río Lerma 154; Tel: 533-1032.

The **María Cristina**, a very pleasant, colonial-style hotel, offers excellent value for its moderate rates. In addition to its 146 rooms, the hotel has a restaurant and bar, a tobacco shop, an in-house travel agent, laundry service, and a garage.

Río Lerma 31; Tel: 546-9880.

There is, in addition, a variety of accommodations offering cooking facilities in this neighborhood.

The **Parioli** has 30 well-furnished rooms with kitchenettes, as well as laundry service and a garage.

Río Po 108; Tel: 533-0154.

Just down the street, the **San Marcos** also has 30 rooms with kitchenettes.

Río Po 125; Tel: 533-2041.

Slightly larger, the **Michelangelo** offers 36 comfortable rooms with kitchen facilities, as well as a garage.

Río Amazonas 78; Tel: 566-9877.

The 48 rooms in the **Silver Suites** are plain but comfortable, and all have cooking facilities. The establishment also has a restaurant and bar, a garage, and laundry service.

Sullivan 163 Bis (near the intersection of Paseo de la Reforma and Avenida Insurgentes); Tel: 566-7522.

The Zócalo area

The beautiful Art-Nouveau lobby, featuring a stained-glass Tiffany dome and old-fashioned cage elevators, is the pride and joy of the **Gran Hotel de la Ciudad de México**, which is conveniently located on the *Zócalo*. The 100 rooms here, on the other hand, are adequate but not nearly as elegant as the lobby. The hotel does offer excellent service, however, as well as great views of the *Zócalo* from the rooms on its upper floors, an in-house travel agent, a restaurant and bar, and a garage.

16 de Septiembre 82; Tel: 510-4040.

The **Majestic** offers pleasant colonial décor in a 16th-century building overlooking the *Zócalo*. Some of its rooms are rather cramped, so a pre-registration check is advisable. There are great views of the historic *Zócalo* area from the rooftop restaurant, and the hotel also has a bar, an in-house travel agent, and laundry service.

Calle Madero 73; Tel: 521-8600; to make reservations in the United States and Canada: (800) 528-1234.

The **Monte Carlo**, a spotlessly clean hotel housed in a 17th-century building, is very popular with visiting foreign students. For about $10 a night you can get one of the large, airy, no-frills rooms surrounding the hotel's courtyard. And the Monte Carlo is only a few minutes' walk from the *Zócalo*.

Uruguay 69; Tel: 521-2559.

Other Choices Downtown

Located just north of Alameda Park, one block west of the Franz Mayer Museum, the **Hotel de Cortés** is housed in a former 18th-century hospice that today is a national monument. Behind its fortress-like façade, the 25 clean, reasonably priced rooms are clustered around a truly lovely tree-shaded patio. It offers, in addition, above-average food and service, and stages a great folkloric show in its courtyard every weekend.

Hidalgo 85; Tel: 518-2181; to make reservations in the United States and Canada: (800) 528-1234.

The large, modern **Crowne Plaza**, part of the Holiday Inn chain, is always pulsating with activity—usually because it's hosting yet another convention or tour group. Located halfway between the Zona Rosa and Alameda Park on Paseo de la Reforma, the hotel has five nightclubs offering top-quality entertainment, which makes it a focal point of nightlife in the D.F. Other facilities and services include a swimming pool, three restaurants, two bars, a disco, an in-house travel agent, a solarium, telex and fax machines, secretarial services, and a garage.

Paseo de la Reforma 80; Tel: 566-7777; to make reservations in the United States and Canada: (800) 465-4329.

The original décor of the **Emporio**, on Paseo de la Reforma near the Zona Rosa, was early Space Age. Redecorated a few years ago, some of the rooms have been left more or less intact, and "garish" is the only word for those, so a pre-registration check is advisable. All the rooms in the Emporio have Jacuzzi baths, however, and the hotel also has a restaurant, a bar in the lobby, telex and fax machines, and a garage.

Paseo de la Reforma 124; Tel: 566-7766.

The ultra-modern **Sevilla Palace**, also on Paseo de la Reforma, has over 400 spacious rooms, a number of expensive boutiques, a rooftop pool, a spa-type health club, a fully equipped gym, restaurants and bars, telex and fax machines, and a garage.

Paseo de la Reforma 105; Tel: 566-8877.

The **Vasco de Quiroga**, which is across the street from the Benjamin Franklin Library (an excellent English and Spanish library affiliated with the U.S. embassy) and a ten-minute walk from the Zona Rosa, boasts just 50 comfortable rooms and lovely colonial décor. It also has a restaurant and bar and offers laundry service.

Londres 15; Tel: 591-0244.

Outlying Areas

A few minutes' walk from the international airport terminal and reached directly via an overhead ramp, the two-year-old **Fiesta Americana Aeropuerto** advertises itself as "the only hotel with its own adjoining airport." Whether or not you consider that an advantage, there are some 270 large rooms here, a nightclub featuring the best in Mexico City entertainment, a bar, a number of restaurants, a gymnasium, an in-house travel agent, telex and fax machines, and a garage.

Fundidora de Monterrey 89; Tel: 762-0199; to make reservations in the United States and Canada: (800) 223-2332.

Owned and operated by Club Med, the **Villa Arqueológica**, located north of the city at the Teotihuacán archaeological site, is a small but comfortable motor inn with a good restaurant and a bar. Tel: 595-60244 or 595-60609; to make reservations in the United States, 800-528-3100; to make reservations in Canada: 514-937-7707.

DINING

Mexico City can boast of at least 30,000 registered restaurants, among which you will find not only regional *restaurantes* featuring exquisite native delicacies (and, often, live music from every corner of the country) but superb international-style dining rooms as well. At the same time, on almost any street corner in the D.F. you will find women selling *carnitas* (chunks of roasted pork), tacos, and enchiladas. Many people say that the best Mexican food is found at the tiny stalls, or *fondas,* in neighborhood markets, but going out to a special restaurant is a national pastime.

Many of the best restaurants in the D.F. were created by folks who had never run one before or who liked to eat, happened to own a prime location for a restaurant, and who then learned the business through trial and error. Other bistros are manned by European chefs who came to Mexico to direct the kitchens at the large international hotels and then fell in love with the country and decided to try their luck with their own establishments. The dining-out scene in the capital has been enriched by their daring. Most owners of the better restaurants have in common a passion for food, people, and a flair for showmanship. As Jane Pearson Fernandez, the owner of the Piccadilly Pub and Sir Winston Churchill's, put it: "Every day you have to put on a show that appeals not only to taste but to all the senses."

The sheer number of dining establishments in the D.F. guarantees a virtually unlimited range of culinary experiences. You can, for example, feast in former haciendas and 19th-century French-style mansions complete with lush gardens and exotic peacocks that will evoke Mexico's colonial past. Or you can embark on a gastronomic journey of the country by eating in the city's *fondas,* where you can sample such regional specialties as *cochinita pibil* (roast pork in barbeque sauce) from the Yucatán; *enmoladas de mole negro* (chicken with black *mole* sauce) from Oaxaca; or *albondigas de armadillo* in *salsa de huitlacoche* (armadillo meatballs in a sauce made with a rare and exceptionally flavorful black fungus). Often the menus will sound like the lyrics to a song in an ancient language: *garnachas* (fried tortillas covered with sour cream and chile sauce); *pambazos* (a fried roll filled with beans, hot sausages, and chiles); *pelonas* (a *pambazo* made in Puebla); *totopos* (the original nacho); or *chicharrones* (fried pork rinds). Even the foreign chefs here have been influenced to some extent by traditional Aztec and Mayan fare. As a result, certain ingredients will show up on the menus of trendy international eateries with some frequency, among which the aforementioned *huitlacoche* (sometimes spelled *cuitlacoche*), which grows on corn; *cilantro* (coriander), which is sometimes referred to as Chinese parsley; and *flor de calabaza,* the flower of the yellow squash plant.

There is an old Mexican saying that goes, *Todo se aregla en la cama o en la cantina,* and translates as, "Everything can be fixed in the bed or in the bar," but which in practice means that more important business details in the D.F. are closed over a lunch table in the Zona Rosa than are concluded in the glass skyscrapers that line Paseo de la Reforma. Recently, these "business" lunches—which often used to wind up as wild soirées, with the tequila being shared liberally with members of the always-present mariachi band—have been replaced by working breakfasts—which is one reason why you may find yourself standing in line for breakfast at your hotel at 8:00 A.M.

(Margarita aficionados should be aware that it's almost impossible to get a U.S.-sized frozen margarita in Mexico City, where they're usually served in Champagne glasses with bits of ice floating around on top. Many Mexicans dining out like to down a couple of tequilas straight instead, with a *sangrita,* or spicy tomato juice, as a chaser. They say it "opens the appetite." Remember, though, that alcohol has an accelerated effect in the D.F. due to the altitude; new arrivals in the city should also be careful not to eat too much.)

The better Mexico City restaurants tend to be on the snobbish side. You can almost always count on excellent service at these establishments, but they will insist on relatively formal dress. (In the *fondas,* on the other hand, you can wear what you like.) When in doubt phone the captain and ask about the dress code—it's better to get this information over the phone rather than at the door.

The prices of most dishes in exclusive restaurants will be less than you would expect to pay in comparable restaurants in big cities in the United States, Canada, or Europe. Imported wines, on the other hand, are pricey and can cost more than your entire meal; most restaurants will have a local wine list, however. Major credit cards are accepted in all D.F. restaurants unless otherwise noted. (Many will attempt to avoid American Express but will acquiesce if it's the only one you offer.)

The restaurants listed below all cater to international guests. They claim to use purified water in all drinks as well as in their ice cubes, and also claim that all vegetables and fruits on their menus are disinfected. A phone number accompanies the listing only if reservations are recommended.

Most restaurants in the D.F. are open from 1:00 P.M. to 1:00 A.M. The locals start to pour in from 2:00 on; to guarantee a table for lunch, get to the restaurant you've chosen by 1:00. Dinner crowds peak at about 9:30 P.M. Many restaurants are closed Sunday evenings; check first.

Zócalo Area

El Danubio, located at Uruguay 3, south of the *Zócalo,* is a serious eatery with an emphasis on large portions of seafood at reasonable prices. You can also order Spanish dishes such as *cabrito Vasco* (Basque-style goat) and French pastry. Popular with middle-class Mexicans, El

Danubío has an impressive cold counter featuring lobsters, crabs, clams, and baby eels.

Café de Tacuba, at Tacuba 28, occupies an historic building filled with colonial paintings and decorated with antique Talavera tiles. The café, which claims to be the first in the country and is renowned not only for "the whole enchilada" but for its *chilaquiles,* tamales, *buñuelos, panuchos, pambazos,* and tacos as well, is especially popular with theatergoers and those attending a performance at the nearby Bellas Artes.

Located southeast of the *Zócalo* at Jesús María 22, within walking distance of the square and near its sister restaurant Don Chon (Regina 159), El Mesón de Alonso is justly famous for such pre-Hispanic palate teasers as *iguana en salsa verde* (iguana in pumpkin-seed sauce), *león en salsa de ajonjali* (puma leg in sesame sauce), *albondigas de armadillo en salsa de nuez* (armadillo meatballs in nut sauce), as well as such delicacies as *tepexcuintle* (prairie dog), stuffed chrysanthemums, ants' eggs, wild boar, snake, and venison. For the less adventurous, the *quesadillas de flor de calabasa* (squash-flower quesadillas) or the *tacos de salpicon de venado* (deer-salad tacos) are unforgettable. The clientele here used to be almost exclusively merchants from different regions of the country who had travelled to the D.F. to sell their produce at the nearby market of La Merced. Today it's not unusual to find jetsetters and foreign ambassadors munching on maguey worms and other rare comestibles and washing it all down with mescal from Oaxaca. No matter who's sitting at the next table, however, El Mesón de Alonso is an indelible experience.

The Hotel de Cortés, at Avenida Hidalgo 85, near Alameda Park, is possessed of a setting so beautiful that it more than makes up for its rather ordinary food. Once a notable convent, this colonial-era building is now an oasis for tired museumgoers in the afternoon. In the evening, the soft lights on the gushing fountain and the sparkling candles on the little tables set up in the patio add to the aura of romance here. In addition, every Saturday night the fixed menu includes an alfresco Mexican folklore ballet.

The Hotel Majestic, at Avenida Madero 73, offers some of the best views of the *Zócalo* in the city from its rooftop restaurant. Sunday lunch, which begins early, includes a splendid buffet of Mexican dishes served casserole-style. They say you don't know the people of Mexico City until you have crowded into the traditional dining room at the **Hostería de Santo Domingo**, which also claims to be the oldest restaurant in the country. The service at this perennially popular establishment is swift, but on Sunday afternoons you still have to wait in a line that stretches down the block. A perfect chow stop for those who have been busy touring the central historic district, the Hostería offers *chiles en nogada* year-round. Located north and west of the *Zócalo* at Belisario Domínguez 72.

That many artists, intellectuals, and other restaurant operators flock to "La Casa Paco," as the locals call it, is all you need to know about the **Fonda de San Francisco**. The fresh flowers on the tables and in the wall recesses are changed every day, and the *sopa de flor de calabaza,* which is served in a squash shell, the crab crêpes, and the delicious *sopa de queso* are as good to look at as they are to eat. Located west of the Monument to the Revolution at José Velasquez de León 126, near the phone company building. Closed Sundays. Tel: 546-4060.

Zona Rosa

Bellinghausen was owned by the Austrian Bellinghausens until 1962, when Chef Enrique Alvarez took over the management of this bustling steak-and-seafood establishment, which is located at Londres 95. Sizable servings of crawfish spiced with paprika and olive oil, shrimps in garlic sauce, and a notable red snapper in a light chile sauce are among the specialties that make this a favorite meeting place of Mexican businessmen. Tel: 511-1056.

When Nick Noyes came to Mexico in 1953 he couldn't find a decent steak to eat, so he opened his own restaurant featuring imported beef. Today, thanks to Nick's creation, **Delmonico's**, at Londres 87, not only can you feed on premium U.S. beef in Mexico City, you can also find strawberry cheese cake and triple bittersweet chocolate cake. A real New York steak house, except that the service is superb. The Sunday brunch here is legendary. Tel: 528-7530.

The owners of **El Olivo**, Manolo Fernandez and Henri Donnadieu, are enthusiastic patrons of the arts: All the paintings on the walls of this trendy establishment are for sale. The two also own the celebrated gay nightclub El Nueve and claim to have pioneered Mexican nouvelle cuisine with dishes such as *chile pasilla* soup with Roquefort cheese and *pollo santo* in acuoyo leaf. A hangout for members of the advertising and fashion worlds by day and a meeting place for the gay community by night, El Olivo is located at Varsovia 13. Tel: 525-3822 or 511-4234.

A number of restaurant critics put **Estoril**, Génova 75, among Mexico's finest restaurants. Oaxacan chef Pedro Ortega learned to cook from his Indian mother, who taught him the recipe for his divine *crepas de huitlacoche* (corn-fungus crêpes), and every Thursday and Friday he prepares her chicken in black *mole* sauce. His *perajil Estoril* (fried parsley) is rumored to have aphrodisiacal qualities. Closed Sundays. Tel: 511-3421.

Named for Luis Buñuel's first film, *An Andalusian Dog,* **El Mesón del Perro Andaluz**, Copenhague 26, used to cater to the capital's filmmaking set. Now it's one of a trio of affiliated outdoor eateries, each with its own front-row seats on the colorful parade of Mexican streetlife. Next door, **El Mesón la Marisqueria del Perro Andaluz** serves seafood. Across the alley, Italian chef Mario Saggese prepares the pasta dishes at his **El Perro D'Enfrente**. Tel: 514-7480.

Focolare, at Hamburgo 87, is known as "the Restaurant of the Three Suns," because it features gastronomic specialties from three distinct regions of the country—Veracruz, Oaxaca, and the Yucatán. It also serves a breakfast buffet (you can eat all you want while a marimba band plays in the background) and a different kind of *mole* sauce every day. Things pick up on Saturday nights, when there's a Mexican folk-dancing show and a simulated cockfight. Tel: 525-1487.

The **Fonda del Refugio**, at Liverpool 166, is often called "the cathedral of Mexican cooking." Known for food that is not too spicy, it offers a large selection of tacos, *chalupas poblanas, gorditas,* and baked chiles, all prepared with natural ingredients. While the Fonda del Refugio doesn't sell bottled drinks, it does offer safe fruit drinks called *agua frescas.* Owner Freddy Van Buren is a purist who personally supervises everything from the killing of the livestock to the creation of his homemade pork sausages. Closed Sundays. Tel: 525-8128.

Located at Hamburgo 117, **La Cucaracha**, a voguish restaurant by day and a candlelit disco by night, is a rather surrealistic establishment where you can find international celebrities, jet-setters, and Mexican luminaries munching on plates of iguana, snake, wild boar, and tacos filled with fried grasshoppers and covered with sauces made from mango, *huitlacoche,* or rose petals. Owner Gregorio Perales, know to his friends as "Goyo," is particular about choosing his customers, but if you make a reservation there is always room for a new aficionado. Tel: 207-2093 or 207-2059.

La Lanterna, Paseo de la Reforma 458, features traditional Italian food; the pasta is made on the premises every day. It's also a great choice if you are dying for a pizza. Try the omelette Vonfihure flambé for dessert. Tel: 511-3757 or 207-4469.

Tons of fresh seafood arrive at **La Marinera**'s kitchen every morning, and Chef Pedro Hipolite Palomares will prepare your lobster in any one of eight different ways. The large and succulent oysters on the half shell here are also a treat. Located at Liverpool 183, this informal place is open 365 days a year, and there are several tables outside for open-air dining.

Passy, a garden restaurant with French décor at Amberes 10, is housed in a late 19th-century mansion on the Zona Rosa's most elegant street. Popular with executives for the past 32 years, the crab pancakes, seafood in a shell, and coq au vin are so good that Passy will, in all likelihood, be serving them for another three decades. Wear a tie. Tel: 511-0257 or 207-3747.

Rivoli, at Hamburgo 123, was for years the undisputed king of French restaurants in Mexico. Built in 1950 and decorated with ornate mirrors, crystal chandeliers, and posh red-velvet Louis XVI chairs, it was intended to rival the great French restaurants in Europe. Though there are now other claimants to the throne, it is still a formal, superior eating establishment. Tel: 525-6862 or 528-7789.

For years it was all but impossible to get a decent Chinese meal in Mexico. That's no longer the case, and **Yi-Yen,** at Hamburgo 140, is one of the reasons why. The Cantonese chef here grows his own bean sprouts, and other authentic ingredients are readily available these days thanks to the relaxation of some of Mexico's import restrictions. Closed Sundays.

Yug, at Varsovia 3, is a neighborhood vegetarian restaurant offering a variety of meatless Mexican dishes. The baker here makes fresh brown bread daily, and papaya, carrot, orange, and alfalfa juice are available year-round. There is also a whole-grain bakery and health-food store on the premises. Tel: 533-3296.

Near the U.S. Embassy
The embassy district is north of Paseo de la Reforma, opposite the Zona Rosa.

There are six Japanese restaurants in the neighbor-hood. **Daruma**, at Río Tiber 50, is the least attractive and has the worst service, but the food here is by far the best available in the D.F. for the price. The place is so popular, in fact, that you probably will have to stand in line for a table if you go between 2:30 and 4:00 P.M.. You should also be aware that if you want to order *sake,* a bottle may cost as much as the rest of your meal. Tel: 511-7902 or 511-8115.

Housed in a beautiful 19th-century mansion at Río Sena 88, its patio framed by classical sculpture and lush greenery, **Les Moustaches** is one of Mexico City's most stunning restaurants. It offers more than elegant décor, however; you quickly get the feeling you have walked into another world as you are ushered to your table. At Les Moustaches everyone is treated like a visiting digni-tary. Start your meal with a smoked salmon soup or a spicy shrimp bisque. End it with flaming baked Alaska or the amaretto soufflé. But don't forget to wear a tie. Reser-vations are recommended; Tel: 533-3390.

Las Fuentes, located at Río Panuco 127, two blocks north of the Monument to Independence, is a roomy, comfort-able, and sparklingly clean vegetarian restaurant—the best of its kind in the capital. French-American owner Phillip Cauthorn, who somehow manages to greet every cus-tomer, takes pride in personally purchasing his produce every day at dawn in the Merced market. The result is the absolutely freshest food in town—and the largest help-ings. There are great breakfasts (from 8:00), and all the prices are very reasonable. Las Fuentes is crowded at lunchtime, but the service is so good that you shouldn't have to wait more than a few minutes, even if the line winds out the door and into the street. There's also a retail shop here that stocks a wide variety of top-grade health foods.

Polanco

You can enjoy the atmosphere of "a thousand and one Arabian nights" and dance until dawn with Mexico's Middle-Eastern community at **Adonis**, Homero 424. The food here—falafel, raw and fried kibbe, tabouli, fish with nuts, stuffed grape leaves dipped in tahini, date pie, and other Middle Eastern favorites—is the real thing. Tel: 531-8081, 531-6940, or 250-2064.

At **Amadeus**, Suderman 336, Chefs Imre Nagy and Paco Riviera give every diner a basket of fresh vegetable bread and seasoned butter to start their Middle-European dinner. Also excellent here are the Black Forest hams, Hungarian sausages, smoked trout, goat cheese, duck soaked in blackberry sauce, and goulash with egg noodles. In addition, the desserts at Amadeus are homemade. Tel: 254-3061 or 245-3081.

Chef Jacques Bergerault came to Mexico in 1957 to open the kitchen of the famed Las Brisas in Acapulco. Today he and his sons run the **Café de Paris**, Campos Eliseos 164, one of Polanco's most courtly establishments, and one especially dedicated to pleasing its customers. In fact, Bergerault himself goes to the market twice a week to find the best available ingredients for his daily specials. If *trucha* (trout) Veronique is not on the menu, ask for it. For a very reasonable price per person the Café de Paris will also send a chef and waiter to cook and serve dinner to you and a minimum of three others anywhere in the city. Tel: 531-6646.

El Parador de José Luis, long an institution in the Zona Rosa, has now brought its Mediterranean food and Spanish décor to Polanco, Campos Eliseos 198. Try their *tapas*. El Parador is also a good place to rest after a strenuous day of shopping in Polanco's expensive boutiques, or to indulge in a serious paella (but give the chef an extra 45 minutes to prepare it). Tel: 545-6465.

Just as the Camino Real can claim to be the best hotel in the D.F., **Fouquet's**, in the Camino Real, can legitimately claim to be the best French restaurant in the city. Superb service at lunch as well as dinner, live music, and spectacular flaming dishes make this a favorite with socialites, diplomats, and members of the Mexican communications industry. Tel: 203-2121.

The **Hacienda de los Morales**, Vásquez de Mella 525, was originally the site of Mexico's first silkworm farm. The colonial-era fountains, chapels, paintings, and furniture here evoke that past, and the hacienda is worth a visit for its architecture alone. Considering all the bustling activity created by the conscientious, fast-moving staff as they serve hundreds of elegantly dressed diners, the food is exceptionally good. Don't miss the cold walnut soup. Tel: 540-3225.

Located in a neo-colonial home at Molière 50, not far from the Polanco hotels, **Isadora** is usually packed for lunch and dinner. Chef Carmen Ortino named her restaurant after the flashy, rebellious dancer because she, like Isadora Duncan, is a passionate performer—of the culinary arts. Reservations are advised, especially if the lovely Carmen is orchestrating one of her seasonal food festivals. A great choice in any season, however, is her ravioli stuffed with *huitlacoche* and covered in a light chile and corn sauce (*raviolis relleno de huitlacoche en salsa de chile poblano*). Tel: 520-7910.

The **King's Pub**, Arquimedes 31, is an authentic English pub where informality reigns. Owner Pepe Meehan likes to play the host. Try one of his "McMeehan burgers," the safe salad bar, and the draft beer. There is also live jazz upstairs in the evenings. Tel: 254-2655.

If you have to limit yourself to just one Mexican restaurant, make it the **Fonda del Recuerdo**, Bahía de las Palmas 39, where four strolling bands play Veracruzano folk music—simultaneously. Not a place to propose marriage, perhaps, but a terrific fun-stop where the fiesta never seems to end. Known for its giant portions (truckloads of fresh seafood from Veracruz arrive daily), the house offers specialties that include a drink called the "torito"—guanabanana and mamey juice mixed with *aguardiente*. The Fonda del Recuerdo has English menus and features everything from tortilla soup to crabmeat turnovers. There's also a babysitter on hand in a tot-lot to entertain your children. Tel: 545-7260.

La Tablita, Presidente Masaryk and Torcuato Tasso, is an Argentinian steak house that serves the choicest cuts of meat prepared with special herbs and red-wine sauce. Dining here is something like eating in a greenhouse; the smell of steak cooking on individual braziers fills an atrium alive with the chatter of shoppers and well-dressed businessmen. Try the cheese turnovers (*empanadas*). Tel: 545-4806 or 531-4119.

El Buen Comer, Edgar Allen Poe 50, a small French bistro in the garage of a private home where the customers all seem to know each other, specializes in quiches and fondues. Their beef Bourguignonne is made with the tenderest morsels of steak. The house wine is from the vineyards of Tequisquiapán, Querétaro. El Buen Comer does not accept credit cards. Tel: 254-3061 or 203-5337.

Sir Winston Churchill's, Boulevard Avila Camacho 67, is not just for those who need a quick fix of bangers and mash. In fact, this oasis in an old Tudor mansion is one of the finest, as well as most attractive, eating places in the city. Inside, the walls are mahogany; the tables are set with fresh flowers and cranberry glass goblets; the fireplace may be roaring. In this regal setting you can indulge in a tender rib eye, a rare piece of roast beef, or a flaming skewer of shrimps in herb butter. Among the many sinful desserts is a cappuccino mousse with whipped cream. If you don't have time for dinner, go for tea. And the Irish coffee is great. Coats and ties required. Tel: 520-0585 or 520-0065.

Lomas de Chapultepec

Lomas is a luxurious residential neighborhood in the western D.F. that begins where Paseo de la Reforma turns southwest beyond Chapultepec Park. Magnificent trees line Reforma here, and beautiful old mansions prevail. The area is about 20 minutes by taxi from the Zona Rosa; your restaurant will call you a taxi for the ride back after dinner.

Columbian-born Guillermo Gomez fell in love with his beautiful partner and wife Elizabeth in Victoria, Canada; then, in a daring moment, they decided to move to Mexico City and try their luck as restaurateurs. The result of their decision is the romantically chic **Isla Victoria**, located at Monte Kamerun 120 in a small mansion on a tree-lined residential street. The menu offers daily specials such as Colombian chicken soup served with capers, cream, and avocado; or *marminto* soup, a cream of mushroom and shrimp soup served in bowls covered with a puff-pastry dome. Dress is semi-formal (chic semi-formal, of course); if you manage to look as if you've stepped out of a fashion magazine you will be treated as an honored guest—even if you're not sporting a tie or a diamond necklace. Children are not allowed. Tel: 520-5597.

San Angel

Located between Avenidas Insurgentes Sur and Revolución at Avenida de la Paz 45, a few blocks east of the Plaza de San Jacinto, **Los Irabien** is one of the very best restaurants in the capital, as well as a convenient stop for breakfast, lunch, or dinner on your way to or back from the lovely colonial villages of Coyoacán and San Angel. The Irabien family is dedicated to excellence and caters to more than just your taste buds. Beautiful works of art, including originals by some of Mexico's finest painters, are discreetly interspersed among the spectacular potted plants, antique Mexican furniture, and carved wooden statues. Walls colored in unusual, subdued hues serve as the perfect background for the many visual treats here. The dining area itself is very comfortable, with every seat offering a fine vantage point of the rest of the room, and a pianist performs at lunch and dinner.

The kitchen is under the supervision of inventive master chef Enrique Estrada. One of his many delicious creations is a liver pâté presented atop a sculpted gelatin, itself a work of art. His *sopa de mariscos* (fish) with Pernod is memorable, as are two dishes from the nouvelle cuisine section, both featuring *huachinango* (red snapper)—*huachinango en nopalitos al mojo de ajo* (spineless cactus leaves filled with filet of red snapper and fried in garlic) and "El Rey del Caribe" (red snapper topped with *huitlacoche* and *flor de calabaza*). Closes at 6:00 P.M. on Sundays. Tel: 660-2382 or 548-1706.

King's Road, located a block east of the landmark San Angel Inn at Altavista 43, is an elegant English pub–type restaurant that specializes in serving some of the best quality beef in the D.F. The prime rib and the U.S.-style steaks are excellent, as are the breaded frog's legs. A pianist provides appropriate background music for all meals. Tel: 660-0883.

Restaurante del Convento

French-born chef and owner Gilberto Armand has created a lovely bistro in a portion of a former 17th-century monastery tucked away in an alpine-type forest protected as Desert of the Lions National Park. Located off the road that runs west to Toluca, a 30-minute drive from the Zona Rosa, it is accessible by car only. Once you arrive, however, the setting is positively exhilarating: sweet mountain air does wonders for the apetite. There are two dining rooms inside the fortress-like structure itself (one reserved for non-smokers), but the lovely garden patio is the best place in which to enjoy the exquisite food here.

Morels with cream is one of the rare treats offered by the Restaurante del Convento (available from June through November). Chef Gilberto's *trucha encapuchada* (fresh trout baked in pastry dough) is also outstanding. Madame Armand contributes to the culinary delights offered with her special recipe for truffles; her pâté and her fruit preserves are also memorable. In addition, most of the produce served is organically grown. The house wine comes from a nearby winery that permits Chef Gilberto to "grow his own wines," and the resulting product is infinitely superior to most Mexican wines. His own recipe for espresso is perhaps the country's finest, and is a perfect complement to the superb dessert the Armands call omelette Noruego—orange cake saturated in Cognac and served with a topping of homemade ice cream and whipped egg whites. You can also buy truffles, preserves, wine, and homemade bread to take home with you; they all taste almost as sensational away from this idyllic setting as they do in it. Closed Sundays. Tel: 570-3158.

NIGHTLIFE AND ENTERTAINMENT

Mexico City after dark can be exciting, but selectivity is the key factor. Keep in mind, however, that the mile-and-a-half altitude in the D.F. tends to make each cocktail about twice as intoxicating as it would be at sea level.

Most nightclubs, like most major restaurants, are closed Sunday evenings.

There is a very informative weekly publication, *Tiempo Libre,* that lists all the current events in the D.F.; the latest edition is available at newsstands every Friday.

Cocktail Lounges and Hotel Bars

Live music in most lounges commences at 8:00 P.M. and continues until the 2:00 A.M. closing time (a few remain open longer). Most of the best cocktail lounges are located in the major hotels.

The **Jorongo Bar** is a perennially popular night spot in the María Isabel-Sheraton, featuring the best in ethnic music (mostly mariachi) and jammed nightly in and out of season. It is also the closest thing to a singles bar in the D.F. Next door to the U.S. embassy at Paseo de la Reforma 325, across the street from the Zona Rosa.

The **Majestic Bar**, on the seventh floor of the hotel of the same name, offers superb views of the Cathedral and the National Palace, especially on weekends, when they are floodlit. With the sounds of mariachi music always swirling through the bar, the Majestic is not the place for intimate conversations, however. In the Hotel Majestic, Madero 73, on the *Zócalo.*

Don't be dissuaded by the sleazy appearance of **Tenampa**—if it's a slice of Mexico City life you're looking for, this is the place. The three or four strolling trios get an early (1:00 P.M.) start at this huge bar, often playing simultaneously as they circulate among the hundreds of tables, and usually wait until the last customer is gone, sometime around dawn, before wrapping it up. Believe it or not, the constant cacophony is tolerable, and as the tequila flows the camaraderie gets mellower. There are always bouncers mingling within and undesirables are prevented from entering, so it's really a perfectly safe scene. Credit cards are not accepted, however. North of Alameda Park on the Plaza Garibaldi.

Le Club, in the Hotel Camino Real, offers a comfortable—yes—clublike atmosphere, with large-screen English-language TV and soft recorded music in the background. Backgammon and chess tables are also scattered about. Open nightly from 9:00 P.M. to 1:00 A.M., except Sundays. In the Polanco district, Avenida Mariano Escobedo 700.

Discotheques

If you are fairly sober and presentable, you'll have no problem getting into any of the capital's discotheques. The normal cover charge is in the neighborhood of 25,000 pesos, and major credit cards (with the exception of American Express on occasion) are accepted. Most discos open at 10:00 P.M., but the real action generally doesn't begin until midnight. Closing time in most cases is 4:00 A.M.

Located in the heart of the Zona Rosa and always crowded, **Can Can** is a popular disco with a congenial clientele, which is usually equally divided between tourists and locals. At the corner of Calle Hamburgo and Calle Génova.

Cero Cero, in the Hotel Camino Real, has been one of the most popular discos in the capital for the last 16 years, and features live as well as recorded music. The psychedelic lighting alone is worth a visit. Mariano Escobedo 700.

The intimate **Disco Club 84**, in the Stouffer Presidente Chapultepec, has a good sound system and sleek, modern décor. Frequented by youthful locals and tourists alike. Campos Eliseos 218, across Paseo de la Reforma from the main entrance of Chapultepec Park.

Located north of the central historic district, **Magic Circus** is off the beaten path a bit, so it's best to take a taxi. The décor and lighting are state of the art, and crowds of young locals congregate here nightly, but those with sensitive eardrums might consider visiting the two other discos, under the same management, that are connected to it: **The Rock Garage** is slightly smaller and features parts of classic cars as tables. The enthusiastic waiters weave in and out of this chic junkyard-like area with surprising efficiency—considering the rather bizarre obstacle course they have to deal with. The entrance to the third member of the family is marked **Privilege**. A bit more toney than the other two, it insists on a dress code: men must wear jackets but need not wear ties; no slacks or shorts are permitted for women. Calle Rodolfo Gaona 3.

News, which is very similar in décor and ambience to the disco of the same name in Acapulco and is, in fact, operated by the same people, is the hippest and largest disco in the D.F. Open only on weekends, from 10:00 P.M. to 4:00 A.M., it is located at Avenida San Jerónimo 252, next door to Mauna Loa, a restaurant, about a half-hour's taxi ride south of the Zona Rosa.

With its ultra-modern décor, creative lighting, and excellent sound system, **Zazzy,** in the Hotel Nikko México, has become the new "in" disco in the D.F. Although it's usually crowded with a pleasant, youngish mix of locals and tourists, there is plenty of elbow room off the dance floor. Next door to the Stouffer Presidente Chapultepec, Campos Eliseos 204.

Nightclubs with Floor Shows

Located on the mezzanine level of the always bustling Holiday Inn Crowne Plaza, **Barbarella** offers two shows nightly, Mondays through Saturdays, featuring nationally known headliners. Popular with both locals and visitors, this modern, comfortable room has a relaxed, friendly atmosphere. You can dance to live music between shows, and snacks are served. Open 9:00 P.M. to 3:00 A.M.; Closed Sundays. East of the Zona Rosa at Paseo de la Reforma 80. Tel: 566-7777.

El Corral de la Moreria, in the Zona Rosa, is an intimate dinner club featuring top-quality Spanish music and flamenco dancing. Dinner doesn't quite match the entertainment, however, unless you're absolutely crazy about Spanish cuisine. Open 9:30 P.M. to 2:00 A.M. Calle Londres 161. Tel: 525-1762.

The massive landmark nightclub known as **El Patio** features national and international headliners every other month or so. When there is a show here (two a night), it is done on a grand scale, and there is always plenty to do afterward. The Patio's neighborhood, centrally located near the *Zócalo,* is a bit seedy but not dangerous; it is hard to find, however, so it's best to take a taxi. Calle Atenas 9. Tel: 535-3904 to check on upcoming events.

Located a few blocks south of the Zona Rosa and one block west of Avenida Insurgentes Sur at Calle Oaxaca 15, colorful **Gitanerias** has been a long-time favorite of flamenco devotees. Two shows nightly at 11:30 P.M. and again at 2:00 A.M.; closed Sundays. Tel: 511-5283.

Las Sillas means "the chairs" in Spanish, and there are over a hundred in this intimate, friendly room—no two alike—for your sitting pleasure. You can dance to live music before and after the midnight show. Open nightly 10:00 P.M. to 3:00 A.M.; closed Sundays. In the Holiday Inn Crowne Plaza, Paseo de la Reforma 80. Tel: 566-7777.

Marrakesh is a huge, very popular, always crowded establishment that is actually four clubs in one: Valentino's for dancing; the Morocco bar for a semi-singles scene; Casablanca for top-quality entertainment; and La Madelon for dinner and after-dinner dancing to live music. Frequented by wealthy locals and visitors alike. Open 9:00 P.M. to 3:00 A.M. nightly. In the Zona Rosa at Calle Florencia 36.

The **Plaza Santa Cecilia** is a traditional Mexican nightclub, with four folkloric shows nightly. The room is huge and the food is good, but patience is needed as the service is not especially swift—to put it mildly. Shows at 9:30 P.M., 10:30 P.M., 12:30 A.M., and 2:00 A.M.; there is a cover charge. Located north of Alameda Park on the Plaza Garibaldi. Tel: 526-2455.

The entrance to **Señorial**, located across the street from the Hotel Galería Plaza in the Zona Rosa, resembles an enormous upended milk container. Its three separate rooms with floor shows conducted simultaneously feature top-quality entertainment, and it's very popular with local businessmen, who often arrive in groups. There is a dress code. Open from 10:00 P.M. to 3:00 A.M., except Sundays. Calle Hamburgo 188.

Stelaris, on the top floor of the Crowne Plaza hotel, is considered by many to be the best supper club in Mexico City. The superb food, excellent entertainment (often internationally known headliners), and spectacular views of the city make this a high-priority choice. There is a dress code. Open nightly 10:00 P.M. to 3:00 A.M.; closed Sundays. Paseo de la Reforma 80, east of the Zona Rosa. Tel: 566-7777.

Dining and Dancing

Chez' Ar, a brightly colored nightclub in the Zona Rosa done up in Mediterranean décor, is a place where fun always seems to prevail. Equally popular with locals and visitors, you can dance to two different combos here from

9:00 P.M. to 3:00 A.M. nightly, except Sundays. Located in the Hotel Aristos, Paseo de la Reforma 276.

The **Restaurante del Lago** in Chapultepec Park is a beautiful dinner-dancing spot with glass walls offering panoramic views of the nearby lake and the spectacular fountain in front of its entrance. The international cuisine is good, and the live music starts at 8:00 P.M. Open from 1:00 P.M. to 1:00 A.M.; closes Sundays at 6:00 P.M. Take a taxi; your waiter will be happy to call you another when you're ready to depart. Tel: 515-9585.

The **Muralto** occupies the entire 41st floor of the Latin American Tower. The great views, which sometimes include the surrounding mountains and the Valley of Mexico, are alone worth the visit. In the evening, the city spread out below appears at its best. The live music begins at 8:00 P.M., and there's a strict dress code for men (tie and jacket). Open 1:00 P.M. to 1:00 A.M.; Sundays until 10:00 P.M. Tel: 521-7751.

Yesterday's, a comfortable, friendly ballroom in the Zona Rosa, is frequented by lots of young to fortyish singles six nights a week. The live music starts at 8:30 P.M. and goes until 1:30 A.M. Mondays through Fridays, until 3:00 A.M. Saturdays; closed Sundays. In the Hotel Aristos, Paseo de la Reforma 276.

SHOPS AND SHOPPING

Mexico City, which generates an abundance of artwork, high fashion, and handicrafts, is also the major market in the country for all types of traditional arts and crafts from outlying regional centers. Glassware and ceramics, for example, are only two of the many types of great buys that are available throughout the D.F.

There are large stores and open-air markets devoted exclusively to regional handicrafts scattered throughout the downtown area, with the products of the various states and regions usually separated into sections in each. At many of the markets Indian women wearing traditional garb will be working their looms on the sidewalks while waiting for customers. This should come as no surprise. Since Aztec times, the *tianguis,* or market, has been the economic heart of the Mexican pueblo, at once a place to barter goods and services, eat the local dishes, and visit with friends. Traditionally, markets are the cheapest places to buy arts and crafts, regional clothing, foodstuffs, herbs, leather bags, and silver.

Only a few of the *mercados* in the D.F. have English-speaking shopkeepers and accept credit cards, however. Still, if you possess a sense of adventure but just don't have the time to travel into the interior of the country, you can pay a guide to take you around some of these; you'll be able to pay for his time and car on the money you save. More important, you'll take home the memory of a real Mexican shopping spree.

Craft and Antiques Markets

The easiest to shop in is the **Centro Artesanal Buenavista** at Aldama 187, just off Insurgentes Norte near the Buenavista station. More like an American supermarket than a crafts market; here the vendors welcome major credit cards, and there's even a place for your guide to sip coffee while you browse through the mammoth warehouse containing more than 80,000 items. If you need gifts in a hurry, the selection of blown glass, brass, ceramics, silver jewelry, tablecloths, regional clothing, and gold (by the gram) is as good as in the Zona Rosa shops. Prices are fixed, and the vendors at the market will pack your purchases efficiently and get them to their destination safely. English is also spoken.

If you're looking for a little adventure and have time to bargain, on the other hand, you will do better at **El Mercado de la Ciudadela**, at the corner of Balderas and Ayuntamiento, just a few blocks south of Alameda Park. Built in a former fortress, the market has two *fondas* where you can take a break and drink a beer or order a *comida*. Oaxacan Indians dressed in red *huipiles* sit on the ground, their offspring crawling around their feet as they work diligently on backstrap looms weaving bedspreads, tablecloths, and serapes. There are dozens of workshops inside the peach-colored walls here, and everything from silver baubles and hand-blown glass to Huichol beaded jewelry and rugs is being crafted as you wander among the many stalls brimming with native handicrafts. Some shop operators will accept Visa or MasterCard, none American Express; most will honor travellers cheques and dollars. English here is limited to the basics, but nowhere else can you find such an economical and varied selection of masks (stall 65), copper, handmade guitars, pre-Columbian reproductions, lacquerware, embroidered *rebozos,* weaving, onyx, and rugs.

In the Zona Rosa itself is the **Mercado de Insurgentes**, with over 200 vendors who know what travellers like and are eager to accommodate them. (The entrances to the market are on Calle Liverpool and Calle Londres.) This is an especially reliable bazaar for purchasing silver jewelry and native clothing. Bargaining is expected, and many stalls accept some cards.

The **Saturday Antiques Market**, on Calle Florencia near the Reforma, is a flea market that sets up once a week in a patio in front of some antique shops. As a rule, antiques are overpriced in Mexico, but there is always the possibility of coming up with that unexpected treasure that makes the hunt worthwhile.

The **Mercado de Antiguedades de la Lagunilla**, or "Sunday Thieves' Market," is located two blocks east of Paseo de la Reforma Norte and the equestrian statue of José Martí, beginning on Calle Rayón and stretching east for dozens of blocks. Amid the tangle of booths selling imported video and audio cassettes, foreign cheeses, hair spray, U.S.-made candy, blue jeans, Ray-Bans, and offbeat items too numerous to mention there are some genuine antiques—and some possibly stolen from churches, so be careful. The vendors know what they have, and there are few bargains as a result, but don't hesitate to quibble over the price of an item.

Clinging to the walls on either side of this labyrinth of stalls are Indians who have brought their wares—masks, bark paintings, wooden fish with pastoral scenes sketched on their sides, and the like—from their villages to sell to the buyers of the various crafts shops. The prices for these goods are generally very reasonable.

The **Bazaar Sábado**, in an old colonial mansion on the Plaza de San Jacinto in San Angel (see the main narrative above), was formed by foreign artists as a place to sell their handmade crafts, many of which are their own conceptions of indigenous Mexican designs. Here, too, however, Indian women squat on the sidewalk in front of the old mansion and sell the real thing for less. If you like to sandwich your shopping around a meal, go for lunch; the bazaar's restaurant is commendable and the marimba band is excellent.

The Government Arts and Crafts Stores
To promote the production of regional arts and crafts as well as to help artisans finance their work, the federal and some state governments run their own shops. **FONART** shops (FONART is an acronym for "National Fund to Promote Arts and Crafts") can be found throughout the

country, as well as at four locations in Mexico City: Avenida Juárez 89, Centro; Londres 136, Zona Rosa; Avenida de la Paz 37, San Angel; and Patriotismo 691, Mixcoac. (Mixcoac is a middle-class neighborhood a few blocks from the Plaza México, the bullring. There's not much here other than the FONART shop, so you'll probably want to take a taxi if you go.) The items for sale vary, but normally there is a good selection of ceramics, jewelry, regional clothing, and glassware. FONART shops accept all credit cards.

The **Tapetes Mexicanos**, at Avenida Insurgentes Sur 2375, between Calles Rey Cuauhtémoc and Altamirano, is the place to buy the world-renowned Temoaya rugs. Created by Otomi Indian artisans using an ancient Oriental technique, these hand-knotted wool carpets are known as "Mexican Persian rugs," and the more than fifty styles and patterns are inspired by Mexican folklore. These rugs are heirloom souvenirs that will last for generations.

Located at Avenida Juárez 44, Centro, in a 16th-century structure that was originally the Church of Corpus Christi, the **National Museum of Folk Arts and Crafts** has a section open from 10:00 A.M. to 2:00 P.M. and again from 3:00 to 6:00 P.M. where you can choose from among the best for-sale display of regional clothing in town. There are also wonderful toys, jewelry, and seasonal arts here; at Christmastime an assortment of *nativitas* is for sale in ceramic or laton versions, and in November the museum has the best *calaveras* (skeletons) in town. At Easter you can choose from the most imaginative papier-mâché *judas* on sale anywhere.

CASART, at Avenida Juárez 18C, Centro, was specifically set up to promote the artisans of the state of Mexico. This is the only place in the D.F. where you can purchase a set of unleaded ceramic dishes from the Valle de Bravo, or find original items from Metepec, where villagers produce charming ceramic pieces.

Michoacán is also a notable producer of crafts, and an excellent sampling of what the state offers can be found at the **Casa de las Artesanías de Michoacán**, located at Campos Eliseos 199 and Temistocles in Polanco, in front of the Stouffer Presidente Chapultepec and the Hotel Nikko México. The region's blue-and-white ceramics (popular with Mexican decorators), copper pots with silver filigree, hand-crocheted table coverings, and carved wood columns and chests are among the many tasteful items for sale here.

The Popular Markets

If it weren't for these *tianguis* (where every shopper gets a wholesale price) it would be impossible for most Mexicans to weather their country's ongoing financial crisis. Although they appear to enjoy making crafts, most Mexicans don't buy them. Instead, they prefer to decorate their homes with imported foreign items.

The **Mercado de Sonora**, at Avenida Fray Servando and Calle San Nicolas, about 6 km (4 miles) due east of Chapultepec Park, sells all you need to cast or uncast a spell, which is why it's affectionately known as "the Witches' Market." There are some 30 stalls here, with vendors hawking amulets, dried bats, good- and bad-luck candles, soap to make you rich, wreaths of garlic to protect your home against the dreaded *envidia* (envy), dried hummingbirds to make a man irresistible to the opposite sex, live animals for sacrificial purposes, medicinal herbs, and decks of tarot cards. The market also abounds with cheap ceramics, toys by the dozen, chickens, ducks, geese, songbirds, iguanas, baskets, and party supplies.

Jamaica, at F. Morazan and Parque Guillermo Prieto, is the final destination for the truckloads of seafood that arrive daily from fishing ports on the Pacific and Gulf of Mexico. Dining areas in the market serve the freshest catch of the day at rock-bottom prices.

The **Mercado Cuauhtémoc**, at Río Lerma and Río Danubio, behind the María Isabel-Sheraton, is a neighborhood fruit and vegetable market where you can sample Mexican cheeses and choose from among a great variety of seasonings, among other things.

Inside the enormous **Mercado de la Lagunilla Unidad de Ropas**, located at Ecuador and Allende, a few blocks northwest of the *Zócalo,* you'll find enough clothing for sale to dress a regiment, including a variety of regional headwear, serapes, flamenco dresses, and authentic peasant skirts and blouses (not to mention such necessities as a chicken suit, complete with papier-mâché mask). You can also purchase tutus and tulle butterfly wings for your ballet-student daughter, as well as Superman, Batman, or Spiderman outfits. If you wish, Señor José Alducin (booths 89 and 90) will outfit you as any bird, complete with real feathers. He also makes normal clothing to order. At Typicos Estelita, in the same market (booth 87), you can transform yourself into a mouse, skunk, elephant, or mariachi musician. Esperanza Garcia (booth 134) sells all kinds of dresses, including eye-catching tango and Charleston outfits. (She also makes clothing for dolls.) Be sure to bring your measurements and a translator, however.

La Lagunilla Mercado de Varios, destroyed in the earthquakes of 1985 and out of business for three years, is operating once again, and its prices for hand-tooled leather bags, portfolio cases, wallets, suitcases, and steamer chests made from hand-worked tin are unbeatable. See Señor Rogelio Mejia in booth 38, Pasaje Comonfort. Nearby is the famed Mexican mask store, **Galería Eugenio,** Calle Allende 84 between Honduras and Ecuador, a treasure house of dragons, goblins, religious statues, and antique carvings.

Department Stores

There are only two department stores in the D.F. worth mentioning. **Puerto Liverpool** is less trendy than the **Palacio de Hierro** (the Iron Palace), but both are hipper than the American entry, Sears. The block-long Puerto Liverpool, with entrances on Avenida Horacio and Mariano Escobedo, the eastern boundary of the Polanco district, is a few minutes' walk north of the Hotel Camino Real. The Palacio de Hierro is located on the corner of 16 de Septiembre and Isabel la Católica, a few blocks southwest of the *Zócalo,* in a huge 17th-century structure. Both stores cater to people of some means, and international credit cards are welcomed. English-speaking sales people are also available upon request at both.

Perisur is the largest, most modern shopping mall in the entire country. It's located just north of the Cuicuilco archaeological site, about a 30-minute taxi ride south of the *Zócalo* via the Periférico Sur, the main highway to Cuernavaca.

The Main Shopping Areas

The Zona Rosa. Calle Amberes, one of the city's loveliest streets, is the location of several quality French restaurants as well as practically being an outdoor mall for designer boutiques: Guess? by Georges Marciano, Express, Aca Joe, Ruben Torres, and Ralph Lauren are just some of the well-known names you'll find here. Also here is Noi, a sophisticated dress shop for petites, and the ubiquitous Benetton. (At most of these boutiques international designer fashions are available for less than half their cost in New York or London.) If you are of a mind to shop for silver where royalty does, **Tane** is the most elegant shop in the country, while **Los Castillos** gives it a run for your money.

Around the corner on Calle Londres is Dancin' and Fiorucci, for everything you ever needed to own in Spandex. Recognizing where their largest market is (70 percent of all Mexicans are under the age of 30), the emphasis in both shops is on youthful, casual attire. The Zona Rosa also has two important women's-wear shops: **Girasol**, at Calle Génova 32; and **Marigen**, at Calle Hamburgo 89. Both sell clothing made from hand-woven Mexican cotton and created by foreign designers, and in both places the clothing is so colorful you could hang it on the wall. Marigen also sells the jewelry of Donna Brown, an American who has expressed her love for her adopted country through her beautiful designs over the last 18 years. Also on Hamburgo, at number 98F, is **Explora**, a terrific spot for safari jackets.

Polanco. The chic shopping district here on Avenida Presidente Masaryk has only recently come into its own. Nevertheless, the temples to designer clothing now number in double figures and include all of the above as well as such notable establishments as Esprit, **Ferroni Collection** (a Mexican operation that uses little Scotch terriers on everything in its line, from shoes to umbrellas), and **Amarras** (which means "to tie" in Spanish and refers to the shop's practice of using the knot as the basic element of design in everything from its bathing suits to shorts and shirts). The Furor Clothing Company is another import from the United States and is especially proud of its cowboy jeans. **Aca Joe**, represented by two shops here (one a sale outlet), is not connected with the U.S. operation of the same name, which means you'll find the originals designed by Acapulco Joe Rank himself.

For sophisticated leather goods in Polanco check out **Regina Romero**. Farther down the avenue in the direction of the Hotel Camino Real is the boutique of **Carlos Demicheles**, perhaps the most exciting Mexican designer on the international fashion scene today.

San Angel. Three of the most elegant shops in the D.F. can be found near the San Angel Inn, where Altavista meets Diego Rivera and Santa Catarina: **Carlos Demicheles** for men's and women's clothing; **Aries** for leather bags, valises, wallets, and portfolio cases; and **Tane** (see also the Zona Rosa) for exquisite silverware. Though they can all be found at other locations throughout the city, it is only here that the shops themselves are treasures of contemporary Mexican architecture. Other shopping meccas on Altavista are **HB Galería** for contemporary art; **Galería Kim** for contemporary art and sculpture; **Farre** for decorator housewares; and **Frattina** for women's designer originals.

Calle Madero. The D.F. is the nation's jewelry-making center. Today the old Calle de los Plateros ("Street of the Silversmiths") is known as Calle Madero, but it remains faithful to its 16th-century origins, and shops specializing in custom-made silver and gold jewelry line the street from the *Zócalo* to Alameda Park.

Bazar Del Centro. An old colonial mansion at Calle Isabel la Católica 30, just south of Calle Madero and a few minutes' walk from the *Zócalo,* has just recently been converted into a very pleasant three-level shopping center called the Bazar del Centro. A prestigious jewelry store from Guadalajara, **Aplijsa**, has opened a branch here with an outstanding assortment of jewelry in all price ranges. Other shops ringing the central patio feature quality silver, leather goods, ceramics, and a great variety of expertly crafted products from all over the country.

Salvador Sandoval, owner of both the Bazar del Centro and Aplijsa, purchased the building in 1985 and redesigned and refurbished the old mansion, retaining as much as possible of the original late 17th-century décor, including the entire façade, the iron railings, the exposed beams, and the brick walls. As a result, there is a dramatic contrast between the rather seedy neighborhood and what awaits behind the Bazar del Centro's massive doors. The central patio has tiled benches under graceful laurel trees, and often, during the day, artists work at their easels in view of the shoppers. In a rear patio are more shops offering an assortment of arts and crafts and a very comfortable pub, the **Cueva de Emiliano**, that offers an ethnic setting and a decent margarita.

As of this writing, only the shops on the ground floor are open, but the second story is due to have its inauguration shortly. An art gallery is planned for a huge area on the third floor, with a 19th-century-style "cage" elevator taking shoppers to the upper levels.

Art Galleries

The **Zona Rosa** is the hub of the D.F.'s many outstanding art galleries, all of which remain open until 8:00 P.M.

Galería Misrachi, Génova 20, features the masters—Tamayo, Siqueiros, Zuniga, Toledo, Coronel—as well as works by contemporary sculptors.

Galería Tere Haas, Génova 2, is staffed by knowledgeable personnel, and specializes in paintings, graphics, and bronze sculptures. Zuniga, Castañeda, Amaya, Montoya, Nierman, among many others.

Galería Hardy, Génova 2J, is filled with contemporary art by talented unknowns and has an excellent art bookstore.

Galería Arvil, Hamburgo 9 (between Florencia and Amberes), sells works by Mexico's finest, including Tamayo, Zuniga, and Toledo. Contemporary originals and prints, and a good art bookstore as well.

Galería del Circulo, Hamburgo 112, has works by Tamayo, Siqueiros, and Clement; prints by Dali and Picasso, among others.

Salon de Arte Plastica Mexicana, Hamburgo 202 and Havre 7, is a government-operated gallery featuring works by young Mexican artists.

Galería Solaris, Estrasburgo 19B, sells paintings, sculpture, etchings, and tapestry by the likes of Bustamante, Sebastian, Griza, and Alcantara.

Galería de Arte Mexicano, Milan 18, offers an extensive selection of work by young Mexican artists.

The **Asian Art Gallery**, Amberes 11, is noted for its fine collection of Oriental artwork, sculpture, jewelry, and handmade crafts.

Galería Honfleur, Amberes 14, sells contemporary paintings, sculpture, ceramics, and silver.

Galería Juan Martín, Amberes 17, has a large selection of strictly modern paintings by a variety of international artists.

Galería Aura, Amberes 38, sells contemporary paintings and sculptures by well-known artists.

Galería Londres Chumacero, Estocolmo 30, has a fine collection of contemporary paintings, sculpture, and ceramics.

Near the Zona Rosa: **Galería Pecanis**, Durango 186, a half dozen blocks south of the Zona Rosa, is a fine gallery featuring the work of lesser-known (but quality) Mexican artists. Contemporary paintings, engravings, and drawings make up the collection. **Casasola**, Praga 16, a few blocks west of Calle Florencia at the western edge of the Zona Rosa, features a great photography collection of old Mexico, especially the Revolutionary period. You can have your purchases mounted while you wait. **Galería Summa Artis**, on the mezzanine level of the Stouffer Presidente Chapultepec, a chic gallery featuring the works of old masters as well as aspiring young artists. Paintings, sculpture, graphics, and signed and numbered lithographs fill out its impressive collection.

SIDE TRIPS FROM MEXICO CITY

CUERNAVACA, TAXCO, PUEBLA, TULA

By Robert Somerlott

The area around the capital offers so much that the problem becomes one of choosing among its many archaeological sites, villages, museums, caves, and colonial towns. In deciding, however, a visitor must be aware that growth has smudged the lustre of some places that were once more attractive.

Toluca, to the west, is an example. Its famed market is commercial and common now, the modernized city itself of little interest. Nearby, the pottery village of **Metepec** retains interest for its traditional ceramics, especially its *pulque* jars, trees-of-life, and earthen casseroles. South of Toluca, **Malinalco**, an Aztec temple site carved out of volcanic rock, is worthwhile for archaeology buffs. But the region as a whole is now of low priority to a traveller.

Cuernavaca, once an automatic choice, still has attractions but must be considered realistically, as we will see. Likewise the famous old silver town of Taxco. The old spa town of Tehuacán should be crossed off your itinerary now that its resort hotel is shabby and neglected.

Two places that have recently awakened to the profits of tourism, Tlaxcala and Pachuca, should be low on the list, although Tlaxcala is an attractive side trip from Puebla for visitors who have the time. Pachuca is simply uninteresting.

There is, however, one rewarding side trip in the area east of Mexico City, on the way to Veracruz on the Gulf Coast: Puebla, an early colonial town with very attractive ecclesiastical architecture, and nearby Cholula, a pre-Hispanic religious center.

Two worthwhile places, the Museum of the Viceregal Period at Tepotzotlán and the archaeological zone at Tula, can be visited either as a side trip from the capital or while you are en route to Querétaro and other northern colonial cities. Both are of somewhat specialized interest. An unusual place north of Tula, and perhaps not appealing to everyone, is Ixmiquilpán, an unattractive town with an ancient monastery that contains some of the most unusual and fantastic murals in Mexico. Like Tula and Tepotzotlán, it is of special rather than general interest.

MAJOR INTEREST

Cuernavaca
Scenic beauty on the trip from Mexico City
Hotels, restaurants, and resorts
Xochicalco ruins

Taxco
Picturesque town scenes
Silverwork
Cacahuamilpa Caves

Puebla
Scenic beauty
Colonial buildings
Imposing archaeological site at Cholula
Folk-art church at Tonantzintla

North of Mexico City
Museum of the Viceregal Period at Tepotzotlán
Toltec archaeological zone at Tula
Ixmiquilpán monastery

Cuernavaca and Taxco are easy to combine in one swing south of the capital. The route can be varied by returning to Mexico City via Highway 55, Ixtapán de la Sal, Metepec, and the Toluca bypass. The small but unusual Aztec temple at Malinalco, an interesting sidelight, is also on this route. The trip, often done in one day, actually crowds two.

CUERNAVACA

The journey by car or bus to Cuernavaca from Mexico City takes from an hour and a half to two hours each way—depending on traffic—using the toll road. The route passes through spectacular mountain scenery; the roadside settlements, on the other hand, look interesting from a distance but are unappealing on closer inspection. It is well worth frequent stops to take in the views as the road first rises to magnificent heights, then plunges into the semi-tropical valley enfolding Cuernavaca.

Cuernavaca, now an industrial city of almost a million people, was a winter refuge that beckoned Aztec nobles, Cortés, Maximilian and Carlota, and a legion of their peers and admirers. Malcolm Lowry brought other aspects of Cuernavaca vividly to life in *Under the Volcano*.

Today Mr. Lowry's famous title is much less appropriate: The great, beautiful volcano of Popocatépetl is obscured by a haze of pollution. Not that the smog is terrible—yet. Every weekend hordes of Mexico City residents flee to this verdant valley to draw breaths of air still relatively fresh, although industrial fumes and exhaust are threatening. The weekend trippers arrive by auto, jamming even the broad highways and overloading all facilities. Cuernavaca is therefore to be avoided on weekends.

Along with traffic and industrialization, other menaces to charm have burgeoned: Kentucky Fried Chicken restaurants, electronic hullabaloo, a babel of signs, a glare of chrome and glass-box architecture. The so-called City of Eternal Spring can grate on all the senses at once. Yet there are attractions here, too, though often muffled or camouflaged.

Cuernavaca presents a paradox to the traveller: Two days can be too much here, and yet two weeks might not be enough. It depends on how you use this annoying city—and how you retreat from it.

The eternal spring of tourist brochures is almost true. In this Eden-like climate, a colony of retired Americans enjoys its comfort barricaded behind walls of high-priced real estate. Their affluent Mexican neighbors, who outnumber them by far, sip Scotch, not tequila, in residences

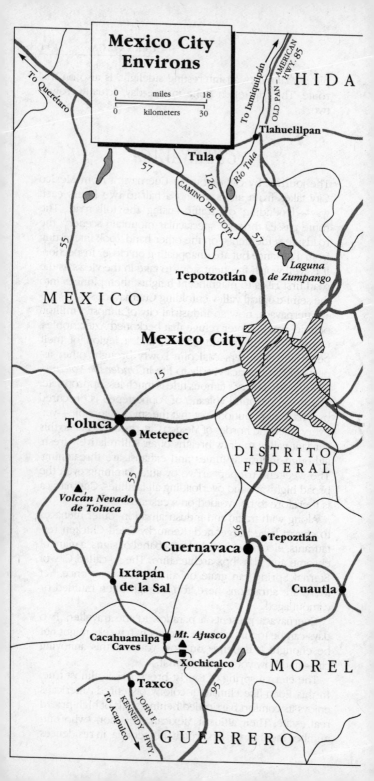

Mexico City Environs

miles
0 — 18

kilometers
0 — 30

where petals float on swimming pools and the servants are well trained.

Visitors will see no more of this than a cascade of bougainvillea tumbling over the outside of a garden wall. Yet a few of the town's inns give a credible imitation of *la dolce vita*—and this is the reason for lingering. Rental houses and apartments, most of them attractive though high-priced, are available on a monthly or seasonal basis. Away from the congestion, life in Cuernavaca can be balmy.

The Central Plaza Area

The main square, or *zócalo,* is a small park whose venerable shade trees and graceful bandstand are an inheritance from a more serene era. This is an inviting spot on weekday mornings or evenings, but bedlam when weekend visitors claim it. Adjacent is a more ample park that's alive with vendors and, sometimes, musicians. (The crafts displayed nearby are not local, and the markup is steep.)

Buildings facing the two public spaces range from ugly to acceptable, and one of them, the **Palace of Cortés,** is the city's most famous structure. This grim pile has been patriotically renamed the Museo de Cuauhnáhuac, recalling the original Aztec name of the city. (Spanish conquistadors found the word as unpronounceable in 1525 as it is now. Cuernavaca, which means "cow horn," was a stab at it.) The palace has been reconstructed so many times that it's hard to guess what it once looked like, although some old photos are displayed inside.

Hernán Cortés ordered its construction in 1527, having just received Cuernavaca as part of his personal fief. In the late 1920s Dwight Morrow, the U.S. Ambassador to Mexico, who had a Cuernavaca residence, hit on the happy idea of commissioning the great Diego Rivera to paint murals in the old palace. Rivera took advantage of the commission to portray Mexico's history from the earliest days of its habitation through the Revolution of 1910, with an emphasis on the events of the Conquest. The results, exuberant and bold, are a national treasure, and the rest of the museum pales in comparison, as most things would.

One long block west of the plaza stands the Cathedral complex. Here again we have a story of antiquity, destruction, and rebuilding. As in the palace, the murals inside outshine the building itself. Very early and naïve frescos show Spanish missionaries bound for Japan in a skiff, as perplexed sea creatures regard them with curiosity. The friars are also shown at their later martyrdom in Nagasaki.

For a simple lunch while exploring downtown, **Marco Polo**, a checked-tablecloth pizzeria facing the Cathedral at Hidalgo 26, is a good choice.

Close at hand, the **Borda Gardens** survive as a relic of the demolished palace of 18th-century silver king José de la Borda. The design is formal but attractive. Fluffy ducks preside at a pool, along one side of which is a *ramada* with paintings portraying the love affair between Maximilian and a local beauty known as La India Bonita. Empress Carlota also resided here at the time, but neither gossip nor history has revealed what she thought of her husband's indiscretions.

The Pyramid of Teopanzolco, an ancient site near the train station, is discussed below under Xochicalco.

Staying in Cuernavaca

Cuernavaca is replete with just-adequate hotels offering basic rooms to weekend visitors at rates too high. A few places, none of them low-priced, are special.

Las Mañanitas, a few blocks from the *zócalo,* is famed for its food, its rooms, and a glorious garden adorned with flamboyant birds. The restaurant is so popular that on weekends it causes traffic to clog the surrounding streets. The suites, with unnecessary but attractive fireplaces, are admirable. Las Mañanitas is a luxury inn.

Between the Cathedral and the *zócalo* in downtown Cuernavaca, Señor Ray Cote, dean of Mexico's innkeepers and founder of the Villa Montaña in Morelia, has opened a luxurious hostelry in a former mansion that only welcomes a few guests at a time. The **Casa Colonial** does not advertise, and is so discreet, in fact, that there is not even a sign. Guests, who will have made arrangements by phone or letter, are ushered into one of the loveliest tropical gardens in Mexico. The kitchen is a gourmet operation, the atmosphere refined but easygoing. Considering the high cost of three excellent meals a day elsewhere in Cuernavaca, this secluded retreat offers much for its price.

In the hills known as Rancho de Cortés, about a fifteen-minute drive north of the center of town via Avenida Morelos, and partially hidden on Calle Francisco Villa, is the **Cuernavaca Racquet Club**, which appears at first to

be a posh country club in the colonial style. The nine
tennis courts, four of them lighted, attract an international
crowd, but the occupants of the forty or so living room-
and-bedroom suites are by no means all tennis addicts.
The dining room, open to non-guests, is quite good, the
service at night late and leisurely.

The **Hostería las Quintas**, much closer to town but still
too far to walk, is less costly than the Racquet Club, less
sporty, and even more beautiful in its tropical garden
setting. The fine public restaurant is a lovely bower of
blossoming shrubs.

Tepoztlán

About 15 miles northeast of Cuernavaca by a good highway is the village of Tepoztlán, with its twisting cobblestone streets, ancient ruins, and Aztec temples clinging to
a steep slope. Tepoztlán kept its pre-Columbian heritage
and language far longer than most villages in Mexico. In
fact, as recently as a few decades ago it was still a magnet
for anthropologists hoping to study the elements of the
earlier culture that survived here.

Today, Tepoztlán's isolation has been shattered by the
outside world, yet despite the intrusion of souvenir
shops, the hamlet remains both antique and primitive.
There's also a 16th-century convent with a small archaeological museum in the village, and interesting ruins at the
end of a steep climb in the hills above town.

The **Hacienda Cocoyoc**, a few minutes' drive from
Tepoztlán, is a big, sprawling resort amid landscaped
gardens, an old aqueduct, and falling water. The hotel has
a nine-hole golf course as well. Prices in this tropical
retreat are just moderate enough to attract weekend
crowds from the capital, but it is lovely on weekdays.
Make sure your room or suite has good ventilation;
Cocoyoc is warm.

The Ruins of Xochicalco

The words "pretty" and "delightful" are not ordinarily
applied to pre-Columbian ruins. At Xochicalco no others
serve so well. The site is beautifully situated in slightly
rolling country broken by hills that are vivid green in the
rainy season, brown and severe in the dry season—but
always impressive no matter what time of year.

Xochicalco commands the heights of Mount Ajusco

some 39 km (24 miles) southwest of Cuernavaca in the direction of Taxco, more than half the distance over a toll road, and all of it paved. In Nahuatl, the Aztec language, the name means "House of Flowers"—highly appropriate, although what the original builders called their city (or themselves) is unknown.

This was not just a ceremonial center, but a true city of at least 10,000 people, and possibly twice that. Although much studied, the ruins remain shrouded in mystery. How did Maya-like figures, carvings, and glyphs arrive in this remote region so far from the main centers of Mayan culture? What kind of people lived here and left their sculptural calling cards? One important point is certain, however: Xochicalco was in flower at a time, about A.D. 700, when northern ceremonial and religious centers had been abandoned, and the flame of culture and learning had all but sputtered out in Mesoamerica. The comparison to European monasteries during the Dark Ages is irresistible. Was this the place where tradition and culture were preserved while barbarians ranged the land? It seems likely. The inhabitants of Xochicalco adopted the styles of earlier civilizations, such as Teotihuacán, changed them somewhat, then passed on these modified traditions as part of the foundation of a new culture, of new ways of life that were established at Tula, quite a bit north of here, in the tenth century. The people of Xochicalco were both keepers and transmitters of that civilization.

The **Temple of the Plumed Serpent**, the site's finest monument, displays superb relief sculpture—flowing lines in stone that are indeed as lithe as a serpent as they curve, coil, and finally rear up in a fierce, dragon-like head. An aristocratic figure, instantly recognizable as Mayan, sits crowned with a panache that blends perfectly with the long rhythms of the whole sculpture.

The site also boasts one of the finest ancient ball courts in Mexico, laid out in the usual shape of the letter I, and over 60 meters (200 feet) long. From the top of a partly excavated mound known as La Malinche, the view down toward a line of circular platforms is striking. A residential section elsewhere on the grounds comes outfitted with a steam bath. Walls and fortifications protect the impressive area now called the Acropolis.

Rambling, evocative Xochicalco is the highlight of any trip to Cuernavaca, but back in the city itself there is a small but interesting pre-Columbian structure, the **Pyramid of Teo-**

panzolco, near the railroad station, that may well be 1,200 years old. At the time of the Spanish Conquest the local inhabitants covered their temple with earth to prevent its destruction at the hands of the Christians. More than a millennium passed, during which time the hill became part of the landscape. Then, in 1910, artillery supporting the rebel Zapata was placed on top of the hill. The repeated firing of the artillery caused a mini-earthquake, dirt and rocks slid away, and the ancient temple was found. Except that it was actually two temples, for one had been built over the other in the traditional manner.

The Cacahuamilpa Caves

Between Taxco and Cuernavaca, and easily reached from either, is Cacahuamilpa (kah-kah-wah-MEEL-pah) Caves (*grutas*) National park. The park's enormous corridors and chambers form the largest known cave system in Mexico, and are comparable in extent to the Carlsbad Caverns in the United States.

The entrance to the caves is an awesome mountainside gap that eerily resembles a gigantic architectural structure. The halls and connecting corridors beyond it unfold like a lunar landscape amid fantastic formations of stalactites and stalagmites.

The Empress Carlota visited these caves in 1866 and wrote on a wall, "Maria Carlota reached this point." Eight years later, a man instrumental in driving her from Mexico, President Lerdo de Tejada, added to the same wall, "Sebastian Lerdo de Tejada went farther." Today, conducted tours, in Spanish, leave frequently from the entrance and last about an hour and a half. Admission is restricted to escorted groups, but those suddenly struck by claustrophobia can turn back at any time and find their own way out.

TAXCO

Located about 50 miles southwest of Cuernavaca, Taxco, in itself a picturesque and photogenic colonial silver town, has been rendered much less appealing to visitors by its own attractiveness and by proximity to the capital. Tour buses, belching exhaust, bear down on its tiny plaza like predatory monsters. Day trips from as far Acapulco, where tourists are misled by promises of exploration of a "colonial gem," fill its streets with bewildered shoppers. What they get instead is hours of travel and about 45 minutes at their destination. The bus driver is bribed to halt at a certain silver shop, then the herding—soon followed by the roundup for departure—begins. The town somehow manages to accommodate these day-trippers, who are, after all, its bread and butter, but much is lost by the crowding.

Another evil effect of living on tourism is the sense one gets that the town is too spiffed up, too conscious of its own image. Taxco, with its uniform white paint and black signs, has an unnatural uniformity akin to the waxy quality of a film set; it does not seem to be a living town. Still, it is undeniably picturesque, even romantic. And while this is especially true of the downtown area—things loosen up farther out—downtown is what everyone goes to see. In fact, that really is all there *is* to see, except for strolls through old neighborhoods that are quaint but unimposing. Such a stroll quickly makes it clear that Taxco's silver wealth did not stay in Taxco, but went to erect mansions elsewhere.

Besides silver, Taxco has another treasure: the **Church of Santa Prisca**, which lifts its magnificent spires to the glory of God and God's self-proclaimed partner, a French miner named José de la Borda.

Taxco is the oldest mining town in North America, and dates back to the days when Mixtec craftsmen hammered its silver into ornaments for Aztec nobles. Of course, the conquistadors were overjoyed to seize its mines, and the serpentine, corkscrew byways of today's town are a reminder of the meandering mining village that tumbled haphazardly down the mountain slope in the 16th century.

The output of silver during those years was substantial but hardly fantastic. Then, in 1716, José de la Borda wandered into town and struck it rich. Grateful, Borda presented the Almighty with the most opulent temple he could concoct. "God gives to Borda, and Borda gives to God," he announced, marking the score even. The church was begun in 1751 and completed in 1758, with the best Mexican architects, painters, and carvers of the day kept busy on it.

Ever since, Santa Prisca (properly called *Santa Prisca y San Sebastián*) has been hailed as the apogee of 18th-century Mexican architecture. In 1945, Manuel Toussaint, Mexico's pioneer art historian, wrote: "A homogenous work of art, and of a beauty which cannot be described, the church of Taxco dominates the delightful town . . . the interior is an astonishing Churrigueresque work of art, madness is held within bounds . . . reason inexorably controls the effect, and fantasy develops just so far as the restraints of reason permit."

Over the decades, the silver in the mountains was steadily mined out. Although Taxco still mines some silver, its modern connection with the metal dates from the 1930s, when William Spratling, a North American writer and artist, introduced silversmithing as a local art and industry.

Buying Silver in Taxco

Taxco's centrally located silver shops are reliable; buyers will not have to worry that some base metal has been palmed off on them. Still, as with anything expensive, you should be cautious; check that the product bears the stamp .925, the government's requirement for purity in silver.

Silver as metal is sold by weight, the price set on the world commodity markets. All costs above weight should involve design and *real* overhead. Some shops on Taxco's Avenida John F. Kennedy add a guide or bus driver's commission without mentioning it. Among the better shops in the *zócalo* area, though, there is little difference in price above weight, and the advantage of buying in downtown Taxco is not price but the range of options, with more than 100 silver outlets to choose from. **Emma**, at Calle Celso Muñoz 4, gleams with a wide selection of smaller gifts and remembrance items. Larger works of quality will be found at **Los Ballesteros**, Calle Soto la Marina 5, and **Los Castillos**, Plazuela Bernal 10. Many other good establishments are sprinkled throughout the area.

Agua Escondida, at William Spratling 4-A, is convenient for lunch or snacks when you're shopping or visiting the sights downtown.

Staying in Taxco

The cottages at the **Hacienda del Solar** are perched atop a mountain in rustic but definitely aristocratic surroundings. Two meals a day are served in its dining room—the city's best restaurant—which is open to the public. The view is magnificent, and the cuisine has accents of Italy.

(You'll need a car or taxi to get up to the hotel from town.)

The **Posada de la Misíon**, also attractive but much less expensive, has colonial style, a convenient central location, and a restaurant.

PUEBLA

In Puebla you feel close to the sky. This sensation stems from more than being in one of the highest cities in the world. Happily, despite the fumes of the ubiquitous traffic, the air here is still unusually clear. But it's really the four great volcanoes towering above the plain—especially Popocatépetl, the Aztecs' "Smoking Mountain," and Iztaccíhuatl, their "White Lady"—that do the most to create this perception of elevation, and their perpetually snow-covered summits do indeed inspire that familiar fantasy of being able to reach out and touch them.

The 95-km (60-mile) drive from Mexico City east to Puebla winds gently through pine-clad slopes and rugged outcroppings of rock that afford spectacular vistas. Puebla stands at the head of a fertile valley athwart the main trade route to Veracruz and the Gulf of Mexico. The location is strategic; every invading army—whether Spanish, French, or American—has had to storm the town on its way to the capital.

The people of Puebla are called *poblanos,* and the adjective *poblano* is especially linked to their tile-encrusted buildings, a style of architectural decoration gone joyously mad with color. They are just as proud of their *poblano* dress and style, and will boast to anyone who will listen that *mole* sauce, made with chiles and rich but not sweet with chocolate, was invented here. Pride is also taken in the city's grid design, in which *avenidas* run east and west, *calles* north and south. This checkerboard of streets was made possible by the fact that there was no native city here before the Spanish arrived—an anomaly in the history of the Conquest—as well as by the fact that the land was flat. In addition, Puebla has more churches than any other place in Mexico, which is either the cause of or the direct result of *poblano* solemnity.

Yes, this is a serious town where eyebrows are frequently raised. Despite the city's apparently staid demeanor, however, a current of passion runs through *poblano* life. The thousands of students at its large univer-

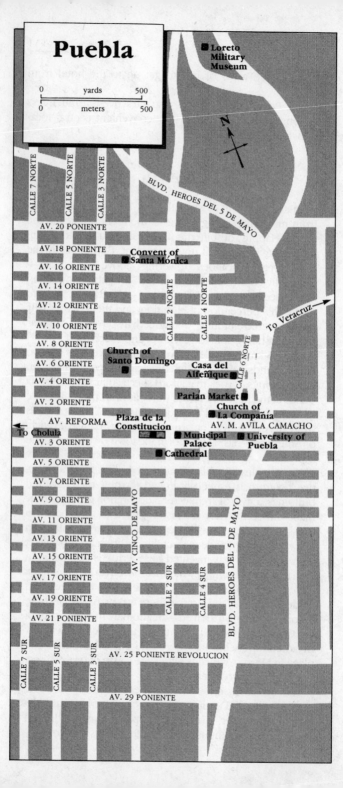

Puebla

0 yards 500
0 meters 500

Loreto Military Museum

N

BLVD. HEROES DEL 5 DE MAYO

CALLE 7 NORTE
CALLE 5 NORTE
CALLE 3 NORTE

AV. 20 PONIENTE
AV. 18 PONIENTE
AV. 16 ORIENTE

Convent of Santa Mónica

AV. 14 ORIENTE
AV. 12 ORIENTE
AV. 10 ORIENTE
AV. 8 ORIENTE
AV. 6 ORIENTE

CALLE 2 NORTE
CALLE 4 NORTE

To Veracruz

Church of Santo Domingo

Casa del Alfeñique

CALLE 6 NORTE

AV. 4 ORIENTE
AV. 2 ORIENTE

Parian Market

Church of La Compañía

AV. REFORMA

Plaza de la Constitución

To Cholula

AV. M. AVILA CAMACHO

Municipal Palace

University of Puebla

AV. 3 ORIENTE

Cathedral

AV. 5 ORIENTE
AV. 7 ORIENTE
AV. 9 ORIENTE
AV. 11 ORIENTE

AV. CINCO DE MAYO

AV. 13 ORIENTE
AV. 15 ORIENTE

CALLE 2 SUR
CALLE 4 SUR

BLVD. HEROES DEL 5 DE MAYO

AV. 17 ORIENTE
AV. 19 ORIENTE
AV. 21 PONIENTE

CALLE 7 SUR
CALLE 5 SUR
CALLE 3 SUR

AV. 25 PONIENTE REVOLUCION

AV. 29 PONIENTE

sity are second to none in the vehemence and violence of their protests. The workers at the auto factory, the largest Volkswagen plant in the world, belong to a voluble and fierce union. The *poblanos,* like the volcanoes around them, are dignified and quiescent—but not always, and certainly not below the surface.

Visitors to Puebla should be prepared to see an abundance of ecclesiastical architecture, impressive and opulent rather than beautiful. There is fine ceramic work here, as well, especially its glazed Talavera ware, and some residences flaunt tile work—gleaming and gay, a flash of fantasy—as exterior decoration. The museums are worth visiting but not worth lingering in. Puebla and nearby Cholula will reward the visitor who spends a day between them, but will only merit more time if you have a car and can explore a larger area.

Downtown Puebla

The city's main attractions lie within walking distance of the *zócalo,* the **Plaza de la Constitución,** a central square that ranks among the most spacious plazas in Mexico. It was planned, as was the whole downtown, by a Franciscan, Fray Julián Garcés, the first Bishop of Tlaxcala, who had been assigned the task of locating a new city. According to legend, His Grace was blessed by the nocturnal visit of two angels whom he watched pace off with pole and line a plain ringed with volcanoes. Thus the city was positioned, and so acquired its full name, Puebla de los Angeles, in honor of its angelic surveyors.

American visitors walking through the plaza usually have no idea they are crossing a spot that should be hallowed ground in U.S. history. It was here, in 1847, that General Winfield Scott seized the city after the battle of Cerro Gordo. While Scott's main force moved on to attack Mexico City, a Colonel Thomas Childs was left behind in Puebla's *zócalo* with a small group of U.S. wounded. Colonel Childs, with foresight, rounded up some cattle and a flock of sheep, then spurred his injured men to barricade their camp. Their work was hardly finished when the Mexican General Santa Anna attacked with 2,500 men, employing artillery and posting snipers on roofs that still overlook the plaza today.

The local populace was jubilant at the imminent destruction of the invaders, cheering the besiegers and wildly ringing the bells of the city's 60 churches and convents. The staunch Americans held their terrible position for 30 days, however, until the approach of a relieving army put Santa Anna to flight.

The bluish-gray **Cathedral** looms over one side of the *zócalo,* a grim shadow on an otherwise lighthearted space. Twin towers, too far apart, impart a stumpy look to the structure. The gloomy exterior hides a splendid nave replete with marble, lovely wrought iron, and admirable woodwork. The **Municipal Palace**, the second most impressive structure on the *zócalo,* was built at the turn of the century in the Spanish Renaissance style—yet another example of the city's long-lived admiration of Spanish models.

It is a relief to turn from the sternness of the palace and Cathedral and discover the totally delightful **Casa del Alfeñique**, located at Avenida 4 Oriente and Calle 6 Norte. The name means House of Almond Cake, and it is indeed quite a confection. Its red tiles are accented by black iron work, and all this is tied together with sugar-colored masonry to create a *poblano* fantasy. Inside is a regional museum, with an emphasis on pre-Columbian history and the indigenous costumes of the area, including *china poblana* dress, the most famous garb of the city.

The **Parián Market** (*mercado*), next to the Casa del Alfeñique, is a cobblestoned mall where crafts and almost-crafts are sold. Ceramics are a good buy here, but buyers should be cautious about the displays of onyx boxes, figurines, bookends, and chess boards—most of the work is imitation and mass produced. The greens and shades thereof, sometimes palmed off as jade, are colored by dye, not nature.

The **Church of La Compañía** at Calle 4 Norte and Avenida M. Avila Camacho, a Churrigueresque riot of decoration, is also the tomb of the original *china poblana,* a not especially fascinating character, but one who looms inordinately large in the city's collective consciousness. She was perhaps a princess, perhaps Chinese, and perhaps kidnapped by pirates who sold her in Acapulco in 1620. She was bought by a Puebla merchant family that later adopted her because of her beauty, sweetness, and virtue. She taught sewing in the Chinese manner, invented the embroidered peasant dress named after her, and was denied her wish to become a nun. Eventually, she devoted an already virtuous life to care of the poor and sick.

The **Rosary Chapel** in the **Church of Santo Domingo**,

two blocks from the *zócalo* at Cinco de Mayo and Avenida 4 Poniente, is the high point of *poblano* religious ornamentation: lustrous goldleaf, brilliant tiles, and enamel dazzle the eye. The sculpted Virgin on the altar, spangled in jewels, seems dressed by Tiffany's.

The **Convent of Santa Mónica** was built in the early years of the 17th century as a sort of retreat where noble matrons could be properly chaperoned when their husbands were out of town. The ladies of Puebla rejected the idea, however, and the building, ironically, became a reformatory for prostitutes. Later it was turned into a convent-college.

The convent went "underground" after passage of the Reform Laws abolishing Church property in 1857, with the nuns remaining secluded in their 39-room establishment. Entrance to the convent was through a secret door in an adjoining house. It was closed by the government in 1934, and is now a museum devoted to religious art and sculpture, as well as to the lives of the sisters. Despite the hocus-pocus of the hidden door, the "secret" was doubtless more widely known in Puebla than is generally admitted today. You can enter the convent at Avenida 18 Poniente 103 just off of Cinco de Mayo.

The **Loreto Military Museum**, in an old fort northeast of downtown, is mainly of patriotic interest to Mexicans, but military and history buffs will find an interesting diorama of the famous battle fought here on May 5, 1862. On that day, badly outnumbered Mexicans, some armed with guns that had seen service at Waterloo almost fifty years earlier, turned back a heavily armed spit-and-polish French army. The battle itself, which is an involved and fascinating story, is remembered throughout Mexico every year on the fifth of May (*Cinco de Mayo*), a legal holiday. To visit Loreto and its sister fort of Guadalupe, take a cab from the *zócalo* or a "Fuerte" bus at Calle 16 de Septiembre and Avenida 9 Oriente. They aren't very far, and the fare will be inexpensive.

Staying and Dining in Puebla

El Mesón del Angel is Puebla's most attractive hotel, with beautiful grounds, balconied rooms, and a very good dining room open to the public. Its bold beams and rock-and-glass walls give it a California feeling, while its location at the edge of the city makes it especially appealing to motorists passing through as well as to business executives visiting the industrial zone. For other visitors, however, it is a long way out.

The **Lastra**, also of the first rank but older and less expensive than El Mesón, is in a quiet neighborhood a little too far from the *zócalo* for easy walking. The roof garden is lovely, and the rooms vary in quality in this traditional but much-remodeled inn. It also runs a good restaurant open to the public.

On the *zócalo* itself, the **Royalty** is a convenient, comfortable, and pleasant choice—depending on which rooms or junior suites are available. Some are cramped and stuffy; the suites are worth the higher rate. At its best, the Royalty is pleasing, and the indoor-outdoor restaurant offers a satisfactory breakfast.

The **Del Portal** is another pleasant if unpretentious hotel in an excellent plaza location. The rooms at the rear, though smaller, are quieter, and the ambience is colonial. The Del Portal has a bar and restaurant.

Poblano food is the specialty of the simple, attractive, and popular **Fonda Santa Clara**, Avenida 3 Poniente 307. The *mole* here is outstanding.

The food at the **Restaurante del Parián**, Avenida 2 Oriente 415, rises above the threats of the "quaint" décor and menus printed on a piece of wood: The coyness, thankfully, does not extend to the fine *poblano* cuisine, with the *adobo* and *pipian* sauces especially noteworthy. (*Adobo* is a tangy blend of cumin, sour orange, chile, and a variety of other spices, as inspiration dictates; *pipian* also varies but starts out with a base of chiles and sesame seeds.)

Regional cooking in Puebla is usually tasty and tangy, but "Continental" dishes seem beyond local abilities. Visitors hungry for international fare should go to the Lastra or El Mesón del Angel, whose rather elegant restaurants are not limited to regional selections, although they do these well, too.

Cholula

The town of Cholula adjoins Puebla, the two now virtually one as a result of growth. In its pre-Hispanic heyday, however, Cholula was a center of trade as well as an important religious center, both a holy city and a place of pilgrimage dedicated to Quetzalcóatl, the Plumed Serpent. Its settlement dates back to 500 B.C., and a city-state, probably a satellite of Teotihuacán, though a very important one that outlived Teotihuacán by centuries, flourished here between A.D. 200–300. Various native conquerers appeared in later centuries.

Cortés, often mistaken for the god Quetzalcóatl by the indigenous people of Mexico, here ordered a merciless slaughter in 1519. He may have misunderstood the intentions of the local people—undoubtedly he was under intense pressure—but at any rate the Spaniards and their Tlaxcalan allies perpetrated a blood bath.

(The name Cholula means "Place the Waters Spring From." When Cortés was threatening the city, its inhabitants appeared to believe that native priests could open the sides of the pyramid to release an avenging water monster, perhaps a flood.)

Because of Cholula's sacredness to the local Indians, the Spaniards saw to it that Christian shrines were erected at almost every other corner of the town. One writer has described Cholula as "blistered with churches." The description is inspired; churches were angrily laid across Cholula like the welts from a lash.

Today, these squat domes and boxy towers swarm around the largest pre-Hispanic structure in Mexico: At least seven immense temple bases were erected here, one atop another, over the centuries, each built at the end of a 52-year religious cycle, according to custom. The result is known as **Tepanapa**, and although it's not as tall as Egypt's Pyramid of Cheops, it's almost twice as large at its base.

From a distance, this pyramid-like structure appears to be a steep, oddly shaped hill, certainly not man-made. A church, dwarfed by this mini-mountain, is perched on top. It is meant to look triumphant; it doesn't. Steps and a trail lead up the side of the "hill" to the church, which, despite its pretty white-and-gold interior, is not worth the climb. But the views in every direction are—they are magnificent. A foot trail on the south slope leads to the entrance of the archaeological zone.

The **Patio of Altars**, in the zone, is enclosed on three sides by curiously modern-looking construction typical of Cholula: Broad stairways flank plain balustrades that are balanced by handsome walls. Bold fretwork designs support large panels, and on two stelae carved in bas-relief there are designs clearly derived from the religious center of El Tajín near Veracruz. Wandering through the three main patios of Cholula, a visitor gets a sense of cosmopolitanism, of ideas and elements brought by pre-Columbian pilgrims who came great distances— though no one knows exactly what attracted these pilgrims to Cholula.

Much of the construction is of adobe brick, with pebble facings overlaid by stucco. This inexpensive technique, still used all over Mexico today with slight variations, does not ensure lasting results without constant upkeep. Thus, the method of construction itself has caused some of the deterioration and shapelessness of Cholula's pyramid. The adobe bricks are believed to have been made at a place about 30 miles distant. According to legend, 20,000 prisoners passed them along to Cholula hand-to-hand, bucket brigade–style.

Miles of tunnels were cut into the great temple base in the 1930s, and these passageways revealed even older construction. Feeble lightbulbs will allow you to find your way, but it is best to carry a flashlight as well. Here and there you'll notice traces of murals on what were once the exterior walls of older temples.

A small museum at the site contains artifacts and an illuminating cutaway model of the pyramid. Studying this before actually exploring the tunnels of Tepanapa is helpful.

In Cholula itself, the **Villa Arqueológica**, next to the pyramid, is a very good hotel, with a pleasant, informal atmosphere and a reliable restaurant. This is also the only really good choice for lunch while exploring the ruins.

Talavera Ware

Talavera ware, both as dishes and as tiles, is almost synonymous with the Puebla area of Mexico, although it is also made elsewhere.

The product, unlike most folk pottery, is durable, which is a quite un-Mexican quality. Fragility, after all, is part of the national fatalism: Dishes will be broken anyhow, so why worry too much or fight too hard to prevent it? Investing in Talavera, on the other hand, demands faith in the future and optimism about the human condition.

Talavera is made of a mix of three clays, which used to be kneaded together for days by men dancing barefoot in clay pits. Today, machines have replaced the Talavera jig in more populated areas. Either way, the mixed clay is ripened for six months, kept under a damp cloth, and rekneaded every few days. (This, too, goes against the national grain, as witness the quick methods of wine- and cheese-making generally used in Mexico.)

Finally, the clay is wheel-thrown or molded, then the tile or vessel is allowed to dry in the shade for days. Slow, low-temperature firing comes next. Prayers are chanted before and during the opening of the kiln, and the Blessed Sacrament is invoked, even in today's highly commercial operations. Every piece is tested to ring true, and those with a faulty tone are thrown away. The glaze applied includes honey; the final product is cream-white. Traditionally, only two colors are used to decorate the piece: always white, with blue or yellow in older works, and a bolder color in modern pieces.

Puebla's Talavera factories will not usually admit visitors, but a few have found on-premises sales to be profitable. Inquire about admission at the Tourism Office, Avenida 5 Oriente 5, beside the Cathedral. Or simply try at **Casa Rugiero**, 18 Poniente 111, or **La Guadalupaña**, 4 Poniente 911.

An especially interesting place to see fine Talavera is in the former convent of Santa Rosa, Calle 3 Norte 1203. A museum here is devoted to arts, crafts, and the kitchen—surprisingly fascinating displays. Not all the pottery is Talavera, but some of the best is. Any Puebla church will also have its own fine examples.

A score of shops in Puebla sell the ware, but not all of it is high quality. Remember: the whiter the base, the better the work. Any piece with smoke marks should be rejected.

Around Puebla

The little parish church in the village of **Tonantzintla**, 3 km (2 miles) south of Cholula, is perhaps the most delightful building in all of Mexico. The modest exterior gives little hint of the richness of craft and imagination that awaits the visitor inside. Local artisans, working in the finest native traditions, have decorated the interior with such a blaze of folk art that entering the church is like stepping into a kaleidoscope. Sly cherubs with Indian features peer from the polychrome murals and gilding, and the power of undiluted primary colors makes the nave radiant, its angels in miniskirts complemented by an abundance of grapes and flowers.

Mexico's smallest state, **Tlaxcala**, is 30 km (19 miles) north of the city of Puebla, its borders following almost exactly the frontiers of the ancient Republic of Tlaxcala, chief ally of Cortés in the conquest of Mexico. The tiny state is walled in by high mountains; views of La Malinche in particular are spectacular here.

The capital city shares the name of the state, and it has two buildings of unusual interest. The **Monastery of San Francisco**, a short walk south of the *zócalo,* may be the oldest church extant in the Americas. The cedar beams and inlaid wood below the organ loft are remarkable examples of carving and decoration, very Moorish in both design and execution.

Not far away stands the famed **Santuario de Ocotlán**, which is frosted with ornately shaped and molded white plaster. The church was built in 1745 to commemorate a purported appearance of the Virgin on the spot two centuries earlier. The interior boasts polychromed and gilded wood carving, the work of Francisco Miguel, an Indian sculptor who devoted 25 years of his life to this glorious achievement.

NORTH OF THE CAPITAL

For an interesting and very full day of sightseeing by car, head north from Mexico City and make a loop that includes the Museum of the Viceregal Period at Tepotzotlán, the Toltec archaeological zone at Tula, and the monastery at Ixmiquilpán, with its strange, almost bizarre murals. Since Ixmiquilpán is of less interest than the other two, it can be dropped to shorten the trip. Also, both the museum and archaeological zone are on the way to Querétaro, so visitors planning to explore colonial Mexico can include both places on their itineraries as they travel northwest.

Tepotzotlán

Tepotzotlán (teh-pote-so-TLAN) is practically a suburb of Mexico City, lying as it does just north of the Federal District on the west side of Highway 57. (It should not be confused with Tepoztlán, however, a town with a similar name located near Cuernavaca.) In 1584 the Jesuits established the Seminary of San Martín here, and it thrived as both a school and missionary center. In the middle of the 18th century the original church and some of the monastery were replaced with the present structure, one of the most impressive examples of Churrigueresque architecture in the Americas. Both the façade and the interior are nothing short of magnificent.

In 1767, shortly after the glorious new seminary was completed, the Jesuits were expelled from Mexico by royal decree. The immense complex they had built at Tepotzotlán was put to various uses, and finally became the **National Museum of the Viceregal Period**. The main buildings were restored to their 18th-century brilliance, and today the great corridors and chambers are filled with the finest examples of colonial art, including paintings, sculpture, furnishings, fabrics, ceramics, and ornaments. One room is a treasure house of ivories brought by galleon from the Orient. The gilded nave of the church, which gleams like Aladdin's cave, has been criticized for its "barbaric splendor," and for good reason. Equally splendid are two smaller, gold-encrusted rooms of the adjacent Holy House of Loreto, which is located to the right of the nave. The whole bewildering spectacle is at once pagan and Catholic, and a treat for the senses.

There's a restaurant in one of the ancient patios, but its service is too leisurely if you are hurrying on to other destinations; a number of small cafés across from the church atrium are better for quick refreshments.

The Ruins of Tula

Tula, once the proud capital of the Toltec Empire, lies 80 km (50 miles) north of Mexico City off of Highway 57, the same road that leads to Tepotzotlán. At Tepotzotlán, however, it becomes a toll road; from there, follow it to the Tula exit, which is clearly marked. The exit road will take you through the modern town of Tula. Follow the signs to "Las Ruinas."

Centuries before the Spanish had even imagined there might be such a thing as a New World, Tula was a fabled city. Legend has it that during its golden age the walls were bejeweled; songbirds would land on your shoulder to serenade you; squashes grew so big that a single one would feed a family for days, and cotton grew in a variety of brilliant colors, so there was no need to dye the cloth later. Sadly, you will find no trace of such wonders today, but what remains is nevertheless impressive in its own right.

Some time around A.D. 900, a nomadic tribe of barbarous people entered what is now Mexico from the north.

This was a period that has since become known as Meso-america's "dark ages," and it is likely that these invaders hastened the decline of the existing civilization. Calling themselves Toltecs, these warrior people began to inter-marry with the vanquished tribes of the region, and in A.D. 968 they established their capital at Tula. Over the next three centuries the Toltecs flourished; their influ-ence on the cultures of Mesoamerica was dramatic. In fact, the civilization of Tula is considered to be one of the greatest of Mesoamerica, the successor to Teotihuacán and the predecessor of the Aztec.

Today, remnants of this bygone glory are evident at the Tula archaeological zone. After leaving the parking area and passing the museum, you immediately come to the **Great Pyramid**. On the north side of the pyramid is a footpath that leads to the top of the structure, where you'll get a bird's-eye view of the whole site. The ruins spread out below you were the inspiration for Chichén Itzá in the Yucatán, and the similarities between the two are everywhere around you—from the type of sculpture that was commissioned, to the architectural design, to the motifs that characterize the relief carvings.

Across the main plaza is Tula's most famed monument, the **Temple of the Morning Star**, with its giant warrior figures exposed to the sky. (The temple is also named for Quetzalcóatl, the legendary Mesoamerican god-hero who was most often worshipped in the guise of a plumed serpent and reached what was perhaps his apotheosis in Tula.) Where they once served as huge columns support-ing a roof, today these statues—each over 15 feet tall and carved in four sections—stand stiffly at attention in full military regalia, their butterfly-shaped shields held closely to their chests. The workmanship is rough and rigid, which only adds to their considerable power. (The pieces of columns at the base of the temple are all that is left of what was probably a meeting hall.)

You will also find two spacious ball courts, a ruin known as the Burnt Palace, and several other structures at Tula. The relief carvings depict stealthy jaguars with out-sized claws, eagles, serpents, and skulls and bones. Every detail is typical of Toltec civilization; this was, after all, a military society, one that was fierce, ruthless, and enam-ored of human sacrifice.

The **Tula Museum** has a collection of ceramics and carvings, but the major pieces here are located outside, not inside.

Bottled soft drinks are also sold at the site, but you'll have to go elsewhere for food.

Ixmiquilpán

Ixmiquilpán (eesh-mee-keel-PAHN) is about 50 km (31 miles) northeast of Tula. To get there, follow Highway 126 along the Tula River; a few minutes past the little town of Tlahuelilpan there is a turnoff to the north, which you take. (You don't want to go to Pachuca.) This will end up joining the old Pan-American Highway 85. Ixmiquilpán is just north of the junction, and the **monastery** is in the center of the town.

In 1555 Augustinian friars founded a church and monastery here, in what had once been one of the capitals of the Otomí civilization. Nothing out of the ordinary was known about these missionaries until two decades ago, when the white paint was removed from a church wall and something truly extraordinary came to light.

As the paint came off, it became apparent that the friars had allowed their church to be frescoed with pagan murals. On panel after panel, Indians were depicted much as they had been in the ancient codices, engaged in life-and-death struggles against monsters. At least one of these dread creatures was a sort of centaur, a horse with arms, hands, and a bow. Elsewhere, twisting vines and other vegetation seemed to be part of the battle.

These murals were painted at a time when convents in Mexico were usually decorated with solemn monochromes. The only subjects deemed fit for display were grim portraits of saints and martyrs accompanied by a few dead flowers copied from prayer books. But at isolated Ixmiquilpán the walls had been allowed to blossom into life.

To this day there is no explaining these murals. When the Inquisition came to New Spain in the middle of the 16th century, the daring missionaries who allowed them to be painted must have had second thoughts and quickly covered the walls with whitewash. Apparently, however, they could not bring themselves to destroy the heretical works completely—and so some of the very few examples of 16th-century native art managed to survive. Today the murals delight the few travellers who know about this out-of-the-way location.

The **Saisa Restaurant** on the highway makes for a pleasant stop, and specializes in well-seasoned food.

The most direct route back to Mexico City from Ixmi-quilpán is on Highway 85, going south. The capital is 155 km (90 miles) distant over a very good road.

GETTING AROUND

Several bus lines serve **Cuernavaca** from Mexico City, all departing from Terminal Central del Sur on Calle General Vicente Guerrero. Autobuses Pullman de Morelos is the most convenient choice because it has a downtown Cuernavaca depot. The second-class line, Flecha Amarilla, also goes to the center of Cuernavaca. All other bus lines halt on the edge of town, and passengers must then take a taxi. Both Pullman and Flecha Amarilla have several departures every hour. Travelling time is just over an hour on weekdays, but less predictable on weekends due to traffic. Seats on the right side of the bus afford better views on the ride from the capital.

A car is a nuisance in the center of Cuernavaca, but you will need one for exploring outlying areas. A wider selection of rental vehicles is available in the capital, but Cuernavaca itself has half a dozen agencies, including Hertz.

Taxco

There is good and regular bus service to Taxco offered by several commercial lines from both Mexico City and Cuernavaca. Driving is also easy, but the last quarter of the trip from Cuernavaca is no speedway. From the capital the trip takes about two and a half hours each way.

Tour buses also depart frequently from Mexico City; the booking is usually done at the travel desks of hotels. Be sure to ask how much time is allowed in Taxco before reserving or paying for a tour.

On any bus going to Taxco or Cuernavaca from Mexico City, the right-hand side as you face front offers a much better view of the scenic mountains south of the Federal District.

Car rentals for Taxco trips are available in Mexico City and Cuernavaca. A car offers a much wider range of possibilities, but is not needed in Taxco itself.

Puebla and Cholula

There is good bus service, first class, from Mexico City to Puebla. Autobuses del Oriente, usually shortened to ADO, has several buses an hour leaving from the Terminal Central del Oriente (TAPO). If you're taking the metro

to the station, get off at the "San Lázaro" stop. The trip to Puebla takes about two hours, and you should try to get a seat on the right-hand side of the bus for the best views on the way. A car is not needed for enjoying downtown Puebla, but service to Cholula can be confusing to newcomers. A taxi, with a price agreed in advance, is your best bet.

Tonantzintla is a short taxi ride from the *zócalo* in Cholula. A car is best for seeing Tlaxcala.

ACCOMMODATIONS REFERENCE

▶ **La Casa Colonial.** Netzahualcoyotl 135, **Cuernavaca** 62000. Tel: (73) 12-1683.

▶ **Cuernavaca Racquet Club.** Francisco Villa 100, POB 401, **Cuernavaca** 62000. Tel: (73) 13-6122.

▶ **Hacienda Cocoyoc.** Kilometer 32.5 Carretera Federal, **Cuernavaca** 62740. Tel: (73) 52-2000. Fax: 9173526003.

▶ **Hacienda del Solar.** Colonia el Solar, POB 96, **Taxco** 40200. Tel: (732) 2-0323.

▶ **Hostería las Quintas.** Avenida Las Quintas 107, POB 427, **Cuernavaca** 62440. Tel: (73) 12-8800.

▶ **Hotel Lastra.** Calzada de los Fuertes s/n, POB 649, **Puebla** 72290. Tel: (22) 35-1501.

▶ **Las Mañanitas.** Calle Ricardo Linares 107, POB 1202, **Cuernavaca** 62400. Tel: (73) 14-1466. Fax: 73183672.

▶ **El Mesón del Angel.** Avenida Hermanos Serdan 807, **Puebla** 72100. Tel: (22) 48-2100.

▶ **Posada de la Misíon.** Avenida J. F. Kennedy 32, **Taxco** 40200. Tel: (732) 2-0063.

▶ **Hotel del Portal.** Avenida Camacho 205 (*zócalo*) **Puebla** 72290. Tel: (22) 46-0211.

▶ **Hotel Royalty Centro.** Avenida Portal Hodalgo (*zócalo*), **Puebla** 72290. Tel: (22) 42-0204.

▶ **Villa Arqueológica.** 2 Poniente 601, **Cholula**, Puebla 72760. Tel: (22) 47-1966 or (800) 528-3100.

THE COLONIAL HEARTLAND

QUERETARO, SAN MIGUEL DE ALLENDE, GUANAJUATO, MORELIA

By Robert Somerlott

Nrth and west of Mexico City lies a pleasant and usually gentle land, ringed by mountains, that is the heart of Mexico. This is the traditional Mexico, where tile-domed churches rise from almost empty fields; where iron-and-tin bandstands and fountains shaded by Indian laurels and pepper trees invite the weary to stop and rest a minute. This is picture-postcard Mexico, the Mexico of song and film. At the mention of such towns as San Miguel de Allende and Guanajuato, a Mexican listener is apt to toss his hands in delight and exclaim, "*Ay, que preciosa!* How beautiful!" At the same time, and perhaps not surprisingly, the cities of the colonial heartland tend to be conservative, wary keepers of a heritage.

Charles Flandrau wrote at the start of this century: "Superficially, Mexico is a prolonged romance. For even the brutal realities—of which there are many—are the realities of an intensely pictorial people among surroundings that, to the Northern eye, are never quite commonplace." Such are the colonial highlands.

This is also where the nation's patriotic soul is en-

shrined (in Mexico it is easy and customary to speak of the soul); this is where the bitter struggle for independence was launched. Half a century later, the final siege against Maximilian was waged here, and then, in 1915, one of the bloodiest battles ever fought on the North American continent took place at Celaya, ending in the destruction of Pancho Villa's army.

MAJOR INTEREST

Colonial architecture and history
Scenic beauty
Handicrafts

Querétaro
Historic sights and buildings

San Miguel de Allende
A largely preserved colonial town
Handicrafts, especially metals
Houses and gardens
Study of Spanish language and arts and crafts

San Miguel environs
The Shrine of Atotonilco
Our Lady of Carmen church in Celaya
The Augustinian monastery at Yuriria
Spas

Guanajuato
Visual drama
The Juárez Theater

Morelia
17th-century architecture
Handicraft marketing centers

The cities of the colonial heartland ring an area known as the Bajío, a vast fertile basin where multinational companies such as Campbell Soup have built packing plants in recent years. It's not unusual to see strawberry fields crowding the houses in some towns.

The Food of the Region

The abundance of fresh farm products in the Bajío has not, unfortunately, fostered an outstanding regional cuisine, perhaps because its agricultural abundance came late, and only with irrigation. Another factor might be that Mexicans in the area are as traditional in their diet as they are in their religion. Except in Morelia, where Tarascan Indian dishes are still produced, no ethnic group has been able to preserve its special ways of cooking.

As a result, the food of the region is very much a cross-section. The better restaurants—and even some inspired cooks in market stalls—hold their own with any in the country, but the traditional dishes lack variety and dash compared with those in other parts of Mexico. Visiting Mexicans often complain, and the more affluent end up patronizing foreign-style restaurants.

There are, however, a few specialties. Celaya, equidistant from San Miguel and Querétaro, produces a caramel confection called *cajeta,* made of goat's and cow's milk, which is packed in wooden boxes and shipped throughout Mexico and abroad. Querétaro cooks work with the *camote,* a relative of the sweet potato, candying it with sugar and lemon juice.

To praise a dessert a Mexican might exclaim, "Good as if made by a nun's fingers!" In the old days the best sweets were made in convents, which preserved Spanish rather than Mexican traditions. Nuns in the larger convents produced almond-paste candy, shaped and colored like little fruits. Today the same recipes are cooked up in home kitchens and appear for sale at fiestas throughout the year. Desserts and chicken dishes enhanced with walnuts and almonds have also slipped out of the convents into private kitchens. *Pollo en nogado,* for example, is a holiday treat made with chicken, walnuts, chiles, and cinnamon. *Ate de Almendra* is a sherry-and-almond glorification of sponge cake.

Chile sauces are less fierce here than in other parts of the country, but it is not macho to admit it; besides, the next restaurant may slip you liquid fire. Beef, except when ground, stewed, or thinly sliced (as for *carne asada*), is often disappointing.

There is a Tarascan touch to the Morelia menu, but the true center for such cooking is west of the colonial region covered in this chapter.

Beverages in the Bajío are not distinct from those in the rest of Mexico. Non-alcoholic *licuados* and *aguas* here do rely a little more on strawberries because they are abundant. The state of Querétaro produces wine, and so does the Dolores Hidalgo neighborhood, but neither area is famous for it.

The Historic Heritage of the Bajío

This fertile region supported a sparse population in pre-Hispanic times. Pottery-making villages flourished as early as 500 B.C., but despite the high art they achieved in clay, they failed to progress to higher levels of civilization.

When the Spanish arrived, they found the land occupied by civilized Otomí Indians in the south, but encountered fierce, semi-nomadic Chichimecs a little farther north. Far to the west the Tarascans, potential rivals of the Aztecs, had established outposts beyond their traditional base.

Silver accounts for the lightning thrust of the Spanish northward. Their hunger for ore from Zacatecas and, later, Guanajuato propelled soldiers and prospectors still breathless from destroying the Aztecs into the Bajío. Simultaneously, missionary priests who had reaped a harvest of souls in the west moved quickly eastward. So the sword and the cross marched together, impelled by different motives.

Silver barons and hacienda owners, often one and the same, multiplied their wealth in the 17th century. Native workers were recruited from afar, and, as they mixed with local folk, lost their identity as Aztecs, Tlaxcalans, or Mixtecs. Intermarriage between Indian and Indian, as well as Spanish and Indian, produced the population that today characterizes the heartland. When a Mexican from the Bajío says he is of a certain descent, he is probably no more accurate about his ancestry than the typical sixth-generation North American.

Prosperity in the 1700s caused the cities of the Bajío to embark on ambitious building programs; most of today's great structures date from that century. The same prosperity fanned the flames of independence, however, and in 1810 a revolt plotted in Querétaro and San Miguel blazed forth from tiny Dolores, now Dolores Hidalgo. During the violence-filled decades that followed, construction nearly ceased, leaving a virtual architectural blank from 1810 until about 1880. With the ascendancy of Porfirio Díaz to the presidency, however, a period of relative calm ensued. Once again, municipal governments turned their attention to dilapidated infrastructures, and a period of zealous rebuilding followed that lasted until soon after the turn of the century—when a new and different kind of revolutionary violence halted everything but destruction and bloodletting.

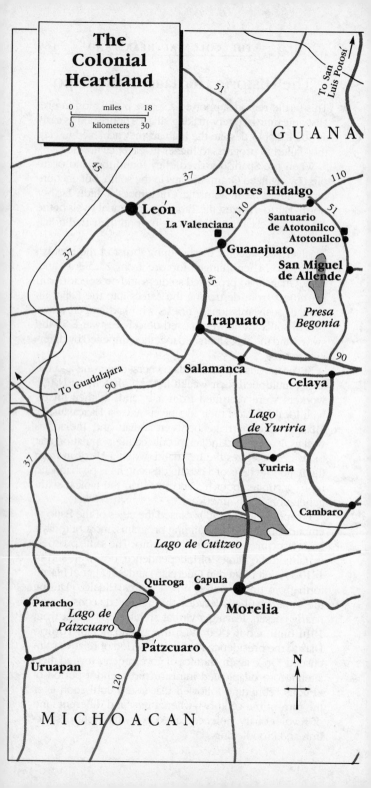

THE CITY OF QUERETARO

Querétaro, prosperous capital of the small state of the same name, is an oft-bypassed beauty. Motorists heading north for the U.S. border or south to Mexico City usually skirt it, sighing as they pass the unattractive industrial suburbs. The impression from a train is little better. Yet Querétaro, in its somewhat staid fashion, has attractions to offer.

Tourists' neglect of the city cannot be blamed entirely on unfavorable first impressions, however. Though worthy and historic, Querétaro lacks the impact of other colonial cities. The flavor is pleasant but not strong, the effect diffused. While it can offer a rewarding two days, and visitors generally like and admire the town, it seldom engenders a passionate attachment.

The first clue that something special awaits is given to travellers approaching from the most popular direction, south, on the Mexico City Highway bypass. At the city's edge traffic abruptly ducks under an 18th-century aqueduct that towers incongruously above the freeway. It happens so quickly, in fact, that most people are oblivious to the extraordinary structure looming over them. The aqueduct, built between 1726 and 1738, has more than 70 arches, some soaring to awesome heights. Once the town's chief source of water, and reputedly the seventh-largest such structure in the world, the aqueduct still supplies the Fountain of Neptune at the center of the city.

Querétaro once stood astride a vital trade route to the Bajío and the silver-rich mountains protecting it. The Otomí people settled here at least a thousand years ago; Aztecs assumed loose control of the city in 1446, turning it into their northernmost allied outpost against the hostile Chichimecs.

The conquistadors swooped down on it in 1531, making a quick alliance with an Otomí chief named Conin, but then the more formidable Chichimecs had to be dealt with. Legend has it that the newcomers and natives agreed to settle ownership by man-to-man combat, a bare-knuckle fistfight. There are variations of what happened next. In one version, there was a melee. In another, even as the champions of either side stood ready, an astounding red-and-gold cross carried by St. James mounted on horseback flared across the sky; the local

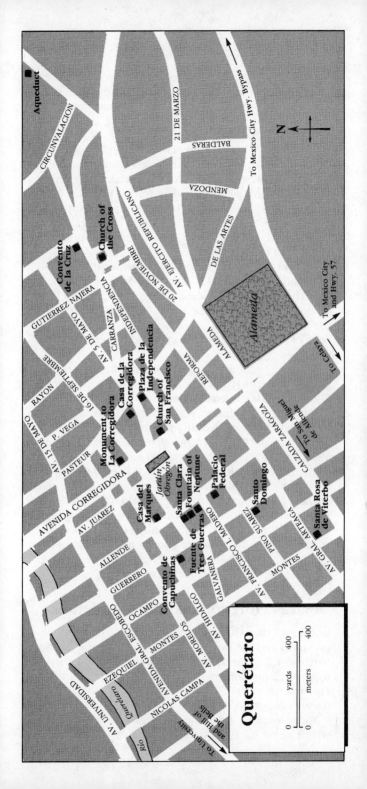

Querétaro

N

To Mexico City Hwy. Bypass

To Mexico City and Hwy. 57

To Celaya

Aqueduct

CIRCUNVALACION

21 DE MARZO

BALDERAS

MENDOZA

DE LAS ARTES

Alameda

Convento de la Cruz

Church of the Cross

GUTIERREZ NAJERA

CARRANZA

20 DE NOVIEMBRE

AV. EJERCITO REPUBLICANO

AV. 5 DE MAYO

INDEPENDENCIA

ALAMEDA

REFORMA

RAYON

16 DE SEPTIEMBRE

Casa de la Corregidora

Plaza de la Independencia

Church of San Francisco

P. VEGA

PASTEUR

AV. 15 DE MAYO

AV DE MAYO

Monument to La Corregidora

AVENIDA CORREGIDORA

Casa del Marques

Jardín Obregón

AV. JUAREZ

ALLENDE

GUERRERO

OCAMPO

EZEQUIEL MONTES

AVENIDA GRAL. ESCOBEDO

Convento de Capuchinas

Santa Clara

Fountain of Neptune

Fuente de Tres Guerras

Palacio Federal

GALVANERA

AV. MADERO

AV. FRANCISCO I. MADERO

AV. HIDALGO

AV. MORELOS

MONTES

NICOLAS CAMPA

AV. UNIVERSIDAD

Río Querétaro

To University and Hill of the Bells

CALZADA ZARAGOZA

To San Miguel de Allende

Santo Domingo

PINO SUAREZ

Santa Rosa de Viterbo

AV. GRAL. ARTEAGA

MONTES

yards 400

0   400 meters

population reportedly converted on the spot. In any case, Querétaro has been a bastion of Catholicism ever since.

In the early 1800s the traditionally cautious town became a den of conspiracy. At the center of this plot to overthrow Spanish rule was Josefa Ortíz de Domínguez, wife of the *corregidor* (mayor). In September of 1810, Doña Josefa, already under house arrest, managed to warn her fellow plotters that their sedition had been discovered and the Spanish authorities were ready to pounce. Her message, which, according to legend, was passed through a keyhole, ignited the revolt. Doña Josefa, usually called *La Corregidora,* is today the greatest female figure in the history of a country of few acclaimed heroines.

In 1848 Querétaro became the provisional capital of the nation while the U.S. Army was occupying Mexico City. The Treaty of Guadalupe-Hidalgo, which ceded half of Mexico's territory to the United States (what are now the states of California, New Mexico, and Arizona, and parts of Nevada and Colorado), was signed here later that year.

Nineteen years after that national disaster, the beleaguered Emperor Maximilian, along with the remnants of his army, was cornered at the edge of town. After a three-month siege, Maximilian was captured, tried, and executed (an event recalled in a painting by Manet). On a happier day in 1917, the constitution that is still in force in Mexico was written and adopted in Querétaro.

The latest incursion into the city has been quite different from the hostile ones of the past. After the earthquakes of 1985, thousands of Mexico City residents sought solid ground and new lives here, enlarging and changing the city even as they adapted to its peculiar rhythms. In return, these newcomers have brought with them a tonic of sophistication, a delight in the performing arts, and a generally faster-paced lifestyle.

Plazas Obregón and Independencia

In colonial days Querétaro, as a major link between the provinces and the capital, came to dominate the artistic tastes of a huge area, developing a gay, exuberant style that was flashier and more sentimental than the capital's. For two centuries it supplied even faraway towns with painters and artisans.

Today touches of this antique extravagance are everywhere to be seen in Querétaro, from its grillwork and balconies to its cornices and doors. The old section of town is an especially delightful place for strolling and discovering these details.

Traffic has been banished from the downtown area, which, while a blessing, is also the cause of many a snarl in outlying areas. Parking lots are hidden from the uninitiated, so the best course is to walk or take a taxi to the main plaza.

The **Jardín Obregón**, spacious and pleasant, is adorned with a bronze statue of the Greek goddess Hebe, swans, gargoyles, and curlicues—all the mandatory signs of civic chic at the turn of the century (other Bajío towns were not nearly so stylish). The character of the city becomes apparent in this square, which is suspiciously tidy and well-ordered. There is a strange paucity of vendors, a lack of the usual confusion and sprawling disorder here. It's as if it were saying, This is a tightly governed town, a slightly gentrified town, a town aware of its image.

On the east side of the square looms the **Church of San Francisco**. Built in 1545, it has endured so much expansion and cosmetic surgery that what remains is little more than a hodgepodge. Still, the dome and tower are splendid. Inside, the nave harbors some dreadful sculpture and one exceptional statue, a polychrome Saint James by the local master Arce, who worked at the start of the 19th century. A glance at the organ loft will reveal a fine iron grille (*reja*) enclosing the choir.

The 17th-century Franciscan monastery next door has become a regional museum that includes the former **Museo Pío Mariano**, with exhibits of war relics, several fine paintings (including two by the famed Baroque master Juan Correa), and a variety of colonial furnishings, among them chairs identical in design and discomfort to those sat upon in conservative Querétaro today. Elsewhere in the museum, huge music books are emblazoned with hand-drawn notations big enough to be read over the choirmaster's shoulder from the loft above.

While the museum's contents may be scant, the building itself is an exhibit, especially the central patio, with its carved arches and domes in the Moorish style (*mudéjar*). The smaller Patio of Novices and the Orange Garden evoke a sense of antiquity and the monastic life. The building as a whole is typically Franciscan, strong and practical, handsome but never extravagant.

Leaving the museum and walking east along a very pretty pedestrian mall, you pass attractive shops with quite ordinary merchandise. This shaded and flowering street leads to the tiny but charming **Plaza de la Independencia**. Here, in bronze, stands the Marqués de la Villa del Villar del Aguila, the benefactor who financed the Querétaro aqueduct. The marqués was also a keen hunter, which accounts for the lean stone hounds that cling to his monument. These particular animals are replacements; the original bronze canines were dognapped.

On the east side of the plaza is the riotous façade of the one-time mansion of Don Tomás Lopéz de Ecala, a display of Querétaro exuberance run amok, with a pair of vulturine eagles signifying the owner's high rank, stone draperies, and tangles of wrought iron. Don Tomás stole part of the park in order to erect this astonishment.

At least a score of other attractive colonial buildings, both religious and residential, enrich downtown Querétaro. For the visitor who chooses to explore it on foot there are countless touches of charm—including a statue of La Corregidora in a vaguely Greek costume but wearing long drop earrings for an added touch of elegance. (The statue is northeast of the Jardín Obregón.) And although sitting and strolling are the town's chief pleasures, Querétaro does have four additional sites of special interest.

The Santa Clara and Santa Rosa Churches

Santa Clara stands gracefully behind its own atrium just west of the Jardín Obregón, with the Fountain of Neptune—the modern terminus of the Querétaro aqueduct—lending it an air of distinction. The fountain, for many travellers, is their introduction to Francisco Eduardo Tresguerras, the Renaissance man of Mexican art. Born in Celaya, 45 km (28 miles) west of Querétaro, in 1759, Tresguerras, with one year of formal art training, became an architect, painter, sculptor, etcher, woodcarver, poet, and musician, and left a legacy of work that remains the pride of the region. His prestige is so great, in fact, that dozens of buildings in various cities are proudly, and falsely, attributed to him by local boosters. As the fountain demonstrates, he possessed a particular talent for warming the cold, often sterile Neoclassical style in which he was forced to build by government decree. (The ruling clique of his day had become embarrassed by the flamboyant decoration of Mexican High Baroque, or Churrigueresque style, and sought to tame and refine Mexican buildings by making them look vaguely Roman. Artistic strangulation generally resulted; Tresguerras saved many new structures from what would have been an otherwise arid fate.)

At Santa Clara he designed the fountain, although he did not create the sculpture. In the last years of the 1790s he redid the dome and tower of the church, and probably created the main altar and interior vaulting as well. The rest of the church, dating from its original construction in 1633, features Baroque ornamentation that is majestic to the point of being sublime.

The church itself is the only surviving structure of a huge religious complex that once stretched all the way to the Jardín Obregón. At one time, 8,000 nuns and their servants found shelter here, in what was one of the richest religious communities in the world. Evidence of that wealth is abundantly obvious in the church's ornamentation and sculpture, the most famous piece of which is the beautiful *La Piedad* by Mariano Arce. That there were hundreds of such communities throughout the country explains in part the genesis of Mexico's anti-clerical laws.

Southwest of the center of town on Avenida General Arteaga, a rather long walk from the main square, stands the imposing **Church of Santa Rosa de Viterbo**, the most unusual of Querétaro's many ecclesiastical monuments. In 1670 three pious young sisters were granted permission to construct cells for their religious devotions. Other aristocratic girls immediately wanted the same fashionable seclusion, and thus began the convent. In time, the nuns became teachers, and the convent became a college. (Of Mexico's tens of thousands of nuns, most were simply ladies in retirement and seclusion, "extra" women in a society that had no use for unmarried ladies of gentility. The teacher-nuns at Santa Rosa were among the exceptions.) The college was eventually housed in its present building, which was completed in 1752. The dome is so ponderous that special flying buttresses had to be added to support it, creating in the process a strikingly theatrical exterior.

Tresguerras was employed to rebuild and redecorate the structure at the end of the century, but it is hard to say how much of the building is his. Certainly he did the outer ornamentation, the dome and tower, and the carvings in the sacristy. In the same room you'll find one of the best murals painted during the colonial period, often attributed to Tresguerras but probably the work of José de Paez. The mural depicts nuns and their pupils in an enclosed garden while lambs carry white roses that turn red upon contact with the blood of the Savior.

The Church of the Cross

The Church of the Cross commands the highest ground in the city, the alleged spot where Saint James stopped the fight between conquistadors and Chichimecs, thereby settling the future of Querétaro. Nowadays the views of the town's roofs and many church towers are almost as dramatic.

The church was for many years headquarters for the missionary priests who went forth on foot to Christianize the vast area of New Spain that is now the southwestern United States. Among them was Father Junípero Serra, whose missionary activities (he founded the California missions of San Diego, San Luis Obispo, San Juan Capistrano, Santa Clara, and San Francisco, among others) have virtually assured him of sainthood while earning the condemnation of Native American rights activists. In the late 1600s the church was also home to over 7,000 mostly scientific volumes—what was probably the largest library in the New World at the time. A century and a half later Maximilian used the adjacent convent as a barracks, only to have it become his temporary prison. Today mementos of the emperor are on display there.

The Church of the Cross itself is a labyrinth of seven patios and rooms that are literally countless due to the fact that many are sealed and buried. The present structure, with expansions and rebuilding, dates from around 1650. Historically and spiritually it is the most important edifice in Querétaro and attracts pilgrims from all over the country, who come to worship at the site of a famed miracle.

According to legend, Fray Antonio Margil de Jesus Ros (1657–1726) was an amazingly devout missionary who, among other feats, walked barefoot from present-day Guatemala to Texas. In a garden at the church he reportedly plunged his staff into the ground, where, like Aaron's rod, it took root. A tree soon sprang up that bore cross-shaped thorns, and it still thrives in the same courtyard alongside some of its offspring. Supposedly, this type of tree will grow nowhere else—which means it not only has to be protected from the usual souvenir hunters but also from seekers of holy relics, who would shred it to its last root if given the chance. The church is located east of the main square at the corner of Carranza and Calle Acuña.

The Hill of the Bells

Whether or not the hill is worth visiting depends on your sense of history and romance. Outwardly it is not much, and the whole site has been called ugly for arguable reasons. But those fascinated by the story of Maximilian and Carlota will want to stand on the spot where their tragedy came to an end and modern Mexico began—or at least was reassured about its survival.

The hill rises between the university and the industrial zone at the northwestern edge of town. The first thing to arrest the eye is a stone colossus of Benito Juárez, harsh and rough, appropriately made of unyielding granite. His words are inscribed below: "Between individuals as between nations, respect for the rights of others is peace."

The memorial to the emperor is down the hill at the spot where he was executed. In death as in life the two leaders do not meet. The Austrian government has erected a chapel here as well, and near its altar are three stone plinths marking the spot where Maximilian, with his two Mexican generals, faced the firing squad. (Juárez once observed that Maximilian was honored to die beside two gallant Mexicans who loved both their church and country.) The chapel is ill-maintained, however, and from the beginning was cheap, even mingy, somehow suggesting that the emperor, for all his glamour, was as great an embarrassment to Austria as he was a plague to Mexico.

Opals

East of the city is one of the world's major veins of opals, a source of every grade of this lovely stone. The mines have been worked for more than a century now, so the supply is not as abundant as it was a few decades ago, when opals were offered on almost every corner of the city. But there is still a supply, and Querétaro remains a cutting and marketing center for them—as well as for amethysts, topazes, and aquamarines from elsewhere.

Evaluating opals is a tricky business, however. Buyers

should always avoid street vendors who have just made "wonderful finds." Perhaps the first dealer you should consult is Señor José Ramirez, owner of his own opal mine, who for many years has had an outstanding shop, **Lapidaria Querétaro**, at the corner of Pasteur Norte and 15 de Mayo. Both loose stones and stones in settings are offered, and lovely imported amethysts and topazes may also be inspected here. The shop is a few minutes' walk northeast of the Jardín Obregón.

To compare prices and quality go to **El Rubí**, a few steps west of the *jardín* at Avenida Madero 3. This is a family affair run by three gracious sisters who are both welcoming and knowledgeable. Again, both set and unset stones are displayed.

The **Sociedad Cooperativa Otomí**, in the center of town at Cinco de Mayo 29, has a much smaller collection, as does **Opalo** at Corregidora 13 Norte, near Sears.

Opals and other stones at these (as well as other) established stores are the only Querétaro specialty worth the attention of shoppers. A better selection of art and craft products will be found elsewhere in Mexico.

Staying in Querétaro

Most of the modern Querétaro hostelries are strung out along Highway 57 to attract motorists travelling to or from Mexico City, and therefore tend to suffer from typical motel monotony, limited service, and isolation. An exception is the attractive **Holiday Inn**, a very well run establishment that more than justifies its slightly higher prices with comfort, décor, and such facilities as lighted tennis courts. The Holiday Inn also has a fine Mexican/international restaurant with a selection of wines, gentle lighting, and music in the evenings. The cheerful coffee shop, La Capilla, serves good breakfasts.

Less complete in its offerings but perfectly acceptable is the **Real de Minas**, part of a motor inn chain popular with Mexican business and government travellers. It, too, is near the highway.

Visitors arriving by bus or train may want a more central location (although the Holiday Inn is especially helpful about arranging transportation). On the Plaza de la Independencia in the historic district is the **Mesón de Santa Rosa**, an elegant and unusual colonial building that has been restored and adapted with taste. The dining room is rather formal, with both food and service seeming more European than Mexican.

Within easy walking distance of the downtown area is the **Senorial**, a conveniently located and modern hotel with protected parking.

The **Hacienda Jurica**, 13 km (8 miles) northwest of the city off of Highway 57, is a fashionable resort hotel that is particularly popular with vacationers from Mexico City. It offers an 18-hole golf course, squash, tennis, even a roller-skating rink. Not all rooms in this 17th-century hacienda are excellent, but most are.

The **Mansión Galindo**, another elegant resort, is located some distance to the southeast on the way to Mexico City. Take Highway 57 east for 37 km (23 miles) to the Amealco exit, and then follow Route 120 another 6½ km (4 miles). After the turnoff, the directions will be clearly marked. The hacienda dates from the 16th century, but not even the viceroys of that era imagined the luxury that Galindo offers today: lighted tennis court, posh nightclub, and so forth. Galindo is popular with the capital's film, TV, and political folk.

Dining in Querétaro

Querétaro has a truly outstanding restaurant in **La Estancia**. Its menu is European but also includes creative variations on traditional Mexican dishes; the service is impeccable. While the evening ambience is romantic, this converted hacienda also has great charm during the afternoon dinner hours. It is located on the northeast edge of town, km 8.5 Carretera Querétaro–San Luis Potosí. Tel: 7-0405. Open seven days a week.

The **Parilla Argentina Fogon Pampero**, near the entrance to the country club on Boulevard Las Americas opposite the bullring, packs in local businessmen for an afternoon feast of, usually, beef. It is a rather plain place, serving large (but not cheap) portions of hearty food.

For a simpler meal or snack while downtown, the **Flor de Querétaro**, a family spot at Juárez 9, Jardín Obregón, offers an inexpensive menu for a set afternoon dinner (the *comida corrida*), as well as à la carte Mexican dishes.

A little fancier is **Fonda del Refugio**, a restaurant and sidewalk café located in the historic zone at Jardín Corregidora 26. The café is popular with the more affluent students from the local university, and outdoor tables here are at a premium. Traditional dishes are satisfactory, the attempts at international cuisine a bit more risky.

The dozen or so hole-in-the-wall counter-in-the-front spots scattered throughout the Jardín Obregón neighborhood are all right for tacos, tortas, and the like. One is much the same as another, but out-of-towners should confine themselves to bottled beverages.

SAN MIGUEL DE ALLENDE

The usual approach to San Miguel de Allende is from the southeast, by car or bus from Mexico City via Querétaro. Above the town the cobbled road suddenly widens into a balustraded overlook, or *Mirador,* where most drivers pause to admire the view. After shooing away the vendors of flimsy rugs, you gaze across a valley toward a pale lake and distant mountains. The town lies directly below, its domes and towers clinging to the slope of the Hill of Móctezuma, a pastel collage.

The collage image is obvious, of course. Everyone knows that San Miguel is an art colony, and one rather self-conscious of the fact. But visitors standing at this spot have been known to fall in love with the town instantly and not always reasonably. And why not. This is the prettiest town in Mexico, although many others are more spectacular, imposing, or exotic. And despite recent growth and urban sprawl, it remains a small city, easy to see and manage.

San Miguel can be "done" in just a few hours by a zealous sightseer with a checklist. Indeed, there are a few marathon bus tours out of Mexico City that offer just such a production-line schedule. However, the town will not reveal itself in a series of snapshots; much of its charm is subtle and indefinite, the whole effect being more than the sum of its parts. Still, energetic folks who do not enjoy sauntering, lounging, or soaking up ambience may grow restless after a day or two here.

San Miguel is a winter haven for a few hundred refugees from the cold and snow of the States and Canada. In summer it is a cool and convenient retreat for people from Texas and the Gulf Coast region. Many of these visitors from the north return year after year, renting houses or apartments or booking the same rooms in favorite hotels, staying a month, or two, or even three. They become possessive of the town, as well as strong supporters of its cultural and charitable activities. Others,

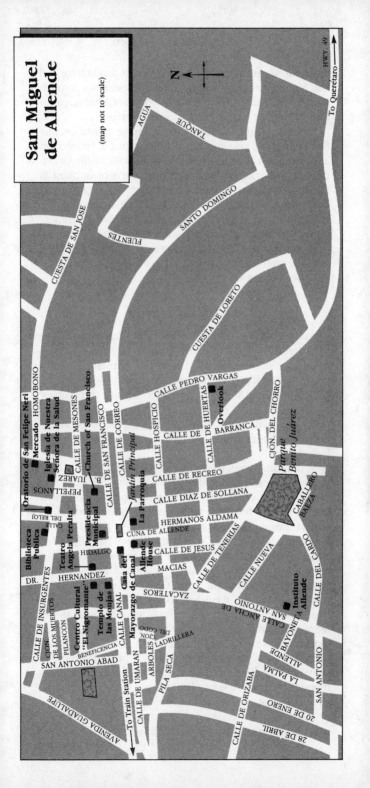

San Miguel
de Allende

(map not to scale)

N

To Querétaro

HWY. 49

AGUA

TANQUE

SANTO DOMINGO

CUESTA DE SAN JOSE

FUENTES

CUESTA DE LORETO

Oratorio de San Felipe Neri

Mercado HOMOBONO

Iglesia de Nuestra
Señora de la Salud

CALLE DE MESONES

Church of San Francisco

PEPELLANOS

B. JUAREZ

CALLE DE SAN FRANCISCO

CALLE DE CORREO

CALLE PEDRO VARGAS

Overlook

CALLE DE HUERTAS

CALLE HOSPICIO

CALLE DE BARRANCA

Jardin Principal

La Parroquia

CALLE DE RECREO

CALLE DIAZ DE SOLLANA

CJON. DEL CHORRO

Parque
Benito Juárez

CABALLERO

BAEZA

Biblioteca
Publica

CALLE
DEL RELOJ

Teatro
Angela Peralta

Presidencia
Municipal

HERMANOS ALDAMA

CUNA DE ALLENDE

DR.

HERNANDEZ

HIDALGO

Casa del

Allende
House

CALLE DE JESUS

CALLE DE TENERIAS

CALLE NUEVA

CALLE DEL CARDO

CALLE DE INSURGENTES

CJON.
DE LOS MUERTOS

PILANCON

Centro Cultural
"El Nigromante"

BENEFICENCIA

Templo de
las Monjas

CALLE CANAL

Mayorazgo de Canal

MACIAS

ZACATEROS

CALLE ANCHA DE

SAN ANTONIO

Instituto
Allende

SAN ANTONIO ABAD

AVENIDA GUADALUPE

To Train Station

CALLE DE UMARAN

CJON.
DEL CORO

ARBOLES

LADRILLERA

PILA SECA

BAYONETA

ALLENDE

LA PALMA

SAN ANTONIO

CALLE DE ORIZABA

20 DE ENERO

28 DE ABRIL

again mostly from the United States or Canada, retire to San Miguel to live on pensions and investments. A much smaller expatriate group actually works for a living, painting, writing, or running small businesses.

There are fears, usually expressed from a distance, that San Miguel has become North Americanized. Indeed, on any given morning during the peak seasons North Americans seem to occupy the south side of the main plaza as surely as they do the Alamo. But visitors wishing to avoid other visitors have only to detour half a block to be solidly back in Mexico. Mexicans outnumber foreigners here by 100 to 1, and all the guest rooms in town would fit easily into a single resort hotel in Acapulco. San Miguel, despite superficial indications to the contrary, is as Mexican as cactus.

The Plaza Area

Visitors standing on the south side of the main plaza facing San Miguel's imposing parish church, **La Parroquia**, will find themselves surrounded by as well-preserved a colonial town as there is. Despite the traffic and overhead power lines, its 18-century character remains surprisingly intact. Much of this is due to the fact that San Miguel was declared a national monument in 1926. Since then, architectural change has been banned, signs regulated, neon forbidden.

At the same time, the preservation of the town is only in part the result of decrees. The 17th and 18th centuries saw the town grow wealthy from commerce and ranching, as well as from the tanneries that lined some of its streets. Eventually it changed its name to San Miguel el Grande (because it was by then the biggest San Miguel, of which there were more than a few, in the region) and assumed aristocratic airs. But civil upheaval and the Industrial Revolution brought ruin to the burghers of the 19th century. Gradually, the silver in the surrounding region was mined out and the silver trains stopped coming; the tanneries found themselves unable to compete in mass markets because the town lacked sufficient water. So San Miguel was bypassed by the times. The old buildings were left standing because there was no need and no money to replace them; cobblestones were left in place by a town that could not afford repaving.

Today almost everything dates from the 1700s, with the exception of an occasional sign of more recent prosperity and the French-influenced details from the turn of the century. (The landscaping, benches, and bandstand of the *jardín* date from that brief period, for example.) And since the town has never been reconstructed as a sort of museum, it is saved from being self-consciously picturesque. In the long run, San Miguel's past misfortune has become our good fortune.

At the edge of La Parroquia's atrium rises a bronze statue of Fray Juan de San Miguel, the barefoot Franciscan missionary who founded the town in 1542, naming it for his own patron saint, the warrior archangel. The full name of the town was San Miguel de los Chichimecas, prematurely honoring those Indians the friar intended to convert. As it turned out, the angel's protection was needed; this was wild country, and the Chichimecs proved so stubborn that Indians from Tlaxcala had to be imported to serve the needs of the Spaniards.

The settlement, located astride the silver trails, thrived. Prosperity, however, meant rebuilding; nothing remains of the 16th-century village. A stone church was erected, then replaced. The oldest walls of La Parroquia may date as far back as 1620, but most of it, except for the façade, was built 60 years later. Today, La Parroquia is the most photographed, most painted church in Mexico, an astonishment of neo-Gothic architecture gone mad—or Mexican.

Ceferino Gutiérrez, a self-taught Indian stonemason, was commissioned in 1880 to create a new façade for the then-conventional church. In love with the Gothic architecture of Europe, he studied drawings, engravings, and postcards, admiring especially the cathedrals of Milan, Chartres, and Cologne. Though he was probably illiterate and knew nothing of drafting, Gutiérrez daily sketched his plans in the sand for workmen to follow, just as the great cathedral builders of Europe once had. The result is, in the truest sense of the word, fantastic. La Parroquia stabs the sky with its turrets and spires; everything is aimed heavenward. But that was the only aspect of Gothic style Gutiérrez grasped. The rest of his façade is massive, brooding, solid as a fortress.

Still, La Parroquia completely dominates the San Miguel landscape, just as its humble builder dreamed it would. Its heavy bells, the largest almost six feet high, give it added authority and act as a constant sound track for the town, sounding early Mass at dawn, ringing rosary, signaling events, arrivals, and departures. The slender clock tower next door, rebuilt by Gutiérrez to match his church façade, adds its own strong bell voice as it announces the quarter hours. (Visitors should be warned that there are about 150 public bells in town. They are all rung on various occasions and sometimes all at once.)

The interior of La Parroquia is less interesting than its façade. There is, however, a remarkable life-sized statue of Our Lord of the Conquest, made by Tarascan converts at Pátzcuaro in the 16th century out of cornstalks and an enduring orchid-bulb glue, in a chapel to the left of the main portal. This powerful figure is venerated by the *conchero* dancers, who perform their ceremonial dances in flamboyant costume accompanied by shell instruments at various religious festivals throughout the year. There are more than 100,000 *concheros* scattered over a wide region that was once Chichimec country, but apart from the religious customs and ceremonial dances that glorify their ancestral heritage, most *concheros* lead ordinary lives. The wild dancing warrior with hair to his waist may be, under his wig, the short-haired bank clerk who changed your money earlier in the day.

Across the narrow street that flanks La Parroquia to the west stands the **birthplace of Ignacio Allende**, the town's most famous citizen. A fine and well-proportioned mansion, there have been ongoing efforts to make it a museum open to the public. Allende himself was an aristocrat, but the "taint" of being born a *criollo*—a Spaniard born in Mexico—condemned him to second-class status in his own country. The Crown's discrimination against Spaniards born abroad gradually nurtured resentment and, eventually, rebellion. Allende, a career army officer, was one of the few trained military leaders among the insurgents and became their general, second in command only to Father Hidalgo. After the rebel forces disintegrated in 1811, however, he was captured, shot, and then beheaded by royalist forces. His beloved hometown of San Miguel el Grande was renamed in his honor by an independent Mexico in 1862.

San Miguel's three leading art galleries are all within a block of Allende's birthplace. Around the corner at Umarán 1 is the **Josh Klingerman Gallery**; facing the side of the church at Cuna de Allende 15 is the **Galería Atenea**; and on the north side of the *jardín* at number 14 is the **Galería San Miguel**. The number of artists living in San Miguel has declined over the last dozen years, but the town remains the nation's second-largest art market, surpassed only by Mexico City.

At the north end of the block-long colonial arcade facing the *jardín* on the west side rises the imposing **Casa del Mayorazgo de Canal**, now occupied by Banamex, the Bank of Mexico. (To visit a colonial mansion in San Miguel, all you need do is step into a bank. There are five of them established in palatial quarters, all located on the street running uphill from the north side of the plaza.) The grand entrance to this 18th-century mansion is on Calle Canal, which heads downhill from the northwest corner of the plaza. The carriage doors seek to overwhelm the caller with the family Canal's importance: the eagle signifies its baronial status, the helmets indicate that ancestors fought against the Moors in Spain. (Two helmets here; both the husband and wife's families earned the distinction and flaunted it.) The residence itself was built sometime around 1740 on top of an older structure, then remodeled some 50 years later. Supposedly, Eduardo Tresguerras did the restyling. Regardless, it is a fine example of the Mexican "severe" style: dark red walls, black wrought iron, white trim and woodwork. All such buildings—and there are many in Mexico—were either built or spruced up around 1800.

The owner of the house at the time of the War of Independence was Colonel Narciso de la Canal, commander of the local Spanish garrison. When the rebels, led by his neighbor Allende and Father Hidalgo, marched on the town, the colonel prudently kept his soldiers in their barracks. Later, when the possibility of his elevation to the rank of count was brought up, serious questions about his true allegiance were raised, and the title remained unconfirmed when the colonel died, under arrest, in Querétaro. His true role in the rebellion is still unknown, but posterity has granted him the title that was withheld in life: His family is always called "the Counts of Canal" in San Miguel de Allende.

One block north of the *jardín,* the **Church of San Francisco** graces the street named after it, an elegant structure with a disturbing note. The delicately carved façade is pure Churrigueresque, its central decoration abhorring a blank spot, its columns tapering illogically toward their bases. (Whenever you see this inverted column in Mexico you can instantly date the structure as being built between 1720 and 1785; the odds against being mistaken are overwhelming.) However, this particular church was caught in a period of stylistic flux. Begun in 1779, its bell tower was still unbuilt when the shift to the Neoclassical swept the country. The always ingenious Tresguerras was brought in from Celaya to design a tower that would express the new style yet blend with the church's existing façade. Though he didn't quite manage this impossible task, he came close. The interior design is also mostly his, and features a nave bathed in light. The Enlightenment, which was late in coming to Mexico, is seen in the most literal terms here. The Church of San Francisco, like many others of the era, was purged of all atmosphere of oppressive mystery.

A block to the north, an open plaza fronts the **Iglesia de Nuestra Señora de la Salud**, the Church of Our Lady of Health. A gigantic seashell commemorating a mass baptism by sea water spans the entrance. In the middle of the shell an all-seeing eye set in a triangle celebrates both the omniscience of God as well as the Holy Trinity. Many people believe, sensibly enough, that the church must specialize in curing diseases of the eye.

The interior boasts two unusual details. An old wooden altar in the right transept has panels showing Jesus the Good Shepherd ministering to his flock while some of the sheep are menaced by a unicorn. The oddity here is the portrayal of a New Testament parable in a Mexican church, where the miraculous usually reigns supreme. There are also four startling paintings of the classic virtues under the dome; while they're not exactly pagan, they're certainly not Roman Catholic, either.

The church itself was built early in the 18th century as a chapel for the college next door, an institution radical enough to have educated several martyrs of independence, among them Allende. This is the only explanation for the odd décor of La Salud.

A block west, the **Oratorio de San Felipe Neri** boasts silverwork designs chiseled into the stone of its façade. The designs are somehow appropriate, for San Felipe Neri stands in a neighborhood where pack trains from distant silver mines once halted for a night's lodging.

This otherwise ordinary church, San Miguel's largest, has two unusual features, neither immediately apparent. Attached to the building is the **Santa Casa de Loreto**. According to Catholic tradition, the house of the Virgin Mary was transported by angels to Loreto, Italy, where it can still be visited today. Here we have a replica of sorts, although some locals would have you believe it's the original. To enter this special sanctorum, walk to the left side of the altar, where impressive gates often bar the way—but an attendant will usually fetch a custodian with a key.

The outer room, the Virgin's drawing room, contains statues of Manuel Tomás de la Canal and his wife, who paid for the chapel; they are buried underneath their statues. After going down a narrow hall lined with Oriental tiles (brought by the Manila galleons to Acapulco), you'll enter a dazzling chamber, the Virgin's bedroom, where even the stonework is gilded. The tile is Spanish Talavera, laid in 1735.

The other unusual feature of San Felipe Neri rarely seen by visitors is the Indian entrance on the east side of the church. To get there, go through the wooden gate, which is almost always open, at the front of the atrium. On the other side is the simple but beautifully carved entrance, with its Indian cherubs and plumes etched in stone. Originally, this was the portal of an older church, which was taken from its humble congregation by legal trickery. In time, a grand new building was raised on the site by the rich *criollo* parishioners. Time has given the story a fittingly ironic ending: San Felipe Neri is once again the main church for the townspeople of San Miguel de Allende, whose ancestors once entered it through what is now the side door.

One block west of the plaza, the convent and church of **La Concepción** dominates its neighborhood. Here the remarkable but unoriginal imagination of Ceferino Gutiérrez is again apparent. His façade for La Parroquia borrowed from several Gothic cathedrals, just as here he recreated the dome of Les Invalides in Paris—not exactly but quite obviously. The dome is a century old; the church goes back an additional hundred years.

Almost all of the massive former convent behind the church has been taken over by the government and turned into a school of the arts, part of the national system. Properly known as the Centro Cultural "El Nigromante," it is generally called **Bellas Artes** and is the focal point of the town's cultural life, especially for music. In addition to its magnificent patio, which is one of the most ambitious such designs in the country, a small covey of nuns is still secluded in a corner of the building, squeezed between the church and the art center. Remarkably, their convent survived the battles and anti-clerical campaigns of the 1920s, and was perhaps the only one in Mexico not to be "opened" by revolutionary troops. The existence of this marooned little convent is still illegal, but nobody seems to care.

Staying in San Miguel

San Miguel has been receiving travellers since the early 17th century, when every week mule and burro trains arrived with silver ore bound for the capital. Today, ancient inns line two streets, and the visitor has a wide selection of hotels whose managements have a good idea of what foreigners want and expect.

Almost all the inns in town are small and have only two stories. (The town's single elevator is looked upon with suspicion.) There is no air conditioning, but then it isn't needed at an elevation of 1,951 meters (6,400 feet). It is best to have quarters within easy walking distance of the main square, the *jardín,* since San Miguel distances are vertical as well as horizontal; the steep hill must be taken into account. A few otherwise good hotels are too far out or too far up.

The **Casa de Sierra Nevada**, one of the country's best and most enjoyable small hotels, occupies four colonial houses, one a true mansion, that have been converted into rooms and suites. Some have patios, roof terraces, and fireplaces, and all are decorated with fine crafts and colonial-style pieces. The tone is refined and international (a former First Lady of the United States is a frequent guest), and the emphasis is on personal service and attention. Guests may have breakfast in the excellent dining room, on a verdant patio, or in their own rooms or on their terraces. A heated swimming pool with club privileges is also available. No credit cards are accepted, but personal checks may be by prior arrangement. The inn is near the center of town, slightly but not formidably uphill.

On the same quiet street, a step higher in topography but a decided step lower in price, is the well-named **Hacienda de las Flores**, a garden inn with restful lawns and a heated swimming pool. The hacienda has a modest entrance typical of San Miguel—noncommital until you are fully inside. But then it opens onto a building and landscape designed to blend in with the colonial town. The rooms—actually junior suites—are attractive in décor, spacious, and have good views. The hotel's intimate lounge is centered around a fireplace. Two meals are included in the daily rate, and since the food is one of the hacienda's attractions, this makes it a good buy. The guests tend to be travel-wise but informal. Children are welcome; credit cards are not.

The same type of knowledgeable clientele is attracted to the more expensive **Villa Jacaranda**, which is located a little farther from the plaza but on a level street. The rooms and suites, some with private patios, are excellent. Classic films are shown in the evening in a friendly lounge. The small heated swimming pool also has a whirlpool.

The **Aristos/Parador San Miguel**, with 56 units, is a giant by San Miguel standards. It stands amidst spacious grounds behind the Instituto Allende, an art and language school on Calle Ancha de San Antonio, about ten minutes' walk from the center of town. There's an adequate pool, which is usually heated in cooler weather. Long-term guests, conscious of value, return every winter to claim most of these pleasant but not luxurious rooms. Several bungalows with kitchens are available by the month. The matter of including meals in the rates changes, and should be settled before registering. The dining room offers well-prepared food for conventional tastes.

Generations of art students and vacationing teachers have chosen the provincial surroundings at the **Posada de las Monjas**, two blocks downhill from the *jardín*. A new section is nicer than the older part up front. The new **Hotel Monte Verde**, two blocks farther from the plaza, combines modern comfort with colonial décor, a flowering central garden, and a good restaurant. The attractive rates make it worth the longer walk.

One of the best buys in town is the unpretentious but more than adequate **Casa Carmen**, located a few steps from the central post office. Heated rooms encircle a pretty patio. Guests return often to this friendly pension for both its rooms and its food.

The **Hacienda Santa María** is at the limit of easy walking distance to town, although the stroll is along a shady and interesting street. The three rooms with private bath are luxurious and beautifully furnished, with fine colonial ceilings and tilework. The three other rooms, which share bath facilities, are not in the same class but are a good value. The ambience at Santa Maria is that of being a guest in a relaxed home characterized by the fine taste of its owners.

Dining in San Miguel

Because of tourism and the presence of the foreign community, San Miguel's restaurants surpass those of neighboring cities in both quality and number. Still, regional fare of distinction is scarce here, and most of the better dining places emphasize "international" food, a cuisine that is sometimes a little vague.

The **Bugambilia**, at Hidalgo 42, is an exception and has clung staunchly to a Mexican menu for three generations. The dishes are classical: *tinga, sopa Azteca,* steaming *caldo de res* with a chunk of chewy stewing beef, *chiles en nogada* sporting the national colors. There is also guitar music in the attractive patio of this former private home, which remains a bit rustic and nicely plain. Closed Wednesdays. No credit cards.

The **Restaurant Casa de Sierra Nevada**, in the hotel of the same name, is managed by a French chef with flair and imagination. The menu, French but not exclusively, changes with the seasons—freshness seems to be the watchword here. Special dishes can be prepared with advance notice. Reservations are advised because the elegant dining room seats only 32 (though other seating is available in the less formal patio; there is also an intimate little bar off the other side of the patio.). Soft classical guitar music; dress code evenings. No credit cards. Hospicio 35; Tel: 2-0415.

The **Villa Jacaranda**, at Aldama 53, also a hotel dining room, displays the various awards for excellence it regularly captures from travel magazines on its walls. The menu is international, the presentation and service meticulous. Besides a cheerful main room with views of the patio there is a glassed-in gazebo that overlooks the leafy treetops of a nearby park. The atmosphere, food, and service justify the fairly high prices.

The **Hacienda de las Flores**, yet another hotel restaurant, offers a carefully chosen menu of the chef's specialties. This is an intimate place, quiet and pleasant, with guitar music on weekends. Reservations are advisable. Hospicio 16; Tel: 2-1808.

Pepe's Patio is popular with the foreign colony, especially for Sunday brunch. It's outdoors, partly sheltered by tile roofs, and resembles a set for *Ramona* or *The Mark of Zorro*. The menu is divided between traditional Mexican and international dishes. Closed Sunday evening and Monday. No credit cards.

The plastic-and-chrome **Café Colón** is not quite what might be called a fast-taco place—though it uses paper napkins—but it is almost un-Mexican in the speed of its kitchen. Its menu is Mexican, with concessions to *norteamericanos* such as hamburgers and milk shakes. San Francisco 21.

La Dolce Vita is a very European-style coffee-and-pastry café, a place to browse through newspapers and magazines. Located on the second patio of Canal 21.

San Miguel tends to call it a night after a late supper. **Mama Mia**, a pizza emporium, at Umarán 8, offers flamenco guitar music in a popular patio and various combos in a smaller bar. **Pancho and Lefty's**, at Mesones 99, has a Texas saloon feeling, complete with a neon beer sign above the bar, and features changing entertainment: jazz, country and western, and combos. The town's discos cater to teenagers, although oldsters in their twenties do not arouse suspicion.

Shopping in San Miguel

Metalwork, especially in tin and brass, is excellent in San Miguel, and a good buy. The town's weavers also offer fine quality, but the selection is more limited here than elsewhere. Furniture making in colonial or provincial style is a local tradition. There is also a wide selection of embroidered clothing, and a small but good selection of leatherware.

Two reputable places create wonderful items in silver: **Beckman** at Hernández Macías 115 and **David**, at Zacateros 53.

There are galleries and boutiques all around the main plaza and in any street within a block of it. Others line Calle Zacateros two blocks west.

The **Casa Cohen**, at Reloj 18, is the country's best maker of cast brass and also offers other items of more than usual interest. **El Pegaso**, a gathering place for coffee drinkers located across from the post office, displays carefully selected clothing and other unusual goods. The **Casa Canal**, at the corner of Canal and the main plaza, is virtually a museum of provincial furniture; it is also a boutique.

Special Events and Studies

There are frequent concerts and musical events in San Miguel, ranging from soloists to symphony orchestras.

The **Chamber Music Festival**, which features internationally known string quartets and offers master classes, is staged every August. A smaller but equally pleasing string festival takes place at Christmastime. Belles Artes (San Miguel de Allende, Guanajuato, Mexico 37700) will be happy to provide information by mail. Several theatrical performances are given each year, some in Spanish, others in English. Art exhibits open with some frequency, of course, in this art colony.

On most Sundays the **Biblioteca Pública** (Public Library) conducts a tour of local houses and gardens—an excellent opportunity to "see behind the walls." Not surprisingly, it's a very popular event. The library is on Calle Insurgentes between Hidalgo and Reloj.

For four decades special San Miguel schools have attracted students who are mostly English-speaking. The Instituto Allende on Calle Ancha de San Antonio offers a curriculum of fine arts, crafts, and Spanish. The School of the Art Institute of Chicago uses the Instituto's colonial-style campus for its study-abroad plan; students and teachers from the Rhode Island School of Design also come to San Miguel every winter. The Centro Cultural "El Nigromante" (Bellas Artes) offers classes in the arts, crafts, and some musical instruction. Two schools specialize in Spanish and related subjects only: the Academia Hispano Americana, at Mesones 4, is quite traditional in its by-rote approach; the newer Casa de la Luna, Cuadrante 2, is more innovative.

AROUND SAN MIGUEL

North of the town is an area dotted with hot mineral springs that bubble from the ground. Naturally, spas and resorts have sprung up here, the most impressive being the **Hacienda Taboada**, at km 8 (5 miles) on the highway to Dolores Hidalgo. This spa offers an Olympic-sized pool with volcanically heated water, 60 rooms done in Mediterranean décor, and all hotel services, as well as horseback riding and free transportation to and from San Miguel. Non-guests are admitted to the rather posh facilities every day from 9:00 A.M. until 6:00 P.M. There are also less costly and much less luxurious spas in the neighborhood, including La Gruta and El Cortijo, both popular with the locals.

Nearby, but quite different from the picnic-like gaiety

of a spa, hulks the **Santuario de Atotonilco**, a huge shrine that is a repository of Mexican folk painting and offers a glimpse into a corner of Catholicism seldom seen. Although the main building was begun in 1754, a medieval grimness and chill seemingly centuries older pervades this sprawling maze of rooms and corridors. (Only the center section is open to the public.) Each year thousands of religious penitents trek to the shrine to attend "exercises," to cleanse themselves and be shriven. Little whips called *disciplinas* are available for those who want them, and discarded crowns of thorns are often found outside.

Inside, in room after room, walls and ceilings are frescoed with naïve but skillful murals charmingly executed. Never have pain, suffering, and penance been portrayed more cheerfully. Sometimes the themes of these murals stray from the religious: The naval battle of Lepanto, for example, appears on a chapel ceiling, and elsewhere legends mix freely with miracles. But the overarching theme is wickedness, remorse, and pain. Here you will confront the dark side of Faith and be reminded of the days when saints mortified their flesh and starved themselves atop pillars.

The village of **Atotonilco** is also historically important, for it was here that Father Hidalgo seized the banner of the Virgin of Guadalupe and proclaimed her patroness and generalissimo of the Mexican forces, an honor she unofficially holds to this day.

Fifty-two km (32 miles) south of San Miguel lies the industrial and commercial center of **Celaya**. In the center of this otherwise uninteresting city stands the masterwork of Eduardo Tresguerras, the **Church of Nuestra Señora del Carmen**, which was erected in 1807. Tresguerras, as architect, sculptor, muralist, and decorator, created a light-bathed interior that proved it was possible to inject warmth into the usually severe Neoclassical style. In a mural that depicts the Judgment Day, the artist himself is shown emerging from a tomb, quite uncertain of his future.

Still farther south, 114 km (71 miles) from San Miguel over paved and pretty country roads—an easy one-day excursion or, alternatively, a stop on the way to Morelia—lies the town and lake of **Yuriria**. The town is noted for its massive Augustinian monastery, whose construction was begun in 1550 and completed in 1568. In the 18th century it was expanded to include a lofty cloister, buttresses, and a new main entrance. Today the building's impact is overwhelming, impressing the visitor as a prime example of the "fortified" religious centers of the early days of the colonial era. Several missionaries who were later martyred in Japan studied here while en route from Spain to the Orient. Ask to be admitted to the bell tower, which commands a sweeping view of the lake and countryside. Unfortunately, there are no especially worthwhile hotels or restaurants in the Yuriria area.

THE CITY OF GUANAJUATO

For most American visitors Guanajuato is little short of astonishing. Few places in the world seem as exotic to northern eyes: narrow, tortuous streets that lose themselves in flower-bedecked plazas; unexpected balconies and bridges; and red-tiled roofs that lie level with the street above. Guanajuato both eludes and inspires description. Travellers speak of similarities to the hill towns of Italy, to southern Spain, even to the Aegean islands—all close to the mark but none quite hitting it. The fact is, Guanajuato retains a peculiar combination of Mexican and European qualities that is unrivalled.

It was once the second-largest city in Mexico, one of the wealthiest in the world, and no place in Latin America could match it for the sheer display of its riches. The treasure that poured from its silver mines is legendary and beyond reckoning. The opulent structures left behind are mostly relics of two eras: the silver-mad 18th century, and just prior to the turn of our own century, when great new strikes again filled the local coffers. As a result of the Mexican fondness for different styles in both these periods, Guanajuato today is a mélange of the Spanish, Moorish, Italian, and French. The styles are not mixed, however. Instead, they stand side by side in happy defiance of each other, bewildering and wonderful all at once.

Guanajuato is sometimes offered as a one-day excursion from Mexico City. Certainly, you can cover the highlights of this compact city in a day, but even so it requires a sightseeing marathon. Instead, at least two full days should be allotted, and twice that would not be misspent. The city's monuments are impressive, but the greatest pleasure is derived from simply wandering among its picturesque plazas and fountains and getting lost in its colorful maze of streets and alleyways.

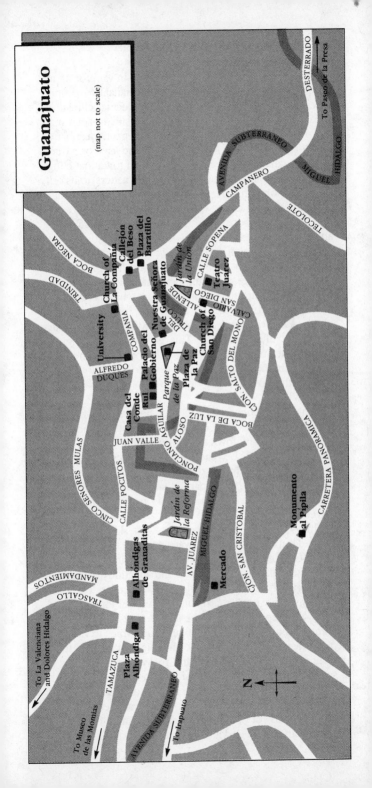

Guanajuato

(map not to scale)

Visitors exploring the town will look in vain for an art gallery or good book store, however. Guanajuato, despite its claims to the contrary, has no intellectual climate to speak of—and this includes the university. In such matters, the citizens are quite unlike the elegant, imaginative buildings of their city. Never having found itself on a trade route, Guanajuato is a closed, provincial town that clings tenaciously to its old ways and, in some matters, to its self-satisfied isolation. The folk who live in this dramatic cityscape did not create it. The state and national governments are the sponsors of the community's performing arts groups, for example.

Guanajuato is also devoutly religious, its Catholicism of a conservative bent. You need look no farther than the Cerro del Cubilete, a looming mountain 13 km (8 miles) outside of the city, for proof. Atop it, at what is reputed to be the geographical center of Mexico, towers a gigantic statue of *El Cristo Rey,* or Christ the King, that dominates the great valley below it. This is not only a religious monument but a striking symbol of the will of the local people, who by a large majority resisted the national laws limiting the power of the clergy.

Guanajuato crouches in a gorge, hemmed in by rock walls. Although it's the capital of the state of the same name, a university town, and a busy city of some 75,000 people, it can only be reached by car or bus. If you come by car, after one initial detour, suggested below, your vehicle should be safely parked and then forgotten during your stay here. Guanajuato is truly an ordeal for drivers.

Almost all traffic enters from the west, skirting the now revived but not especially rewarding ghost town of Marfil. At the edge of town, the **Carretera Panorámica**, a skyline drive that offers a spectacular introduction to the city, veers sharply to the right and is easy to miss. The road climbs steeply toward a titanic statue of El Pípila, a local hero of independence. At the statue, near stands heaped with souvenirs and junk, is a place from which to view the magnificent gorge. The city, the high hills with their fortified mines and scarred and rocky slopes—all this is spread out below in a spectacular panorama.

Silver was the only excuse for building a city in this improbable place, but of silver there was plenty. In fact, the monarchs of Spain were deluged with silver for the better part of two and a half centuries, and fully half of it came from this inhospitable canyon. The first major lode was discovered in 1548—just 20 years after the town was founded—a bonanza that was only the beginning of its long and happy affair with the metal.

From the statue of El Pípila, the Panorámica winds eastward and down, debouching in a neighborhood known as **La Presa**, where the streets are lined with edifices financed by the city's last great windfall from silver, at the end of the 19th century. Many are sumptuously French Romantic and Italianate, so grand it is hard to imagine them as formerly private homes.

Just past this district is the entrance to the **Avenida Subterráneo Miguel Hidalgo**. Some years ago, to relieve traffic, the city utilized a number of mine tunnels and an old riverbed to create an underground thoroughfare that runs through the heart of the city. As a result of serendipity, the engineers also managed to create an unusual visual experience for visitors: The thoroughfare twists among the foundations of the town, its roof reinforced by a tangle of old mine cables embedded in concrete and stone. The effect is at once romantic and eerie, and will stay with the visitor long after the many meals eaten and shops visited are forgotten.

The Avenida Miguel Hidalgo ends near the city market, an area where a car or taxi becomes a definite encumbrance. The market, which bears an incongruous resemblance to an Italian railway station, offers a profusion of foods, goods, and gimcracks. The crafts mezzanine is worth the climb, if only for a view of the jumbled colors below. The merchandise offered here includes fake antique bells, machine-made cloth, and mass-produced figurines appropriate as prizes at a shooting gallery and little else. The sad truth is, there are no worthwhile crafts in Guanajuato and no surviving craft tradition to speak of.

The Alhóndiga de Granaditas

A block up the hill from the market is the broad esplanade behind the Alhóndiga de Granaditas, where every year the Cervantino, an international festival of performing arts honoring the master, Miguel de Cervantes, is staged. The festival, which is held in the late autumn, once glittered with the stars of the music and dance worlds. During the six years when Carmen de López Portillo was First Lady of Mexico in particular, it enjoyed bountiful patronage; she even arranged the restoration and scrubbing up of part of the city to improve its setting. These days, artists still come to the festival from a score of countries, but it nevertheless seems to have lost its glitter.

Short farces and skits from Spain, some by Cervantes, are performed by students during the Cervantes Festival. These romps are essentially mime shows, and the broad jokes are funny without language. These *entremeses,* as they are called, were written to be played as comic relief between the acts of Spanish dramas.

The fortress-like **Alhóndiga de Granaditas**, one of the most prominent buildings in Mexican history, looms over the esplanade. Originally built as a granary, it served as a refuge for royalist supporters when Hidalgo's rebels attacked the city in 1810. With the confrontation threatening to swing in favor of the royalists, Juan Martínez, a miner from San Miguel who would be known to history as El Pípila, tied a broad flagstone to his back, and, so shielded, braved enemy fire to set the wooden doors of the granary aflame (an action that cost him his life). Rebels surged into the building, where a hand-to-hand struggle and, ultimately, a butchery of the Spaniards ensued. The few survivors retreated step by step to the roof, only to be slain there. Even this was not the end of the horror, however. Days later, after 247 unarmed Spanish soldiers had been imprisoned in the building, a screaming mob broke in and murdered them to the last man.

The slaughter changed the public's perception of the uprising. Spaniards throughout the country rallied in support of the Crown. When they finally recaptured Guanajuato, they retaliated with a blood bath, killing every man, woman, and child they could get their hands on. If it hadn't been for a local priest, who stepped between the executioners and their intended victims, holding aloft a cross as his only weapon, the massacre might have spread to other towns in the Bajío. But, as it was, the bloodshed in the Alhóndiga helped polarize Mexico for generations to come.

After the revolt ultimately failed, the heads of its leaders—Hidalgo, Allende, Jiménez, and Aldama—were sent back to Guanajuato and hung from iron hooks at the corners of the Alhóndiga, where they remained for ten years. Only the hooks remain today.

A crafts museum has been set up in the building, its gaiety a welcome but odd note. In addition, Guanajuato painter Chavez Morado has dramatized its violent history in a series of powerful murals. There are also historical exhibits here, none of them especially fascinating but one, a collection of small-town studio photographs, ordinary at first glance but remarkable when studied, definitely worth closer inspection. It is a sweet and touching album of the city—newlywed couples stiff in their finery, awkward soldiers, miners with their hair slicked down for the occasion, and so on.

Around the City

Emerging from the Alhóndiga and turning right, walk toward Calle Pocitos and the university. At Pocitos 47, now a museum, is the house where the muralist Diego Rivera was born. The collection, not surprisingly, is meagre, consisting of some old furniture and early Rivera practice pieces. What *is* surprising is not that the museum is modest, but that it exists at all—for years Rivera was *persona non grata* in his hometown. The town fathers despised the great painter for being an atheist, a leftist, and a mocker of the church and society. Pious Guanajuato, which resisted the revolution Diego glorified, never forgave the sinner, and never had second thoughts about forcing his family, wicked liberals all, to leave the city. The little museum, needless to say, is of recent vintage.

The **Museo del Pueblo de Guanajuato**, Pocitos 7, was once the home of a noble Spanish family. On display are a number of good provincial paintings of the colonial era, as well as works by Hermenegildo Bustos, a strong 19th-century talent.

The many broad stairways of the University of Guanajuato sweep upward toward a towering structure that is a less-than-happy mixture of Spanish colonial architecture and something else. The pale university structure dominates a portion of the cityscape, an odd reversal of roles in light of the fact that the university has always been subservient to the interests of the city and its politicians. The school is tame and traditional.

Nearby is the lovely **Church of La Compañía**, an 18th-century Jesuit contribution to the city's beauty and an admirable example of Baroque architecture as it began to flower into the more elaborate Churrigueresque style. A block to the east, the way widens into the Plaza del Baratillo, where sunlight plays on a fountain that Maximilian gave to a city that entertained him lavishly. Students live on the upper floors of the old buildings in this neighborhood, and much of the university's rather sedate social life is centered here. In addition, the University of Guanajuato produces some of the best *estudiantinas*, student musical groups akin to glee clubs, in the country. Students in the romantic beribboned costumes of Old Spain sing through the streets at least once or twice a month.

Turning right and circling back, you'll come upon the **Jardín de la Unión**, one of the loveliest and most inviting little plazas in Mexico. As public squares go, this is a mere postage stamp, but the leafy low-branched laurels form a canopy that shades its pretty benches of painted iron. On the southwest side of the plaza, two adjacent buildings present façades that exemplify the richest architectural periods of the city's history: the exterior of the Teatro Juárez is a Neoclassical dream, while next to it rises, a little feebly, the weathered Church of San Diego, an exquisite late-18th-century Churrigueresque fantasy in stone. In different languages the two façades proclaim the same thing: the affluence of their builders.

The **Teatro Juárez** is such a delightful building that only a curmudgeon would call some of it a little silly. The green columns of its façade, quarried locally, ascend majestically behind bronze lions. On the roof are eight allegorical female figures, also bronze. Interestingly, these Hellenic ladies were the work of one W. H. Mullen of Salem, Ohio, and were purchased in the 1890s, an era when Mexico renounced all things Mexican.

The lavish interior is a marvel as well, its ceiling resembling a carpet out of the *Arabian Nights*. The stage curtain was reportedly copied from a backdrop at La Scala a century ago. Throughout the building the details and furnishings are ostentatious, overdone, and yet somehow perfect. The sightlines from the boxes of honor are so bad that half the stage remains obscured; no matter, its occupants were royally displayed to the rest of the house.

Porfirio Díaz, "president" of the so-called republic from 1877–1880 and again from 1884–1911, attended the opening night here, arriving by special train with his whole cabinet and a good part of the capital's diplomatic corps. Across the street, in the Posada Santa Fé, there hangs today a painting of that special occasion. In it, the distinguished spectators are not looking at the Italian singers on stage, but, naturally, at each other.

Back outside, Calle Sopeña makes for an interesting stroll toward Avenida Juárez and the market area as it heads northwest and slightly downhill past the Hotel San

Diego. Branching off it are the narrow alleyways and "pocket" plazas that give Guanajuato such character. No matter where you walk in the city, however, you'll probably notice markers with the dates 1885 or 1905 on them; these indicate the high-water lines of disastrous floods that hit Guanajuato in those years. (The river has since been diverted.)

The parish church of Nuestra Señora de Guanajuato, on Parque de la Paz, was erected in 1671 and has suffered so many changes that little is left of distinction. Housed in one of its chapels, however, is a statue of the Virgin Mary that purportedly was hidden in a cave in Spain after the Moors invaded in A.D. 714. The statue was rediscovered eight and a half centuries later, undamaged by time and dampness, and was therefore declared miraculous. It was bestowed on the city by Philip II, who was grateful for the flood of silver pouring in, in 1557. The plain wooden figure is enhanced by a gemmed gown and a golden diadem weighing almost five pounds.

Across the Plaza de la Paz, which the great church flanks, is the handsomest town house in Mexico, once the palace of the Conde de Rul, a Midas among millionaires. Not surprisingly, the ubiquitous Tresguerras was the architect of this severe, august mansion with its clean lines and perfect balance. The stone, a soft rose color, was the best the area had to offer. (The handsome patio is usually open for inspection.)

The grace of Tresguerras's simple design is made all the more striking by the close juxtaposition of the green and grandiose Palacio del Gobierno, its ornate decoration proclaiming its own importance.

The renowned **Callejón del Beso**, or Alley of the Kiss, is a passageway and set of steps flanked by flowering balconies. A local legend tells of kisses snuck over balcony railings, a cruel father, and a girl whisked away to a convent. The alley is located just north of the Plaza del Baratillo.

The biggest indoor drawing card for visitors to Guanajuato is the **Museo de las Momias**, or mummy museum, located next to the cemetery about half a mile west of the Alhóndiga. In fact, its turnstiles have proved to be the most profitable installation in town since the days of the first silver mine. About 60 "examples," as the cadavers are called, stand posed for inspection behind glass display cases. The exhibits are not mummies in the Egyptian sense, however, but corpses that have undergone a sort of tanning process due to chemicals in the ground before being dug up and thrust into show business.

The **Presa de la Olla** is one of two dams creating artificial lakes in a rustic setting. Picnickers come for the shade and breezes at the lakes, and rowboats are also available for rent. The park area is located at the southeast corner of town at the end of Paseo de le Presa.

The revived ghost town of Marfil, just west of the city, no longer has much to offer. Once it was rich beyond measure, a place where bullfights were staged in the private patios of mine owners' mansions. Opera companies were imported to perform in the same spaces.

Almost adjoining Marfil to the southwest, the **Hacienda San Gabriel de Barrera** boasts lovely gardens with French-inspired landscaping. The remaining estate buildings are of some interest, but the gardens outshine everything else in the neighborhood.

The Silver Mines and the Silver King's Church

The **Valenciana Mine**, profitable and operating today, plunges 530 meters (1,738 feet) into the mountainside above Guanajuato. Old service buildings made of stone and tile remain, and visitors may look down a shaft whose mouth is supposed to represent the Crown of Spain. Far below, a black maze of tunnels twists and turns like the roots of a gigantic tree. This was once the world's richest vein of silver, yielding fully one-fifth of all the silver circulating in the world for nearly a century, and yielding its owners, first the Conde de Valenciana and then his son-in-law the Conde de Rul, unimaginable wealth.

Because it is an operating mine, visitors are not allowed to descend into the shaft of the Valenciana. Conditions and schedules for visits to other mines in the area change frequently; for up-to-date information, inquire at the state tourism office, located at the corner of Avenida Juárez and Cinco de Mayo. (Local guides will also have current information.)

Across the street from the Valenciana mine stands the church of the same name, which was begun by the Conde de Valenciana and continued by the Conde de Rul with a little compulsory help from their mine workers during the second half of the 18th century. In the course of construction, silver dust and Spanish wines were added to the mortar, inspiring the comment that the count was not only bribing the Lord but "getting Him drunk at the same time." Nevertheless, the finished product reveals both wealth and superb craftsmanship. Connoisseurs of stone sculpture praise the elegant relief work around the church's main portal; the façade and interior carving are airy, and the pulpit is a masterpiece.

Staying in Guanajuato

Guanajuato's somewhat narrow range of hotels does not include any of the finest in Mexico. The **Posada Santa Fé**, built in 1862, faces the lovely Jardín de la Unión, an ideal location from which to explore the city. Rooms vary, and the first one offered you should not automatically be accepted. The interior rooms, untouched by sun, seem positively polar on winter nights. The hotel is nonetheless gracious, and its stately public rooms are rich with the charm of Old Spain transported to Mexico.

The **Hotel San Diego**, across the square from the Santa Fé, is in the same moderately priced bracket. Its better rooms have patios or balconies with views of the town, the rooftop terrace is inviting, and the cellar-style bar romantic. There's also a dining room with a fine view from the two tables at the corner window, but the vista is the only reason for trying to eat there; the hotel is much better than the restaurant. The hotel's bar can be lively at times.

Although the **Hostería del Fraile** has 36 rooms, it feels like an intimate pension. It also has precipitous stairs, and the outside rooms tend to be noisy while the inside ones are cramped. Still, its excellent location near the Jardín de la Unión and its pleasing details make this converted 17th-century mint a satisfactory inn, and one with reasonable rates.

The difference between moderately priced hotels and budget accommodations in Guanajuato is not a step but a plunge. Travellers trying to cut costs would be advised to do it in other cities rather than here.

The more expensive and mostly newer hostelries are found along the road that leads to La Valenciana. Guests without a car will have to depend on the bus or wait, sometimes a while, for a taxi to arrive after one has been called.

As its name suggests, the **Castillo de Santa Cecilia** is a castle, albeit more Disney than medieval. Spacious lawns, gardens, terraces, a heated pool, and a nightclub push up the rates for good rooms. The hotel is more cheerful than its battlements would suggest, however.

The **Parador San Javier**, the largest of the hillside establishments, is a modern hostelry with colonial touches, and boasts all the necessary conveniences of a high-quality inn. Some rooms have fireplaces. There's also a large pool, a disco, and a cocktail lounge. The place is a favorite of Mexico City people exploring the provinces in style.

The **Motel Guanajuato**, like the Parador San Javier, offers its guests panoramic views from a perch high above the town. It is modern and comfortable, as well as a little plainer and less expensive than its neighbors (although it does have a pool and quite a good restaurant).

On the opposite side of the city, near Marfil, the **Hotel San Gabriel de Barrera**, situated across a country lane from the famous gardens, is not cheap but is still an excellent value for those with a car who do not mind a ten-minute drive to the center of town. Everything is spacious at this former hacienda, and the terraces overlook gardens and flowerbeds. The rooms, public and private, are airy and bright. There are tennis and swimming facilities as well.

Dining in Guanajuato

Visitors must keep in mind that they have come to Guanajuato for attractions other than its cuisine. There are no really good restaurants here. Expect sustenance, not delight, from the town's dining establishments. Guanajuato cares little about the capricious tastes of tourists, and the local cookery lacks flair and imagination as a result.

The sidewalk café at the **Posada Santa Fé** is happily situated so that customers can ignore the mediocre fare and concentrate on the scene in the Jardín de la Unión instead. Nearby on the same plaza, the Casa Valdez is passable for snacks, breakfast, and a hearty soup. The best buys, however, are soda fountain items and postcards.

The **Tasca de los Santos**, at Plaza de la Paz 28, presents a Spanish-style menu featuring *fabada* and *paella*. It's not outstanding, but the low prices are some consolation.

El Claustro, on the Jardín de la Reforma, is tricked out like a Spanish tavern (Guanajuato seems to draw out the

Spanish side of Mexicans), and the stage-set atmosphere attracts students. Egg dishes are the safest bet here.

Other downtown eateries are pretty much alike. Order simply and be patient. At the hillside hotels your chances are better. The Motel Guanajuato runs the best, most reliable kitchen in the region. The coffee shop at the Parador San Javier seems better than the dining room, perhaps because its simple décor prevents expectations from rising too high. **Venta Vieja de San Javier**, across from the Parador, appeals more to the eye than the palate. The quality is not as high as the prices, but it offers more verve than most places.

As in most things, Guanajuato is restrained when it comes to nightlife. The Castillo Santa Cecilia offers decorus dancing every night except Sunday, with a minimum charge designed to cover supper and the entertainment. **El Pozo**, the club in the Parador San Javier, presents fairly good late-evening entertainment in an unusual setting where patrons may gaze at a built-in waterfall.

MORELIA

Morelia, the most stately and handsome of Mexico's cities, is like the Roman god Janus or certain masks on Mayan temples: It faces two directions at once. That's because Morelia is among the most Spanish of Latin American cities: It looks like Spain, and sometimes it even *feels* like Spain, which is unusual in Mexico. Yet almost in its backyard are the communities and culture of the Tarascan Indians. Despite its profuse craft markets, its patriotic nods to pre-Columbian culture, and even its geography, however, Morelia remains solidly colonial in appearance and Mexican in its style.

In recent years Morelia has burgeoned into a city of about half a million people, spilling over its old boundaries and creating a ring of suburbs, developments, and industrial zones that isn't of much interest to the traveller. Inside this ring, however, lies another world.

Founded by Don Antonio de Mendoza, New Spain's first and greatest viceroy, in 1541, and christened Valladolid in honor of his home town, the city, a one-time Tarascan village, was designed to be the center of government and religion for a vast area (the modern state of Michoacán, of which present-day Morelia is the capital, constitutes only a part of that region). The city grew

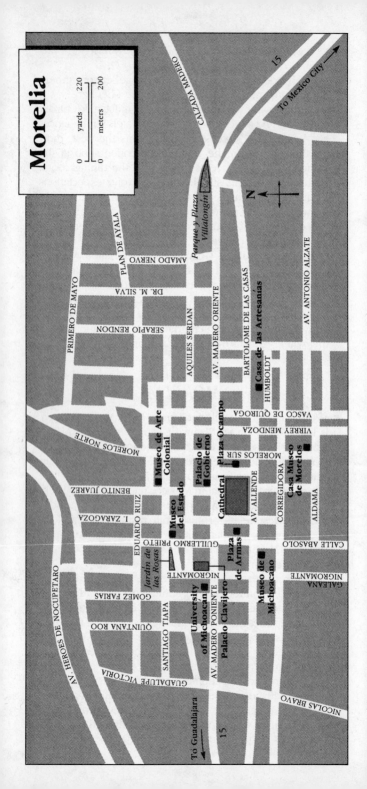

Morelia

yards 0 220
meters 0 200

slowly, however, and it wasn't until the middle of the 17th century that it truly started to flourish. Even then, the optimism and foresight of its architects and builders, who laid out their little provincial town with a practicality and spaciousness that are remarkable to this day and must have been revolutionary more than three centuries ago, was amazing. The results are obvious to anyone who has spent time in Mexico's other colonial gems: Unlike most of its contemporaries, Morelia is not only well-preserved, it actually works. Its plazas and public buildings accommodate modern-day crowds easily and efficiently, and its lovely streets even allow you to get around by car.

The first glimpse you get of this old city is of the domes, towers, and pinnacles of the imposing yet graceful **Cathedral**. Begun in 1640 but not completed until 1744, its design was intended to be Plateresque, a style of decoration based on silver plate, from the beginning. During a century of construction, while a variety of architectural styles swept New Spain, the builders of Morelia's Cathedral stuck to their plan, almost the only ones in the country to do so. The result is a beautiful example of Baroque ecclesiastical architecture made out of trachyte, a brown volcanic rock warmed by rose overtones. Carved overlays and low reliefs, not to mention a number of broad, plain areas, accent the six statues around the main portal. In addition to its two graceful towers it has an exceptional dome. While it is true that Mexico is a land that bubbles with domes, this one is special; from inside, it seems to float above the nave, giving an impression of height far greater than it can actually claim.

Although Morelia never became as rich from silver as its founders had hoped, the Cathedral once boasted a communion rail made of the precious metal. In 1858 the Bishop of Morelia refused to pay a war assessment, however, and as a result his precious railing was ripped out and melted down. But the church has other treasures: paintings by a number of outstanding colonial artists, as well as what is perhaps the best pipe organ in Latin America—a treat for both the ear and eye. Every May a festival is held in the Cathedral to take advantage of this marvel, with organists from many countries coming to play. In fact, Morelia has a rich musical heritage: Among other distinctions it can claim the first conservatory founded in the New World. Today, a celebrated boys' choir helps to continue the tradition.

The Plaza de Armas Area

The **Plaza de Armas** (also called the Plaza de los Mártires, in honor of Mexico's slain patriots), a lovely square with a bandstand that is, in its modest way, as perfect as the Cathedral, is the heart and hub of Morelia. This is the place to stroll, lounge, meet friends, and listen to band concerts. The ambience is idyllic and inviting.

Also inviting, however, are the sidewalk cafés under the arcade across the street, where newspapers are read, politics discussed, and students from the University of Michoacán, unusually purposeful for their age, hurry by.

The **Palacio de Gobierno**, the state capitol, faces the Cathedral. Although an 18th-century structure, it could be a hundred years older. (Morelia seems always to have been wary of new-fangled architecture.) Inside, murals by one of Mexico's outstanding painters, local product Alfred Zalce, dramatically illustrate scenes from Mexico's history.

Behind the Cathedral and plaza, at the corner of Guillermo Prieto and Santiago Tapia, is the **Museo del Estado**, the state museum. The building itself and the murals inside are better than the displays, which include the complete stock of a Morelian pharmacy circa 1868, Tarascan jewelry, and other artifacts.

An even better building houses the **Museo de Michoacán**, also on Allende, just across Calle Abasolo. This former residence boasts beautiful Michoacán woodwork, starting with the front door. The arches are also unusually effective, as is the stairway. The structure, not the collection of historical items it houses, is the attraction.

Not far away, at Avenida Morelos and Iturbide, is the **Casa de Morelos**, the home of the hero for whom the city was renamed. Of all the early figures in Mexico's struggle for independence, José María Morelos was the most brilliant. Born in what was then Valladolid in 1765, he became a laborer on a hacienda when a young man. By almost starving himself to death he managed to make it through the Colegio de San Nicolás in his home town and became a priest. The revolt of 1810 was a call to greatness for Morelos, who emerged from obscurity to become the military genius of the rebellion. In a relatively short period of time, he raised, trained, and armed 9,000 men using captured equipment, and then gained control of virtually all of western and northern Mexico. Morelos, who stood hardly five feet tall, cast a long shadow over

Mexican history, both in his words and by his deeds, and Valladolid was renamed in his honor in 1828. The small museum is representative of a humble house of the hero's day.

Several impressive buildings are located a block west of the plaza. The **Colegio de San Nicolás de Hidalgo** is the second-oldest college in the New World, and the oldest one extant. The patriot Father Hidalgo studied and taught here, as did Morelos and Agustín de Iturbide, who would later proclaim himself Emperor of Mexico. The University of Michoacán, which now occupies part of the old building, is a descendant of the venerable institution.

The **Palacio Clavijero**, which now houses a massive state library and industrial school, dates from the 17th century and is located across the street from San Nicolás. Its patio is magnificent and a must-see for visitors. At the end of the second block heading north, you'll come to the lovely **Jardín de las Rosas**—which isn't named for its abundant flowers. The Templo y Conservatorio de las Rosas (the Church and Conservatory of the Roses) is the mellowed building across from this square. Once a girls' boarding school, it is now home to the Morelia Boys' Choir, and their singing can often be heard coming from this, the oldest music school in the Americas.

Three blocks east of Las Rosas stands the **ex-Convento del Carmen**, now a government-sponsored cultural center. Construction on the convent was begun in the late 1500s and continued for almost two centuries, producing a building of enormous proportions. The stairway and domed ceilings are especially noteworthy. Midway between the church and the ex-convent, the little **Museo de Arte Colonial** has an interesting series of displays, including a collection of religious figures made from cornstalks and sugar cane.

The Plaza Villalongín Area

The Parque and Plaza Villalongín, the most attractive strolling area in Morelia—high praise in a city where street after street vies for the attention of the visitor—is located about half a mile east of the Cathedral on Avenida Madero. The small plaza itself is attractive, though a visitor can only marvel at the dreadfully kitsch sculpture of Indians and fruit here. The kindest word for it is memorable.

Beyond the plaza stands an aqueduct that was begun in 1785, an immense project designed to carry water more than a mile from the surrounding hills. Here you'll also find a shady promenade leading to the fanciful **Sanctuary of Guadalupe**, a church that's a bit of Morocco somehow Christianized and made Mexican. The neighborhood is woodsy, and a favorite Sunday spot for local families.

The Monarch Butterflies

In an awe-inspiring migration, 100 million monarch butterflies make their way annually from Canada and the United States to winter in Michoacán's mountaintop forests of pine and oyamel trees. A visit to the groves at this time of year will be an unforgettable experience.

The most popular point of departure for the sanctuary is the little mountain town of **Angangueo** in eastern Michoacán, about 200 km (124 miles) east of Morelia. From the town, trucks carry passengers part way up a rugged and scenic slope, which is then followed by an arduous climb up a steep path to the groves. The altitude will probably make it necessary for you to pause frequently along the way in order to catch your breath. Go slowly.

The scene that waits to greet you is worth the effort. On top, the forest will be literally coated with monarchs, and the muted sound you hear will be the rustling of millions of wings.

If the trip is made from Morelia, you should be on the road no later than 7:00 A.M. However, the experience is worth turning into a more leisurely trip. If you decide to do so, you can stay overnight in clean but simple accommodations in Angangueo itself at the **Posada Don Bruno**. Very good accommodations—and butterfly-viewing arrangements—are also available at the gracious if slightly faded **Hotel Spa San José Purua**, on the rim of a canyon 45 km (20 miles) from Angangueo. The spa has thermal pools and offers a spectacular view that includes a waterfall.

Staying in Morelia

When it comes to accommodations, there isn't a great range of choices in Morelia, but comfort, charm, and—in one case—luxury are available.

The city is walled off to the south by the steep slopes of the Santa María hills. On their crest, reached from the city via Calle Galeana, is a quiet neighborhood with lovely

views and two secluded hotels. Both establishments are located a little more than 3 km (2 miles) south of town, past the Parque Juárez, and across the Periférico, the main highway. Calle Tangaxhuan, a winding road, leads up the hill.

The **Villa Montaña** is one of the country's better inns. It commands a spectacular day and night view of the city and the long valley in which it lies. Its bungalow units have all the comforts, including fireplaces, and some guests spend a good part of the winter here even though it isn't an inexpensive haven. Its restaurant is outstanding; see Dining below.

Across the road, the **Posada Vista Bella** is less luxurious and less expensive, but quite satisfactory. It also offers, in addition to its regular units, a number of apartments for weekly or monthly rental, and has a restaurant.

Downtown, just off the main plaza, is the charming **Posada de la Soledad,** a former monastery that has been modernized with skill and taste. The patio garden, around which the hotel is built, is noted for its serene beauty. Not all of its 60 rooms are desirable, though; a few should be avoided because of kitchen noise, others because of left-over monastic chill.

The **Best Western Hotel Virrey de Mendoza** is Morelia's traditional choice for a good hotel on the plaza. Its style is colonial, the building old but well maintained. The dining room under its covered central court is filled most nights.

The **Calinda Morelia Quality Inn,** 6 km (4 miles) south-east of town on the Periférico and across from a shopping center, is modern and well planned for comfort and convenience. Its guests are more likely to be prosperous business travellers than tourists and, consequently, its rates are designed for expense accounts, but the trained staff does make every effort to offer value for your money.

The cocktail lounges of the major hotels provide what entertainment the city has to offer, mostly piano music, with an occasional combo making an appearance.

Another alternative is to stay in scenic Pátzcuaro, just to the west—see the Western Highlands chapter—and use it as a base for day trips to Morelia.

Dining in Morelia

The Villa Montaña keeps a fine restaurant and bar with a good wine selection. Non-guests should make reservations (small children are not welcome); Tel: 4-0179. The menu is international—regional cookery appears to be taboo here.

Those who wish to sample the traditional dishes of the region will do well in the flowering patio or equally charming dining room of the **Posada de la Soledad**. Their special *sopa Tarasca* has the right zing, and the Pátzcuaro whitefish is delicate and flaky.

The **Grill d'Enrique**, at Hidalgo 54, has some style and is best with local specialties. Quail, when available, is skillfully prepared (*cordóniz al carbón*), and the appetizers are tasty. The chicken dishes are also good choices.

Los Comenzales, a simple, low-priced patio restaurant at Zaragoza 148, is devoted entirely to both Michoacán and more general Mexican cooking. Its fare is hearty rather than delicate, but the lengthy menu offers a good sampling of regional dishes. Try, for instance, *uechepos,* a slightly sweet cornmeal bread, or the little triangular tamales called *corundas. Ate Moreleon,* the most famous dessert item of the region, may appear in the form of any fruit paste: pineapple, guava, mango, or papaya.

The cafés under the arcade near the Cathedral are more for snacks and sodas than for meals, but within their limits all are pleasing. Don't even think of trying to order when they're busy, however. Coffee or anything in a bottle will get to you; ordering anything else will be testing your luck.

Shopping in Morelia

Morelia specializes in crafts from the various nearby Tarascan communities. Good quality can be found in a variety of stores, but the best choice is the fabulous popular arts market at the **Casa de las Artesanías** in the former Convent of San Francisco, two huge floors crammed with items from all over the state. While buying here is not as exciting as going to a craft village and making your own discoveries, you will probably not find better bargains anywhere. The prices reflect real market value, and the selection is excellent. The only thing missing is the thrill of the hunt.

Michoacán lacquerware is an especially good buy here because the work is genuine and as lasting as this rather fragile craft can be. (In recent years there has been a lot of "forged" lacquerware—glossy auto paint sprayed on cheap wood—making the rounds. It takes a sharp eye and a bright light to spot the real thing.) On the other hand, you'll probably want to avoid the guitars; for those you must go to Paracho and search. (**Paracho**, noted for its woodcarvings and musical instruments, is a small town about an hour-and-a-half drive west of Morelia. While its specialty is guitars, other quality hand-crafted string instruments are also available.)

GETTING AROUND

Querétaro

Querétaro has no commercial airport. There is daily rail service from Mexico City, leaving the capital early in the morning and returning in the afternoon. Trains to all points leave from Mexico City's central station on Avenida Insurgentes Norte. Breakfast is included in a first-class ticket (which you'll want), a box lunch on the return trip. Morning travellers should be at the dining room the moment it opens, for better service.

First-class bus service, which is faster than the train, is the usual choice for those not driving. There is good and frequent service to Querétaro, which is a major hub for almost all routes north and west, with about eight different buses leaving the capital every hour. All depart from the Central Caminero del Norte, also called the Terminal Central del Norte; the station is on Avenida de los 100 Metros, quite a way out on Insurgentes Norte.

Taxis are cheap and easier than trying to drive in town. Walking is also easy on the flat paving stones of this almost flat city. (Be sure to bring comfortable, thick-soled shoes, however.)

San Miguel de Allende

One first-class bus leaves Mexico City every morning for San Miguel, arriving about four hours later. The line is Tres Estrellas del Oro. Second-class bus service, also available, likewise departs from the capital's Terminal Central del Norte. Purveyors include Flecha Amarilla and Herradura de Plata. Both first- and second-class buses leave every few minutes for Querétaro; San Miguel passengers failing to make a direct connection can go to Querétaro and change there.

A dawn train, first class, from the capital (central station on Insurgentes Norte) arrives in San Miguel early in the afternoon; it is pleasant but slow.

There is little reason to have a car in San Miguel itself, but driving is the most practical way to explore the countryside. Car rentals are best arranged in Mexico City, however—rentals in San Miguel are uncertain and often unsatisfactory.

In town, thick-soled, comfortable shoes are essential. Taxis are cheap and can be found near the *jardín* (they will seldom respond to phone calls).

Guanajuato

A car is a great convenience for getting to Guanajuato and a nuisance afterwards (except for guests at the outlying hotels). The nearest airport is in León, 50 km (30 miles) distant. Bus travel is the usual choice from Mexico City (see Querétaro and San Miguel de Allende above). Second-class Flecha Amarilla has more daily trips to Guanajuato than any other line. Tres Estrellas de Oro is better but offers less frequent service. Buses to and from San Miguel de Allende arrive and depart frequently. From the capital or Guadalajara insist on a direct (*directo*) bus.

Stout walking shoes are mandatory. Taxi service is cheap, courteous, and as efficient as the cramped streets will permit. There are also bus tours of the city, although they're usually conducted in Spanish only. Hotels will arrange for guide service if desired.

Morelia

The Morelia airport is serviced daily from the capital by Aeroméxico. Car rentals are available at the airport, as are taxis and minibuses.

Regular bus service is from the Terminal Central del Norte. Destinations include Guadalajara, Guanajuato, Pátzcuaro, and, of course, points in between. Visitors travelling directly to or from the capital will want to go via Toluca, the fastest, most scenic route.

Train service to Mexico City is available but not recommended. There is also daily rail service to the famous **Pátzcuaro** (see The Western Highlands chapter), but buses are a more dependable alternative for this short trip 40 km (25 miles) to the west.

Morelia is mostly flat, and thus an easy city for walking. Taxis are cheap and plentifuly, but fares should be settled in advance to avoid unpleasant surprises.

ACCOMMODATIONS REFERENCE

▶ **Aristos/Parador San Miguel de Allende.** Ancha de San Antonio 30, POB 85, **San Miguel de Allende** 37700. Tel: (465) 2-0392.

▶ **Best Western Hotel Virrey de Mendoza.** Portal de Matamoros 16, **Morelia** 58000. Tel: (451) 2-0633 or (800) 528-1234.

▶ **Calinda Morelia Quality Inn.** Avenida de las Camelias 3466, **Morelia** 58270. Tel: (451) 4-1427 or (800) 228-5151.

▶ **Casa Carmen.** Correo 31, **San Miguel de Allende** 37700. Tel: (465) 2-0844.

▶ **Casa de Sierra Nevada.** Hospicio 35, **San Miguel de Allende** 37700. Tel: (465) 2-1895. Fax: (465) 2-2337.

▶ **Castillo de Santa Cecilia.** Camino a la Valenciana s/n. POB 44, **Guanajuato** 36000. Tel: (473) 2-0485.

▶ **Posada Don Bruno.** Calle Principal, **Angangueo,** Michoacán. Tel: Angangueo 26

▶ **Motel Guanajuato.** Camino a la Valenciana s/n. POB 113, **Guanajuato** 36000. Tel: (473) 2-0689.

▶ **Hacienda de las Flores.** Hospicio 16, **San Miguel de Allende** 37700. Tel: (465) 2-1808.

▶ **Hacienda Jurica.** POB 338, Highway 57, northwest of **Querétaro** 76100. Tel: (463) 8-0022.

▶ **Hacienda Santa María.** Calzada de la Presa, **San Miguel de Allende** 37700. Tel: (465) 2-0040.

▶ **Hacienda Taboada.** Kilometer 8, Carretera a Dolores Hidalgo, **San Miguel de Allende** 37700. Tel: (465) 2-0850.

▶ **Holiday Inn Querétaro.** Carretera Constitución 13 Sur. **Querétaro** 76010. Tel: (463) 6-0202 or (800) 465-4329.

▶ **Hostería del Fraile.** Sopeña 3, **Guanajuato** 36000. Tel: (473) 2-1179.

▶ **La Mansion Galindo.** Carretera 57, Amealco exit. POB 16, **San Juan del Río** 76800. Tel: (467) 2-0050.

▶ **Mesón de Santa Rosa.** Pasteur Sur 17, Plaza de Armas, **Querétaro** 76000 Tel: (463) 4-5781.

▶ **Posada de las Monjas.** Canal 37, **San Miguel de Allende** 37700. Tel: (465) 2-0171.

▶ **Hotel Monte Verde.** Voluntarios 2, **San Miguel de Allende** 37700. Tel: (465) 2-1814.

▶ **Real de Minas Querétaro.** Constituyentes 124 Poniente, POB 77, **Querétaro** 76010. Tel: (463) 6-0444.

▶ **Hotel San Diego.** Jardín de la Unión 1, POB 8, **Guanajuato** 36000. Tel: (473) 2-1300.

▶ **Hotel San Gabriel de Barrera.** Carretera Marfil, **Guanajuato** 36000. Tel: (473) 2-3980.

▶ **Parador San Javier.** Plaza Aldama 92, **Guanajuato** 36000. Tel: (473) 2-0626.

▶ **Hotel Spa San José Purua.** Carretera Conocido, POB 23, **Michoacán** 61471. Tel: (725) 3-1544.

▶ **Posada Sante Fé.** Jardín de la Unión, POB 191, **Guanajuato** 36000. Tel: (473) 2-0084.

▶ **El Senorial.** Guerrero Norte 10A, **Querétaro** 43700. Tel: (463) 4-3700.

▶ **Posada de la Soledad.** Zaragoza 90. **Morelia** 58000. Tel: (451) 2-1888.

▶ **Villa Jacaranda.** Aldama 53, **San Miguel de Allende** 37700. Tel: (465) 2-1015.

▶ **Villa Montaña.** Calle Galeana, Santa María Hills, POB 233, **Morelia** 58090. Tel: (451) 4-0179.

▶ **Posada Vista Bella.** Calle Galeana, Santa María Hills, POB 135, **Morelia** 58090. Tel: (451) 4-0284.

THE WESTERN HIGHLANDS

GUADALAJARA AND PATZCUARO

By Robert Cummings

Robert Cummings has lived in Mexico for the past five years. He has written many travel articles, and is currently at work on a novel.

The sophisticated residents of Mexico City have always looked upon Guadalajara as the overgrown village where their country cousins live, friendly folk who strum guitars by day and perform hat dances by candlelight in a land of swaggering cowboys and blushing señoritas.

Everyone knows the stereotype is silly, but it persists because it bears a grain of truth. More than most large cities, Guadalajara *is* a collection of villages. There are strong neighborhood loyalties here, a sense of closeness to the parish churches, and, in the midst of modernity, a love of and yearning for the soil. Songs about *mi tierra,* "my land," and *mi ranchita,* "my little ranch," never lack for listeners, and often bring a tear to the eye of these transplanted city dwellers. After all, this is the state of Jalisco, and Jalisco means ranches, cattle, and crops. There's a secret rodeo buckaroo lurking inside many a banker and attorney here, one that usually bursts forth as soon as the music starts.

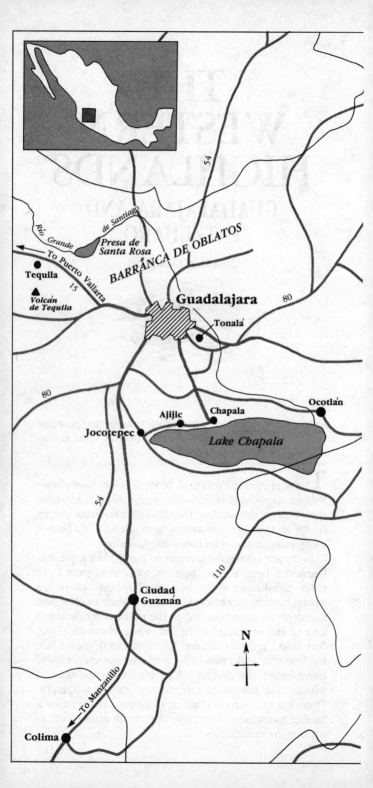

The Western Highlands

0 miles 35

0 kilometers 55

JALISCO

León

37

80

GUANAJUATO

Irapuato

To Mexico
City

La Piedad

90

15

Zamora

MICHOACAN

Zacapu

Quiroga

Lake
Pátzcuaro

Tzintzuntzán

YACATECAS
ARCHAEOLOGICAL
ZONE

40

37

Paracho

Janitzio

Angahuán

Paricutín

Pátzcuaro

Opepeo

Uruapan

Santa Clara
del Cobre

Río Cupatitzio

120

Guadalajara is the chief metropolis of the Western Highlands and the gateway to the mountains that surround it on every side but the east. The grassy ranch country of Jalisco, from which Guadalajara drew its early wealth and cowboy traditions, crinkles into hills just south of the city, ridges that frame Lake Chapala, the largest and most northerly of the highland lakes.

Southeast of Chapala the forested mountains of Michoacán rise sharply, becoming the peaks that cradle Mexico's loveliest lake, Lake Pátzcuaro. It was along these shores that the Tarascan civilization arose eight centuries ago; the mountain villages remain Tarascan to this day.

(Far to the north and west of, and a world apart from, Lake Pátzcuaro, Jalisco's booming coastal resort of Puerto Vallarta caters to sun-worshippers and deep-sea fishermen from around the globe. See the Pacific Resorts chapter below for a closer look at it and some of its nearby smaller sister resorts.)

This crescent-shaped region, with spirited Guadalajara at one tip and colorful Pátzcuaro at the other, offers visitors some of Mexico's richest discoveries, in colonial history, native crafts and cultures, and urban diversions.

MAJOR INTEREST

Guadalajara
Las Cuatro Plazas
The Cathedral
Government Palace
Degollado Theater
Regional Museum
Orozco murals at Instituto Cultural Cabañas
The Church of San Francisco area
The ceramic centers of Tlaquepaque and Tonalá
Mariachi music
The Liberty Market
Nightlife and entertainment

Around Guadalajara
Oblatos Canyon
Tequila
Lake Chapala area

The Tarascan Country
Scenic beauty
Picturesque town of Pátzcuaro

Eleven Patios craft market
Lake Pátzcuaro
Tzintzuntzán colonial town and archaeological site
Craft villages around Pátzcuaro
The city of Uruapan
Paricutín volcano

GUADALAJARA

Guadalajara is Mexico's second-largest city, and almost as populous as Chicago. But unless you're caught in rush-hour traffic, you're likely to feel that it is much smaller. Maybe it's because there are no urban canyons, no skyscrapers, and even the moderately tall buildings are few and far apart.

It is true that there are more guitars per city block in Guadalajara than any other city would dream of listening to. And it's also true that despite the encroaching urban pressures and crush, these country cousins really are the friendliest people in the Mexican Republic. Or perhaps it's just that they're the heartiest. In Jalisco it is sometimes hard to determine where heartiness ends and friendliness begins. The question becomes further confused by courtesy. The *tapatíos,* as the people of Guadalajara are nicknamed, are polite, smiling, and even courtly—insofar as the demands of surviving in the modern world permit.

Their style, however, can be confusing at times. You will be invited cordially, even enthusiastically, to "my house, which is *your* house," but you'll never learn the address. This is no more hypocritical than a friendly backslap at the club; it's merely a manner, a way of making life pleasant and gracious while staying safely uninvolved.

Perhaps *tapatío* cordiality, and the love of country values, is rooted in Guadalajara's unusually stable past. Founded soon after the Conquest on productive, gently rolling land, Guadalajara was bypassed by many of the storms of Mexican history. After some initial atrocities in the 16th century, ranch servitude, though hardly an enviable condition, here involved little of the suffering inflicted on native populations elsewhere in New Spain. The region also escaped the brutality of invasions, the social upheaval, and the violence that much of the country endured. Where other regions of the country were forced to

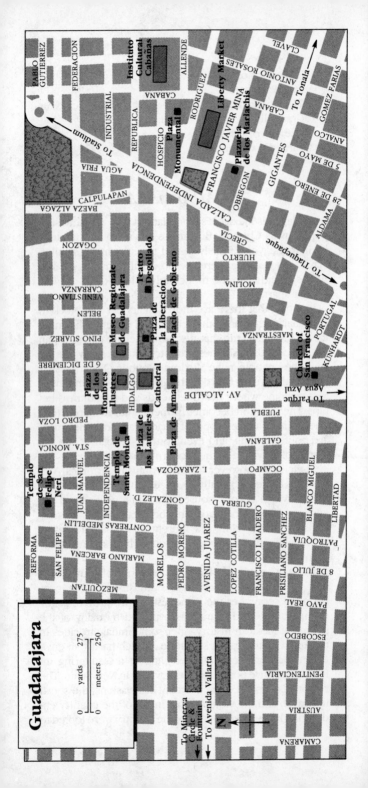

Guadalajara

0 | yards | 275
0 | meters | 250

N

Pablo Gutierrez
Federacion
Instituto Cultural Cabañas
Allende
Cabana
Republica
Industrial
Hospicio
Plaza Monumental
Agua Fria
Calpulapan
Baeza Alzaga
Calzada Independencia
Rodriguez
Francisco Javier Mina
Liberty Market
Plazuela de los Mariachis
Obregon
Grecia
Huerto
Molina
Antonio Rosales
Cabana
Gigantes
28 de Enero
Aldama
To Tonala
Gomez Farias
Analco
5 de Mayo
Clavel
To Tlaquepaque

Ogazon
Venustiano Carranza
Belen
Pino Suarez
6 de Diciembre
Museo Regionale de Guadalajara
Plaza de la Liberación
Teatro Degollado
Palacio de Gobierno
Plaza de los Hombres Ilustres
Hidalgo
Cathedral
Plaza de Armas
Plaza de los Laureles
Maestranza
Church of San Francisco
Portugal
Kunhardt
To Parque Agua Azul

Reforma
San Felipe
Pedro Loza
Sta. Monica
Templo de San Felipe Neri
Juan Manuel
Independencia
Contreras Medellin
Mariano Barcena
Templo de Santa Monica
Av. Alcalde
I. Zaragoza
Gonzalez D.
Guerra D.
Puebla
Galeana
Ocampo

Mezquitan
Morelos
Pedro Moreno
Avenida Juarez
Lopez Cotilla
Francisco I. Madero
Prisiliano Sanchez
8 de Julio
Blanco Miguel
Libertad
Patroquia

To Minerva Circle & Fountain
To Avenida Vallarta
Pavo Real
Escobedo
Penitenciaria
Austria
Camarena

To Stadium

bow to sword and cross, Guadalajara had a chance to cultivate graciousness and romance—and it did so in abundance. Spain was remote, the life here casual.

Not surprisingly, its problems and dislocations have been more recent, and have come as a result of growth and industrialization. Its major problem has been trying to reconcile its own explosive growth with its slow-paced, gracious traditions. Sometimes it manages to succeed; often it doesn't. For all that, Guadalajara remains a pleasant, livable, charmingly robust city.

Las Cuatro Plazas

The Four Plazas are at the heart of downtown Guadalajara. The city, realizing it has to yield to modernization, has nevertheless made major efforts to preserve the traditional grace and dignity of its historic center. The large area set aside as a result is impressive, and occupies about a dozen city blocks.

A good place to start exploring is the **Plaza de Armas** on the south side of the Cathedral at the corner of Morelos and Avenida 16 de Septiembre. This is a small, formal park where nothing distracts from the ornate bandstand, forged in Paris at the turn of the century, and today a fanciful reminder of the Art Nouveau style that Mexican travellers brought back from France. Concerts are held here every Thursday and Sunday evening, and it is truly a pleasant place to linger on a wrought-iron bench, to enjoy the almost perpetual spring of Guadalajara, and to study the domes, towers, and balustrades of the Cathedral.

On the east side of the plaza stands the stolid **Palacio de Gobierno**, or Government Palace, its 18th-century Baroque façade unusually severe. Inside is a dramatic mural by native son José Clemente Orozco. The subject, which enfolds the viewer like a net, is Father Hidalgo's abolition of slavery in Mexico, an act that was proclaimed from this very building.

The **Plaza de los Laureles**, which fronts the Cathedral, is not named for its laurel trees, but rather for the wreaths reserved for Mexico's heroes. Its fountain, bubbling in the sunlight, adds a touch of life to this public space of stone.

The **Cathedral** stares at the plaza with its two big round windows. An ungainly building, it is said you can count fourteen distinct styles in the hash of its architecture. But *tapatíos,* having grown up with it, love it and proudly show it off to visitors. Actually, the ponderous structure is seen to best advantage at night from Avenida Juárez, when the yellow lights on its towers lend it a magic glow. Inside, there are a number of good paintings, especially *The Assumption of the Virgin* by Murillo at the entrance to the sacristy.

In front of the Cathedral you can hire a horse and carriage for a tour of the neighborhood.

North of the Cathedral a Doric rotunda graces the shady **Plaza de los Hombres Ilustres**. Behind it to the east, housed in a dignified old seminary building, is the **Museo Regional de Guadalajara**. The highlights of the collection—and worth careful study—are the pre-Columbian figurines from the Western Highlands region. Fashioned by anonymous village sculptors, many are powerful representations of women at once fierce and compassionate; the animal figurines are also touched with genius. The second floor houses a collection of European painting (mostly Spanish) that was assembled from the 19th-century collections of rich *tapatíos*. While most are not masterpieces, they are skillful, and revealing of local tastes of the era.

Leaving the museum, turn left and walk east along the **Plaza de la Liberación** toward the imposing **Teatro Degollado**, another source of local pride. Inside are murals inspired by Dante's *Divine Comedy,* gleaming chandeliers, and a profusion of gold leaf. It is the home of the Guadalajara Symphony Orchestra and the Ballet Folklórico of the university. The orchestra is well worth hearing, the ballet a blaze of color.

Continuing east, you can stroll through the long, narrow **Plaza Tapatía**, a model urban mall adorned with fountains and sculpture. The long thoroughfare is also a fitting build-up to the city's great treasure at its eastern end, the **Instituto Cultural Cabañas**, also called the Hospicio Cabañas.

Erected in 1801 as an orphanage, the building was the design of the talented Spanish architect-sculptor Manuel Tolsá, who was imported to head Mexico's first formal academy of the arts. While it's a fine and interesting building, no one pays much attention to it; the murals inside are what make it celebrated.

Working with a dark palette, chiefly grays and blacks, which fit the atmosphere of its old chapel, José Clemente Orozco painted these frescoes in 1938 and 1939. Making spare use of details—a few thrusting lines portray a war horse, arrogant and apocalyptic, or what must be the sharpest barbed wire in the world, fangs of metal— Orozco managed to create a powerful protest against war and violence. The centerpiece of this breathtaking vision is his *Man of Fire*, painted on the interior of the dome high above. To be viewed properly it should be viewed as the artist saw it. For this, the Institute provides benches so that visitors can lie down and gaze straight up. You shouldn't feel hesitant about this. The Institute also provides mirrors; by all means use both methods. Either way, you'll feel as if you've come face-to-face with the gates to the inferno.

If you only have time to see one thing in Guadalajara, it should be this chapel with its brilliant murals.

Markets and Mariachis

Just south of the Instituto Cultural Cabañas, facing Calzada Independencia, sprawls the **Liberty Market** (*Mercado Libertad*)—actually a complex of many markets of many types. While no one should miss it entirely, don't expect too much.

Visitors to the market should look for its color and life rather than merchandise. While there are displays of local weaving, glass, and leather goods, most are not first rate, examining the goods is frowned upon, and the bargaining that goes on could teach lessons to sharks. Serious buyers will do better elsewhere. Serious hagglers for whom the hunt is worth more than the prize will find paradise, on the other hand.

At the southern end of the market is the old church of San Juan de Dios and, nearby, the **Plazuela de los Mariachis**, the famous "Mariachi Square." Here, at the many sidewalk cafés, customers may order drinks, food, and their favorite song. Day and night the musicians stroll among the tables or linger on the sidelines waiting to be hired. There is no charge for listening to what others have requested, but if you decide to become a patron yourself, ask the price in advance (this is not ordinarily a bargaining situation).

Mariachis are said to have originated in Guadalajara, and purists claim the city still has the best. Although they started out as string groups, featuring violins and a variety of guitars, these days their hallmark is brass. A traditional performance begins with a *sinfonía,* a gay little tune unconnected to the melody that will follow; this serves as an introduction, as well as the signature of that particular band. What follows is usually lusty and exuberant music, with hints of sadness and disappointment. While almost all mariachi musicians are accomplished instrumentalists, most usually are not talented vocalists. As a consequence, there is a mariachi tone that is a little harsh, a little hoarse, and decidedly rough and masculine. The *gritos,* shouts often done in falsetto, are essential to a good performance.

Mariachi music is composed for streets, squares, and spacious patios. Open air is as characteristic of the performance as the mariachis' flamboyant adaptation of cowboy clothing. Customers are often part of the act, joining in or even performing solo, using the hired band as accompaniment. It's not unusual for a host, or even more frequently a guest, to leave a private party, drive to the square, and bring back a carload of mariachis to play for an hour—or a night.

Mariachi music is heard all over Guadalajara. Aside from the plaza, the best bands can be heard in nearby Tlaquepaque in the *zócalo* (El Parián) and at major Guadalajara hotels. The nightclub groups, however, tend to sweeten their tone.

The Church of San Francisco

The **Barrio de San Francisco**, a corner of the downtown area five blocks south of the Plaza de Armas, is notable for two contrasting examples of ecclesiastical architecture, as well as for an old-fashioned garden that is both shady and welcoming.

The Church itself, with a handsome Baroque façade that is at once ornate yet highly controlled, is probably the finest religious structure in Guadalajara. Across the street is the small **Chapel of Our Lady of Aranzazú**, with its exquisite interior and splendid altar screens.

The nearby **Plaza de las Sombrillas** (Square of the Parasols) is a good place to sit at a café table, enjoy the passing life of the street, and admire the sparkling fountain.

Sports and Spectacles

The Guadalajara bullring, or **Plaza Monumental**, is as good as any in the country, famed for its great international stars and dazzling pageantry in the winter season. In warm Guadalajara, where early afternoon skies are almost always clear, it is important to get a seat in the shade, however. The bullfights are held on Sundays.

During the summer the Sunday thrills are at the **charreada**, Mexico's version of a rodeo, where the beauty of the costumes and horses is almost as important as the skill of the competitors, or *charros*. The stadium is near one of Guadalajara's parks, Agua Azul.

Cockfighting is a national passion, often an occasion for reckless betting, and not always to the taste of visitors. Matches are held on Sundays at noon and again at 7:30 P.M. There are special fights on holidays. The Plaza de Gallos, where these furious combats occur, is on Calzada de la Revolución in the direction of Tlaquepaque.

Staying in Guadalajara

The **Hotel Fiesta Americana Guadalajara** is one of the most luxurious and modern hotels in Mexico: helicopter service from the airport to the roof; glass elevators; panoramic views of Guadalajara from every room. There is also a nightclub and a lively bar with music. The hotel is located on Minerva Circle, at the north end of the city, but there is fast transportation to the downtown area.

The **Holiday Inn**, a little farther out at the Plaza del Sol, west of Minerva Circle, is a modern and attractive motel complex with gardens, balconies, terraces, and all the other amenities of a first-rate operation. The rates are moderate for an inn that has lighted tennis courts and a sauna and whirlpool. The music in the hotel's nightclub is an added bonus.

The **Malibu**, a satisfactory motel not far north of Minerva Circle, is popular with families and Mexicans traveling on business.

There aren't many attractive hotels in downtown Guadalajara. The colonial-style **Hotel Francés**, behind the Government Palace, is the most charming, its cocktail lounge a cheerful gathering place with music and an international flavor. Some of the inside rooms overlook air shafts, but guests who have been lucky enough to get rooms facing the street are enthusiastic about the hotel. The rates are reasonable, and parking in a public establishment two blocks away is provided.

The **Hotel De Mendoza** is also centrally located, and on a tranquil street. All the rooms are airy and comfortable, the décor provincial with a colonial feeling. While it is slightly more expensive than the Francés, the space and ventilation are better.

The **Calinda Roma**, part of a chain of hotels, is located at the edge of the historic district on Avenida Juárez halfway between the Cathedral and the Liberty Market. It has convenient basement parking, good rooms in a new wing, and a rooftop pool. The hotel, which offers senior citizens discounts, is popular with tour groups.

Dining in Guadalajara

Typically, Jalisco fare is ranch fare—hearty, rather plain, with the emphasis on meat and fowl. Local cooks have a patronizing attitude toward vegetables. An à la carte order in the typical Jalisco restaurant is apt to be a slab of meat, some tortillas, chile sauce—and nothing else.

Cabrito, roast kid, is a regional specialty. So is *birria,* a hearty plate with chunks of goat, pork, or mutton, and sometimes all three in combination. It is best barbecued; most Guadalajara restaurants steam it. On the other hand, *carnitas* (chunks of roast pork), a staple in Mexico, are reputed to be superior here. Another local favorite is *pozole,* half soup and half stew, made with hominy and pork and topped with onions, lettuce, and radish slices.

Mexican cuisine at its absolute best is presented at **La Hacienda**, a smart and sophisticated restaurant in the Hotel Fiesta Americana. Its serious rival in this field is **Río Viejo**, a handsome Guadalajara town house romantically furnished with antiques, located at Avenida de las Américas 302, a few blocks north of Avenida Vallarta in midtown.

Closer to Avenida Vallarta, with less atmosphere—but also costing less—**Los Otates**, Avenida de las Américas 28 at the corner of Morelos, serves traditional Mexican food with few surprises.

Most fine restaurants in Guadalajara pride themselves on their European or "international" dishes. The two most elegant restaurants in town are French—**Lafayette** in the Hotel Camino Real (Avenida Vallarta 5005, near the Malibu) and **Place de la Concorde** in the Hotel Fiesta Americana. There is a dress code at both.

Less formal and much less expensive is **La Fuente**, located in a town house in a pleasant neighborhood at Avenida Plan de San Luis 1899. To get there head north from Minerva Circle on López Mateos and turn right at the Colombus Fountain. International menu.

La Copa de Leche, in the center of town at Juárez 414, was for years famous as the city's finest restaurant. It has since been surpassed more than once, but remains a traditional standby. Good Mexican food and other dishes are served on the second floor. There's a different menu downstairs, mostly seafood and steaks, the former better than the latter.

In the Hotel Francés, El Molino Rojo, on the first floor, is a good value for lunch and breakfast. Visitors looking for convenience food should try Sanborn's at Vallarta 1600, where the craft items are as well selected as the clean, well-prepared food.

For nighttime entertainment and perhaps a taste of the region's famed tequila, the two most popular places are El Parián, the courtyard in the main square in Tlaquepaque (see below), and Plaza del Mariachi near the Liberty Market. They are both authentic rather than fancy.

All the major hotels have bars with entertainment. The best show with traditional music and, of course, a hat dance is at the Holiday Inn. Its two rivals are El Pueblito Cantina in the Hotel Hyatt Regency across from the Plaza del Sol, which presents fine mariachi music; and La Pergola in the Hotel Sheraton, located near Parque Agua Azul a short distance from the downtown area by taxi.

Atop the Hotel de Mendoza, located in the center of town at Venustiano Carranza 16, you'll find the welcoming El Compañario, with twinkling panoramic views of Guadalajara and dancing after 9:00 P.M. Only couples and mixed parties are admitted, however.

The Copenhagen is a cheerful spot to listen to a good jazz trio from 9:00 P.M. on. The Copenhagen serves food (paella is the house specialty) but a meal is not mandatory. You'll find it in the center of town off Parque Revolución at Marcos Castellanos 140.

The Hotel Francés bar is inviting for its conversation, background music, and convivial atmosphere. The "disco" next door is actually a modest nightclub with live music for dancing or just plain listening.

Shopping in Guadalajara

To find a wide range of crafts at fair prices, you should first visit the Casa de las Artesanías de Jalisco, a state museum devoted to the popular arts. Located in the Parque Agua Azul, it offers a range of work, which provides a basis for comparison. There's another branch at the corner of Avila Camacho and 16 de Septiembre. In both places the quality is good, prices reasonable.

Tlaquepaque and Tonalá

San Pedro Tlaquepaque (Tlah-keh-PAH-keh) is no longer a separate town but a continuation of the city to the southeast. Once famed as a pottery village, much of it has been turned into a psycho-ceramic nightmare heaped with crimes against taste committed in clay. Three-fourths of the stuff is dime-store junk, both gaudy and fragile, with glazes that threaten lead poisoning. In the middle of this mess you can find some good pieces, but you can also be dazed by the junk and give up quickly. Fortunately, the glassware is better than the pottery, and local glassblowers achieve some beautiful shades of red.

Shops and galleries in the pedestrian mall on Independencia have much the best offerings, and there's some imaginative work in metal and paper to be found here as well. The "antiques" on sale are also attractive, although usually manufactured last week. The **Ken Edwards** shop presents the most appealing, whimsical earthenware in town.

The **Museo Regional de la Cerámica**, at Independencia 237, will give you an idea of what you wish you could find along the streets outside.

Tlaquepaque buses, so marked, run along Calzada Independencia with some frequency. By car, you head south on Calzada Independencia Sur and turn left on Calzada Revolución. At the traffic circle you keep to the left of a gasoline station and stay on Revolución. You'll see signs for Tlaquepaque ahead. A right turn takes you to the central plaza, El Parián.

Tonalá, a ten-minute drive from Tlaquepaque, has managed to keep its sincerity. Maybe it's because the town actually makes things, rather than just selling them. Stoneware is especially good here, thanks to a recent tradition established by U.S. designers Ken Edwards and Jorge Wilmot. Wilmot's pieces, which are much more durable than the many imitations, are stamped with a "W." The glossy black pottery that looks like Oaxaca ware but is actually made in Tonalá competes in every respect with the more famous work produced in the south.

Many Tonalá creations can also be found in Tlaquepaque and Guadalajara, but it takes a little searching. The

studio of designer **Jorge Wilmot**, however, is located at
Morelos 80, not far from the Cathedral.

Buses to Tonalá run along Calzada Independencia, and
are clearly labeled. To get there by car, head east on
Carretera Los Altos and take the "Zapotlanejo Libre" exit.

AROUND GUADALAJARA
Barranca de Oblatos

This canyon (*barranca*) is an impressive 610-meter
(2,000-foot) slash in the earth that has been cut over the
ages by two rivers. In addition to its sheer beauty, it's
interesting for the fact that its climate changes as the
gorge deepens, becoming positively tropical by the time
you reach the bottom. As a result, fruits such as papayas
flourish here, and are harvested for the markets back in
Guadalajara. For those interested in experiencing the
phenomenon, a cable car makes the descent to the bottom and back.

The "Barranca" bus runs north along Calzada Independencia Norte to the canyon rim and the point from which
the cable car departs. If you're driving your own car,
follow Independencia 11 km (6 miles) north until you
reach the canyon (it's actually northeast but is marked
"north"). Taxis, which are not expensive, are another
option, and can be hailed on Independencia; they'll be
available at the canyon for the return trip.

Tequila

The town for which the famous liquor is named lies 57
km (36 miles) northwest of Guadalajara. It is not interesting enough to warrant a special trip, however, unless
you're already passing that way on Highway 15, the
coastal route that heads north to the Arizona border. In
that case, it is worth a stop to tour one of the distilleries,
which are usually open to the public until 2:00 P.M.

A more interesting demonstration of the distilling process can be seen right in Guadalajara itself at the big
Tequila Sauza bottling plant, located at Avenida Vallarta
3273. Tours are conducted daily from 10:00 A.M. until 2:00
P.M., with courtesy samplings of the deliciously piquant
stuff offered to visitors.

To get to the Sauza plant, take the Parque Vial or Plaza
del Sol bus on Juárez to the far (west) side of Minerva

Circle. Then walk a few blocks farther west on Vallarta. Because taxis are not expensive, however, it's more convenient to hail one westbound on Juárez and tell the driver you want to go to Tequila Sauza. For the return trip, taxis are easy to find outside the bottling plant or near Minerva Circle.

Lake Chapala

It is an easy trip from Guadalajara, about an hour south by car or bus, to Mexico's largest lake and its shoreline villages. The excursion is worth making for visitors with the time, but be sure to explore Guadalajara first. The badly polluted lake is too dirty for swimming, almost useless for boating, and its fish died long ago. Only the magnificent views survive.

The town of **Chapala** has some attractive turn-of-the-century houses fronting the lake, worth a thirty-minute walk or so. The villages farther west, Ajijic (ah-hee-HEEK) and Jocotepec, lost much of their innocence—and with it most of their charm—a generation ago. The area is heavily advertised as a place for "bargain retirement" and "bargain winter retreats." Actually, the bargains vanished at about the same time as the Chapala whitefish. Rentals here are expensive, hotel rates not low, and the restaurants and stores usually overpriced.

As almost everyone knows, a large colony of U.S. and Canadian retirees lives along the lake, enjoying the climate, the views, and each other's company. Over the years they've also established such things as an enterprising English-language community theater, a weekly journal, and a chili cookoff.

In Chapala the traditional place for a drink or lunch overlooking the lake is the **Beer Garden** at the foot of the main street; it's the roofed terrace on the right as you approach the head of the pier. The view and drinks are fine, the food only so-so.

For a meal, or even an overnight stay, at Lake Chapala, much the best choice is the **Posada Ajijic** in the dusty village of the same name about a ten-minute drive west along the lake from Chapala. The bar and dining room offer pleasant views of the lake, and, while the service may be chaotic, the lodge maintains the best kitchen in the area. The guest rooms all have a rustic charm.

Buses are reputed to run along the lakeside highway. Their reliability, on the other hand, may be gauged by the large number of hitchhikers, both Mexican and foreign, you'll see thumbing their way between the villages.

PATZCUARO
AND THE TARASCAN
COUNTRY

The lakeside town of Pátzcuaro (PAHTZ-kwah-ro), situated just west of Morelia (see the Colonial Heartland chapter) and about halfway between Mexico City and Guadalajara, is the spiritual capital of the Western Highlands region, and possibly Mexico's most purely Indian city. A city of almost 60,000 (at times it seems much smaller), it is, in the minds of many travellers, the heart of the most scenic corner of Mexico. For such people, no other region can equal Pátzcuaro and its environs for alpine beauty, and only the Mayan settlements in the southeastern part of the country can rival it for being exotic and picturesque. The Tarascan people themselves, often under even greater pressure to change than the Maya, have been almost as successful in preserving their traditional ways, their language, and their artistic heritage.

The Tarascans (also known as the Purépecha) are an ancient people. According to legend they were one of the tribes that migrated into the region with the Aztecs. When they paused at Lake Pátzcuaro, so the legend goes, the Tarascans went into the water to bathe. The Aztecs seized the opportunity to abscond with the Tarascans' clothes, and so began the undying enmity between the two peoples. In time, gods, speaking through hummingbirds, commanded the Tarascans to build a city on the shore of the lake. It was a thriving center by the time the Spanish arrived, and managed to survive the atrocities committed by the conquistadors—atrocities that are remembered by the Tarascans to this day.

There is one archaeological zone of medium interest in the region, Tzintzuntzán, as well as some smaller cities. Volcano buffs may want to visit the desolate world left behind by the eruption of Paricutín, Mexico's youngest volcano. In addition, the semi-tropical city of Uruapan is less than an hour's drive away.

Some travellers also use Pátzcuaro as a base for visiting Morelia, a short journey to the east (see the Colonial

Heartland chapter), preferring the lakeside town's serenity and lower prices.

Pátzcuaro is in high country, located at an elevation of
2,190 miles (over 7,000 feet); a warm sweater is a necessity, as will be a windbreaker on many occasions.

Pátzcuaro Town

The town rambles down the slopes of several hills toward
the big lake of the same name. Its steep roofs of red tile
jut out over carved beams, giving it a slightly Oriental
atmosphere, while its cobblestone streets lead to the two
plazas around which the life of the town revolves.

The **Plaza Chica** (little plaza) is the first one you see on
arrival and is officially named the Plaza Gertrudis Bocanegra, after a local heroine of the War of Independence.
The municipal market, which has some good handicrafts
near the fruits and vegetables, starts at the square's southwest corner. Like Indian markets throughout Mexico, it is
commercial, bustling with life, rundown, and colorful.
Facing it on the north is a 16th-century Augustinian
church that now houses the drafty **Biblioteca Pública**.
Inside you'll find a dramatic fresco depicting the region's
history painted by Juan O'Gorman, one of Mexico's leading muralists in the middle decades of this century.

A block to the south lies the **Plaza Grande**, known
formally as the Plaza Vasco de Quiroga. This square is the
community's spacious and comfortable outdoor living
room, a place where towering ash trees at least a century
old provide dappled shade as well as a stately reminder
of the forests at the town's edge. There's also a sense here
that the town is on its best behavior; all is quietly
Tarascan, and the sidewalk cafés are pleasant rather than
lively.

Friday is market day. Early in the morning Indians from
the surrounding countryside pour into town to sell and
buy. They walk, they come by canoe, or they lead burros
loaded down with pottery, lacquerware, cloth, carved
wood, and hammered metal. Many of the women wear
the traditional skirt made of yard upon yard of homespun
wool, a garment that can weigh as much as 30 pounds.
Pleated accordion style, the skirts are gathered in back
and held by a belt so that they spread outward like a fan.
Their shawls, or *rebozos,* are often distinctive to a particular village. Paracho women, for instance, favor a scarf with

a brilliant fringe designed to resemble the plumage of a hummingbird.

The serape, carried folded during the day, is a masculine item. Serapes tend to be dark in Pátzcuaro, coarse in texture, and relieved by simple designs in red. Male fiesta wear, which you probably won't see at the market, is usually an intricately embroidered shirt complemented by a hat decked out with gay ribbons.

Tarascan jewelry is also handmade, usually out of hammered silver fashioned into hollow globes and a variety of other shapes; various shades of crimson beads are also popular.

A short walk uphill from the two squares and market is a spacious open area that was the center of town centuries ago. In 1540 the Pope decreed that a cathedral be built in Pátzcuaro, and grandiose plans were drawn up. Only a portion of the nave was erected, however, before a terrible earthquake struck the town, damaging the new structure. The Bishop of Michoacán, alarmed by this turn of events, decided to move his see to Valladolid (now Morelia). Today, the cathedral, which is known as the **Basílica de Nuestra Señora de la Salud** (Our Lady of Health), remains standing as a relic of that bygone age, and still serves the local community. It also houses a revered image of the Virgin made out of corn paste. A bit farther to the south is La Compañía, another church built in the 1540s.

The **Museo de Artes Populares**, near La Compañía, was originally built in the 16th century as a Jesuit seminary. Today the museum inside is small but delightful, and boasts an antique kitchen, exquisite crafts, and a gracious patio.

La Casa de los Once Patios, the House of Eleven Patios, half a block east of the plaza fronting the Cathedral, was once a Dominican convent and is now a hive of crafts workshops, studios, and salesrooms. The sheer volume of work on display—including lacquerware, woven goods, pottery, woodcarving, embroidery, lace, and metalwork (especially copper)—makes it worth a visit.

A lookout, or *mirador,* on the shoulder of **El Estribo**, the extinct volcano that walls off the town to the south, is well worth checking out for spectacular views of the lake and its seven islands. To get there, follow the cobblestone road that twists sharply upward from the Plaza Grande for a distance of about 4 km (2½ miles); it will end at a small park, which also makes a nice spot for a picnic.

Staying in Pátzcuaro

There are no deluxe hotels in Pátzcuaro, but there are several good places to choose from.

The fanciest by far is the **Best Western Posada de Don Vasco**, a motor inn on the edge of town. It has a tennis court, cocktail lounge, what little nightlife the town offers, and a bowling alley (separate charge). As the most modern place in town, it is also the most expensive.

The **Mesón del Gallo**, in the center of town adjacent to the Plaza Grande, is a smaller operation with a little pool and garden area. The rooms can be cold in the winter, however.

The **Hotel los Escudos**, on the main plaza, is cheerful and simple. The rooms are not large, but all have fireplaces.

The **Posada de la Basílica**, near the Cathedral, is easily the most charming of the local inns. At once rustic and homey, it also has fireplaces and a big patio that lets in the winter sunshine. The management is helpful and friendly.

Dining in Pátzcuaro

Whitefish, delicate and flaky, is the specialty here; ask for the *pescado blanco*. Trout (*trucha*) is always fresh. The *sopa Tarasca,* rich and spicy, but not peppery, makes an excellent first course.

Local restaurants, almost all of them located in hotels or inns, tend to be small, adequate, and pleasant, but not special. Service can be casual.

Los Escudos, the dining room in the hotel of the same name, is satisfactory. Its neighbor, **El Patio**, is in the same category, and also inexpensive.

The restaurant in the **Posada de la Basílica** offers a good breakfast and lunch, as well as romantic views of the town—an almost Oriental panorama of steep tile roofs with quaintly upturned corners. A meal here will taste twice as good at a window table.

The **Don Vasco**, at the Best Western, is more elaborate than other places—not because it offers better food, just a more attractive room. Traditional entertainment is presented twice a week, including the famous Tarascan Dance of the Old Men.

Lake Pátzcuaro

This beautiful mountain lake is about 20 km (13 miles) long from north to south. Its irregular shoreline is dotted with Tarascan villages, and the scenery is made even more interesting by the islands that break the lake's surface.

The largest and most famous island is Janitzio, easily identifiable by the colossal statue of patriot José María Morelos—who deserved something better than this ungainly stone—that crowns its summit. The island itself is the favorite destination for launches leaving regularly from the Pátzcuaro pier. The boat trip is lovely, the destination dubious. Nowadays, Janitzio is utterly commercialized, one junky shop after another, their ranks broken only by risky eateries. The island was once justly famed for its annual Day of the Dead celebration on November 2. It is now entirely a tourist event and a crush; worse than spoiled, it has become offensive.

Likewise, the colorful fishermen with "butterfly nets" who were once emblematic of the region have all but vanished, except for arranged appearances in front of tour groups.

Tzintzuntzán and Quiroga

The drive north on Highway 40 along the eastern shore of the lake, on the other hand, is still a pretty trip. Tzintzuntzán (tsin-soon-sahn), 21 km (13 miles) from Pátzcuaro, was once the capital of the ancient Tarascan kingdom. When the Spanish arrived they estimated the population at 40,000—most of whom were soon liquidated or scattered.

Today the main points of interest are clustered around the southern entrance to the town.

The parish church is mellow and splendid. It was once the headquarters of Bishop Vasco de Quiroga, the most brilliant and sympathetic figure to emerge in New Spain in the decades immediately following the Conquest. After an outstanding career as a lawyer in the colony, a career that attracted the attention of Charles V, Don Vasco was chosen to mitigate the sufferings that had recently been inflicted upon the Tarascans. In order to employ the power of the Church in his task, Don Vasco took holy orders at a time when most men were ready to retire. He was sixty-eight and a bishop by the time he arrived in Tzintzuntzán, and he quickly set about creating (or perhaps reorganizing) a communal and quite utopian society. As a result of his humane efforts, the bishop is still remembered as *Tata,* or "Father," by the people of the region.

Upon entering the huge atrium of the church the visitor is immediately confronted by a reminder of the bishop—gnarled and venerable olive trees, which Don Vasco planted despite laws forbidding native production of olives. Also around the atrium are a number of small outdoor shrines, an echo of the long-ago times when the Tarascan people would purify themselves before entering their temples. The façade of the church is richly Plateresque, a beautiful example of the early handling of European themes by native artists. Adjoining the churchyard is the studio of Luis Mandel Morales, an outstanding potter. His *Taller Alta Temperatura,* a ceramics workshop, is remarkable, if a bit hard to find. One of the small boys who frequent the church grounds will be happy to guide you to it for a tip, however.

On the other side of the highway rise the heights that are now protected as the **Yácatecas archaeological zone**. These ruins, which functioned as a sort of Acropolis of the Purépecha people in the 15th century, consist of five temple platforms. Unfortunately, the intervening centuries have not been kind to this "Place of the Hummingbirds." Still, the temple platforms remain an impressive sight, the views of the surrounding countryside even more so.

The village of Tzintzuntzán itself is not attractive, but displays of the inexpensive local pottery here are worth examining.

Quiroga, a few minutes' drive to the north, is of interest primarily for its main-street shops, which feature the town's fine lacquerware and woven furniture.

The Craft Villages

Villa Escalante, more commonly called **Santa Clara del Cobre**, is located 16 km (10 miles) south of Pátzcuaro. Bishop Quiroga introduced the art of coppersmithing to the region in the mid-16th century, and Santa Clara has thrived on it ever since. Here you'll find copper in every imaginable shape and form. There's also a little museum in town with prize-winning examples of the local specialty.

Opepeo, which is situated on the road to Santa Clara, is home to many skilled wood-carvers and furniture makers.

Capula, a 40-minute drive north and east of Pátzcuaro, is, like Tzintzuntzán, not an especially pretty village, but it does produce the most imaginative pottery in the region. To get there, take the highway connecting Quiroga and Morelia. The village will be at the end of a side road heading north from the highway, about halfway between the two larger towns.

Uruapan

Uruapan (oo-roo-AH-pahn), a verdant semi-tropical city noted for its blossoms and luxurious foliage, is located some 62 km (38 miles) west of Pátzcuaro, and the scenic drive from Pátzcuaro may be the best reason for visiting it. In only a few minutes the scenery will change from stately pine forests to lush hillsides checkered with coffee and banana plantations, as well as groves of lemon and orange trees.

At the northern entrance to town lies **Eduardo Ruíz National Park,** which protects the headwaters of the Río Cupatitzio. Shady paths and rustic bridges make this a lovely place for a walk. At the end of the trail a cascade foams and seethes over rocks and ledges.

At the same end of town is a small museum that displays and sells local crafts, notably the lacquerware for which Uruapan is known. Another museum, located on the main plaza, is housed in a fine 16th-century building; the collection inside includes antique and modern Tarascan craft work.

Uruapan, despite its relatively fast pace, remains graciously provincial. It is still Tarascan enough to take pride in its local color; the annual fair, where locally produced crafts and toys are displayed, ranks among the best in Mexico, drawing a crowd during Palm Sunday week.

The **Mansión del Cupatitzio** is a hotel in a converted and expanded hacienda overlooking the national park. The rooms with park views are the best. The pool is well-maintained, the restaurant satisfactory. The hotel is about a ten-minute walk from the *zócalo.*

Downtown on the *zócalo* itself, the **Best Western Plaza Uruapan** occupies a parcel of land that is part of a shopping mall. Ask for a room on the top floor for views of the town and surrounding mountains from a private balcony. The bar, restaurant, and weekend disco are favorites with local businesspeople and commercial travellers.

La Pergola, a restaurant on the *zócalo,* is an unhurried spot with a broad menu, but the broadly national dishes show the kitchen off to the best advantage.

Paricutín, the now-dormant volcano that raised havoc when it was born in a cornfield in 1943, is 39 km (25 miles) north of Uruapan. To get there, head north on Highway 37, the road to Paracho, for 18 km (11 miles), then turn left onto the road that leads to Angahuán. The village of Angahuán, where more Tarascan than Spanish is spoken, is at the end of the road about 19 km (12 miles) to the west. A guide will usually be waiting outside the village—the most convenient way to see the volcano. If no guide is on duty, drive into the center of the village and someone will soon approach you. Just beyond town, but a little tricky to find, is the departure point for tours of the area, complete with a place to rent horses and very basic overnight accommodations.

There is no access by car to the volcano itself, or to the villages it destroyed. Instead, it's a short ride by horseback (or a long hike) to the lava beds, a weird and lunarlike landscape. Of the first village, only part of the town church remains, the building buried in lava but the tower rising eerily above the blackness. Most visitors turn back after seeing this bizarre sight. To visit the crater itself requires an early morning start; the round trip, by horseback, takes most of a day. The ride to the village should not be daunting to inexperienced riders, however; the horses are gentle and know the routine.

Paracho, the first town north of Uruapan past the turnoff for Argahuán, is famous for its wood carvings and stringed musical instruments, especially guitars.

GETTING AROUND
Four airlines fly directly between Guadalajara and the United States: Western, American, Mexicana, and Aeroméxico (the latter two also have frequent flights to Mexico City and other cities in the country). From Guadalajara there are daily westbound flights to Puerto Vallarta. Transportation into the city from the airport is by cheap minibus or rate-controlled taxi. Airport buses will also pick you up at your hotel and take you to the airport for departure.

The only train service to the capital that can be recommended is the night train, *El Tapatío.* It leaves Guadalajara at 7:55 P.M. and arrives in the capital the next morning at 8:10 A.M. (There's another evening train, but you'd be better off to avoid it.) Passengers should not buy the cheapest ticket, however, which is misleadingly called "first class." A choice of roomettes and bedrooms is available; the service is fair, the dining car adequate. The incoming train from the capital leaves Mexico City early in the evening and reaches Guadalajara twelve hours later. The *Del Pacifico* winds between Guadalajara and Mexicali on the U.S. border—a trip of about 33 hours. The only rail depot in Guadalajara is on Avenida Washington, 15 blocks south of the Liberty Market near the Parque Agua Azul. *El Tapatío* arrives and departs in Mexico City from the central station on Calle Buenavista off Insurgentes Norte.

Car rental agencies at the airport include Arrendadora de Automobiles, S.A., Albarran; Auto Arrendadora Nacional; Avis de Mexico; Hertz de Mexico; Alal; Budget; and Quick. All of these companies have offices in the city as well.

Except in the central historic district, distances in Guadalajara are too great to be covered easily on foot. Taxis are plentiful, however, and not expensive. An excellent bus system runs from the center of town to the Minerva Circle hotel area and beyond. There's also good bus service to Tlaquepaque and Tonalá, and destinations are marked on each bus.

Although there is regular bus service to Lake Chapala, the problem is getting around once you're there. The trip, therefore, is probably best made by car or tour bus. The outstanding tour bus company is Panoramex, which calls at hotels throughout Guadalajara.

ACCOMMODATIONS REFERENCE

▶ **Posada Ajijic.** 16 de Septiembre, **Ajijic.** Tel: (376) 5-3395.

▶ **Posada de la Basílica.** Arciga 6, **Pátzcuaro,** Michoacán 61600. Tel: (454) 2-1108.

▶ **Best Western Plaza Uruapan.** Ocámpo 64, **Uruapan,** Michoacán 64430. Tel: (452) 3-3700, or 3-3813; or (800) 528-1234.

▶ **Best Western Posada de Don Vasco.** Calzada de las Américas 450, **Pátzcuaro,** Michoacán 61600. Tel: (454) 2-0227 or (800) 528-1234.

▶ **Calinda Roma.** Avenida Juárez 170, **Guadalajara** 44100. Tel: (36) 14-8650; in U.S. (800) 228-5151.

▶ **Hotel los Escudos.** Portal Hidalgo 73, **Pátzcuaro,** Michoacán 61600. Tel: (454) 2-1290.

▶ **Hotel Fiesta Americana.** Avenida Vallarta and López Mateos, **Guadalajara** 44100. Tel: (36) 25-3434 or (914) 633-1545.

▶ **Hotel Francés.** Maestranza 38, **Guadalajara** 44100. Tel: (36) 13-1190.

▶ **Holiday Inn.** Boulevard López Mateos and Avenida Mariano Otero, **Guadalajara** 44100. Tel: (36) 31-5566 or (800) 465-4329.

▶ **Hotel Malibu.** Vallarta 3993, **Guadalajara** 44100. Tel: (36) 21-7888.

▶ **Mansión del Cupatitzio.** Adjoining Eduardo Ruíz National Park, **Uruapan**, Michoacán 64430. Tel: (452) 3-2060.

▶ **Hotel de Mendoza.** Venustiano Carranza 16, **Guadalajara** 44100. Tel: (36) 13-4646.

▶ **El Mesón del Gallo.** Dr. Jose María Coss 20, **Pátzcuaro**, Michoacán 61600. Tel: (454) 2-1474.

THE COPPER CANYON
RIDING THE CHIHUAHUA-PACIFIC RAILWAY

By Robert Cummings

It has been called the most scenic railroad trip in the world. No doubt there are rivals and other claimants, but it's hard to name one. The Chihuahua-Pacific weaves, snakes, and climbs through as wild and spectacular a countryside as you are ever likely to visit. High in the Sierra Madre of northwest Mexico, south of Ciudad Juárez and western New Mexico, the train skirts the brink of deep canyons, then rolls into the immense Copper Canyon (*Barranca del Cobre*) itself. Upon seeing it a rush of adjectives floods the mind—breathtaking, awe-inspiring, incomparable. In fact, four Grand Canyons could be dropped into this vastness, which is why it's sometimes called "the Grander Canyon."

There are two ways to do this trip. First—and the most usual way—is simply as an exciting rail journey. You get aboard at either end of the line (but preferably the southern terminus near **Los Mochis**, in the state of Sinaloa on the Gulf of California) and pass through a series of titanic canyons, getting out now and then to catch your breath and gape at the spectacular scenery that stretches as far as the eye can see. Then you detrain at the other end of the line, **Chihuahua** inland to the northeast, or Los Mochis to

To Ciudad Juarez
45

Chihuahua

28

To Ciudad Juarez
10

Matachic

CAMPOS MENONITAS

Laguna Bustillos

16

Cuauhtémoc

C H I H U A H U A

Río Papagochic

Laguna de los Mexicanos

■ **Basaseachic Falls**

San Juanito

Sisoguichi

Caves of Comachi

Río Conchas

Creel

Lake Arareco

Cusárare

Divisadero

Basihuare

Bahuichivo

BARRANCA DEL COBRE

Parque Natural

Cerocahui

Río Septentrión

Río Urique

S I E R R A

■ **Batopilas Canyon**

N

M A D R E

Presa Miguel Hidalgo

O C C I D E N T A L

El Fuerte

To Mexicali

S I N A L O A

Río Fuerte

Los Mochis

15

To Mazatlán

GULF OF CALIFORNIA

The Copper Canyon Area

| 0 | miles | 40 |
| 0 | kilometers | 60 |

the southwest. If the train is on schedule, the trip takes 13 hours, but 15 is not unusual. It doesn't really matter, however, because the trip is worth taking no matter how long it takes. Nevertheless, spending 13 to 15 hours, even in a comfortable coach, with stops too few and too brief, hardly does justice to the magnificence of the canyon, and totally omits the surrounding area. If that's the only way your schedule permits, by all means do it.

On the other hand, an unhurried trip with overnight stops is far better. The Copper Canyon can and should be considered as a short vacation destination of unusual interest and beauty, something more than an excuse for a spectacular train ride. Ideally you should allow three or four nights for exploring the canyon itself, not counting time spent in Chihuahua or Los Mochis. Even one overnight along the way is better than a straight-through trip, which may leave you physically tired and mentally dazed from taking in too much scenic beauty at a single stretch.

If it is to be one overnight, **Divisadero** is the halfway point of the trip and very appealing. On the other hand, **Creel**, five and a half hours from Chihuahua, has more local attractions. Visit both if possible.

A ticket on the daylight *especial* permits unlimited stops in the same direction. A one-way ticket costs about $40, and there's a 15 percent surcharge for stopovers. Seats on the train are comfortable, and there is a dining car, usually with an observation bubble. Frequently the heating system doesn't work or is inadequate, so in cold weather you might want to carry a lap robe. Recently a number of new deluxe coaches have been added, but few things about the Chihuahua-Pacific are certain or permanent. At the frequent five-minute stops along the route vendors hawk hot coffee, cocoa, and soft drinks.

The Railroad Itself

This seemingly impossible route, which was gouged out of ancient rock, thrown across plunging gorges, and bored through towering mountains, was the dream of one Albert K. Owen, a visionary who longed for a railroad connecting Texas to the Gulf of California, partly in order to service a utopian community he was building at what would be the line's southern terminus. Launched more than a century ago, it was an impractical idea, even for the Gilded Age, but Owen sank large amounts of money into it. The beginning and end of the line presented no problems; the land there was flat. But in between was the formidable Sierra Madre.

Fortunes were devoured trying to make the link. Finally the best engineering and financial minds in the United States pronounced the railroad an impossibility. The enterprise was shelved and almost forgotten. Only the first section, from Chihuahua to Creel, was put to use.

In the years after the Revolution Mexico gradually began to acquire ownership of her own railroads, and in 1939–40 bought out the last of the foreign companies, among them the Chihuahua-Pacific. Mexican engineers studied and debated the ambitious project for 13 years before announcing their solutions to the daunting problems blocking the completion of the railroad.

The biggest one, of course, was the 260-km (161-mile) stretch through the Copper Canyon, a land of rugged mountains and bottomless gorges that was inhabited only by the primitive Tarahumara Indians and a handful of missionaries. For eight years the construction work inched along. Thirty-nine bridges were built to span the chasms of the canyon, and 86 tunnels were dug through its mountains. Finally, in 1961, the line was opened, making it possible to take what would soon be known as "the Train Ride in the Sky."

The Tarahumara

The railway did not replace a road; there were—and are—no through roads in the region. In fact, the surrounding countryside had been virtually isolated since the earliest days of its habitation. As a result, when the construction crews first encountered the local Tarahumara Indians, they found themselves among a Stone Age people.

The Tarahumara you will encounter are a sturdy people with sharply defined features and long coarse hair, which the men wear bound in a headband. They also wear rough white shirts and the *tapote,* a kind of loincloth. They are fabled runners who will hunt a deer by chasing it until the animal drops of exhaustion, and their strength is as great as their stamina. A favorite Tarahumara game involves kicking a small ball while running a footrace; participants will run as much as 150 miles without a real rest, a feat of endurance that covers several days and nights.

Today, many of the Tarahumara still live in caves and

follow the seasonal migration patterns of their ancestors: In the summer they live on the high cliffs, but retreat to the canyon depths when winter comes, moving from colder to milder temperatures as they descend over a mile to the bottom.

Taking the Train

First-class trains, known as the *especial,* make the trip daily, one southbound from Chihuahua, the other north-bound from Los Mochis. They pass near the little town of Divisadero, but there is no exchange of passengers be-tween them. In other words, you'll have to wait about 24 hours at any stop along the line for the next train. And because the entire trip (without stopovers) takes longer than daylight lasts, you'll have to make a round trip to see everything in daylight. (Most travellers choose not to do this, although it can be a convenient plan depending on your next destination.) The best way to see the canyon is to take the *northbound* train, either from Los Mochis or El Fuerte, about 80 km (50 miles) to the northeast. If you must leave from Chihuahua and do the trip straight through, you'll probably be disappointed when falling darkness obscures the views while you're still in scenic country. The longer days of summer will lessen this prob-lem somewhat.

(There is a third possibility for travellers coming from the north: a train from **Mexicali**, on the U.S. border with Baja California Norte. The train has sleeping cars and makes the run to Los Mochis, where it stops on a siding so the sleeping cars can be added to the Copper Canyon Special, in about 24 hours. In Mexicali, the **Hotel Castel Califia** is satisfactory; the **Holiday Inn**, which is more expensive, is better. This option, not surprisingly, is espe-cially popular with travellers from Southern California, who often go as far as Creel, stay overnight, and take a return train the next day. The first leg of the trip, from Mexicali, is of limited interest, however.)

Most travellers use Los Mochis, a modern agricultural center, as their boarding point. The town was founded in the last century by Albert K. Owen, the same man who pioneered the Chihuahua-Pacific Railroad, and was envi-sioned as a socialistic utopian settlement, grand in scale, noble in purpose. The present reality is different; Los Mochis is a prosperous but unexceptional community. For those who linger here a day or two, there is a small coastal resort beginning to be developed nearby that's enjoyable and holds much promise for the future: Topolibampo offers a pleasant beach, swimming, and boat rentals for fishing. There are no recommendable accommodations, but drinks and snacks are available.

There is no major airport in town, but feeder service is provided by the smaller aircraft of Aero California out of Guadalajara; Tel: (36) 25-6035. The nearest regular airport is in the resort town of Mazatlán; the bus connections from Mazatlán to Los Mochis are also good.

The **Santa Anita** in Los Mochis offers comfortable accommodations at moderate rates. A travel service in the hotel specializes in Copper Canyon excursions.

If you are planning on staying overnight in the canyon, it is *essential* to have confirmed hotel reservations before you step aboard the train. Once en route, your alternatives are limited; hotels are few and there are no roads to take you to the next town if the first one is fully booked.

The train leaves the Los Mochis station at 6:00 A.M. If you have driven, hotels at either end of the line will arrange car storage. You can also have your car shipped from Los Mochis to Chihuahua. (The vehicles do not go on the passenger train but on a freight that follows.) The cost is steep, however: about $250 to transport a compact model.

An alternate boarding point is the town of **El Fuerte**. Founded as a mission in the 16th century, then a vigorous mining town in succeeding centuries, today it is a quaint colonial town located on the Río Fuerte in the middle of good fishing and hunting country. El Fuerte has the **Hotel Posada**, a sister hotel of the Santa Anita in Los Mochis. The train leaves town at 8:00 A.M., and you won't have missed much by avoiding the Los Mochis–El Fuerte leg.

East of El Fuerte the train begins its long ascent into the Sierra Madre Occidental. Soon the fertile coastal plains of Sinaloa give way to a spectacular landscape of cliffs and buckled escarpments carved into a jumble of shapes by millions of years of wind and water. The whole complex is vast, a cluster of canyons of which the Copper is merely the greatest. As you look out the window of your coach or observation car, the average crest you see will be nearly 2,000 meters (6,500 feet). Several will rise to 2,800 meters (9,000 feet) or more, soaring above gorges that drop completely out of sight. The most spectacular contrast of this sort is the upthrust of **Mohinara Mountain**, which towers some 3,700 meters (over 12,000 feet) above the rocky canyon bottom. The canyon floor itself enjoys a semi-tropical climate, while the heights above are often snow covered.

At about 12:30 P.M. you arrive in remote **Bahuichivo**, having crossed the state line into Chihuahua. There is a short stop here for sightseeing; it is also the first possible overnight break in the trip—and a good one. The **Misión Cerocahui**, also part of the Santa Anita operation, offers accommodations, food, guides, and a warm welcome to the back country. Situated in a quiet valley in the middle of inspiring scenery, it has a hacienda atmosphere, and sends a bus to meet the train, a trip of about 30 minutes.

The fertile valley is carpeted with apple and peach orchards, and boasts a gentle climate. In 1690, Juan María de Salvatierra, the first European to see the region, was so enchanted that he established a mission here. Today, Cerocahui offers riding, hunting and fishing, two mines open to the public, a sparkling waterfall, and lofty mountain peaks. In addition, guests can take a motorized excursion down to the lovely Río Urique or visit the mission school, which gives you a chance to meet the shy Tarahumara. The charm of the hotel is further bolstered in the winter months by the pot-bellied stoves that are used to heat it.

From Cerocahui the train climbs through more spectacular country, plunging into tunnels and seeming to fly over bridges. The illusion of flight is powerful when the bridge is narrower than the train and nothing but space is visible between you and a stream hundreds of feet below, but the sensation is beautiful rather than frightening.

Divisadero is the halfway point of the trip, and the view is so overwhelming that a 15- to 30-minute stop is made. The great canyon winds around a big bend in the river here, making it even more dramatic. From a promontory you can see the opposite rim a mile away. Beyond that are still more peaks and mesas. The air is bracing, the whole prospect magnificent.

The **Hotel Cabañas Divisadero-Barrancas** is perched on the very edge of a sheer cliff commanding a view across the canyon and of a pine forest below. The log-and-stone cabins with fireplaces, and the rugged dining room, have an almost ski-chalet-type atmosphere. The hotel is part of the Exelaris Hyatt chain, and fairly expensive. It will arrange trips to Indian villages and into the canyon, as well as to a nearby waterfall.

Creel, a town with a frontier spirit, five and a half hours from Chihuahua, is the next major stop. Situated high in the Tarahumara Mountains, the most forbidding part of the Sierra Madre Occidental, this logging village straddles the track. Nearby, huge stacks of lumber await shipment, scenting the crisp mountain air with an aroma of pine.

Creel is also known as the Indian capital of northern Mexico because of the concentration of Tarahumaras in the region. Roads, most of them quite rough, stretch out to all the major canyons from here, providing access to Tarahumara villages, fantastic rock formations, a remarkable waterfall, mountain lakes, and old Jesuit missions.

The most difficult, yet rewarding, trip from Creel is to **Basaseachic Falls**, which the state of Chihuahua advertises as one of "nature's greatest wonders" (it has another one, of course, in Copper Canyon). Here, the Basaseachic River plunges 1,000 feet into Camdamena Canyon—said to be the highest single-drop waterfall in North America. You can reach this great silver ribbon of water by heading northeast from Creel to Cuauhtémoc, from there by four-wheel drive to Matachic, then southeast to Choncheno, where you can hire pack animals or hike to the falls—all together a trip of five hours one-way.

Another local attraction, but more easily reached from Creel, are the "mushroom rocks" located outside of the Indian village of Basihuare, 38 km (24 miles) from town. There you'll find a huge mountain dotted with outcroppings of rock, some reaching a height of 66 meters (215 feet), that have been eroded by weather and beautifully colored by minerals in pinks and whites, making them seem as if they have "sprouted" from the side of the mountain.

Also nearby, about 20 km (12 miles) from Creel, the Jesuit mission of **Cusárare** remains much as it has since it was founded in the 17th century. The interior, decorated with pigments made by the Tarahumara, is known for its life-size paintings. Abandoned in 1767, the mission was only recently restored to service.

Other points of interest around Creel include the caves of Chomachi; the village of Sisoguichi, with its 16th-century Jesuit mission; and **Lake Arareco**, a marvelous spot for swimming or rainbow trout fishing.

Another highlight of the surrounding area is the village of **Norogachi**, about 77 km (48 miles) from the Creel station. Sunday is fiesta day, when large numbers of Tarahumara dressed in traditional costume congregate here, giving the village a pre-Columbian air. Farther along the same road you'll come to the deep gorges of **Batopilas Canyon**, which boasts the most beautiful of the many canyon floors in the region.

(Creel *can* be reached by a day's ride over rough roads from Chihuahua City, and small aircraft can be landed on a packed-earth landing strip outside of town. Many people from the United States drive to Creel, do some exploring, then take the train to the Pacific coast, having their vehicle shipped after them or stored in Creel to await their return.)

Creel also has a wider range of accommodations than the other stops along the line. The best buy is the **Parador de la Montaña**, a comfortable establishment with private baths and a very good restaurant and bar. The Parador is close to the center of town, just west of the plaza. Across the tracks from the station, the simple **Hotel Nuevo** is clean and pleasant. The owner will be happy to help in arranging trips to the canyons, and knows the best fishing spots in the area. The **Copper Canyon Lodge** is rustic but well equipped; it has stone fireplaces and a pleasing dining room, and also arranges excursions to the many scenic attractions in the region. The Lodge provides bus transportation to and from the station—about a 30-minute drive.

Boarding the train the next afternoon, you'll arrive in **Chihuahua**, a large and thriving city, later that evening. The Cathedral here is a fine 18th-century structure, and there are a number of good museums in town, including a regional museum (in an Art Nouveau mansion) and the Museum of the Revolution, located in the one-time home of Pancho Villa.

There is a wide selection of hotels to choose from, as well, the most luxurious being the **Exelaris Hyatt Chihuahua**. Also in the center of town, and less expensive, is the good if unremarkable **Posada Tierra Blanca**.

Chihuahua offers regular air service to other major cities in Mexico, as well as first-class bus service to a variety of destinations. Aeroméxico is the chief air carrier, with flights to Mexico City. A dozen major bus lines have arrivals and departures at the Camionera Central, which is about a mile northwest of the city's center.

Tickets and Reservations

You need both a ticket and seat reservation for the Copper Canyon train. It is easier to deal through an agent than directly with the railroad. However, information, tickets, and reservations can be obtained from: Jefe, Ferrocarril Chihuahua al Pacífico, Apartado 46, Chihuahua, Chihuahua; or Jefe, Ferrocarril Chihuahua al Pacífico, Los Mochis, Sinaloa.

In Los Mochis, Flamingo Travel Service in the Hotel Santa Anita is helpful. Tel: (681) 2-1213; telex: 53254 HOBAME. In Chihuahua, the travel agency in the Hotel Exelaris Hyatt, Viajes Gulliver, is especially good. Tel: (14) 16-1270; telex: 349618.

Those wishing to take the train from Mexicali should contact: Jefe, Ferrocarriles Nacionales, Mexicali, Baja California Norte. Information is also available from Mexamerica, S.A., Boulevard Benito Juárez, Mexicali 2210; Tel: 6-3455. Travellers from Southern California might want to contact Bananafish Tours, 707 30th Street #6, San Pedro, California 90731. Tel: (213) 548-6841. The fare from Mexicali to Chihuahua, including roomette, is about $150 one-way.

ACCOMMODATIONS REFERENCE

▶ **Hotel Cabañas Divisadero-Barrancas.** POB 661, **Divisadero**, Chihuahua. Tel: 2-3362.

▶ **Hotel Castel Calafia.** Calzada Justo Sierra 1495, **Mexicali**, Baja California Norte 21230. Tel: (656) 8-3311.

▶ **Copper Canyon Lodge.** Creel, Chihuahua. Reservations, Hotel Santa Anita, Box 159, Los Mochis, Sinaloa. Tel: (681) 5-7046.

▶ **Exelaris Hyatt Chihuahua.** Avenida Independencia 500, **Chihuahua City**, Chihuahua 31000. Tel: (141) 6-6000; in the United States and Canada: (800) 228-9000.

▶ **Holiday Inn.** 2220 Boulevard Benito Juárez. **Mexicali.** Baja California Norte. Tel: (656) 6-1300; in the United States and Canada: (800) 465-4329.

▶ **Misión Cerocahui. Cerocahui**, Chihuahua. Tel: (681) 5-7049.

▶ **Hotel Nuevo. Barrancas del Cobre**, Railway Station, **Creel**, Chihuahua Tel: (141) 600-22.

▶ **Parador de la Montaña.** Calle López Mateos 41, **Creel**, Chihuahua. Tel: (145) 6-0085.

▶ **Hotel Posada del Hidalgo.** Hidalgo 101, **El Fuerte**, Sinaloa. Tel: (681) 3-0242.

▶ **Posada Tierra Blanca.** Avenida Independencia and Niños Héroes, **Chihuahua City**, Chihuahua 31000. Tel: (141) 50-000.

▶ **Santa Anita.** Leyva y Hidalgo. **Los Mochis**, Sinaloa. Tel: (681) 5-7046.

THE BAJA CALIFORNIA RESORTS

LOS CABOS

By Susan Wagner

Susan Wagner, the travel editor of Modern Bride *magazine for ten years, has been on the staff of* Travel & Leisure *magazine, has written a guidebook to Acapulco, and is a member of the Society of American Travel Writers. She attended graduate school in Mexico and returns there frequently.*

Baja California is so unusual—and the car trip from one end of it to the other so demanding—that it really calls for its own separate guidebook. We recommend a couple of good ones in the Bibliography. (You would also be smart to write or call the foremost "Baja" bookstore, John Cole's Book Shop, 780 Prospect Street, La Jolla, CA 92037; Tel: (619) 454-4766.)

However, while we do provide some (very limited) background on the peninsula itself, it is for the resorts at Los Cabos, "the Capes," at the southernmost tip of the peninsula, that we provide details. That's because most visitors to these resorts choose to fly rather than drive down the peninsula from California.

The hotels and resorts at Los Cabos are concentrated on a ruggedly beautiful coast that stretches from the town of San José del Cabo, the commercial center of the area, to Cabo San Lucas, the resort-like town to the south and west of it, and this is the area on which we focus our attention.

MAJOR INTEREST

Baja California
Rugged natural beauty
Unusual plants and wildlife
Deep-sea fishing

Los Cabos
Isolated resort hotels
Small-town resort atmosphere in Cabo San Lucas
Natural scenic beauty
Sunsets
Deep-sea fishing
Scuba diving
Sightseeing by boat

Baja California

If you travel the highway that stretches from Tijuana, just over the border from San Diego, south to Cabo San Lucas at the tip of the peninsula, you'll experience 1300 km (800 miles) of rugged, sometimes forbidding terrain that is never less than spectacular and often is heart-stopping. This slender piece of land is only 30 miles wide at its narrowest point and no more than 140 miles at its widest. With the Pacific Ocean to the west and the long, narrow Sea of Cortés (known as the Gulf of California in the United States) to the east, a stunning beach or lovely seascape is never far away. The waters off Cabo San Lucas, where the two meet, are among the world's most fertile fishing grounds. Their junction is marked by a natural arch-shaped rock formation called El Arco; no trip to Cabo is complete without taking a boat out to see it.

People who haven't spent a lot of time here tend to think of Baja as an 800-mile-long cactus garden. It is true that dozens of species—many of which cannot be found anywhere else in the world—flourish here, including 80-foot-high cardons, the world's largest cactus, and the *damiana,* a plant alleged to possess curative and aphrodisiacal properties (and which can be slipped into a margarita). Nevertheless, the Baja peninsula is the kind of place where smart visitors travel with a pair of binoculars at the ready. Around any corner you may come upon sea lions basking on the rocks offshore, gray whales frolicking in a pristine bay, or fish jumping clear of the deep-blue waters.

The indigenous people who lived here before the Conquest were unaware of the highly developed cultures that had flourished on the mainland before the arrival of the Spanish. Hernán Cortés himself came to the peninsula in 1535 and lived here searching for gold and pearls until 1537. In 1847, after the United States had claimed the rest of Alta California as its own, it decided not to acquire Baja because it didn't feel the desolate desert land was worth keeping. In fact, except for the chain of missions built by the Jesuits, Franciscans, and Dominicans during the colonial era, the human imprint on Baja California is of relatively recent vintage.

It all started to change when Baja became a territory in 1931 and a state in 1952. (Baja California Sur became a separate state in 1974.) But until the Benito Juárez Transpeninsular Highway (Mexican Highway 1) opened almost two decades ago, much of this immense desert wilderness remained a dusty, isolated backwater. (Previously, most of the distance to Cabo was unpaved—or nonexistent—and only four-wheel-drive vehicles could make the trip with any reasonable assurance of getting to their destination.) Today Highway 1, though only two lanes, is a smooth ride all the way down. The peninsula is still sparsely populated, however, and its primitive natural beauty is still largely unspoiled. In fact, Baja California is one of the few places in the world that remains unmarred by vast road and rail networks, ports, or power lines. Though pockets of development are growing at the northern and southern ends of the highway, most of Baja is still a paradise for naturalists and a world apart from "civilization" for the rest of us.

Because of its remoteness, visitors should bring plenty of cash or traveller's checks with them, as well as call ahead to ask if hotels can be paid with credit cards. Many fishing charters, meals, car rentals, and hotel accommodations still have to be paid in cash, and patchy phone communications can make it difficult to get credit approval at those places that do accept cards.

Down the Peninsula to Los Cabos

If you have the time to drive the length of the peninsula without hurrying, you are in for long days full of scenic treats.

The trip begins with a bang at Tijuana in Baja California

Norte. The city that gained prominence as a wild and woolly border town still has the bawdy nightlife that first attracted people from north of the border, but it has also cleaned up its act and worked to provide visitors with something to do during the day as well. Today Southern Californians flock across the border as much to shop— and at the same time enjoy a taste of Mexico—as they do to party. Others head farther south and buy condos or "summer homes" in places like Ensenada, about 85 km (50 miles) down the coast from Tijuana, a bayside town that is also a popular port of call for cruise ships.

The rugged part of the Baja peninsula, a vast and for the most part remote area dotted by private airstrips, begins below Ensenada. (The American hunters and fishermen who discovered Baja in the 1940s and 1950s still get here in the same ways they did before Highway 1 was built.)

In the northern part of the state of Baja California Sur (after Highway 1 swings east across the peninsula), Santa Rosalía, Mulegé, and Loreto—where a giant resort catering to tennis players has been built by Fonatur, the government agency in charge of the development of tourism—are all showing signs of becoming popular vacation spots.

La Paz, the capital of Baja Sur, is growing as well, and was the first Baja city to be discovered by the "outside" world after sportsmen and fishermen started coming here over 30 years ago. (The old Los Arcos hotel bar was John Wayne's favorite place to watch the fishing boats come and go.) La Paz is still a sporting paradise, but today one with a few conspicuous touches of the good life thrown in. Its picturesque seaside drive is lined with first-rate restaurants and hotels, including Los Arcos and La Perla for accommodations; and La Paz-Lapa (a Carlos 'n' Charlie's place), Campanario (on the second floor above the town's favorite disco), and L'ecuyen du Roy (a tasteful French restaurant) for food. Of course, fishing is still the main thing on everyone's mind, but for those who like their fish to be filleted and broiled before they see it, excursions to the unpopulated, exquisitely beautiful islands in the Sea of Cortés, such as Espíritu Santo, make for unforgettable days. In addition, Mazatlán, across the Sea of Cortés from the tip of the peninsula, is linked to Baja by overnight car ferry from here. A ferry also connects La Paz with Los Mochis, the gulf terminus of the Copper Canyon train.

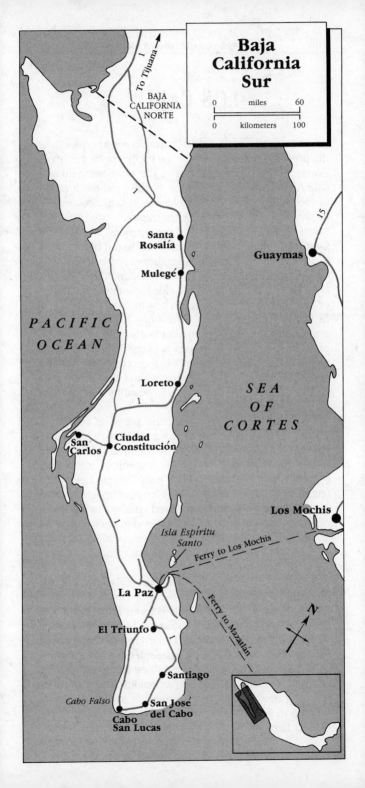

Baja California Sur

| 0 | miles | 60 |
| 0 | kilometers | 100 |

To Tijuana

BAJA CALIFORNIA NORTE

Santa Rosalía

Mulegé

Guaymas

PACIFIC OCEAN

Loreto

SEA OF CORTES

San Carlos

Ciudad Constitución

Los Mochis

Isla Espíritu Santo

Ferry to Los Mochis

La Paz

Ferry to Mazatlán

El Triunfo

N

Santiago

Cabo Falso

San José del Cabo

Cabo San Lucas

LOS CABOS

Los Cabos, the premier Baja California resort area, lies at the tip of the peninsula where the Pacific meets the Sea of Cortés. Here, Highway 1, one of the most beautiful seaside highways anywhere in the world—and the location of most of the area's top-drawer resort facilities—travels 37 km (23 miles) between the region's two principal towns, Cabo San Lucas and, to the northeast, San José del Cabo. Vermilion mountains seem to rise out of the ocean itself, and just behind them endless terra-cotta-colored desert landscapes stretch to the horizon. The visitor to Los Cabos can rent horses and ride for miles in the desert or take solitary strolls on virgin beaches that stretch as far as the eye can see. Rock formations jutting out of the water and a shoreline that is alternately craggy and gentle provide spectacular seascapes at every turn. **El Arco,** an arch-shaped rock formation off the coast, has become one of Mexico's scenic trademarks, and the pink dawns and soft sunsets that bathe it are so beautiful they can take your breath away.

Exquisite beauty lies under the water as well. The waters off Los Cabos are teeming with marine life and provide a gorgeous payoff for scuba divers. In fact, life under these waters is said to be as scenic as it is above. (One of the deep underwater canyons has been protected as a marine refuge.) Hundreds of species of fish can be found here, and sharp-eyed visitors can see many of these species without having to don their scuba or snorkeling gear. In addition, porpoises, whales (between January and March), seals, and sea lions are also common sights in these coastal waters.

Before Highway 1 opened, this part of Baja was accessible only by air or water, and the only hotels were posh fishing "camps" for wealthy fishermen and Hollywood celebrities who could afford to arrive by private plane or yacht. Even today, Los Cabos is the kind of place where fishing charts and boat rental schedules are integral parts of hotel brochures and where fishing fleets and private airstrips are listed among their amenities. In fact, the area has long been known to fishermen as Marlin Alley, and several thousand blue, black, and striped marlin are boated here every year. Swordfish, sailfish, dolphinfish,

tuna, sierra (a large mackerel-like fish), black snook (a warm-water pike), and other species are also among the sportfishing prizes here.

Not surprisingly, life in Los Cabos seems to run on a fisherman's schedule. Everyone gathers around the hotel verandah in the late afternoon to watch the boats come in with their catches and to listen to the day's fishing yarns over drinks. Early-morning fishing trips mean that dinner is generally served early and partying doesn't stretch into the wee hours. Most social life centers around the hotels, but much of the fun here is to dine in hotels other than your own.

The Los Cabos climate is ideal for fishermen and non-fishermen alike. The average annual temperature is 24°C (75°F), with hot days and cool nights (be sure to bring a light sweater or shawl). Some hotels used to close in summer when limited diesel-generated electricity ruled out the use of air conditioners, but today most hotel rooms are air-conditioned and only the Twin Dolphin closes (for the month of September).

Most of the activities in Los Cabos can be found just off Highway 1 between Cabo San Lucas and San José del Cabo, or in either of the two towns. Vast parcels of land lie between the hotels along this stretch, and the properties can't be seen from the highway (most are recessed to avoid "visual" pollution). The area's single drawback is the fact that developers have managed to fence off major portions of these beautiful beaches, all of which are supposed to be open to the public. (The national law making beaches a part of the public domain doesn't seem to apply here.) Access to others is so well disguised that anyone new to the area doesn't stand much of a chance of finding his or her way. Ask at your hotel for directions.

A final word about beaches. Though all are stunningly scenic, not all are good for swimming because of strong undertows. Ask at your hotel before you dive in.

San José del Cabo

San José del Cabo, the location of the Los Cabos airport, is the area's major banking and business center. Though the population of the town is listed as 18,000, looking at it for the first time you'll probably wonder if everyone has "gone fishin'"—which, in all likelihood, they have. Like everything else down here, this quaint little town is spread out. Most of the shops, boutiques, and restaurants, however, can be found on either side of Boulevard Mijares, the main street, or around the town's small plaza.

The tranquil face of San José del Cabo belies its relatively eventful history. The town had its own mission and presidio in colonial times, when Cabo San Lucas was still a village inhabited largely by Pericue Indians. The local priest was slain by marauding Indians, however, who then proceeded to discourage early settlers of the area from staying. Pirates, who plundered Spanish galleons arriving from the Philippines, were another thorn in the side of settlers.

To explore a quieter San José del Cabo today, begin where the gardened Boulevard Mijares meets the plaza and stroll the six blocks to the Town Hall.

La Casa Vieja, Boulevard Mijares 27, one of the nicest shops in town, sells women's resort wear by Josefa and Girasol, as well as a good selection of decorative items. Even if you're not buying, the interior of the old house is worth a stop.

Damiana, hidden away behind the plaza garden, is the most charming restaurant in the area, and also has a more sophisticated touch than most places in Los Cabos. Lunch here is served in a sunny patio, and dinner is served indoors in what was once the main room of this 18th-century structure; the thick adobe walls keep it cool by day, and candlelight makes it romantic at night. Lobster, abalone, and shrimp are the house specialties. Oenophiles also enjoy trying the Baja wines on Damiana's wine list. (The Santo Tomás Winery, located just outside Ensenada in Baja California Norte, produces chenin blanc, Pinot noir, and cabernet sauvignon.)

Tropicana, a sports bar/restaurant popular with the locals, specializes in seafood, which is served in a shaded, breezy room inside or out back in a garden.

Añuití, near the Presidente Hotel on the southwestern edge of town, is pure romance. Looking like a transplanted Florida conch house—short on décor but long on natural beauty—the restaurant perches on the banks of an estuary that is alive with waterfowl and other wildlife. Ask for a table on the screened porch so you don't miss any of the action while you're having lunch. (A tour of the estuary can also be arranged.) At night there is nothing here but candlelight and the sounds of nature. As at almost every other dining establishment at Los Cabos, seafood stars on the menu at Añuití, which is also a popular spot for Sunday brunch.

San José to Cabo San Lucas

The **Presidente Los Cabos,** just outside of town, is the first of about a dozen widely separated resort properties between San José del Cabo and Cabo San Lucas. But the Presidente is the place to stay if you want to be near the commercial district in San José, or if you want to dance. **Cactus,** one of the best discos in town (located in a separate building just outside the hotel's front door), is small but vibrates with energy.

The hotel itself resembles a colonial village. Tiled walkways lace the grounds, and the large pool area is usually the center of activity here. Rooms are medium-sized and comfortable. There is also an 18-hole golf course in the vicinity, and the beach is a short walk away. Guests who like their nightlife a bit more informal than what the hotel has to offer head over to **Barlovento,** a bar in the nearby convention center where a convivial young crowd gathers to drink beer and dance.

The **Hotel Palmilla** has been the darling of knowledgeable resort travellers since the 1950s. Designed and built by the son of a former president of Mexico, it sprawls over 1,000 acres and heads the string of hotels just off the highway to Cabo San Lucas. The rooms and suites are large and comfortable, and most have balconies. (Many also have patios where you can share a scenic breakfast overlooking the ocean; fresh orange juice and warm rolls can be requested along with your wake-up call.) Fluffy robes and giant towels add to the appeal of the large tiled bathrooms.

Guests at the Palmilla often feel as if they are members of a private club. The hotel offers personalized service (there are three employees here for every guest) that makes them feel at home the minute they step in the door (even though there are no telephones or TVs here). Not surprisingly, many return year after year (and a few have even married in the private chapel just up the hill). Tennis and paddle-tennis courts, horseback riding, and croquet are a few of the sports offered on the premises. (A modern scuba-diving operation—already the best in the area—has just been started up by the hotel.) The Palmilla also has its own fishing fleet and its own private airstrip, and its beach is one of the nicest stretches of sand in Los Cabos.

For a perfect vacation in an idyllic setting, the Palmilla has that certain something that other hotels and resorts at Los Cabos lack.

You have to have an eagle eye to find **Da Giorgio's**, a few miles west of the Palmilla. Standing atop a hill on the same side of the highway, this popular restaurant serves up homemade pasta, pizza baked in brick ovens, and a variety of other Italian dishes. Drive out to Da Giorgio's in the daylight if you plan to dine here after dark, however—the sign is small and the turnoff is easy to miss.

The **Cabo San Lucas Hotel**, about five miles farther down the road in the direction of Cabo San Lucas, is sometimes referred to as "El Chileno" because it stands at the head of Chileno Point. Situated on a 2,500-acre estate fronting Chileno Bay and a very pretty beach, this massive hotel facility has the mark of the visiting fishermen who made it famous: Everything is on a grand scale and has a solid he-man look about it. (It also has its own private airstrip.) The rooms and suites are spacious, and some have fireplaces. Of course, everyone gathers in the bar in the late afternoon to sip margaritas and watch the fishing boats come in. The dining room, which overlooks the ocean, is one of the most picturesque in the area. (You'd be wise to stick with the bar; the food leaves a bit to be desired.)

The hotel's own fishing fleet is anchored five minutes away. There is also shooting on the premises. One of the most interesting boutiques in the Los Cabos area is located in the lobby of the hotel and carries a well-chosen selection of exotic treasures and jewelry from the Orient. Be prepared to settle your bill at the Cabo San Lucas with cash or traveller's checks.

As you travel along this stretch of road, stop at the roadside lookout point just before you get to the Twin Dolphin Hotel to watch the surfers.

The posh **Twin Dolphin**, located about halfway between San José del Cabo and Cabo San Lucas, has the look of a businessmen's private sporting club, with an unusual modern architectural style and a surrounding desert landscape and cactus garden that make it unique. Its comfortable rooms and bungalows overlook the ocean, and graceful sculptures dot the property and stand guard over the pool. The bar, with its comfortable leather furniture, paneled walls, and soaring ceilings, resembles an old-fashioned gentlemen's club, and the dining room has a high ceiling that gives it a touch of elegance and formality.

The facilities at the Twin Dolphin are top of the line, and include an 18-hole putting green, two tennis courts that are lit for night play, a fishing fleet of nine boats, and

two miles of marked nature trails. The sophisticated international resort crowd that would just as soon do without nonstop nightlife loves it here. The Twin Dolphin operates on a full American plan and is closed for the month of September. Credit cards and personal checks are not accepted, and the hotel's no-tipping policy makes life even easier (a 15 percent service charge will be added to your bill).

Playa Santa María, next door to the Twin Dolphin, is one of the most beautiful beaches in the world. Although developers have fenced it off to deter visitors, a rugged path that begins behind the hotel's potting shed leads down to it, and the aggravations of the rocky path and its brambles are all but forgotten once you reach the shore. In the distance, mountains tumble into the water at either side of the moon-shaped bay, and the swimming and snorkeling conditions are almost always perfect. Watching the sun set from here is more than memorable. Bring your snorkeling gear, pack a picnic (but be sure to bring your refuse back to the hotel), and make an unforgettable day of it.

The buildings along the highway become more numerous as you approach Cabo San Lucas, and you will find at least half a dozen restaurants scattered on both sides of the main road in the vicinity of the Pemex station at the outskirts of town.

Candido's, on your left as you near town, is a large Cabo San Lucas–style *palapa* with a skylight and adobe walls. Popular with an older crowd of condo-owners from the United States as well as locals, it is known for its meat entrées, including lamb chops, filet mignon, and porterhouse steaks. The tiny bar with comfortable rattan chairs is also a nice spot for an after-dinner drink. Credit cards are not accepted, and the restaurant is closed from June to October.

Cilantro's, on the beach next to the Melía San Lucas, serves up largish portions of nouvelle cuisine with a Mexican flair. Mesquite-broiled lobster, chicken in black-bean sauce, and homemade tortillas are among the specialties here, and the food in general is outstanding; the bar is made from an old boat that washed ashore. At night a band plays sixties music, and the candlelit atmosphere is ideal for romance or conversation with other diners. Lunch is a different matter entirely—you can rent a Hobie Cat, a windsurfing board, or even play volleyball on the beach between courses.

Estela's, up a small hill a block from the beach in front of the Marina Sol condominiums, is a pretty spot to linger over a drink and enjoy the soft breezes. A *palapa* covers the tiny bar and restaurant area, and the menu is not much bigger than a postage stamp. No matter. The beautifully lit cactus garden (with its statue of King Kong) serves as a front lawn and helps give the place a special look and feel. Somehow, Estela's manages to seem upscale and away from it all in spite of the fact that it's just a few minutes off the highway.

If there is truly elegant dining to be found outside of a hotel in Los Cabos, **Alfonso's** is the place. Located in the two-story home of Alfonso Fisher on Calle El Medano, one block from the Melía, everything here, from the food to the décor, bears the special touch of its owner. The menu changes every other night, according to what is fresh or in season, the presentation is impeccable, and the service is first-rate. A typical six-course dinner might include clams vinaigrette, cream of zucchini soup, shrimp cocktail, an entrée, and your choice from a dessert tray— all for $30 (not including wine and tip). And for those who can't tear themselves away, the upstairs rooms with little balconies overlooking a lush garden have been turned into a bed-and-breakfast. Reservations are a must; Tel: 3-0709.

Back on the highway, pandemonium reigns at **Squid Roe**, a two-story Quonset hut decorated with neon on the outside and bizarre memorabilia inside. Find a seat at a picnic table and let the good times roll—everyone will drop by for a drink sooner or later, and the beat goes on almost until the sun comes up.

The **Melía San Lucas**, on Medano Beach right beside Cilantro's, is one of the newest hotels in town—for the moment. The rooms, lobby, and pool area are done up in tropical décor and are especially pretty, and the poolside *palapa*-style restaurant is a lovely place to dine after dark.

The **Hotel Hacienda**, located on a pretty beach at the outskirts of town, is another old Los Cabos favorite. Travellers who aren't looking to spend top dollar and want to be near town like the Hacienda, which is also the only hotel in the area with its own shopping mall. The rooms and suites are simply furnished but comfortable (though in need of a bit of refurbishing), and the beach, where you can do just about any water sport you can think of, is only a few steps away.

Cabo San Lucas

Cabo San Lucas itself is a delight. In the old days, the moneyed crowd that stayed at the posh hotels along the highway rarely saw this little town except from the water. Today new buildings are going up everywhere, the shopping has become first-rate (by Baja California standards), and there's more than enough to see and do.

As is the case in Cabo San Lucas, however, the population of 14,000 doesn't all seem to be home at the same time, though the town does wake up considerably when the cruise ships and ferries glide into its tiny harbor. Even then, however, the one traffic light here—one of only two in the entire area—seems superfluous. At the same time, though everything seems to be scaled down in size, Cabo San Lucas is nonetheless spread out. There is a cluster of small businesses where the road enters town from the northeast; a second cluster of stores and shops up the hill on Avenida Lázaro Cárdenas; and a third concentrated around the harbor.

The **Hotel Mar de Cortez**, located on the edge of the downtown area on Lázaro Cárdenas, is the place to stay if you're looking for economical accommodations in the middle of things. The locals call this clean, no-nonsense establishment the Mar De (pronounced MAR-day), and though its rooms don't offer much in the way of ocean views, it is popular with old-timers and fishermen alike.

Some of the best shopping in Cabo San Lucas is located within easy walking distance of the Mar De. **Zen-Mar**, on Lázaro Cárdenas, is owned by a Oaxaqueno who has original folk-art pieces from his native state made to order. **Mama Eli's**, perhaps the area's best shop for decorative items, is located in a large, newly restored building on the far side of the plaza.

The closest thing to a U.S. style shopping mall in Cabo San Lucas is the **Plaza Candido**, on Lázaro Cárdenas near the Hotel Mar de Cortez. Located in a modern building, it boasts two floors of quality shops, including Maraca, Guess, the Cotton Club, and La Bamba, all of them offering an assortment of resort wear. In addition, **El Porton del Angel**, on the second floor, has a tastefully chosen collection of contemporary decorative items.

Farther along Boulevard Marina, the beach road, in the direction of the Hotel Finisterra, you'll come to the terracotta-colored **Nekri**, one of the best places in Los Cabos

to shop for folk art and decorative items with flair.
Nearby, the **Galería El Dorado** is a contemporary art
gallery that also sells more typical Mexican souvenirs.

The cavernous **Giggling Marlin**, located downtown on
Boulevard Marina, is one of the liveliest restaurants in the
area. Old-timers and those on a budget love it here—and
for good reason. The beer seems to flow from breakfast
on, and once the sun sets there is usually a crowd dancing
under the indoor *palapa*. Elsewhere in the restaurant
there's a stall where a friendly local will help you arrange
for a fishing boat, and a silver shop is open almost around
the clock. The Giggling Marlin is even more informal
than Squid Roe, and the fun goes on till dawn.

Romeo and Julieta, an Italian restaurant located in a
colonial-style home one door down from Boulevard Marina on Subida del Cerro (a sheet that runs through the
residential section of Pedregal), serves up delicious homemade bread and pizzas baked in a brick oven, as well as
some of the best Italian specialties in town.

You'll find another mini-mall with four stores—Sol
Aire is the best, with an assortment of souvenirs, jewelry,
and resort wear—at the corner of Boulevard Marina and
Calle Cabo San Lucas, where Boulevard Marina takes a
sharp turn to the left.

The harbor is where the cruise-ship passengers debark
and from where most of the fishing boats leave. As a
result, it can get quite congested—especially in the early
morning as the fishing fleets prepare to head out for the
day. There is, in addition, an open-air market, or *tanguis,*
spread out here in which you'll find a variety of silver
jewelry, T-shirts, and other stuff for sale. Bargaining is a
must, however—prices for some items will differ as
much as $20 from one stall to the next.

The **Galeon**, a Spanish restaurant overlooking the harbor, features live piano music in the evenings.

The **Hotel Finisterra** (Land's End), high above the ferry
terminal, is another popular golden oldie that appeals
both to tour groups and fishermen alike. Built on various
levels up the hillside (some rooms and public areas are
situated below the lobby), the Finisterra is the place to stay
if you want to be within walking distance of the fishing
boats and town yet still have that feeling of being away
from—or above—it all. Comfortable and moderately
priced, the Finisterra is planning to double its size in the
coming year, adding rooms on the beach, a new lobby,
banquet rooms, and a nightclub, all of which should make

its personalized service, award-winning food, and locally famous bar—don't pass up the opportunity to watch a sunset from here—that much more popular.

The restaurant in the **Faro Viejo Trailer Park** is one of the best-kept secrets in town. That's because while everyone has heard about it, only a handful of locals know how to get there. If you plan on going for dinner, be sure to make a trial run in daylight. The restaurant is located in a residential area behind the entrance to town at the corner of Matamoros and Ildefonso Green, but much of the road is unpaved and some of the potholes in it could swallow a Volkswagen. Your efforts will be rewarded once you get there. The food is good and the oasis-like décor surprisingly pleasant. Lobster and spare ribs are among the house specialties that keep customers coming back.

Nightlife in the Los Cabos Area

Nights in Los Cabos seem to end early, and most nightlife centers around the hotels. There are two discos, however: the **Cactus** in San José del Cabo next to the Presidente Los Cabos and the **Oasis** on the road leading into Cabo San Lucas. A third, tiny, open-air disco can be found near the trailer park in downtown Cabo San Lucas. In addition, both Squid Roe and the Giggling Marlin have live music and dancing till dawn.

Sports in the Los Cabos Area

There are any number of sports options in Los Cabos, but fishing is the top attraction. If your hotel doesn't have its own fleet, here are a few outfits that can arrange anything from a 22-foot *panga* (skiff) to a fully equipped ocean cruiser.

- Los Pices. El Presidente Los Cabos; Tel: 2-0211.
- Fleet Solmar. Hotel Solmar (downtown Cabo San Lucas); Tel: 3-0022.
- Hotel Twin Dolphin. Tel: 3-0140
- Hotel Palmilla. Tel: 2-0583.
- Cortez Aqua Sports. Tel: 3-0506.
- Finisterra Tortuga Fleet. Tel: 3-0000.

Almost all boats leave from the Cabo San Lucas harbor. The price for a group of four for the day will be in the

$250–$350 range, and most hotels will be happy to help you arrange to share.

Canoeing, parasailing, snorkeling, windsurfing, jet skiing, and water skiing are also available. If your hotel doesn't have them, call Cabo Acquadeportes at the Hotel Hacienda, Tel: 3-0117; or see Mike at Cilantro's (next to the Melía San Lucas).

Chileno Bay (the location of the Cabo San Lucas Hotel), Punta Palmilla, and Playa Santa María (next to the Twin Dolphin) are the best places to snorkel. Scuba-diving excursions to see coral beds ranging in color from red to white, underwater caves, and the largest coral reef off the west coast of the Americas can be arranged through Amigos del Mar, Tel: 3-0022; or Buzos del Cabo, Tel: 3-0747. The truly dedicated sometimes rent a boat and fish, scuba dive, and snorkel all in the same day. In addition, the giant waves at Costa Azul Beach, halfway between San José del Cabo and Cabo San Lucas (just before you get to the Twin Dolphin), are perfect for surfing.

Hunting trips for white dove and quail can be arranged through the travel agent at your hotel. Duck and goose shooting is also superb here.

Excursions in the Los Cabos Area

One of the most popular excursions takes you by boat past hundreds of unconcerned sea lions to **El Arco**. Boats leave from the Cabo San Lucas harbor, and a round-trip costs $5.00.

You can also arrange for the boat to leave you at **Playa del Amor**, a sparkling stretch of white sand where you can dip your toes in the Pacific, walk a few hundred yards up the beach, and then dip them in the Sea of Cortés (The boat will pick you up at a prearranged hour.) If it's solitude you seek, however, don't do this on a Sunday or when a cruise ship is in.

Viajes Los Cabos and other travel agencies in the area offer trips to Buena Vista and the **East Cape area**, about an hour and a half north and east of Cabos San Lucas, where you can visit a game refuge, stand at the point where the Tropic of Cancer crosses the peninsula, and see a wide variety of cacti. The trip includes swimming and lunch at the Rancho Buena Vista Hotel, which has bungalows spaced along walkways and a large pool. It also has hot mineral waters, but the spa facilities are not operating as of this writing. Other trips or excursions that can be arranged include the village of Santiago, where there's a small zoo; the old lighthouse at Cabo Falso; the picturesque copper-mining town of El Triunfo; a number of mission churches in the area; and sunset cruises of the bay leaving from the Cabo San Lucas harbor. Contact the travel agent at your hotel to arrange these and similar tours. Most will leave from your hotel lobby.

Finally, the Finisterra, the Palmilla, and a number of other hotels can arrange guided horseback tours of the beaches here—an exhilarating way to enjoy the truly spectacular scenery in Los Cabos.

GETTING AROUND

The easiest way to get to Los Cabos is by plane. (All flights arrive at the San José del Cabo airport.) Aero California flies to Los Cabos from Los Angeles and Tijuana; Aeroméxico from Mexico City; Mexicana from Los Angeles, Denver, Seattle, Mexico City, and Puerto Vallarta; Continental from Los Angeles; and Alaska Airlines from Los Angeles.

For the moment, ferries are not running between Cabo San Lucas and Puerto Vallarta. Ferry service between La Paz and Mazatlán has only recently been reinstituted; as of this writing schedules remain undetermined. The one-way fare for the 16-hour trip will cost in the neighborhood of U.S. $20 (depending on the accommodations you choose). Add another $25 if you take a car.

Once you arrive in San José del Cabo, you can either rent a car or take a taxi to your hotel. If you're going to rent a car, it's best to do so at the airport (Budget, Hertz, and others have desks there), as Cabo San Lucas is about 20 miles distant. A *colectivo,* shared with others, will cost you about $4.00.

Cabs can be called from most hotels, and are usually vans. The average taxi fare between San José del Cabo and Cabo San Lucas, a 30-minute ride, is about $14.00. There is also a taxi stand at the plaza in Cabo San Lucas.

Remember: Baja California Norte is on Pacific Standard Time (the same as Los Angeles and Vancouver), but Baja California Sur is on Mountain Standard Time (the same as Calgary and Denver)—one hour earlier than Mexico City. Be sure to take this into consideration if you have to make a flight connection; airline representatives often forget to do so.

ACCOMMODATIONS REFERENCE

Some hotels at Los Cabos do not accept credit cards. Some have good swimming beaches on the premises, others offer them nearby; check with your travel agent if this is a concern. Most hotel booking offices are located in the United States, as it takes about two weeks for a letter to reach Los Cabos. The rate ranges given here are projections for December 1989 through Easter 1990. Unless otherwise indicated, rates are for double rooms, double occupancy. The telephone area code for Los Cabos is 684.

San José del Cabo

▶ **Hotel Palmilla.** 4577 Viewridge Avenue, San Diego, CA 92123. U.S. $200–$260. Tel: 800-854-2608 in the United States; in Canada: 800-854-6742.

▶ **Presidente Los Cabos.** Boulevard Mijares 2, P.O. Box 2, San José del Cabo, Baja California Sur, Mexico 22340. U.S. $105–$120. Tel: 2-0038; in the United States and Canada: 800-325-5000.

Cabo San Lucas

▶ **Cabo San Lucas Hotel.** P.O. Box 48088, Los Angeles, CA 90048. U.S. $80–140. Tel: 3-0123; in the United States: 800-421-0777; in Canada: (213) 205-0055.

▶ **Hotel Finisterra.** Baja Hotel Reservations, 4332 Katella Avenue, Los Alamitos, CA 90720. U.S. $85–$95. Tel: 3-0000; in the United States: 800-347-2252; in Canada: (213) 598-1381.

▶ **Hotel Hacienda.** P.O. Box 48872, Los Angeles, CA 90048. U.S. $38.50. Tel: 800-421-0645 in the United States; in Canada: (213) 205-0015.

▶ **Hotel Mar de Cortez.** P.O. Box 1827, Monterey, CA 93942. U.S. $23–$31. Tel: 3-0032; in the United States and Canada: (408) 375-4755.

▶ **Melía San Lucas.** Playa El Medano, Cabo San Lucas, Baja California Sur, Mexico 22340. U.S. $150–$170 (not including a 15 percent surtax and 10 percent service charge). Tel: 3-1000.

▶ **Twin Dolphin.** 1625 West Olympic Boulevard, Suite 1005, Los Angeles, CA 90015. U.S. $100. Tel: 800-421-8925 in the United States; in Canada: (213) 386-3940.

THE PACIFIC RESORTS

By Susan Wagner

Some of the world's most sophisticated and glamorous resorts, as well as some of its most scenic, are to be found on Mexico's Pacific coast. A combination of summer-like temperatures year-round, plenty of sunshine, broad sandy beaches, and lively nightlife has made these resorts, collectively, the country's major drawing card for international travellers. While those travellers who want to combine a bit of archaeology with their sun, sea, and sand tend to congregate in the Caribbean resorts of the Yucatán peninsula, and sportsmen/sybarites who relish being surrounded by all the comforts of home head for Los Cabos at the tip of the Baja peninsula, the international traveller looking for a mix of sun and fun, bustling activity and peaceful serenity is drawn to the exciting string of resorts that dot the Pacific coast from Mazatlán down to Huatulco. And though the personality of each of these resorts differs from those of its sister resorts, they do share one thing in common: Almost everything a visitor will want to see or do is located on or just off the coast road that runs through town.

We cover the Pacific resorts in geographical order, from Mazatlán in the north to Huatulco in the south. For those thinking about driving to one or more of these spots, Highway 15 heads south from Nogales on the U.S. border and passes through Mazatlán on its way to Tepic, in the state of Nayarit, where Highway 200 becomes the principal coastal route, linking the rest of the Pacific resorts all the way down to the Guatemalan border.

Mazatlán is the resort for those who put an emphasis on sports and would rather not worry about dressing up or doing anything too fancy. It's a hodgepodge of things to see and do, and although they're all here, you have to find them. If you want to arrange for a fishing charter boat or a windsurfing lesson, go to the Hotel El Cid's sports center on the beach; if you just want to lie on a beach with plenty of company, head for the beach in front of the Playa Mazatlán or the Costa de Oro; if you like beaches that are a bit more quiet, put on your best bathing suit and head for the Camino Real Hotel; and if you don't want to see *anybody,* just travel north and pick your spot. Hunters, fishermen, and surfers like Mazatlán because it's the kind of resort that makes no demands.

Puerto Vallarta is perhaps the quintessential Pacific resort, combining the outgoing friendliness of a small town with first-rate amenities. It's a favorite with discriminating travellers from the West Coast who are used to beautiful beaches and enjoy strolling around the town and dining in its charming restaurants. The shopping is terrific as well; some of the resort wear for sale here is made by local designers, and new malls are springing up everywhere. In addition, a sprawling new marina complex has added an extra touch of glamour to the town that Taylor and Burton first put on the map.

Popular with affluent young couples from Mexico as well as abroad, beautiful, remote **Careyes** is a resort where you probably won't leave the premises. The resort's horseshoe-shaped hotel sprawls around the pretty little beach, and just about every water sport you can think of is available here. The complex, which includes the hotel, several restaurants, condos, and a number of private homes, was built by a European, and Italian design touches are evident in its sleek facilities.

Tenacatita, a huge complex hidden away at the end of a winding road off the coastal highway to the south of Careyes, is another resort hotel on a small bay. It's a modern, comfortable place, ideal for those who wish to spend a few lazy days on a flat, sandy beach in the middle of nowhere.

Barre de Navidad, a few miles farther down the coast in the direction of Manzanillo, is a grown-up fishing village that has retained some of its charm in spite of the fact that, for the moment at any rate, it is stuck somewhere between what it once was and what it might yet become.

Manzanillo, due west of Mexico City, is a resort where

your choice of hotel will determine what kind of vacation you have. Elegant, Moorish-style Las Hadas (where much of the movie "*10*" was filmed) sits high on a hill like the regal dowager she is. Affluent travellers from around the world who want to unwind in a self-contained resort far from the madding crowd return here year after year. Other, less formal resorts line the road leading into town. Be forewarned, however: nightlife and shopping are not the chief attractions of Manzanillo.

Ixtapa/Zihuatanejo, on the long stretch of coast between Manzanillo and Acapulco (but closer to the latter), is a laid-back version of Acapulco. With its "Hotel Row"— a string of soaring high-rise structures lining Palmar Bay, one of the most gentle bodies of water in the country— Ixtapa is also a modern mega-resort in the making. Zihuatanejo, one bay to the south, is an old fishing village where those who prefer a more casual atmosphere come to vacation. In this friendly and charming little town (about four miles from Ixtapa over a paved road) you never have to wear anything more than cutoffs, a T-shirt, and sandals.

Acapulco is the queen of Mexican resorts, and as such is one of the world's most famous playgrounds, as well as one of Mexico's largest cities. The Las Brisas residential section in particular is a haven for sophisticated pleasure-seekers, movie stars, statesmen, and just plain folks who like to relax by day and party by night in the sprawling private villas overlooking the bay. Elsewhere in town, the wide variety of restaurants and glittering shopping malls is hard to beat in any resort anywhere, as is the colorful array of discos.

Puerto Escondido and **Puerto Angel**, east of Acapulco and south of Oaxaca City, are slated for further development, but for the moment they are mostly visited by youngsters on a budget and hearty fishermen and retirees who arrive in their RVs and don't need glasses for their beer. Still, the fishing and surfing *are* great, and both towns boast beautiful beaches that are ideal for swimming. Neon lights and TV, on the other hand, are especially scarce.

Finally, **Huatulco**, with its nine glorious bays, is the newest star on Mexico's resort map and is being developed by Fonatur, the all-powerful government tourism agency, in much the same manner as Cancún and Ixtapa were before it. As of this writing, there's a beautiful Club Med here; a Sheraton that is only partially completed; and another hotel that promises to be ready for the 1989–1990 season (we'll wait and see). Shopping and dining outside the hotels hasn't been developed as yet, but the fresh air and exquisite scenery more than make up for the lack of citified pleasures.

MAZATLAN

Mazatlán, on the Pacific coast due east of Los Cabos, is unique among Mexican resorts. For one thing, it's closer to the United States than any other major Mexican resort (and closer to Texas than it is to Acapulco). At the same time, it's a muscular, macho-looking place—but one with a soft side. The perimeter of the seaport area is rough-and-ready, and the town itself is no-nonsense and busy. In this guise Mazatlán is a tropical port for beer drinkers of all ages.

Most visitors don't see this commercial side. Nevertheless, Mazatlán is one of Mexico's leading ports (it's the largest seaport between San Diego and the west coast of Panama), and is the home port for the country's biggest shrimp fleet—as a glance at any restaurant menu in town will reveal. Fortuitously situated at the mouth of the Sea of Cortés, it is also considered the deep-sea fishing capital of the mainland (over 5,000 billfish are boated here every year, some of them world records), and is home to one of the country's largest breweries, Pacífico. Finally, it is one of the few Mexican resorts on the national rail network.

In spite of its commercial importance, however, Mazatlán has that other, softer side, which manifests itself as a carefree, informal attitude in both its dress and manners. It's the kind of place where mariachis will strike up the band in a parking lot (or anywhere else that moves them, for that matter) and people will start to dance on the sand; where you can take your surfboard on a bus; live in cutoffs; and go to bed early and not miss much. In February it's also the scene of one of the best *carnavales* in the country. Rodeos, masked balls, fireworks, and parades are all part of the merriment as Mazatlán turns topsy-turvy for a week. (But be sure to reserve early if you want to join in the fun.)

A visitor's typical daily schedule here revolves around sports and the great outdoors. In fact, Mazatlán was one of the first Mexican resorts to attract visitors in substantial numbers—and has been successful at keeping them coming back—because there *is* so much of everything for everybody, including space (with almost 30 miles of beaches in the area). Among the many activities offered here, duck, pheasant, and dove shooting are especially good (the season runs concurrently with the high tourist season, December–March, with another month on either side), and it is also one of the few Mexican resorts to allow surfing. In fact, surfing is Mazatlán's ace in the hole, and the beach at Los Pinos, in front of the old Spanish fort, is known in surfing circles as "The Cannon."

MAJOR INTEREST
Zona Dorada resort-hotel area
Deep-sea fishing
Hunting
Surfing

The less-than-eventful history of Mazatlán—which in Nahuatl means "Place of the Deer"—is in keeping with its laid-back personality. In the decades following the Conquest, the Spanish garrison in the area was stationed 15 miles away at Villa Unión, and Mazatlán itself was used merely as a sentinel post. In the 19th century the troops of Napoléon III were based not here but at Malpica, a few miles away, and gold and silver were mined at towns farther inland such as Rosarío, Copala, and Pánuco. In fact, the first municipal government here wasn't established until 1837.

But it was an event out of the Keystone Kops that finally put Mazatlán on history's map. In 1914, during the Mexican Revolution, General Venustiano Carranza's forces set out to destroy the fort on top of Icebox Hill (*Cerro de la Nevería*) with a homemade bomb fashioned from dynamite, stones, and nails packed in pigskin. Instead, the pilot overflew the target and the airsick bombardier dropped his charge on a downtown street—thereby earning Mazatlán the questionable distinction of being the second city in the world to be aerially bombed.

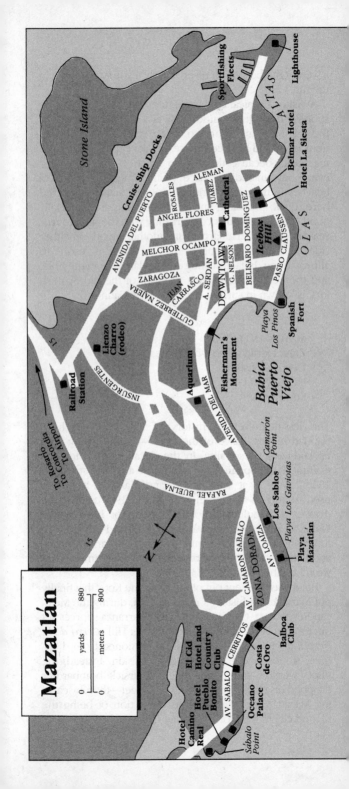

It wasn't until the 1950s, however, when it was discovered by deep-sea sportfishermen, that Mazatlán truly came into its own. Happily, the emphasis on the outdoor sporting life has prevailed ever since.

Together, the hard-working city and good-time resort cover much of a 15-mile-long peninsula. Most visitors to Mazatlán congregate along the coastal strip that stretches from the old lighthouse on the southern tip of the peninsula to the new condominiums in back of the beaches to the north. The center of action, however, is located on the strip of high rises between Valentino's Disco on Camarón (Shrimp) Point and the posh, private Balboa Club to the north—the Zona Dorada, or "Golden Zone." From here, the strip of popular seaside hotels that extends north to the Hotel Camino Real at Sábalo Point is also hot. And the area on the other side of the tiny bridge north of the Camino Real is slated for development as well; in fact, a number of condominiums are already up, and more are under construction.

All of this is relatively spread out in comparison with most Mexican resorts. As a result, the beaches in front of the Zona Dorada have a fresh-air feel about them. And, as is the case in all of Mexico's resorts, everything you'll need is on or just off the beach road, which here is called Avenida del Mar south of Camarón Point, changes its name to Avenida Camarón Sábalo north of the point, and becomes Avenida Sábalo Cerritos north of the Zona Dorada.

Olas Atlas, at the far southern end of town just before the old lighthouse (the second-tallest in the world after Gibraltar's), is where the fishing fleet is berthed. The seaside Belmar and La Siesta hotels here, the first tourist accommodations in Mazatlán, are still popular with budget travellers as well as with fishermen who want to be near the fleet.

El Centro, Mazatlán's downtown area (and a busy one by Mexican resort standards), is inland from Olas Atlas and south of the Fisherman's Monument, which faces the Bahía Puerto Viejo on Avenida del Mar and has become the city's most famous landmark.

The curving strip of coast that follows Avenida del Mar north from the old Spanish fort to Camarón Point—the beginning of the Zona Dorada—was the resort-strip successor to Olas Atlas. Now itself eclipsed by the Zona

Dorada and points north, it still boasts a variety of restaurants and other places of interest to visitors.

We begin with the older parts of town.

Olas Atlas

This is where, in the 1940s, it all began. Back then, celebrities such as Ernest Hemingway and Katharine Hepburn would watch the sun set into the Pacific from their rooms at the Hotel Belmar as their fans back in the States wondered where they had disappeared to. The fishing fleets were just a lengthy cast away, and nothing but empty beaches, beaches, and more beaches spread out to the north. The **Hotel La Siesta**, another establishment with lots of charm, was located on the waterfront nearby. Today both of these hotels are funky in an old-fashioned way—though La Siesta is the more picturesque of the two—and remain popular with an older crowd of budget travellers. These are *not* what anyone nowadays thinks of as resort hotels, however. La Siesta, at Olas Atlas 11, has a pleasant outdoor restaurant shaded by soaring palms and a big paneled bar where fishermen gather to drink Pacífico from the local brewery. The beach is just across the road.

Otherwise, this part of town is of little interest to anyone except fishermen and those who have come to eat at the one-and-only **Shrimp Bucket**, the flagship restaurant of the ever-popular Carlos 'n' Charlie's chain. Local businessmen, fishermen, and tourists alike flock to this place, especially at lunchtime, and the portions of meat, fish, and poultry are large—as are the drinks. No one comes here for a *quick* bite to eat, however: El Shrimp Bucket is all about animated conversation and hearty, drawn-out meals. For non-fishermen who want to watch the sunset and see the day's catch on display, it's also a great place to stop in for a drink before heading out to the pier. (And you can pick up a fisherman's box lunch here every morning at 6:00 A.M.) The Shrimp Bucket is also located in the Hotel La Siesta.

While you're in the neighborhood, drive or take a taxi to the top of Icebox Hill for panoramic views of the entire city. Originally a military observation point, the hill got its name in the days before electric refrigeration, when local fishermen would store their catches in ice-filled caves in its side.

Downtown

The Centro, or downtown, district, north of the Olas Atlas neighborhood, is only for the curious—at least until a giant restoration project is completed. (The restoration that already has been completed, however, has added immeasurable charm to what had been an area of interest to residents only.) The municipal market at the corner of Avenida Juárez and Calle Ocampo sells predictable Mexican souvenirs that can be bought elsewhere in less time than it takes to bargain for them here. The Angela Peralta Opera House, on Calle Carnaval, was built in the 19th century and has recently been restored, but there's little to see unless a performance is taking place. The new Museo de la Ciudad, which recounts the history of Mazatlán, is housed in an old building a half block up from Olas Atlas. The giant late-19th-century Cathedral on the *zócalo* is cool and imposing but of relatively recent vintage. Taking time to explore this part of the city during the day, therefore, should be weighed against the loss of equivalent beach, sun, or fishing time. Combining a sunset stroll with dinner in one of the downtown restaurants is much the better alternative.

Located in one of the few colonial homes in Mazatlán, **Casa de Tony**, at Mariano Escobedo 111, near the Hotel La Siesta, is at the top of the list if it's gracious, refined dining you're looking for. The menu features Continental cuisine, with a variety of meat and seafood dishes, and the courtyard with fountain makes for an especially romantic change of pace. Reservations are advised; Tel: 5-1262.

La Negra, hidden away at Calzada G. Najera 220, is a tiny family-run place and one of the city's best-kept dining secrets. A favorite with locals, it's the kind of cozy, reliable restaurant that makes everyone feel at home, and to which, sooner or later, everyone goes. Seafood is the specialty here, and La Negra is open for dinner only.

From the Spanish Fort to Camarón Point

The coastal strip along the Bahía Puerto Viejo was the site of the first true resort action in Mazatlán. Today it's the location of the main airline offices, the aquarium, and several popular restaurants. (Mazatlán dines earlier than other resorts, by the way. Prime time for lunch is between

1:30 and 2:00; dinner is usually eaten between 8:30 and 9:00.)

El Marinero, a plain, family-style seafood place near the Mexicana Airlines office, looks more like someone's home than a restaurant, and caters to those who like quality in their food but don't want to pay extra for ambience or décor. Occasionally it offers live entertainment (usually mariachis). Local businessmen have been coming here for years.

Everyone who comes to Mazatlán soon hears about **Señor Frog's,** on Avenida del Mar, but not everybody tries it. Maybe that's because you have to be in a party mood to enjoy this place to its fullest. Cruise-ship passengers, some direct from the ship, arrive revved up and ready, and many stay right through lunch and into dinner. Forget about having a quiet conversation or sparking a little romance on most nights in season—and don't come at all unless you're prepared for a raucous, rowdy time. And whatever you do, don't wear your best white shirt or dress; the waiters here sometimes like to play games with Spanish wine *porrónes.* If you don't know how to open your throat when they "shoot" from high above your head, the wine will end up running down the front of whatever you're wearing—all in the spirit of good fun, of course.

El Patio, near the Fisherman's Monument, is also informal and lively, though the decibel level is noticeably lower than at Señor Frog's. It does a variety of seafood, meat, and chicken dishes well, and also includes a few Mexican dishes on its menu. Diners so inclined can watch the disc jockey at work selecting the soothing old-time dinner music.

The Mazatlán Aquarium, one long block east of Avenida del Mar on Avenida de los Deportes (turn off just before Rolf's Restaurant), offers those who don't scuba dive a look at the marine life that inhabits the waters around Mazatlán. A film on the history of the town is shown in the adjacent auditorium. The small garden and zoo outside are also worth the time it takes to stroll through them.

Valentino's Disco, at Camarón Point, is a pretty, long-time favorite with locals and tourists alike, and has a nice view of the ocean in addition to its lively nightlife.

The Zona Dorada

The "Golden Zone," an oval-shaped sliver of land bordered by Avenida Camarón Sábalo to the east and Avenida

Rodolfo T. Loaiza to the west, is the heart of Mazatlán's modern resort district, as well as the site of the most popular beach in town.

Los Sábalos, a gleaming white stucco hotel on the beach at the southern end of the zone, is surrounded by a bright green carpet of grass, and its arched windows, clay tennis courts, health club, geometrically shaped pool, and beach club give this medium-sized resort an edge over its competitors. In addition, the hotel's beachside restaurant, **Joe's Oyster Bar**, is one of the best places in town to have a beer and watch the sunset. Kick off your shoes, order a Pacífico, and get ready for the Big Show.

The **Playa Mazatlán**, a sprawling complex with more than 400 rooms (most with balconies), is farther north along the beach from Los Sábalos and is considered to be one of the top hotels in town. Although it has its own shopping mall, the main reason for its popularity is its strategic location: The beach out front, the Playa Los Gaviotas, is the best in town. The hotel's Mexican Fiesta Night, also the best in town, ends in a shower of fireworks.

Shopping should not be the main reason you come to Mazatlán. Most places feature quantity rather than quality and cater to a beer-drinking crowd that likes to take home crazy shorts and T-shirts. The handful of shops and boutiques that do offer a tasteful selection of items are for the most part located in or near the Zona Dorada on Rodolfo Loaiza or Camarón Sábalo. (The siesta is observed by these shops between 2:00 and 4:00 P.M.)

The **Mazatlán Arts and Crafts Center**, on Rodolfo Loaiza across from the Los Arcos motel, is a small colonial-style brick mall with over 20 shops. The shoe shop upstairs and outside sometimes carries crazy huaraches in bright colors. Just inside the main entrance, the **Boutique Nueva** has a particularly good selection of resort wear and accessories to match, and the shop under the stairs at the back offers an excellent selection of folk art from around the country. **Tequila Charlie's**, in the mall's patio, is a friendly, informal place where shoppers can stop for a light meal or quick snack; occasional folkloric performances and other shows are also part of the appeal of this place.

The **Mercado Viejo**, at Rodolfo Loaiza 303, across the street from the Playa Mazatlán's front door, is not a market, even though it looks like one. Colonial-style arches lead into this shop's spacious showroom, which is chock-a-block with attractive ceramic pieces from Tlaquepaque, near Guadalajara. Painted figurines and lacquerware are also good buys here.

Casa Roberto, in the Playa Mazatlán mall, has some real antiques among its many excellent copies. Their collection of decorative items is also different from and better than that found in most other shops in town. **Designers' Bazaar**, across the street and a few doors to the south, has two floors of attractive resort wear as well as a number of whimsical sculptures by Sergio Bustamante.

Sea Shell City, Rodolfo Loaiza 407, is a sight in itself. This two-story structure filled with nothing but seashells is as kitschy as kitsch gets—just about anything you can think of that can be made from shells is lurking somewhere on the premises. In fact, Sea Shell City is so bad it's good. (Don't miss the seashell curtains on the second floor.)

Mr. Indio, Rodolfo Loaiza 311, is the modern steel-and-glass antithesis of Sea Shell City. A branch of the first tasteful handicraft shop in town, it carries attractive brass, copper, and silver decorative items and jewelry, all of which are beautifully displayed.

Casa Loma, located six blocks from the Balboa Club at Avenida Gaviotas 104, is a few minutes' taxi ride north of the Zona Dorada. With its plush red velvet and dark wood, this small restaurant in a frame house is an anachronism, both in appearance as well as personality. The popularity of the Casa Loma's Italian specialties has been tested over a dozen years, and the people are still coming back. (The place is so popular, in fact, that the owners can afford to close it from June to October.) Casa Loma is for people who like to eat early, however: Closing time is 10:00 P.M. Tel: 3-5398.

From the Balboa Club
North to the Camino Real

The Balboa Club, a private club with lovely screened rooms overlooking the beach at the northern end of the Zona Dorada, is an upscale oasis for yuppies of all ages. (A letter of introduction from a member will get you a room.)

The **Costa de Oro**, a large, modern, first-class hotel, is also located on this pretty stretch of beach. The Costa de Oro has two swimming pools, two restaurants, a bar, and tennis courts.

The **Restaurant Tlaquepaque**, across the beach road, is an unusual dining establishment, with its own pool where you can swim up to the bar for a drink between courses of a traditional Mexican meal.

El Cid Hotel and Country Club, about a quarter of a mile north of the Balboa Club, is the undisputed king of Mazatlán resorts as far as size and facilities are concerned. With over 600 rooms (making it one of Mexico's largest resort hotels) on both sides of Avenida Camarón Sábalo, the beach road, it is a center of action with a tranquil façade. The 18-hole championship golf course is right outside the front door, and El Cid also has Mazatlán's best tennis and water-sports facilities. Inside this huge complex you'll find a bunch of restaurants and bars, a nightclub, squash and racquetball courts, and a health club. The Super Duck, a water taxi, makes the run from the beach in front of the hotel to nearby Los Venados (Deer) Island every two hours; the trip takes about 20 minutes. For a day of sun in primitive, secluded surroundings there, complete with a pretty beach and tide pools, pack (or rent) your snorkeling gear, pack a picnic, and hop aboard.

The **Caracol Tango Palace** disco in the Hotel El Cid is one of the hottest spots in Mazatlán for dancing and staying up late. Built in a three-tiered, circular shape that gives the place its name ("The Snail"), this multi-million-dollar extravaganza looks like a set for "Miami Vice." The clientele is mostly affluent young trendsetters, but anyone is welcome so long as they dress the part: no shorts or cutoffs here.

The restaurant in the **Los Arcos** motel, across the beach road from the Holiday Inn, is popular with both visitors and locals. Mouth-watering marlin tacos, a great shrimp *ceviche,* and a Mexican décor with antiques from the old mining town of Concordia keep packing them in under the big *palapa* here.

The **Oceano Palace,** up the beach road a bit, is a friendly place favored by the 20–30-year-old crowd. And if they're not staying here, they seem to end up spending the day around the bar and swimming pool. The grounds here are smaller and the hotel offers less in the way of frills than some of the others in town, but it is simpatico throughout.

The **Hotel Pueblo Bonito,** the next hotel up the beach and next door to the Camino Real, looks like a terra-cotta-colored colonial village. Everything about it is right, especially the location. The rooms here are tastefully decorated, and all have an ocean view, direct-dial telephones, color television, and fully equipped kitchenettes.

The deluxe **Camino Real** hotel stands apart from the other resort hotels in Mazatlán on its own promontory, Sábalo Point, overlooking the ocean at the northern end of the resort action. The extra few minutes it takes to get downtown are compensated for by myriad features: You can wake up to birdsong and fall asleep to the sound of waves; it has its own tiny beach where swimming conditions are almost always perfect; and the atmosphere here is relaxing, thanks to the absence of itinerant vendors and gaggles of people watching the parasailers. Though the rooms are just average, clean and standard-sized, the public areas in the Camino Real are outstanding. The attractive lobby bar is lively and especially good for watching the sunset.

It is unusual for a relatively small hotel like the Camino Real to have not one but two restaurants that rate so highly with the locals. The more formal of the two, **Lafitte**, on the second floor, is considered to be one of the finest restaurants in town, and the candlelit dining room with French touches is truly elegant. The superb service makes the excellent food here taste even better. **Chiquita Banana**, a few steps up from the beach, is a lively place to lunch and an informal yet charming place to dine to the sound of waves and soft live music at night. Although the restaurant is under a *palapa* and open to the night air, it somehow manages to be chic as well as sensual, with the atmosphere of a private beach club.

Few restaurants in town are as romantic as **Señor Pepper's Supper Club**, across the beach road from the Camino Real. The candlelight and lace, polished wood and brass, and soft jazz music make it perfect for intimate conversation, and dining here never fails to put you in a mellow mood.

Sports in Mazatlán

Mazatlán is made for sportsmen. Almost every hotel has a water-sports center, and most will be happy to arrange everything. If yours doesn't, or won't, go to El Cid Hotel; theirs is right on the beach.

Mazatlán is the deep-sea fishing capital of the mainland, and the odds of catching Something Big here are stacked in the fisherman's favor. Striped marlin season runs from December–April; black marlin, May–June; sailfish, May–November. Tuna, dorado, bonita, yellowtail, sea bass, and a host of others can be caught year-round. Boats can be rented at most hotels. (The size of the boat will determine the cost.)

Scuba-diving and snorkeling excursions can be arranged at your hotel. Los Venados Island, just off the beach from the Playa Mazatlán and El Cid hotels, about a 20-minute ride by water taxi, is one of the best places in the area for both activities, but you'll have to rent your equipment before you get out there.

Parasail rides are available on Los Gaviotas Beach in front of the Playa Mazatlán.

Tennis players congregate at the Camino Real, Los Sábalos, and El Cid hotels.

There are two golf courses in Mazatlán. The Casa Club at El Cid is an 18-hole championship course that winds right through the main hotel zone. The Campestre Club, 20 minutes away on Highway 15 in the direction of the airport, is a nine-hole course.

Horses can be rented in Los Gaviotas, a residential neighborhood five minutes by taxi from the hotel zone. The stables are near the Casa Loma restaurant.

As we noted, this is one of the only resorts in the country that permits surfing on town beaches. The waves are best at Los Pinos, on Paseo Claussen north of the fort, or in front of Valentino's Disco.

Charreadas, Mexican rodeos, are staged at Lienzo Charro on Avenida Insurgentes, near the bus station; watch for announcements around town.

Excursions from Mazatlán

Anyone who likes getting out of a resort and into the countryside for a change of pace has a number of destinations around Mazatlán to choose from.

The "country tour" offered by most hotels includes three of the most picturesque villages in the area. **Concordia,** an hour to the east, is centuries away in feeling. The town, which is over 400 years old, is today a crafts center where leather goods, wooden furniture, pottery, and tiles are made.

Copala, northeast of Concordia on Highway 40, is an old mining town with cobblestone streets and a history that dates back to 1571. You can get steeped in the past here while dining in one of the tiny restaurants in town such as **The Butter Company** or **Daniel's.**

Villa Blanca, which is beyond Copala on the same road, looks like a Swiss village transplanted to the foothills of the Sierra Madre.

Allow a full day for a tour of all three places.

Rosarío, southeast of Mazatlán on Highway 15, was founded in 1655 and is another of the mining towns where Mexico's silver wealth was dug from the ground. (Ironically, its cathedral has a splendid altar made of gold.) Stops along the way include the thermal springs at Aguacaliente and at Villa Presidio, the first settlement in the area.

Touring the **Teacapán Lagoon**, farther south of Mazatlán, is an unforgettable experience. This long, narrow body of water stretching along the coast for nearly 100 km (60 miles) has been likened to the Amazon because of the vegetation that grows along its banks. The tour includes stops at the thermal springs of Aguacaliente and the old mining town of Rosarío. There is also a break for lunch on a primitive beach lined with palms where you can go beachcombing and swimming. Allow eight hours for the tour.

Still farther south, the unspoiled swamps around **San Blas**, in the state of Nayarit, are laced with mangroves and freshwater springs that bubble into the sea, and the whole area is a haven for naturalists and bird watchers. Boat tours of this tropical wilderness wind through a network of natural canals that lead deep into the jungle, and the waters are clear and teeming with fish. The trip includes a stop in the picturesque port town of San Blas itself, with its 400-year-old fort. Set aside a full day for this tour.

Both tours are offered by Marlin Tours (Tel: 3-5301) and Deerland Tours (Tel: 2-6385). Most hotels in Mazatlán will also be able to arrange them for you.

The Marlin and Deerland outfits will also be happy to arrange trips out to either **Chivos** (Goat), **Pájaros** (Parrot), or **Stone** island for a day of sunning and swimming. (Pájaros Island is just off the beach in front of the Oceano Palace hotel; Stone Island is a 20-minute boat ride from the cruise-ship pier.) Have your hotel pack a lunch and ask the boatman to come back for you at an appointed hour. You can also catch the water taxi to these islands from the beach in front of El Cid.

Finally, you can take a cruise of the bay on the motor yacht *Fiesta*. Cruises leave daily at 11:00 A.M. from the pier near the lighthouse, and tickets can be purchased from any hotel travel agent as well as at their office at José María Canizales 5.

GETTING AROUND

Mexicana offers direct service to Mazatlán from Seattle (daily), San Francisco (daily), Denver (four times a week), Los Angeles (daily), and Dallas-Fort Worth (four times a week). Aeroméxico flies direct to Mazatlán from Tucson (daily, with stops in Hermosillo and Los Mochis). And Continental flies direct to Mazatlán from Houston (five times a week). Other major U.S. carriers will be happy to connect you with one of these flights. It's a four-hour flight from Seattle; two and a half hours from Los Angeles and Houston; and eight hours from New York (with a connection). The connecting flight from Mexico City to Mazatlán (which usually involves an overnight stay) is an hour and a half.

The Rafael Buelna Airport is about a half-hour's ride from the hotel zone, and you'll find a number of car-rental agencies there, Hertz, National, and Avis among them. *Colectivos* are the only other option. If that's the way you decide to go, bite the bullet and be patient as yours drops other passengers off along the way.

Mazatlán, as we've already noted, is one of the few Mexican resorts you can reach by rail. Trains leave daily from Nogales and Mexicali on the U.S. border, with connections to Guadalajara and Mexico City. The *Tren Bala,* or "Bullet Train," leaves Mexicali at 9:30 A.M. every morning and arrives in Mazatlán at 8:20 A.M. the next day. There's an hour layover north of Hermosillo in the afternoon as you wait for the train from Nogales; then the two trains combined continue on their way to Mazatlán and, at the end of the line, Guadalajara. There is café and bar service on the train, and for a little extra passengers can reserve a sleeper with its own bathroom. The one-way fare to Mazatlán, depending on your choice of sleeping arrangements, will run between $25–$35.

Tres Estrellas de Oro offers express air-conditioned bus service to Mazatlán from either Mexicali or Tijuana (four times daily from the latter). The trip takes approximately 26 hours, and the one-way first-class fare is about $35.

If you plan on driving, you'll probably enter Mexico at Nogales and head south on Highway 15 through Guaymas and Culiacán. Ferry service linking Mazatlán with La Paz, 380 km (235 miles) to the west on the Baja peninsula, has been reinstituted recently, but schedules remain undetermined as of this writing. The cost for the 16-hour over-night trip across the Sea of Cortés varies according to the accommodations you select; cabins for two or four are available, and a one-way ticket will cost you in the neighborhood of $20. Add an additional $25 if you take your car (depending on size).

Once you're in Mazatlán, getting around is a breeze. With the exception of the Zona Dorada, most hotels in a given part of town are within walking distance of each other. Taxi rates are slightly higher here than in other resorts in Mexico, however, and there are no meters (rates are set by zone), so check the rate before you get in. (Most hotels will post the going rates on a placard outside the lobby.) If your destination is not a well-known landmark, call before you go and get the name of the nearest one.

Another option is to hop aboard a *pulmonia*—or "pneumonia," as the locals call them, because they are open to the air—the jaunty little golf cart–like contraptions. These charge about one-third to one-half less than taxis, but be sure to check the rate before boarding nevertheless (again, there are no meters). Allow more time if you decide to go this route, and don't forget to bring a scarf if it's a windy day.

Mazatlán is also one of the few Mexican resorts where it's easy to get around by bus. Yellow buses can be flagged down along Avenida del Mar and Camarón Sábalo, but not all go all the way downtown. Watch the signs on the front of the bus: "Centro" buses go downtown; "Sábalo-Cerritos" buses operate in the hotel zone (*zona hotelera*) only. Gray buses travel the same routes, and the fare is a few centavos less, but the ride is less comfortable. On both types of buses, pull the cord for your stop.

Mazatlán is on Mountain Standard Time (the same as Denver and Calgary), which is one hour earlier than Mexico City.

ACCOMMODATIONS REFERENCE
The rate changes given here are projections in U.S. dollars for December 1989 through Easter 1990. Unless otherwise indicated, rates are for double rooms, double occupancy. The telephone area code for Mazatlán is 678.

▶ **Camino Real**. P.O. Box 538, Mazatlán, Sinaloa, Mexico 82110. U.S. $92–$124. Tel: 3-1111; in the United States and Canada: 800-228-3000.

▶ **El Cid.** P.O. Box 813, Mazatlán, Sinaloa, Mexico 82110. U.S. \$105–\$115. Tel: 3-3333; in the United States: 800-525-1925; in Canada: 800-344-0293.

▶ **Costa de Oro.** P.O. Box 130, Mazatlán, Sinaloa, Mexico 82110. U.S. \$40–\$50. Tel: 3-2005.

▶ **Oceano Palace.** P.O. Box 41, Mazatlán, Sinaloa, Mexico 82110. U.S. \$50–\$70. Tel: 3-0666.

▶ **Playa Mazatlán.** P.O. Box 207, Mazatlán, Sinaloa, Mexico 82110. U.S. \$60–\$70. Tel: 3-1120; in the United States: 800-222-4466; in Canada: (213) 228-5588.

▶ **Pueblo Bonito.** P.O. Box 6, Mazatlán, Sinaloa, Mexico 82110. U.S. \$95–\$115. Tel: 4-3700; in the United States: 800-262-4500; in Canada: 800-654-5543.

▶ **Los Sábalos.** P.O. Box 944, Mazatlán, Sinaloa, Mexico 82110. U.S. \$76–\$85. Tel: 3-5333.

▶ **La Siesta.** Olas Atlas 11, Mazatlán, Sinaloa, Mexico 82110. U.S. \$20. Tel: 12-3344.

PUERTO VALLARTA

Puerto Vallarta, on the Pacific coast due west of Guadalajara, looks like a movie set: Sprawling white stucco houses with red-tiled roofs, bougainvillaea spilling over their walls, are stacked on a hillside overlooking the ocean. The tiny, compact town, complete with a bandstand and seaside promenade, is nestled at its base. To the west, the perfect Pacific sunset, with palm trees silhouetted against an orange-pink sky, happens just about every evening out over the Bahía de Banderas, Mexico's largest natural bay.

Puerto Vallarta, or "P.V.," has been the darling of the California crowd ever since Taylor and Burton made headlines here in the early 1960s during filming of *The Night of the Iguana.* People from the West Coast and elsewhere love the easygoing way of life, which rarely requires getting dressed up, and though there are plenty of sophisticated facilities in and around town, Puerto Vallarta remains less citified than some of her sisters on Mexico's Pacific Coast.

Like most Mexican resorts, P.V. has a coast road that threads its way into, through, and out of town past dramatically scenic cliffs, beaches, and rock formations. And while Guadalajara is only 380 km (240 miles) to the east, *tapatíos* (as Guadalajarans call themselves) have several Pacific playgrounds to choose from and, therefore, are not overly concentrated here. As a result, much of the land south of town and vast stretches beyond Nuevo Vallarta, a hotel/condo complex 13 km (8 miles) north of town, are still relatively undeveloped and promise to remain so for at least a few more years.

MAJOR INTEREST

Small old town with cobblestone streets
Restaurant row
Bahía de Banderas sunsets viewed from hillsides
   or cliffs
Shopping
Jungle restaurants
Horseback riding along the beaches
Boat trips to isolated beaches

Unlike many of the resorts on the Pacific coast, Puerto Vallarta did not start out as a fishing village in the 1500s. Founded in 1851, P.V. is, in fact, a relative youngster—by Mexican standards. It remained unknown to the outside world until the 1950s, when Mexicana Airlines began to offer regularly scheduled flights into town. In the 1960s, after Highway 200, which linked it to the rest of the country, was inaugurated, Puerto Vallarta became even better known.

The influx of Americans and Canadians began in earnest after Burton and Taylor catapulted Puerto Vallarta into international fame. By the end of the decade, one area overlooking the Río Cuale—which divides the town into northern and southern halves—was even nicknamed "Gringo Gulch," in recognition of the many vacation homes that had been built by foreigners there. Today clusters of condos and time-sharing units are going up on either side of the river and, as a result, vacationers and sometime residents are more widely dispersed than they were in the old days.

At the same time, condo shills are P.V.'s one flaw. Tucked away in doorways and alleys along the major streets in town, they usually lure passersby with the promise of a free meal or complimentary sightseeing excursions. Don't fall for this unless you're in the market. Even if they do make good on their promises chances are that you'll waste valuable sun time inspecting the property.

Getting around Puerto Vallarta couldn't be easier. Everything is built around the Bahía de Banderas, which extends as far as Punta de Mita to the north and Cabo Corrientes to the south. The greatest concentration of hotels and two marinas are found north of the Río Cuale, toward the airport. The major shops and restaurants as well as a few small hotels are located downtown. Just beyond the Playa de los Muertos (or Beach of the Dead), the town beach south of the river, the coast road begins to climb. Three major hotels—the Camino Real and Garza Blanca, on the beach, and the Coral Grand above the beach (you get to the water via an elevator)—as well as numerous condominiums line the road all the way to Mismaloya Beach and beyond. Unique jungle restaurants are situated off the road and up the hill to the east of Mismaloya, where *The Night of the Iguana* was filmed and where a new hotel is now under construction.

You can walk safely anywhere in town, but rubber-soled shoes are a must: hard, leather soles slip on the cobblestone streets and smooth sidewalks. Bring a flashlight with you as well if you plan on venturing into town at night: the curbs in P.V. are unusually high and hard to see in the dark. Streetlights, when they exist, are dim.

From the Airport to Town

These days, this is the hottest area in Puerto Vallarta. Almost all the major hotels, most of the major shopping malls, and a good many of the largest construction sites are spread out along this stretch of Highway 200, which here is called the Carretera al Aeropuerto and which runs from the airport to Avenida México, just north of the center of town. New places to stay, shop, and dine are springing up like mushrooms along the road, among them Christine's, P.V.'s most opulent disco; Bogart's, its most outrageous restaurant (both in the Krystal Vallarta); the Plaza Caracol and Plaza Marina, two of its biggest shopping complexes; and the Villa Vallarta Mall, one of the town's best places to shop.

A giant new complex, the Marina Vallarta, with 442 acres and two miles of beachfront some five minutes (by taxi) south of the airport, is well underway along this stretch. (This chic new marina should not be confused with the marina and ferry terminal a few miles farther down the road in the direction of town. The latter is where the local fishing boats dock and charter fishing boats can be arranged. If you're taking a taxi from the airport, specify the Marina *Vallarta*.) The Plaza Marina shopping mall mentioned above is already off and running, and new Hyatt and Marriott hotels are under construction nearby. A golf course is also under construction here, which should make the golfers who now have to drive or take a taxi 25 km (15 miles) to the Flamingo course north of town happy. When the Marina Vallarta is completed it will also have tennis facilities and a beach club.

To get a feel for how it will all look when it's completed, stop for lunch at **Las Palomas Dorado**. A branch of one of the town's most popular downtown restaurants, Las Palomas is far from noisy traffic and has a certain chic look to it. Customers can choose between the air-conditioned bistro-like atmosphere inside or head out to the umbrella-shaded tables overlooking the marina outside. Salads and light entrées are the bill of fare here, and the private yachts moored nearby will allow you to imagine, if only for the duration of your meal, that you're a part of the international yachting scene. **Galería Uno**, the best art gallery in town and a Puerto Vallarta landmark, also has a branch in the marina mall.

The **Krystal Vallarta**, about ten minutes south of the airport on the airport road, one of the prettiest hotels in P.V., is favored by a fairly upscale clientele. This complex, built by the Gershenson family and run by them as the "Posada Vallarta," was taken over by the Krystal chain after the elder Gershenson's death. The solid construction, tasteful layout, and beautiful decorative touches here are proof that superb craftsmanship exists in this world—even if wealthy individual owners seem to be the only ones who will still spring for it.

From the outside the Krystal Vallarta looks like a colonial village. Suites and villas (the latter perfect for families) border beautiful gardens and are linked by cobblestone streets. The beach—where swimming conditions are nearly always perfect—is just a few steps away. (Puerto Vallarta, by the way, is one of the few resorts that allows horseback riding on its beaches. Horses can be rented a short distance from the hotel. If you're lucky, you might even catch a crazy game of donkey polo.) Non-guests can enjoy poolside dining al fresco at the Krystal, which is also a tranquil place to lunch—except on the days when a cruise ship is in (cruise-ship passengers who don't head for town tend to congregate here). Finally, Mexican Fiesta nights are sensational in this lovely setting—catch one if you can. They are held once a week, usually on Tuesdays, and include traditional music, colorful folk dances, rope tricks, and typical Mexican food.

Christine's, P.V.'s best disco (see Nightlife below), and **Bogart's**, a lavish restaurant, are part of this complex. Bogart's is a dress-up kind of place filled with fountains, shimmering mirrors, peacock chairs, and plants. The Continental cuisine is complemented by a number of Moroccan specialties, and soft piano music provides a romantic atmosphere for your meal. Reservations recommended; Tel: 2-1459.

The **Fiesta Americana Condesa Vallarta**, farther south on the airport road in the direction of town, is popular with group travellers. The soaring seven-story lobby with its *palapa*-style roof immediately puts guests in a party mood, and the free-form pool is so big that there's an island in the middle of it. Better yet, every room has a view of the bay (and the Puerto Vallarta sunsets), and just about any water sport you can think of can be arranged on the beach in front of the hotel.

Farther to the south, the **Plaza Las Glorias**, midway between the airport and town on the airport road, is a horseshoe-shaped hotel complex arranged around a palm-shaded pool. The rooms overlooking the pool area are spacious and especially nice, and the poolside bar and dining area is a charming oasis when the noontime sun gets too hot.

The sprawling **Plaza Vallarta Beach and Tennis Resort**, next door, home of a John Newcombe Tennis Center, is the best tennis/hotel facility in town. Although most guests come with groups, it is surprisingly easy for non-guests to get court time. Three of the seven courts are under a roof, so you can play all day, and some are lighted for night play.

The **Villa Vallarta Mall**, a few steps away in the same complex as the Plaza Las Glorias and Plaza Vallarta, makes for a pleasant shopping experience. Fiorucci and Mar y Mar, two of the best boutiques for women's resort wear in town, are here, as are Gucci and Cartier. In addition, just about any toilet article or sundry can be found at the air-conditioned supermarket on the street side of the mall. The **Place Vendôme**, P.V.'s most popular French restaurant, is located just outside the door. Reservations are needed; Tel: 2-4448, ext. 150.

Just beyond the mall, Avenida México, which is lined with hotels, branches off from the airport road and heads into town. Most of the hotels along this stretch are set back from the road so that their "front doors" are right on the beach, and the beach they share is one of the best in town.

The **Buenaventura** is a little jewel of a hotel within easy walking distance of town. Everything about it is compact, clean, and efficient—yet the Buenaventura has a big-time-resort look and feel about it. The pool area is located on the other side of a small bridge in a palm-shaded garden, and the hotel remains popular with Mexican business-men and European visitors, who go for its harmonious mix of atmosphere and proximity to town—a bit of every-thing for those who like to be near the action.

The neighborhood between the Buenaventura and town along Avenida México has an unhurried feel to it that eases visitors into the hustle and bustle of the con-gested downtown area. **Alfarería Tlaquepaque**, at the cor-ner of Avenida México and República de Chile, looks as if it's an old garage but is in fact one of the last old souvenir shops in Puerto Vallarta. Anyone who likes looking for typical old-fashioned ceramic or glass souvenirs will love poking around this place. Christmas is a particularly good season to browse for decorations and unusual crèche figurines. Take a Handiwipe to clean your hands with after you've finished shopping, however; it would be impossible for anyone to keep this profusion of merchan-dise free of dust.

The North Side

Roughly speaking, the downtown north side (meaning north of the Río Cuale) encompasses the area from the point where Avenida México hits the cobblestones and turns into Paseo Díaz Ordaz, the seaside drive, to the river. Paseo Díaz Ordaz, the streets parallel to it—Mo-relos and Juárez—and the side streets between Calle 31 de Octubre and Calle Galeana constitute the main down-town shopping and dining area. The downtown area from Calle Galeana to the river also has some upscale shops and restaurants, but is largely commercial. This is where you'll find most of the airline offices and banks, as well as the open-air souvenir market. Much of the north side is tough on the ears and the feet. Its streets are too narrow for the number of vehicles using them and the cobblestones don't make for comfortable walking. Still, no one seems to care.

Restaurant Row, which begins at Calle 31 de Octubre and extends along Paseo Díaz Ordaz to what was once the Oceano Hotel, at the corner of Calle Galeana, is one of the most popular areas in town to shop, dine, and people watch. Popular restaurants in this neighborhood include such old favorites as La Cebolla, Roja, Il Mangiare, and Monte Carlo. It's not hard to make a choice; just look in their windows until you find the one that seems right. In addition, Aca Joe, Ruben Torres, Guess, and Express are just a few of the popular boutiques along this busy stretch. (Because many of the better designers and artisans in the country have homes here, Puerto Vallarta merchandise generally has a unique look.)

The big star on the north side, however, is **Carlos O'Brian's Pawn Shop and Restaurant**. Merrymakers of all ages often begin their evenings in the restaurant here and end them in the bar, where the décor runs to old photographs recalling the Mexican Revolution and crazy memorabilia hanging from the ceiling. To describe this place as "action-packed" would be an understatement. The "action" is amazing (maybe one of your shoes wrapped in potato tinfoil and placed on your plate) and the "packed" is a fact—every night. Chances are good that there'll be a line at the door any time after 8:00 P.M., but the wait is worth it. Carlos O'Brian's captures the spirit of Puerto Vallarta as no other place does.

Las Palomas, on the corner of Díaz Ordaz and Calle Aldama, is open all day. Painted pink and decorated in colonial style, and open to the street and bay, it's a local favorite. (Try to wangle a table near the window in the bar; it's one of the best places in town to watch the sunset.) The small dining room on the other side of the bar is lit by candles at night, and simple Mexican meat and fish dishes are featured. The quality of the meal here often depends on the mood of the chef, but the strategic location couldn't be better for those who like to people watch. (There is another branch of the restaurant in the Marina Vallarta north of town.)

Sunsets in Puerto Vallarta are an event that shouldn't be missed. Purists like to watch them from places like El Set in the Hotel Conchas Chinas out on the highway south of town; Le Kliff, even farther out at Boca de Tomatlán; or Chez Elena in the Cuatro Vientos Hotel on the hill above Restaurant Row. Those who just want to enjoy the view without the benefit of food and drink can plop down on a bench along the seaside promenade, or *malecón*.

Chez Elena, Matamoras 520, a friendly, old-fashioned kind of place, is also one of P.V.'s most sophisticated restaurants. The Continental cuisine here is served in an air-conditioned dining room, and after dinner you can drift upstairs to a club that offers dancing and a show. Chez Elena is the place to go downtown when you want to get away from the crowds and enjoy the view. Reservations are advisable; Tel: 2-0161.

The former Oceano Hotel, at the corner of Paseo Díaz Ordaz and Calle Galeana, and across the street from the statue of a boy riding a seahorse—Puerto Vallarta's best-known landmark—is where everyone used to meet before it began to be turned into condominiums. Though its lobby bar is long gone, the colonial-style restaurant is still intact. Simple Mexican dishes and Continental cuisine are served in an informal atmosphere, and live music accompanies dinner in the evenings. Reasonable prices and its vantage point overlooking the street make it one of the best places in town to have breakfast or lunch—as well as to get a feeling for what the old days in P.V. were like. The new name of the restaurant is **Tequila**, but it will be a long time before anyone calls it anything other than the Oceano.

Some of the most interesting shops in town are located on Morelos and Juárez, the first two streets up from and running parallel to Díaz Ordaz.

Galería Uno, at Morelos 561, is one of the finest art galleries in the country. Owned by Jan Lavender, an American who has made Puerto Vallarta her home, it sells paintings and sculptures by Latin American artists for serious collectors. Visitors from throughout the world congregate here to see works by the likes of Manuel Lepe, Miguel Angel Rios, and Colunga, and it is safe to say that every celebrity who comes to town passes through here at least once. (There is another branch of the gallery at the Marina Vallarta.) The Galería Uno print and poster gallery is in the Plaza Malecón at the corner of Paseo Díaz Ordaz and Calle 31 de Octubre.

Retin A users can find the Mexican-made version of the cream at **Farmacia Vallarta**, which is nearby on Morelos. The price is one-fifth of what it goes for in the United States or Canada.

St. Valentin, down the street at Morelos 574, is one of the best shops in town for decorative items and offers bowls, platters, and other original tableware (along with whimsical folk art) from Oaxaca. Don't let the unimpressive façade deceive you; the collection here is quite extensive. **Villa Maria**, at Juárez 449 B, also has an exceptionally good selection of decorative and gift items.

Vallarta Mia, one of the most original boutiques in town, is on the south side of Aldama between Díaz Ordaz and Morelos. (There's no name on the door, and the narrow entrance is a few steps up from the sidewalk, so it's hard to find.) Necklaces and bracelets made from what look like the painted rubber rings of jelly jars, silver conch belts in all sizes, and other avant-garde accessories are some of the items for sale here.

Suneson's, Morelos 593, carries pieces by the famous Taxco silversmiths Los Castillo in addition to a wide selection of other top-quality silver jewelry, and is one of the best such shops in town.

The market at the corner of Calle A. Rodríguez and Morelos, near the New Bridge, offers a plethora of typical Mexican souvenirs. Take time to bargain; it will be worth it, even if the vendors are fairly sure you can't find it elsewhere.

The Bridges

Downtown Puerto Vallarta is divided into a north side and a south side by the Río Cuale, which is crossed by two narrow bridges. Locals call the one nearest to the bay the "New Bridge," and it's open to one-way traffic heading south. The "Old Bridge," three blocks to the east, carries traffic going north toward the airport.

The **Paseo Río Cuale** meanders through the parklike Isla Río Cuale under both bridges. If you have to go from one bridge to the other this is the place to do it. (Access to the little island is provided by a short staircase at either bridge.) The lush foliage down here also makes it the perfect spot to cool off on a hot day. The noises of the traffic above are subdued, and shoppers can browse to their hearts' content in the stalls and boutiques that line the promenade.

Le Bistro, one of Puerto Vallarta's most enjoyable restaurants, is located at the river's edge on the Isla Río Cuale near the Old Bridge. Popular with affluent tourists and locals alike, the enameled walls and black-and-white floors give this place a sleek California look. Soft candlelight at night, an imaginative menu, stylish service, and soft jazz music in the background make Le Bistro a must at least once during your visit. Reservations are necessary; Tel: 2-0283.

The South Side

The part of town south of the bridges to the Restaurant El Dorado has a slightly slower pace than the areas north of the bridges, and there seems to be less of everything here—except fun.

The **Molino de Agua**, where an atmosphere of Old World charm prevails, is a pretty hotel on the beach, perfect for those who don't like to stay in high-rises. Bungalows and rooms surround a garden, with a walkway leading to the beach.

A new seaside promenade links the end of the New Bridge with **La Palapa**, a rustic open-air restaurant on the Playa de los Muertos, the town beach. The promenade has a good view of the small hotels bordering the beach, and the ten-minute stroll to the restaurant is pleasant and interesting.

A number of good boutiques and galleries line the streets that run perpendicular to the promenade. One of the best is **Modas Delia**, Ignacio L. Vallarta 277, whose specialty is white cotton resort wear characterized by its beautiful thread work and embroidery.

Many locals claim that **Los Angeles**, a tiny restaurant hidden away in the Suites Rogers at the corner of Ignacio Vallarta and Basilio Badillo, serves up the best breakfasts in town. Home-style pancakes and waffles are its specialty (the recipe for the pancake batter is so secret that only the owners know it), along with huevos rancheros, chilaquiles, and other standard Mexican breakfast fare. Los Angeles also offers light lunches and dinners.

Daiquiri Dick's, on the promenade overlooking the bay at Olas Altas 264, was one of the first restaurants to become popular in P.V. More recently it's been taken over by a young California couple who appreciate good food and have managed to create a refined atmosphere at one of the most desirable locations in town. It's the kind of place where you linger over your meal and try to soak up the ambience of an evening that you'll long remember. Seafood and meat dishes with a light California touch are the specialties, and you can either eat outside a few steps from the bay or under a roof set farther back from the promenade. No matter which you choose, however, Dick's will have a breeze when other places in town don't.

The **Playa de los Muertos**, which was (unsuccessfully) renamed the Playa del Sol a few years ago, is congested with sunbathers and vendors. You can rent a Sunfish or an inner tube here, or simply opt for a *palapa* and chair and watch the parade go by. Be forewarned, however: Mariachis may strike up the band at a moment's notice, and the place goes crazy on weekends.

El Dorado restaurant is the last stop as you head south along the Playa de los Muertos. Though everything about it leaves something to be desired, the overall experience of eating in such a friendly place more than makes up for that. The chicken soup here is the best, and the hamburgers and grilled fish specials are also local favorites. The laid-back ambience is often undermined by the vendors who stroll in and out (as does the house cat), and everyone seems to check in sooner or later to check it out.

The Highway to Mismaloya and Beyond

The coast road (Highway 200) begins to climb beyond the Playa de los Muertos as it heads in the direction of two major hotels: the Camino Real and the Garza Blanca. Both are perfect for those who don't mind being away from the hustle and bustle of town, and though they are worlds apart in atmosphere, each offers the ultimate in privacy and comfort.

The **Camino Real** is about ten minutes south of town by taxi but seems to be even farther, in part because there are no other hotels nearby. The beach out front seems endless, and swimming conditions are ideal. The trademark modern architecture of the Camino Real chain—in this case a stylish arc-shaped building with thick adobe-style walls and arches—and the lush vegetation surrounding the place make this hotel even more appealing to an upscale clientele of all ages.

El Set, a funky, rustic-looking place in the Hotel Conchas Chinas between town and the Camino Real, is one of the best places in the Puerto Vallarta area to have a light meal and watch the sunset.

Many repeat visitors consider the **Garza Blanca**, which is just off the highway, about a five-minute ride beyond the

Camino Real, the crème de la crème of resort hotels in Puerto Vallarta. The screened-in apartment-like bungalows, each with a spacious sitting room and separate bedroom, face an exceptionally beautiful beach and crystal-clear (if somewhat shallow) water, and lying in the sun with your favorite book or strolling the flower-lined paths that crisscross the grounds is the order of the day here. For those looking for an even more exclusive setting, the hotel's property rambles up the hill and across the beach road to a cluster of villas, some of which have private pools. The Garza Blanca's attractive dining room overlooking the beach and bay is open to non-guests.

Farther south along the beach road the only points of interest are condos and a few restaurants. The **Coral Grand Hotel dining room** along here, for example, is considered to be one of the town's finest, with tasteful décor, exquisite table settings, and a lovely view of the ocean. Frequented by discriminating locals and visitors alike, the Coral Grand is for those looking for good food served in a quiet, refined, air-conditioned setting. Dinner is accompanied by soft piano music, and on weekends there is dancing at the bar outside.

Sitting high atop a cliff overlooking Boca de Tomatlán, where the Río Tomatlán empties into the bay, **Le Kliff**, on the bay side of the road, is aptly named. Tablecloths and candlelight make this open-air restaurant a somewhat more elegant spot for romance than some of its neighbors in this area, and the views of the sunset are truly out of this world.

Chee Chee's, half a mile south of Le Kliff and just before Mismaloya Beach (where *The Night of the Iguana* was filmed), is a Polynesian-style "jungle" restaurant. A steep, winding bamboo staircase leads down through the overgrown hillside to the restaurant and then continues on down to a swimming pool and a dock extending into the bay. Women guests here often feel as if they should be wearing a Dorothy Lamour-type sarong, and the staircase, while a boon for photographers, with a breathtaking vista around every corner, is not for the weak of heart: People of all ages find themselves huffing and puffing on the way back up.

Mismaloya, the locale that put P.V. on the map, is just before Boca de Tomatlán, and these days is the site of a huge hotel/condo complex under construction. While you can almost drive down onto the beach, for now it's best to settle for the views from the coast road.

Jungle Restaurants

Puerto Vallarta offers an exotic dining experience that few other resorts can match: jungle restaurants. There are several south of town where you can combine a day of sunning, swimming in a rushing river, and strolling through the lush vegetation with a good meal (lunch only). **Chico's Paradise** was the first one on the scene and still offers a bit more than the rest, including a woman who demonstrates how to make tortillas and a couple of tiny gift shops. The Río Tomatlán is down the hill from the restaurant, but it sometimes disappears completely during the dry season.

Chino's, at the end of a bamboo bridge spanning the Tomatlán, is the best bet. They make a special drink here that will slow you right down, while dedicated sunbathers often climb the boulders in the river to tan.

Eden is the most remote and primitive of these jungle restaurants. Signpost boulders painted with serpents and apples lead you up one of the most winding roads you'll ever travel. It is open only during the high season, however (the road is washed out during the rest of the year).

Most of the hotels will be happy to arrange outings to these restaurants (going in a group will add to the fun), or you can drive on your own (look for the small signs along the coast highway past the Camino Real). If you decide to take a taxi (about 50 minutes to Eden), ask the driver to return at an appointed time. (Chico's and Chino's often have taxis waiting out front.) Once you get there, be very careful about walking around; the rocks in the river are slippery and it's an understatement to say that adequate safety measures have not been taken. A meal at any one of these places, however, is an unforgettable experience.

Nightlife in Puerto Vallarta

Puerto Vallarta nights are mellow, and you never have to get dressed up in anything more than jeans and a T-shirt unless you go to one of the more formal restaurants or to Christine's disco in the Krystal Vallarta.

The discos here are smaller and less flamboyant, with fewer videos and gimmicks, than those at other resorts, but they're no less fun. **Christine's** is currently number one, with laser lights, a sound system, and other features that surpass those of her sisters in Ixtapa and Cancún.

Capriccio, up the hill overlooking the Playa de los Muertos, is the former number one. Most disco devotees drop into both during the course of an evening, however.

If you just want a drink and quick dance you can go instead to **Ciro's** on Restaurant Row. Most of the major hotels north of town also offer live music in their bars.

Sports in Puerto Vallarta

Just about every water sport can be found here, along with two things that you won't find at most other resorts: donkey polo and hunting.

Scuba-diving and snorkeling equipment can be rented in town or at most hotel beaches. Once you get it, head for Yelapa and Los Arcos in the south, or Punta de Mita in the north. Any of these excursions can be arranged at the beach or at **Paradise Divers**, 443 Olas Altas; **Divers de México** on Díaz Ordaz near Carlos O'Brian's; or at the **Dive Shop**, Díaz Ordaz 186.

Deep-sea fishing in the waters off Puerto Vallarta is also good. November to May are the months to catch sailfish, marlin, rooster fish, red snapper, snook, sea bass, tuna, and bonito. You can rent a boat through a travel agent, across from the Hotel Rosita downtown, or at the marina and ferry terminal (*terminal marítima*). Fresh-water fishing excursions to the Canyon de Peña Reservoir, 113 km (70 miles) south of Puerto Vallarta, can also be arranged. If your hotel doesn't have a travel agent head downtown or to the Krystal Vallarta.

Riding horses along the beach is a treat that cannot be found in many other resorts; horses can be rented on the major beaches north of town.

Hunting excursions for wild boar, wild turkey, duck, dove, quail, and pheasant can be arranged through Aventuras Agraz; Tel: 2-2969.

Until the new golf course at the Marina Vallarta is finished, the only course in the area is Los Flamingos, an 18-hole championship course that meanders around the inlets of a beautiful lagoon, located some 13 km (8 miles) north of the airport.

Most hotels in P.V. have tennis courts. If yours doesn't, head over to the the Plaza Vallarta, with its John Newcombe Tennis Center, north of town.

Sports buffs from the States who find themselves missing a daily diet of televised sports should check out El

Torito Bar & Restaurant, Avenida Nicolás Bravo 29; pick up a calendar of games to be broadcast at the door.

Excursions from Puerto Vallarta

There are a number of excursions available for those who want to get away from the getaway in Puerto Vallarta. The following sailboat cruises leave from the old marina and ferry terminal north of town.

The *Serape* or the 60-foot *Vagabundo* will take you on a beautiful day trip south along the coastline to **Yelapa**, a cluster of open-air buildings on a beach where you can sun, swim, or take a guided walk to a jungle waterfall that cascades 150 feet into a crystal-clear pool (the latter is for the hearty traveller only). A number of ramshackle *palapa*-style restaurants on the beach here serve snacks and fresh seafood.

The trimaran *Bora Bora* cruises to **Las Animas**, another beautiful beach south of Boca de Tomatlán, and one that is accessible by water only. Fishing en route and snorkeling once you get there are part of the fun.

The trimaran *Cielito Lindo* takes vistors to **Huancaxtle**, north of P.V. in the state of Nayarit, a primitive fishing village fronted by a deserted beach where you can sun, fish, and sail.

The catamaran *Shamballa* sails to Quimixto Beach, which is located between Las Animas and Yelapa.

There is also a day trip available to **Rincón de Guayabitos**, a primitive beach in the state of Nayarit. The tour includes lunch, stops at small villages, and an exhibition of Huichol Indian art that mostly consists of whimsical "paintings" woven out of concentric circles of fine yarn.

GETTING AROUND

The following airlines service Puerto Vallarta's Gustavo Díaz Ordaz International Airport from the United States: American (connecting in Dallas), Continental (connecting in Houston), Aeroméxico (connecting in Mexico City), and Mexicana (connecting in Dallas; one daily nonstop from Chicago). As of this writing Alaska Airlines offers direct service to Puerto Vallarta from its hubs on the West Coast.

Private taxis are not permitted to carry passengers from the airport into town. Your best bet are the combis (vans), which charge about $3.00 for the trip from the airport to the hotels on the beaches north of town. If business is slow, you can pay a little extra (about $4.00) to have the van to yourself. Buy your tickets at the counter at the airport before boarding, however.

Unless you're planning on leaving town frequently, there's no need to rent a car in Puerto Vallarta; the best way to get around is by taxi. A taxi from the hotels on the airport road into town costs about $3.00. Public buses, while not very comfortable, are convenient. They stop every two blocks along the beach road but can be flagged down. Look for those saying "Pitillal," "Las Juntas," or "Ixtapa."

Guadalajara is a five-hour drive over a good highway. The bus (first-class) takes about seven hours. The bus station in Puerto Vallarta is on the corner of Insurgentes and Basilio Badillo, south of the Río Cuale.

ACCOMMODATIONS REFERENCE

The rate ranges given here are projections for December 1989 through Easter 1990. Unless otherwise indicated, rates are for double rooms, double occupancy. Puerto Vallarta is in the Central Standard time zone; the telephone area code is 322.

▶ **Hotel Buenaventura.** P.O. Box 8-BV, Avenida México 1301, Puerto Vallarta, Jalisco, Mexico 48300. U.S. $55–$64. Tel: 2-3737; in the United States: 800-458-6888; in Canada: (714) 494-8129.

▶ **Camino Real.** P.O. Box 95, Avenida México Zoo, Puerto Vallarta, Jalisco, Mexico 48300. U.S. $100–$120. Tel: 2-0002; in the United States and Canada: 800-228-3000.

▶ **Coral Grand Hotel.** P.O. Box 448, Puerto Vallarta, Jalisco, Mexico 48300. U.S. $160. Tel: 2-5191; in the United States and Canada: (409) 756-1802.

▶ **Fiesta Americana Condesa Vallarta.** P.O. Box 270, Playa Los Tules, Puerto Vallarta, Jalisco, Mexico 48300. U.S. $110–$120. Tel: 2-2010; in the United States and Canada: 800-223-2332.

▶ **Garza Blanca.** P.O. Box 58, Playa Polo Maria, Puerto Vallarta, Jalisco, Mexico 48300. U.S. $185–$395. Tel: 2-1083; in the United States and Canada: 800-331-0908.

▶ **Krystal Vallarta.** P.O. Box 94, Avenida de las Garzas, Puerto Vallarta, Jalisco, Mexico 48300. U.S. $115–$130. Tel: 2-1459.

▶ **Molino de Agua.** P.O. Box 54, Ignacio L. Vallarta, Puerto Vallarta, Jalisco, Mexico 48300. U.S. $50. Tel: 2-1907.

▶ **Plaza Las Glorias**. Playa de Las Glorias, Puerto Vallarta, Jalisco, Mexico 48300. U.S. $110–$130. Tel: 2-2224; in the United States: 800-342-AMIGO; in Canada: (713) 448-2829.

▶ **Plaza Vallarta Beach and Tennis Resort**. P.O. Box 36, Playa de las Glorias, Puerto Vallarta, Jalisco, Mexico 48300. U.S. $70–$100. Tel: 2-4360.

CAREYES

Situated on a pretty, isolated bay a little more than half-way between Puerto Vallarta and Manzanillo, the **Hotel Costa Careyes** is an elegant place to unwind—*Italian* style.

MAJOR INTEREST

Isolation with sophistication
Water sports

If you're the kind of person who craves fast-lane glitz, this sophisticated but secluded resort, with its clientele of affluent couples from Mexico, Europe, Canada, and the United States, may not be the place for you. If, on the other hand, you can handle a kicked-back pace in a beautiful setting, you may just think you've stumbled onto a little bit of heaven.

The sprawling resort property here—with eight miles of Costa Careyes beachfront—is owned by an Italian banker who fell in love with the spectacular beauty of the place and decided to develop it—tastefully—with a hotel, condominiums, and private homes. (Club Med's Playa Blanca resort is just up the beach.) The end result is very chic; everything at the Costa Careyes has the feel of Big Money, and the Mexican décor is overlaid with a patina of Italian designer style. The hotel itself is built in a horse-shoe shape on a flat stretch of ground facing the beach. All rooms have balconies with a view of the Pacific or the central patio area, and guests can choose between swimming in the pool or the ocean. The water-sports center is one of the best in the country, with windsurfing, sailing, scuba diving, or snorkeling available, and horseback excursions on the beach can also be arranged. (Polo is the real name of the equestrian game here, however, with two polo fields operated by a member in good standing of the Oak Brook Polo Club.) In addition, there are three restaurants—El Mirador, a sushi bar in the woods; the hotel dining room overlooking the ocean; and a beachside restaurant on the Playa Rosa, a couple of minutes' walk away—but absolutely *nothing* to do off the premises. (There are also no television sets or telephones to interrupt the reverie.)

At Careyes you have to know how to entertain yourself. If you do, a few days here will make you feel as if you've been away for months.

GETTING AROUND

Guests at Careyes usually fly into Manzanillo, about 100 km (60 miles) to the south and east. The hotel is an hour's drive from the Manzanillo airport, where car rentals are available. The highway turnoff for the hotel is also clearly marked. A taxi to the hotel will cost about $30. An air taxi, which the hotel or a travel agent can arrange, is about $50 per person. The landing strip for the latter is about ten minutes from the hotel, and the hotel will be happy to pick you up.

ACCOMMODATIONS REFERENCE

The rate range given here is a projection for December 1989 through Easter 1990. Unless otherwise indicated, rates are for double rooms, double occupancy. Careyes is in the Central Standard time zone; the telephone area code is 333.

▶ **Hotel Costa Careyes.** San Patricio 87, Careyes, Jalisco, Mexico 48980. U.S. $180–$420; full American plan. Tel: 7-0010; in the United States and Canada: 800-543-3760.

TENACATITA

If you've ever wanted to know what it's like to vacation in the middle of nowhere, this is the place to find out—though it's hard to imagine that you would come to Mexico just to come here. The Hotel Los Angeles Locos de Tenacatita is aptly named—only "crazy angels" know where it is; if you're not looking carefully, you'll never find it. Nestled on a beautiful bay off Highway 200, south of Careyes and north of the Manzanillo airport, the hotel here is announced by a few small signs along the road that point the way to the big red billboard at the turnoff to the hotel's access road. If you blink, however, you can miss them all.

Though the choice to put a hotel on the graceful curve of this lovely bay was a sane one, it's the snaking mile-and-a-half-long access road through thick jungle that makes the whole prospect of the place seem totally crazy.

MAJOR INTEREST

Superb bay and beach
Utter isolation

The property, now managed by the Fiesta Americana chain and called the **Fiesta Americana Los Angeles Locos**, was originally built by a Mexican labor union that wanted to provide restful vacations for its members. (Shortly after this workingman's paradise was completed, the union had to turn it over to the Fiesta Americana.) The result was a low-rise deluxe hotel with 250 rooms arranged around a central pool area (there are two pools here). Most rooms overlook the ocean, and all have balconies, television, and comfortable rattan furniture. There are, in addition, three open-air restaurants offering Mexican and Continental cuisine; four tennis courts (lighted for night play); and horseback riding along the wide, sandy beach, which is caressed by shallow water and gentle waves. A tiny disco with live entertainment (sometimes) is the only other distraction from the beauty and solitude in Tenacatita. However, most guests choose to fall asleep to the sound of waves and wake up to birdsong.

With the nearest "action" of any kind located over an hour to the south in Manzanillo or two hours to the north in Puerto Vallarta, the Crazy Angels of Tenacatita is for those truly seeking serenity in a remote paradise.

GETTING AROUND
The hotel is about 80 km (50 miles) northwest of Manzanillo and 160 km (100 miles) southeast of Puerto Vallarta. The taxi fare from Manzanillo is more than the one-way plane fare to Manzanillo from Guadalajara, but you can rent a car at the Manzanillo airport. For an additional charge of $22 per person, one-way, the hotel will send a combi to the airport to pick you up—perhaps your best bet (arrange in advance through the hotel or a travel agent).

ACCOMMODATIONS REFERENCE
The rate range given here is a projection for December 1989 through Easter 1990. Unless otherwise noted, rates are for double rooms, double occupancy. Tenacatita is in the Central Standard time zone; the telephone area code is 333.

▶ **Fiesta Americana Los Angeles Locos.** P.O. Box 7, San Patricio-Melaque, Jalisco, Mexico. Minimum stay: 3 days May–December 22, from U.S. $228 per person; Minimum stay: 7 days December 23–April, from U.S. $822; full American plan. Tel: 7-0220; in the United States and Canada: 800-223-2332.

BARRA DE NAVIDAD

Barra de Navidad, 60 km (35 miles) northwest of Manzanillo on Highway 200, is a little fishing village that is well on its way to becoming a mini-resort. In the old days, it used to be the kind of place where carefree travellers would rent hammocks, sleep on the beach, and dine in rustic restaurants on just-caught seafood. Today it has become a bit more sophisticated but, fortunately, retains much of its original barefoot charm. The town, which is largely residential, is the kind of place its residents take pride in, and they can be seen washing the cobblestone streets in front of their homes on most afternoons. The surrounding terrain is flat, with scrubby undergrowth and the occasional orchard, but nevertheless scenic.

MAJOR INTEREST

Fishing-village atmosphere

The **Hotel Cabo Blanco**, on the edge of town, looks like a plush country club and is part of a pretty, developed (for this part of the coast) complex called Pueblo Nuevo that also includes condos, tennis courts, a yacht club, and a canal that leads to the ocean. The hotel itself has a pleasant restaurant and offers comfortable rooms. **Pancho's**, at Avenida Lopéz de Legaspi 51, on the beach, serves up tasty seafood and is a fun place to dine, but be sure to bring cash—no credit cards are accepted here.

The dark-sand beach in Barra de Navidad is wide and attractive; the hotel's beach club is a five-minute drive from the hotel itself. Waterskiing, scuba diving and snorkeling, windsurfing, or sportfishing boat rentals can all be arranged here. The hotel also has the area's only tennis courts.

After a few days here you'll feel as if you know everybody in town. With this kind of hospitable atmosphere, it's only a matter of time before Barra de Navidad becomes a resort destination that is more talked about.

GETTING AROUND

It's essential in Barra de Navidad to have a car in order to get around. In other words, if you don't drive here on your own, chances are you won't spend any time here. Cars can be rented at the airports in Puerto Vallarta, Manzanillo (the closest air gateway), or Guadalajara (see their respective "Getting Around" sections for further information).

ACCOMMODATIONS REFERENCE

The rate range given here is a projection for December 1989 through Easter 1990. Unless otherwise noted, rates are for double rooms, double occupancy. Barra de Navidad is in the Central Standard time zone; its telephone area code is 333.

▶ **Hotel Cabo Blanco.** Armada and Pueblo Nuevo, Barra de Navidad, Jalisco, Mexico 48987. U.S. $35–$45. Tel: 7-0182.

MANZANILLO

Manzanillo is the only Mexican resort to have become a movie star before it was a well-known destination. In fact, the movie *"10"* catapulted it onto the map with even more effect than the gala opening of Las Hadas, a few years earlier, which was attended by celebrities from around the world.

Before Las Hadas, Manzanillo was nothing more than a sleepy tropical port surrounded by fertile farmland. The few visitors who came to town were likely to be deep-sea fishermen, and the biggest decision anyone ever had to make was whether to eat the large tangy oysters from the bay or the small sweet oysters from the Laguna Cuyutlán on the other side of town.

Highway 200, the road linking Manzanillo to Puerto Vallarta, about 280 km (175 miles) up the coast, opened about a dozen years ago, however, and things haven't been the same since. (In the interim, two more highways linking it to Guadalajara have been built as well.) With miles and miles of beautiful beaches, excellent weather (Manzanillo is on the same latitude as Hawaii), and a number of first-class hotels and resorts in addition to Las Hadas, Manzanillo is the perfect getaway for those who want to unwind in an exotic setting without the hustle and bustle of some of Mexico's larger vacation destinations.

MAJOR INTEREST

Las Hadas resort

Manzanillo's fresh-faced appearance belies its importance: It is one of the busiest commercial seaports in Mexico, and is connected by rail to cities throughout the country. It is also one of Mexico's major deep-sea fishing ports, and lies at the heart of one of the most fertile agricultural areas in the country—lush papaya, banana, and coconut plantations stretch for miles inland from the coast.

Cortés named the small settlement he found here for the beautiful blossoming apple trees of the surrounding area, and soon after established Latin America's first shipyard in order to build boats for the further exploration of New Spain and the Philippines. (In fact, he found the area so much to his liking that he eventually made his home here.) By the end of the 16th century Manzanillo was one of the New World's leading ports, with an emphasis on trade with the Orient. But as Spain's fortunes in the New World declined, Manzanillo was all but forgotten by the rest of the world.

That all began to change in 1974 when Antenor Patiño, a Bolivian tin magnate, unveiled Las Hadas. Other hotels have followed, but, overall, the growth of Manzanillo as a destination for international travellers has been slower than in other Mexican resorts.

The ten beautiful miles of the beach-fringed Bahía de Manzanillo run in a graceful curve from northwest to southeast. Downtown Manzanillo, where the major banks, airline offices, and cinemas are located, is at the southeastern end of the bay. Las Hadas is located at the opposite end. The smaller scallop-shaped Bahía de Santiago lies immediately to the west of Las Hadas, and the two bays are separated by the Península de Santiago. To the north and west of Santiago Bay are the Playa de Oro, the finest black-sand beach in Mexico; the airport; and the coastal highway leading to Barra de Navidad and points north, including Puerto Vallarta. Most of the things that visitors like to see and do are spread out along the seven-mile stretch between Las Hadas and the downtown area. Pockets of development surround each resort complex in the Manzanillo area—among them Las Hadas, Club Maeva, and Club Santiago—but miles of relatively unspoiled beaches lie between each pocket. Other attractions here are also spread out—so spread out, in fact, that it's best to rent a car if you plan on spending any time exploring; the roads in and around Manzanillo are good and getting around is easy.

From the Airport to Las Hadas

The ride from the airport to Las Hadas is a long (almost 48 km/30 miles) but scenic one that passes through lush banana and coconut plantations. If excursions to nearby towns and villages are on your itinerary, this will be a good time to watch the road signs and get a feel for the lay of the land.

What most visitors think of as Manzanillo starts at **Club Santiago**, on the **Playa Miramar** (the first beach you'll see on the trip in from the airport). Club Santiago offers a variety of accommodations in a posh, country club–like setting, including one- to six-room beachfront villas, secluded cottages, and spacious condominiums. The huge pool has a shaded swim-up bar, and guests can dine on the beach at Oasis (where Mexican and seafood dishes are the house specialties) or dance till they drop at the club's lively disco. There are also a nine-hole golf course and six tennis courts on the premises. The greatest attraction at Club Santiago, however, is the marvelous seclusion it offers.

Body surfing is popular at Playa Miramar itself. To the east and south, following the curve of the bay in the direction of Las Hadas and town, the **Olas Atlas** and **Santiago** beaches are especially pretty and unspoiled.

Just down the road from Club Santiago in the direction of town, about a 20-minute drive from the airport, you'll come to **Club Maeva**, a picturesque and self-contained resort hotel spread over 90 acres. Its 200 compact blue-and-white villas, each one capable of accommodating up to six people, are clustered around the resort's beautiful gardens. Available by the day or the week, their no-nonsense design—bright blue tiles cover the floor and built-in couches and beds keep the living areas uncluttered—seems to have been arrived at with families in mind. You can also buy groceries at the supermarket on the premises and prepare meals in your villa's kitchenette.

Guests at Club Maeva tend to congregate around the pool, which is one of the largest in the country (they sometimes hold water-skiing exhibitions in it); a pedestrian walkway leads over the coast road to the beach on Santiago Bay. The 12 tennis courts here are lighted for night play, and special activities for children are staged throughout the grounds. In fact, Club Maeva strikes the first-time visitor as a "user-friendly" playland where the whole family feels at home from the moment it arrives—which is why they keep returning year after year.

Farther south and just off the highway at the crossroad leading to the Fiesta Mexicana Hotel, you'll come to the popular **Carlos 'n' Charlie's Colima Café**, one of the chain of un-serious and much-loved restaurants started by Carlos Anderson. In the Manzanillo area this is the place to go if you're in a rambunctious mood. The prevailing attitude is "Come in and join the fun" (although it's not as boisterous as some of its brethren in other Mexican resorts), and the ribs, chicken, beef, and fish dishes can satisfy even the heartiest appetite.

La Audiencia Beach

Playa de Audiencia, a graceful moon-shaped beach and bay at the point of the Santiago peninsula, is one of the best places to sun and swim in the Manzanillo area. (Though it's most commonly reached by water, you can also drive to it.)

La Audiencia got its name from a meeting that Cortés reputedly had on the beach here with local Indians—its only claim to fame besides its great natural beauty. Nestled in a protective inlet (within the larger Santiago Bay), the waves are even gentler than they are elsewhere in Manzanillo; in fact, because the swimming and snorkeling conditions here are so ideal, it has become a favorite destination of many of the excursion boats operating out of Manzanillo. (Any of the tour outfits in town that offer such an excursion will be happy to pick you up at your hotel and deposit you at the boat dock.) La Audiencia is a wonderful hideaway for those who are looking for undisturbed sunbathing in tranquil surroundings—and Las Hadas is just around the point.

Las Hadas

It is entirely appropriate that *Las Hadas* translates as "the Fairies" in Spanish—the guests at this exquisite resort often feel as if they are vacationing in nothing less than an enchanted fairyland. The architecture of Las Hadas is a unique blend of Moorish, Mexican, and Caribbean elements that have been combined to create this gleaming white stucco village perched on a hill overlooking Manzanillo Bay. And while Señor Patiño built the place to meet the high standards of his wealthy and discriminating friends, he also priced it so that others could enjoy the luxury and beauty that prevail here. (Las Hadas is now under the management of the Westin Hotel group.)

Everything at Las Hadas is on a grand scale, and the luxury has been built in from the ground floor up. (The Pete and Roy Dye–designed golf course, for example, cost five and a half million dollars to build.) All the rooms and suites have an ocean view, and some have large private patios. Inside, the marble floors and tiled baths keep these spacious rooms and suites cool and inviting. The two swimming pools are attractively decorated with mosaics, and exquisitely carved fountains dot the landscaped walkways that lace the complex. If you get tired of walking to the beach or the pool, a chauffeured golf cart (Las Hadas uses a noiseless model so that other guests won't be disturbed) will respond to your summons.

The 90-slip marina at the foot of the hill looks like a showroom for the latest luxury yachts, and its arcade offers the best shopping in the entire area. The larger of the two pools, which is a few steps from the beach, is so large that a suspended bridge crosses over it and the two landscaped islands in the middle of it. Throw in a waterfall and swim-up bar and it's easy to see why this is one of the most spectacular pools in the country. The lovely beach nearby rings a small bay, and every morning the beach attendants put up small white tents to provide their pampered guests with shade.

The open-air **El Terral**, where Dudley Moore and Bo Derek shared a romantic dinner, is one of the most charming restaurants at Las Hadas; **La Cartouche**, the piano bar/disco that also appeared in the movie, is where you'll find the nightlife. **Hermosa Cove** at the Las Hadas marina is also fun, and live mariachi music livens up most nights here.

Manolo's, a popular garden-style restaurant in the Salahua neighborhood across the coast road and three blocks south of the Las Hadas turnoff, is a long-time Manzanillo favorite with few frills except for its salad bar. Steak and seafood are the specialties here.

Club Las Hadas, an orange-roofed condominium complex just down the road in the direction of town, looks like a hilltop Mediterranean village. A maze of cobblestone streets links these luxury condo units, and the entire complex overlooks Las Hadas and its marina. The **Villas del Palmar**, a cluster of luxury villas within the larger Club Las Hadas complex, is situated on the edge of Las Hadas' 18-hole championship golf course and has the atmosphere of a private club. The décor of each villa is contemporary Mexican, and each has its own verandah that is perfect for star-gazing on warm, flower-scented evenings. Best of all, guests at both the Villas del Palmar and Club Las Hadas have privileges at Las Hadas' facilities, including the golf course.

In the same neighborhood, **El Pueblito** is an attractive condominium hotel perched atop another hill overlooking Las Hadas, the golf course, and Club Santiago. For those who would just as soon avoid paying top dollar for the view (and can forgo a few of the frills), it's one of the better options in the area. The one- to three-bedroom suites have private balconies and sunken tubs, and the pool has its own swim-up bar and bridge (though it's not as big as the pools at Las Hadas or Club Maeva). A shuttle bus takes guests to the Playa Santiago a few minutes away.

From Las Hadas to Town

Almost everything that a visitor will want to see, do, or arrange can be found along the seven-mile stretch of beach—the **Playa Azul**—that rings Manzanillo Bay. With its gentle curves and gentler waves (more so the closer you get to town), it has become a magnet for hotels and restaurants, which can be found on either side of the highway and become more concentrated as you near town. The dining establishments and discos along this stretch are as informal as they come—you're not likely to find the fast-track Mexico City crowd here. Generally speaking, Manzanillo doesn't attract night owls, serious shoppers, or those who like to be "seen."

Ostería Bugatti, on the coast road at the Las Brisas intersection, was one of the first restaurants on the scene and is still one of the most popular. Locals like the garden setting and tend to linger around the piano bar after dinner. Those who like to dance can drift over to the restaurant's disco and sway to lively salsa and rock rhythms until the wee hours of the morning.

El Vaquero, which is also located at the Las Brisas intersection, serves up its beef with a special flair. Customers choose their steak by cut and weight, and it is then prepared to order on a special charcoal grill.

If you stay to the right at the intersection, you'll soon enter the Las Brisas zone on Avenida Lázaro Cárdenas. The **Club Roca del Mar** is a pretty condominium-style hotel with a strategic location on the southeastern corner of Manzanillo Bay. Small and modern, with a friendly family atmosphere, it is a delightful place to spend a few days.

The **Hotel La Posada**, right next door to the Roca del Mar and across the road from the yacht basin (where you can charter fishing boats), is the kind of place where you can let it all hang out, relax in the sun on the beach with your favorite book, and enjoy the gorgeous Pacific sunsets over a cold drink. The sandals crowd who have the time to travel through Mexico by car or RV loves this place, and guests and locals alike stop here to enjoy the hearty, cooked-to-order American-style breakfasts and catch up on the latest gossip: The large living room/dining room is the kind of place where you can put your feet on the table without worrying. Burt Varlemann, the owner, is a Dutchman who came to Manzanillo years ago and decided to stay, and he goes out of his way to make his guests feel right at home. (The bar even works on the honor system!)

Downtown

There is little reason for visitors to head into downtown Manzanillo. Those who do usually visit the small municipal market, where sundries and souvenirs are sold, then stop for a drink at the **Bar Social**, Calle 21 de Marzo and Juárez, on the *zócalo* (also known as the Jardín Alvaro Obregón). The **Hotel Colonial**, Avenida México 100, is a throwback to the days when only fishermen came to Manzanillo and the beaches were all but ignored.

Nightlife in Manzanillo

Nightlife and shopping in Manzanillo can be summed up in a few words: There isn't much of either. What little nightlife there is centers around the hotels and a few restaurants. **La Cartouche** at Las Hadas; **The Club** at Club Maeva; and the **Oasis** at Club Santiago are the most popular of the hotel nightclub/discos. **Osteria Bugatti**, at the Las Brisas intersection, has a piano bar as well as a lively disco. **Coco's**, another lively local favorite, is on the strip in Salahua, across the coast road and three blocks south of the Las Hadas turnoff.

Las Hadas and Club Santiago also stage colorful Mexican Fiesta nights once a week; call their front desks for the day, time, and location.

Shopping in Manzanillo

As we've noted already, Manzanillo is not a shoppers' paradise. Most hotels have one or two boutiques; **Elena's** in the Roca del Mar, with a selection of gifts, sportswear, and decorative items, is one of the best. Las Hadas also has one or two top-of-the-line shops, but even there the selection is limited.

The **Plaza Santiago**, a small mall at the Las Hadas marina, has a handful of good shops. Jaramar II for handicrafts, Bye Bye for informal resort wear, and Tane for exquisite silver pieces are three of the best. **Rubén Torres**, located in a snazzy glass structure on the beach side of the coast road at kilometer 13 (heading in the direction of Las Hadas and the airport), sells resort wear for men and women in a variety of bright colors.

The municipal market downtown on Avenida Cinco de Mayo is the place to bargain for typical souvenirs.

Sports in Manzanillo

Manzanillo is yet another Pacific Coast paradise for sportsmen—though water-sport centers are not as visible here as they are in other resorts. At the same time, chances are good that you won't be approached on the beach by enterprising young locals hustling their water-skiing boats or parasailing rides. Windsurfing boards can be rented at the Roca del Mar, and the conditions at its end of the bay are usually gentle enough for even the greenest beginner.

Of course, fishing was responsible for Manzanillo's early popularity and remains one of its biggest draws. Sailfish and marlin (Manzanillo bills itself as the "Sailfish Capital of Mexico") are the prize catches here, and November and December are the best months to go for them. Other great game species such as sea bass, mackerel, giant tuna, and yellowtail are abundant year-round, with October–March being the busiest season. Your hotel will be happy to arrange a charter boat for you at the marina across the street from the Hotel La Posada; the price will usually include bait and tackle.

Most of the major hotels and resorts in Manzanillo have tennis courts. If yours doesn't, there are six at Club Santiago and 12 at Club Maeva (six of them lighted) open to the public. Call in advance for reservations, however (see the "Accommodations Reference" list below for telephone numbers).

The Pete and Roy Dye championship golf course at Las Hadas also makes tee times available to the public; here, too, you'll want to call in advance, however.

Excursions from Manzanillo

Colima, about 100 km (60 miles) northeast of Manzanillo, is the capital of the small state of the same name. In the nearby colonial town of Comala visitors can choose from among a selection of painted furniture, pottery, and wrought iron at the Mercado de Artesanias. The principal attraction in Colima itself is the **Museum of Dance, Masks, and Popular Arts of Western Mexico,** in the Fine Arts Institute at the corner of Calle 27 de Septembre and Manuel Gallardo Zamaro; the museum also has a selection of folk art for sale. The travel agent in your hotel or in downtown Manzanillo can arrange the trip if you decide not to drive yourself.

More adventurous travellers can head for the primitive seaside town of **Cuyutlán,** about 48 km (30 miles) south of Manzanillo, most of it over Highway 200. The lagoon and beautiful unspoiled beach here are reason enough to pack a picnic and make the trip, but the lucky visitor may reap a dividend: Every spring between March and May, especially as the moon waxes full, the beach here is subject to repeated visitations of the mysterious *Ola Verde,* or "Green Wave," a wall of water that sometimes reaches heights of 30 feet or more.

If your hotel does not have a travel agent, contact **Bahás Gemelas** at Las Hadas; Tel: 3-1000 or 3-0204.

GETTING AROUND
You can drive good highways from either Puerto Vallarta or Guadalajara to Manzanillo, but flying is by far the most convenient way to get there. Most international carriers, however, do not offer direct service to Manzanillo, which means that more often than not travellers will be routed through either Mexico City or Guadalajara, with some connections through the former requiring an overnight stay. Two carriers that do offer "direct" service to Manzanillo are Mexicana and Aeroméxico. The former offers a daily flight (with the exception of Saturday) from Los Angeles via Guadalajara, as well as four flights a week from Dallas-Ft. Worth (only the Saturday and Sunday flights are non-stop). Aeroméxico flies to Manzanillo from Los Angeles (via Guadalajara) seven days a week. It's a 4½-hour flight from L.A. and a 3½-hour flight from Dallas.

The airport is a long ride—about 48 km (30 miles)—to the major hotels, so relax and enjoy it; the plantations you'll pass along the way are lush and lovely. There are a number of car-rental agencies right at the airport (Avis and National among them), as well as a few in town. A taxi from the airport will cost about $15; a combi will make the same trip for about $4.50.

Once you've settled in, taxis or rental car are the best way to get around. Taxis are plentiful and easy to hail; if you don't find one waiting outside your hotel door, ask the hotel to call one. There's also a taxi stand downtown across from the *zócalo* on Avenida Morelos. As is the case any time you decide to take a taxi in Mexico, establish the price *before* you get into the cab.

ACCOMMODATIONS REFERENCE
The rate ranges given are projections for December 1989 through Easter 1990. Unless otherwise indicated, rates are for double rooms, double occupancy. Manzanillo is in the Central Standard time zone, and the telephone area code is 333.

► **Club Las Hadas/Villas del Palmar.** P.O. Box 51, Manzanillo, Colima, Mexico 28200. U.S. $85–$115. Tel: 3-0888/3-0575.

► **Club Maeva.** P.O. Box 442, Manzanillo, Colima, Mexico 28200. U.S. $60–$75. Tel: 3-0395; in the United States: 800-262-2656; in Canada: (619) 452-2639.

► **Club Santiago.** P.O. Box 374, Manzanillo, Colima, Mexico 28200. Condos U.S. $82–$115; villas $155–$290. Tel: 3-0413; in the United States: 800-525-1987; in Canada: (303) 740-7644.

► **Hotel Colonial.** Avenida México 100, Manzanillo, Colima, Mexico 28200. U.S. $15–$20. Tel: 2-1080.

► **Las Hadas.** P.O. Box 158, Manzanillo, Colima, Mexico 28200. U.S. $125–$150. Tel: 3-0000; in the United States and Canada: 800-228-3000.

► **Hotel La Posada.** P.O. Box 135, Manzanillo, Colima, Mexico 28200. U.S. $44. Tel: 2-2404.

► **El Pueblito Hotel and Villas.** Avenida del Tesoro, Fracc. Las Hadas, Manzanillo, Colima, Mexico 28200. U.S. $65. Tel: 3-0440.

► **Roca del Mar.** P.O. Box 7, Manzanillo, Colima, Mexico 28200. U.S. $80. Tel: 2-0805.

IXTAPA/ZIHUATANEJO

Ixtapa/Zihuatanejo, 210 km (130 miles) northwest of Acapulco on the Pacific Coast, offers the best of two worlds. It is both old and new, and is really two destinations in one—visitors so inclined can get double their money's worth.

This resort duo is somewhat difficult to describe. The destination is called Ixtapa. The airport, however, is called Zihuatanejo and is located just outside the town of the same name. Ixtapa is sprawling and modern—it didn't even exist before the early 1970s—and is where most visitors stay, shop, and play after dark. Zihuatanejo, on the other hand, dates to the 16th century and is where most visitors dine and play during the day, as well as where the resort's business is conducted. The umbilical cord linking the two is a smooth, gently sloping highway, with little in the way of development along its four-mile length, that runs inland between the two towns.

Ixtapa/Zihuatanejo may be one of the most relaxing resorts in the country. It is certainly the best resort for parents with young children because of the gentle waves here and the unbroken vistas on most beaches, as well as for disabled travellers, due to the generally flat terrain. And experienced travellers will tell you that Ixtapa has Acapulco's fine weather (the average year-round temperature is 26°C/78°F) without that famous resort's crowds. (The best weather coincides with the high season, December–April, and temperatures are generally a few degrees cooler than they are in Acapulco. The rainy season stretches from June–October, but the showers usually wait until evening.) Those who like life in the fast lane, on the other hand, won't find it here. Instead, the ambience is laid-back, and you get the feeling of being delightfully marooned in the midst of the great outdoors.

MAJOR INTEREST

Mix of especially relaxing resort pace with good shopping and dining

Ixtapa
Superior beach along hotel strip
Shopping

Dining
Nightlife

Zihuatanejo
Tranquil small-town atmosphere
Secluded beaches

Ixtapa/Zihuatanejo is situated on a 25-mile-long coastline of scalloped bays and beautiful beaches that runs in a northwest-to-southeast direction, with Ixtapa to the west and north of Zihuatanejo. Ixtapa's dazzling hotel zone lies on the Bahía del Palmar, which is edged by an expanse of flat beach known as the Playa del Palmar. The coast is broken at the far (western) end of the hotel zone by the small mouth of the Laguna del Ixtapa and then continues in a westerly-northwesterly direction to Punta (Point) Ixtapa. This undeveloped western stretch of coastline is scooped out into coves and inlets and has a number of unspoiled beaches, including (from east to west) Playa Don Juan, Playa Juan de Dios, and Playa Don Rodrigo. Playa Las Cuatas, on the near side of the point, is a pretty beach with rock formations that will remind you of a Bermuda beach. Playa Quieta (a Club Med beach) and Playa Linda are situated on the far side of Punta Ixtapa. **Playa Quieta** is the departure point for the 15-minute boat trip to Isla Ixtapa (also called Isla Grande). **Playa Linda**, the farthest beach from the Ixtapa hotel zone, is backed by trees that provide delicious (and welcome) shade virtually at the water's edge. It's a perfect place for mid-week picnics, but gets crowded on weekends.

At the other end of Ixtapa, Playa Hermosa, a crescent-shaped beach in front of the deluxe Camino Real hotel, is perhaps the prettiest of all the beaches in the area. (You have to enter through the hotel to get there, however.)

The more than 400-year-old Zihuatanejo is a five-minute drive to the east and south over a highway carved into the hills. The tiny town is situated on its own bay, and the downtown beach, though sometimes sprinkled with seaweed, is shaded in places and friendly everywhere. Few tourists sun here, but the passing parade on the seaside promenade, or *malecón,* is always fun to watch. Playa La Madera is a broad, flat stretch of dark sand that begins just southeast of town, but you can't walk to it directly from town because of a channel that leads inland at a point just north of it. A road behind the beach climbs a hill to smaller hotels such as the Catalina, Irma, and

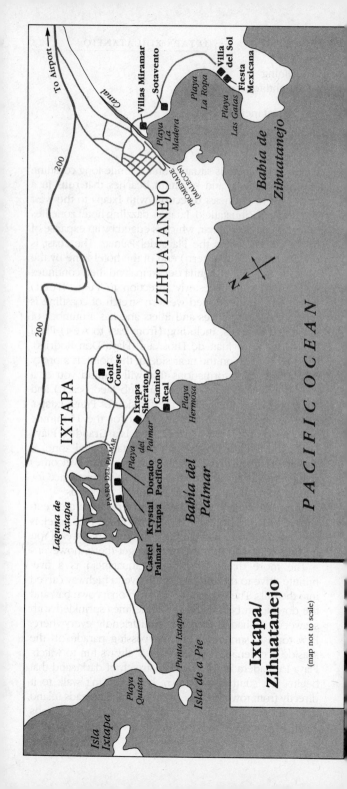

Ixtapa/Zihuatanejo

(map not to scale)

To Airport

Canal

200

200

IXTAPA

Golf
Course

PASEO DEL PALMAR

Ixtapa
Sheraton

Camino
Real

Playa Hermosa

Playa
del
Palmar

Bahía del
Palmar

Castel
Palmar Ixtapa

Krystal
Ixtapa

Dorado
Pacífico

Laguna de
Ixtapa

Punta Ixtapa

Isla de a Pie

Playa
Quieta

Isla
Ixtapa

ZIHUATANEJO

PROMENADE (MALECON)

Villas Miramar
Sotavento

Playa
La Madera

Playa La Ropa

Playa
Las Gatas

Villa
del Sol

Fiesta
Mexicana

Bahía de
Zihuatanejo

N

PACIFIC OCEAN

Sotavento, and the Villas Miramar is at the bottom of the hill just across the street from the beach.

Along the curve of the Bahía de Zihuantanejo to the south, Playa La Ropa, a favorite of international travellers and the location of the Villa del Sol and Fiesta Mexicana hotels, is named for the clothes that washed up on it after a long-ago shipwreck, and is a five-minute drive from town over a scenic, rolling road.

Playa Las Gatas, accessible only by water, is still farther south and is lined with tiny restaurants where you can rent chairs and have a snack, but has less-than-ideal swimming conditions because of its rocky bottom. It is a good beach for diving and snorkeling, however, and there's a dive operation right on the beach.

IXTAPA

Ixtapa is a baby on the Mexican resort scene—but what a baby. Selected for development 15 years ago by the government computers at Fonatur, Ixtapa was built with the comfort and convenience of large groups of travellers in mind. This is one place in Mexico, for example, where you can drink the water and not worry about the ice cubes, because the hotel zone has its own water purification plant.

About a dozen large high-rises border Palmar Bay; it takes about 30 minutes to walk the length of Paseo del Palmar, the road that serves as the spine of the hotel zone, from the Ixtapa Sheraton at the eastern end to the Posada Real at the western tip of the point. The beach is at your back door along this stretch, the waves are gentle, and the water temperature warm, so you can dive right in without shocking your system. It is also one of the few stretches of beach in the country that is lit for nighttime strolls (although you should stick to the beach in front of the hotels).

The Ixtapa shopping district, which is easily accessible from any of the hotels in the zone, is a maze of modern malls on the other side of Paseo del Palmar. The Palma Real golf course at the eastern end of the hotel zone—an 18-hole Robert Trent Jones–designed course—is also an easy walk from any of the major hotels here. (From the Sheraton you can walk to the first tee of the Palma Real in minutes.)

Staying in Ixtapa

The **Camino Real** is the crème de la crème of Ixtapa hotels. Big, breezy, and beautiful on its own promontory on the eastern side of the bay, it stands apart from the other hotels here not only in terms of its location but in its architecture as well. Built into the hillside above the **Playa Hermosa**, its graceful, crescent-shaped beach, the Camino Real resembles a vast expanse of bronze-colored bleachers. There are four freshwater pools here, complete with fountains and an aqueduct (the six suites in the hotels have their own private pools), seven restaurants and bars, a disco, four tennis courts, and an indoor shopping mall. But perhaps the one feature that makes the Camino Real so outstanding is the fact that even the smallest room has, in addition to an ocean view, its own terrace-like balcony where you can dine under the stars, relax in a hammock, or read in a chaise longue. In fact, the room and the balcony together have many of the amenities of a small cottage. Even the decorative touches are first class; so many guests have asked if they could buy the lamps and bedspreads in their rooms that the hotel soon plans to offer them for sale in the shop downstairs. And yet, in spite of its size and attention to detail, you will never feel as if you're just one more guest of a big operation at the Camino Real.

A few minutes' walk to the west, the towering **Ixtapa Sheraton** heads the row of hotels that comprise Ixtapa's hotel zone along the **Playa del Palmar**. The Sheraton itself is an attractive, large, American-style operation where efficiency and cleanliness are very evident. And the glass elevator is a favorite with guests. The Sheraton is also closer to the Palma Real golf course than any other hotel in the zone.

The **Dorado Pacifico**, one of the costliest hotels ever built in Mexico, is also one of the few privately-owned hotels in the country. The lobby and public areas are cool and spacious, with marble floors and comfortable chairs in bright colors, and the butterfly-shaped pool with swim-up bar is just a few steps from the ocean. Inside, the contemporary polished-wood décor lends the Dorado Pacific a plush, tropical feel. **Giuseppe's**, where you can enjoy the Italian specialties of the chef and watch the passing parade on Paseo del Palmer as you dine, is located right in front of the hotel.

Everything about the **Krystal Ixtapa** is upscale, including Bogart's, a branch of the well-known chain of restaurants of the same name, and Christine's, its dazzling disco. Each room here has its own private terrace, climate control, and closed-circuit television, and there are five bars and restaurants as well as lighted tennis and racquetball courts. In addition, their weekly Mexican Fiesta Night, which combines lively folkloric shows with traditional music, Mexican food, and rope tricks, is one of the best in town. (Check with your own hotel for the day and time, as well as how to make reservations.)

Dining in Ixtapa

Almost all the major hotels in Ixtapa have one or more air-conditioned restaurants, but trying those outside your own hotel is part of the fun of vacationing here. **La Hacienda**, for example, overlooks the Paseo del Palmar and is a perfect place to stop for a late breakfast or early lunch.

Bogart's, in the Krystal Ixtapa, is by far the most outrageous restaurant in town. The experience begins on the sidewalk out front, where someone dressed like Aladdin greets diners and escorts them between two flaming torches to the front door. Inside it looks like a set from *Casablanca:* Everything—costumes, carved screens, peacock chairs, and more—could have been lifted from Rick's. A fountain dominates the center of the room and soft music from a white piano at the end of the room provides the perfect accompaniment for a memorable dining experience. Pretend you're Bogie or Bacall and dress up for this one. Reservations advised; Tel: 4-2618.

Montmartre, on the second floor of the Galería Ixtapa overlooking the Paseo del Palmar (see "Shopping" below), is a wonderful surprise. This breezy, informal place looks like a plain but attractive room in somebody's home. It offers French food prepared by French-trained chefs, with an emphasis on seafood. However, if you're the kind of person who likes juicy steaks without fancy sauces, you'll find those here, too. Montmartre was one of the first restaurants on the Ixtapa scene, and its popularity has grown along with that of the resort.

Villa Sakura, a few steps off of the Paseo del Palmar, has more than a touch of Japan; in fact, it looks as if part of the country had been transplanted here. Be sure to take the time to stroll through the Japanese garden outside with its small bridge and waterwheel. Inside, waitresses in kimonos serve at the bar, and some dishes are prepared at your table by *teppanyaki* chefs.

Getting to **Carlos 'n' Charlie's** is like following the clues in a treasure hunt. (It's hidden away at the far western end of the hotel zone next to the Posada Real.) Once you find it, however, the ambience is pure barefoot vacation and the décor rustic Polynesian. The dining room is under a *palapa* and crazy memorabilia hang from the ceiling: You half expect Trader Vic to wander into the bamboo bar at any minute. The fun begins as soon as the front door opens around noon and keeps rolling until 4:00 A.M. The beach is a step away, so you can take a dip in the ocean or soak up the sun between courses of lunch, and after dinner you can dance in the tiny open-air disco on the premises, which opens at 9:00. Late-nighters who have already dined elsewhere often stop here for a pre-dawn hamburger.

Los Mandiles stands alone in a corner of the new shopping plaza, its décor an odd combination of colonial style with neon touches. Informality reigns with the beer-drinking crowd at the bar, however, and the Mexican food is wonderful. You can dine either inside or out on the porch.

Mac's Prime Rib, overlooking the strip on the second floor of the Patios shopping mall, is one of the new places in Ixtapa where everybody goes; its specialty is roast beef.

O.k.'s, also on the second floor of the mall and also new, is another popular hangout with locals and visitors. The big bar, booths, and tables are surrounded by a 1940s-style décor in soft pastels. Seafood (including an oyster bar) and meat entrées are the specialties.

Nueva Zelanda, a circular cafeteria in the middle of Ixtapa's shopping complex, is the perfect place for a light snack. The *licuado de papaya*s and *sincronizado*s (hot wheat tortillas with ham and cheese) here are delicious and will keep your stomach from growling until dinner. Hamburgers, sandwiches, and enchiladas are also on the menu. The place is kept spic-and-span and the prices should bring a smile to your face. (Zelanda began in a closet-sized space in Zihuatanejo where local businessmen still gather for late breakfasts and lunches.)

La Esfera, in the Camino Real, is another dress-up place. The refined dining here, either inside in air-conditioning or outside on the patio, is unusual for Ixtapa (the staff, including the maitre d' and hostess, are all dressed impeccably in white) and the Continental cuisine is reliably good. You'll pay for the location, however. Reservations advised; Tel: 4-3300.

Standing by itself on Paseo de la Roca, just past the Camino Real, the **Villa de la Selva** is Ixtapa's chic-est restaurant (in spite of its disappointingly average food). Tables are placed a discreet distance apart on one of two terraces surrounded by lush vegetation. The romantic candlelight, beautiful table settings, and tropical ambience put the Selva a cut above the rest—and the prices don't reflect it. Come here to watch the sunset, stay through dinner, and enjoy one of the most memorable evenings of your life. You'll need a reservation, however; Tel: 4-2096.

Ixtapa is growing by leaps and bounds, and new restaurants seem to spring up by the minute. For the moment, however, **El Faro** is the only place with a panoramic view of the entire bay. Unfortunately, finding it isn't easy if you're driving yourself. If you are, head for the Camino Real and turn just before the entrance to the hotel. Then climb the hill to the condo development called Pacifico El Faro all the way at the top. Parking is an adventure due to the steep incline of the parking lot, but the trip is worth it. The dining area is open to the sea breezes and has a refined atmosphere; the spectacular view here serves as the décor as soft piano music fills the air. Seafood is the specialty at El Faro and everything is fresh. Prices tend to be on the high side, but the good food and above-it-all location will make them easier to swallow. Reserve a table by the railing if you can; Tel: 4-3373.

Shopping in Ixtapa

In a very short time Ixtapa has grown into one of the best shopping destinations in the country. In fact, so many new malls have gone up in the hotel zone that it's hard to figure out where one ends and the next begins. When they're all completed Ixtapa will have over 300 stores and boutiques, and will give Cancún a run for its shopping money. Resort wear is the purchase of choice here, with handicrafts running a close second. (Surprisingly few stores in Ixtapa carry the usual Mexican souvenirs.)

Los Puertas, Ixtapa's original mall, is directly across the Paseo del Palmar from the hotels; newer malls have been built around and behind it. To help sort it all out, here are a few of the shops to look for.

In Los Puertas itself, **Galería Florence** has a good selection of paintings and sculpture.

To the left of the Puertas complex, in the **Galería Ixtapa**, near the Joy disco, **Fernando Huertas** sells original designs in cotton as well as a few antiques and a small collection of well-chosen folk art.

Terra-cotta-colored IxpaMar, behind Los Patios, has the best folk-art store in town, **El Amanecer**.

Fiorucci is located in the Galería Los Arcos. **Aca Joe** was one of the first to set up shop in Los Fuentes across the way. Ralph Lauren and Benetton (both stocked with goods made in Mexico) are there as well, as are **Luisa Conti**, an Italian designer who carries original costume jewelry and sweaters; and **Wanda Ameiro**, a well-known Mexican designer. In Los Patios, Maroc and Chiquita Banana, on the first floor, and Nature Crafts on the second, all offer pretty, decorative items.

Nightlife in Ixtapa

Ixtapa is the center of the area's nightlife. Though its nights end earlier than they do in Acapulco, this former early-to-bed area has nonetheless become a favorite of those who love late nights.

Christine's, at the Krystal, one of a chain of well-known discos, is sensational. The crowd is generally well dressed and the place itself is attractive and exciting. Even the entranceway is dramatic: You walk in under trees strung with Christmas lights and Victorian-style lampposts line the way. Inside, video screens, flashing lights, balloons, smoke, and other gimmicks are the rule, but conversations can actually be carried on. Though for the most part the crowd will be under 30, people of all ages feel comfortable here. In other words, Christine's is worth the hassle at the door and the hefty cover charge—at least for one evening.

Near the Galería Ixtapa, **Joy**, with its tiered, high-tech Miami-disco look, has a sophisticated atmosphere. Though it's less pretentious than Christine's, it's no less fun.

The hotels in Ixtapa occasionally feature international entertainers. Mexican Fiesta nights also are held at different hotels during the week (watch for signs at the various hotels or check with your own hotel). In the low season, live music adds excitement to many a lobby bar. When you hear it, be sure to stop—you never know when a party might break out.

ZIHUATANEJO

Zihuatanejo is long on charm. Now a resort as well as a fishing village, it got its start back in the 1500s, when it was an important center for New Spain's trade with the Orient. (In Nahuatl *Zihuatan* means the "Place of the Women"; it is believed the Cuitlalteca tribe that lived here was ruled by matriarchs. Until Ixtapa came along, however, Zihuatanejo was little more than a remote haven for adventurous budget travellers who loved the barefoot lifestyle here. Although it now serves as Ixtapa's commercial center and the resident population has swelled to some 30,000, Zihuatanejo has managed to hold on to its charm and cozy feeling.

The town's small hotels, restaurants, and shops line cobblestone streets and alleyways. It's both easy and rewarding to spend a couple of days exploring Zihuatanejo—it's the kind of place where you can get to know everybody in town if you want to. (You'll never have to dress in more than cutoffs and a T-shirt to do it, either.)

Scenic scalloped bays and inlets—some flat, others backed by hills and cliffs—link Zihuatanejo's three beautiful but very different beaches, all ringing the bay to the east and south of town. **Playa La Madera**, closest to town (there is also a beach in front of town), is the smallest beach in Zihua. There isn't much to see or do here, but one of the town's coziest small hotels, the Villas Miramar, is a few minutes' walk down the beach. Up and over the hill, a 10-minute ride from La Madera, **Playa La Ropa**, a barefoot kind of place, the sort where celebrities come to get away from it all, is lined with small hotels and bungalows (such as Las Urracas) and is as peaceful a place as you could ever hope to find. (Accommodations at Las Urracas Bungalows, which are right on the beach and shaded by lush foliage, are simple, but finding the owner is hard—so we're leaving you on your own here. Once you do rent, however, you're "in" forever.) The Villa del Sol and Fiesta Mexicana hotels are located about halfway down the beach, and the beach club at the Villa del Sol is the place to arrange your water-sport activities. **La Gaviota** restaurant, at the end of La Ropa, is a great place to swim and grab a bite to eat. The third beach, beyond La Ropa, is **Playa Las Gatas**, which is accessible only by boat. Once the private bathing place of a Tarascan Indian princess, today it's the most undeveloped beach of the three (though you can arrange diving and snorkeling excursions here)—just a few seaside restaurants and the spectacular private mansion of Hector Rebaque, Mexico's Formula I racing champion.

Staying in Zihuatanejo

Puerto Mio, the first stage of what will eventually be a large hotel/condo development in the Zihuatanejo marina, is over the small bridge at the western end of the town's *malecón* (just past the Hotel Trés Marías), a five-minute walk from downtown Zihuatanejo in the direction of Ixtapa. Everything about this place—for the moment, at any rate—is intimate and tasteful. All the rooms have a view of the bay, and the tiled bathrooms are cool and pretty. The tiny dining room overlooks a small beach littered with stones. If it's pure romance you're looking for in an accommodation, you couldn't do better than the Puerto Mio.

There are several budget hotels in the middle of town; the **Hotel Zihuatanejo** and **Hotel Avila** are among the cleanest and best. **Sotavento**, the first hotel on the scene here and tops as far as tranquillity goes, stands apart from it all high on a hill overlooking La Madera beach. You pay for the tranquillity, however, with its remoteness from town (about a ten-minute walk going down; forget about walking back); think about renting a car if you plan on staying here.

Villas Miramar is a colonial-style accommodation with 12 charming rooms surrounding a small pool and a couple of additional suites across the street on La Madera beach. The bedrooms have vaulted ceilings with fans, and the toilets and stand-up marble showers are in separate rooms. New, clean, small, and friendly, Villas Miramar is favored by experienced resort-goers.

The **Villa del Sol**, on La Ropa beach, is a beautiful, rustic, 17-room property patronized by an international clientele. The owners are Germans who came here, fell in love with the natural beauty of the area, and built the kind of hotel they thought would be right for the place. The property is tastefully done, with a seaside bar and restaurant and comfortable split-level rooms with a Polynesian décor. (The bathrooms and bedrooms are a few steps up from the sitting area.) La Ropa—the center of the Zihuatanejo beach action—is just outside the door. All things considered, the exotic feeling here more than makes up for the Villa del Sol's location away from the off-the-beach action. Rent a car if you're the impatient type; otherwise, the front desk will be happy to call a cab, which will take about ten minutes to arrive. (There are sometimes cabs at the taxi stand on the corner to your left.)

The **Fiesta Mexicana**, a small new property, is located right on La Ropa beach—its dining area is literally one step from the sand—and is the place for those who like to have the ocean right at hand.

Dining in Zihuatanejo

Coconuts, Avenida Agustín Ramírez 1, in town, is the essence of Zihua. Visitors like it and the locals love it—the bar is one of their favorite hangouts. If you want to find out who's in town and what they're doing, this is the place to do it. Take time for a drink at the bar and then move over to a table under the stars (most of the restaurants in Zihuatanejo are open-air). You'll find as much company as you want here, or you can have a quiet, intimate dinner. Reservations are advisable, especially if you plan on dining late; Tel: 4-2518.

El Castillo, at Calle Ejido 25, is another local favorite. The bar is in a tiny room off the main dining room, but no one seems to mind that it isn't very comfortable; people come just to hang out. The dining room itself is short on décor but long on good food (pepper steak and lentil soup are the chef's specialties). The manager is Swiss, and European touches are evident in both the food and service. However, El Castillo usually comes as a wonderful surprise—especially at night when the streets are dark—because it's so hard to find. Save yourself some aggravation and have a taxi take you. Reservations are advisable; Tel: 4-3850.

The restaurant at the **Villa del Sol** is open to the public. Tiny, under a *palapa,* and almost on the sand, it feels like a private club and is especially lovely at dinnertime, when candlelight, soft music, and the murmur of the waves accompany your meal. Informal elegance and European touches prevail. Be sure to reserve in season, however; Tel: 4-2239.

There are, in addition, two pretty, informal restaurants on the hill between La Madera and La Ropa, both with views of the bay. **The Bay Club** offers soft jazz in an outside patio/bar, as well as candlelit dinners in an upstairs dining room. **Kon-Tiki,** a little farther up the hill, is a Polynesian-style place with lots of bamboo and rattan that serves a variety of Mexican dishes. It's also the place to go if you need a quick fix of televised sports from the States.

Other, less formal restaurants worth a try downtown include El Sombrero, La Bocana (a family-style place popular with local businessmen), and La Casita. **La Sirena Gorda,** on the *malecón,* is a good place to watch passersby at breakfast time.

Excursions from Ixtapa/Zihuatanejo

You can sail away aboard the 36-foot catamaran *Tequila* for a three-hour cruise of Zihuatanejo Bay, with stops for swimming and snorkeling. The boat leaves from the Zihuatanejo pier at the end of the *malecón.*

The *Fandango,* which also leaves from the pier, takes visitors on a romantic moonlight cruise of the bay.

Excursions to Isla Ixtapa from Playa Quieta include a seafood lunch, snorkeling, and swimming. Once you get there, you can follow the path to the other side of the island, where you can sun and swim in front of the island's only restaurant.

A countryside tour (which is offered by almost every hotel in town) takes you to a typical Mexican fishing village untouched by time. Coconut, mango, papaya, and lemon plantations line the road en route.

All cruises and tours can be booked at your hotel, or with a local travel agent in advance.

GETTING AROUND
Most international air carriers do not offer direct service to Ixtapa/Zihuatanejo, which means that more often than not travellers will be routed through Mexico City, with some connections requiring an overnight stay. Among the airlines that do fly "direct" to Ixtapa/Zihuatanejo, Mexicana offers six flights a week from Los Angeles via Puerto Vallarta, weekend flights from Chicago and Dallas-Ft. Worth (the former via Puerto Vallarta and the latter via Manzanillo), and two additional flights during the week (Monday and Thursday) from Dallas-Ft. Worth via Guadalajara; Continental offers a daily flight from its Houston hub; and Aeroméxico offers a daily flight from Miami via Mexico City. Ixtapa/Zihuatanejo is a 5-hour-and-40-minute flight from Chicago; just over 5 hours from Miami; 4½ hours from Los Angeles; 3 hours and 45 minutes from

Dallas-Ft. Worth; and 2½ hours from Houston. The flying time from Mexico City to the Zihuantanejo airport is approximately 50 minutes.

Budget, Dollar, Fast (Jeeps), and Hertz all have desks at the airport.

Combis also make the trip from the airport to the hotels in Ixtapa and Zihuatanejo. Don't buy a round-trip ticket, however. Taking a regular taxi back to the airport will gain you some sun time.

You can drive to Zihuatanejo from Acapulco in about three hours; the bus (Estrella de Oro is the best line) takes about five hours. There are no flights between the two resorts.

Driving to Mexico City takes about eight hours. (The quickest route does *not* go through Acapulco.) The bus takes 12 hours.

With a little effort, you can walk just about everywhere in the Ixtapa hotel zone; buses make the run from the zone to downtown Zihuatanejo, with stops outside most hotels, but there is no set schedule.

Taxis are the easiest way to get around, and the major hotels will have cabs waiting outside. The taxi stand in Zihuatanejo is in front of the Canaima restaurant on Calle Juan Alvarez, which runs parallel to the *malecón*. (If you head into town at night, be sure to take a flashlight—the streets are ill lit.)

If you go to La Ropa or La Madera, ask your cab driver to come back for you at an appointed time; or you can walk to the taxi stand behind the Fiesta Mexicana. Don't count on finding a cab during lunch hour (between 2:00 and 4:00 P.M.), however.

If you go to more remote restaurants such as The Bay Club or Kon-Tiki, the management will be happy to call a taxi when you're ready to leave.

If you rent a car for the day, be sure to visit the opposite ends of the resort—Las Cuatas and Playa Quieta to the west of the Ixtapa hotel zone and La Ropa to the east of Zihuatanejo. Also, the road from The Bay Club to La Ropa is one of the area's most scenic drives.

ACCOMMODATIONS REFERENCE
The rate ranges given here are projections for December 1989 through Easter 1990. Unless otherwise indicated, rates are for double rooms, double occupancy. Ixtapa/ Zihuatanejo is in the Central Standard time zone, and the telephone area code is 743.

▶ **Hotel Avila**. Juan Alvarez 8, **Zihuatanejo**, Guerrero, Mexico 40880. U.S. $45. Tel: 4-2010.

▶ **Camino Real**. Playa Hermosa, **Ixtapa**, Guerrero, Mexico 40880. U.S. $100–$150. Tel: 4-3300; in the United States and Canada: 800-228-3000.

▶ **Dorado Pacífico**. Paseo del Palmar, **Ixtapa**, Guerrero, Mexico 40880. U.S. $120–$125. Tel: 3-2025.

▶ **Fiesta Mexicana**. Playa La Ropa, **Zihuatanejo**, Guerrero, Mexico 40880. U.S. $77–$105. Tel: 4-3776.

▶ **Ixtapa Sheraton**. Paseo del Palmar, **Ixtapa**, Guerrero, Mexico 40880. U.S. $150–$224. Tel: 4-3184; in the United States and Canada: 800-334-8484.

▶ **Krystal Ixtapa**. Paseo del Palmar, **Ixtapa**, Guerrero, Mexico 40880. U.S $120–$130. Tel: 4-2618; in the United States and Canada: 800-231-9860.

▶ **Puerto Mio**. Playa del Almacen, **Zihuatanejo**, Guerrero, Mexico 40880. U.S. $85–$140. Tel: 4-2048.

▶ **Hotel Sotavento**. Playa La Ropa, **Zihuatanejo**, Guerrero, Mexico 40880. U.S. $64–$80. Tel: 4-2033.

▶ **Villa del Sol**. Playa La Ropa, P.O. Box 84, **Zihuatanejo**, Guerrero, Mexico 40880. U.S. $130–$150. Tel: 4-2239.

▶ **Villas Miramar**. Playa La Madera, P.O. Box 211, **Zihuatanejo**, Guerrero, Mexico 40880. U.S. $40–$60. Tel: 4-2106 or 4-2616.

▶ **Hotel Zihuatanejo**. Agustín Ramírez 32, **Zihuatanejo**, Guerrero, Mexico 40880. U.S. $60. Tel: 4-3661.

ACAPULCO

Acapulco is Mexico's glamour resort, its special brand of outrageous, unabashed fun unlike anything you'll find elsewhere. Other resorts may have scenic beauty and fine facilities, but it is the people of Acapulco, who go out of their way to make sure every visitor has a good time, that make it special. In fact, Acapulco just may be the party capital of the universe. And while daytime here is glorious—there are 360 days of sunshine every year—it is the nightlife that is truly legendary. No one ever asks what you did during the day, but seemingly everyone will exhibit an interest in what you did—or are going to do—after dark.

In spite of the fact that the good times have been rolling since the 1950s, when the highway down from Mexico City opened and international flights began to arrive, what is now a third generation of waiters, boat boys, car attendants, and so on does not seem to have tired of the merriment. Smiles, pranks, and jokes still come naturally, and if you smile back, you'll find it goes a long way.

At the same time, Acapulco has been accused of welcoming only the young. The accusation is unjust. As long as they're not wearing brown shoes with crepe soles, anyone can have the time of his or her life here, whether the goal is to party or simply to relax. The trick is in knowing *what* you want and *where* to find it. Ninety-nine percent of the time Acapulco will have it.

MAJOR INTEREST

Large-resort variety of activity
Legendary nightlife
Cliff divers at La Quebrada
Sunsets and laid-back lifestyle at Pie de la Cuesta and Coyuca Lagoon
Shopping, especially for resort wear and handicrafts

One of the world's most beautiful bays, the Bahía de Acapulco has been compared with Rio de Janeiro's, and it's easy to see why. The first glimpse of it, at Puerto Marqués as you come into town from the airport, never fails to take your breath away—regardless of how many times you've seen it.

The famous beaches ringing this beautiful bay come in all shapes and sizes, with rough or gentle waves, *palapas* and palm trees, secluded or action-packed. Finding one that suits your own particular style is easy. The beaches between the Club Presidente and Acapulco Plaza hotels, as well as Playa Caleta and Playa Caletilla in Old Acapulco, are the most congested and lively. The rest are more tranquil and perfect for relaxing. No matter which you choose, however, you can count on the sun being strong in a resort this far south; sunbathers should proceed with caution and be sure to use double doses of sunscreens.

For all the fun available here, those who seek a vacation far from the madding crowds can have it. If this is what you have in mind, rent a private villa in the posh Las

Brisas residential section or stay at the Hotel Las Brisas. If you want serious privacy at more reasonable prices, you can stay up in Old Acapulco or at Ukae Kim way to the northwest in Pie de la Cuesta and sun at places like Beto's Beach Club at Barra Vieja, off the airport road before it starts to climb Las Brisas hill.

In addition to being Mexico's most glamorous resort, Acapulco is also one of its largest cities, with over a million Mexicans residing here. The area near the port is still the commercial center (though it looks like a seedy tropical town), and the Mercado Municipal is one of the country's biggest and best. Fishermen with old-fashioned nets still head out from the port at dawn, and the same tacky souvenirs that were the resort's original take-home treasures can still be bought at street stalls near the *zócalo*.

The weather is Acapulco's ace in the hole. Sunshine is more dependable here than at the other resorts, and the average annual temperature is 27°C (80°F). In fact, only the humidity varies noticeably from one season to the next. Locals consider it cold when they have to wear long-sleeved cotton shirts, and no one would be caught dead in a jacket, tie, or socks unless going to a special private party or one of the top hotel restaurants.

"The Season" runs from the middle of December to Easter (when the humidity is usually at its yearly low). But even in the rainy season—May to October—showers are short and usually fall at night; the foliage is at its most photogenic then as well, and the clear blue skies are often painted with rainbows. Prices for everything go down after Easter, but the same kinds of fabulous fun and activities prevail year-round. The only time things might slow down is late September or early October, when improvements are made in anticipation of the coming season, but this pause is imperceptible to most visitors.

Daily schedules follow those of most tropical places. If you want to conduct serious business, plan on doing it between 10:00 A.M. and 1:00 P.M. Business people generally get up early to take advantage of the cooler temperatures, and have breakfast around 10:00, as the temperature begins to heat up. Likewise the best time to play tennis or golf is early in the morning or late in the afternoon. Lunch is eaten between 2:00 and 5:00 P.M. Dinner usually begins around 9:00 P.M., unless you're going to a private home, where cocktails normally are served around 10:00 and dinner at midnight or later. Discos are at their frenetic best between midnight and 2:00 A.M. It's worth resetting your body clock to take advantage of it all.

Day and night bring different pleasures and are linked by delicious (and life-sustaining) siestas. If you take one and then go out later, you'll feel as if you're getting two days for the price of one. If you dine at 6:00 P.M. and go to bed early, on the other hand, you'll be missing half of the fun that is Acapulco's hallmark.

Gourmet dining à la Paris or New York, or even Mexico City, is unfortunately *not* an Acapulco specialty. If you like delicate food with intricate sauces, you won't find it here—or in any Mexican resort, for that matter. The best eating here is generally simple seafood and meat dishes with fresh tropical fruit for dessert. So unless you're dying for French, German, Italian, Japanese, or Chinese food, all of which can be found in Acapulco, when you select a restaurant you'll really be choosing what kind of atmosphere you like to dine in.

When it's time to get ready for dinner, remember that, in matters of dress, Acapulco is one of the most permissive places in the civilized world. You can wear a ball-gown to breakfast, stay in your bathing suit until way past midnight, or walk around in a disguise of some sort and no one will bat an eye. Anything goes, as long as you make an attempt to cover the important places. Well-put-together resort wear will get you in anywhere; the flashier it is, the faster you'll get in.

Finally, it won't take long to discover that Acapulco is a place where you can shop until 4:00 A.M. (Many discos and some restaurants even have stores where you can shop until dawn.) Competition from resorts such as Ixtapa and Cancún has forced retailers to take notice and upgrade both the merchandise sold here as well as the stores where it is displayed. Not surprisingly, Acapulco seems to have risen to the challenge overnight: Malls with good shops—the sparkling, air-conditioned Plaza Bahía is one example—are springing up all over town.

The best buys here are resort wear, handicrafts, and decorative items. Some of the resort wear sold might shock your grandmother, but most of it can be worn back home without causing a ruckus.

With no conscious plan in mind, Acapulco has developed into a series of pleasure pockets.

The Acapulco Princess and Pierre Marqués hotels are at the center of the action in the area lying between the

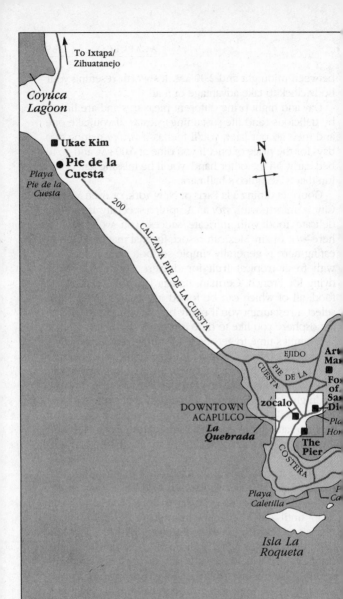

To Ixtapa/
Zihuatanejo

*Coyuca
Lagoon*

■ **Ukae Kim**
● **Pie de la
Cuesta**

*Playa
Pie de la
Cuesta*

200

CALZADA PIE DE LA CUESTA

N

EJIDO

PIE DE LA

CUESTA

Art
Ma

Fo
of
Sa
Di

*Pla
Hor*

**DOWNTOWN
ACAPULCO**

zocalo

*La
Quebrada*

COSTERA

**The
Pier**

*Playa
Caletilla*

P
Ca

*Isla La
Roqueta*

*PACIFIC

OCEAN*

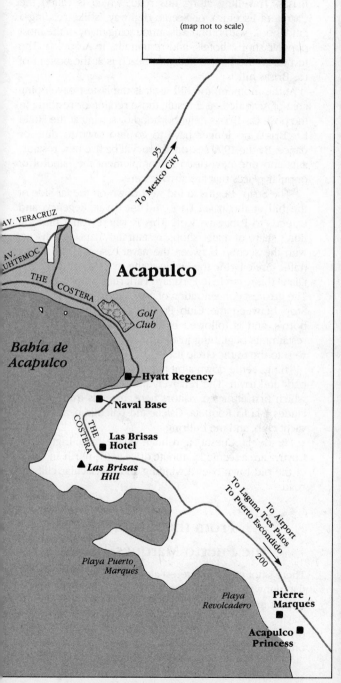

Acapulco
Area

(map not to scale)

To Mexico City

95

AV. VERACRUZ

AV. CUAUHTEMOC

THE COSTERA

Acapulco

Golf
Club

*Bahía de
Acapulco*

■ **Hyatt Regency**

■ **Naval Base**

THE COSTERA

■ **Las Brisas
Hotel**

▲ *Las Brisas
Hill*

To Airport
To Laguna Tres Palos
To Puerto Escondido

200

*Playa Puerto
Marques*

*Playa
Revolcadero*

■ **Pierre
Marques**

■ **Acapulco
Princess**

airport and the bottom of the hill on which presides Las Brisas. Travelling along this road, which is called the Carretera Escénica, or Scenic Highway, is like reading a guidebook, with billboards announcing many of the most popular shops, hotels, and restaurants in Acapulco. The turnoff to the Puerto Marqués beach is at the bottom of Las Brisas hill.

At the moment, the hill itself is the fastest developing area of Acapulco. As a result, those renting or residing in the posh Las Brisas neighborhood or staying at the Hotel Las Brisas no longer have to go into town to dine or dance. By the 1990 season, there will be five new restaurants and one new disco to complement the handful of popular places that are already here.

"The Strip" begins to the west down on the far side of the hill at the naval base and the Hyatt Regency, and extends to Papagayo Park. This is where you'll find the lion's share of malls, shops, restaurants, bars, and discos, with the section between the naval base and the Diana traffic circle being the liveliest (the stretch west from the Diana traffic circle to Papagayo Park runs a close second). The greatest concentration of good stores is found on the Strip between the Club Presidente Acapulco and Sanborn's, and is followed by a string of amazing seaside restaurants beginning just past Sanborn's and extending west to the traffic circle itself.

Things settle down a bit between the underpass to the park and town. The relatively tranquil old part of town, which first attracted visitors here, extends from and includes Isla La Roqueta, Caleta and Caletilla beaches, the yacht club, and the bullring.

Pie de la Cuesta, a fishing village, and Laguna de Coyuca are a scenic 15-minute drive to the north and west of the old town over a winding and spectacular cliffside road.

From the Airport to the Puerto Marqués Turnoff

There's not much of interest along the stretch of pancake-flat highway (the Carretera Escénica) that leads from the airport to the coast road. Not much, that is, unless you're staying at the Acapulco Princess or Pierre Marqués hotels, or you have a tee time at one of the two 18-hole championship golf courses that lie between them.

Many people who stay at the **Acapulco Princess** never venture off the premises. Built to resemble an Aztec pyramid, this bustling self-contained resort offers its guests an air-conditioned shopping mall; fresh- and salt-water pools; a broad beach (unsafe for anything but wading, however); horseback riding; eight restaurants; and a disco. With over 1,000 rooms, it's also one of the largest hotels in the country.

The Princess is typical of what makes Acapulco hotels different from others around the country. Most of the rooms here are more spacious, and the public areas larger, than you'll find at other resort hotels. Similarly, the pool areas are bigger and more exquisitely gardened. And the range of services and facilities available is generally more extensive than you'll find elsewhere.

The **Pierre Marqués**, its sister hotel, is "next door" across the two golf courses, and has more of a laid-back atmosphere than its much larger neighbor. The rooms and suites at the Pierre Marqués are linked by sprawling lush green lawns and peaceful gardens, and you can sun at either one of its two pools or on its beautiful beach (part of the longest beach in Acapulco). When you want action, just hop the shuttle bus over to the Princess (all amenities are interchangeable). The Pierre Marqués is for those vacationers who want to get away from it all.

As the coast road begins to climb west toward Las Brisas you'll get a glimpse of tiny **Puerto Marqués**, where pirates once hid from Spanish warships, off to the left, Today the beach there is a relatively undeveloped spot where Mexican vacationers on a budget spend the day swimming or floating around the quiet bay in an inner tube or on a Sunfish. Coming here to spend a day away from *gringos* can be a refreshing change of pace, but never do it on Sunday and be prepared for the swarms of kids who try to hustle business (they're on commission) for the beachside restaurants. Those who like to play the "I-was-there-when" game had better check out Puerto Marqués soon, because it, too, is slated for serious development in the near future.

The Hill between Puerto Marqués and the Hyatt Regency

This is the hottest area in Acapulco today—it seems as if every time you look there is something new to see and do on this hill. Restaurants, shops, discos, even a new tennis club—all have been built or are under construction within the last year. No wonder: The views of the bay are spectacular, and Las Brisas residents are a natural target for ambitious entrepreneurs. When it's all completed (supposedly) in 1990, this new crop of pleasurable distractions promises to revive Acapulco's original glamour at the same time as it gets the really upscale crowd to leave their villas and enjoy Acapulco by night again.

Madeiras, one of Acapulco's most popular restaurants with a view, is near the top of the hill not far from Fantasy, Acapulco's most sophisticated disco. **La Vista Mall**, which looks like a Mediterranean village, is nearby, as are Miramar, another elegant restaurant with a great view; the new King's View restaurant; and Los Rancheros, a long-time favorite popular with budget travellers.

Although you have to take your patience with you and sometimes bite your tongue over brusque treatment at the door, it seems that everyone wants to eat at **Madeiras**. Don't bother trying to get in if you haven't booked in advance; their policy is a strict "reservations only" one, and they're busy enough to enforce it. In fact, those who want to be sure of getting a reservation often call from home before getting on the plane. During the high season you'd be wise to book three days in advance. There are usually two seatings: opt for the later one, at 9:30, if your appetite can hold; Tel: 4-4378.

Once you're in, however, dining here is quite pleasant; little details make it special. Some of the exquisite tableware, for example, has been designed by Los Castillo, the country's leading silversmiths. (A variety of beautiful pieces, some made with new techniques arrived at through a collaboration of Japanese and Mexican silversmiths, is on sale in the shop near the entrance.) And if you reserve a table by the railing, you'll like this restaurant even more. The four-course meals are prix fixe, and the menu features what is fresh at the market, with a choice for every course.

Miramar, nearby, offers the same view as Madeiras but in a bigger building. In fact, Miramar looks like the living room of someone's oversized mansion. A slightly older crowd than at Madeiras congregates here, which probably explains why the atmosphere in its open-air dining room is more formal. Give yourself time to have a drink in the bar and then head downstairs to make your entrance. Reserving a table by the railing (although all tables have a view) will make the dining experience even more memorable.

Until recently, the "Big Three"—Madeiras, Miramar, and Los Rancheros—had a virtual monopoly on panoramic views of the bay (the exception was Coyuca 22 on the other side of town). Today's diners have a much wider choice, however. **Palenque,** just across the street from the disco Fantasy, stages a typical Mexican Fiesta Night, complete with folkloric dances and cockfights, in a pretty, colonial-style setting every night of the week.

Charlie's Chili, "The Grill on the Hill," in La Vista Mall on a promontory overlooking the bay, is a cool lunchtime getaway and an especially pleasant and informal place, with a fine view, for dinner.

Fantasy, the most dazzling of all Acapulco's discos, is just down the road from the mall and Madeiras. Floor-to-ceiling picture windows give dancers a spectacular view of the bay, and the walls are lined with plush velvet booths. Confetti, laser lights, and fireworks set off from the roof so that they cascade in front of the windows are just some of the tricks used to keep the place jumping, and visitors seem to love the glass elevator and the lingerie shop on the second floor. Popular with a glitzy, slightly older Beverly Hills–type crowd, Fantasy is an experience you won't soon forget, even if you're not one of them.

There's a special treat for serious art collectors just up the hill from Fantasy. Sculptor Pal Kepenyes has designed a new home for himself in which to exhibit his work. The house, a work of art in its own right, has been featured in the pages of *Architectural Digest* and promises to be recognized in many more publications. This versatile artist, who also designs jewelry and objets d'art, can be visited by appointment; Tel: 4-3738 or 4-4738.

King's View, a half mile down the hill in the direction of town, is a cozy little restaurant with—you guessed it—a view that is worthy of a king. It offers a slouchy living room kind of comfort and a limited selection of light entrées and snacks.

Grazziel, a bit farther on, is a new Italian restaurant that looks as if it belongs on a Mediterranean hillside. A tiled foyer leads into a pleasant dining room downstairs. The feeling is that of a bit of Italy transplanted to Acapulco.

A list of coming attractions on the hill would have to include **Extravaganza,** a new disco owned and to be operated by Tony Rullan, Acapulco's Disco King, that will be just that; and **Casa Nova,** by the people who brought you Coyuca 22. Located on a promontory across from the front door of the Hotel Las Brisas, the Casa Nova's customers will have a choice between dining under the stars on one of three outdoor terraces or inside in air-conditioned splendor.

The posh Las Brisas residential section begins just below Madeiras. Anyone who believes that Acapulco's popularity is declining should wangle an invitation to a party in one of the many extraordinary villas here.

Everything they say about **Las Brisas** itself, in the same neighborhood, is true. Built on a hillside, the hotel has probably entertained more celebrities than any other resort property in the world, and it's so private that guests have to wait at a reception building for the ubiquitous pink-and-white Jeeps to take them to their rooms. Many of the rooms (which here are called *casitas,* or "little houses") have their own private pool, and the management makes sure each one gets fresh flowers every day. Morning rolls and coffee arrive through an unobtrusive window in one of the walls (so you can sleep as late as you like), and a fruit plate will be waiting in the minifridge when you come back after a day in the sun. Little things like this make Las Brisas one of the most relaxing and private resort hotels anywhere (although if you truly want to guarantee your privacy, check to make sure that your pool isn't visible from the *casita* above you).

In keeping with its exclusive character, Las Brisas does not allow non-guests to dine at either of its two exquisite restaurants, **Bella Vista** and **La Concha Beach Club** (reached via a winding road through the residential section). And it's also one of the few places in Acapulco where guests seldom venture into town or even onto the Strip. For shoppers, La Vista Mall is a few minutes away by taxi, as are Madeiras, Miramar, and the disco Fantasy. For honeymooners or couples who want to be left alone, Las Brisas is the ultimate resort accommodation.

Los Rancheros, a long-time favorite serving Mexican food, is located down the hill in the direction of the Strip but has the same spectacular view as the more expensive places higher up the hill. Offering lunch and dinner in an informal atmosphere, Los Rancheros is a great bargain on the cook's good days. Just going for a margarita at sunset is a much safer bet, however—at least until they find a new cook.

THE STRIP

The Strip, where the beat goes on almost around the clock, is the pulsing heart of Acapulco. About 80 percent of the city's restaurants, discos, and boutiques are on or near it, and anyone who loves being in the middle of the action will want to stay in one of its hotels. Also, if you're looking to buy *anything* while you're in Acapulco, chances are you'll be able to find it here—even if it's tucked away among a host of other distractions.

Generally speaking, the Strip is the section of Avenida Costera Miguel Alemán (usually just called the Costera) that stretches along the bay from the naval base and the Hyatt Regency at the foot of the hill down from Las Brisas west to the Radisson Paraiso Acapulco and the underpass at Papagayo Park. The string of beaches fronting the Strip sparkles from sunup to sundown, and then the restaurants and discos take over and keep things going until dawn.

Until a few years ago this whole stretch was divided into unmarked pockets of action separated by private homes or empty tracts of land. Now, with breathtaking speed, almost all of these homes have been or are being replaced by hotels and malls, and the empty lots are giving way to other kinds of development.

From the Hyatt Regency to El Presidente

The Hyatt Regency; Regina's and Kycho's, two fine restaurants; and Baby O, Magic, and The News, three lively discos, get the Strip off to a sensational start. All are clustered near the naval base, which is tucked away at the bottom of Las Brisas hill. The base is off limits to all but naval personnel, except when the *Cuauhtémoc,* Mexico's "tall ship," is in port.

There are two Hyatts in town, so for the one next to the base tell your taxi driver that you want the Hyatt *Regency,* not the Hyatt *Continental.* The **Hyatt Regency** has a canny combination of qualities that enables it to be all things to all people. Financiers stay here when international bankers' meetings are held in Acapulco, and conventioneers and just plain folks also like it because it's recessed from the highway and therefore quieter than

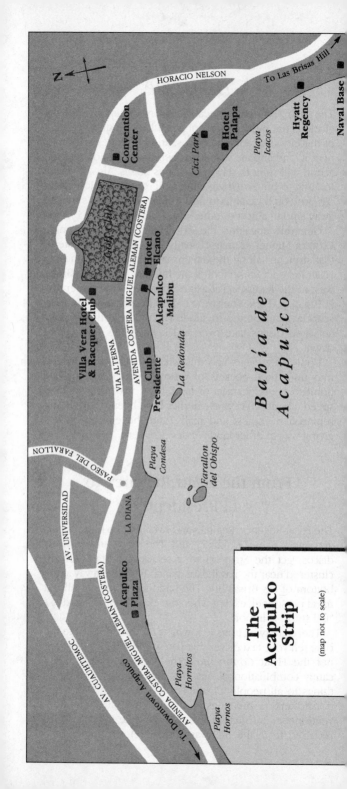

N

HORACIO NELSON

To Las Brisas Hill

Naval Base

Hyatt Regency

Hotel Palapa

Playa Icacos

Convention Center

Cici Park

Golf Club

Hotel Elcano

AVENIDA COSTERA MIGUEL ALEMAN (COSTERA)

Villa Vera Hotel & Racquet Club

VIA ALTERNA

Acapulco Malibu

Club Presidente

La Redonda

Bahía de Acapulco

PASEO DEL FARALLON

AV. UNIVERSIDAD

LA DIANA

Playa Condesa

Farallon del Obispo

Acapulco Plaza

AVENIDA COSTERA MIGUEL ALEMAN (COSTERA)

AV. CUAUHTEMOC

To Downtown Acapulco

Playa Hornitos

Playa Hornos

The Acapulco Strip

(map not to scale)

some of the other hotels on the Strip. A fresh-water pool and a beach with good swimming conditions, two restaurants (Neptuno, its beachfront seafood restaurant, is a favorite lunchtime meeting place for local businessmen), and a small shopping mall make this a self-contained resort. If it has a flaw, it's that the rooms themselves are quite plain and in need of refurbishing.

Keep two things in mind if you decide to stay here: 1) the hotel grounds abut the naval base, so you'll want to reserve a room on the beach side of the hotel in order to get an ocean view (naval maneuvers can also get noisy, especially on a Sunday when you're trying to sleep in); and 2) use room service for breakfast or find a place off the premises—the coffee shop on the lobby level leaves a lot to be desired. On the other hand, **La Cascada**, also on the lobby level, is a pretty Mexican-style restaurant (watch out for the burro that strolls through on occasion).

Regina's, in front of the naval base, is a favorite with locals who want to splurge and dine in elegant surroundings. Its Continental cuisine—the quality varies widely from night to night—is served by waiters dressed in black tie, and classical music adds to the refined ambience. Reserve a table in the air-conditioned dining room; there are plenty of other restaurants in Acapulco where you can dine outside, but air-conditioned non-hotel restaurants like Regina's are at a premium. Reservations are advised; Tel: 4-8653.

Kycho's is informal, even a bit crazy. Partyers from Baby O, across the street, pop in when the disco's snack bar doesn't offer enough in the way of sustenance, while other diners come to sandwich a meal between multiple games of backgammon. Kycho's serves up good, sensible food and occasionally has smoked salmon—a rarity in Acapulco. Wednesday night is fun night here: A Mexican Bingo-type game called Loteria, backgammon tournaments, and a bit of everything else goes on as you dine, making you feel as if you're a member of the club.

Acapulco disco-goers are accustomed to checking out two or three spots a night, and **Baby O** is always one of them. In fact, disco diehards invariably end up here to let their hair down with a younger crowd after a warmup, say, at Fantasy. As a result, there's usually a line at the door; come prepared to wait. The choice tables are on the dance-floor level, and of those the choicest are the banquettes against the wall facing the dance floor and the "caves" at each side of the dance floor. Squeezing as many people as possible into a banquette or "cave" is the modus operandi, so don't wear anything you can't afford to have wrinkle. Videos, electronic message boards, and other disco tricks are part of every evening. If you happen to be in Acapulco at the end of February or beginning of March when their Pajama Party is held, don't miss it (even if you have to buy a pair of pajamas at the door). The pillow fights, costumes (or absence thereof), and uninhibited pandemonium will make you feel as if you've landed a supporting role in a movie's party scene.

Magic and the new **News**, two other hot discos, are also on the Strip near Baby O (see "The Discos" under "Nightlife" at the end of the Acapulco section).

Cocula, at the sign of the sombrero, down the Costera a piece in the direction of town, offers informal Mexican dining at its best. Have a drink in the unobtrusive air-conditioned bar under the steps (a secret the locals seldom reveal) while you wait for a table under the stars. The only view is of traffic on the Costera, but Mexican-food lovers don't seem to mind; the do-it-yourself chicken-and-beef taco plates and Bohemia beer are guaranteed to make you want to order seconds. (A second Cocula in El Patio shopping center, across from the Hyatt Continental farther down the Strip, serves the same fare but isn't half as much fun.)

The **Hotel La Palapa**, a soaring structure on the beach behind the CiCi amusement park, is favored by Canadians and groups, and has nothing but mini—truly mini—suites. It does have the best beauty salon in town for manicures and pedicures, however. (False nails and the niceties of their maintenance haven't arrived yet in most Mexican resorts, so bring your own fakes and glue in case you need emergency service.) The pool is a few steps from the ocean, and the hotel itself offers tranquillity just off the beaten track of the Strip at reasonable rates. For those who don't mind getting their elegance elsewhere, La Palapa is a good bet.

Back on the Costera, **CiCi**, a water-oriented park for children, is enclosed by a wall painted with blue-and-white waves. Inside you'll find a pool with a wave-making machine, water slides, and a dolphin show. The Convention Center across the way is equipped to accommodate everything from an opera to a rock concert, but unfortunately its beautiful gardens and buildings are rarely used. Watch the marquis for special performances.

Something new and different in Acapulco—a feat most

people had written off as impossible—has been built just a few doors down from CiCi. **Antigua**, a colonial-style shopping complex, is up and running, and **Issima**, one of the best boutiques in town, heads the lineup of shops here. There are also rumors that a Hard Rock Café will be opening in the mall soon.

The newest and very best place to shop for upscale decorative items in Acapulco is a hideaway called **Nina's Bodega**. Nina, a vivacious writer who covers local events and the party circuit for the *Mexico City News,* is the proprietor of this spic-and-span warehouse tucked away on an unpaved back road five minutes from the Costera. (The best way to get there is to have Nina herself pick you up, but if you insist on finding it on your own, ask your cab driver to take you to La Garreta, Acapulco's oldest cemetery. Nina's unmarked bodega is just across the street.) Her merchandise—some old, some new—consists of tastefully selected ceramics, furniture, antiques, and miscellany ranging in price from $10 to $3,000, and it's the place to check out if you're looking for an original piece. (Nina will be happy to arrange its shipment back home.) Meeting Nina and browsing through her giant shop is one of Acapulco's best treats. The warehouse is open by appointment only; Tel: 4-0007.

The restaurant in the **Hotel Elcano**, a block off the Costera across from the golf course between the Convention Center and El Presidente, is one of the last vestiges of the "good old days" in Acapulco. The open-air beachfront dining room serves delicious seafood with a Spanish flavor, the setting is tranquil, and the price is just right. In fact, people who have been coming to Acapulco for years love the Elcano precisely because it is one of the few places on the Strip where you can escape the crowds and take a step back into yesteryear. Avoid it on Sundays, however.

The **Acapulco Malibu**, another of the town's best-kept secrets, is a five-minute walk down the Costera from the Elcano in the direction of town. The Malibu is a time-sharing hotel; that is, it rents rooms when their individual owners aren't in residence. Really the only small hotel on the Strip, it was built by a Texas millionaire and his partners, who intended it to be a chic hideaway in the midst of the high-rise hotels and condominiums. The rooms are large and octagonal, and most balconies have a view of the ocean. **Tabasco Beach**, a beachfront restaurant outside the hotel, is a pleasant spot for a quick breakfast, lunch, or sunset drink. The beach, a few steps from the small pool, is uncrowded—or at least it will be until the new high-rise next door is completed. The cozy, family-style atmosphere at the Malibu is refreshing, and the friendly staff will make you feel at home from the moment you walk in the door. (In fact, your chances of receiving a telephone message here are far better than they are in most of the larger hotels.)

The **Villa Demos**, a popular Italian restaurant with a dining room in a sprawling tree-shaded patio; the Gallery, the best gay nightclub in town; and **Alfredo's Tennis Club** and **Tiffany's Tennis Club** are behind the Pizza Hut on Lomas del Mar, the street where the Villa Vera Hotel & Racquet Club is located.

The Gallery has the best, most opulent transvestite show in town. Non-gay visitors usually check out the scene at least once—the "girls" here look as good as real showgirls in Las Vegas.

The **Villa Vera Hotel & Racquet Club** is the snazziest hotel on or near the Strip. Only minutes inland from the Costera, it resembles a dazzling piece of Beverly Hills transplanted to Acapulco. The clientele ranges from serious tennis players (the tennis facilities are easily the best in town) to the well-heeled set seeking plush accommodations and privacy in a beautiful setting far from the crowds—but not so far that they can't partake of the action on the Costera when the mood strikes. Every one of the 90 rooms is different: some have their own pools and many have sunken baths. The dining room, with grand views of the bay, is one of Acapulco's most popular places for breakfast, lunch, and dinner, and the main pool is a favorite hangout of the trendy singles crowd (it offered the first swim-up bar in the country). Beach nuts can use the facilities at the Maralisa, its sister hotel down on the Costera in the direction of town, but most people find the scene at the pool too riveting to leave.

The hotel, which is now owned and managed by a bright young American woman, prides itself on the kind of service that only such modest-sized establishments can offer. Attention to detail is evident in everything, and guests are carefully looked after. The Villa Vera is the kind of place that allows guests to make of it what they want. And the fact that everything—*including* the guests (who apparently come here *after* going through a weight-loss program back home)—is easy on the eyes and ultra-luxurious makes it that much more appealing. As a result, a good percentage of the guests are repeat visitors who request a specific room when making a reservation.

At the top of the same hill, on the Carretera Panorámica, the Italian palazzo–style **El Campanario**, the highest restaurant in town, offers 180-degree views of the bay. This is a wonderful place for a drink, but when the restaurant gets crowded diners may have to get their patience out. The menu features Continental cuisine, but you might want to have dinner elsewhere until it gets a new chef and works the kinks out of its service. By day, on the other hand, it's an oasis for anyone who likes to relax around a pretty pool (massages are available in the changing rooms). The light lunch fare is tasty and the spectacular location seemingly puts you miles above the hustle and bustle.

Down on the Strip again, at the bottom of the hill, you'll find **Fiorucci's** and **Anna's**, a boutique featuring the best in original Mexican fashion, just across the street.

From El Presidente to the Diana Traffic Circle

This is Acapulco's epicenter, and the action really picks up as the Costera climbs toward the El Presidente and Condesa del Mar hotels. Gucci and **Aca Joe**—probably the most popular unisex store in town—as well as Rubén Torres, Voban, and Dancin' are just a few of the "name" boutiques crammed in between some of Acapulco's best-known restaurants along this stretch. All sell colorful resort wear. Voban also carries great bathing suits and accessories.

Sanborn's, the drugstore/cafeteria that no one seems to be able to do without, stands at the top of the hill. Only a handful of locals know that superb malted milkshakes are served in the downstairs restaurant here.

Carlos 'n' Charlie's, king of Acapulco's fun restaurants, is just across the street. Unless you're a well-known celebrity, however, you'll probably have to stand in a first-come, first-served line to get in. That fact doesn't seem to deter anyone, and crowds of all ages and nationalities begin to arrive by car, taxi, and horse-drawn carriage as soon as the door opens at 6:00 P.M. The "Cluck, Moo, and Oink" items on the menu give you some idea of what to expect once you get inside, and waiters' pranks and jokes are an integral part of the total dining experience. In fact, nothing is serious here except the no-nonsense food. Fair portions of chicken, ribs, and fish are the most popular items. With all the activity and people-watching going on in the dining room, few customers notice the passing scene on the Costera below. Stop in the air-conditioned bar before dinner; chances are you'll stay longer than you planned.

When you step into **El Fuerte del Virrey**, on Roca Sola just behind Carlos 'n' Charlie's, you step into another world. A private museum is located just off the bar below the dining room, complete with a collection of paintings, costumes, and memorabilia from the decades around the turn of the century. (Diners can request a tour before or after dinner.) Upstairs, the rococo dining room recalls all the splendor of colonial Mexico. Although the prices for its Continental cuisine are on the high side, the total experience offered by this elegant restaurant makes for a memorable night out. Reservations are advised; Tel: 4-3321.

Pepe & Co., a popular restaurant and piano bar that for years was just a few doors from Carlos 'n' Charlie's, has moved to the beach behind the Acapulco Plaza. An air-conditioned Friday's has taken its place here and is in full swing.

Stern's, a great place for one-stop gift shopping, is located a few doors farther down the Costera at the entrance to the Plaza Condesa mall, and offers a tasteful selection of silver jewelry and decorative items (which they'll be happy to pack and ship for you).

The beachfront restaurants that have captured the hearts (and stomachs) of Acapulco vacationers for so many years begin just west of Sanborn's. **Beto's Safari Bar** is popular with beer-drinking youngsters and budget travellers, but the open-air restaurant on the lower deck is another of the well-kept secrets in town. The prices at the latter are moderate and the food decent, but it's hard to resist the romance of a candlelight dinner under the stars with the Bahía de Acapulco just a stone's throw away. Ask for a table near the railing so you can watch the moonlight shimmer on the water.

Beto's, a separate establishment next door, is one of the oldest and best of these beachfront restaurants. Located at the bottom of a short staircase leading down from the Costera, it somehow manages to look like the verandah of a private home. There are dining rooms on either side of the stairs and luncheon service under *palapas* on the sand. Be sure to try one of the dishes here that are hard to find elsewhere: *quesadillas de cazon* (fried tortillas filled with baby shark meat) or *pescado a la Talla* (marinated grilled fish)—a local specialty. Beto's also offers live music during the week, and while there's no formal dance floor, no one will stop you from dancing if the spirit moves you. (That's another one of Acapulco's most endearing traits: Once someone starts to dance, everyone else will try to get in on the act.)

Most restaurants along this stretch offer food service on the beach. The left side of Beto's beach is frequented by the local gay community, but there's plenty of room for everyone.

Mimi's Chili Saloon (no beach service here) is a powder-blue hoot that promises and delivers dynamite two-for-one strawberry and mango margaritas at "happy hour"—but if you drink half of one you might not make it home. It's better to have a hamburger with an order of French fries or onion rings on the side along with your margarita. In fact, everything from the hot dogs to the potato skins and country-fried chicken at Mimi's is designed to make you drool. This is the place to go when you're dying for American-style fast food (McDonald's hasn't arrived in Acapulco yet).

There's no restaurant on this planet quite like **Paraiso**, a few doors down from Mimi's. One of the pioneers of Acapulco's special tongue-in-cheek style of fun, Paraiso is the kind of place where anything can happen at any time. A woman may find herself attracting admiring wolf whistles one minute, then have a lei of fresh flowers thrown over her head as a chimpanzee puckers up to give her a sloppy kiss the next. The live salsa and rock and roll music gets everyone feeling friendly in a hurry (and out on the dance floor sooner or later), and heaven help you if they find out it's your birthday or anniversary—you just may be picked up, chair and all, and carried off to the bandstand to the great amusement of the other customers. The drinks are big here, the *palapas* keep you cool, and the party lasts well beyond sunset. Hefty portions of lobster, shrimp, meat, and red snapper (*huachinango*) are the specialties of Paraiso, and lunch is the busiest time; if a conga line to the beach starts to form, forget your inhibitions and jump in.

Two art galleries—**Sergio Bustamante** and **El Dorado**—a few doors down from Paraiso on the opposite side of the street, sell a variety of whimsical animals and other sculpture. **Marti**, everyone's favorite sporting-goods store, is nearby and can't be missed. **Marbella,** a new shopping center at the Diana traffic circle, promises to attract even more people to the area. **Eve,** the only disco in Acapulco whose wall opens to the great outdoors, is a few doors away. While the crowd at Eve can include anybody and everybody, the beachfront dance patio is unbeatably romantic.

The Diana, as it is known, where traffic circulates around a fountain topped by a statue of the huntress with her bow, is one of Acapulco's busiest intersections. Highway 95, the road from Mexico City, meets the Costera here, and it's the location of the only big gas station in town. (There are only three major gas stations in the entire area: one at the bottom of the hill before the residential neighborhood of Las Brisas; the one here; and a third at the western end of town where the winding road to Pie de la Cuesta begins.)

From the Hyatt Continental to the Radisson Paraiso Acapulco

El Patio, across from the Hyatt Continental west of the Diana, was one of Acapulco's first malls. Gucci; **Thelma's,** a long-time Acapulco favorite that makes clothes to order; and **Marietta's** are just a few of the good boutiques along this stretch of the Strip. Marietta, a Scandinavian beauty who married a local boy, designs cotton dresses with a unique European/Mexican flair (she also designs to order), and the popularity of her store has prompted her to set up shop in a number of other locations around town. Victor Salmones, a popular local sculptor with an international following, has a good gallery in the neighborhood, and the **Galería Rudic,** which sells paintings by Mexican artists to serious collectors, is across the way.

Just beyond the Hyatt Continental to the west, the **Acapulco Plaza,** with over 1,000 rooms and suites in three towers, a shopping mall with over 50 stores, four tennis courts, and two pools, is the biggest hotel on the Strip. In spite of its size, however, the management somehow keeps the service personalized, and because all the public areas (including the free-form pools) are especially spacious, you never get the feeling of being crowded. Not surprisingly, the Plaza has everything that a visitor on vacation could want. **Maximilian's,** one of two "gourmet" restaurants in Acapulco, is the only air-conditioned one on the beach (reservations advised; Tel: 5-9050), and **Los Arcos**, an air-conditioned Mexican-style restaurant with a great make-your-own-taco platter, is a more than pleasant place to eat. The Oasis health club on the third-floor level of the hotel is just that—no children allowed, so the only noise you hear is the sound of adults working off last night's dinner; you can also order up a light snack here or sun bathe to your heart's content.

The rooms in the main tower are the most convenient. Though the suites in the smaller towers have their own registration desk, they are a considerable distance from the restaurants and the entrance to the hotel's beach (something you'll notice if you leave your sunscreen behind in your room). If you do end up staying in one of the smaller towers, try to avoid the west side of the Catalina Tower—the music from the lively lobby bar makes taking that all-important siesta a virtual impossibility.

The **Acapulco Plaza Mall** has two floors of good boutiques. Diva, Mar y Mar (the big Mar y Mar store is across the street), Banana Republic, and **Pasarela** (for glitzy Mexican-style evening clothes and accessories) are a few of the top ones here. In addition, Pasarela sells beautiful (but expensive) hand-beaded dresses.

Papacito's Last Call and Barbecue, tucked away in a corner of the mall at street level, is one of a handful of places in Acapulco that can be enjoyed by the late-night crowd that doesn't like discos. The place has a modern look and offers a macho sort of comfort, with sofas where you can order drinks and snacks. Their frozen margaritas are marvelous and the fajitas are superb. The non-stop live music will last until 3:00 or 4:00 A.M. here—even if you don't.

The Acapulco Plaza has a sports center where everything from scuba diving to deep-sea fishing excursions can be arranged, and the hotel's beach is one of the best places to try the parasail rides for which Acapulco is famous.

Pepe & Co. is now in a Polynesian-style place behind the Plaza, having been transplanted to the beach here from its old location on the Costera, but its piano bar is still a favorite with late-nighters. Chacon, the pianist, has a loyal following of people who like to hum, sing along—or even grab the mike when they get sufficiently inspired.

Plaza Bahía, on the Costera a few doors down from the Acapulco Plaza, is the first and only air-conditioned non-hotel mall in town, and, not surprisingly, was an instant success. Baby O, for trendy resort wear and accessories; Galería 10/10 for decorative items; and Bazaar, which offers a varied assortment of souvenirs and objets d'art, are among the best shops on the second floor. Taxi and Regina Romero are among the better ones downstairs.

ACAPULCO OFF THE STRIP
The Underpass to Town

After the Radisson Paraiso, which is located a bit to the west of the Acapulco Plaza, the Costera goes underground a few minutes farther west to accommodate Papagayo, a sprawling park with games for children and a cable car that connects it to the beach. The best thing about this piece of prime real-estate, however, is the aviary, which is a wonderful place to keep cool on on a hot day.

Super Super (which has everything from shampoo to suntan lotion, along with food, wine, liquor, and film), Gigante, and Commercial Mexicana, the three best supermarkets in town, are just to the west of the Papagayo underpass and across the street from **Playa Hornos**, a palm-shaded beach beloved by Mexican vacationers, who rent beach chairs nearby and cool off in thatched-roof restaurants such as Sorocco.

You'll feel as if you're in France when you step into **Normandie**, on the corner of the Costera and Calle Malespina next to the Sol de Acapulco office. This unassuming establishment has a time-tested reputation for excellent food; some even say it's the best French cuisine in the country. Fresh-from-the-market ingredients are used for the imaginative appetizers and entrées, and the eclectic décor somehow manages to be relaxing. You can choose to dine on the patio or inside in air-conditioned comfort—but only for dinner, and only from December to Easter (it's closed the rest of the year).

The **Mercado Municipal**, five long blocks inland from the Costera near the Sol de Acapulco office, is one of the most colorful open markets in the country, and local residents depend on it for everything from food to magic potions. Strolling through its crowded aisles will give you an idea of what life in this tropical port behind all the glitz and glamour is like. The best way to enter the market is through the flower section. Ask your taxi driver to leave you at the corner of Ruiz Cortínes and Diego Hurtado de

Mendoza. If you do the driving, look for the sign just past the Sol de Acapulco that reads "San Jeronimo, Pie de la Cuesta, Zihuatanejo, and Mercado." Turn right and get ready to sit: the narrow street is always congested. Park wherever you can just before Ruiz Cortínes, and give the attendant a few pesos to watch your car.

Although it doesn't appear to be the case, the market *is* divided into sections. If you are looking for something in particular, learn its name in Spanish and ask directions. Handicrafts and souvenirs are in the covered area next to the flower section toward the back, which is a good place to begin any exploration of the market. The market itself is at its best in November and December, when whimsical Christmas-tree ornaments can be bought for pennies, and bargaining is part of the fun. Saturday between 10:00– 11:00 A.M. is prime time throughout the year. If you just want to have a quick look, go on a weekday morning around 10:00, and ask your taxi driver to accompany you inside.

The **Museum of Acapulco** is housed in the Fort of San Diego, which overlooks the Costera from its hill above the cruise-ship pier. Though its name means "place where the reeds were destroyed" in Nahuatl, Acapulco has had a relatively uneventful history. It became a ship-building center for New Spain's trade with the Orient after the Conquest, and though pirates came on occasion to plunder its shores, no major war or uprising has ever touched the city.

After the Spanish departed in the aftermath of the War of Independence, Acapulco was all but abandoned for the next hundred years. It was only after the first road from Mexico City was pushed over the Sierra Madre del Sur in 1927 that Acapulco began to awaken. Highway 95, the first superhighway, was inaugurated in 1955, but the real fun began in 1964, when direct international flights began to bring a host of celebrities and jet-setters into town.

A broad staircase across from the cruise-ship pier leads from the Costera to the museum, where the story of the fort and the town's history are displayed in a series of air-conditioned rooms that were once used to store ammunition. The clever design (created by experts at the Museum of Anthropology in Mexico City) is in many cases as interesting and avant-garde as the exhibits themselves. And though it only takes a few minutes to see everything, it's well worth a stop. The museum is open from 10:00 A.M. to 6:00 P.M., Tuesdays through Sundays.

Downtown

There are few good reasons for visitors to check out downtown Acapulco. It looks like any tropical port, complete with a central plaza, or *zócalo,* and mandatory bandstand where concerts are held on Sundays; a church (Nuestra Señora de la Soledad) with a charming exterior; and some major banks and stores, including Woolworth's, another branch of Sanborn's, and Emil, a no-nonsense clothing store for both sexes. If you want to change a large amount of currency, you'll save some money by doing it at one of the downtown banks. **Terraza de las Flores**, overlooking the plaza, is the best German restaurant in town. It is also the only one, but its red cabbage, schnitzel, sauerkraut, and potatoes are in fact delicious.

The Artisans' Market, sometimes called the Flea Market, is full of the typical souvenirs that you may already have found along the Costera. It's located behind the Woolworth's on Calle Velasquez de León.

Samy's closet-sized shop at Calle Hidalgo 7, two blocks west of the church, is the darling of knowledgeable residents and visitors alike. At first glance there doesn't appear to be much in the way of merchandise here, but the affable owner, Armando, will whip up anything from a pair of pants to an elaborate costume in no time (he also offers his own reasonably priced line of resort wear, Linea Sol). The store itself needs some refurbishing, and the temperature inside can become unbearable on humid days, but that doesn't seem to bother a surprising number of people you often see mentioned in the social column and business pages. Samy's specialties are cool summer caftans in gorgeous colors and lightweight shirts and pants for men. (A chat with him as he takes your measurements will also fill you in on all the local gossip.)

Fishermen mend their nets, much as they always have, across from the *zócalo* at the corner of Costera and Calle Iglesias. You can rent deep-sea fishing boats at Pesca Deportiva, opposite the *zócalo* next to the municipal pier, or *muelle.*

Old Acapulco

Old Acapulco—the peninsular area that includes **Playa Caleta** and **Playa Caletilla**, as well as Isla La Roqueta (see Excursions, below)—looks much the same today as it did in the days when Acapulco was rehearsing for international stardom. You'll find the bullring, Plaza Caletilla, in this part of town, as well as the world-famous Acapulco *clavadistas,* or cliff-divers. The men who make their daring leaps from a 150-foot-high cliff at **La Quebrada** dive several times each day—once in the afternoon and two or three times at night. You can watch these spectacular athletes in comfort from the bar at the Hotel Mirador or, for a small fee, from La Perla, a nightclub. You can also watch from the steps in the cliffside park near the hotel. The "show" is free, but you will want to contribute when the divers pass the hat. Ask at your hotel or call the Mirador for the times of the performances.

PIE DE LA CUESTA

Pie de la Cuesta and Laguna de Coyuca are for those who like their scenery minus a backdrop of multi-million-dollar high-rises. The fishing village of Pie de la Cuesta is one of the best places in Acapulco to go on Sundays, and one of the best places to watch the sunset any day of the week.

The area is a scenic 15-minute drive north and west of downtown along Calzada Pie de la Cuesta, which overlooks the ocean. There's a turnoff leading to what was once the old airport road—and which is now lined with ramshackle restaurants—after the road comes down out of the hills. If you've come to see the sunset, choose one of the restaurants on the beach side, rent a chair or a hammock, order your coco loco, and get ready for one of the world's finest shows.

The entire area is a world apart from the glamorous resort just over the hills to the south. Many children still get to school by dugout canoe, and in some places the waterways are made impassable by lily pads. The long, flat stretch of beach here is unspoiled and beautiful, but the surf is too strong for swimming.

The **Coyuca Lagoon**, behind the beach, is a nature preserve much loved by bird watchers, fishermen, and filmmakers (*Rambo II* was just one of the movies filmed here), as well as a water-skier's idea of heaven (and the perfect place to learn how to drop one ski). **Tres Marías** is the local cognoscenti's favorite hangout. Order your lunch in advance (it will be waiting for you at the prearranged hour) and claim a hammock or lounge chair. And whether you waterski or not, be sure to ask one of the boatmen to take you on a tour of the waterways at the end of the lagoon. "Broncos"—small motorboats for one or two—and inner tubes can also be rented.

If you're only coming out for the day, be sure to arrange for a taxi driver to pick you up at an appointed time.

If you fall in love with the place (a distinct possibility), on the other hand, you can stay overnight at **Ukae Kim**, an attractive 18-room hotel on the beach side. Reserve a room overlooking the ocean—the beds are on raised platforms so you can catch the view. There is also a small restaurant and beachclub at Ukae Kim—all far from the crowds—and the absence of telephones or television sets will guarantee that your reverie won't be interrupted. Non-guests can use the beach club for a small fee, which includes a towel and lounge chair.

NIGHTLIFE IN ACAPULCO

Acapulco's nightlife enjoys an international reputation, and ranges from sassy to sophisticated. There is truly something here for everybody; all you have to do is pick and choose.

You can dine and dance at romantic air-conditioned rooftop restaurants such as **Techo del Mar** in the Condesa del Mar hotel; **Windjammer** (La Fragata) in the Radisson Paraiso Acapulco; and, in season, **La Joya** at the Hyatt Continental. All of these still have the feeling of days gone by and attract an older crowd that likes touch dancing.

Nightclubs such as **Banneret** in the Calinda Acapulco Quality Inn and **Mil Luces** in the Hyatt Regency offer floor shows with big-name entertainers. **El Fuerte**, in front of the Hotel Las Hamacas, on the Strip just before you get to town, is for those who like it spicy and Spanish, flamenco-style.

The Convention Center offers the occasional spectacle; watch the marquis outside for upcoming events.

The Discos

Acapulco's discos rank as one of its leading attractions, and you're definitely missing something if you don't go at least once. They're at their best between 12:30 and 2:00 A.M. on a weekend night. Otherwise, they're open every night of the year from 10:00 P.M. until the last customer goes home (except for Boccaccio, a few doors down from Baby O in the direction of town, which closes "early" at 4:00 A.M.). Try to come with a partner of the opposite sex. Some discos have big crowds waiting, especially in season, but if you're well dressed and well behaved (and good at staring doormen down) you're likely to get in sooner than the rest.

Once you're inside, tip the maitre d' or waiter right away to ensure a good table and good service. If you can't get into the disco of your choice, try another one. They're all crazier and zanier than anything back home.

Fantasy, Baby O, Magic, and The News are the current favorites.

Just beyond the Hyatt Regency in the direction of town, **The News**, Acapulco's newest disco—for the moment— has managed to do something different. While other discos look small, this one is large, and prides itself on being upscale and "civilized." On a good night The News packs in some 2,000 souls, but there's plenty of room for everbody. Two giant bars, a restaurant, and a "Champagne room" (you have to buy three bottles of domestic Champagne or one imported bottle in order to sit there) are just part of the fun.

Magic, across the Costera and a little bit closer to town, has been redecorated and now caters to a more affluent crowd of young people than before, making it one of the best values in town. Private tables and plush banquettes give it the feeling of a nightclub. The sound system is one of the best in town; lasers, confetti, and other gimmicks liven up the party even more from time to time, and a snack bar will soon be ready for business.

(Fantasy and Baby O are discussed earlier in this section, under "The Hill" and "From the Hyatt Regency" respectively.)

A slightly older crowd of regulars remains loyal to **Boccaccio** (back across the Costera), which still has most of the features that once made Acapulco's discos unique: balloons, confetti, streamers, and the like. Unfortunately, when laser lights and video screens infiltrated the scene, much of the anything-can-happen spirit of Acapulco's discos was diluted. Most discos in town include a sprinkling of the above to add a bit of excitement, but Boccaccio has a party spirit that is a bit more contagious than the others.

Koko's, on the site of the late Tequila A Go Go at the western end of the Patio shopping mall, has been popular since the day it opened. And no wonder. For starters, the entrance is sensational—it even lights up as you walk in—and the interior has a clean, ultra-modern look about it, with comfortable chairs and one of the few dance floors in town that you can walk around.

SPORTS IN ACAPULCO

Most major hotels have sports centers where you can arrange just about every major water sport. In addition, water-skiing boats are available at every major beach, as are parasail rides. Jet skis can be rented by the hour on the beach behind Mimi's Chili Saloon. The same goes for Broncos (one- or two-person motorboats).

Windsurfers and sailboats can be rented on the beach behind the Hotel Malibu and Diana traffic circle. Scuba diving and snorkeling excursions can be arranged at Arnold Brothers or Divers de México, both on the beach side of the Costera just before town. Surfing is not permitted on the beaches along the Strip, so diehards take their boards out to Playa Revolcadero, south and east of town beyond the Acapulco Princess.

Fishing boats can be chartered through your hotel or at **Pesca Deportiva**, across from the *zócalo* near the municipal pier; Tel: 2-1099. Sailfish, marlin, tuna, mackerel, and snapper are all prize catches in the waters around Acapulco. Divers de México (Tel: 2-1398) will be happy to arrange you a spot on a boat shared by others.

The area's two championship golf courses are located between the Acapulco Princess and Pierre Marqués hotels, and a nine-hole public course can be found across from the Hotel Elcano along the Costera.

The bravest bulls and greatest bullfights are usually not seen in the tropics. Acapulco's **Plaza Caletilla**, however, offers the best of any Mexican resort—largely because it has the biggest potential audience. The season runs from December through Easter, and the seats by the railing (*barerra*), in the shade, are the best. Tickets are sold at the Motel Kennedy, a few feet off the Costera near Big Boy (Tel: 5-8540), or can be arranged through your hotel.

EXCURSIONS FROM ACAPULCO

The catamaran *Aca Tiki* takes guests on day and sunset cruises of the bay. The boat (which claims to be the world's

largest sailing catamaran) leaves from the pier near the
Fort of San Diego, and the cruises are popular with an
international clientele as well as wealthy locals. Reserve in
advance to avoid disappointment; Tel: 4-6140 or 4-6786.
Sunset cruises include drinks (Mexican brands), dinner,
and a folkloric show that the operators claim can't be seen
anywhere else in town.

Those who want to do it the way the locals do it can sail
around the bay on the *Fiesta,* the *Bonanza,* or the *Hawai-
iano* at rock-bottom prices; each has its own pier past
town on the way to Caleta Beach.

Ferry boats take passengers from the Caleta pier to **Isla
La Roqueta,** where you can lunch at **Palao,** which also has
its own tiny bay where you can take a dip between
courses. Palao serves tasty, simple seafood and meat
dishes, occasionally accompanied by marimba music. After lunch you can take a scenic walk through the jungle,
with breathtaking views of the ocean along the way. More
energetic travellers can climb up to the lighthouse. In
addition, the main beach at Roqueta, a favorite Sunday
excursion for visiting Mexicans, is a ten-minute walk from
the restaurant when the boardwalk is in good repair.
Otherwise, it's about five minutes by boat.

GETTING AROUND

A number of international air carriers link Acapulco with
cities in the United States. While many flights are direct,
few are non-stop, however, and often passengers will
have to deplane and go through customs in Mexico City.
Those carriers that do fly non-stop to Acapulco include
Continental, which offers daily flights from its hubs in
Newark and Houston, and American and Delta, which
offer daily flights to Acapulco from Dallas-Ft. Worth. Aeroméxico (from New York) and Mexicana (from Chicago
and San Antonio) offer daily "direct" service to Acapulco,
with a stopover in Mexico City for customs. It's a 6-hour-
and-45-minute flight from Newark; 5 hours and 40 minutes from Chicago; almost 4 hours from San Antonio; 2
hours and 40 minutes from Dallas-Ft. Worth; and 2½
hours from Houston.

Getting from the Acapulco airport into town is no cup
of tea, either. Private taxis are not allowed to pick up
passengers at the airport, so you're stuck with taking a
combi or a bus. Your best bet is to call your travel agent
or hotel before leaving home and arrange to be picked
up by private car. If, on the other hand, you do take a

combi or bus, only buy a one-way ticket: taxis are allowed to take departing guests *to* the airport (the fare is about $10). Watch to make sure your luggage is loaded, but if you're traveling with a companion have him or her get on and claim a seat while you wait. Finally, be prepared to be patient; invariably, the combi or bus will make many stops before it drops you off. The good news in all this is that the trip in from the airport is scenic. Try to get a seat on the left side of the bus for the best view.

Acapulco is 420 km (260 miles) south of Mexico City. Driving over the superhighway, Highway 95, a toll road (tolls are minimal), takes about five hours. Those who prefer a more scenic, leisurely trip travel the "old road," making stops in Taxco and Cuernavaca. This route takes 7–12 hours, without the stops.

Buses—Estrella de Oro (the luxury line) and Estrella Roja—operate several runs daily between Acapulco and the D.F., and fares are rock bottom. The trip, however, takes at least eight hours. If you decide to do it, travel first-class—you can afford it.

Getting around Acapulco itself is a breeze. Now that there are parking meters on the Costera, however, using taxis makes life infinitely simpler. Otherwise you have to come back from the beach every hour and plug 1,000 pesos into the meter. If you don't, zealous traffic cops will take your license plate.

Taxis in large numbers cruise the Costera day and night. Fares are set by zone and are usually posted on placards outside hotel lobbies. An average point-to-point fare will be in the neighborhood of $1.50–$3.00. "Sitios"—those taxis that have paid for the privilege of standing in front of specific hotels—cost a bit more. Rates go up as the night gets later, but are generally far less than rates back home.

City buses do run from downtown to the naval base and beyond, but their schedules are erratic. Look for the large yellow shelters with blue public phones—they're the stops. Also, during rush hour the ride is far from comfortable and you'll want to watch your purse or wallet.

ACCOMMODATIONS REFERENCE

The rate ranges given here are projections for December 1989 through Easter 1990. Unless otherwise indicated, rates are for double rooms, double occupancy. Acapulco is in the Central Standard time zone, and the telephone area code is 748.

▶ **Acapulco Malibu.** Avenida Costera Miguel Alemán 20, P.O. Box 582, Acapulco, Guerrero, Mexico 39868. U.S. $84. Tel: 4-1070.

▶ **Acapulco Plaza.** Avenida Costera Miguel Alemán 22, Acapulco, Guerrero, Mexico 39868. U.S. $125–$135. Tel: 4-0333.

▶ **Acapulco Princess.** Playa Revolcadero, P.O. Box 1351, Acapulco, Guerrero, Mexico 39868. U.S. $105–$200. Tel: 4-1300; in the United States and Canada: 800-223-1818.

▶ **Las Brisas.** Carretera Escénica 5255, P.O. Box 281, Acapulco, Guerrero, Mexico 39868. U.S. $175–$200. Tel: 4-1580; in the United States and Canada: 800-228-3000.

▶ **Hotel Elcano.** P.O. Box 430, Acapulco, Guerrero, Mexico 39868. U.S. $80. Tel: 4-1950.

▶ **Hyatt Regency.** Costera Miguel Alemán 1, Acapulco, Guerrero, Mexico 39868. U.S. $110–$150. Tel: 4-2888; in the United States and Canada: 800-228-9000.

▶ **Hotel La Palapa.** Fragata Yucatán 210, Acapulco, Guerrero, Mexico 39868. U.S. $85–110. Tel: 4-5363; in the United States and Canada: 800-528-1234.

▶ **Hotel Pierre Marqués.** P.O. Box 474, Acapulco, Guerrero, Mexico 39868. U.S. $170–$240. Tel: 4-2000; in the United States and Canada: 800-223-1818.

▶ **Ukae Kim.** Pie de la Cuesta, Acapulco, Guerrero, Mexico 39868. U.S. $50–$60. Tel: 800-544-2785.

▶ **Villa Vera Hotel and Racquet Club.** Lomas del Mar 35, P.O. Box 560, Acapulco, Guerrero, Mexico 39868. U.S. $165–$330. Tel: 4-0333; in the United States: 800-333-8847; in Canada: 800-268-7041.

PUERTO ESCONDIDO, PUERTO ANGEL, HUATULCO

Oaxaca's tropical, largely undeveloped southern coast is Mexico's newest resort hot spot. Long a favorite destination for those travelling Mexico by car or RV, for deep-sea fishermen, and for avid surfers in search of the Perfect Wave, Puerto Escondido and Puerto Angel were, until recently, just dots on a map, the kind of places where some telephone numbers only had one digit; Huatulco wasn't even marked on most maps.

That is all changing—and in a hurry. Fonatur, the huge government agency in charge of developing resorts, got the name of Huatulco out of its computers and has plans to turn it into a billion-dollar, 52,000-acre mega-resort by the year 2010; if it succeeds, Huatulco will become the biggest resort in the country, and Puerto Escondido and Puerto Angel to the west will boom in its wake.

In the meantime, these are wonderful destinations for travellers who like to be the first on the scene, who can entertain themselves and don't mind going to bed early, and who are looking to spend time in a natural paradise surrounded by jungle-covered mountains, beautiful beaches, and crystal-clear waters.

PUERTO ESCONDIDO

Until 20 years ago a tiny fishing village east of Acapulco that no one outside of town had heard of, Puerto Escondido was "discovered" by the backpacking set in the late 1960s and has been gaining in popularity ever since. Today it's the kind of place that's big enough to have the basic amenities you expect in a resort—airport, car-rental agency, hotels, and places to eat—but, at the same time, small enough so that people will remember your face (if not your name) the second time they see you.

Built at the water's edge, the main street of Puerto Escondido is about eight blocks long and is lined by most of the small shops, restaurants, and hotels the town has to offer. There are also several smaller hotels on the hill behind town—an area that seemingly overnight has become dotted with construction sites. In fact, new businesses are springing up every month, and it's only a matter of time before this "hidden" port is found.

The **Best Western Posada Real**, a mile from the airport on Boulevard Benito Juárez, sits—for the moment—on its own promontory overlooking the ocean (the area is slated for development in the near future). Its air-conditioned rooms all have balconies, television sets, and telephones, and conditions on the beach below are ideal for swimming and windsurfing.

The **Hotel Santa Fé**, on the town beach at the end of the row of shops, has two dozen rooms—not all have a view of the ocean—and a pleasant pool area shaded by palm trees.

The **Paraíso Escondido**, tucked away near the town beach at Calle Unión 10, looks like somebody's country estate. The lovely gardens surrounding the pool area and the colonial-era furnishings contribute to the appeal of this small hotel.

The **Fiesta Mexicana**, on Emerald Beach in Bacocho, a nearby residential neighborhood also slated for development, is one of the newest hotels in Puerto Escondido and offers air-conditioned rooms with balconies and an ocean view, and also has a pool and a disco.

There are, in addition to these quality establishments, a number of small, rustic hotels lining the beach that have long been popular with fishermen and a younger crowd not especially fussy about where they sleep. The Hotel Las Palmas, Hotel Nayar, and Rincón del Pacifico are three of the best among these. Guests at these places don't need reservations—they just arrive.

The number and variety of places to eat in Puerto Escondido is surprising. For now, most are located on or near Pérez Gasga, the main drag. Surfers like to hang out at **Perla Flamante** and **Cheko's & Willie's Lobster House**. Elsewhere, the craze for Italian food has hit; **Viandante**, the **Spaghetti House**, and **Da Ugo** are the most popular. **La Marfa**, Playa Marinero and Calle del Morro, serves up seafood dishes with a Spanish flavor, while **Las Mariposas**, Juárez 208, offers Continental cuisine. **La Estancía**, a simple steak-and-seafood place on Pérez Gasga, also has live music on occasion.

If shopping is the reason you've come to Mexico, you'll do much better elsewhere. If, on the other hand, a few trinkets are all you're looking for, Puerto Escondido can take care of your needs. There are tiny shops, most selling resort wear and handicrafts, scattered all over town. Three of the best are: **Anita's** for resort wear, and **La Bamba** and **Alberto's** for silver jewelry.

Over the years Puerto Escondido has developed a reputation as a surfing hot spot. Most surfers congregate at **Playa Zicatela**, south of town, to ride waves that seem to have rolled in from as far away as Hawaii; you'll find many of them hanging out at the Bungalows Delfines, on Cerro de la Iguana above the beach, after a long day on the water.

More than just surfers frolic on the waters off Puerto Escondido, however. Deep-sea fishermen have known about the place for decades, and boats—most of them *pangas,* or skiffs—can be rented on the town beach. Just ask the nearest friendly-looking fisherman. Windsurfing, snorkeling, and scuba diving are the other favorites here. For information on locations and equipment rentals, contact the Hotel Santa Fé (Tel: 2-0170) or Deportimundo, at the marina.

PUERTO ANGEL

The fishing village of Puerto Angel, which is even smaller than Puerto Escondido, is located about an hour's drive to the east of the latter via Highway 200, a good paved road. The "scene" here, such as it is, is about two or three speeds slower than "laid-back," and the accommodations range from simple and straightforward to rustic and communal. Puerto Angel still attracts a good-sized crowd of American and European "hippie-wannabes" who revel in the slow pace, paradisiacal setting, and low cost of living.

For those who want to stay a night or two, there are just a few mini-hotels—for the moment, at any rate. The **Hotel Angel del Mar**, on the hill overlooking the Playa Panteón, and the **Hotel Soraya**, across the street from the town pier overlooking Puerto Angel's wide, crescent-shaped bay, are the favorites. The Soraya is the "fancier" of the two, with air conditioning in some rooms and double beds, but both are clean, pleasant, and inexpensively priced.

HUATULCO

Huatulco promises to be the last—and biggest—jewel in Mexico's resort crown. By the time its nine pristine bays and 20 miles of stunning beaches east of Puerto Angel are fully developed in the next century, it is expected to have a population in excess of half a million people, with enough hotel rooms to accommodate more than two million visitors annually. At the same time, Huatulco will not be subjected to the kind of willy-nilly development that has characterized some of Fonatur's other pet projects. New zoning rules established by the agency mandate that buildings here must be colonial-style and have tiled roofs, with none taller than six stories (in order to blend in with the magnificent jungle backdrop). In fact, over half the acreage here is to remain undeveloped, left in its pristine state as a nature preserve.

That is all in the future, however. For the moment, Huatulco is little more than a construction site hacked out of the lush Oaxacan coastal jungle—which some refer to, appropriately, as the Emerald Coast. Everywhere you look something new—a hotel, an office building, a restaurant—is going up at breakneck speed. The small downtown area in Santa Cruz Huatulco (the original fishing village here; the larger resort is simply called Huatulco) has a spanking new marina for private yachts and will soon have a shopping plaza where handicrafts are sold as well. It's also the location of the **Posada Binniguenda**, a colonial-style accommodation where anyone in town on business seems to stay. The Binniguenda has a lovely patio with a fountain, a pretty swimming pool, and a restaurant and bar.

Most of the luxury resort development has been confined to the Bahía de Tangolunda, the easternmost of Huatulco's nine spectacular bays. This is where you'll find **Club Med**, for example, already up and running in its own brightly colored building. This particular facility is a departure from some of the other Club Meds in that its rooms are larger, with an ingenious sliding wall for privacy, and each has its own spacious terrace. Of course, the major attractions for Club Med guests in Huatulco—apart from the natural beauty of the place—are the sports, in this case water sports. Swimming, surfing, windsurfing, snorkeling, sailing, and fishing are all available here, and club-owned boats will take day-trippers to secluded and almost surreally beautiful beaches for picnics and other fun.

Elsewhere on Tangolunda Bay, the 310-room Veramar and the 345-room horseshoe-shaped Huatulco Sheraton are due to be completed by December 1989.

EXCURSIONS FROM
THE OAXACA RESORTS

The most common excursion from any of these places is a trip to one of its sister resorts along this stretch of coast. Puerto Escondido is 440 km (250 miles) east of Acapulco via Highway 200. Puerto Angel is another 80 km (50 miles) east of Puerto Escondido via the same highway. And Huatulco is 50 km (30 miles) east of Puerto Angel, again via Highway 200.

Day trips to **Oaxaca City**—one of Mexico's most colorful Indian centers and a serenely beautiful colonial city in its own right—and the splendid archaeological ruins at Monte Albán, about 250 km (150 miles) to the north, can be arranged through a travel agent. The trip can be made by car or bus via Highway 131, but flying up from Puerto Escondido (a 45-minute flight) is much the better alternative.

Day trips to the nature preserve at **Chacahua**, where there's an experimental crocodile farm, as well as trips to other beaches in the area can also be arranged through a travel agent. For further information contact Excursiones García Rendón, Boulevard Benito Juárez, Puerto Escondido, Oaxaca, Mexico 71980 (Tel: 2-0114); Viajes Moar, Pérez Gasga 100, Puerto Escondido, Oaxaca, Mexico 71980 (Tel: 2-0315); or Excursiones García Rendón, Manzana 31, La Crucecita, Santa Cruz Huatulco, Oaxaca, Mexico 70900 (Tel: 4-0025).

GETTING AROUND

International air service into Puerto Escondido and Santa Cruz Huatulco (Puerto Angel does not have an airport) is infrequent—at best. Instead, most flights come from Mexico City (Mexicana and Aeroméxico are the chief carriers) or Oaxaca City (Líneas Aéreas Oaxaqueñas); the flying time in either case is under an hour. In addition, Mexicana offers one "direct" flight a week from Los Angeles (with a stop in Mexico City; passengers do not have to deplane).

For those staying at Club Med in Huatulco, there are charter flights from five cities in the United States: Call Club Med for further information; Tel: 800-528-3100.

You'll have to rely on buses or taxis once you arrive at the airport in either Puerto Escondido or Huatulco; there's also a Budget Rent-a-Car desk at the Posada Real in Puerto Escondido. Once you get to your hotel, be prepared to do a lot of walking; taxis are scarce, although they can be found with patience. They can also be hired by the hour for sightseeing excursions of the wild and beautiful coast in this region, but some ability to communicate in Spanish is a must.

ACCOMMODATIONS REFERENCE
The rate ranges given here are projections for December 1989 through Easter 1990. Unless otherwise indicated, rates are for double rooms, double occupancy. The Oaxaca resorts are in the Central Standard time zone; the telephone area code is 958.

Puerto Escondido
▶ **Hotel Nayar.** Avenida Alfonso Pérez Gasga, Puerto Escondido, Oaxaca, Mexico 71980. U.S. $35–$40. Tel: 2-0113 or 2-0319.

▶ **Best Western Posada Real.** Boulevard Benito Juárez, Puerto Escondido, Oaxaca, Mexico 71980. U.S. $70. Tel: 2-0133.

▶ **Hotel Fiesta Mexicana.** Boulevard Benito Juárez, Puerto Escondido, Oaxaca, Mexico 71980. U.S. $86. Tel: 2-0115.

▶ **Las Palmas.** Avenida Alfonso Pérez Gasga, Puerto Escondido, Oaxaca, Mexico 71980. U.S. $18. Tel: 2-0230.

▶ **Paraíso Escondido.** Calle Unión 10, Puerto Escondido, Oaxaca, Mexico 71980. U.S. $40–$50. Tel: 2-0444.

▶ **Rincón del Pacifico.** Avenida Alfonso Pérez Gasga 100, Puerto Escondido, Oaxaca, Mexico 71980. U.S. $40. Tel: 2-0056 or 2-0193.

▶ **Hotel Santa Fé.** Calle del Morro, Puerto Escondido, Oaxaca, Mexico 71980. U.S. $40–$45. Tel: 2-0170.

Puerto Angel
▶ **Angel del Mar.** APO 40, Pochutla, Oaxaca, Mexico 70900. $35–$40. Tel: (905) 536-3341 in the United States and Canada.

▶ **Hotel Soraya.** Calle Virgilio Uribe, Pochutla, Oaxaca, Mexico 70900.

Huatulco

▶ **Club Med Huatulco.** P.O. Box 154, Santa Cruz Huatulco, Oaxaca, Mexico 70900. Rates upon request. Tel: 800-528-3100 in the United States and Canada.

▶ **Huatulco Sheraton.** Huatulco Sheraton Resorts, c/o María Isabel Sheraton Hotel and Towers, Paseo de la Reforma 325, Mexico D.F. 06500. U.S. $80–$120. Tel: 1-0055; in the United States and Canada: 800-325-3535.

▶ **Posada Binniguenda.** Boulevard Benito Juárez 5, P.O. Box 44, Santa Cruz Huatulco, Oaxaca, Mexico 70900. U.S. $55. Tel: 4-0080.

▶ **Hotel Veramar.** Domicilo Conocido, Santa Cruz Huatulco, Oaxaca, Mexico 70900. Rates upon request (the hotel is scheduled to open in December 1989). Tel: 1-0220 or 1-0284.

THE GULF COAST
THE STATES OF VERACRUZ AND TABASCO

By Robert Cummings

The coastal lowlands of Veracruz and Tabasco are wedged between the Bay of Campeche (off the Gulf of Mexico) and some of Mexico's steepest mountains. It is verdant, flower-filled country, with vanilla and coffee plantations perched on the low shoulders of mountains to the northwest, steamy rubber country to the southeast—the center of the first great Mesoamerican civilization, the so-called Olmec, which in the language of the Aztecs meant "the people of rubber"—and cattle ranches hacked out of the jungle in between.

The people of the region, with the exception of a pocket of Totonac Indians in northern Veracruz, share a number of qualities that set them apart from highland Mexicans as well as from the people of Chiapas and the Yucatán. The Caribbean influence is strong here, the impact of African cultures over the centuries more noticeable than in other parts of the country. At the same time, writers of popular songs delight in the area. Veracruzanos are reputed to be languorous but passionate, tolerant but fierce; these extremes often seem to resonate in the region's music, while its traditional dances can shift from courtliness to sudden abandon. It is also rumored elsewhere in Mexico that people from the Gulf Coast region are given to crimes of passion—an unsubstantiated rumor but one that makes them appear both dangerous and attractive. Katherine Anne Porter seemed to accept the notion of the archetypal Veracruzano when she wrote, "They carry on their lives of alternate violence and lethargy with a pleasurable contempt for outside opinion." While she may have overstated the case, the people of the region do impress the visitor with their confidence and self-assurance.

Foreign travellers have never come to the Gulf Coast in great numbers, but Mexican vacationers, searching for bargains, beaches, and the exotic, swarm to the Gulf, where they quickly notice the regional differences. The coast dwellers are darker complexioned, they drink rum instead of tequila, and their speech is lisping and clipped. And where does that odd music come from?

MAJOR INTEREST

City of Veracruz
Fortress-prison of San Juan de Ulúa
Beaches
Fiestas

North of Veracruz
Mountain town of Jalapa
Totonac ruins at Tajín and Zempoala
Sportfishing and skin diving at Tuxpan

South of Veracruz
Lake Catemaco scenery
Olmec park at Villahermosa
Regional birds and lush vegetation

The historic port city of Veracruz, on the coast east of Mexico City, is the primary gateway for the Gulf Coast region. From Veracruz, we consider the coast north as far as Tuxpan, and then south, including Lake Catemaco, as far as the Villahermosa area in the state of Tabasco. Villahermosa is also the jumping-off point for the Palenque archaeological site and San Cristóbal de las Casas, the capital of the state of Chiapas (see Mayan Mexico).

You should be warned beforehand, however: The climate in this part of Mexico is intensely hot from May through September. In addition, in August the *nortes,* or "northers," common to the hemisphere arrive with little warning and drench the entire region, bending trees and sending the temperature plummeting in the process. Usually, fine weather will follow in the wake of a *norte.*

The best time to visit is from November through March. Even winter doesn't necessarily bring better weather, however—one reason why the Gulf Coast's beach resorts have been eclipsed by their younger Pacific and Caribbean cousins.

THE CITY OF VERACRUZ

Veracruz is the most piquant of Mexico's cities as well as the most European of its ports, and was nicknamed "Little Havana" in the days before Cuba turned forbidding. Actually, it was never so free-wheeling, although it has always been a sailor's haven. To quote Katherine Anne Porter again, who had a bad time in Veracruz in her youth: "It is in fact to the passing eye a typical port town, cynical by nature, shameless by experience, hardened to showing its seamiest side to strangers."

In those days, maybe. Today, not really. Veracruz has been scrubbed up a lot in the last decade, which has enhanced its charm without lessening its zest. It is far more high-spirited than bawdy, and still a city flirtatious in every way.

Veracruz is also a town of balconies. Wandering down any street, you'll be distracted and delighted by them— long and narrow, short and obtrusive, many embellished by orange and yellow flowers that are startling in their vividness when seen against the pale-colored walls typical of the city's architecture. The women of Veracruz—some of the loveliest in Mexico—step onto their balconies to call to street vendors, to summon their children playing outside, or simply to dry their long black hair in the sunshine.

The Plaza de Armas

The *zócalo,* also referred to as the Plaza de Armas or Plaza de la Constitución, is a vibrant public space (although in the heat of the day it may turn languid) set off by a lacy iron bandstand, slender coconut palms, and tropical flowers so vivid they seem unreal. Most of the area is closed to vehicular traffic, the better to saunter, promenade, or, at fiestas, to dance. Arcades shelter the cafés around the edges of the plaza, and a table here is an observation point for a never-ending show, of which the spectators themselves are a major part. The *zócalo* in

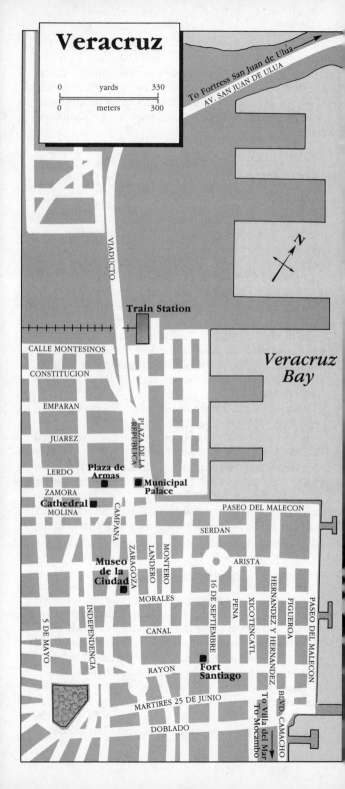

Veracruz

0   yards   330

0   meters   300

To Fortress San Juan de Ulúa

AV. SAN JUAN DE ULUA

VIADUCTO

N

Train Station

CALLE MONTESINOS

CONSTITUCION

EMPARAN

JUAREZ

LERDO

ZAMORA

MOLINA

Plaza de Armas

Cathedral

Veracruz Bay

PLAZA DE LA REPUBLICA

Municipal Palace

CAMPANA

PASEO DEL MALECON

SERDAN

ARISTA

Museo de la Ciudad

ZARAGOZA

LANDERO

MONTERO

MORALES

CANAL

RAYON

16 DE SEPTIEMBRE

PENA

XICOTENCATL

HERNANDEZ Y HERNANDEZ

FIGUEROA

PASEO DEL MALECON

Fort Santiago

5 DE MAYO

INDEPENDENCIA

MARTIRES 25 DE JUNIO

DOBLADO

BLVD. CAMACHO

To Villa del Mar

To Mocambo

Veracruz is a crossroads not only of the city but of the Caribbean and the world beyond. At any moment you might spot a group of Russian or Norwegian sailors or maybe the polyglot crew of some ship registered in Liberia, wandering along shady arcades, as French and Italian tourists, looking chic in their new tropical outfits, stop to check their maps—with everything being photographed by a party of Japanese.

The row of cafés on Calle Miguel Lerdo, which is closed to traffic, begins with the venerable **Prendes**, the city's oldest seafood restaurant and still the best. While spending half an hour at an outside table here you can have your shoes shined, hear a marimba concert, purchase a hammock, test your strength, buy a lottery ticket, hear a recitation of patriotic poetry, admire the bunches of fantastic balloons sold by vendors in the plaza, or watch the world go by. On the other hand, if this sounds a bit overwhelming, you can always retreat to the quiet of the dining room.

If Prendes, as proper as its garrulous elderly waiters, seems too stiff, you can move down the row of cafés, taking a half step down the social ladder at every doorway. The voices gradually grow louder, the spirits flow more freely, and the last watering place on the block, while not raunchy, is certainly déclassé.

Cutting back across the *zócalo,* circling the bandstand, and passing the vendors of gardenias and bubble-blowing pipes, you will come to the greatest local sidewalk institution of all, the **Gran Café de la Parroquia**, which faces the unpretentious parish church, now a cathedral. Here, at any hour of the day from 7:00 A.M. until 1:00 A.M., you'll find a noisy potpourri of Veracruzanos. As patrons struggle to be heard over the din, waiters circle the café in pairs, one with a steaming pot of coffee, the other with hot milk. Spoons bang or tinkle on glasses as customers signal for milk to be added to their cups of black brew. "Coffee must be sweet, hot, and strong as love," Veracruzanos will remind you at every chance. It is an old saying that applies to this colorful city as well.

The coffee is excellent. Then again, it has to be—many of the men who drink it here also grow it, pack it, or ship it by the ton. Others busily concern themselves with oil or beef deals, both major contributors to the region's prosperity. But not everyone arrives with a briefcase. Store clerks come to read their newspapers hurriedly, while students from the university gather to argue, joke, and plot their intrigues.

The Gran Café serves breakfast and snacks as well, but the coffee ritual is its chief drawing card. Endless cups of coffee and endless talk help pass the long hours until the sun goes down and the city cools off.

The church across the street, La Parroquia, needs paint both inside and out, as do seemingly half the buildings in Veracruz. Of course, the salt spray from the sea only a block away has something to do with this, as do the city's torrential rains, *nortes,* and hurricanes. In a climate such as Veracruz's even the most vivid paint soon fades to a pastel color, and eventually to an indistinct gray. The church, which was dedicated in 1734, adds a softening touch of antiquity to the plaza, but it is not particularly interesting in itself. But then, very few buildings in the city are. There is little in the way of art here outside of the art of living.

The Malecón

The *malecón,* which starts two blocks northeast of the *zócalo,* near a spot where crab sellers hawk their wares at the top of their lungs, is the city's long, winding shore drive. At the head of it, a long pier dotted with trashy curio shops and so-so seafood restaurants juts into the harbor. A monument nearby reminds the visitor that Veracruz was the first "European" city to be established in the Americas, as well as the site of the first democratic (European-style) assembly. You can also hire a boat here to take you around the harbor or across to the fortress of San Juan de Ulúa (see below). Both are good, short trips; longer voyages tend to be hot and tedious. (An exception is the trip to Isla de Sacrificios, which is worth making if you'd like to try the beach there. The island, a sandy, desolate little key, is 30 minutes away by launch. Do not make the trip, however, on a windy day.)

The pier is interesting by day, but especially romantic and colorful at night, when lovers and families alike go strolling, pausing to watch sidewalk artists, gape at jugglers, or listen to whatever troubadour happens to pass by.

As the *malecón* curves south it becomes the Boulevard M. Avila Camacho, which eventually leads to Villa del Mar, the most popular beach in the city. This is a place for sunning, wading, swimming, and playing games in the sand. The facilities are simple, but Villa del Mar is never-theless inviting. There's also a public swimming pool here.

Mocambo and Boca del Río

About 9 km (6 miles) south of the *zócalo,* beyond Villa del Mar and just outside the city limits, stretch the sands of Mocambo, a better beach than Villa del Mar and a well-developed resort zone: In addition to its fine hotels, there are chair and umbrella rentals here. Food and drink, including the locally famous *coco locos*—coconuts ad-dled with gin—are also available. The clean, freshwater pool is open to the public.

Boca del Río, a fishing village situated still farther south along the coast, is a community doomed to be swallowed by the encroaching city before long. In the meantime there is swimming near the mouth of the Río Jalapa, although fishing remains the chief attraction. Information about prime spots and renting tackle can be obtained at the Hotel Veracruz Calinda Quality Inn in town. You might also want to check out one of the rustic open-air restaurants near the river for a fresh fish dinner while you're here.

The Forts

There is little in the way of conventional sightseeing in Veracruz, certainly not enough to fill a day unless, in true Veracruzano style, you spend an hour in a café before and after each attraction.

One of the few sights in town, the **Fortress of San Juan de Ulúa,** squats in the harbor like some grim, ugly curios-ity. Although it looks close from the comfort of a café seat near the plaza, it's actually a long walk in the Veracruz heat. A taxi is a better idea, and it's easy enough to find one to take you back downtown once you get there. Or you can take a launch from the pier.

The castle was begun in 1528 on the island where Juan de Grijalva, the first Spaniard to land at what is now Veracruz, had come ashore a decade earlier. During the century that followed, the fort did the town little good, as Veracruz became the victim of one raid after another by the likes of pirates such as Drake, Hawkins, and Agro-monte. The worst catastrophe occurred in 1683, however, when Lorencillo, a merciless buccaneer, captured the sleeping town. The inhabitants were herded into the church and held there for four days—during which many died—while his men methodically sacked their homes.

Finally, after other protective measures had failed, in 1746 the entire town was encircled by a wall with seven gates—one of them reserved exclusively for use by the Viceroy of New Spain. The illusion of security was just that, however. Although Veracruz did manage to hold out for years during the War of Independence, thereby earning a measure of infamy as the last Spanish stronghold in Mexico, the seemingly impregnable gates and ramparts of San Juan de Ulúa itself nevertheless fell easily to French bombardment in 1838, and were taken by U.S. troops in 1846. They also offered little protection when U.S. forces landed again in 1914, capturing Veracruz and killing 200 Mexicans in the process—an incident known locally as the Massacre of Veracruz. (Although Veracruzanos are too polite to mention it to visitors from the United States, they have not forgotten.)

When it wasn't being stormed by foreign invaders, this fierce-looking but impotent dinosaur did long service as a much-dreaded prison. High tides would sweep through the lower levels, forcing prisoners to crouch or stand with seawater up to their chins; such food as was provided would be lowered to prisoners by rope through manholes on the roof. Not surprisingly, incarceration here amounted to a virtual death sentence. Even today the atmosphere is dank and heavy, and while there are fine views of the city from the fort's roofs and battlements, an hour's visit is enough for most people.

A much smaller and less interesting redoubt is found in the center of town, on Calle Rayón and 16 de Septiembre, about six blocks southeast of the main plaza. This fortress, which was dedicated to Saint James and so is known as the Baluarte de Santiago, is all that remains of the old city walls and gives the visitor an idea of Spanish defenses in New Spain. The cramped museum inside is of minimal interest.

The nearby **Museo de la Ciudad**, at Zaragoza 397, is worth a short visit. The sidewalk outside the museum is inset with tiles recounting the exploits of Cortés in this region—images that were borrowed from Aztec codices. The museum itself is housed in a gracious old building that dates from the 19th century, and its interior, one of the best in the city, gives a sense of what life among the wealthy of Veracruz was like a century ago. An Olmec head, not one of the greatest, is displayed downstairs, along with other artifacts and relics, including a number of wonderful clay pieces from the area. Upstairs a group of 26 life-sized wax figures portrays typical styles of dress for Carnival (Mardi Gras) in Veracruz. If nothing else, it's a gaudy and alluring advertisement for this raucous fiesta.

Staying in the City of Veracruz

Veracruz is a magnet for weekend vacationers from Mexico City. The climate and beaches may not compare to those of Cancún or Acapulco, but Veracruz is much closer and cheaper. Hotel reservations are essential if your stay includes a weekend. While the city has so many hotel rooms that *something* is always available (except during Carnival or Holy Week), third-choice rooms in Veracruz can be depressing.

The first decision to make is between the beach and the plaza areas. The best hotels at either location are about equal in comfort. On the other hand, economy is much better practiced downtown. Whatever your choice, however, air conditioning is essential any time of year.

The **Hotel Emporio**, centrally located on the harbor, is the traditional first choice. It offers balconies with most rooms, splendid views, three swimming pools, a restaurant, and a nightclub. The management is experienced and willing to help with boat rentals, fishing information, and tours of the region. It is expensive only by the standards of downtown Veracruz.

The **Hotel Colonial**, on the *zócalo,* is the city's best value. Many of its rooms are equipped with refrigerators, and all are air conditioned. Ask for a room with a balcony. It also has a sidewalk café and an indoor pool.

The **Prendes**, on the *zócalo* above and behind the famed restaurant of the same name, is rather basic but has all the essentials. Some of the larger rooms, called "suites," are much the best.

The sprawling **Hotel Mocambo**, with its terraces that seem to wander off to the sea, is the grande dame of the waterfront inns. And, like the Emporio, it is expensive only by local standards.

Newer and more costly is the **Playa Paraíso**, on the beach near Boca del Río. While it is slightly more modern and luxurious than the Mocambo, it is also less gracious in style. The views of the Gulf from the hotel are lovely, however.

Dining in Veracruz

The word here is seafood, of course. The best-known regional sauce, *veracruzana,* is made from tomatoes, onions, olives, capers, garlic, and mild chile peppers. Cooking with fruits and the use of banana leaves as a wrapper is also common. Although the state is an important producer of cattle, local beef is usually not to the taste of foreign visitors.

The **Prendes** on the *zócalo,* all animation outside and serenity within, is the reliable standby.

La Bamba, formerly Lorencillo, at Boulevard Avila Camacho, near Rayón, overlooks the harbor. There's a South Seas touch to both the décor and the menu in this casual but very fashionable, elegant spot.

El Pescador, Zaragoza 335, has wood paneling that's presumably meant to resemble the interior of a stateroom on an old luxury liner, and a collection of flotsam— kegs, belaying pins, nets, lanterns, and so on. The seafood is good here.

You can find an exception to the usual Veracruz seafood menu at the **Submarino Amarillo** (Yellow Submarine), Boulevard Avila Camacho at the foot of Rayón. This upscale family restaurant is modeled after a typical U.S. steak house. The brick-and-clapboard Submarino features thickly sliced steaks that are tender—unusual in a region that range-feeds its cattle.

La Paella, located on the *zócalo* at Zamora 138, attracts travelling student types who appreciate the hearty set *comida,* usually four courses, at a thrifty price.

Veracruz Nightlife and Fiestas

Veracruz seems to wake up about an hour after the sun sets. That's when the *zócalo* begins to pulsate, couples drift toward the *malecón,* and the sidewalk cafés become lively with music. More formal—and costly— entertainment is provided at the Emporio, the Mocambo, and the **Torremar,** a resort hotel located on the beach near the Mocambo.

Veracruz also boasts the most famous **Carnival** in Mexico. While it is not on the scale of the annual celebration in New Orleans, it remains happier, safer, and cheaper. Of course, the city turns delightfully mad, the floats are glorious, and the dancing never stops. Hotel reservations must be made, paid, and confirmed months in advance, however. Although the last three days are the climax of the celebration in Veracruz, most visitors try to arrive a week before Ash Wednesday.

After the fireworks of Carnival, the city rests a little during Lent, then explodes again during Holy Week. The Easter crowds here are also enormous, so arrangements must be made far in advance for then as well.

NORTH FROM THE CITY OF VERACRUZ

Buses will do for point-to-point travel to major destinations along the coast north of Veracruz, but a car will be needed if you really want to explore the region, an area much visited by Mexicans but seldom seen by foreign visitors.

The coast here is dotted with small, rustic beach resorts, especially between Nautla and Tecolutla. It's also a fisherman's paradise; various annual tournaments are a major attraction of the region. Accommodations and restaurants are uniformly simple and economical.

Jalapa

Jalapa (pronounced hah-LAH-pah, and also spelled Xalapa) is an easy day's excursion from Veracruz, or can be visited en route to or from Mexico City.

Poised high above the Gulf in the foothills of the Sierra Madre Oriental, some 100 km (62 miles) northwest of Veracruz, Jalapa was once the site of a thriving pre-Columbian town. It came into its own, however, as Veracruz became Mexico's most important port. With its relatively temperate location, Jalapa offered escape from the tropical fevers that plagued the lowlands around Veracruz, and eventually became the capital of the state for reasons of health. Even after the old tropical diseases were eradicated in the lowlands, Jalapa remained popular because of its comfortable climate and scenic beauty. To this day its mountain breezes promise rejuvenation to sun-struck inhabitants of, and visitors to, the coast.

Here, where the easterlies off the Gulf collide with the Sierra massif, light rainfall is frequent and persistent—a local weather phenomenon known in Spanish as *chipi-chipi,* for its pattering sound. The abundant moisture,

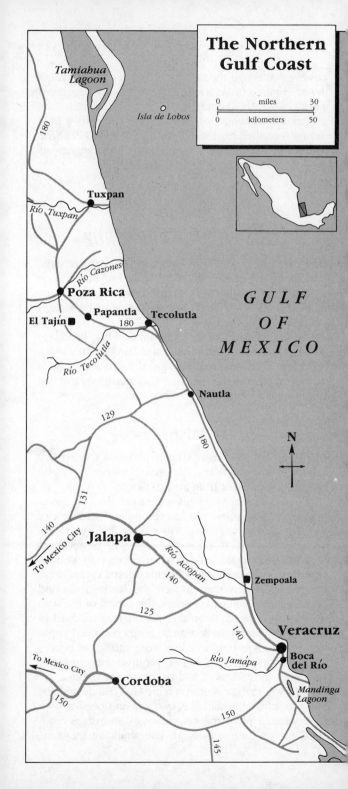

The Northern Gulf Coast

Tamiahua Lagoon

Isla de Lobos

180

Tuxpan

Río Tuxpan

Río Cazones

Poza Rica

Papantla

El Tajín

180

Tecolutla

Río Tecolutla

GULF
OF
MEXICO

Nautla

180

129

131

140

To Mexico City

Jalapa

Río Actopan

140

Zempoala

125

140

Veracruz

To Mexico City

Córdoba

Río Jamápa

Boca
del Río

Mandinga
Lagoon

150

150

145

N

good soil, and mild climate of the region are ideal for plants of all kinds, and the town, as a result, resembles nothing so much as an open-air floral conservatory where blossoms seem to explode into vivid color. Jalapa is justly famous as the "Flower Garden of Mexico."

It has also flowered in other ways. The University of Veracruz, in particular, has helped make Jalapa a lively cultural center famous for its theater, dance, and the best regional symphony orchestra in Mexico. In addition, the relatively new **Museo de Antropología**, on the campus of the university, has a collection of pre-Hispanic art that is, according to many experts, second only to the national museum's vast collection in the D.F. Among its fascinating exhibits are a number of curious (and some think magical) wheeled "toys," smiling figurines of many different shapes and sizes, and a variety of ancient Olmec sculpture. There are also three giant carved Olmec heads on the campus itself. The university is located on the southwest edge of town just off the highway to Mexico City.

Although Jalapa, like Rome, was built on seven hills, it feels more like the older neighborhoods in Naples, with its sloping streets twisting sharply into hidden alleys and courtyards lined by pastel-colored houses. One of the greatest pleasures it affords visitors is simply wandering around its main plaza area and discovering such attractive spots as the lively and informal **Café Escorial** on Pasaje Enriquez. The nearby Agora, a center for the performing arts and favorite gathering place for students, is always busy with music, conversation, and the sale of records, tapes, and books.

Those who would like to spend more time in this delightful city should consider checking in at the very good **Hotel María Victoria**, located in the center of town behind the Government Palace, or the older but equally comfortable **Hotel Salmones**, which is also centrally located on Zaragoza. Both have, in addition, clean and more than adequate restaurants.

Zempoala

The ruins of Zempoala are a short distance west of Highway 180, about 40 km (24 miles) north of Veracruz. It's an easy excursion from the city; if you have a car, a visit can be combined with a trip to Jalapa, or else as the first stop on a trip along the northern Gulf Coast.

Zempoala was the first Indian city that Cortés and his

men saw after their miserable bivouac on the beach of what is now Veracruz. The Spaniards were literally starving when they were befriended by Totonac warriors and led to this jungle city, and many of them initially mistook its gleaming stucco walls for silver. It was also here that Cortés found his first friends among the native people, although the friendship between them would soon turn sour. But that still lay in the future when a delighted Bernal Díaz wrote in 1519: "We were struck with admiration. It looked like a garden with luxuriant vegetation." The local ruler, known to history as Chicomacatl and to the Spaniards as the "fat chief," welcomed the white men as allies against the Aztecs and presented Cortés with an obese bride—a lady whom Cortés "received with courtesy."

Today, enough of the center of ancient Zempoala remains to give us an idea of pre-Hispanic life, although all but traces of its residential neighborhoods have long since vanished. It's clear, however, that it was the Totonac capital, a city of some 30,000 people who called it the "Place of Twenty Rivers" because of the nearby tributaries of the Río Actopan, and that it rose to prominence about A.D. 1200 when Toltec warriors, advancing outward from the central highlands, pushed the Totonacs off their traditional lands and into this less fertile, less healthful region.

The base of its great temple is still in remarkably good shape. (When you multiply 13, the number of its tiers, by four, the number of its sides, you get 52, the mystical Mesoamerican number.) It was on these steps that Cortés had a violent encounter with Chicomacatl after the Totonac chief protested Cortés's decision to destroy the stone idols atop the temple base; Cortés held a blade to the chief's throat while his soldiers carried out the destruction.

The upper platform of the Temple of the Chimneys, east of the main plaza, gives the best view of the site, and from here you can locate another temple and a path leading to it through a field of sugarcane. There are still painted decorations in the latter structure, making it worth the short walk from the Temple of the Chimneys.

The whole area, shaded here and there by low, graceful palms, is open for roaming and exploration, and the small "museum" on the site is worth a glance.

Papantla and El Tajín

Farther north, Highway 180 turns sharply inland near Tecolutla, and after about 20 km (13 miles) comes to

Papantla, 225 km (140 miles) northwest of Veracruz in the heart of vanilla country. Vanilla plants are temperamental and demand endless pampering and coaxing. Until this century the world depended on the patience of Papantla's farm workers, mostly Totonac Indians, for this remarkable flavoring. Sadly, the discovery of inexpensive artificial vanilla extract all but ruined the economy of this corner of Mexico.

There is, however, still a demand for the real thing, so the vanilla farmers hang on. Papantla also benefits from tourism, with visitors coming to see the archaeological zone at El Tajín, as well as to view the famous *voladores,* or "flying dancers." The dance, at once a religious rite and a beautiful spectacle, is performed every Sunday at noon. In it, four colorfully costumed men symbolically dressed as eagles and macaws leap from a tall pole to which they are attached by ropes tied to their ankles and make 13 swooping revolutions around the pole before touching ground (the four fliers multiplied by the 13 revolutions create the sacred number of 52).

Papantla is a charming little city, still countrified and quite Totonac. The *zócalo* is a small jewel; just up the hill from it a striking concrete relief sculpture depicting the history of El Tajín and the Totonacs adds an unusual aspect to the scene.

El Tajín is the best of the town's several inns. You'll want to pay a little extra for air conditioning, which is easily affordable at the hotel's modest rates. Its simple and straightforward restaurant puts out adequate meals.

Travellers bound for the archaeological site of El Tajín who want better accommodations can continue northwest past El Tajín to **Poza Rica**, where the **Hotel Salinas** offers larger and better-appointed quarters and a more extensive menu. Unfortunately, this medium-sized city is a raceway of traffic and, in addition to the carbon monoxide, is often plagued by the smell of oil from nearby refineries hanging heavy in the air. For travellers with cars it is perhaps a better idea to leave Veracruz early, take a quick look at Papantla, spend a few hours at El Tajín, and then continue on to the pleasant river town of Tuxpan (see below), which has a number of good hotels, for the night.

El Tajín, a bit west of Papantla, is the most spectacular pre-Hispanic center on the Gulf Coast, and surely ranks among the finest in the country. Named for both lightning and the Totonac rain god, it was founded early in the

Classic era, about 200 B.C., and reached its zenith from
A.D. 600–900 under the influence of the Toltecs, before
being abandoned in the 13th century (which was considerably later than were most great Mesoamerican ceremonial centers).

Today, the **Pyramid of the Niches** here is a startling
sight, unexpected and strange. Emerging from the lush
jungle that surrounds the site, it is not particularly lofty,
like so many Mesoamerican pyramids, but its design
nevertheless catches the imagination. Constructed in six
tiers, the pyramid is stepped back like a wedding cake.
Each of its sides is covered by row upon row of recessed
rectangles, or "niches," adding up to a total of 365—one
for each day of the solar year (the exact number and
their meaning are still debated). The pattern is continued around the four sides of the pyramid, six layers of
heavily outlined rectangles, dynamic and strong. The
changing light of day constantly shifts the emphasis,
creating different depths and shadows as the sun moves
across the sky. Perhaps these openings are simply orna-
mental, a rhythmically repeated decoration—no one is
really sure. What is clear, however, is that builders
throughout El Tajín's history were fascinated by niches,
even though their use varied over time. One of the most
common motifs was to use the niche as a frame for an
important design element—the serpentine image of the
rain god, for example. Nevertheless, over the centuries a
significant change occurred in this approach. The early
work is serene and confident; the later relief sculpture,
on the other hand, has a tense, even frantic quality, and
sacrifice and self-mutilation begin to enter the picture.
Portraits of the death god are numerous at El Tajín.

The Pyramid of the Niches is built on top of an older but
similar structure that dates to about A.D. 300; archaeologists speculate that the more recent structure was built
perhaps three centuries later, but the origins of El Tajín's
early builders remain obscure. There are, in addition, a
dozen other structures, including ball courts, scattered
across the compact site, as well as an unknown number
that are still covered by earth and tropical vegetation.
Fortunately, excavation continues at the site, and each year
more of its mysterious but fascinating past is revealed.

Sometimes *voladores* perform their spectacular flying
dance in the main plaza at El Tajín. For those lucky
enough to catch such a performance, it is the perfect—
not to mention original—setting.

Tuxpan

Tuxpan (TOOSH-pan), a pleasant fishing port rather recently made prosperous and prodded into the 20th century by the discovery of oil, lazes along a riverbank some 58 km (36 miles) northeast of Poza Rica. The feeling of an "oil town" is almost totally absent here, with the exception of what amounts to a virtual second city built by the national petroleum company, PEMEX, between Tuxpan and its beach near the mouth of the Río Tuxpan.

There are no attractions of particular interest to be seen here—although the colonial church and bridge are handsome. Nor is there much of anything to do other than saunter along the river admiring the palm trees and the view. For all its lack of specific attractions, however, Tuxpan is nevertheless quietly enjoyable, with much color and life on display in and around its two main plazas.

Launches serving as ferries ply the Río Tuxpan, affording a pleasant little boat ride with good views of the town. In the village on the opposite bank you'll find the Mexican-Cuban Friendship Museum, located on the spot from which Fidel Castro returned to Cuba in a fishing boat; the rest, as they say, is history. The boat is being restored (or perhaps re-created) for visitors, but only great admirers of Castro are likely to enjoy the museum, which consists almost entirely of early photographs of Fidel and his fellow revolutionaries.

The Tuxpan beach, **Barra del Norte**, is easily reached by bus or car from town. The beach has good sand and warm, shallow water; the facilities are simple but adequate. The beach itself resembles the more famous ones at Padre Island in Texas.

Tuxpan is perhaps best known for its **sportfishing**. Information is available at the Club de Pesca (Tel: 40-406). The annual tarpon tournament is held in June. In addition, skin divers enjoy the **Laguna de Tamiahua** and **Isla de Lobos** north of town. Tuxpan is a good headquarters for expeditions to both.

The new **Hotel Sara** is the town's best, with tastefully decorated rooms that have balconies and views. It is about three blocks uphill from the center of town, and has a cheerful restaurant.

On the main street a block above the river boulevard is the comfortable **Hotel Plaza**, which is older than the Sara and a bit worn but still a good buy. The Plaza's restaurant features seafood and has good breakfasts.

Fischer Restaurant, at the western edge of downtown facing the river, is Tuxpan's best restaurant, high-priced but attractively situated.

SOUTH FROM THE CITY OF VERACRUZ

Travelling south and east along the coast from Veracruz you find green, level ranchland speckled with brahman cattle. These pastures have been wrested from the jungle, and defending them is a never-ending struggle. Now and then the horizon is broken by mountains tumbling down toward the sea.

By car or bus, the trip around the Bay of Campeche—as this southwesternmost part of the Gulf is called—is both lovely and pastoral. But there are only two destinations of interest in this region: the Lake Catemaco area and, farther east in the state of Tabasco, Villahermosa. For most travellers the towns along the route will be of little interest.

Catemaco

Both the town and lake are an easy one-day trip from Veracruz, lying just 145 km (90 miles) southeast of the city over a good road. There's also fast and frequent bus service to both.

The lake, which was created in prehistoric times by the eruption of a cluster of volcanoes, is an impressive body of fresh water some 16 km (10 miles) long. Two imposing volcanoes, **San Martín** and **Cerro Blanco**, both long extinct, rise to the north, forming a frontier of sorts: This is the northern limit of the tropical rain forest on the continent. Travellers will notice the change as they head southeast, with the greens becoming deeper and the timber taller with every hour of driving.

Lake Catemaco is sometimes hailed as the most beautiful in Mexico. Certainly it is a contender for the title in a country where lakes are few. The town huddled on its western shore has some color and zest, although it is not pretty. A walk along the lakeside promenade under the majestic trees can be pleasant, even romantic. In addition, enjoyable boat rides are offered from the town dock. The Iglesia del Carmen is interesting for its collection of *milagros,* drawings and photographs about miracles experienced by pilgrims to this shrine.

The most evident pilgrims here, however, are the middle-class residents of Veracruz treating their families to a weekend at the lake. As a result, many of the hotels in town have kiddie waterslides and such.

The **Playa Azul,** located west of town on a gravel road, faces the lake and has extensive lawns and its own dock, as well as a dining room. The rather modest accommodations are priced above value, and a car is necessary to get around. The rooms farthest from the driveway are the best.

For those without a car, the **Berthangel,** on the south side of the *zócalo* in town, is tidy and safe, with pleasant balconies—about as well as you can do here despite the rather cramped quarters. It also has a coffee shop.

Unfortunately, meal times tend not to be joyful occasions in Catemaco. The small restaurants on the lakeshore offer limited menus of freshwater fish along with guitar music and lake views. The Hotel Catemaco on the *zócalo* has good ice cream, however.

Not far from town are some beautiful waterfalls, and one, **Salto de Eyipantla,** that is truly spectacular. Before setting out, inquire about directions and road conditions; washouts are common, the mud often deep, and warnings rarely posted.

Youngsters in Catemaco celebrate a year-round Halloween, and some establishments are named for *brujas,* or witches. Masks and skeletons are brought out to celebrate an annual reunion of sorcerers held on the slopes of Monte del Cerro Blanco. The tradition inspires children to dress up and caper as witches regardless of the season, a surprising show in streets and plazas, even along roadsides.

VILLAHERMOSA

The name Villahermosa means "pretty town," but most writers have begun their descriptions of the city by declaring that the name is deceptive, that the place is unpretty, even ugly. That declaration is no longer accurate; Villahermosa is beginning to live up to its name.

Located some 485 km (300 miles) southeast of Veracruz, this sleepy, depressed old Tabasco town boomed because of oil, a windfall prosperity that resulted in tacky

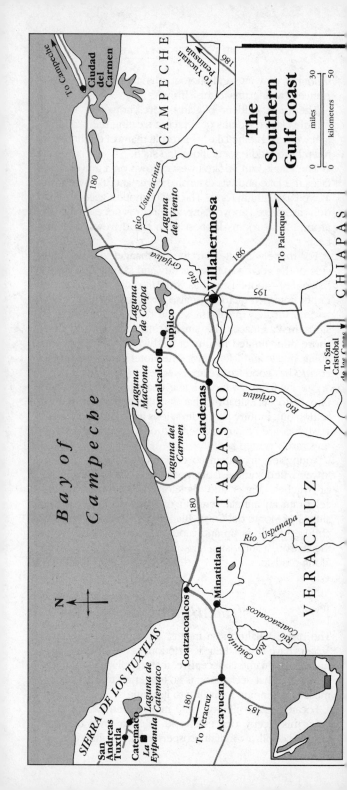

overgrowth. In the 1960s the old run-down town was transformed into the modern run-down city. But since then Villahermosa has been consolidating its prosperity, building and remodeling. Unfortunately, inflation came with wealth, and Villahermosa remains one of the more expensive cities in Mexico.

Still, it offers what travellers to the region need: attractive, if sultry, surroundings for those visiting the city's remarkable archaeological park-museum, its more conventional regional museum, and its zoo. It is also a convenient gateway to Maya country, with **Palenque** less than a two-hour drive from the city (see the Chiapas section of the Mayan Mexico chapter).

In addition, the many lagoons, rivers, and inlets nearby support an abundant birdlife, attracting bird watchers from near and far. Not surprisingly, the plumage of the tropical species that flock to the region is often gorgeous, and flamingos, toucans, and parrots make for a resplendent natural show.

In Villahermosa itself, café life centers on the Plaza de Armas, with the **Café del Portal** being the traditional gathering place. The downtown area has many blocks closed to traffic, and visitors can stroll down streets lined with buildings designed in a simple but distinctive Caribbean style.

Parque-Museo de La Venta

La Venta, the greatest of the Olmec centers, was established before 1200 B.C.—perhaps at about the time of Moses—and reached its zenith in 800 B.C., becoming the fountainhead of art and culture in ancient Mesoamerica, predating the rise of the Maya by centuries. Everyone has seen pictures of the colossal Olmec stone heads sitting out in the jungle, but government officials felt that La Venta and the other Olmec centers were too remote for most visitors. As a result, the great sculptures produced by this mysterious and surprisingly advanced culture were assembled and brought to an open-air museum in Villahermosa; smaller works went to the city's regional museum.

Instead of simply setting out a row of statuary, however, a Mexican poet-savant by the name of Carlos Pellicer Cámara designed a "natural" environment in which these works might be seen as their creators had intended. Starting with a parcel of land along the **Laguna** de las Ilusiones, Pellicer created, in effect, an Olmec jungle.

The environment is perfect, at once a frame for and an extension of the sculpture. Monkeys caper about in the trees; browsing deer look up, hesitate, then vanish into the thickets; the snarl of a jaguar (safely caged) underlines the fact that the Olmec were "jaguar people," with themes featuring the great felines an important aspect of their art. Small details have been considered as well. For instance, instead of directional signs, naked footprints that look as if they've dried in the clay paths point the way.

Perhaps the best way to visit the park is simply to stroll through it, coming upon the huge heads, altars, and other great monoliths by surprise, and gradually growing used to the Olmec "line" and concept of monumentality without worrying about specific meanings and relationships. Then walk through it a second time with the official guidebook and map in hand (these are sold at the entrance).

Of all the monuments in the park, Colossal Head #1 evokes the most comment. Carved almost 3,000 years ago, this single boulder was somehow transported some 112 km (70 miles) through the jungles to the original La Venta site—despite being over 3 meters (9 feet) high and more than 2 meters (6 feet) in diameter, and weighing 44 tons. Yet, according to experts, the great stone was somehow moved without the help of wheels or draft animals.

You will read and hear endless speculation about the heads, especially the three magnificent examples in the park. Are they kings? Beheaded ball players? The simple truth is that nobody knows. Even the best and most official printed material contains much speculation presented as fact. The carved altars, for example, may be something else—thrones, perhaps. While some of the sculptures have stronger explanations than others, visitors to the park are free to speculate on their own while contemplating the beauty and haunting power of these ancient stone sculptures created many centuries before Periclean Athens.

The Regional Museum of Anthropology

This museum, one of the best in the country (and an adjunct of CICOM, the Centro de Investigaciones de las Culturas Olmeca y Maya), is the perfect complement to La

Venta park. The museum is filled with artifacts from a variety of locations, but the emphasis—and the best collection—deals with the surrounding region: Olmec and Mayan objects, including beautiful copies of Mayan codices. You should allow about two hours for viewing its extensive collection of artifacts, maps, exhibits, and photographs. The museum, open daily, is located on the banks of the Río Grijalva, just west of the Prolongación de Ocampe, an extension of Villahermosa's *malecón*. Tours begin on the second floor.

The Villahermosa Zoo

Adjacent to the Parque-Museo de La Venta and likewise stretching along the esplanade bordering the Laguna de las Ilusiones is a delightful public garden that is also home to the equally delightful Villahermosa Zoo. Here you'll find jungle animals and birds in a lush, tropical setting that is in no way artificial. The bands of monkeys, in particular, attract crowds of fascinated, wide-eyed children.

Behind the zoo runs the long esplanade with its lovely views of the palm-fringed lagoon—a perfect place to find the stray breezes that occasionally stir in this tropical city.

The park-museum, zoo, and beautiful Laguna de las Ilusiones are grouped together on the west side of the city, occupying a broad area northeast of the prominent corner of Paseo Tabasco and Boulevard Adolfo Ruíz Cortines.

A Day Trip to Comalcalco

The ruined Mayan city of Comalcalco, situated at the very limit of Maya country some 60 km (37 miles) northwest of Villahermosa, was in pre-Hispanic times a satellite of Palenque. Comalcalco is somewhat of an oddity in that it was constructed of brick—the only important Mayan center so built. Though the site has been badly ravaged by time, some elaborate structures survive, as do some fine examples of stucco art inspired by Palenque.

While the site itself is only of medium interest, the drive through the surrounding cocoa-growing countryside, which is still inhabited by the Maya, will add a great deal to the value of the excursion. A little past the halfway point from Comalcalco stands the village church of Cupilco, a cheerfully gaudy example of folk art and decoration featuring a profusion of flowers and angels.

Staying in Villahermosa

The outstanding hotel here is also the city's newest, the **Holiday Inn Tabasco Plaza**, east of the Parque-Museo in a new residential and shopping district. One of the best operations in Mexico, it reflects Villahermosa's recent prosperity and burgeoning internationalism, with refrigerators, balconies, and spacious rooms furnished with quiet good taste. The dining room is excellent for well-prepared regional and Mexican dishes as well as international-style entreés, and the bar has entertainment. The hotel's atmosphere is elegant but relaxed.

The **Exelaris Hyatt** is in the same fairly expensive price range without being as luxurious or gracious, although it is a decidedly first-rate hotel. It has a dining room, coffee shop, and nightclub; located near the zoo in Juárez, just off Paseo Tabasco.

The **Hotel Cencali**, a comfortable establishment situated in a gardenlike neighborhood near the Laguna de las Ilusiones, offers its guests (mostly tourists) good rooms and attractive tropical grounds. The restaurant, with a bar and entertainment, can also be recommended.

The **Miraflores**, located downtown on Calle Reforma (part of the pedestrian mall closed to traffic), has air conditioning, a bar, and a restaurant. This is a rare operation in Villahermosa—an inexpensive hotel that is still acceptable. It will do.

Because of a steady stream of business traffic, much of it international, Villahermosa's hotels are crowded and reservations absolutely essential.

Dining in Villahermosa

The first choice for good food and service in town is the Holiday Inn Tabasco Plaza's serene but gleaming dining room.

Los Guayacanes, which overlooks the river on the grounds of the regional museum, is somewhat romantic and serves good seafood.

Capitán Buelo is a riverboat restaurant that serves lunch, in two sittings, on two separate trips; the first departs at 1:30 P.M., the second at around 3:00. You do this for the boat ride, not the food, but the meal is better and less expensive than you would expect from this kind of operation. Get the boat at Malecón and Zaragoza.

Leo's, at Paseo Tabasco 429, became so popular as a

result of its service, informality, and substantial fare—
beef and pork tacos, pastries, all-American hamburgers
with fries, and the like—that a second one has been
opened in Mérida.

Los Pepes, centrally located at Madero 610, is the best
of the open-front cafés and serves regional food at inexpensive prices. The ceiling fans help some, but nothing
open to the outdoors is very appealing on a torrid day.

GETTING AROUND

Veracruz

All major airline service is via Mexico City. Mexicana is the
chief carrier, with three flights to and from the capital
daily, plus four flights a week to Los Angeles with a
Mexico City stopover. The Mexicana office in Veracruz is
on the corner of Serdán and Cinco de Mayo. Aerotur, a
feeder airline, has flights to Villahermosa, Mérida, and
Ciudad del Carmen in the state of Campeche. Ground
transportation to and from the airport is by taxi, *colectivo,*
or rental car. For the return trip from the city to the
airport, however, the *colectivo* is not always reliable.

Intercity buses arrive and depart from the Central
Camionera, which is located about 4 km (2½ miles) from
downtown Veracruz and is accessible by taxi or city buses
running south on Avenida Cinco de Mayo. (They're
marked "Camionera" in white paint on the windshield.)

First-class buses (the ADO line) arrive and depart every
few minutes for the capital. Buses *from* the capital depart
at the Terminal de Autobuses de Oriente (TAPO) near the
San Lázaro metro station. There is also good service from
Veracruz to Lake Catemaco, Villahermosa, Tuxpan, and
Jalapa (which is on the northern route to Mexico City).
There is, in addition, a special night bus to Mérida, another to Oaxaca. It takes about 14 hours to reach Mérida,
a little less than 12 to Oaxaca. A trip to the capital takes
about seven hours.

Four trains a day run between Veracruz and the capital,
two departing each city in the morning, one via Jalapa and
the other via Córdoba. The trip takes about 12 hours.
There's also a night express, with Pullman cars, via Córdoba, that leaves both cities at 9:30 P.M. and arrives at the
other end of the line at around 7:40 A.M. Travellers taking
the night express have a choice of accommodations, and
tickets should be purchased well in advance. The night
sleeper, called the "Jarocha," offers the best service.

The better highway to Veracruz from the capital is the southern (toll) route, Highway 150D, via Puebla and Córdoba. The alternate route, via Jalapa on highways 140 and 129, is both longer and slower. Both routes, however, offer spectacular mountain scenery.

A choice of car rental agencies is available in Veracruz, but none is of international reputation. Service at the airport and in the city is offered by Auto Laurencio, Autos Panamericana, Renta de Carros Veracruz, and Valgrande Rent a Car. Major credit cards are accepted. However, there is no real need to have a car in the city. Public transportation is both fast and frequent, and taxis are plentiful.

Villahermosa

Daily flights by Aeroméxico and Mexicana connect Villahermosa to Mexico City, Mérida, Tuxtla Gutiérrez, and Cancún. Price-controlled taxis provide ground transportation from the airport to the city, which is about 10 km (6 miles) distant.

ADO is the best bus line linking Villahermosa with Veracruz, as well as Mérida, Palenque, and San Cristóbal de las Casas. The trip to Mérida takes about nine hours. The daily express bus to Oaxaca is about an 11-hour trip.

None of the city's dozen car rental agencies is known internationally. Two of the larger are Arrendadora de Autos Usumacinta, at the airport and the Hotel Cencali in town, and Tabasco Auto Rent, which is also at the airport and in town, the latter at the Hotel Viva, Paseo Tabasco 1201. Both offer a variety of models, and both accept credit cards.

Tour buses leave regularly for the archaeological zones of Palenque and Comalcalco and have pickup service at all the major hotels.

Highway 180 is the best road to Veracruz and points north and west; it also runs into Campeche and points east via the coast. Motorists heading east on this route, however, are dependent on the ferry at Ciudad del Carmen, and are therefore at the mercy of the weather. The inland route, Highway 186, is the more dependable route to the Yucatán Peninsula.

ACCOMMODATIONS REFERENCE

▶ **Berthangel**. Zócalo, **Catemaco** 95870. Tel: (294) 3-0089.

▶ **Hotel Cencali**. Carretera 180, **Villahermosa** 86040. Tel: (931) 2-6000.

▶ **Hotel Colonial**. Zócalo and Miguel Lendo, **Veracruz** 91700. Tel: (293) 2-0193.

▶ **Hotel Emporio**. Malecón and Xicoténcatl, **Veracruz** 91700. Tel: (293) 2-0020.

▶ **Exelaris Hyatt Villahermosa**. Avenida Juárez 106, **Villahermosa** 86040. Tel: (931) 2-7862; in the United States and Canada: (800) 233-1234.

▶ **Holiday Inn Tabasco Plaza**. Paseo Tabasco 1407, **Villahermosa** 86040. Tel: (931) 3-4400; in the United States and Canada: (800) 465-4329.

▶ **Hotel María Victoria**. Zaragoza 6, **Jalapa** 91000. Tel: (281) 7-5600.

▶ **Miraflores**. Reforma 304, **Villahermosa** 86040. Tel: (931) 2-0022.

▶ **Hotel Mocambo**. Carretera Mocambo, POB 263, **Veracruz** 91700. Tel: (293) 7-1661.

▶ **Playa Azul**. Carretera Sontecomapan, **Catemaco**, Veracruz 95870. Tel: (294) 3-0001.

▶ **Playa Paraíso**. Boulevard Veracruz Mocambo, Boca del Río, **Veracruz** 91700. Tel: (293) 7-8399.

▶ **Hotel Plaza**. Avenida Juárez 39, **Tuxpan**, Veracruz. Tel: (783) 4-0838.

▶ **Prendes**. Zócalo, **Veracruz** 91700. Tel: (293) 2-0153.

▶ **Hotel Salinas**. Boulevard Ruíz Cortines 1000, **Poza Rica**, Veracruz. Tel: (782) 2-0706.

▶ **Hotel Salmones**. Zaragoza 24, **Jalapa** 91000. Tel: (294) 7-5351.

▶ **Hotel Sara**. Garizurieta 44, **Tuxpan**, Veracruz. Tel: (783) 4-0010.

▶ **El Tajín**. Domínguez 104, **Papantla**, Veracruz. Tel: (784) 2-1062.

OAXACA

By Celia Wakefield

Celia Wakefield has lived in Mexico for many years, the past 13 in San Miguel de Allende, and travels extensively throughout the country. She has written articles for The Atlantic, Saturday Review, Christian Science Monitor, Newsday, *and* Punch. *She is also the author of* High Cities of the Andes.

The city of Oaxaca (wuh-HAH-kah) lies about 300 miles southeast of Mexico City geographically; in spirit it is a world away. There could be no more complete change from the frenetic traffic, bustle, and pollution of the capital than this lovely city in the Sierra Madre del Sur.

Some cities keep their essential character in spite of the passing of time. Although Oaxaca has mushroomed in size in recent years, it is still a semi-tropical oasis of quiet charm, a place where visitors return again and again to unwind in its gentle, springlike climate. Nobody seems to be in a hurry here, but there is always something to do— especially outside the city limits proper, whether it's visiting the native crafts villages for which the region is justly famous; exploring the magnificent archaeological sites at Monte Albán, Mitla, and elsewhere; or using the city as a way stop for vacations on the beaches of Puerto Angel, Puerto Escondido, or Huatulco (see the separate chapter on Pacific resorts for a more detailed look at these and others).

MAJOR INTEREST

Oaxaca City
Main plaza and Cathedral
Church of Santo Domingo

Regional Museum of Oaxaca
Rufino Tamayo Museum
Saturday market

Outside the City
Monte Albán
Mitla
Craft villages

OAXACA CITY

Oaxaca is easily reached by plane, train, bus, or car from Mexico City, though each of these may have its disadvantages: the seven-hour drive is through uninteresting country; the plane flight may be canceled for mysterious reasons; the train may be late or the bus crowded. Any of these inconveniences will be forgotten, however, once this pleasant city is reached.

Oaxaca takes care of its guests in small but important ways. At the airport a *colectivo* van pulls up to carry passengers to their hotels for a minimum fee. (If it doesn't turn up instantly, wait for it; taxis charge five times as much.) A few years ago the city banned all vehicular traffic from the central downtown plazas. Now pedestrians amble freely under huge trees, rest in the shade on white wrought-iron benches, and listen to marimba music at the rococo bandstand. Shopkeepers, passersby, and neighbors on park benches are liberal with information; old-fashioned courtesy has not gone out of style here.

How long will you want to spend in Oaxaca? There are several museums, churches, and markets to be explored, as well as two separate excursions to the important archaeological sites of Monte Albán and Mitla. Three days should therefore be the minimum. Travellers with special interests in crafts or archaeology will want to allow a day or two extra for visits to small weaving and pottery villages, or to the less well known archaeological sites at Culiapán, Zaachila, Dainzú, Lambityeco, and Yagul.

Oaxaca is a city of about 300,000 people nestled in a valley at an altitude of a little over 5,000 feet. Actually, there are three Oaxacas: the state, the city, and the valley of the same name. In conversation, "Oaxaca" may refer to both the city and the surrounding valley, which includes the craft villages and archaeological sites most visitors come to see.

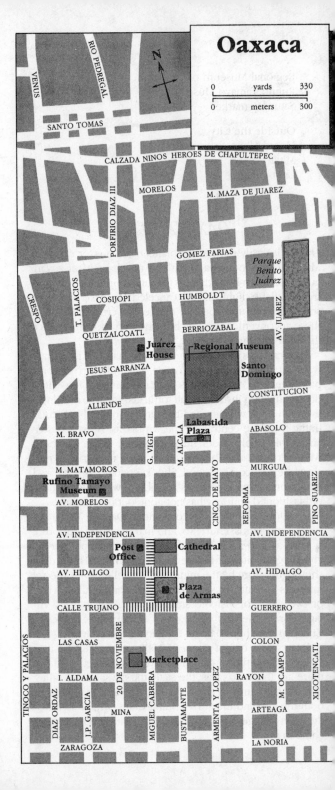

Oaxaca

| 0 | yards | 330 |
| 0 | meters | 300 |

VENUS

RIO PEDREGAL

SANTO TOMAS

N

CALZADA NINOS HEROES DE CHAPULTEPEC

MORELOS

M. MAZA DE JUAREZ

PORFIRIO DIAZ III

GOMEZ FARIAS

Parque Benito Juarez

CRESPO

T. PALACIOS

COSIJOPI

HUMBOLDT

AV. JUAREZ

QUETZALCOATL

BERRIOZABAL

Juarez House

Regional Museum

JESUS CARRANZA

Santo Domingo

CONSTITUCION

ALLENDE

M. BRAVO

G. VIGIL

M. ALCALA

Labastida Plaza

ABASOLO

M. MATAMOROS

MURGUIA

Rufino Tamayo Museum

CINCO DE MAYO

REFORMA

PINO SUAREZ

AV. MORELOS

AV. INDEPENDENCIA

AV. INDEPENDENCIA

Post Office

Cathedral

AV. HIDALGO

AV. HIDALGO

Plaza de Armas

CALLE TRUJANO

GUERRERO

TINOCO Y PALACIOS

LAS CASAS

20 DE NOVIEMBRE

COLON

I. ALDAMA

Marketplace

RAYON

M. OCAMPO

XICOTENCATL

DIAZ ORDAZ

J.P. GARCIA

MINA

MIGUEL CABRERA

BUSTAMANTE

ARMENTA Y LOPEZ

ARTEAGA

ZARAGOZA

LA NORIA

The valley was inhabited as long ago as 9000 B.C. In time, the Zapotec Indians developed an advanced civilization here, trading with the equally advanced Olmecs on the Gulf Coast, and built a number of impressive ceremonial centers. Foremost among these was the great center of Monte Albán, which had been founded around 800 B.C. by a pre-Zapotec culture. The Zapotecs dominated the valley from around the birth of Christ to A.D. 800. Their eventual decline was hastened by the arrival of the warriorlike Mixtecs from the north, who did not so much subdue the Zapotecs as assume the reins of an exhausted culture. Toward the end of the 15th century the fierce Aztecs made their presence felt, building a fort in the center of the valley and controlling its trade and tribute. Details of these migrations and shifts in power are obscure, but the Zapotecs, who were the first to leave an imprint on the Valley of Oaxaca, survived, and theirs is the language most often heard in its markets today.

The Spanish appeared on the scene in 1521, but it was some years before they were able to subjugate the indigenous population and establish a city on the spot where the Aztec fortress had been. As W. H. Prescott wrote in his classic *History of the Conquest of Mexico:* "Cortes obtained a grant of an extensive tract of land in the fruitful province of Oaxaca, where he proposed to lay out a plantation for the Crown. . . . He soon had the estate under such cultivation that he assured his master, the Emperor, Charles the Fifth, that it was worth 20,000 ounces of gold." In 1529 the emperor gave Cortés the title of Marqués del Valle de Oaxaca.

The Dominican friars were instrumental in building the colonial city, and by 1575 there were 160 churches in the valley. At the same time, the province flourished economically. Silkworms were imported from Spain, and silk spinning was profitable until the China trade undercut it. Cochineal dye from the region was in demand until the advent of artificial dyes in the 19th century. Cattle ranching and wheat farming were both suited to the mild, dry climate of the valley. Oaxaca prospered, in part because it supported very few people. As the population increased over the centuries, however, the forests were cut down and the once-rich soil was eroded away. Today, it is one of the poorest states in Mexico.

Oaxaca is also famous as the birthplace of two of Mexico's most important political figures. Benito Juárez, a full-blooded Zapotec, was prominent in the reform movement of the 1850s and instrumental in the 1860s in ridding Mexico of the foreign rule of the Emperor Maximilian. In 1867 he became the first and (so far) only Mexican president of pure Indian descent, and he has been revered as his country's Abraham Lincoln since his death in 1872. The house where he worked as a servant in Oaxaca City is maintained as a small museum. Local legend has it that he did not die but rather disappeared into a lake in his native town of Guelatao, from which he will emerge some day to lead his Zapotec tribesmen once again.

Porfirio Díaz, another *oaxaqueño,* rose to prominence from the other end of the social spectrum, having always known wealth and influence. Although he governed his country as president for thirty years, from 1877–1880, and again from 1884 until the second year of the Revolution in 1911, his accomplishments have not been so honored in Oaxaca, where he is usually thought of as a ruthless dictator not deserving of memorials—though you will find a few streets named in his memory.

The Plaza de Armas

The Plaza de Armas, or *zócalo,* actually consists of two public squares, the large Plaza de la Constitución and the smaller Alameda de Leon, which is surrounded by the Cathedral, a number of government buildings, and the post office. The Cathedral, which was begun in 1553 and finally finished in the 19th century, is squat rather than soaring, solid rather than elaborate. It almost seems to huddle on its site, its two flying buttresses ready to ward off the vicious earthquakes that have struck the city more than once. Nevertheless, the colonial clock on its façade still keeps good time.

The enormous main plaza is surrounded by arcades with café tables set out under them. These are occupied from breakfast to late evening by people eating, listening to music, gossiping, reading newspapers, or simply nursing cups of coffee as they while away the hours. On a typical day there is much to watch here. A couple of jugglers entertain with brightly colored balls. A guitarist squats at the curb, tuning his instrument. Two women, their *rebozos* worn looped around their heads turban-style, walk slowly side by side, the big flat baskets on their heads balanced off-center in apparent defiance of gravity. The roses inside are a deep burgundy, all perfect, all halfway between bud and flower. Elsewhere, a small ragged boy recites a poem at the top of his lungs. It goes on, stanza after stanza; payment is hoped for. Two businessmen sitting on a nearby bench huddle over a handful of legal forms. A couple of girls giggle, their heads together, as they turn the pages of a glossy magazine. For many, the best seats from which to take this all in are the tall chairs meant for shoe shines, spaced like thrones at the edges of flowerbeds and sidewalks. Business thrives. Unless the customer is wearing running shoes, he seems to need a shine every hour or two.

The air in Oaxaca is soft, the climate mild, neither sultry nor cool (although a sweater or light jacket will come in handy in the early morning and evening). Against the sky over the *zócalo* float bunches of balloons arranged in the shapes of fanciful animals. The balloon vendors seem to float as well, wandering from spot to spot, seldom making a sale. Oaxaca's vendors in general are businesslike without being offensively pushy. They have apparently learned that "no" may actually mean "no," whether the prospective buyer is looking at a woven rug, an engraved machete, or a colorful necklace.

Church of Santo Domingo and the Regional Museum

The Church of Santo Domingo is located five blocks north of the *zócalo,* and the city has again shown good taste in keeping traffic out of the surrounding area. The church was begun by the Dominicans in 1575 and finished about a century later; the Baroque façade was added another hundred years after that. The intricate ornamentation everywhere evident, however, makes it surprising it was ever finished at all. Dazzling golden scrollwork covers almost every inch of the interior, including the eleven chapels. Especially remarkable is the many-branched Tree of Jesse, a series of 35 detailed relief figures illustrating the lineal descent of Christ.

The **Regional Museum of Oaxaca**, housed in the attached convent, has as its great prize the treasures from Monte Albán. Visitors who see nothing else in the city usually find their way to the **Tomb 7 collection**, discovered in 1932. The magnificent jewelry on display, which dates from about A.D. 500, consists of gold, conch shell, turquoise, amber, obsidian, onyx, and glass worked into elaborate pieces by the superb ancient craftsmen. (The filigree necklaces are often used as models for the jewelry sold in Oaxaca's downtown stores.) Like so much else in Oaxaca—the rococo bandstand, the fine embroidery work, and the marimba music with its extra trills and flourishes—the jewelry from Tomb 7 is above all elaborate and complex, suggesting that Indian craftsmen centuries ago may have originated the long artistic traditions of the region.

The Rufino Tamayo Museum

A plaque in the Rufino Tamayo Museum tells the visitor, in less-than-perfect Spanish, French, and English: "This museum is dedicated to the millenary art which flourished in the area called now-a-days the Republic of Mexico, art entirely inspired (with the exception of Occidental Mexico) by Pre-Columbian religions and myths, which represents the deified forces of nature: the sun, the wind, the water, and a multitude of other natural phenomena. But if, in our time, the pieces exhibited in the niches of the museum impress its visitors, it is not for religious feelings, because the religions of ancient Mexicans, a long time ago have been forgotten. Rather they are moved by the aesthetic rank of the works, their beauty, power, and originality."

The plaque goes on to emphasize the point: "It is the first time that a Mexican museum exhibits the relics of Indian past in terms of aesthetic phenomena, in terms of works of art."

The pieces in this museum were assembled by Rufino Tamayo, one of modern Mexico's most admired painters, from his private collection and donated to the city of Oaxaca, his birthplace. Tamayo took care that the public would see the objects at their best: There are no catchall display cases of "black pottery from the valley" or "human figures, various" here. Instead, each piece has received careful consideration, is described individually, and is mounted against a background—light blue, perhaps, or rose, or orange—that brings out its beauty. The museum, near the *zócalo* at Morelos 503, is housed in an old mansion with a flower-bordered patio. The convenient benches around the patio are a good place to rest and admire the pre-Columbian figures of men playing musical instruments, the Colima dogs yapping in unison, a man in a coyote mask, or a fierce jaguar carved out of jagged volcanic rock. The Rufino Tamayo Museum is what a museum should be and often is not: a place for quiet contemplation and unhurried reflection.

The Saturday Market

Outdoor markets are a way of life in Mexico, and the market in Oaxaca is one of the biggest and best known. Although it operates every day, it really comes alive on Saturdays, when farmers, crafts people, and merchants from the small villages of the great Valley of Oaxaca stream into town. D. H. Lawrence was so intrigued by the spectacle, in fact, that he devoted a chapter of *Mornings in Mexico* to it. In those days, some sixty years ago, Indians almost always travelled by foot or burro, arriving loaded with goods for sale or to barter. "A little load of firewood, a woven blanket, a few eggs and tomatoes," Lawrence wrote, "are excuse enough for men, women and children to cross the foot-weary miles of valley and mountain. To buy, to sell, to barter, to exchange. To exchange, above all things, human contact."

Today's participants are as likely to arrive by truck or ancient car as by burro or on foot. The city has also cleaned up and somewhat de-romanticized the market. Food is no longer spread out haphazardly on the ground. Merchants are assigned stalls, and their wares are exhibited on wooden stands, shielded from the sun and rain by lengths of old canvas. What was once a wide-open area of color and activity has been turned into a maze of alleys, with here and there an open patio, making it easy to get lost. As is always the case in Mexican markets, the same types of goods are displayed together. Next to the sugarcane vendor is another sugarcane vendor and next to him another. There seems to be no special competitive atmosphere; instead, it's much like a single department store where dresses or kitchen utensils are lumped together.

There is an endless variety of things to choose from here, from shoelaces to coconuts. Still, for the visitor—especially one with a camera—the food area is by far the most interesting. All of this food comes from the surrounding countryside in trucks, by mule, or on someone's head, and the minute it arrives, it is arranged artistically, best side outward, in small piles (*pilas*) of five, in mountains of gleaming color, or in bundles or baskets.

The food area may be splendid, but to get to it you have to walk through alley after alley of uninteresting pots and pans, tapes of rock music, men's pants, and automobile parts. Do not go to the Saturday market, therefore, expecting a primitive Indian scene. Approach it, instead, as a remarkable chance to see how impressive a massing of objects can be: a hundred cold gray machetes, a thousand plastic shoes, a glittering mound of blood-red tomatoes, a barricade of papayas, a million dried shrimp in baskets shining golden in the sun.

One more word of advice: The market should not be visited in the early morning, despite the fact that this may be recommended to you. The vendors will still be streaming into town then, and many of the stalls where they display their wares are not yet open. The best time to go is about 10:30 A.M.

Shopping in Oaxaca

Oaxaca City is noted for the variety of its local crafts— serapes woven in muted colors and intricate patterns; unusual green and black ceramics; machetes with elaborate designs incised into their handles; delicate filigree jewelry. The serious shopper will have a wide selection to choose from, and the way to go about it will depend on your personality and frame of mind. Anyone who loves to bargain will head for the market, where the first price mentioned is always far higher than the final price. The aficionado of cottage industries, on the other hand, will head for the outlying crafts villages. The best of these are **Teotitlán del Valle** (on the way to Mitla) for weaving, and **Atzompa** for green pottery, or **Coyotepec** for black. The black pottery, which is unique to this area, is left unglazed and fired in subterranean ovens so that the smoke colors the clay. Tours to these villages can be arranged in town, and there are also frequent buses from the second-class bus station at the end of Calle Trujano. For those with their own cars, these places are all a short distance from town over good roads.

Anyone who dislikes discussing price, however, will be best served in a shop, and Oaxaca has some good ones.

Yalalag de Oaxaca, at the corner of Avenida Morelos and Macedonio Alcalá, is excellent for black pottery and woven goods.

Victor's, at Porfirio Díaz 111, is a 17th-century monastery that has been converted into a shop. The stark, battered building seems about to collapse, but the store boasts a large selection of woven goods, ceramics, and cut paper. **El Tecolote**, nearby, offers ceramic figurines and a variety of woven goods.

There are two shops located at Calle 3 and Alcalá, on the pedestrian mall one block from the Hotel El Presidente. Here, **Copil** has the best collection of masks, while **Itandehui** sells a variety of colorful things that make good gifts, including dolls and glassware.

El Cosijo, on Calle García Vigil, is a store with imagination, where the unusual offerings include fanciful figurines and big papier-mâché skeletons decorated with feathers.

Finally, **Colibri**, at Crespo 114, is a new store with an excellent collection of ceramics and weaving. The proprietors have also been handing out the best detailed map of the city available, and if they continue to do so, that in itself will be a reason to drop in. (Most city maps, including the one given out by the tourist bureau, are small and virtually impossible to read.)

Even in Oaxaca's stores, however, there is an undercurrent of bargaining. Any customer who buys more than one item has a reason to ask for a discount, which usually runs about 10 percent off the marked price.

Staying in Oaxaca City

The **Presidente** is probably the most romantic, and certainly the most historic, hotel in Mexico. It was originally the Convento de Santa Catalina (c. 1576), and when it was tastefully remodeled and converted into a hotel some years ago, no expense was spared. Today it's a labyrinth of patios, ambulatories, and shadowy corridors. The junior suites are decorated in bright yellow tile, with locally woven wall hangings. The single rooms tend to be a little monastic, perfectly adequate but not as nice as the doubles and junior suites. The building itself is a veritable museum, and offers its guests a tangible sense of Oaxaca's colonial past. It also has the usual modern conveniences—swimming, dancing, a nightclub, and convenient parking outside. By Oaxaca standards the Presidente is expensive, but not by international or even national standards. It is especially popular with Europeans, so the atmosphere tends to be international, but the jeans-and-sandals set is also welcome.

The **Victoria** sits high on a hill outside of town and has a beautiful view of the Valley of Oaxaca. Its guests frequently fly down from Mexico City, then rent a car for the sake of convenience and sightseeing. There are two sections to the complex; the newer—and much the better—one features bungalows with slick pine furniture, walk-in closets, and refrigerators. The Victoria also has a restaurant, bar, disco, and swimming pool, and is less expensive than the Presidente, though still high priced.

The **Fortín Plaza**, a neighbor of the Victoria, opened in 1987. The front rooms get the best view here, and the interior decorating features much white tile and marble, with Mixtec motifs. It also has a swimming pool and tennis courts, as well as a restaurant overlooking the pool. Although slightly less expensive than the Victoria, the Fortín Plaza attracts affluent Mexicans from the D. F. as well as locally.

The **Misión de los Angeles**, a ten-minute drive from the center of town, is tropical, lazy, and spacious, with beautiful and extensive grounds ideal for strolling. The suites here have fireplaces and old-fashioned furnishings, and the hotel has a dining room, a nightclub, and, on weekends, a disco. The Misión appeals to an older crowd, many of them retirees from cold climates. It's in the same price range as the Victoria, but not quite as good.

The **Calesa Real**, two-and-a-half blocks north of the *zócalo,* is a former colonial town house with 77 units and a central patio. The rooms are simple but charming, and there's a secure parking lot next door. Moderately expensive.

The **Señorial** is right on the *zócalo,* and also has a secure parking facility for guests (located at the rear of the hotel). Behind its colonial façade is a modern and busy, though somewhat impersonal, hotel. However, many visitors find it comfortable as well as convenient. The units vary greatly in size; the rates are moderate.

The **Mesón del Rey**, near the center of town, is a good bet for the budget-conscious traveller, providing small rooms at reasonable rates. The management is courteous and pleasant as well. The hotel, though modest, is not a haunt of the backpack set.

The **Marqués del Valle** is a dowager that has been deteriorating for a couple of decades, its rooms a bit threadbare, the baths big and old-fashioned. Its public spaces are a hodgepodge of posters stuck on marble columns, cigarette dispensers, and soft-drink vending machines. Still, it is right on the *zócalo,* and its café tables are always occupied. The rates are moderate but not a bargain.

Dining in Oaxaca City

Oaxaca has its specialties, among them tamales wrapped in banana leaves and a Oaxaca version of *mole,* the chocolate-chile sauce more often associated with Puebla. Also notable here is the *comida corrida,* the fixed-price meal of several courses served during the midday lunch hour (a good way to get a well-balanced dinner from soup to dessert for a reasonable price).

There are a number of good hotel restaurants in Oaxaca. The food at **El Presidente** is definitely international, with few traditional Mexican dishes on the menu. As one of the chain of Presidente hotels, it has the advantage of expertise from the capital, and may bring in a guest chef to supervise from time to time. The food is beautifully presented in a manner worthy of the hotel's colonial style. The sauces, especially, are rich and elaborate, the garnishes attractive.

The **Victoria**'s Mixtec-decorated restaurant also caters to foreign tastes, with traditional Mexican dishes modified to suit North American palates. Looking out on the panoramic view of the valley, the diner here can enjoy what D. H. Lawrence described as the "gleaming, pinkish-ocre of the valley flat, wild and exalted. . . ."

The kitchen of the **Fortín Plaza** specializes in seafood. Meals are served on a terrace overlooking the swimming pool, with soft tango music as an accompaniment from four to eight every day except Sunday.

The **Calesa Real** is the most Mexican of the hotel restaurants, in both atmosphere and menu, with few concessions to the tourist. The pork and chicken dishes are especially tasty, and its prices are moderate.

The restaurant at the **Hotel Monte Albán,** opposite the Cathedral, is only mediocre; the best reason for going there is the evening show of regional dancing, which, in spite of its amateurism—poor soundtrack, overlong intermissions—is an excellent opportunity to see traditional dances from various towns in Oaxaca state staged with grace and enthusiasm. There is a small admission charge; dining is not required.

In addition, Oaxaca has a handful of very good restaurants that are not in hotels. The best one is also the newest, a dream of period atmosphere, delicious cuisine, and sensible, friendly service: the **Del Vitral,** listed in *Gastrotur,* a Mexican gourmet magazine, as "the best restaurant in Oaxaca and the southeast of Mexico." It's a short distance from the *zócalo* on Avenida V. Guerrero, where it occupies the second floor of a magnificent turn-of-the-century mansion. An imposing staircase leads up to a balcony, a dining room facing the street, and the "stained glass" room to the left. The stained glass, which gives the restaurant its name, runs along one whole side of the room, an enormous window that is decorated with fountains, cupids, and trees. It was created by European craftsmen for the wealthy Zorrilla family, whose descendants own the restaurant and have refurbished it to splendid effect: a pale rose décor, opulent draperies, and huge chandeliers are just some of its elegant touches. The best thing about Del Vitral, however, is the fact it has not become "Continental" and snobbish. The menu is listed in Spanish, not French, and many of the dishes are from old Oaxaca recipes. Prices are high but not outrageous.

One restaurant that has been doing well for a good many years now is **El Asador Vasco**, located on the second floor of a building on the west side of the *zócalo*. It caters to a European crowd, and serves steak, chicken, and fish as well as a few regional dishes. Try for a table overlooking the plaza; it's an expensive place, but you're paying partly for the view—as well as for the musicians who wander among the tables. Reservations are important; El Asador Vasco can get very crowded and rushed (Tel: 6-9719).

The **Catedral**, at García Vigil 105, one block from the *zócalo*, is pretty, airy, and comfortable, with tables set out in a small courtyard. It offers a lengthy menu with an emphasis on meat: eight different steak entrées along with chops and chicken; it's also a good place for the *comida corrida*. At night there is piano music, and its prices are reasonable.

The **Tipica de Oaxaca**, in Labastida Plaza, between Alcalá and Cinco de Mayo, offers typical regional fare at modest prices. **La Fontana**, across the street, is a pleasant and cheerful family operation that also features Oaxaca-style cooking.

Doña Elpidia's, located seven blocks from the center of town at Miguel Cabrera 413, has been serving noonday dinners for half a century. Behind her plain door (Doña Elpidia doesn't bother with a sign) is a lovely courtyard filled with birds and flowers—and there are guard dogs on the roof. The hours are from 1:00 to 5:00 P.M. only, during which a five-course *comida corrida* is served; it's a wonderful opportunity to enjoy a real Mexican family-style meal.

Finally, and especially for the younger crowd, **Los Guajairos**, at Alcalá 303, serves a good meal that's accompanied by pop music at dinnertime.

OUTSIDE THE CITY
Monte Albán

At the majestic ruins of Monte Albán, a 10-km (6-mile) drive southwest of the city, everything is enormous and austere, the ambience of the site enhanced by the sheer mass of the stone structures and the perspective lent by the surrounding mountains. As anyone who has ever visited Monte Albán knows, it's not surprising that people should come from all over the world with the express purpose of seeing the ruins. The groups of tourists who walk to and fro here are dwarfed by the scene; but then, a crowd of thousands would be dwarfed by this scene.

Monte Albán is the only pre-Columbian necropolis in Mexico. The hill on which it stands, 1,300 feet above the Valley of Oaxaca, was flattened and shaped by the original builders and then used as a base for the construction that ensued. Today, grayish masses of stone—stairs, columns, platforms, colonnades, halls, and passages—surround the central plaza in all directions. Below ground, more than two hundred tombs where the dead were buried along with their "companion sculptures" (which were meant to accompany them on their journey to the other world) have been found. The earliest writing known in Mexico (glyphs) was also found at Monte Albán.

Monte Albán's precise origins are uncertain. Construction of the site seems to have begun about 800 B.C., and it might have been an early center of the Olmec culture; although no artifacts from that civilization have been found at the site, the presence of the flowing "Olmec" line in some of the sculpture suggests that they might have been there. The *danzantes,* in the so-called **Temple of the Dancers**, low relief sculpture carved out of hard stone, remain from this period. These are stone slabs with engravings of human figures in strange positions. Their appearance suggests the jaguar motif in Olmec art. After Monte Albán I, however, there was little further stone sculpting at the site, and pottery took over.

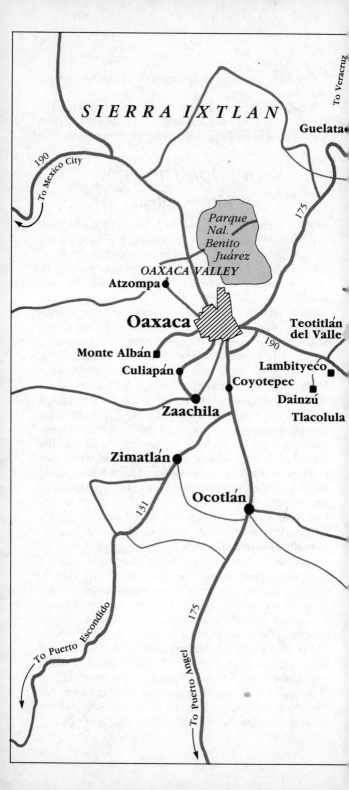

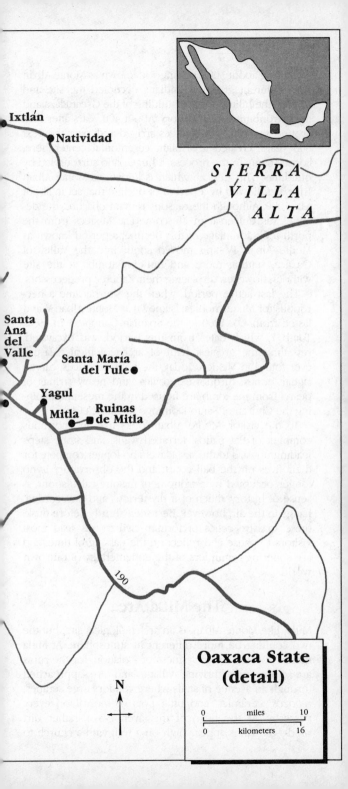

Ixtlán

Natividad

SIERRA VILLA ALTA

Santa Ana del Valle

Santa María del Tule

Yagul

Mitla   Ruinas de Mitla

190

Oaxaca State (detail)

N

0	miles	10
0	kilometers	16

Starting about 300 B.C., a period known as Monte Albán II, a different group of Indians occupied the site and leveled the hilltop for the building of the Great Plaza and the **astronomical observatory**. About 400 years after that, around A.D. 100, the Zapotecs arrived and, over the next 800 years, created a brilliant ceremonial center here, constructing, in the process, a huge patio surrounded by buildings. This period, which is known as Monte Albán III, was followed by a period of decline that set in about A.D. 1000. Although the reasons remain obscure, the decline was universal in Mesoamerica. Mixtecs from the north took advantage of this decline, a period known as Monte Albán IV, and moved south into the Valley of Oaxaca, settling there and building tombs at the site without, however, displacing their Zapotec predecessors.

The last active period, when the site became a necropolis for Mixtec nobles, is known as Monte Albán V, and lasted from A.D. 1200 to the Spanish Conquest. In 1932, Tomb 7, which dates from this period, was excavated, revealing the greatest haul of archaeological treasure ever found in Mexico. Today, the gold necklaces, carved jaguar bones, turquoise mosaics, and heavy strings of pearls from the tomb are housed in the museum adjoining the Church of Santo Domingo in Oaxaca City.

To the visitor, Monte Albán looks like an enormous complex of flat patios, terraced walls, and stone steps leading upward to the sky. Players no longer compete for their lives on the ball court, and the observatory is no longer occupied by astronomers making calculations. A sense of history, much of it mysterious and unrecorded, hangs in the air, however. Best seen shortly before dusk, these massive relics of former civilizations lead most visitors to pause and reflect on the passing of time, and are sobering reminders of the ephemerality of our own world.

The Mitla Area

Mitla, like Monte Albán, is an archaeological site, but the two couldn't be more different in atmosphere. At Mitla there is no feeling of vastness or isolation, for the ruins are close to a thriving village and are approached through an avenue of stalls where vendors urge serapes, *rebozos,* ceramics, and little pots of mezcal on every passerby. At the head of this avenue—or rather dirt road—the ruins appear high on a hill, with a church to one side. Even at the entrance to the site, however, wares are offered insistently.

To get to Mitla requires more time and effort than the half-hour's drive to Monte Albán. The daily tours from the Presidente, Victoria, and Marqués del Valle hotels, minivans of eight passengers with a trained guide along to explain things, are your best bet. It's also possible to get there by bus, which makes for an interesting excursion and gives you a chance to mingle with passengers who often speak an Indian dialect rather than Spanish and carry their children tenderly on their laps. (Children receive particular attention in Mexico. They are uniformly well behaved—except some of the spoiled, rich city kids—and seldom ill treated. Fathers seem to take as much practical care of them as mothers, and older children mind the younger ones. Charles Flandrau, who visited Mexico early in this century and wrote a classic account of his experiences, suggested that all children should be Mexican until the age of fifteen.)

Along the 40-km (25-mile)-long road to Mitla there are turnoffs to Dainzú, Lambityeco, and Yagul (archaeological ruins), as well as the textile-craft villages of **Teotitlán del Valle** and **Santa Ana del Valle**. It would be easy to extend your visit to Oaxaca beyond the normal three days in order to spend some time visiting any or all of them.

The three archaeological sites would be more crowded than they are were it not for the ruins at Monte Albán and Mitla. **Dainzú**, with some carvings dating from about 500 B.C. to A.D. 1000, boasts a number of large patios and buildings, as well as 50 sandstone slabs bearing bas-reliefs of ball players in action. **Lambityeco**, which dates from about A.D. 700, is noteworthy for its stucco busts of Cociojo, the Zapotec rain god, along with its portraitlike human heads. **Yagul** contains an acropolis comprising a cluster of tombs and palaces, as well as a great fortress situated on the crest of a hill. There are also a number of stone mosaics similar to those at Mitla, with which it was contemporary, and its ball court is the largest in the valley.

Two other sites, although not on the road to Mitla but on a side road south from Oaxaca, are nevertheless worth visiting separately. At **Culiapán**, in addition to a pyramid and Zapotec tomb, there's a handsome 16th-century monastery and church. **Zaachila**, a small village and the last Zapotec capital in the valley, boasts a huge unexplored pyramid that dominates the center of the town.

The two crafts villages on the road to Mitla produce some of the most elaborate handwoven textiles in Mexico. The *huipiles,* a sleeveless blouselike garment for women, are woven in complicated patterns on pale or colored backgrounds, and often have embroidered overlays and bright fluttering ribbons. Connoisseurs can even identify the town of origin: in Teotitlán del Valle, for instance, doves, fish, and flowers are combined in a variety of artful designs. Likewise, chemical dyes, not the primitive cochineal and vegetable dyes, are used to produce unusual shades of red, purple, and green. The serapes worn by Zapotec men are less elaborate, although they're sometimes designed with strident patterns for sale to tourists. The most attractive are woven out of undyed gray or black wool, and feature figures of animals, birds, or abstract patterns in pale colors.

If your time is limited, instead of going to these individual crafts villages take the Mitla tour on a Sunday, when the town of **Tlacolula**, on the way, is crowded with buyers and sellers attending its weekly market. Wares from all the nearby villages are brought to town and then sold up and down the dirt road in front of the local church. Tlacolula is also a mezcal-producing center, and the stores will offer tiny glasses (your choice of sweet or dry) as a softening-up gesture. (If you buy a bottle of mezcal, don't be surprised to find a worm at the bottom—it's traditional for this particular beverage.) There's a gypsy-like air to the Tlacolula market, and everyone seems to wear their brightest skirts, shirts, and shawls.

Every tour bus or taxi that heads out this way also makes an obligatory stop to see the **Tule tree** at Santa María del Tule. What kind of a tree warrants such attention? Well, it's a superlative tree, the oldest living thing in Mexico—2,000 years old, according to some naturalists. It's also an ahuehuete tree (*Taxodium mucronatum*), which is variously translated as a water cypress or sequoia. While they're larger in girth than American redwoods, they're not as tall. A smaller tree of the same species, known as *el hijo,* "the son," grows nearby (it's only 500–600 years old). The older tree is usually surrounded by crowds of onlookers—foreign, Mexican, Indian, children as well as adults—staring with concentrated interest. But what else can be done with such a landmark? It's even too big to photograph, unless you're carrying a wide-angle lens.

Mitla was a shrine long before the extant ruins were constructed, and was probably inhabited a thousand years before the beginning of the Christian era. The latest explorations here show that it probably emerged in its present incarnation during the period known as Monte Albán I, but its greatest development occurred later, possibly at the time of Monte Albán's decline, when it was rebuilt by the Mixtecs and dedicated to Mictlán, the Lord of the Underworld. It remained in full flower until relatively late, and was still in use at the time of the Spanish Conquest.

Today the ruins seem almost perfectly preserved (actually, much of the site was destroyed after the Conquest to build a sugar mill and churches), and seem to indicate a secular rather than religious use, with many of the structures dating back to about A.D. 1400. (Much older structures are still being explored in a larger area encompassing the town.)

The style of construction at Mitla is also different from that found at Monte Albán. There is no relief carving, for example, and all the decoration is in the form of geometrical mosaics that are precisely cut and fitted into walls. The effect is akin to stylized embroidery, beige on beige, monochrome and repetitive, set in a surrounding area of sand-colored rock. Here and there the effect may be broken by a scarlet or bright blue flower that has gained a foothold in a crevice of the latticelike patterns. In the courtyards enclosed by these elaborately worked walls are a number of heavy columns; put your arms around a certain column, legend has it, and the space between your hands will reveal how long you have to live. (Because the column tapers toward the top, however, it would seem that a taller person can expect a shorter life.)

In the village of Mitla there is, surprisingly, a pleasantly simple restaurant aptly called **La Sorpresa** (The Surprise). It has been there for years, not advertising much but serving good, plain food, mostly North American style, with some Mexican dishes on the menu for variety.

GETTING AROUND

Oaxaca is easily reached from Mexico City. Both Mexicana and Aeroméxico make the 50-minute flight several times daily. There is also a night train with Pullman accommodations. Buses make the trip in 10–12 hours, and Highway 190, for those driving the seven hours from the D. F. to

Oaxaca, is a good one. There are no direct flights to Oaxaca from outside of Mexico, however.

The beach resorts are a half hour's flight from the city itself. Puerto Escondido is served by Aerovia Oaxaqueños, Huatulco by Mexicana. Puerto Escondido can also be reached by car or bus over a spectacular mountain road that dives down to the the tropical Pacific coast by way of Pochutla and Puerto Angel. The direct Oaxaca–Puerto Escondido Road, on the other hand, is still unimproved in places.

The city of Oaxaca is easily explored on foot. Taxis are always available near the Cathedral, and rental cars can be obtained from Avis at the airport, or from Hertz at Bustamante 620.

Guided tours to the surrounding villages and archaeological sites leave from the Presidente, Victoria, or Marqués del Valle hotels. A *colectivo* van from the Mesón del Angel (Mina 518) takes passengers to Monte Albán and picks them up later for the return trip back to the city.

The first-class bus station is at Niños Héroes de Chapultepec near Emiliano Carranza, but most of the buses to the surrounding villages leave from the second-class station across the railroad tracks at the end of Calle Trujano.

For the trip to the airport seats in a van can be reserved at the office on Valdivieso near the *zócalo*.

When to go? The big tourist season is from January to March, but this is caused as much by North Americans' desire to escape the snow as it is by the belief that summer in Oaxaca is unpleasant. Summer *is* warmer, and there are brief tropical rains almost daily from June through September, but the altitude eliminates the sultry tropical heat you would expect at this latitude.

There are a number of famous fiestas in Oaxaca, particularly the "Night of the Radishes," on December 23. To visit the city at Christmastime you must make reservations long in advance, however.

ACCOMMODATIONS REFERENCE

▶ **Calesa Real.** García Vigil 306, **Oaxaca** 68000. Tel: (951) 6-5544.

▶ **Fortín Plaza.** Venus 118, **Oaxaca** 68040. Tel: (951) 5-7777.

▶ **Marqués del Valle.** Portal de Claveria, **Oaxaca** 68000. Tel: (951) 6-3295.

▶ **Mesón del Rey**. Trujano 212, **Oaxaca** 68000. Tel: (951) 6-0033.

▶ **Misión de los Angeles**. Calzada Porfirio Díaz, POB 17, **Oaxaca** 68050. Tel: (951) 5-1500.

▶ **El Presidente,** Cinco de Mayo 300, POB 248, **Oaxaca** 68000. Tel: (951) 6-0611.

▶ **Señorial**. Portal de Flores 6, **Oaxaca** 68000. Tel: (951) 6-3933.

▶ **Victoria**. Pan-American Highway, kilometer 545, POB 248, **Oaxaca** 68000. Tel: (951) 5-2633.

MAYAN MEXICO
THE YUCATAN PENINSULA AND CHIAPAS

By Robert Somerlott

"Whatever country this is, it is not Mexico."

The journalist John Kenneth Turner wrote this after visiting the Mayan region at the beginning of this century, and he was by no means the first to express the opinion. It is an observation that springs more from the senses than from any single political or even economic fact. Nevertheless, wars have been fought and lives sacrificed to support or discredit such a view. In the Yucatán, these are fighting words.

From the foreign visitor's viewpoint, on the other hand, the contrast offered by the Mayan region is simply another example of the Mexican republic's diversity. And what diversity it is! Anyone who spends time in the southeastern region of the country will soon understand what Turner meant. The people here call themselves *yucatecos,* not *mexicanos,* and, after 3,000 years of history, are part of a cultural legacy that, if not wholly independent, is quite different from that of the rest of the country.

To which a Mexican might well reply that Hawaii is part of the United States, as little as it resembles Vermont or Montana.

Even so, the sense that this is another world persists. Whereas most of Mexico is a topographical tumult, with rugged mountains plummeting down to lush valleys and, even in the most barren regions, distant ridges and peaks looming against the horizon, the tortilla-flat Yucatán Peninsula is so unbroken that normally insignificant hills are considered major heights. Likewise, to foreigners as well as the majority of Mexicans, the plant, animal, and bird-life here is nothing less than exotic. Spider and howler monkeys romp—and sometimes rampage—through the trees (a howler monkey chorus is unforgettable). Brocket deer, which resemble tiny antelope, appear in clearings, then vanish, while parrots and parakeets flash gold, red, and green through the foliage. Where the topsoil is thick enough, tropical trees such as kapok, ebony, and rosewood flourish. Zapote trees produce not only the chicle used in chewing gum but also wood so strong and enduring that zapote beams still support the stones in Mayan temples after 1,000, and in some cases 2,000, years.

On the rim of the classic Mayan region to the south, in the state of Chiapas, in highland Guatemala, and in western Honduras, craggy sierras rear up to elevations of 4,000 meters (13,000 feet). In the high, temperate valleys of such ranges the highland Maya still tend their corn (maize) patches, much as they have for centuries. And while this corner of the Mayan world outwardly resembles other parts of Mexico, its atmosphere is altogether different.

Still, it was not in these friendly highlands that the magnificent Mayan centers flourished. Instead, with few exceptions, the flowering of Mayan civilization took place on the peninsula to their north, on a flat, featureless limestone shelf covered with a veneer of thin soil and tangled with stunted vegetation. It was—and is—raw, calcareous land, newly liberated (in geologic terms) from the sea—and a sense of the sea still lingers. Yet from this meager, infertile soil sprang one of the most advanced civilizations to arise in the Americas, as well as some of mankind's greatest achievements. The ruins of ancient cities and ceremonial centers here rival any the Old World has to offer, and strike modern eyes with their beauty and originality.

MAJOR INTEREST

The greatest Mayan ruins
Uxmal
Chichén Itzá
Palenque (in Chiapas)

Smaller but important Mayan sites
Kabah
Sayil
Labná
Mayapán

The city of Mérida (gateway to Uxmal, Chichén
Itzá, and other Mayan sites)

San Cristóbal de las Casas and its environs in
Chiapas

Besides these attractions (and in addition to the celebrated beach resorts of Cancún, Cozumel, and Isla Mujeres, which, along with the nearby Mayan sites of Coba
and Tulum, are covered in another chapter), this region
offers other delights: sparkling waterfalls, sweeping
ocean views, mysterious caves, a score of lesser but
fascinating archaeological zones, handsome native crafts,
and colorful villages.

Although more than twice the size of the six New
England states, the area that shares the Mayan heritage
(including parts of Guatemala and Honduras) is set apart
from the surrounding area by mountains, jungles, and
swamps. Even today, despite the advent of jet planes and
high-speed highways, the region is (or was until quite
recently) a curiously isolated corner of the world. For the
Maya themselves, of course, it simply was and still *is* the
world. But outsiders living here have always felt this
isolation.

"Yucatan is not an island," wrote Friar Diego de Landa
in 1566, "but mainland. . . . It is not seen from ships until
they come very close." The friar had to explain this even
though he was addressing some of the best-educated
men in Spain and a quarter of a century had passed since
one of the decisive battles of the Conquest had been
fought on the site where the Mérida cathedral stands
today. But because the region lacked silver and gold it
had remained on the periphery of its Spanish rulers'
collective consciousness.

Forty years earlier, Hernán Cortés, after conquering the
Aztecs, had rashly decided to traverse this country over-
land. The consequences of his decision, which were faithfully recorded by Bernal Díaz, make for one of the most
grueling travel accounts of all time, a succession of days
in which all the Spaniards seemed to do was slash, chop,
stumble, sweat, and pray.

The wilderness was so dense and inaccessible, in fact, that they had to institute stern ordinances in order to keep their Indian converts (and labor supply) corraled. In 1552 Governor Tomás Lopez decreed that "the Indians must not live off in forests, but come into the towns together . . . under pain of whipping or prison." So came about the hundreds of villages in the region that travellers can still see, each with its own outsize church crumbling away.

Despite prolonged assault on their language and customs, there remain about two and a half million native speakers of Maya today, the language fragmented into a dozen dialects that are not always mutually understandable. (University courses in Maya are offered by the state from time to time, but these seem to be token efforts.) Nevertheless, after more than four centuries of being besieged, the Maya have kept their ways surprisingly intact, and a cultural gulf still separates them from their Yucatec or "ladino" neighbors. (A Yucateco is supposedly anyone native to the area, but the word often does not include the Maya—who are the most native of all. Instead, the Maya mysteriously call themselves *mestizos,* people of mixed blood, and describe all "Europeanized" folk around them as "ladinos." Mexicanos, a subgroup of the ladinos, are those who come from other parts of the country.) While the most obvious differences are in language and dress, religious differences, which are not instantly apparent, become clear on closer acquaintance.

Long treatises have been written on the distinctive Mayan way of life. Perhaps just one difference, concerning machismo, will illuminate the hundred other contrasts with mainstream Mexican ways. The Mayan male needs a woman to grind his corn and bear his children—he is incomplete without a wife. But he finds romantic love foolish and sexual conquest dishonorable. Success with several women would earn him no credit; in fact, Casanovas are considered contemptible. Similarly, a Mayan male is free to show affection to his wife in public without sacrificing his machismo; he has no need to display a masculine superiority or aloofness. At the same time, his dignity will not allow him the exuberant camaraderie most Mexican men enjoy with their male friends.

All of this is so different from the arrogant pride of mainstream machismo that the emotional understanding between the Maya and their neighbors is often tenuous. Some of the most basic words in life—"sex," "love,"

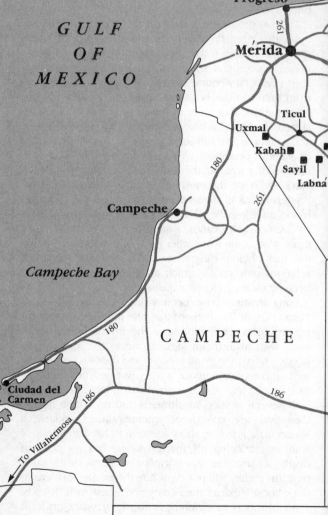

The Yucatán Peninsula

0   miles   40
0   kilometers   70

GULF
OF
MEXICO

Progreso

261

Mérida

Ticul

Uxmal

Kabah

Sayil

Labná

Campeche

Campeche Bay

180

261

CAMPECHE

180

Ciudad del
Carmen

186

186

To Villahermosa

CHIAPAS   GUATEMALA

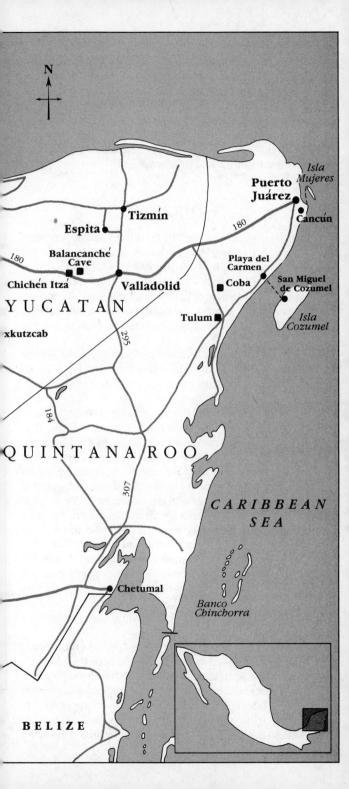

"honor," and "success"—become blurred in translation. As a result, the Maya and the more aggressive, acquisitive people around them have seldom communicated clearly except through violence. And although peace has long been maintained, the distance between them remains. For all that, the Maya are a friendly, gracious people with a lively curiosity about strangers.

MERIDA

Mérida, tropical and Caribbean, is the Yucatán Peninsula gateway for visits to Uxmal, Kabah, and some lesser but fascinating ruins. It is also a possible headquarters for a day trip to Chichén Itzá (although it is much more satisfying to stay overnight at that magnificent site). Three days are enough to glimpse the highlights of the Mérida area. Five days are more reasonable, and a week is not too much.

Mérida has two nicknames, and both are clichés—"the Paris of the West" and "the White City." Neither is accurate, but both contain a germ of truth about this curious town.

From the beginning, the city, which was established in 1542, looked across flat country toward the sea. The markets for the raw materials taken from the jungle around it, including hemp and lumber, lay in Europe, not Mexico, and events in Spain loomed far larger here than the goings on in remote Mexico City. In the 19th century, when hemp exports brought great wealth to Mérida, the city sent its sons to Paris for cultivation; over time they brought back the French manners and styles that are still in evidence today. In fact, strolling or riding along Mérida's Paseo Montejo, its most elegant avenue, evokes not only France but far more the old French neighborhoods in Algeria. Here are the curlicues, fancies, and fripperies of both Paris and Tangier. Yet the "Frenchness" of Mérida is merely a patina; ultimately, the hemp barons adopted a style, not a civilization.

As to its reputation as "the White City," when the Spaniards first stumbled out of the jungle here they found a town called Tiho (the Mayan *T'hó*). This native settlement, which was constructed of gleaming limestone, impressed them as both splendid and lovely. So, with the perversity of their tribe, they promptly destroyed it. Francisco de Montejo the Younger, the chief destroyer, gazed upon the havoc his men had wrought and nostalgically recalled the white stone heaps of a Roman ruin near the Spanish town of Mérida. Hence the name of the new city that was built with the stone blocks of the old.

While the walls of Mérida are no longer uniformly white, the local people make up for it with their clothing. Plump Mayan women billow like clouds in their *huipiles,* pale tunic-like dresses tipped by rainbows of embroidery (pronounced locally as "ipiles"). The men are usually clad in white trousers and loose white *guayabera* shirts. When the main plaza is thronged with scrubbed people in their scrubbed clothes, Mérida is still "the White City." (Like the Maya people, who always bathe more than once a day, Mérida takes pride in being "the cleanest tropical city in the world." Perhaps this is true, although the market area somewhat belies the claim.)

Plaza Mayor

The main square, variously called the Plaza Mayor, Plaza Principal, Plaza de la Independencia, and Plaza de Armas, is at the intersection of Calles 60 and 61, the geographic and commercial heart of the city. (Mérida, like most towns the Spanish built from scratch, was laid out as a grid: odd-numbered streets run east and west, even-numbered ones north and south.) This spacious plaza, with its tall, dignified laurel trees, is the ideal place to linger and get accustomed to the tempo of the city. Like so many things in the city, even the laurels have a Caribbean connection. They were originally sent from India, and were intended to embellish Havana. After they were salvaged from a shipwreck off the Yucatán coast, however, they were planted here. (Yucatecos have always been quick to snatch any gift from the sea.)

The Cathedral, which is on the plaza, was begun in 1561 and is the oldest still in use in Mexico. Unfortunately, its age and size are its only real claims to distinction, as is the case with all the extant colonial buildings in Mérida; they offer nothing special.

The Montejo family—father, son, and cousin—and their successors were the Spanish conquerors (some would say plunderers) of the Yucatán. Their palace, built in 1549, originally occupied the whole south side of the square. Today it is greatly reduced in size and serves as a bank. Its façade, however, is the single colonial landmark in Mérida that merits careful inspection.

In 1841 John L. Stephens, the modern discoverer of the ancient Mayan cities, strolled into Mérida's plaza, where this building instantly "arrested" his attention. As he later described the relief carving he saw that day: "The subject represents two knights in armour with visors, breast-plates and helmets, standing upon the shoulders of crushed naked figures, probably intended to represent the conquering Spaniard trampling upon the Indian."

Stephens was accurate but kind. In actuality, the relief is one of the most arrogant representations ever commis-sioned for a private residence, and the skill of the Mayan slave-artists who did the carving only makes the whole matter worse. To see this relief is to see the brutal atti-tudes of the conquerors starkly revealed. Looking at it another way, you might say that even Diego Rivera, mas-ter propagandist for Indian rights, never created a more scathing indictment of the conquistadors.

Nearby, caryatid-like Amazons, fierce but busty, lurk at windows, where they uphold royal escutcheons. Again, the stonework is as admirable as the idea is repellent.

The Conquest was neither as easy nor as complete as the Montejo façade pretends, however. The Maya resisted the Spaniards with greater fierceness and success than the Aztecs, at first repelling the invaders entirely, then battling for three years before their defeat at Tiho. Even then their acquiescence was no sure thing, and skirmish-ing continued for more than a century. In fact, a "final" surrender didn't come about until 1697.

But even as John L. Stephens was studying the Montejo palace, trouble was brewing among the people who had been "crushed" by the conquering stone foot. In 1846 the Maya arose with such ferocity that only the cities of Mérida and Campeche held out in what became known as the "War of the Castes." The terrified whites implored Spain, England, and the United States to accept the Yuca-tán as a colony. Finally, a Mexican federal army rescued them in 1848, retaking the burned haciendas. Sporadic violence continued until 1901, however.

On the opposite side of the plaza, a world away from the savagery portrayed on the façade of the Montejo palace, is the leisurely society of Mérida's sidewalk cafés. It's true that the city is a center of industry and commerce; somehow, things must get done. Yet in its cafés unhurried patrons who are obviously men of affairs have seemingly endless time and endless coffees served as *grecos*—triple strength with hot water on the side. Here, haste is frowned upon, and voices and gestures are modulated, although the nearby streets bustle with people in a hurry.

The **Parque Cepeda Peraza**, at the intersection of Calles 58 and 59, two blocks from the Cathedral, is another shady spot for lingering over coffee or a cool drink. It's also an international crossroads for archaeology buffs— many of them young and travelling on tight budgets—the kind of place where you can witness unexpected reunions of people who last saw each other in Cuzco or Crete. Tourists sit scribbling postcards, music echoes from a cantina in a nearby patio, and Mérida's only aristocratic church, the Iglesia de Jesús, mellows in the tropical sunshine.

Around Mérida

The appeal of Mérida does not lie in inspecting its local monuments. On heavily advertised city tours, guides struggle to fill up two or three hours, driving through gentrified neighborhoods, holding passengers captive in overpriced craft shows, and turning them loose on their own in the municipal market. It is far better, instead, to stroll the downtown area on your own or ride in one of the horsedrawn carriages that lend color to the city.

The **Paseo de Montejo** is lined with imposing homes and spacious gardens, a reminder of how patrician the rulers of this city have always been. Mérida is probably the only city in Mexico where old families trace their history not just to the Conquest, but to a specific conquistador. They have not intermarried with the Maya—although their men have certainly interbred. Nor have they formed marital alliances with the many immigrant Levantine merchants who dominate the city's dry goods business.

At the intersection of Calle 43 and the Paseo stands one of the most opulent and rococo of the old mansions, now the local **Museum of Anthropology**. The collection of Mayan artifacts, including a variety of stunning jewelry, is excellent, while the building itself is a different kind of treat.

Staying in Mérida

The **Holiday Inn** in Mérida lives up to its name, conjuring a spirit of cheerful leisure. The service is excellent, and its large and well-maintained swimming pool is especially welcome after hours of exploring ruins. Located in a

quiet flower-filled neighborhood just off the Paseo, the
hotel is convenient to fast transportation downtown. The
clientele is international, as are the dining room, its two
coffee shops, the cocktail lounge with entertainment, and
the disco. It also has a lighted tennis court. Higher priced
than other Mérida hotels, the Holiday Inn is still a top
value.

El Conquistador, located in an expensive and busy
commercial neighborhood halfway between the downtown area and the outskirts of the city, offers new and
very good rooms and suites with private balconies on
the Paseo de Montejo. Although it's more than walking
distance from the center of town, transportation along
the Paseo is good. It also has an indoor pool and a
restaurant.

El Castellano is a modern high-rise near the center of
town, two blocks west of the main plaza. Rooms vary in
size, but some of the best are on the upper floors, with
panoramic views of the city spread out below. They are
also quieter, almost hushed. There are also ample public
rooms, a pool, and a restaurant.

The **Hotel Dolores Alba** is a smaller, friendly, family-
run establishment in a converted town house three
blocks east of the main plaza on Calle 63. The rooms are
basic, but the atmosphere is pleasant. Not all rooms are
air conditioned, however, and some are small. Get the
best or go elsewhere; the *good* accommodations here,
though, are a bargain.

The **Hotel Colón**, located a block northeast of the plaza
at Calle 62, has enough charm to compensate for its
rather plain rooms. Stay in the newer, air-conditioned
wing if you can.

The **Gran Hotel** on the lively Parque Cepeda Peraza
downtown is a favorite of students and thrifty travellers of
all ages. Inside, the old building is adorned with the
owner's eclectic collection of antique sewing machines,
phonographs, radios, and curios. The hotel, like the collection, is left over from another age. Despite the noise
and reliance on ceiling fans, its guests seem to be happy
with its personality.

Dining in Mérida

Yucatecan cuisine, which is spicy and rich, has little to do
with the usual fare of Mexico, except for their common
reliance on corn and chiles as basic ingredients. Mari-

nades, seldom used in the rest of the country, add tantalizing hard-to-recognize flavors to many dishes here. Foods prepared in a tangy, sour orange marinade are a particular specialty. In addition, the word *pibil* appears frequently on menus and refers to the traditional barbecue pits of the Maya (although *pibil* cookery in restaurants is usually done by steam). Chicken and pork (*pollo* and *cochinita*) so prepared are tender and succulent. Lime soup (*sopa de lima*) is a rich chicken broth made glorious with lime juice and spices, then garnished in a hundred different ways. Sometimes it has pieces of chicken, tortilla chips, chopped tomatoes, and onions (creativity is the soul of a good *sopa de lima*). Foods served *escabeche* have been soaked in a marinade of onions, vinegar, and whatever spices inspiration dictates. Finally, the Lebanese and Syrians have been settled in the Yucatán for so long that many of their national dishes have also became standard fare here.

Los Almendros, a traditional Mérida favorite, is located two blocks north and four blocks east of the Plaza Mayor on the Plaza Mejorada. This rather plain establishment nevertheless presents a fine sampling of Yucatecan cuisine. For an introduction to the regional fare, the combination plate is a good choice, giving the diner about four selections, including the region's famous sausages. Here and in other regional restaurants, however, you should treat the side sauces with respect; while the cookery is not fiery, the sauces may be molten lava.

Rather more elegant is **Las Palomas**, on Calle 56 between Calles 55 and 53, a 19th-century Spanish-Moorish town house that has been converted into a very good restaurant serving Yucatecan and European dishes.

The **Chateau Valentín** is a distinguished restaurant with impeccable service and a selection of international and Yucatecan offerings (although the regional fare has been somewhat adapted). Piano music adds to its elegant ambience. Calle 58 number 499. (This is in the Holiday Inn neighborhood, not downtown as its address might suggest.) Reservations advised; Tel: 5-5690.

For snacks, short orders, and good but rather standard desserts, **Leo's** at Paseo de Montejo 460A, Calle 37, is modern, casual, and inexpensive.

The best Lebanese food in town is found in the hacienda atmosphere of **Alberto's Continental Patio**. Lunch and dinner from an international menu are served in this early 19th-century mansion.

Shopping in Mérida

The city market, a short walk south from the main plaza, is a crowded, bustling, somewhat confusing maze of stalls and counters heaped high with what the region has to offer. Articles made of henequen cord take a hundred different forms here, from the obvious such as shopping bags, mats, and hammocks to some quite surprising and imaginative neckties and belts. The rugs are both unusual and durable.

On the other hand, the best hammocks are made not from henequen but from linen, and built to last a lifetime. Besides the usual one-person size, you can choose from matrimonial hammocks, family hammocks, and hammocks that seem to be designed for community siestas.

Much of the embroidery on display is machine-made, but it is so intricate that the method of manufacture hardly seems to matter.

Mérida is one of the great centers for Panama hats, but the best, unfortunately, are not displayed in the market. The city's most famous hat shop is **La Casa de los Jipis**, located on Calle 56 between Calles 65 and 67. Some of the hats here are among the best in the world, so don't be surprised if the prices seem high.

Gold filigree, crafted much as it was in pre-Hispanic times, is offered in many shops. Caution is advisable here, however, for traditional Yucatecan gold work is only 10-carat, not 14 as is often claimed. In some shops true 14-carat is sold, and these will be happy to give a written or printed guarantee.

Guayabera shirts are a Mérida specialty and can be found in a score of shops. Jack, at Calle 59 number 505, has an especially large selection. The loose-fitting cotton *guayabera* is worn for its coolness, and you'll be disappointed to find you've acquired one that's warm because of the overuse of synthetic fiber in the cloth, so buy carefully.

Finally, there are good craft and popular arts stores to be found at the entrances to major archaeological sites near Mérida; while the prices will be a little touristy, they won't be larcenous.

Excursions from Mérida

If your time is limited you *can* see Uxmal, Kabah, Sayil, and Labná in a one-day excursion, but it won't allow you to appreciate them fully. Uxmal by itself is enough to take in at one go, although it can be combined with Kabah. But that really should be the limit. (See the Getting Around section below.)

Mayapán and Ticul can also be combined in a one-day excursion. **Mayapán**, which flourished in the 13th and 14th centuries, was an important Mayan city in the centuries leading up to the Conquest; unfortunately, not a great deal of it remains. **Ticul**, where native dress is still worn, is known for its handicrafts, especially its pottery and embroidery. Although both places are interesting, time should be allowed for them only after the major sites have been explored.

An excursion to the old port of Progreso, north of Mérida, is hardly worth the effort. Similarly, the city of Campeche, a two-and-a-half-hour trip south, does not live up to its colorful publicity.

To sum up, the archaeological zones nearest Mérida, in descending order of importance, are: Uxmal, Kabah, Sayil, Labná, Mayapán, and, for handicrafts, Ticul. Magnificent Chichén Itzá is a possible one-day trip from Mérida, but is better left as an overnight (at least) excursion. On the other hand, it's an easy overnighter from either Cancún or Cozumel.

The late Mayan site of **Tulum** (too-LOOM), on the Caribbean coast, was a Mayan trading center from A.D. 1200–1450. Although it makes for a convenient excursion from Cozumel, and is easy enough from Cancún, it does not, in spite of its lovely setting, quite justify a five- to six-hour drive from Mérida itself. Travellers between Mérida and the Caribbean resorts, however, will find Tulum a delightful bonus.

UXMAL

The first U.S. traveller to visit this imposing ruined city was John Lloyd Stephens, who wrote in 1843, "We entered a noble courtyard with four great façades looking down upon it, each ornamented from one end to the other with the richest and most intricate carving... presenting a scene of strange magnificence."

Magnificence indeed! At Uxmal (oosh-MAHL) gigantic masks of snouted rain gods are crowded upon each other in emphatic profusion; mosaics of amazing intricacy enfold whole buildings; boldness of conception is combined with the most delicate technique. Invariably, the visitor is struck by the deluge of carved symbolism applied to Uxmal's palaces, pyramids, and temples. At the same time, the decoration is daring and radical; potentially disagreeable combinations of geometric and floral patterns are instead magically combined to achieve a sublime harmony. Such designs often convey a sense of modern, rather than classical, orchestral music, with its discord, contrasts, and unexpected yet pleasing shifts of rhythm.

This great center was rebuilt several times over the centuries, so it is impossible to date its structures with any exactness. Its zenith, however, occurred between A.D. 600 and 900. The latest confirmed written date at the site is A.D. 909; its temples and courtyards were probably abandoned soon after that—for reasons that remain unknown.

Near the entrance to the site rises the imposing **Temple of the Magician** (*Pirámide del Adivino*). The Magician was constructed in five different stages, and its exact function is unknown. (The name refers to a magical dwarf-like figure in Mayan folklore.) A single mask on the temple suggests the influence of the central highlands people. But the Toltecs, who greatly changed the architecture of the Yucatán, never occupied Uxmal; it remains pure Maya. The three-room sanctuary atop the Magician offers a breathtaking view of the site and the surrounding jungle.

The **Nunnery Quadrangle** (*Cuadrángulo de las Monjas*), immediately behind (to the west of) the Magician, is often hailed as one of the most beautiful structures, or complex of structures, in the New World. The four buildings that compose it are a triumph of decoration in stone. The work is mosaic, but on a scale not usually associated with mosaic art. Individual pieces may be over three feet in length and so heavy that one man could never have lifted them into place.

The four structures of the Nunnery may have served as a residence for priests; at least that is the tradition. The modern explanations of its name, however, are illuminating, if perhaps inaccurate: It was so named because nuns make lace and the stonework is lacy; or because the atmosphere within its walls suggests the serenity of a convent.

The ball court, located just south of the Nunnery, seems to have been constructed to accommodate a small—

doubtless elite—group of spectators. A little farther south the small and, at first glance, plain **House of the Turtles** (*Casa de las Tortugas*) is likely to be overlooked amid the grandeur of the rest of the site. In its own sober way, however, this structure is a masterpiece, at once pure in its proportions and discreet in its decoration (with the exception of the carved turtles that adorn the frieze on its upper ledge). The molding, especially, is beautifully managed, and the symbolism throughout is connected with rain and agriculture.

The **Palace of the Governor** (*Palacio del Gobernador*), which takes its name from the crowned figure in the center of the structure, is located next to the House of the Turtles and dominates the site. Set upon a stone platform and built in three sections, it is regarded, like the Nunnery, as one of the masterpieces of Mesoamerican architecture. The designs on its façade were inspired by weaving and the decorative arts and combined with a variety of snakeskin patterns and representations of the rain god (in total, some 20,000 mosaic elements were used in the frieze).

The three sections of the palace are joined by corbeled "arches." Although they are not true arches in an architectural sense, they are as close as the Maya came to achieving that engineering feat, and are often called "Mayan arches." They were created by gradually projecting stone blocks outward from each side until the arch came to a peak, but since they were not efficient in supporting weight, the Maya would reinforce them with a beam near the top. Today many of the beams have fallen or rotted away, but the holes cut for them remain.

In addition, two sculpted works stand at the base of the broad stairway leading up to the palace—a two-headed jaguar on a small platform that is perhaps a throne, and a phallic column that is an oddity in this otherwise classic Mayan site. (Phallic sculpture was rarely used to decorate lowland Mayan centers, although other examples are found at Uxmal, most notably serving as rainspouts. Instead, the theme seems to have been imported from the Veracruz area, where such work is not unusual. Plumed serpent representations at Uxmal also suggest faraway influences that seem to have come late and had little effect on the basic style.)

The **Grand Pyramid** (*Gran Pirámide*), a few steps west of the palace, is in poor condition, and so is the small

Temple of the Parrots (*Templo de las Guacamayas*) that sits atop it. The dedication here is to the sun. The pyramid is easy to climb, however, and affords both views and excellent photo opportunities.

A bit to the west is the ruined **Dovecote** (*El Palomar*). The nine triangular works of masonry that top it are fanciful Mayan roof combs, which were often added to rather squat structures to create the illusion of height and grace. Like all of Uxmal, they were once painted in brilliant colors.

Three outlying groups of structures are in ruined condition, some of them little more than rubble. They include the North Group (*Grupo del Norte*), the Cemetery Group (*Grupo del Cementerio*), and the House of the Old Woman (*Casa de la Vieja*); beyond that lies the quite unerotic Temple of the Phalli (*Templo de los Falos*).

Uxmal is 77 km (48 miles) south of Mérida via a good paved road. If your itinerary only allows for a one-day excursion, you should leave Mérida early in the morning so that any climbing you do at the ruins is over before the hottest part of the afternoon. (See the Getting Around section below.) In addition, every night a well-designed and dramatic sound-and-light show is presented. There are two performances, one just after sunset in Spanish, a later one in English. (The English version is usually too late for visitors returning to Mérida.)

There are good hotels with restaurants for overnight stays at Uxmal, and all of them are helpful in arranging further exploration of the area. None is inexpensive, however.

The **Villa Arqueológica**, at the entrance to the ruins, follows the solid format of this chain, which is Club Med connected but very unlike Club Med in personality. Tennis court, bar, restaurant, pool, air conditioning, and pleasant grounds.

The **Hacienda Uxmal**, across the highway from the ruins, is gracious, tropical, and colonial. Long verandas, ceiling fans, and wicker furniture lend it a hacienda feeling.

The **Misión Uxmal**, part of the Misión chain, is modern and comfortable and has air conditioning. The better rooms also have balconies and striking views. Its popularity with tour-bus groups is an indication of its value, but it's less personal than the other hotels here. Located a mile from the archaeological zone.

Kabah

The fanciful city of Kabah (kah-BAH), located on either side of Highway 261, lies some 22 km (14 miles) south of Uxmal. A visitor approaching the zone from Mérida and the north will suddenly see a remarkable structure rising above the low, spiky vegetation on the left side of the road. This is the famed **Palace of the Masks**, also known as the Codz Pop (*Coiled Mat*) because of its vast array of masks with twisty noses, which vaguely resemble the curving lines of Mayan mats.

Even after the exuberant decoration of façades at Uxmal, this structure comes as a surprise. The entire façade is covered with masks of the rain god—row upon blank-eyed row, and mostly noseless now. Here is stone clamoring for rain, the most insistent statement made by any Mayan temple. The masks, like the decorative work at Uxmal, are in actuality large-scale mosaics: Each mask comprises 30 separate carved and dressed stone elements, and there are some 250 masks. Obviously, the labor involved in running the "mask factory" must have been enormous. You will need a lot of imagination, however, to restore the Palace to its former glory.

Kabah, which was contemporary with Uxmal, thrived between A.D. 600 and 900, when, for unknown reasons, it was abandoned. There are nine more or less excavated structures here, two of which are three-building complexes. One of the most intriguing is located across the highway from the Palace of the Masks: **The Arch**, a white limestone structure standing stark and alone, is a beautiful work of corbeling that spans a distance of more than 5 meters (15 feet). According to anthropologists, it once served as a monumental gateway to a road or processional route that ran all the way to Uxmal. These roads, of which there were more than a few in the region, were impressive achievements, as they cut through dense jungle and crossed treacherous swamps. The Spanish, arriving more than six centuries after the arch was built, proved woefully inferior to the Maya when it came to building roads.

The **Temple of the Columns**, a long ripple of carving, is related artistically to the House of the Turtles in Uxmal, both making extensive use of engaged columns as decoration. A front terrace once served to catch rainwater for a nearby cistern.

The soil around Kabah is ungenerous, yielding stingy corn crops to slash-and-burn farming, which the Maya practice today much as they did in the heyday of this ceremonial center. All the more reason, therefore, to stand in awe of the religious and cultural forces that drove the Mayas' magnificent impulse to build here and elsewhere in the Yucatán.

Sayil, Xlapak, and Labná

Three other interesting Mayan sites can be included in a trip from Uxmal.

Sayil (sah-YEEL) is a neighbor of Kabah. To get to this site, head south on Highway 261 for 5 km (3 miles), then turn left. This road, which is marked "Oxkutzcab," takes you to Sayil 4 km (2 miles) farther on.

The Sayil archaeological zone is famed for its Palace, a seventy-room, three-story, terraced structure. Though it is huge and massive, the lightness of its design counteracts any bulkiness, giving it instead a feeling of elegance and airiness. A broad stairway rises gracefully to divide the structure; elsewhere, round columns, well-spaced doors, and lovely friezes impart a pleasing rhythm to its lower floors. Among the site's curiosities are sculptures of the "upside-down god," which are variously described as diving, falling, and descending. The Chac (rain god) masks and accompanying scrollwork are particularly beautiful. Carved stelae date from about A.D. 850, Sayil's heyday. Another stela, probably much older and perhaps not even Mayan, is an exaggerated phallic figure. The site, which was abandoned in the tenth century, seems to have been inhabited as far back as A.D. 200, to judge from the ceramic evidence. There are several (out of several hundred) buildings accessible to the public; the rest are still locked in the jungle.

Xlapak (shlah-PAHK) is 7 km (4 miles) farther along on the road to Labná and makes for a quick visit, since there remains only one temple at the site; but it is an almost perfect structure. Three great stone masks dominate the center of the symmetrical, beautifully proportioned temple—not rare but somewhat unusual in Mayan architecture. The building dates from about A.D. 800.

The small but quite wonderful ruins of Labná are just 4 km (2 miles) east of Xlapak; there will be a sign indicating a parking area and path to the right.

Three major structures survive at Labná. The chief one, or **Palace**, is almost 165 meters (535 feet) long at the base of its terrace and two stories high. Besides the stern masks of the snouted rain god, you can see here examples of the Mayan "hut theme"—a sculpted representation of what seems to be a thatched dwelling. A date corresponding to A.D. 862 is inscribed on the extended nose of one of the Palace's rain gods, possibly the last carving done at the site before it was abandoned.

The Mirador, rising just south of the Palace, displays an elegant roof comb; the severe complex nearby is called the East Building.

The famous **Labná Arch**, often called "the Gateway," is a fantasy in stone. A corbeled arch is stepped up to an almost Gothic point, and is flanked by sculpted latticework and a small room on either side. It is an altogether delightful monument, and one that once connected two courtyards.

Labná was a major religious center, and probably an important market center as well, with a resident population that approached 3,000—an estimate partly based on the capacity of the 60 cisterns that were dug to supply it with water in the dry season. The water works can still be seen, although the site has long been abandoned.

The Loltún Caves

These caves (*grutas*) comprise a series of dramatic chambers and corridors that honeycomb the limestone crust in this region and were known to ancient hunters as early as 2,500 B.C. These prehistoric visitors left behind a variety of stone artifacts, as well as the remains of animals they had killed. Later on, the mysterious atmosphere, strange rock formations, and stalactites and stalagmites appear to have inspired a certain amount of religious awe among the Maya. Eventually, glyphs and steps were carved at the entrance, and a sculpted sentinel was placed nearby—a figure thought to date from 300 B.C.

Lights have since been installed in the caves, but only enough to illuminate the surroundings without compromising their mystery. You may only enter, however, with a guided tour group. The tours, which are conducted in Spanish, leave from the entrance at 9:30 A.M., 11:30 A.M., and 1:30 P.M., Tuesday through Sunday; allow two hours for the full tour.

The caves are 20 km (12 miles) east of Labná on the

road to Oxkutzcab (oosh-coots-cahb). They can be visited as part of an excursion to Labná or when exploring Mayapán and Ticul.

Tours leaving from the Uxmal hotels cover all the above sites in a day, including Kabah, though sometimes omitting the caves. Such a trip allows for a cursory glance at everything, but is far too rushed for true archaeology buffs, photographers, and anyone else who simply might want the time to absorb the strange and unusual things they have encountered.

A better trip would be: a full day at the Uxmal ruins, ending with a late lunch and perhaps a swim. Return to the ruins for the sound-and-light show in the evening, and stay overnight at an Uxmal hotel. The next day return to the ruins to reexamine its memorable corners, then go on to Kabah. A third day could be devoted to the other sights of the region, including the caves in the morning, and ending either at an Uxmal hotel or back in Mérida that afternoon.

CHICHEN ITZA

This sprawling ceremonial center thrusts itself up from the jungle about 120 km (75 miles) east of Mérida on Highway 180, not quite halfway to Puerto Juárez (Cancún and Isla Mujeres). The architecture here is dynamic, full of force and energy in ways that nothing else in the Mayan world prepares the visitor for. The lively structures at Uxmal, for instance, authoritatively but serenely occupy the ground on which they rest. They are so self-contained that it doesn't matter that they crowd each other; in a sense, they provide their own framing. But at Chichén Itzá the great monuments each seem to insist on—and get—their own space. As with skillfully done stage sets, the illusion they create exceeds their physical dimensions. In fact, Chichén Itzá is so theatrical that dazzled visitors often call it perfect, the most beautiful of all the Mayan ruins. While no site is "perfect," what Chichén may lack in depth and subtlety it does make up for in drama.

It is quite easy to get lost at Chichén Itzá, literally as well as artistically. This does not mean that a guide is necessary. Most visitors will want to move at their own pace, taking time to form their own impressions; it is difficult to absorb a running commentary while trying to grasp the purely visual aspects of such alien and majestic surroundings. On the other hand, it is wise to acquire a detailed guidebook to the ruins. The government handbook issued under the INAH (Instituto Nacional de Antropología y Historia) imprint, on sale at the entrance to the site, is invaluable.

Chichén Itzá (pronounced chee-CHEN eet-SAH) roughly translates as "place at the rim of the well of Itzá." Identifying the people known as Itzá is not terribly important for fully appreciating the site. Knowing about the well, however, is crucial, for that is where the whole story begins.

The northern Yucatán, for all intents and purposes, is without rivers or lakes. The torrential rains of summer disappear as quickly as they fall, running to the sea or vanishing beneath the limestone underlying the soil. Instead, there is a huge and complex system of subterranean rivers in the Yucatán, but for the most part their life-giving waters are inaccessible. Here and there the limestone has caved in, creating natural wells or sinkholes called *cenotes*. To the ancient Maya a cenote was literally the wellspring of life and a sacred gift from the gods.

The great cenote at Chichén Itzá, the **Sacred Cenote**, is the most awesome of these sinkholes, a gaping mouth in the earth roughly 60 meters (190 feet) in diameter, and slightly more oval than circular. Sheer or undercut sides drop 20 meters (65 feet) or more to the surface of the water, which fills it to a depth of some 11 meters (35 feet). The cenote is so unexpected and is surrounded by such solitude that it would seem menacing even without the stories every visitor hears. It's not unusual to see people stand at the little temple platform on the rim, glance down at its murky waters, blink, and take a step backward.

In pre-Hispanic times the cenote was a magnet for Mayan pilgrims who came to this spot to implore or appease the rain god. Dredging it in modern times has brought up a trove of sacrificial objects, including gold, silver, copper, polished jade, and more grimly, about 50 human skulls, some of those belonging to young children. The latter must be kept in perspective, however. The cenote was a center of sacrifice for at least 1,000 years. A victim every 20 years does not suggest that maidens were hurled into the depths seasonally, as some writers have imagined and certain guides still insist today.

In time the mystique and life-giving power of the cenote impelled the Maya to erect a ceremonial center

not far away, and it flourished during the latter stages of
the Classic period, from about A.D. 600 to 900. At that
point, the region was overrun by a people known as the
Itzá. The Itzá were allies, or perhaps cousins, of the
warlike Toltecs of the central highlands, whose great
capital was Tula (they might even have *been* Toltecs; this
is a subject for scholarly debate). At any rate, under their
influence a new ceremonial center, strategically located
between the Sacred Cenote and the older Mayan city, was
built after A.D. 900.

Chichén Itzá, as it exists today, is a mostly Toltec-
inspired creation built by Mayan skill and labor—"Maya-
Toltec" is as good a term as any. Toltec domination in the
Yucatán was effective but brief, a case of "the flies conquering the flypaper." They were assimilated; they disappeared. Yet during their short tenure they revived the
greatness of Mayan art, as Chichén Itzá attests.

Visitors to the site are often so eager to begin exploring
that they forget to stop at the Service Unit located at the
entrance. This is a mistake. You can get the latest orientation information there, as well as schedules that give the
hours when interiors of certain temples are open.

The Northern Zone

The effect of the northern complex, more Toltec-Tula, is
instantaneous and powerful, so theatrical that the word
"operatic" immediately suggests itself. Where other Mesoamerican ceremonial centers seem to have been constructed more for the benefit of the gods than for the
impression they created on humans, Chichén Itzá is nothing less than a gigantic and obviously intentional show.

El Castillo, the **Pyramid of Kukulcán**, holds center
stage. Kukulcán is the Mayan name for the Plumed Serpent, the Mexican priest-god folk hero who was also the
Quetzalcóatl of the Toltecs and then the Aztecs, and besides being a temple the structure is a literal calendar in
stone. Its original steps coincided with the days of the
solar year, a type of symbolism not unusual in Mesoamerica; time cycles and months were numbered in terraces
and panels. To this day, in fact, you can witness a curious
byplay of shadows on the temple steps at the time of the
equinox, with some observers able to see a representation of a serpent during a precise 34-minute period at
sunset. Others, watching the same thing, remain skepti-

cal. In any case, the structure reveals a knowledge not only of architecture but of astronomy as well.

The pyramid rises in perfectly proportioned stone terraces of diminishing size, which contribute to the illusion of height. (The structure followed the tradition of placing one temple atop an older one after a 52-year cycle. The first Toltec religious structure here was dedicated to the sun.) Eager and heat-resistant visitors who have no tendency to claustrophobia can enter the pyramid and climb an irregular stairway to the top, where they will discover, besides a magnificent view, a rather crude but powerful jaguar sculpture, apparently a throne, cut from a single piece of limestone and painted with vermilion cinnabar. The bared teeth are made from white flint, the eyes from green jade (as are the large discs representing spots on the body).

To the northwest of El Castillo lies the great **Ball Court** (*Juego de Pelota*), the largest in Mesoamerica. There appear to have been various versions of this ceremonial game. Courts were always built in an I shape, thereby creating "end zones," and scoring at first may have involved cornering a hard rubber ball at either end. Later, stone rings were added to the side walls, and a player could win the contest by knocking or kicking (not throwing) the ball through one of these small hoops. The improbability of managing this is clear: A player who actually "scored" won all the clothes and jewelry worn by the spectators. It is often assumed, as a result of certain carvings, that those who lost the game were "sacrificed." This interpretation is Eurocentric, however; it's just as likely that the *winners* could have merited what was seen then as an honor.

A paved path to the Sacred Cenote begins to the east of the ball court and runs past the easily identified **Temple of the Jaguars**.

East of the path, the **Temple of the Warriors** (Templo de los Guerreros) and the **Group of the Thousand Columns** (*Grupo de las Mil Columnas*) are second only to El Castillo in impressiveness, and second to none in their fascination for visitors. In addition to comprising a huge complex of courtyards, platforms, terraces, and colonnades, the two signify a sharp change in the life of Chichén Itzá. Prior to their construction, small interior rooms were adequate to meet the needs of its inhabitants. At a certain point, however, there appears to have been a sudden demand for roofed areas and meeting halls protected from the rain—proof, according to some experts, that a large new military aristocracy had developed among the Toltecs. In fact, just such a warrior elite is depicted in full regalia in carvings located throughout the site.

The so-called Market (*Mercado*) was more likely a stone stage used for dance or theatrical performances. Just to the east of it efficient steam baths were built, and were no doubt used for both the ritual purification of priests as well as to accommodate the personal fastidiousness of the Maya.

Chichén Itzá seems to have been a gathering place rather than a continuously inhabited city, although it obviously could accommodate a large number of people. In addition to its many ceremonial buildings, there is a well (not the Sacred Cenote) capable of supplying water year-round, and seven other ball courts (although not all were in use at the same time).

Over the years scholars have avoided public speculation about life at Chichén Itzá in its glory days. But one, Jacques Soustelle, has ventured to the edge of conjecture. Discussing the northern zone, Soustelle writes: "One is tempted to group the buildings . . . under two headings: the religious and ritual center, with the great ceremonial ballcourt, the Temple of the Jaguars, and the sacrificial monuments; and the meeting place of the Itzá warriors . . . whom one can imagine strolling through the colonnade and beside the pool on their way to the small ballcourt. The Temple of the Warriors, with the vast pillared hall before its façade, serves as a transition between the two centers, the one religious and the other secular, military and no doubt commercial."

Soustelle's speculations, whether wholly accurate or not, dovetail with the site's design and help a visitor's imagination re-create the life that went on in the northern zone.

The Southern Zone

This area, which is called Old Chichén (*Chichén Viejo*), was the older ceremonial center that the northern "Maya-Toltec" zone replaced, and is done in the classic Mayan *Puuc* style, much in the manner of Uxmal (although Toltec embellishments were added to some of the buildings at a later date). While it is a fascinating and beautiful place, it does not have the instant impact of the northern group, in part because of its subtler style of architecture, but mostly because the positioning of the structures does not result in the breathtaking vistas and contrasts that later Toltec planning afforded.

El Caracol (*The Snail*) is the most immediately striking structure in the neighborhood. (Because a snail's shell is spiral-shaped, anything that winds upward—a road or stairway for instance—is likely to be called a *caracol* in Spanish.) The structure has an interior stairway that spirals upward and was probably used by ancient stargazers. In fact, the four apertures facing the cardinal directions at the top of the structure seem to confirm that it was constructed as an observatory. Although imposing and surprising, El Caracol is less than beautiful, and inspired Mayanist J. Eric Thompson to observe that the building "stands like a two-decker wedding cake on the square carton from which it came."

Indisputably lovely, on the other hand, is the ruined **Nunnery** (*Edificio de las Monjas*) and its adjacent Annex. (The modern name is simply a bit of Spanish fancy.) In 1868 an eager archaeologist set off a an explosive charge inside the Nunnery to speed his search, and did irreparable damage to the structure. The entrance to the Annex is through the mouth of a stone monster.

Nearby, the exuberant decoration of the "Church" reminds viewers that the ancient Maya abhorred a design vacuum. Half a dozen other, lesser structures, each with its own mysteries, are scattered elsewhere around the area.

Staying near Chichén Itzá

Mayaland, adjacent to the archaeological zone, is the usual favorite. Its bungalows are especially attractive, and most of the rooms are very comfortable, though a few seem cramped. Ask for a private balcony. It also has a pool and a dining room and cocktail lounge. In addition, the hotel staff is very helpful and skilled in making travel arrangements in the region.

The **Hacienda Chichén** keeps its cottages open only in the winter. It is also located at the archaeological zone, and is almost as attractive as the Mayaland.

The **Misión Inn Chichén Itzá** is in the nearby village of Pisté. Besides the usual amenities it has a children's zoo. Many families and tour groups choose the Misión, even though it is slightly more expensive than the Mayaland and Hacienda.

Also in Pisté is the unpretentious **Dolores Alba**, which offers adequate accommodations at attractive prices. If air conditioning is available (check first) it is worth the extra charge.

Some travellers, especially students, choose to stay in the small town of **Valladolid**, 40 km (25 miles) east of Chichén Itzá. The town's attractions consist mostly of hotel rooms for the thrifty and good bus service to the ruins. In addition, there are some very old colonial buildings here, and a cenote that is used as a public swimming pool.

El Mesón del Marqués, on the Valladolid plaza, is a former colonial residence with a number of new rooms. Most of its rooms, old or new, are air conditioned, and there is a pool. Its patio restaurant is also pleasant. A popular arts shop here offers a good selection of regional handicrafts. The **Hotel San Clemente**, also facing the plaza, has less character but is at least as comfortable as the Mesón del Marqués.

The Balancanché Cave

This is an adventure for the dedicated involving some squeezing and crawling through narrow passages. Visitors who were less than delighted by the interior stairways at Chichén Itzá will definitely want to skip it. Others may find it rewarding.

The subterranean passages here contain sacred urns dedicated to the Toltec rain god, and are believed to have served as a refuge during times of invasion. In addition, a pond at the end of a main passageway is home to blind fish. Cameras are banned, as are small children, the latter for good reasons: The cave is eerie and tomblike.

The cave lies almost 5 km (3 miles) northeast of Chichén Itzá. Admission is with a guide only; arrangements may be made at the entrance to the archaeological zone.

PALENQUE

"The temples of Palenque ... are exquisite rather than imposing; refined, rather than massive. They are quite

content with the earth they stand on, and do not, like their predecessors, reach for the sky. Like precious jewels, they are beautiful and complete in themselves. The earlier gods, if they were gods, in the sculptures of Tikal, Copan and elsewhere seem to represent great natural forces, the forces that caused the maize to grow and the rain to fall; these gods here at Palenque are members of an elegant aristocracy that rules gracefully over the destinies of men."—Louis J. Halle, Jr.

The site at Palenque (pah-LEHN-keh), in the rain forests of northern Chiapas, is compact and remarkably harmonious. Although its structures do not all date to the same period, they are of a piece and share a common aesthetic tradition. This is thought to be the most beautiful cluster of pre-Columbian buildings in the Americas. To find its rivals, you will have to travel to Greece or Southeast Asia.

For centuries Palenque was the proverbial "lost city in the jungle," known only through vague rumor and manuscripts that were as obscure as the city itself. In 1786, however, a Captain Antonio del Río was sent to investigate. After weeks in the jungle he and his men found what they were looking for and immediately set about driving spikes into the stucco sculpture in order to hang up their hammocks and armor. They also dug a quite useless trench, doubtless seeking treasure, then gave up after del Río had "discovered all that was to be found." The captain, while perpetrating this archaeological mayhem, observed that the natives were "sullen and suspicious." He was one of the rare visitors who did not like Palenque.

The next Europeans to set eyes on the ruined city were John L. Stephens and his friend Frederick Catherwood, the English artist and architect. After hacking their way through the jungle with the help of native guides, the two stumbled upon the ruins in 1840 and were so delighted by their find that they fired the last of their gunpowder into the air.

Although the original name of this Mayan ceremonial center is unknown, we do know that it was the capital of a large Late-Classic (after A.D. 600) kingdom. The modern name, which was borrowed from the nearest town, means "palisade," and otherwise seems to have no connection to the ancient city that dominated this corner of the world with its knowledge and culture. When, near the end of its reign, some fortifications were built, it seems that Palenque was already doomed. It fell, for reasons unknown, in A.D. 800, the first great Mayan city-state to fail and be abandoned to the jungle.

Today the ruins nest on a narrow shelf of forested land high enough to provide sweeping views of jungle, meadows, and, in the distance, flat savannah stretching toward the sea. It is, above all, a green world, with every shade from olive through emerald to chartreuse present. The site is also compact; there's no need to hire a guide. Do stop at the information center at the entrance to inquire about hours and regulations, however, as well as to buy the official INAH handbook to the ruins. Once inside the zone, it is important to remember to move in a leisurely manner. Not only are you in the tropics, but the subtleties of Palenque do not reveal themselves at a glance. If at all possible, two days should be allowed for the site; the pleasure lies not only in seeing, but in absorbing and relating. Palenque is alien and distinctive even to travellers familiar with other Mayan sites. A good plan, therefore, is to use the first day for exploring the Great Palace, the Temple of the Inscriptions, the Temple of the Lion, and Temple XII. The rest can wait for the second day.

Most visitors coming along the path from the entrance are drawn immediately to the **Great Palace**, which is readily identifiable by its four-story tower, leaving the structures on their right for later. A wise choice; the Palace is the best introduction to Palenque.

The Palace

Much of this complex, which surmounts a huge rectangular platform, was the creation of Lord Pacal, the most famous ruler of Palenque. Ascending to power in A.D. 615 as a 12-year-old boy, he is said to have ruled until his death at the age of 80—a period that coincides with Palenque's most marvelous work. Augustus Caesar once boasted that he found Rome brick and left it marble. Lord Pacal's achievement was every bit as impressive: He found Palenque humble and left it magnificent.

Additions were made to the Palace by Pacal's son, Lord Kan Xul. Indeed, some of the finest reliefs here date from his reign, and the work merits close examination. Unfortunately, much of it has been eroded over the centuries and some destroyed. Visitors will need to do some restoration in their imaginations to appreciate fully the achievements of the Palenque stone carvers.

The landmark tower is often called the **Observatory** and probably was used for both stargazing and keeping an eye on affairs on the plain below. The climb to the top, where there is often a refreshing breeze stirring through the windows, is not difficult, and the views of the flat green world spread out to the horizon are unforgettable. From here it's also immediately apparent that only the central area of Palenque remains—or at least that is all that has been uncovered.

A new surprise awaits around every corner of the Palace complex—altars and thrones, hidden stairways, reliefs in stone and stucco. After a few hours you will even develop a sense for the unique Palenque line— smooth, serene, and quietly understated.

The **Temple of the Inscriptions** is perched dramatically above its green jungle backdrop on stone terraces stepped one atop another. Though beautiful in its own right, the structure is best known for the discovery made here in 1952 by the Mexican archaeologist Alberto Ruz Lhuiller. Noticing some holes in the temple floor and suspecting they were handholds, Ruz had a huge slab raised, which revealed a hidden stairway blocked with rubble. While the passage was being cleared, Ruz also discovered the skeletal remains of five or six youths—apparently the sacrificial companions of a master who had been entombed beyond. But, of course, everyone knew that Mesoamerican pyramids and temples were never used as burial crypts. This wasn't Egypt, after all.

To everybody's surprise, however, a sepulchral vault was eventually uncovered, with the figures of the Nine Lords of the Night standing solemn watch in the chamber. When, after immense difficulty, the beautifully carved slab lid of the huge stone coffin was removed, Ruz found the skeleton of a large man as well as an extraordinary jade mosaic funerary mask. We now know, after decades of trying to decipher the ancient Mayan glyphs on the sarcophagus lid, that the bones are those of Lord Pacal. (At the same time, Ruz made another interesting discovery: From the sarcophagus a sort of pipe, or hollow molding, wound up the stairs to the temple—apparently so that Lord Pacal could maintain postmortem communication with the world he had departed.)

As was usual at that time, everything in the tomb was whisked off to Mexico City, and all is now on view at the National Museum of Anthropology. But the monolithic casket lid would not fit up the narrow, twisting stairs, and so it remains in Palenque, proof that the tomb was built before the temple.

Near the Temple of the Inscriptions is the much smaller Temple XII, accessible by a hillside path, which means it isn't necessary to descend the steep steps of the Inscriptions, as most visitors do. This lesser temple is somehow connected with death; at least the main stucco decoration remaining portrays a death god. From here a short, steep path rejoins the main path from the entrance.

A group of four temples, each distinctive but all related in style, is a good start for the second day's viewing. This group is located just southeast of the Great Palace across a narrow stream, and includes the temples of the Sun, the Cross, the Foliated Cross, and Temple XIV.

The small **Temple of the Sun** is a treasure. Besides being valued for its lovely proportions, it contains a masterpiece, a carved panel of Pacal deified. The **Temple of the Cross** is the tallest of this group, with a crumbling but still glorious roof comb. The temple itself almost seems to serve as a pedestal for the architectural element above. The **Temple of the Foliated Cross** and **Temple XIV**, badly damaged, nevertheless offer examples of beautiful carving. Considered as a whole, the quartet embodies the genius of Palenque, with the roof panel and roof comb of the Temple of the Sun, especially, speaking volumes about their creators.

The Northern Group

North of the Great Palace complex are five structures that share a single base. Unfortunately, they're in sad condition, but the view from here of the surrounding plain is lovely, and it's still possible to imagine how they once might have looked. Nearby, the **Temple of the Count**, named for a German nobleman who lived in the structure for a time and made extensive drawings of the ruins here in the early decades of the 19th century, is in slightly better condition. While this group is too damaged to be compared to its better-preserved neighbors, it is worthwhile to linger here: There's an ineffable atmosphere that is likely to haunt you for a long time to come.

The small **Palenque museum** is located near the Northern Group, and its collection, while not extensive—the best has gone elsewhere—boasts some beautiful carving, ceramics, and bits of stucco decoration.

Staying and Dining at Palenque

Five miles by paved road from the archaeological zone is the unlovely town of Palenque. Seeing this modern settlement after visiting the ruins is enough to make anyone pessimistic about human "progress." Fortunately, there are far better accommodations closer to the site.

Staying at the **Chan Kah Cabañas**, a group of cottages about 4 km (2½ miles) from the ruins, will enhance your visit to Palenque. The Maya-style bungalows here are so well designed and ventilated that ceiling fans provide enough cooling; there's also a stream-fed pool. Try for a cottage near the river. The alfresco restaurant is just adequate.

The **Hotel Nututun Viva**, less expensive than the Chan Kah, has a beautiful, woodsy location on the river 5 km (3 miles) south of town on the way to the ruins. The hotel is good and very popular, but some rooms are dark and damp; there is air conditioning, however. The dining room has a delightful river view, and the food can be recommended. While the hotel advertises swimming in the river, the rocks and shallow water make this an uninviting prospect.

The **Hotel de las Ruinas**, about a ten-minute walk from the entrance to the archaeological zone, offers basic motel accommodations, ceiling fans, and a restaurant.

Two hotels in the town of Palenque are geared to student and archaeological tour groups. **La Cañada**, with both cottages and rooms, has attractive grounds and a thatched-roof restaurant that's quite good. The **Casa de Pacal** is modern, air conditioned, and uncharming, but a good buy.

Located on the edge of town on the way to the ruins, the restaurant **La Selva** is a jungle fantasy mansion come true, a marvel of thatch, knotted twine, and polished wood. The menu is extensive, the food carefully prepared, and there's entertainment and dancing in the evenings.

(For how to get to Palenque, see Getting Around at the end of the chapter.)

Agua Azul

Visitors to the Palenque area who have extra time, or who are driving on to San Cristóbal de las Casas, should stop at the lovely series of cascades (*cascadas*) known as Agua Azul. To get there, follow the Ocosingo road 58 km (36

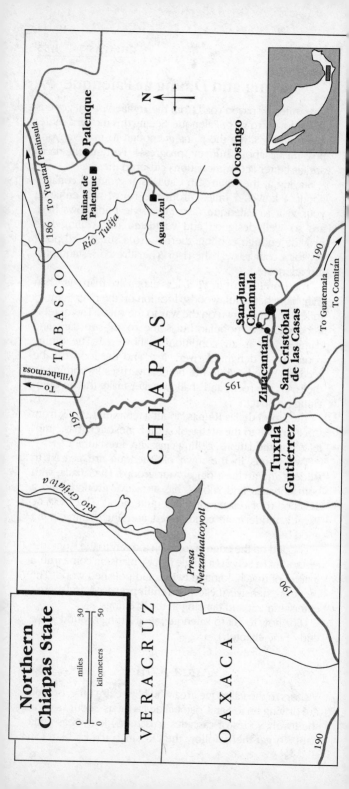

miles) south from Palenque town, then turn right onto the dusty side road, which requires patience and a bit of skill but is only 4 km (2½ miles) long.

At the end of the road, the waters of the Río Tulija swirl and plunge through a web of cataracts and rapids. It is possible to follow the riverbank upstream past several foaming cascades, where the perpetual mist from the falls gives the foliage a special lushness and little rainbows form when the sun shines. In all directions the mountains of the Sierra Madre de Chiapas serve willingly as a spectacular backdrop.

There's not much in the way of facilities at the little park, and the mist and dampness make it a less-then-ideal spot for picnics. (There are drier, more comfortable places farther from the tumbling, swirling water.) Nevertheless, it's an excursion well worth the time and effort. And the road from Palenque past the falls turnoff and all the way south into San Cristóbal de las Casas is extraordinarily scenic.

SAN CRISTOBAL DE LAS CASAS

The mountain-ringed city of San Cristóbal de las Casas is situated at the southwestern edge of Mexico's Mayan region, in the center of the state of Chiapas. Here, in the fastness of the Sierra Madre de Chiapas, the native settlements sprinkled throughout the region seem almost like outposts. And, in a sense, that's exactly what they are. Ages ago the highland Maya pressed no farther; they decided that their world ended here.

Most travellers will like San Cristóbal as a stopover. Those bound by car for Guatemala from central Mexico should certainly take the highland route, Highway 190, which goes through San Cristóbal, rather than the sultry and uninteresting Highway 200 along the Pacific coast: The scenery will more than make up for the extra distance. Likewise, motorists covering Mexico in a great loop from the Yucatán back to Oaxaca will also want to stop here. As a sole destination on what is a long journey, however, San Cristóbal is a doubtful choice for most travellers. Still, a few will be enchanted by this odd, tucked-away town and will end up staying and exploring the surrounding region for as long as possible. The only way to tell which group you fall into is to go there.

The first signs that you're approaching San Cristóbal de

las Casas appear along the roadside—groups or families of Maya gathering or carrying firewood, waiting for rides, plodding patiently toward unknown destinations. Physically these highland Maya look much like their cousins in the Yucatán: short, sturdy, dark, with rather coarse jet black hair and expressive almond-shaped eyes. But their garb is noticeably different. This is cool country, after all. No gauzy *huipiles* for these ladies; instead, their clothing is dark and plain. It is left to the male to be the peacock, a role he embraces.

In fact, the different groups of the region can be told apart by the costumes the men wear. The Zinacantecos, for example, stand out in their beribboned straw hats, pink-striped serapes, and scarves soberly checked in gray but trimmed with magenta tassels. Even in winter they are likely to be barefoot, although at times you'll see them wearing *huaraches* made from discarded automobile tires. The Chamulas, on the other hand, sport white hats big enough for a Hollywood cowboy; under these hats, they wear a bright kerchief that is wrapped around the head for warmth in winter, used as a sweatband in summer, and serves as an accessory in all seasons. Their serapes, which are worn over white tunics and white knee pants, are among the most beautiful in Mexico, with their long fringes, and are usually woven of thick wool left a natural or bleached white (although they are sometimes dyed black).

The ancestors of both these Mayan groups were quite possibly the builders of Palenque and other lowland centers in the Classic period. If so, they were probably dispersed and became refugees in the mountains after their magnificent cities were abandoned in the ninth and tenth centuries. They encountered the Spanish for the first time when Diego de Mazariego established San Cristóbal in 1528. His successor unleashed a reign of terror in the region, but the Maya's suffering abated after the arrival of the Bishop of Chiapas, Bartolomé de las Casas, and 35 fellow Dominicans in 1545. The bishop was a vigorous and effective defender of Mayan rights, and even managed to get some of the worst laws against them repealed. As a result, the town was renamed for him during the era of anti-clerical reform in Mexico in the 19th century, becoming simply "Las Casas"—a name that is often still used today.

The town held onto its isolation and old ways for centuries, traditions that were more common to Guatemala than Mexico. Racial purity was maintained along with sharp class distinctions. Politically, San Cristóbal resisted independence, resisted union with Mexico, resisted *all* change. In 1890, as a punishment, the state capital was shifted to Tuxtla Gutiérrez, which subsequently outdistanced San Cristóbal in both size and wealth—though not in interest for travellers.

The racial and caste divisions are obvious even today in San Cristóbal. This is much more a city surrounded by Indians than an Indian city, and the easy cultural assimilation of Oaxaca or Morelia is virtually unknown here.

Around the Zócalo

The dark reds and oranges of tile roofs, steeply sloped because the summer rains here are torrential, are what most visitors first notice about San Cristóbal. It is also a place of whites and pastels, pale lavenders warming to pinks. And everywhere, in any direction, you have the sense of being hemmed in by mountains, as well as of distance.

Situated on the north side of the *zócalo,* the old cathedral has a Plateresque façade and some antique statuary. The building dates from the 16th century, with later additions—a big structure but not a major one.

A very helpful government tourism office can be found on the south side of the *zócalo,* opposite the cathedral. Nearby is the 16th-century home of Diego de Mazariego, which is older than the cathedral but done in the same style.

In addition, there are pleasant strolls in every direction from the plaza; the destinations matter less than the cobblestone streets themselves, which are lined with quaint façades that offer glimpses of gracious courtyards. The homeowners of San Cristóbal appear to have taken special pride in the ironwork decorating their houses; it is unusually good.

The **Church of Santo Domingo** is located five blocks north of the *zócalo* at the corner of Calzada Lázaro Cárdenas and Calle Nicaragua and is the finest colonial building in the region. Its style was borrowed from a number of 16th-century churches in Guatemala, and its interior is embellished by a masterpiece of a pulpit and some extraordinary gilded screens.

Outside is a Mayan market, and on a bright, sunny day a stop here leaves you with the impression of walking into a rainbow, of sparkling colors blending and clashing. The vendors, mostly women, wear delicately embroidered blouses, bold sashes, and, in their hair, yarn that is almost Chinese red, and their offerings include brocade and embroidery work, leather goods, hammocks, bags, and jewelry. Children, bright-eyed miniatures of the vendors, scamper and play among the displays.

Part of the church is now used as a museum (open mornings), and next door there is a shop offering the same kind of goods found outside, but in greater variety: handsome shirts, belts, decorated arrows, and a limited selection of pottery. Prices in the shop are comparable to the prices outside.

The municipal market, located just north and east of Santo Domingo, is less interesting for its merchandise than for its customers: In every aisle appear faces that might have been models for the carvings at Palenque or Uxmal.

Staying in San Cristóbal

Visitors in the winter will definitely want a room with a fireplace, an adequate supply of wood, and—equally important—sufficient kindling. All the hotels in town are colonial and provincial, and some are even rustic.

The **Posada Diego de Mazariegos**, an inviting provincial inn with ample rooms (some with fireplaces) arranged around large patios, occupies two converted colonial buildings a block from the *zócalo*. The dining room is also the town's best restaurant. Added attractions include a bar, a coffee and pastry shop, and friendly service. Convenient parking, not easy to find in San Cristóbal, is provided.

Even lower priced, although not quite as good, is the **Hotel Español**, also centrally located, and also with a dining room and charming patio garden. All the rooms have fireplaces, but they vary greatly otherwise.

Just outside town is the inviting **El Molino de la Alborada**, a hacienda-style establishment with cottages. It's a small, intimate inn, with a fine kitchen to serve its guests. It also has a good stable—as well as an airplane landing strip. El Molino is especially appealing to visitors with time to explore the countryside and the native villages, as well as simply to relax. The rates are quite reasonable considering all that is offered.

Exploring the San Cristóbal Region

Casa Na Bolom, at Calle Vicente Guerrero 31 in San Cristóbal, a small, privately run museum, is a center for visiting anthropologists and archaeologists investigating the area. It is owned and supervised by Gertrude Duby, herself an anthropologist and the widow of Frans Blom, who is celebrated for his explorations and studies of the Chiapas highlands. Museum tours are conducted, and a donation is expected. In addition, maps of the surrounding countryside can be bought at Na Bolom and the staff there is generous with their knowledge of the region and its people. El Molina de la Alborada is also helpful and expert in making excursion arrangements for its guests.

Native villages, lovely lakes, and forested mountains— all lie within reach of San Cristóbal de las Casas. **Zinacantán** and **San Juan Chamula** are two of the more interesting rural centers of the highland Maya, and the Chamula Sunday market is especially lively and colorful. In both places the inhabitants in their quaint clothing will strike the visitor as exotic.

The lakes of the **Lacandon Forest** are also accessible from San Cristóbal, though a fairly long trip by car; allow a full day. To get to the Lacandon area, drive to the town of Comitán, 86 km (54 miles) southeast via the Pan-American Highway. Fifteen km (9 miles) south of Comitán you'll come to the village of La Trinitaria, where you turn left onto the paved road that leads to Lagunas de Montebello National Park; the park lies 36 km (23 miles) farther on. After entering the park the road forks. Go left to the **Colored Lakes**, which are lovely, tranquil, and startling in their contrasting colors.

There are 16 lakes in the park, but those off the right fork are not as accessible from the road. If you take that fork, however, after almost 16 km (10 miles) you'll come to **Dos Lagunas**, two especially beautiful bodies of water surrounded by forest. It is advisable to return to San Cristóbal for the night.

The San Cristóbal region is crisscrossed by bridle trails. Arrangements for renting horses may be made at El Recoveco, a shop on the San Cristóbal plaza. Reservations are taken at 7:00 P.M. for the next morning; information about trails and maps are also available. In addition, most local hotels will be happy to arrange horse rentals and provide relevant information.

Advice and help with all excursions in the region can be obtained at the Tourism Office on the *zócalo* in San Cristóbal.

GETTING AROUND

Mérida

Mexicana Airlines offers flights connecting Mérida with Mexico City; it also flies, via Cozumel, to Miami and Dallas-Fort Worth. Aeroméxico links Mérida with Mexico City, Villahermosa, and Miami. Aerotaxis Bonanza offers small-plane service from Mérida to Chichén Itzá, Cozumel, and Cancún. The Mérida airport is a 15-minute ride from the main plaza and is served by price-controlled taxis. An airport bus (marked "Aviacion") departs from the corner of Calles 67 and 60, downtown.

All buses to other cities arrive and depart from the central terminal on Calle 69 between Calles 68 and 70. There is good first-class service to all major destinations, with ADO one of the larger and better lines.

The train from Mexico City, via Palenque, has sleeping cars, but even so it is suitable only for travellers with endless time, patience, and fortitude.

Most Mérida hotels have travel desks or offices that are happy to offer options for exploring the area. These hotel services also tend to be more reliable than the little storefront agencies that pepper the city.

Bus tours are another dubious option and tend to be mass movers, highly regimented, and overly fast-paced. Other guided tours with more than seven passengers are also questionable. In fact, nothing larger than a station wagon or minivan is recommended. Private cars with guides are available at Sindicato de Guía; Tel: 3-2602.

A number of major car-rental agencies have offices in Mérida in order to serve visitors who want to go at their own pace; expect costs somewhat higher than in the U.S. and Canada, however. Public transportation by bus is available to all major sites; schedules can be obtained through hotels or at the Tourism Office, Teatro Peón Contreras, Calle 60 between Calles 57 and 59; Tel: 4-9290 (the staff there is most helpful).

Chichén Itzá

The first-class buses between Mérida and Cancún also serve Chichén, which is just off the highway linking the two cities. Most buses stop at the entrance to the ruins, while a few stop at the nearby village of Pisté, where taxis to the ruins are available. You can also use the sidewalk from Pisté to Chichén—about a 20-minute walk. Travellers coming by bus or car from Isla Mujeres and Cozumel get to Chichén via the very good Cancún-Mérida highway. Chichén is about 200 km (125 miles) west of Cancún.

In addition, you can fly to Chichén Itzá with Aerotaxi Bonanza out of Mérida, or with Aero Caribe/Aero Cozumel from the Caribbean resorts.

Palenque

The nearest commercial airport is in Villahermosa, 151 km (94 miles) to the northwest on the Gulf Coast. There are car rentals available in Villahermosa as well, and the ADO line offers good bus transportation to the site. (It is a two-hour drive from Villahermosa to Palenque.) Those with cars may wish to continue south on the beautiful mountain drive to San Cristóbal de las Casas after exploring Palenque. (See the Getting Around section for San Cristóbal below.) For the adventurous, there is Pullman rail service to Palenque from Mexico City as well as from Mérida. The posted length of the trip from the capital is 24 hours—which seems to be more a speed record than the reality. The train sways and shimmies, and while part of the trip—through jungle—is interesting, more of it is dull.

At Palenque, *combi* buses ply the road from town to the ruins with reasonable frequency, and taxis will respond to phone calls from area hotels.

For exploring the ruins, tennis or running shoes will do nicely; boots are not necessary. A sun hat and insect repellent are advisable, however.

San Cristóbal de las Casas

There is no commercial airport at San Cristóbal, but Tuxtla Gutiérrez, 93 km (51 miles) to the west, has regular daily flights to and from Mexico City. In addition, cars may be rented at the Tuxtla airport. There is minibus service from the air terminal to the bus depot, where you can catch the ADO bus for San Cristóbal. The road to San Cristóbal climbs steeply, so it takes about two hours to make the journey by car, a little longer by bus.

There is regular bus service from San Cristóbal to Guatemala City, with connections from there to most Guatemalan towns. The border is 172 km (106 miles) southeast from San Cristóbal. Buses also run regularly between San

Cristóbal and Palenque, a distance of 207 km (128 miles). Travellers planning on coming from Oaxaca by car should prepare for a very long day's journey of about 630 km (390 miles).

ACCOMMODATIONS REFERENCE

▶ **La Cañada.** Calle Cañada 18, **Palenque** 29960. Tel: (934) 5-0102.

▶ **Casa de Pacal.** Calle Juárez 8, **Palenque** 29960.

▶ **El Castellano.** Calle 57 513, **Mérida** 97000. Tel: (992) 3-0100.

▶ **Chan Kah Cabañas.** Kilometer 31 Carretera a las Ruinas, POB 26, **Palenque**. Tel: (934) 5-0014.

▶ **Hotel Colón.** Calle 62 483, **Mérida** 97000. Tel: (992) 3-4355.

▶ **El Conquistador.** Paseo de Montejo 458, **Mérida** 97000. Tel: (992) 6-2155.

▶ **Posada Diego de Mazariegos.** María Adelina Flores 2, **San Cristóbal de las Casas** 29200. Tel: (967) 8-0513.

▶ **Hotel Dolores Alba.** Calle 63 464, **Mérida** 97000. Tel: (992) 1-3745.

▶ **Hotel Dolores Alba.** Two kilometers east of Highway 180, **Chichén Itzá**. In Mérida, Tel: (992) 1-3745.

▶ **Hotel Español.** Avenida 16 de Septiembre and Primero de Marzo, **San Cristóbal de las Casas** 29200. Tel: (967) 8-0045.

▶ **Gran Hotel.** Parque Cepeda Peraza, **Mérida** 97000. Tel: (992) 1-7620, or 4-7622.

▶ **Hacienda Chichén.** Zona Arqueológica, **Chichén Itzá**, POB 407, Mérida 97000. In Mérida, Tel: (992) 1-9212.

▶ **Hacienda Uxmal.** Zona Arqueológica, **Uxmal**, POB 407, Mérida 97000. In Mérida, Tel: (992) 1-9212.

▶ **Holiday Inn.** Avenida Colon and Calle 60, POB 134, **Mérida** 97127. Tel: (992) 5-6877; in the United States and Canada: (800) 465-4329.

▶ **Mayaland.** Zona Arqueológica, **Chichén Itzá**, POB 407, Mérida 97000. Tel: (985) 627-77.

▶ **El Mesón del Marqués.** Calle 39 203 (Parque Central), **Valladolid** 97780. Tel: (985) 6-2073.

▶ **Misión Inn Chichén Itzá.** Pisté, Yucatán 97000. Tel: Piste 4.

▶ **Misión Inn Uxmal.** Zona Arqueológica, **Uxmal** POB 407, Mérida 97000. Tel: Uxmal 1, or (992) 4-7308.

▶ **El Molino de la Alborada.** Periférico Sur s/n, POB 50, **San Cristóbal de las Casas** 29200. Tel: (967) 8-0935.

▶ **Hotel Nututun Viva**. Carretera Agua Azul, **Palenque** 29960. Tel: (934) 5-0100.

▶ **Hotel de las Ruinas**. One kilometer east of the archaeological zone, POB 49, **Palenque** 29960. Tel: (934) 5-0352.

▶ **Hotel San Clemente**. Calle 41 206, **Valladolid** 97780. Tel: (985) 6-2208.

▶ **Villa Arqueológica**. Zona Arqueológica, **Uxmal**. Tel: (99) 6-2830; in the United States: (800) 258-2633; in Canada: (514) 937-7707.

GUATEMALA

By Robert Somerlott

In the first installment of the epic *Star Wars* trilogy, Princess Leia flees to a hiding place in a remote galaxy, somewhere on the nether edge of the universe. For the film's director the problem was where—on earth—could such an alien landscape be found? Eventually, he decided that the perfect background would be Tikal, the great ruined Mayan city hemmed in by the Guatemalan jungle. As a result, at least a few viewers were startled to recognize the towering Temple of the Giant Jaguar when it appeared on-screen. The choice was brilliant. Until intergalactic travel becomes possible, Tikal is about as far removed from our own world as one can get.

To a lesser degree, the same can be said for much of Guatemala. In a world growing smaller and more homogeneous, Guatemala has managed to keep its character, its color, and its oddity. In a sense, a visitor to it has an opportunity to sample time travel, to see a vanishing way of life. Not everywhere in the country, of course, and perhaps not always for long. Still, there remains an element of fantasy in this picturesque land, where reality has often been brutal.

For travellers who have become intrigued by the Maya in Mexico, a trip into Guatemala is a rewarding excursion. While the modern political boundary between the countries may separate two very different and sometimes antagonistic governments, in the Mayan view of time the separation is merely a recent development. The Maya recognize the frontier only as they are forced to. In the remote jungles straddling the border there is a constant flow of people, ideas, goods, and news in both directions. Despite a profusion of dialects and other differences, the indigenous folk are one people, far more like each other than they are akin to their Mexican, or ladino, neighbors.

The Mayan presence in Guatemala is strong. You will see them everywhere, a flashing display of color, their embroidered and appliquéd clothing as flamboyant as the plumage of the country's profusion of tropical birds.

MAJOR INTEREST

The ruined city of Tikal
The Mayan people and their crafts
Scenic beauty, including Lake Atitlán

Museum of the city of Guatemala (Mayan carvings)
A boat trip on the Río Dulce
The ruins of Mixco Viejo and Quiriguá
The city of Antigua

For a small country, Guatemala is unusually diverse in its scenery and climate. The terrain includes jungles, high mountains, temperate highlands, savannah, and a desert. Although it's about the same size as Ohio and almost half the size of the United Kingdom, such comparisons are misleading for the traveller because fully a third of the country is accessible only on horseback or by safari. Most of its attractions, with the exception of Tikal and the Río Dulce, are clustered in the pleasantly cool highlands in the south, so you can see a great deal of Guatemala in a short time. Tours planned and sold by agents or airlines tend to be either five- or eight-day trips. Five days hardly offer time enough to cover the highlights, but an eight-day tour, whether packaged or independent, is not unreasonably crowded for sightseeing. Another day or two might be added for the Río Dulce or other out-of-the-way excursions.

Such tight scheduling allows little leisure for appreciating and absorbing this quite foreign land, however, and rules out some pleasant experiences—such as watching a sunset on Lake Atitlán for the second or third time or seeking out picturesque villages. Still, the colorful surface of Guatemala can be skimmed in a little more than a week, which is about what most travellers will choose to devote on a first visit. Inevitably, some of them, charmed by the country, will return for much longer visits.

A great cordillera of lofty peaks and ridges thrusting south from Mexico forms the rugged backbone of Guate-

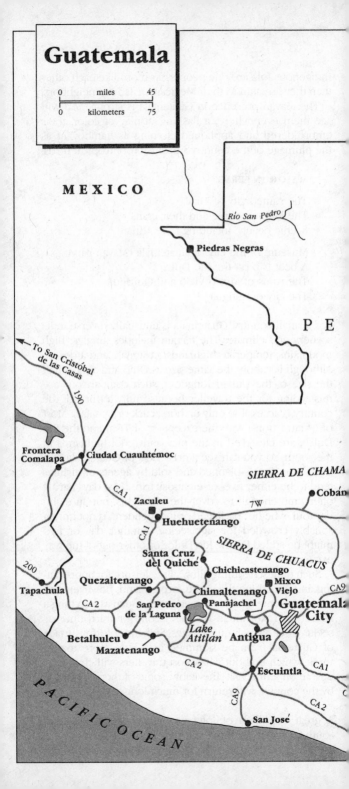

Guatemala

| 0 | miles | 45 |
| 0 | kilometers | 75 |

MEXICO

Río San Pedro

■ Piedras Negras

P E

← To San Cristóbal
de las Casas

190

Frontera
Comalapa

● Ciudad Cuauhtémoc

SIERRA DE CHAMA

● Cobán

CA 1

■ Zaculeu

7W

● Huehuetenango

CA 1

SIERRA DE CHUACUS

● Santa Cruz
del Quiché

● Chichicastenango

■ Mixco
Viejo

CA 9

Quezaltenango

Chimaltenango

Guatemala
City

200

● San Pedro
de la Laguna

Panajachel

● Tapachula

CA 2

Lake
Atitlán

Antigua

● Betalhuleu

● Mazatenango

CA 2

CA 1

● Escuintla

CA 9

CA 2

PACIFIC OCEAN

● San José

mala. Along the Pacific these mountains link up with an ancient chain of volcanoes that almost edge the ocean, leaving only a narrow shelf of lush tropical land that is broken by swift rivers pouring down from the highlands. No roads run along this coastal shelf; instead, all highways here lead inland and upland.

Higher up on the slopes lies coffee country—some of the richest in the world—and, higher still, long valleys wind among mountain peaks. Here are huddled the cities most travellers visit: Guatemala City, Antigua, Panajachel, and Chichicastenango. Surrounding these are orchards of peaches and apples as well as truck farms and pastures. But above all, this is corn (maize) country. No slope seems too steep or discouraging for a Mayan farmer to plant this venerated cereal. The rainy season in the highlands lasts from May through October, but even in those months the climate up here is pleasant rather than sultry.

On the northern side of this mountainous spine, which here begins a gradual descent to the lowlands below, are more coffee plantations. Soon, however, the land starts to fall away more sharply, and eventually becomes the wild, inhospitable region known as the **Petén**. Jaguars, often feeding on wild pigs, still inhabit this jungle, and bands of monkeys chatter and howl in the dense foliage.

The Petén is the root of the Yucatán Peninsula, a little less flat than the Yucatán proper, but just as tangled, torrid, and wet. It was here, where opportunities would seem poorest, that the Classic Maya raised their magnificent city of Tikal.

The Maya

Little is known about the first human inhabitants of Guatemala; the area's subsequent history, however, is linked to that of southeastern Mexico, for geographically it is the same region.

Mayan civilization was definitely established here before 300 B.C., flourished, like much of Mesoamerica, between A.D. 300 and 900, and then suddenly declined. No one knows why, though there is of course a lot of scholarly speculation (see the Bibliography).

In the highlands of Guatemala groups of semi-nomadic Indians appeared at various times, fought, mingled, and interbred with the local populace. The "pure Maya" of these highlands are a myth. Throughout its human history there were various Indian peoples in Guatemala—as there still are—but the Maya were so dominant that it is simpler for the purposes of this discussion to lump them all together.

When the Spaniards arrived in 1523, along with their Indian allies from central Mexico, they found a large population warring among itself. The subsequent conquest of the region was led by Pedro de Alvarado, an especially bloodthirsty and gold-hungry lieutenant of Cortés. The Spaniards, abetted by local treachery and feuds, not only defeated the Maya but also drastically reshaped their whole society. The educated ruling class of the Maya was annihilated; the surviving peasants were forced out of their rural dwellings and herded into Spanish-style towns that bore a strong resemblance to labor camps; and Spanish Catholicism was imposed on the indigenous population, often with the aid of fire and the lash.

Mayan resistance, often passive but occasionally violent, proved to be more than a match for the Spanish, however. When native gods were officially abolished, the people simply renamed them after Christian saints. Here, as elsewhere throughout Mesoamerica, paganism and Catholicism ran like parallel lines, never meeting but always closely related and often indistinguishable.

The Maya maintained their identity, as they do today, through the force of tradition, which is summed up by the Spanish word *costumbre*. Although it usually translates as "custom," the word implies immeasurably more. *Costumbres* are not exactly at the heart of their religion; indeed, they are far more *in*flexible than the Maya's faith. Perhaps the word "kosher" comes closest to conveying some sense of the power of *costumbre*.

After the Conquest, Spanish colonial society in Guatemala was rigidly divided into castes. For almost four centuries there existed a form of apartheid here, although it was somewhat diluted because Spaniards were neither as puritanical nor as consistent as the Afrikaners have been. Guatemalan independence from Spain, achieved early in the 19th century, made little difference in the lives of most Guatemalans.

Today, in Guatemala, blood and custom continue to serve as the basis for the division of society, even though the edges are a bit more blurred. The segment of the population known as ladinos controls almost everything. Originally, the word "ladino" described someone who was crafty and cunning, a city slicker. Some Maya people will tell you it still means that, although in everyday parlance it refers to all Guatemaltecos who are "Europeanized." A ladino wears shoes, of course, and maybe a charcoal gray suit during business hours. Generally speaking, he is modern, regards mechanical and material progress as blessings, and admires novelties. Most ladinos are partly or entirely of European descent; skin color and features are important in Guatemala, although not as basic to classifying a person as proper shoes or a proper frame of mind.

In Guatemala, ladinos often tell you that an Indian is simply someone who chooses to call himself so. This pretense to equality, however, will not become a reality until the day all ladinos suddenly go blind. Guatemala is, above all else, a caste-conscious country. While there are no separate public facilities here, there are certainly separate bank accounts. Still, people on either side of this social and financial chasm are almost always courteous and gracious to visitors.

Guatemalan Food and Drink

Restaurant food throughout the country tends to be a blending of European and North American cuisine. In fact, you could travel extensively in Guatemala without ever suspecting that there exists a national cuisine. To sample local food you must therefore look for places advertising a *comida típica.* Such an establishment will usually call itself a *comedor* (eating place) rather than a *restaurante,* which is more pretentious sounding to the ears of most Guatemalans.

Chuchitos are little tamales with a spiced meat stuffing; *pepian* is a fricassee with squash seeds in a rich, dark sauce; another unusual item is *guisquil,* a pearlike vegetable that grows on vines. *Pacaya,* also native to the country, is a vegetable with an unfamiliar, rather harsh tang. Bananas, fried, mashed, or prepared any number of other ways, play a major role in Mayan cookery. Black beans, too, are prepared in various ways. Beef, except in expensive restaurants, is often tough, so it is usually cooked by simmering it in *guisados,* which are stews, or *caldos,* soup broths. Many foods usually considered Mexican are also standard in Guatemala, including enchiladas, guacamole, and *ceviche.* Corn tortillas are a national staple.

Local wines, which are usually concocted with grape

concentrates, orange pulp, and the like, should not be considered; imported vintages are expensive, so ask about price before you order to avoid a later shock. Good Guatemalan beer helps to offset the lack of wine, however. Gallo and Cabro, both medium light, are the most popular brands. Medalla de Oro, which is higher priced, is not really better. Moza, a rich, dark beer, is excellent but not always available. Local rum and *aguardiente,* both distilled from sugarcane, are commendable, and the local vodka is smooth enough. The prudent will stay far away from the native whiskey.

GUATEMALA CITY

Guatemala City, la Ciudad de Guatemala, may be the hub of the country but it is certainly not its heart. As the major transportation center of the country, the capital becomes the inescapable destination of most travellers. The best visit is a brief one, however; most of one day will do nicely, and even that is not necessary unless there's a delay involving your flight to Tikal. Hotels in Antigua and Panajachel (other important sites in Guatemala; see below) will arrange to have a driver and car meet you at the airport, or you can rent a car at the airport, convert some currency, and be on your way, skipping the city.

While this might make it sound as if the capital is a dreadful place, it really isn't—except perhaps in rush-hour traffic or by the glare of neon at night. In fact, Guatemala City has good hotels and restaurants and three worthwhile museums. But then, it's probably not what you came to see.

The city is also not the best jumping-off point for visits to the surrounding countryside. Both the attractive town of Antigua and the delightfully located lakeside town of Panajachel, as we will see, are better choices.

Guatemala City teems with more than two-and-a-quarter million people packed into a space never meant to accommodate such an onslaught. You can see some impressive buildings downtown, but beyond them spreads an ocean of urban sprawl. Likewise, parks are too often inundated by waves of hurrying humanity. The city's saving grace is that much of this humanity is Mayan, which enables you to see wonderfully expressive faces and, sometimes, the flair and flash of native costumes.

Around in the Capital

Tours of the city sold by hotels are of dubious value, mainly because much time is wasted on uninteresting monuments. It is better to hire a cab by the hour at an agreed-upon price, or to take a series of cabs and be on your own.

Before setting out, however, you should know that Guatemala City is divided into twenty-one zones. A street address without a zone number is insufficient, since names and numbers may be repeated from zone to zone. Although addresses can sound complicated, they are logical and easy to find with a map.

Your exploration of the city should begin with the **Parque Aurora**, near the airport on the south side of the city, Zona 13, between 7 Avenida and 11 Avenida. Museums, a zoo, a racetrack, and an extensive handicraft market make this park a center of interest and activity.

The Museo Nacional de Arqueologíca y Etnología is often referred to by its old name, the **Museum of the City of Guatemala**, and is housed in a gleaming white modern building. The architecture is totally Spanish-Moorish, which is odd because the museum's contents are almost totally Mayan. This is more than just an incongruity; it's also a telling comment about the divided nature of the country.

For all that, the museum's extensive collection of Mayan carvings, the largest in the world, is magnificent. One of its highlights is a throne from the jungle city of Piedras Negras. In addition, masterworks in ceramics—masks, figurines, and a variety of containers and vessels—rival the achievements in stone. Many of the objects on display—or others like them—were the accessories, the fittings and utensils, found at Tikal. Studying them here makes it easier to reconstruct that magnificent city in the mind's eye. The ethnological section of the museum, which is devoted chiefly to native costumes, is also interesting and well presented.

Across the street, the **Museum of History and Fine Arts** merits a short visit because of its fine interior, especially the main ceiling, and the paintings of Carlos Mérida; its historical section, however, is limited.

The handicraft market, located behind the Museum of History, has work for sale from every part of the country. If nothing else, the prices here will give you a standard of comparison for shopping elsewhere; work of higher quality, especially fine weaving, can be found outside the capital. The colorful atmosphere and gay marimba music are the market's best offerings.

The zoo, just north of the market, is, with the exception of its flamboyant native birds, nothing special.

Two other museums in the capital are also worth a visit. The **Museo Popol Vuh** occupies the sixth floor of a highrise building known as the Edificio Galerías Reforma, Torre 2 (Zona 9 at Reforma 8). Its display of polychrome vessels, including a number of large burial urns, is dazzling. The items were once in a private collection, and great care went into choosing every piece. All the Maya-inhabited regions of the country are represented, and although works created between A.D. 150 and 900 predominate, there are also earlier and later examples of the Maya's pre-Columbian artistry.

Quite different, but just as delightful in its own right, is the **Museo Ixchel**, where the textile arts of Guatemala, especially weaving and embroidery, are honored. The clothing on display in this museum is gorgeous, and the whole show so imaginatively presented that it rises far above the usual crafts display. In addition, this valentine of a museum is located in one of the city's better neighborhoods, 4a Avenida 16-17, Zona 10, about a fifteen-minute walk from the Museo Popol Vuh.

If you have extra time, the Relief Map (*Mapa en Relieve*) may prove interesting. This is a sprawling rendering of the country, 40 by 80 meters (125 by 250 feet), in somewhat exaggerated relief (the volcanoes, as shown here, would tower over Mount Everest in the real world). It's a painless and unusual geography lesson, and useful if you're about to set out to tour the country. You'll find the map in the pleasant Parque Minerva, Zona 2.

A number of city landmarks, though touted by guides and local advertisers, have little interest or charm. These include the grim National Palace, the Metropolitan Cathedral, and the National Theatre—all of them, at best, just time-fillers. Guatemalans are also extremely proud of the municipal buildings in their Civic Center; these structures are modern, functional, and handsome.

Staying in Guatemala City

The capital has good hotel accommodations in all price ranges except the very cheapest, which are miserable. A room tax of 17 percent will be added to your bill, and the charge is not always announced in advance. You should inquire beforehand.

In an attempt to avoid congestion, which sometimes overtakes them anyway, the newer and more luxurious hotels are located outside the center of the city. The better neighborhoods are Zonas 4, 9, and 10. A hotel in Zona 1 is likely to be economical but noisy, and there is little advantage to being in this, the old central area.

Throughout the country national taste favors the sleek, streamlined, and unmistakably modern; the more North American the better. International travellers, on the other hand, seem to prefer more charm and less plate glass. Both types of hostelries are mentioned here.

The **Camino Real-Biltmore** is excellent—as it should be for the prices it asks—and has restaurants, three bars with live entertainment, tennis courts, a gym, and swimming pools in assorted sizes. (Guatemalan luxury hotels, by the way, put a premium on sports and body-conditioning facilities.) The Zona 10 location of the hotel is in an upper-class neighborhood.

The **Hotel El Dorado Americana** is a multi-storied block of masonry and glass that the Ministry of Tourism often features in its publications to represent "modern Guatemala." The hotel has everything the Camino-Biltmore has—bars, restaurants, and swimming pools—only fewer of them. In other words, this is a fine international hotel, with prices to match.

The **Conquistador Sheraton**, expensive but less so than the Dorado or Camino Real, surprises guests with its flourishing orchids in the lobby. While it has most of the amenities, it does not feature all the gym and sauna facilities of its somewhat more lavish competitors. It does have a good location in Zona 4, however.

The **Plaza**, also in Zona 4, is straightforward and a couple of notches above basic at a moderate price. Ask for a room overlooking the swimming pool; the rooms facing the parking lot can be noisy.

The **Hotel del Central** is located in Zona 1 near the Cathedral. It's an inn rich in wood paneling and wrought iron; everything is hushed and gentle—except the streets outside (although the night traffic does eventually die down). The parking garage is convenient, the carpets good, and it's not hard to imagine you've been transported to Spain. The location explains its bargain rates.

In the same moderate bracket, and with the same problems of noise and congestion, is the **Pan American**. In the

Art Deco era the Pan American was the capital's leading hotel. Today, if some of its elegance has faded, it makes up for it with an abundance of charm. The hotel, located at 9a Calle 5-63, Zona 1, is comfortable and a good value.

The **Posada Belén**, a quiet, friendly, and welcoming little inn, is the city's best pension. Although it, too, is located in the center of town, in Zona 1, its street is spared the worst of the racket. The management, in addition, is happy to help with tours and excursions.

Dining in the Capital

The restaurant in the Pan American, though not exactly elegant, offers a good introduction to Guatemalan cuisine and also serves a variety of foreign dishes, good coffee, and fine pastries at modest prices. The waiters are decked out in traditional village attire, and the woven wall hangings are added attractions.

The posh neighborhood around the Camino Real-Biltmore in Zona 10, **La Zona Viva**, or "lively zone," is where you'll find the dining, dancing, and cabaret world in Guatemala. While it is far from the equal of Paris or Rome, it is surprisingly chic for Central America. There are not many rich people in Guatemala, but those who have money seem to have a lot of it, and they spend it freely. They also all seem to know each other, and where they meet is New York, Paris, or here in La Zona Viva.

Le Rendezvous, 13 Calle 2-55, Zona 10, is a transplanted bit of Montmartre, more bistro in style than haute cuisine, and offering indoor or patio service. It's very good, very French, and fairly expensive.

The **Puerto Barrios** is tricked out like a Spanish galleon, but the seafood is much better than the pirate rigging would indicate. The steaks are good, the shrimp and lobster better.

Martin's offers fare that is uncommon in Guatemala, including such items as frog's legs and rack of lamb. Broiled salmon, also offered here, is an exotic item in Central America. Reasonable prices have helped keep this august establishment, located at 13 Calle 7-65, Zona 9, popular for almost two decades.

Located not in La Zona Viva but across the street from the Conquistador Sheraton is **Estro Armónico**, mostly French and as warmly provincial as its flickering hearth. While it is less expensive than the better establishments of the more fashionable zone, it is not inexpensive.

All the leading hotels in Guatemala City have satisfactory restaurants. The best in the deluxe category, in the Sheraton, is the **Restaurante de las Espadas**, which specializes in broiled steaks, fish, and shrimp. It also has style and panache. Among the moderately priced hotels, the dining room of the **Hotel del Centro** is a good choice. The food isn't quite as Spanish as the décor, but the atmosphere is genteel and comfortable.

TIKAL

Tikal, the grandest of the ruined Mayan cities, is nothing less than awe inspiring. Here, in the tangled and almost impenetrable jungle of northern Guatemala at the base of the Yucatán Peninsula, you suddenly come upon the greatest human achievement of the Stone Age. For Tikal *is* a Stone Age creation, even though its magnificent structures were raised in the first centuries of the Christian era. Its builders used no metal tools, no draft animals, and no wheels (consequently, no pulleys). In order to accomplish these feats of engineering and construction, an army of laborers and artists had to be recruited, trained, and maintained not for just a few years, but for generations— an achievement as amazing as the buildings themselves.

To date, three thousand buildings have been mapped near the Great Plaza of Tikal. Foundations of about ten thousand stone structures are known—impressive enough when read about, but mind-boggling when you are actually there in the jungle.

Tikal began to take shape around the **Great Plaza** about 2,000 years ago on a site that was probably selected because it was higher than the surrounding swamps. The city reached its zenith of art and activity between A.D. 500 and 900, when it had at least 50,000 inhabitants. Then, suddenly and inexplicably, it was abandoned to the jungle.

Some dates at the site can be confirmed. Temple I, better known as the **Temple of the Giant Jaguar**, bears a Mayan glyph corresponding to A.D. 741, which tests have confirmed as the probable date of construction. The steep, graceful temple, Tikal's most famous monument, rises a lofty 52 meters (170 feet) above the East Plaza and looms almost as high above the Great Plaza.

Nearby are the plazas, terraces, and other buildings, including the tallest in the ancient Americas, **Temple IV**, which rises over 65 meters (212 feet) from its base to the

tip of its roof comb, and even looks down on those giants
of the jungle, the ceiba trees (which were sacred to the
Maya).

Tikal is simply too vast and complex for a detailed
discussion here, however. Those planning to explore the
city should arm themselves with archaeologist William R.
Coe's clear and definitive guide *Tikal: A Handbook of the
Ancient Maya Ruins,* published by the University of Penn-
sylvania Museum, Philadelphia, and in Guatemala by Editorial Piedra Santa. While it is usually available in English
at the Tikal museum or in the town of Flores, it is safer to
purchase it in advance. (For getting to Tikal, see the
Getting Around section at the end of this chapter.)

Staying at Tikal

Visitors have a choice of staying at the Parque Nacional
Tikal itself or in **Flores**, the small capital of the Petén, an
island town in Lake Petén Itzá that's connected to the
shore by a causeway. Two other little towns, Santa Elena
and San Benito, are located nearby on the mainland.

Accommodations at Tikal itself are Spartan and not
always available. Despite the low quality of these facilities,
however, being a twenty minutes' walk from the ruins has
its advantages. Besides the convenience, there's the jungle, itself an attraction. With its cacophony of bird and
animal cries it seems to be a living, breathing entity at
night. The experience has much to recommend it.

(Moonlight not only transforms the jungle but works
magic on the ruins. Tikal is magnificent under a full
moon, and although the zone is usually closed at night,
exceptions are made. Spend a night or two if possible in
Tikal or Flores. More extensive tours than the usual packages provide can be arranged there. In addition, a limited
number of Jeeps are available for private exploring.)

The **Jungle Lodge** is the best of the rustic few. As any
guest will quickly surmise, however, it was not built as a
hotel. When the modern archaeological excavation was
organized at Tikal, the Lodge was constructed as staff
housing, with materials brought in by pack animals. Today some rooms are in a main building, others are huts.
Quarters with a private bath are few and cost more; there
is no hot water. The Lodge does have a bar and a simple
restaurant, however. The rates, though not high, are less
modest than the accommodations. (The hotel is listed as
the Posada de la Selva in directories.)

A good second choice at about the same price is the tiny **Jaguar Inn**. Although it's primitive, meals are available. Reservations are made by telegraph, they wire acceptance, then you make a deposit.

The **Tikal Inn** offers simple huts with thatched roofs and half-wall dividers. There's an eternally empty swimming pool doomed by water shortages and regulations on the grounds here, but perhaps it's the thought that counts. You can also eat in its plain but overpriced restaurant.

The Flores/Santa Elena/San Benito area is an hour away with good transportation. With one exception the better hotels in the area are adequate but not luxurious. There is a certain oddity, even simple charm, about these hotels, however, and you do not entirely lose the sense of being in the jungle.

The **Savanna** is pleasant, tropical in atmosphere, and clean, and offers simple but comfortable rooms as well as—for the area—a good restaurant. Its rates are very reasonable, the staff helpful. The **Hotel Maya Internacional** is a collection of bungalows, thatched and stilted like lake dwellings, which indeed some of them are. As a result, it has a South Seas B-picture atmosphere. There's a pretense of hot water in the showers, and the walls are thin. The dining room, overlooking the lake, will do.

At one end of the lake the Guatemalan government has begun a development called Touricentro. The **Villa Maya** recently opened there has two swimming pools, tennis courts, air conditioning, and a miniature golf course, which makes it the fanciest hostelry north of Guatemala City, and priced accordingly. While such amenities are fine, in the past few people minded missing putting practice for the opportunity to explore Tikal. In short, the Villa Maya dilutes the whole experience. Nevertheless, a Camino Real hotel is now under construction at Touricentro.

If you have the time, boat rides on the lake are easy to arrange and an enjoyable way to spend an afternoon while you're in the area.

OTHER MAYAN RUINS IN GUATEMALA

Any archaeological zone in Guatemala will seem a bit anticlimactic after Tikal, and in fact the sites that dot official maps are mostly of minimal interest, or else too remote to repay the trouble involved in getting there. However, three other ruin sites can be recommended to enthusiasts, with the obvious reservation: None is another Tikal.

Quiriguá (kee-rhee-GWAH) is famed for its carved monuments, some of the finest in the Mayan world. It is not a large site, and the remaining buildings are of secondary interest, but it is the location of the largest carved Mayan monolith known—Stela E, nearly 11 meters (36 feet) tall and weighing some 65 tons. Almost a quarter of this massive stone remains buried, and the narrative carving on it is fascinating. Scattered elsewhere around the site, a dozen smaller works boast equally intricate detailing. Quiriguá is a little more than three hours from Guatemala City by car, about 206 km (128 miles) of that being paved road. Highway CA 9 heads northeast from the city to the vicinity of Los Amates, at which point you take a dirt cutoff for 3½ km (2.2 miles). You'll want to pack a lunch before heading out, however, including anything you might want to drink. (You can also visit Quiriguá on the way to the Río Dulce; see below.)

Mixco Viejo (MEESH-ko vee-EH-ho), the capital of the Pokomam Maya, a warlike people who fought and were eventually defeated by the conquistadors, was still a thriving urban center when the Spanish arrived in 1525, although it had been established many centuries earlier near the end of the Classic era. Today it's a beautiful ruins site, and less well known than it should be. There are two Mayan ball courts here, one that's particularly impressive; a major temple structure; and a number of pyramids and platforms. In addition, it's only 50 km (31 miles) north-northwest of Guatemala City, most of that over a paved road and the rest improved. You should allow an hour and a half by car for this beautiful drive— think of it as offering a good opportunity for a picnic and one of the prettiest short trips you can take in Guatemala. If you are driving, however, make sure you have a good map with the two turnoffs marked by your hotel or the tourist office. (Bus travel to Mixco Viejo is not a practical option.)

Zaculeu (sah-koo-LEH-oo) is situated in Guatemala's far western highlands near the modern city of **Huehuetenango**—a very long one-day excursion from Guatemala City, or a slightly easier one from Panajachel (see below). Huehuetenango (way-way-te-NAN-go) itself is 264 km (164 miles) northwest of the capital. The Zaculeu archaeological zone is just outside the town. Allow 3½ hours each way from the capital.

Zaculeu, occupied for at least a thousand years before the arrival of the Spanish, has divided stairs, dancing platforms, and other signs of influence from Mexico. Structure I is an impressive stepped pyramid with a temple atop it. There is also a handsome ball court here. More than forty structures are officially listed, but most are only grassy mounds today. Although the site is interesting and the surroundings attractive, this is a trip for dedicated enthusiasts, or for those seeking a good excuse to visit another region of Guatemala.

The **Hotel Piño Montano**, just outside Huehuetenango, is a motel-type establishment with a restaurant and pool in a garden setting—simple but satisfactory for those looking for a night's lodging here.

Travel agencies in the major hotels in Guatemala City offer regular tours to Quiriguá, Mixco Viejo, and a number of lesser sites. Clark Tours (see Getting Around below) also makes such arrangements and will be happy, in addition, to advise visitors about seeing Zaculeu, a site too remote to be included in most standard itineraries.

Copán

Located not in Guatemala but just across its eastern border in Honduras are the magnificent Mayan ruins at Copán, generally considered one of the half dozen greatest Classic Maya centers. The trip is an ordeal, however, and casual travellers usually skip it. Archaeology buffs, on the other hand, will probably not want to miss it.

Bus tours (see above) from Guatemala City leave early, and often return after dark. Unfortunately, much of this long day is spent in transit, with hardly enough time for the ruins themselves. The far better (and much more expensive) option is small-plane charter service, which is available through most large hotels and major travel agencies.

To visit Copán by car, take CA 9, the Atlantic Highway (see the Río Dulce section below). Turn south onto CA 10 near the Río Hondo and follow it for 42 km (26 miles). You then turn left (northeast) onto Highway 21, a poor road, which will take you to the border of Honduras, 43 km (27 miles) farther. There will be customs and immigration formalities at the border. Copán is another 13 km (8 miles) from the border via Honduras Highway 20.

The simple **Hotel Marina**, in the village of Copán on

the main plaza, has adequate accommodations and a restaurant. The electricity is cut off at about 9:00 P.M., however.

The trip, which takes about four and a half hours each way (from Guatemala City), can be combined with a visit to the ruins at Quiriguá to make a two-day archaeological excursion, with an overnight in Copán.

ANTIGUA

Antigua, on first sight, reveals nothing of its former glory. It's a pretty town, 20 km (12 miles) west-southwest of Guatemala City, and is manicured and buffed for visitors, which it receives in abundance and with a gracious nod. It's also decorous and proper, and its people are quite aware that this is *the* (living) national showcase.

The wide cobblestoned streets here are lined by colonial façades that you think must be old yet don't seem to have aged. These structures are, for the most part, single-story with red-tiled roofs, and this imparts a uniformity of height and style to some neighborhoods that makes them seem harmonious, if a bit monotonous. As a result, the profusion of flowering vines throughout the city adds a welcome touch of disorder. And everywhere you look the silhouette of a mountain looms in the background.

Because Antigua seems to have been created by a Latin American Norman Rockwell, with what some people see as a slightly artificial prettiness, it is difficult for many visitors to fathom the cataclysmic past behind its genteel present. On the night of September 10, 1541, the original capital of Guatemala was obliterated by fire and then a terrible deluge of water released from the crater of a nearby volcano. The survivors dragged themselves to the apparently safe valley here and founded Santiago de los Caballeros de Guatemala, Saint James of the Knights of Guatemala, as Antigua was then called.

The new capital, which was cradled in a valley dominated by three immense volcanoes, grew to become an important center of Spain's New World empire, next to only Mexico City and Lima in power. The city's business was to exploit—however ruthlessly—the whole Maya region, and in so doing it became a metropolis of some 60,000 people.

Then the omens of wrath began. Several times in the

early 18th century an irritable volcano by the name of Mount Fuego belched forth lava and ash, burying some inhabitants alive. Earthquakes set the town's massive arches trembling. According to contemporary accounts, Antigua descended into a vicious cycle of crime, violence, and oppression. There appears to have been a cruel Old Testament justice to what fate had in store for the town and its citizens.

In the summer of 1773 the earth came alive again and literally shook the city to death—not a quick death, but rather a prolonged agony that lasted over a month, followed by week upon week of deadly aftershocks. Adobe walls melted under torrential rains, and plague soon haunted the ruins. The governor, believing the valley to be cursed, ordered an evacuation and removed himself and his capital to what is now Guatemala City, which was formally declared the new capital in 1776. (Exactly two centuries later the quake of 1976 would almost level *that* city.)

The archbishop fought the governor to save the old town but was himself forced to move. A few determined survivors nevertheless hung on among the ruins of Santiago. Gradually, a new town arose from the devastation; in the 19th century it began to prosper from the coffee trade and became known as Antigua Guatemala, "Old Guatemala."

Exploring Antigua

The town is laid out on a grid, with the north-south thoroughfares called *calles* (streets) and the east-west ones called *avenidas* (avenues). The point at which "north" (*norte*) becomes "south" (*sur*) and "east" (*oriente*) becomes "west" (*poniente*) is the cathedral on the south side of the plaza.

The tourist office, also located on the south side of the plaza, in what was once the Palace of the Captains-General, is manned by a staff that is most helpful and has a repository of up-to-the-minute information.

Sightseeing here is mostly a matter of inspecting ruins while you wander through tidy, quaint neighborhoods. Antigua has been preserved as a monument to earthquakes, and the city takes a perverse pride in these lingering echoes of destruction. The ruins are impressive, though a little melancholy in the bright sunshine, and soon you begin to think of Shelley's Ozymandias. It's a fascinating, if not exactly jolly, way to spend time.

There is little point in detailing the sights: You start with the shell behind the present cathedral and continue around town. The **Church and Convent of Santo Domingo** is worth a brief mention because it was once huge and fantastically rich. A silver statue of the Virgin once here was reportedly the size of a tall woman, and a silver altar lamp was said to be so weighty it took three men to raise it. (After one earthquake the Virgin was fruitlessly bribed with a crown of jewels.) The **Convent of the Capuchinas**, much of it still standing, affords memorable views from its roof.

The **Convent of San Francisco** is itself an ancient rubble heap, but the adjacent church survived the frequent devastation and contains an extensive collection of votive paintings, signs, letters, and photos proclaiming the miracles performed by Brother Pedro de Betancourt, a 17th-century holy man who's entombed here. Those needing his intercession in their own affairs rap on the tomb to get his attention; the knocking is frequent, gentle, but persistent.

There are also two museums in Antigua. The venerable **University of San Carlos** has an uninteresting collection of colonial objects, but the building housing it boasts a lovely patio and an antique feeling. The nearby Museum of Santiago has little to recommend it other than its rough, almost Medieval architecture.

Staying in Antigua

Antigua's inns tend to be high priced for what they offer; nevertheless, the town is often short of rooms, so reserve ahead.

One reason for the town's popularity is its admirable location, which is excellent for staging excursions into south-central Guatemala. Knowledgeable guides and drivers are available in town, and attractive villages can be found nearby with their help.

The **Hotel Aurora**, conveniently located four blocks from the cathedral, offers the best value in accommodations in Antigua, although it's not the most luxurious in town. This spacious old residence, which is built around a flower-filled patio, now houses a carefully run family operation and has all the necessities, but offers no public rooms or luxuries other than its own atmosphere and service. Breakfast is served.

The **Hotel Antigua**, another colonial gem, at least in décor, is far more luxurious. Its beautiful lawns frame a swimming pool and a children's wading pool near nicely spaced bungalows, and the colorful parrots in the gardens, lovely but raucous, are rivaled in beauty by the many rose bushes, trees, and hedges on the grounds. In addition, the dining room is cheerful and tastefully decorated. The hotel is also proud of its Sunday buffet, which is accompanied by music. Actually, Sunday is the least attractive day of the week at the hotel, because then it's crowded with day-trippers from the capital. Nevertheless, the inn is a rarity in Guatemala, and rare things tend to be expensive, as this hotel is—but not outrageously so. The inn is a five-minute walk south from the plaza.

The **Posada de Don Rodrigo** is a series of high-ceilinged rooms and a restaurant and bar clustered around several shady patios in the center of town. This old residence is historic, heavy on atmosphere, and a little too heavy on shadows, but it is nonetheless a handsome inn. Only avid marimba music aficionados should accept quarters facing the main patio, however—at least on weekends. There are also considerable differences in size, light, and ventilation among the room choices. No one section of the inn is best in its entirety, so look at the individual room offered before registering. The rustic dining room is colorful, but the food is unexceptional. The Posada de Don Rodrigo is moderately expensive.

The **Ramada Antigua** is mentioned because of the frequent scarcity of rooms in Antigua. To stay here is better than having to journey back to Guatemala City, and the hotel is not terribly overpriced, but this apricot-colored cube of cement at the edge of town gives the impression that several conventions are just ending or threatening to begin. It is popular with the business and government crowd from Guatemala City, who enjoy the tennis courts and the illusion of being in North America. The Ramada is on the Ciudad Vieja highway at the southwest edge of town.

Scattered around Antigua are a number of modest pensiones and rooming houses that accommodate travellers looking for economy over a long term and students studying Spanish in Antigua (Antigua beckons language students of all ages, many of whom live with local families).

Dining in Antigua

El Sereno, the most stylish restaurant in Guatemala, welcomes you with candlelight, crystal, and a lovely fountain. The food, which has gourmet aspirations, is French and international, with some transfigured native dishes. The restaurant is expensive but memorable. Reservations should be made by calling 032-00-73. El Sereno's elegant entrance will be found at 6 Calle Poniente 30; closed Monday and Tuesday.

Doña Luisa Xicotencatl seems to have something of everything, including a devoted following of students and young people from the capital. The courtyard is an especially convivial place, but a number of the tables upstairs have striking views of the nearby volcanoes. You check off your choices on a long paper menu, which includes such fare as chile con carne, sausages, Reuben sandwiches, pies, and cakes. The food is fair, the atmosphere casual, the prices moderate. 4 Calle Oriente 2.

Welten, unlike its name, is Italian, and the fare classic. The patio environment here is pleasantly floral and ferny, the wrought iron handsome. Prices range from moderate to expensive.

Alom La Creación, in the Ramada, presents international specialties with a German emphasis. It's only open from 7:00 P.M. until 11:00 P.M. but claims it won't turn you out until you're ready to end the night. **Las Chimeneas**, in the same hotel, is a standard operation, with piano music and (usually) good service that becomes rushed on weekends. Both Ramada restaurants are at the expensive end of the scale.

Shopping in Antigua

Tourist prices tend to prevail in Antigua, but there are also some good buys and fine merchandise here, especially at the weaving market located next to the Jesuit church, 6 Avenida Norte and 4 Calle Poniente. Those searching for interesting textiles should also visit the nearby village of **San Antonio Aguas Calientes**.

Jade is an Antigua specialty. The founder of the jade art and industry here is **Jades** (HA-dess), a large, beautiful shop at 4a Calle Oriente 34 (there are also a number of interesting working studios in the building). Guatemalan jade is the real stone, by the way, and it's risky to buy it off the street unless you are highly knowledgeable; you can rely, on the other hand, on an establishment like Jades, which specializes in exquisite stones, finely set, but has many other items of interest, including woven cloth and the best available coffee beans.

After checking out Jades, pause at the tempting candy shop on the opposite side of the street across from the gas station, where chocolate is served in all its glory and many of its forms. This street, 4a Calle Oriente, also has several other worthwhile handicraft shops, all of them located between Jades and the main plaza.

Mayan women frequently come into Antigua to sell their work or their possessions on the streets. It's a mistake to turn away automatically; you just might miss the best buys in town.

LAKE ATITLAN AND PANAJACHEL

Half a century ago Aldous Huxley pronounced Lake Atitlán to be "the most beautiful of the world." Virtually every ad, brochure, and discussion of the lake begins with the great man's encomium. In fact, in the lakeside town of Panajachel you can find the Huxley quote printed in at least four different languages, at once challenging and offending countless travellers. (It seems that everyone has a personal candidate for "the most beautiful," and though the lakes are scattered from Finland to California, none ever seems to be Atitlán.)

Regardless of which is fairest of them all, Lake Atitlán, in all its changing moods, *is* unforgettably, hauntingly beautiful. It is a broad sweep of water some 26 km (16 miles) long and 18 km (11 miles) wide, and is framed by massive symmetrically shaped volcanoes whose eruptions created the basin in prehistoric times. The lake is relatively clean and remains good for water sports, but it is mainly enjoyed for its beauty, whether it's in the late morning, when a daily wind freshens and lightens its deep blue color, or in the early evening, when the rising mist tints it silver. At any time of day, however, lake-watching is a local pastime.

A dozen towns and villages, heavily Mayan and linked to each other by launches, hug the shoreline, although roads run between most places. (The Maya prefer to have their feet on the ground. They are neither fishermen, good swimmers, nor canny boat builders: *No es costumbre*. The lake is merely the limit of their cornfields. Accordingly, they do not create legends or sing songs about it, and its waters are not viewed as a resource.)

Panajachel

Of the lake settlements at Atitlán, the most interesting to travellers is Panajachel (pahn-ah-hah-CHELL), the only one with facilities for visitors. The town itself winds, sprawls, and ambles along the northeastern shore of the lake, as casual in its layout as it is in its approach to life. Being more Mayan than ladino, Panajachel has little of Antigua's tidiness, quaintness, and squared corners. There are no ruins, monuments, or museums here. Instead, Panajachel draws visitors because of the beauty of its setting, the interesting variety of its people (both native and foreign), and the careless atmosphere of easy living that prevails. In addition, as a headquarters for exploring the countryside, it is more centrally located than Antigua, and its accommodations are a better value.

Panajachel carries no heavy burden of history. There was a good-sized native population here when the Spanish marched into the region, but after one bloody battle the struggle was over, and only the resistance of custom and stubbornness remained to confound them. The town became a center for the Franciscans, who converted the local folk after a fashion. Otherwise, life, which chiefly meant raising corn, continued along its age-old path.

In our own century the lake has increasingly attracted tourists and vacationers alike. Day-trippers come from Guatemala City, travelling 115 km (72 miles) each way. Europeans, especially younger ones, also come in noticeable numbers, usually after visiting Tikal. (Many seem to be taking vague sabbaticals.) In addition, foreigners and wealthy people from the capital have bought or built homes here. These substantial holiday or retirement houses are planted comfortably between the commercial district and the shore.

There is also a small coterie of North American and European transients, mostly young, who maintain a '60s lifestyle reminiscent of the vanished world of San Francisco's "Hashbury." You might call them "post-hippies," but the term somehow seems too emphatic. At any rate, they hang up their wind chimes, play their bamboo flutes, and contemplate the lake at sunset with great seriousness. The backpackers among them gaze uncomprehendingly at Maya folk carrying loads in much the same way. (The Maya do it more efficiently; they have tumplines circling their foreheads to brace the burden.) A number of artists and writers are also drawn to the lake. While the mix of people is not homogeneous enough to be convivial, Panajachel is probably the liveliest little town in Central America.

The town's center, like the lifestyle it encourages, is somewhat haphazard. Street names are rarely posted and frequently change. The heart of town is located at the corner of Calle Principal, the main street, and Calle Santander, which runs toward the lake. Along Calle Principal you will find a slow-service bank, a peaceful enough pool hall, and a stand where delicious Topsy ice cream is sold. The **Maya Palace** craft shop, an excellent store, is still operating even though the old hotel of the same name has become an office building. You'll also find a book exchange, a chocolate shop, and some restaurants and snack shops along the main street.

The evangelical church on Calle Principal is far livelier than the pool hall, in part because Protestant missionaries have flocked to Guatemala in recent years and enjoyed great success. The authorities seem to like this particular foreign import: The missionaries take a less jaundiced view of the Guatemalan government than the Catholic liberation theology movement. Politics aside, you'll probably be startled to hear "Rock of Ages" pounded out on an electric keyboard and backed by guitars as a fervent congregation sings along in Spanish and Mayan.

Walking down Calle Santander toward the lake, you pass several blocks of cloth displays. Visitors are invited, even urged, to inspect the wares, but are not badgered. The overall effect is flamboyant and dazzling, and the quality often high—here and there you'll come across machine-made junk—but in the face of such a profusion of merchandise it is hard to concentrate.

The town's beach on Lake Atitlán is a pleasant, busy place, but more for strolling than sunbathing, as much of it is gravel and dirt. The swimming is best in the morning before the breezes stiffen and turn the water choppy (there is better swimming nearby at the Hotel Visión Azul beach). Still, you can always consider the merchandise offered by perambulating vendors here as you enjoy a cool drink in one of the beach's open-fronted restaurants, or even take a boat ride.

Instead of renting a boat, however, most visitors take the mail launch (really a passenger launch) across the lake to

San Pedro de la Laguna. The roofed launch carries a couple of dozen people, mostly Maya, on each trip. Mayan women, who are often uneasy away from land, seem to draw comfort from hand-lettered signs posted by the captain: JEHOVAH OUR GOD IS UPON THE GREAT WATERS, one plaque announces in Spanish; BE NOT AFRAID! another urges. Obviously, this is an evangelical boat.

Its destination, San Pedro, is also evangelical. Here, little wooden steeples, one after another, poke sharply at the sky, for the town was converted en masse, then splintered into sects, some of them Pentecostal. Elsewhere houses seem to climb upon each other as they struggle to hold the hillside; the inhabitants of San Pedro are jammed together, apparently by choice and custom. You will also see horses and mules carrying loads here, the animals replacing men and women as beasts of burden, which is definitely not *costumbre,* and may be a result of the new religion. Men's shirts are a good buy if you can find them for sale. Women's clothing is characterized by fairly good embroidery on machine-made cloth.

The San Pedro trip takes about two hours. Other boat rides are available at Panajachel, including a circumnavigation of the lake, which starts in the morning. On all of these trips, the views are beautiful and the Mayan passengers a delight.

Staying in Panajachel

The hotels in town will be happy to offer advice and help with nearby excursions, hiring guides or drivers, and bus schedules.

The **Cacique Inn** (kah-SEE-kay), located near the southern edge of town on the Sololá road, a continuation of the main street, is a fine value. The rooms, which have attractive stone fireplaces, are grouped around a swimming pool and a well-kept garden; the dining room is probably the best restaurant in the area, and serves international food with some local touches; and the inn itself is relaxed and very well run. In addition, you can walk from the Cacique to the center of town.

The **Hotel Atitlán**, about a mile south of town past the Cacique Inn, has lovely grounds with gardens featuring topiary sculpture. The views from the hotel are also impressive, which makes the bar an ideal place for a drink at sunset. The dining room, with alamo beams, is more stately than cheerful, however, and the food is only satisfactory. There are no fireplaces in the rooms, and town is a long walk away. Nevertheless, the views and the serene, secluded surroundings justify the high prices of this handsome inn.

The **Hotel Visión Azul** seems to have been carved out of the same coffee plantation as its neighbor, the Hotel Atitlán. This is a comfortable choice, with lawns and a number of rooms offering panoramic views of the lake and surrounding mountains. It is also simpler than its elegant neighbor, and therefore less costly.

The **Rancho Grande Inn** is located in town, not far from the beach. The accommodations here are bungalows set in a garden, good but not special. A hearty cooked breakfast is included in the price. The only public room is the dining room at breakfast time, and the management is not especially good about information and arrangements. The hotel does offer privacy and a fine location, however.

The **Hotel del Lago** overlooks the beach and was obviously designed with vacationers from Guatemala City in mind. Thick-pile carpets climb right up the sides of the bar, and the volcanic stone seems to come in a variety of designer colors. All the rooms have balconies and wonderful views of the lake, but the top-floor rooms are the best. The hotel also has a restaurant, a nightclub, a swimming pool, and two curio shops—and it is expensive.

The **Hotel Galindo**, on Calle Principal, proudly advertises its patio garden, which is a veritable jungle. Unfortunately, its rooms are small and far from bright, but it does have two things to recommend it: a location downtown and low rates. The Galindo also rents out several lakeside cottages with kitchens.

Dining in Panajachel

All the dining spots here are informal, and most of them at least a little rustic.

The **Cacique Inn**, although its menu is limited, has the most consistent kitchen in town. Of the other hotels, the **Atitlán** is really selling its surroundings more than its food, which is only satisfactory. The views are lovely.

La Fontana, on the main street, offers Italian-style cooking, with indoor and outdoor service. Both the service and the surroundings are pleasing.

El Bistro, on Calle Santander, features lake bass, salads, chicken, and steaks, and seems to take its food very seriously. Tables are set up in a small dining room and an adjacent garden. El Bistro is located about halfway between the main street and the beach.

The murky **Last Resort**—it will take a few minutes for your eyes to adjust to the gloom—is mainly a bar. Late in the evening it draws a young (and sometimes not-so-young) international crowd. The food runs to such offerings as ribs and pizza, and the sandwiches are generous—a welcome surprise, because Guatemala is the land of the stingy sandwich and the scant taco. It's hard to find in daylight, however, even though it's just off Santander not far from the public school. At night look for a bulb burning outside, or trail a likely-looking patron (the clientele will quickly become identifiable).

The **Circus Bar** is located in a Hansel and Gretel–style house near the center of town. The bar does serve food, mostly snacks, which are good enough as well as inexpensive, and has live music many nights.

In addition, several eateries have been tacked up along the beach. Most of them are breezy places where you can enjoy something cool while watching the lake and beach. One of them, **Los Pumpos,** is worth trying for lunch. The building is cobbled together out of split bamboo, thatch, and, it sometimes seems, glue. Hanging inside are stuffed fish, nets, oars, glass pendants, and all manner of flotsam. If the Swiss Family Robinson had opened a café, this would be it.

CHICHICASTENANGO

Despite the side effects of increased tourism, Chichicastenango, about 20 km (12 miles) north of Panajachel, remains the quintessential Mayan town, at once a confluence of paganism and Catholicism, of folklore and ancient traditions culled from the entire highlands region. There are no numbers or names along the cobblestoned streets here—and it hardly matters. This is a small place, and everybody knows how to get everywhere; as a result, you will not need a hired guide.

The market tradition of Chichi, as the town is often called, dates back to the pre-Columbian era. People from a wide area have always come here to buy, sell, or trade. Others come merely to watch the transactions—

not only foreigners but Mayan villagers themselves, for whom this is, and always has been, life and excitement. One writer has described Chichi as "anthropology in action."

The main market is held on Sunday, but preparations for it begin on Saturday afternoon (a smaller market is held on Thursday). Some visitors feel that the market is conducted for their benefit, that it's a craft show for tourists. And while it's true that ladino merchants are there to deal and give customers what they want, another market, where cheap kitchenware, needles, dyes, and furnishings for primitive dwellings are sold, is operating at the same time. Your eyes should not be held entirely by those who want your attention; the sideshow is truly the main event.

After checking out the market you should visit the local church, **Santo Tomás**. The rites here are not performances for the benefit of curious onlookers, and neither are they voodoo rituals. This is folk Catholicism, practiced with candles and overhung by acrid incense. The chants, prayers, and costumes of the devout are strange, even alien, and Santo Tomás is a grim place fraught with an almost palpable aura of belief and magic.

There's also a small museum in town, nicely done, but it will occupy you no more than half an hour. The real museum is Chichi itself.

If you want to stay overnight you'll find the **Mayan Inn** to be outstanding. Although it faces the plaza, its terraces afford lovely views of the valleys around Chichi. The dining room is also very good, and the comfortable rooms are made charming and personal with a selection of antiques and native art. A marimba band plays in the patio on market days; its musicians are as good as everything else about this inn, which is well worth the fairly high tariff charged.

Less expensive, but with less personality, is the attractive and colonial **Hotel Santo Tomás**. It, too, has beautiful views and lovely grounds, and the comfortable dining room serves well-prepared food.

The **Posada Chugüilá** is, unfortunately, no better than the room you get, which can vary from cramped to spacious. Some have fireplaces; ask for one of those, even in a heat wave—they're the best the inn has to offer. The patio is comfortable; the restaurant serves hearty, rather heavy fare.

THE RIO DULCE

The relatively new Atlantic Highway (Carretera al Atlántico), designated CA 9, has created fast, easy access to a region of Guatemala that was, until recently, little known or explored by foreigners. Although the highway heads in a northeasterly direction toward the Caribbean coast, in the minds of most travellers it seems to go *down,* dropping in its course from temperate highlands to rainforest and the steamy tropics. The trip is usually made for one reason—to see the jungle and the somnolent Río Dulce as it meanders from Lake Izabal into the Gulf of Honduras and the Caribbean. (The river is also a possible stop on the way by car or bus to the ruins at Tikal.)

At minimum, this is an overnight trip from Guatemala City; driving time is a little over four hours each way. Some travellers will wish to combine this excursion with a visit to the Mayan ruins at **Quiriguá**, which are located not far from the highway. (The Quiriguá turnoff is near the Texaco station at Los Amates, kilometer 205.)

For the Río Dulce, however, you continue on CA 9 past the Quiriguá turnoff until, just past the town of Morales, you reach the junction with the road to Frontera, where you turn left (north). About 34 km (21 miles) farther on lies El Relleno, a small settlement at the water's edge—and not on most maps. There is a good general store there, Tienda Reed; Mrs. Reed, who speaks English, can help with car storage and advice.

Once that is settled, all that's left is to hire a launch from among those you'll see moored nearby. In choosing a launch, however, be sure to select one with a strong motor. Some of the boats are underpowered, and although they manage the trip, what should be a leisurely excursion can become a slow boat to nowhere as the motor fights the current. You'll also want to agree upon a price in advance—it's usually not the first price suggested. The whole trip takes a little more than two hours, including a short stop at Castillo de San Felipe, a 17th-century fortress built to fend off pirates. The boatman should understand that the castle stop is included in the price.

El Golfete, downstream, is a broadening of the river that seems more like a tropical lake. On the north bank is a reserve for those fantastic creatures, the manatees, or sea cows, which can weigh up to a ton. (Distant sightings of manatees by sailors may have been the origin of the mermaid legend.)

Soon the river narrows and then enters a gorge. Mangroves, their twisted, clawlike roots gripping the riverbank, line either side. Kekchi Indians have built a few primitive villages in the jungle here, their thatched huts with peaked roofs appearing every now and then in a clearing. But human intrusion into this region is, for the most part, barely noticeable, the silence broken only by the cries of a multitude of birds or a breeze rustling the tangled foliage.

Lívingston, the small town at the mouth of the Río Dulce, gives an appearance of gaiety with its cheerfully painted wooden houses and corrugated metal roofs, but it's not really interesting unless you can stay long enough to become acquainted with its people, a mélange of Caribs, ladinos, Kekchis, Lebanese, Chinese, and East Indians.

The surrounding area has not been notably successful in promoting itself as a beach resort—other Caribbean resorts outdo this narrow strip of coast in both facilities and atmosphere, nor is Lívingston cheap for what is offered—but there is good skindiving, swimming, sailing, and fishing here.

Staying in the Río Dulce Area

Perched on a hill above the boat landing in Lívingston, the luxury **Tucán Dugu** is a striking building with white walls and tropical thatch. It also has a swimming pool and a beach. Jungle motifs and rich woodwork contribute to the exotic atmosphere of this expensive accommodation.

The **Casa Rosada,** also in Lívingston, is much more modest but shares the Caribbean flavor of the Tucán Dugu. While there isn't a full restaurant operation here, a cooked breakfast is served. Reservations and payments can be made by telegram; rates are reasonable. (The Casa Rosada will not accommodate children.)

Upriver, at the El Relleno–Río Dulce crossing, the **Turicentro Marimonte** is a good hotel and resort situated on the banks of the river. The Marimonte has a swimming pool and marina, and is popular with boating enthusiasts from Guatemala City. It also has a satisfactory restaurant.

About a mile downstream is the quite special **Hotel Catamarán,** which is situated on a small island in the river. The Catamarán caters to visitors wanting to explore the Río Dulce and surrounding jungle, as well as those simply in search of a South-Seas atmosphere in a relaxed environment. Its swimming pool and marina are well maintained, the food is good, and the rates are a good deal for such an attractive and unusual jungle inn. The Catamarán will also be happy to arrange for your transportation from the capital.

GETTING AROUND

Getting There

Citizens of the United States may obtain a Guatemalan tourist card, required by law, for a small fee by presenting proof of citizenship (passport, birth certificate, or voting registration) at airline check-in counters, Guatemalan consulates, or border crossing stations; naturalized citizens may need their certificate of naturalization. British Commonwealth and Canadian citizens should apply in advance, with a passport and round-trip ticket in hand, at a Guatemalan consulate.

Entering Guatemala with an automobile requires an additional permit as well as proof of ownership. There will be another small fee for the former, and still another for fumigating the tires of your car and squirting a whiff of something inside.

There are three possible entry points into Guatemala from the north. (Unless you have been exploring Mexico in your own car, however, crossing into Guatemala by automobile will prove both costly and time-consuming.) Coming directly from Mexico by car, you can take either the lowland coastal route, Highway 200, through Tapachula, or the highland road, Highway 190, from San Cristóbal de las Casas, which crosses into Guatemala near Ciudad Cuauhtémoc. The highland route is cooler and much more scenic. If you choose the latter, you'll soon understand why Guatemala, with its pine-clad mountains and long auto tunnels, is sometimes called "North America's Switzerland."

A third possibility is to enter through Belize. This route should not be attempted in a conventional car, however; stick to four-wheel-drive vehicles with high wheel bases if you have your heart set on this option (even then, it will be a long, bumpy, exhausting trek).

Air service from abroad to Guatemala City, which has the country's only international airport, is frequent and dependable. Both Pan Am and Eastern, with flights from New York and Miami, link Guatemala with the United

States, Canada, and Europe. Mexicana, the Mexican national airline, offers a daily flight to Guatemala City that leaves Mexico City at 6:30 A.M. In addition, two airlines not widely known outside of Central America also deserve consideration. Aviateca, the Guatemalan national airline, flies to Guatemala City from Miami, Houston, New Orleans, Los Angeles, and Mexico City, and has good service, an admirable safety record, and a thorough knowledge of its home country. At times it also offers reduced fares and attractive travel arrangements, including special rates on hotels and car rentals. Lacsa, the fine Costa Rican operation, flies to Guatemala City from New York and Los Angeles (with a stop in Cancún), and often attracts passengers away from the bigger carriers with its discount fares. (Lacsa is a favorite with Latin American travellers.)

Currency

The national monetary unit is the *quetzal* (ket-SAHL), named for the shy jungle bird beloved by the Maya. A *quetzal* is divided into one hundred *centavos*. The currency is relatively stable; you should be able to change back to dollars or other major currencies without incurring startling losses.

The Guatemala City airport, La Aurora, is a convenient place to exchange currency—especially since banks in Guatemala can be quagmires of bureaucracy. Small denominations of U.S. dollars are generally accepted throughout the country, but usually not at a favorable exchange rate. Hotels and better shops almost always accept U.S. dollar travellers checks, but again, you pay a small penalty.

Credit cards are accepted at establishments dependent on tourism, including the better hotels, restaurants, and car rental agencies.

Telephoning, Local Time, Electric Current

The international telephone code is 502; the capital area code is 2. There are several other area codes used within the country.

Guatemala is on Central Standard time (the same as Chicago and Winnipeg) year-round, but does not change over to Daylight Saving Time.

Electricity in Guatemala is supplied at 110 volts, alternating current, the same as in the United States, Canada, and Mexico. The same type and sizes of sockets and plugs are also standard in all four countries.

Travelling in Guatemala

A rental car is a pleasure but not a necessity in Guatemala. You will find Avis, Hertz, Budget, Dollar, and National at both the airport and in Guatemala City. If you decide to rent a car from one of these outfits, make sure you're not paying double for insurance. Many credit-card companies cover such insurance, or at least a part of it, automatically (check with your own card-issuing company). Once you rent the car, stay with the attendant as it's being checked for damages prior to taking it; be sure that every dent and missing hubcap is properly noted, or else you may end up paying for them.

Those who wish to know more about packaged tours to Guatemala should contact Clark Tours, 7 Avenida 6-53, Edificio El Triángulo, 2nd floor, Zona 4, Guatemala City, C.A.; Tel: 310-213. Clark is the oldest and largest company in the field. The international travel company Wagon-lits may also have some attractive tours, and Aviateca, the Guatemalan national airline, is usually helpful. Most hotels in the major cities will arrange for cars, drivers, and guides.

There is good, regular bus service from the capital to Antigua, Chichicastenango, and Panajachel. Bus service to the Río Dulce region, on the other hand, is less than convenient, and the bus trip to Tikal is not only an ordeal, it's boring.

First-class buses are your best bet. You can reach **Antigua** in an hour on the Preciosa line, 15a Calle 3-37, Zona 1. Buses depart hourly from 7:00 A.M. to 8:00 P.M.

Panajachel service is provied by Rébuli, 20a Calle 3-42, Zona 1. Rébuli offers regularly scheduled departures from 5:00 A.M. to 4:00 P.M. Panajachel is a four-hour journey one way.

The **Chichicastenango** bus, also a four-hour-trip one way, is for early risers. Buses leave at 4:30, 5:00, and 5:30 A.M.; service is provided by Reinita de Utatlán, 20a Calle and 4a Avenida, Zona 1.

The 14-hour endurance run that ends at Flores (**Tikal**) begins at 17a Calle 8-46, Zona 1. The line is Fuentes del Norte, and the bus goes via the **Río Dulce**, so it's possible to break up the trip. The stretch from Guatemala City to the river is the easy part (see below for more on Tikal).

Second-class buses are often antique school buses that were retired from service in the United States long ago, and stop anywhere you can flag them down. Baggage goes on the roof, birds and animals travel inside with the people. Still, they are satisfactory, even an adventure, for good-humored travellers going a short distance. After a while, however, the smells, pushing, crowding, fumes, and general slowness of the proceedings lose their charm.

In almost all Guatemalan towns buses arrive and depart from a central street near a main corner. Inquire locally.

Getting to Tikal

The easiest and most practical way for travellers to get to Tikal is by plane from Guatemala City. Aviateca offers regular morning and afternoon flights (the planes accommodate either 6 or 24 passengers) to the nearby town of Flores. From there you can get a bus, taxi, or combi to take you to a hotel or, if you so choose, the ruins themselves.

The ruins are also accessible by car, with the most common route starting in the capital and ending some 12 hours later. The least rugged vehicle available in Guatemala that is practical for the trip is a Suzuki model, and looks something like a Jeep. Bus transportation over the same route is also available, but the inexpensive fare is no bargain when you figure in the day lost and the considerable discomfort (not to mention the boredom). An Aviateca flight is much the better choice.

Half-day tours of Tikal by Jeep or minibus, with lunch included, can be purchased in Guatemala City. You return to the capital in the afternoon. While this is better than nothing, it's hardly good enough. Not only will you be rushed at the ruins and miss much of what is best about them, you'll also miss the once-in-a-lifetime experience of nightfall and sunrise in the jungle.

Whichever way you choose to go, you should take a few items along with you: insect repellent; a sun visor or hat; a flashlight for viewing darkened chambers; and binoculars. The latter need not be especially powerful—the details you want to bring closer are not far away, just high up.

If you're arriving by plane and plan on going exploring as soon as you get there, be sure to eat a good breakfast before departing the capital; food is not served on the plane.

ACCOMMODATIONS REFERENCE

▶ **Hotel Antigua.** 8a Calle Oriente, **Antigua.** Tel 032-0217.

▶ **Hotel Atitlán.** Camino a Sololá, **Panajachel**. Tel: 062-1441.

▶ **Hotel Aurora.** 4a Calle Oriente 16, **Antigua**. Tel: 032-0288.

▶ **Posada Belén**. 13 Calle A 10-30, Zona 1, **Guatemala City**. Tel: 51-3478.

▶ **Cacique Inn**. Calle Embarcadero, **Panajachel**. Tel: 062-1205.

▶ **La Casa Rosada. Lívingston**. Contact by telegraph.

▶ **Hotel Catamarán. Río Dulce**. Tel: (Guatemala City) 32-4829.

▶ **Camino Real-Biltmore**. Avenida Reforma 14-01, Zona 10, **Guatemala City**. Tel: 33-4633; in the U.S.: 800-228-3000.

▶ **Hotel del Centro**. 13 Calle 4-55, Zona 1, **Guatemala City**. Tel: 81-281.

▶ **Posada Chugüilá. Chichicastenango**. Tel: 056-1134.

▶ **Conquistador Sheraton**. Vía 5, 4-68, Zona 4, **Guatemala City**. Tel: 31-2222; in the U.S.: 800-325-3535.

▶ **Posada de Don Rodrigo**. 5a Avenida Norte 17, **Antigua**. Tel: 032-0291.

▶ **Hotel El Dorado Americana**. 7 Avenida 15-45, Zona 9, **Guatemala City**. Tel: 31-7777; in the U.S.: 212-757-2981.

▶ **Hotel Galindo**. Calle Principal, **Panajachel**. Tel: 062-1168.

▶ **Jaguar Inn. Tikal**. Contact by telegraph.

▶ **Hotel del Lago**. Calle Rancho Grande, **Panajachel**. Tel: 062-1555.

▶ **Hotel Marina**. Gonzalez Bocanegra 100 ZP3, **Copán**, Honduras. Tel: 526-7676 (country code: 504).

▶ **Mayan Inn. Chichicastenango**. Tel: 056-1176.

▶ **Hotel Maya Internacional. Santa Elena**. Tel: 081-1208.

▶ **Pan American**. 9a Calle 5-63, Zona 1, **Guatemala City**. Tel: 26-807.

▶ **Hotel Piño Montano**. Kilometer 259, Pan American Highway. **Huehuetenango**. Tel: (Guatemala City) 310-761.

▶ **Plaza**. Vía 7, 6-16, Zona 4, **Guatemala City**. Tel: 63-173.

▶ **Ramada Antigua**. 9 Calle Poniente y Carretera a Ciudad Vieja, **Antigua**. Tel: 032-0011; in U.S. 1-800-2RAMADA.

▶ **Rancho Grande Inn**. Calle Rancho Grande, **Panajachel**. Tel: 062-1554.

▶ **Hotel Santo Tomás. Chichicastenango**. Tel: 056-1061.

▶ **Tucán Dugu. Lívingston**. Tel: (Guatemala City) 31-5213.

▶ **Savannah. Flores**. Tel: Call "Operator, Flores."

▶ **Posada de la Selva** (Jungle Lodge). **Tikal**. Tel: (Guatemala City) 76-0294.

▶ **Turicentro Marimonte**. **El Relleno–Río Dulce**. Tel: (Guatemala City) 31-4437.

▶ **Tikal Inn**. **Tikal**. Contact by telegraph.

▶ **Villa Maya**. **Flores**. Tel: Hotel Maya Internacional 081-1208.

▶ **Hotel Visión Azul**. **Panajachel**. Tel: 062-1426.

THE
YUCATAN
CARIBBEAN
RESORTS

By Susan Wagner

The Yucatán peninsula is one of Mexico's most exotic areas. Though part of the mainland, for much of its history it has been isolated geographically as well as psychologically from the rest of the country. Today, linked to the outside world by superhighways and international flights, the Yucatán somehow manages to remain apart, retaining the mystery of its long and fabulous past.

Over a thousand years ago the peninsula was the center of the great Mayan civilization. Only now, however, are the mysteries of that civilization being explained (archaeologists recently deciphered the key to the ancient Mayan glyphs). Names that conjure up this ancient glory—Chichén Itzá, Uxmal, Labná, Kabah, Tulum, Cobá—dot the map of the Yucatán and tantalize travellers who have the time to make detours. Those who don't have the time, can still hear the ancient Mayan language spoken in the streets of the Yucatán's towns and villages, see natives wearing the traditional *huipil* (a white shift with embroidered neck and hemlines), and eat dishes made from ancient recipes such as *pollo pibil* (chicken seasoned with *anchiote,* a local herb, wrapped in banana leaves, and cooked in a hole in the ground).

The Yucatán peninsula comprises three states: Quintana Roo, encompassing the eastern third of the peninsula, including Cozumel, Isla Mujeres, and Cancún; Yucatán, which takes in much of the northern third of the peninsula and includes the charming colonial city of Mérida as well as two of the country's most important archaeological sites, Chichén Itzá and Uxmal; and Campeche, the little-developed state encompassing much of the western third of the peninsula. It is easy to understand why many travellers, including resort-goers, prefer the Yucatán to other parts of the country. The exceptionally calm and clear waters; the feeling of being in an unspoiled place that one gets in spite of the small pockets of development; and the sense that you are surrounded by living history make the Yucatán virtually irresistible.

CANCUN

Cancún looks like Miami, acts like Mexico, and delivers the best of both: the kind of endless beaches that you fantasize about in wintertime dreams; turquoise water that comes in a painter's-palette of different shades; beautiful white sand that doesn't burn the feet; an assortment of luxurious resort hotels; and enough nightlife and sports activities to keep even the most energetic traveller satisfied. For snorkeling or scuba diving enthusiasts, Cancún is among the world's top dive sites. And then there are the Mayan ruins.

MAJOR INTEREST

A day at any beach
Snorkeling
Shopping at the Plaza Caracol
Dinner at a lagoon-side restaurant
Ruinas del Rey
Xel-há National Park
Mayan ruins at Tulum

Nothing in Cancún is middle-aged—it's either centuries old or brand-new. That's because, developed from scratch, with an eye on the comfort and convenience of large groups of tourists, Cancún was built to be the flagship of

Fonatur's string of modern mega-resorts. Things that are difficult to do or to get to in other resorts are easily accessible in Cancún. It's also a place where you can drink the water and eat the salads. In fact, a water-purification plant is part of the basic infrastructure, and special care is taken in many other ways to avoid visitors' getting sick.

Scarcely 15 years old, Cancún has already made it to the big time, with over one million guests visiting annually, and the end nowhere in sight. Though its popularity may have made some taxi drivers and hotel employees brusque, life here generally goes along at a leisurely Mexican pace, with plenty of fun thrown into the bargain.

The Hotel Zone lies along a slender island that resembles the number seven. The island itself is connected to the mainland by two almost invisible bridges, one at each end of the "seven," with the Caribbean to the east and north and two lagoons to the west of, or inside, the long stem of the "seven." This narrow spit of land (never more than a quarter of a mile wide) has 14 miles of some of the world's most exquisite beaches. If you stay in the Hotel Zone, one of them is never more than a few minutes away.

Cancún's beautiful white-sand beaches aren't the area's only draw, however. Mexican tourists like the sleek steel-and-glass sophistication of the place, as well as the duty-free shopping. European visitors go for the unspoiled natural setting provided by the Nichupté and Bojórquez lagoons, the nature preserves in the middle of the Hotel Zone, and the unspoiled countryside that stretches for miles beyond the resort area. And U.S. and Canadian visitors like the great variety of things to do. Isla Mujeres, for example, a relatively undeveloped island much loved by Mexican vacationers, is a short ferry ride away, and Cozumel just a 15-minute flight (or a two-hour car-and-ferry trip). Cancún is also the resort gateway to some of Mexico's most splendid archaeological sites. Chichén Itzá, Tulum, and Cobá are just some of the Mayan sites that are within easy daytrip distance (for Chichén Itzá see the Mayan Mexico chapter).

The whole Cancún area is undergoing a construction boom, one that was underway long before Hurricane Gilbert hit in the fall of 1988. Most of the hurricane damage was repaired in a matter of months, and new places to stay, shop, and dine are opening up every day. Giant hotel, condo, and time-sharing complexes now stand side by side in the Hotel Zone, with the density increasing as the Paseo Kukulcán, the main drag, nears Punta (Point)

Cancún at the very elbow of the "seven." The boom, which represents the second phase of Cancún's development (based on the overwhelming success of the first), is almost completed. A clue to just how big it has been is the fact that Sotheby's real-estate department has a branch here. Miraculously, though, construction noises have not drowned out the birdsong, and hotels and restaurants along the road are generally tranquil.

The Yucatecan vegetation, on the other hand, is low and scrubby, which gives the older hotels as well as the newer ones a somehow unfinished look. The beaches and glittering shopping malls make up for the lack of tall, lush foliage, however. Chances are, as you're stretched out on a beach or searching for bargains, that you won't even miss it.

Paseo Kukulcán, named after the Mayan version of the Toltec serpent-god Quetzalcóatl, begins in Cancún City at its junction with Avenida Tulum, the main downtown thoroughfare, and runs due east across the "top" of the "seven" to its elbow at Punta Cancún, where it then swings to the south. This is the center of the area's action, and the elbow is its heart. (Things are a bit quieter farther south on the seven.)

Cancún City, at the western end of Paseo Kukulcán, is also booming. Hotels, shops, and restaurants are springing up all over town and figure to compete with those in the Hotel Zone before long.

If you drive north through town, you'll reach first Puerto Juárez and then Punta Sam, both departure points for the ferries to Isla Mujeres.

Avenida Tulum is a wide two-lane road that leads south from Cancún City to the airport and, in order, Puerto Morelos (the departure point for ferries to Cozumel), Akumal, Xel-há, and Tulum. It is lined with beach resorts and promises to be the next "in" spot. Puerto Aventuras, for example, a giant complex surrounding a marina about an hour's drive south of town, will have branches of Cancún's most popular restaurants in addition to its slips for private yachts.

CANCUN ISLAND
From the Bridge to Punta Cancún

Paseo Kukulcán, the spine of the Hotel Zone, begins downtown, where it branches off perpendicularly from

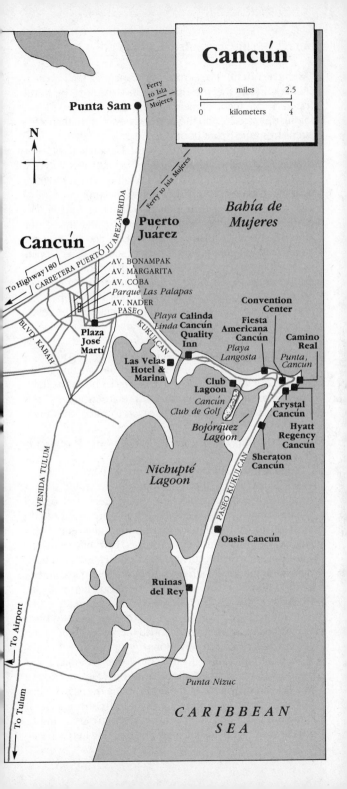

Cancún

| 0 | miles | 2.5 |
| 0 | kilometers | 4 |

Punta Sam

Ferry to Isla Mujeres

N

Ferry to Isla Mujeres

Puerto Juárez

Bahía de Mujeres

Cancún

To Highway 180

CARRETERA PUERTO JUAREZ-MERIDA

AV. BONAMPAK
AV. MARGARITA
AV. COBA
Parque Las Palapas
AV. NADER
PASEO

Playa Linda

Calinda Cancún Quality Inn

Convention Center

Fiesta Americana Cancún

Playa Langosta

Camino Real

Punta Cancún

BLVD. KABAH

Plaza José Martí

PASEO KUKULCAN

Las Velas Hotel & Marina

Club Lagoon

Cancún Club de Golf

Bojórquez Lagoon

Krystal Cancún

Hyatt Regency Cancún

Sheraton Cancún

AVENIDA TULUM

Nichupté Lagoon

PASEO KUKULCAN

Oasis Cancún

Ruinas del Rey

To Airport

To Tulum

Punta Nizuc

CARIBBEAN SEA

Avenida Tulum. The stretch of Cancún Island west of
Punta Cancún was the first area in Cancún to be developed. Today, many of the most popular places are located
along this stretch, and the beach is never more than a few
steps from the "front door."

Las Velas Hotel & Marina, on the lagoon side of Paseo
Kukulcán, just before the bridge, is one of a very few
deluxe hotels in Mexico to offer an all-inclusive program.
(All-inclusive prices include deluxe accommodations—
ask for a room with a Jacuzzi—all meals and snacks,
unlimited beverages, entertainment, sports instruction
and equipment rental, a gym, a pool, and all tips and
taxes.) Guests here feel as if they're staying in a colonial-
style village and can take advantage of two beaches—one
for water sports and one for resting and relaxing—as well
as a freshwater pool. (A small lagoon is a few steps away;
the Caribbean beach, Playa Linda, is just across the road.)
The daily schedule of activities available at Las Velas includes water sports, aerobics, and dance classes, as well
as arts and crafts and Spanish lessons.

Extasis, one of the newest discos in Cancún, is also
nearby. For the moment, there seem to be more lights
and action on the outside than there are inside, but this
huge place only needs a big season to catch on. Condo
owners and locals who like to dance but want to avoid the
crowds at Christine's and La Boom, nearby, are slowly
discovering Extasis.

The **Calinda Cancún Quality Inn**, on the ocean side of
Paseo Kukulcán, is the first hotel on the other side of
bridge. A moderately priced establishment, and one of
the first on the scene, the Calinda has many advantages in
addition to its location. A marina for sightseeing boats
(including excursions to Isla Mujeres) is within easy walking distance over the bridge, as is the **Plaza Náutilus**, a
new shopping mall with over 70 good boutiques. Guests
at the Calinda, many of whom arrive on charter flights
from the States, are friendly and give the impression that
they know each other. A new tower has recently been
completed next door, and is much the better choice for a
room when making reservations.

Step into **Maxime's**, next to the Hotel Casa Maya, just
up the beach from the Calinda, and you'll feel as if you're
in a French provincial home far from the tropics. (In fact,
this was once the home of a mayor of Cancún.) Floral
wallpaper, French country furniture, soft music, and of
course the French cuisine itself make dining here a pleas-

ant change of pace—even if you find the price of the soothing, lacy ambience on your bill.

The **Club Lagoon**, about halfway to Punta Cancún on Nichupté Lagoon, is something entirely different. This small hotel is an oasis among the larger resort properties and offers a degree of tranquillity and intimacy that some of the others can't. The décor has a preppy look, and it's the only hotel in town that feels as if it's a private club. The rooms have patios where you can read and relax, and there are a surprising number of facilities for such a small place. The bar on stilts overlooking the lagoon is one of the prettiest places in town to watch the sunset, and the cheery outdoor restaurant is one of the best places to have breakfast.

Carlos 'n' Charlie's, a branch of the ubiquitous restaurant chain, overlooks the lagoon but doesn't make much of the view. No matter. Everybody goes to this restaurant at least once, and no one seems to care that the raised dining room gets hot (despite the ceiling fans); the crowd, the waiters' pranks, and the funny menus make customers forget the temperature, and the live music keeps the place jumping. No reservations here, so be prepared to wait in line, especially on weekends. You're sure to make new friends while you wait.

The old **Pok-Ta-Pok Golf Club**, now called the Cancún Club de Golf, is on the lagoon side on one of the arms of land that separates Laguna Nichupté from the smaller Laguna Bojórquez. The 18-hole course, which was designed by Robert Trent Jones, winds around Mayan ruins and beautiful homes, and is open to the public; Tel: 3-0871.

Jalapeno's, in La Hacienda, a sidewalk shopping center, offers an all-you-can-eat breakfast buffet that's guaranteed to fill you up for the day. Their lunch is good too. And after your meal you can take a dip in their pool.

Sometimes it seems as if half of Mexico is wearing Hard Rock Café T-shirts. In Cancún, the **Hard Rock Café** is hidden away in the Plaza Lagunas Mall, across the street from the Fiesta Americana Cancún (not to be confused with the Fiesta Americana Plaza), but its popularity makes it easy to find—just follow the crowds. The dark, panelled walls, blue-and-white checkered tablecloths, the best hamburgers in Cancún, and the snappy English-speaking waiters and waitresses are some of the reasons for its success. They don't accept reservations here, however, so be prepared to wait in line—though there are usually no lines at lunchtime.

At the Point

The area around Punta Cancún is where you'll find the greatest concentration of large hotels, the best and biggest shopping mall, and the Cancún Convention Center, all of which combine to make this the most exciting area in town.

The **Fiesta Americana Cancún**, just west of the point on the Bahía de Mujeres, looks like a pastel-colored Mediterranean village, and is especially popular with tour groups. All its rooms have sea views, balconies, and mini-bars, and Friday López, a friendly bar with soft jazz music, is near the front door. The Plaza Caracol mall, the Costa Blanca mall, and the Hard Rock Café are all a few minutes' walk away.

The **Plaza Caracol** is a sight in itself. One of Mexico's newest malls, it's an air-conditioned delight with two floors of the best boutiques in town as well as several good restaurants. The décor is sleek and modern, and most of the merchandise is top drawer. **Whitefield's, Julio,** and **Suceso's,** all on the second floor, are among the better boutiques here, and Aca Joe and Fiorucci can be found on the first floor, along with LuLu's Parfumerie and Enny Cano, the shop of one of Mexico's top designers. Best of all, if you find yourself on a shopping spree and run out of pesos, there's a money exchange at the base of the escalator.

Savio, an Italian restaurant in the mall with a green, white, and gray Art-Deco décor, is a good place to stop for a drink while you're shopping. **Karl's Keller,** which specializes in German cuisine, and the **Casa Salsa,** where Mexican specialties are served up with a Mexican floor show in the evenings, are also located in the mall.

Costa Blanca, a pink-and-white open-air mall next door to the Plaza Caracol, has a small but good selection of stores; the silver shop here is one of the best anywhere. **La Mansion,** also in the mall, is another place that offers Mexican food with a lively floor show.

The Convention Center, almost at the point itself, is distinguished by its circular design and a soaring sculpture, and was one of the first structures built along this stretch of the zone. **El Parian,** the mall surrounding it, was the first and only place to shop on the island until just a few years ago. Today it's the site of frequent special events, including a colorful folkloric dance performance almost every night; watch for signs around town for other events. There's also a beautiful **archaeological museum** tucked away in the Convention Center. This is the place to learn about the area as well as to see some of its ancient Mayan treasures.

Daddy O, a new five-million-dollar disco with the latest in laser light technology, is across Paseo Kukulcán from the Convention Center.

The 1988 hurricane did serious damage to the beaches of the three hotels on the point, but they are being reconstituted and should be in good shape by the 1989–1990 season.

The **Camino Real** virtually sits on the point by itself, surrounded by the Caribbean on three sides. Slightly recessed from the hustle and bustle around it, the Camino Real has its own man-made lagoon as well as a pool and four lighted tennis courts. All rooms have private balconies with an ocean view, and all are equipped with minibars. (Some rooms even come with king-sized beds.) This is also one of the best places in Cancún to snorkel—if you have the patience required to wade out to the end of a rock jetty.

The **Hyatt Regency Cancún** is situated just around the point from the Camino Real. Its 14-story atrium aside, the pool is the real pièce de résistance here. Tiled lounges and tables (for drinks) are built into it so that guests can tan, cool off, and read the paper all at once. The bar area upstairs overlooking the ocean is also fun (it's linked to the Krystal Cancún pool still farther around the point). Note: There are two Hyatts in town. The Hyatt Caribe Cancún, a smaller, moderately priced hotel, is a few minutes to the south. Specify the Hyatt Regency when you get in a taxi.

Everyone seems to stop in at the **Krystal Cancún** next door sooner or later. Maybe it's because there's a certain mystique about the place. Then again, when the live music starts to play in its lobby bars (usually in summer) this is one of the liveliest spots in town. Something always seems to be going on in the pool area as well, and all sunbathers have to do is pull up their chairs to get a view of the action on the beach below.

The Krystal is also the location of the first **Bogart's** in Mexico, and the word about this outrageous restaurant has spread fast. Though it is no longer unique (others have opened in Ixtapa and Puerto Vallarta), the layout of this one somehow makes it seem classier than its brother restaurants. The décor is Moroccan, complete with peacock chairs, shimmering pools and fountains, and live piano music, and the effect is convincing enough to make you want to dress up to play the part. The prices may be high, the service a bit snooty, and the food not as good as it should be on some nights, but it's worth checking out all the same.

The first **Christine's**, another knockout, also made its debut in the Krystal. The founders borrowed many of their ideas from Acapulco discos, combined them with state-of-the-art electronics, and then launched this winner (which eventually became the flagship of a chain of discos). The crowd is better dressed and a few years older here than in other discos in Cancún, and the line out front, the steep cover charge, and the rude treatment dished out at the door don't seem to discourage anyone.

From the Krystal to Punta Nizuc

The long stretch of Paseo Kukulcán that runs from the Mauna Loa Shopping Center south to Punta Nizuc, where Club Med is located, is the scene of the greatest amount of construction in Cancún. As you round the point coming from town, or drive up from the airport past Punta Nizuc, it quickly becomes apparent that it will be chock-a-block with giant resort hotels in no time flat. (Most of the structures on the ocean side of this stretch are condos or hotels. Shopping centers are sprinkled in among the hotels on the lagoon side.)

The **Sheraton Cancún** is located a few minutes' ride south of the Krystal. Low and spread out, this self-contained resort hotel is built in the shape of a Mayan pyramid. If it's peace and quiet you crave, ask for a room at the southern end of the building. During the day the sprawling pool with swim-up bar is the center of the action, but the Sheraton also has a small but good shopping arcade, a fitness center, six lighted tennis courts, and several restaurants.

The **Oasis Cancún**, with over 900 of its eventual 1,200 rooms open, is already up and running. When completed, it promises to be a self-contained city, with an enormous pool, an exquisite stretch of beach, and a clientele comprised of Europeans and group travellers.

Two of the most popular restaurants in town are also located on this stretch overlooking Laguna Bojórquez: Orquideas and Gypsy's Pampered Pirate. Both offer Polynesian-style décor under thatched roofs, and both serve up plenty of candlelit tropical romance. **Orquideas** is a bit more elaborate, its dining room on a porch overlooking the water; ask for a table near the railing. **Gypsy's Pampered Pirate** is less formal but just as romantic. Most of the restaurant is on stilts facing the water, but the room is relatively closed and there isn't much of a view.

Lorenzillo's, nestled in the southern corner of the lagoon, looks like a hut where a pirate might have stored his loot (legend has it that the real Lorenzillo *was* a pirate in these parts). Reserve a table outside overlooking the water, but go early and stop for a drink at the bar. This was one of the first restaurants on the scene and locals are loyal to it, so if you want to find out what's happening in town, this is the place to find out.

The **Ruinas del Rey**, one of the Hotel Zone's most interesting attractions, is a little past midway between Punta Cancún and Punta Nizuc. Watch for a small sign on the lagoon side and follow the dirt road to this small archaeological site. The ruins are surrounded by lush vegetation, and you will feel as if you've discovered them yourself. (You'll also forget—at least for a while—that there are so many new and modern buildings close by.) There is a small entry fee, and for a nominal price the guard will give a brief tour of the site (in Spanish).

Just across from the entrance to the ruins a set of stairs leads up through the jungle to a pleasant restaurant overlooking Paseo Kukulcán and the sea. This, too, offers a quiet change of pace. The only traffic out here is the cars of sightseers who stop at the lookout point across the road and trucks heading to the many construction sites nearby. Inside, fishnets and nautical memorabilia stand in for décor. If you don't have a car, the restaurant will have a taxi pick you up, or you can arrange your own and have the driver return at an appointed time.

Sports in Cancún

Cancún is a haven for water-sports lovers. Coming here without a snorkel mask would almost be as big a mistake as forgetting your bathing suit. If you do bring your own mask, you'll be able to enjoy some of the world's most glorious underwater sights—while others are still waiting in line to rent equipment. Waterskiing, deep-sea fishing, jet-skiing, scuba diving (and excursions), parasailing, windsurfing, Hobie Cats, and even kayaking—all can be arranged at a number of marinas. If your hotel doesn't have a water-sports center the following will be happy to help you: the Hotel Playa Blanca (which offers wind-surfing lessons); the Hotel Caribe Mar; the Hotel Viva; the Hotel Casa Maya; the Aquaquin Marina at the Camino Real (Tel: 3-0100); Scuba Cancún (Tel: 3-1011); Pez Vela (Tel: 3-0952); or Marina Jet Ski (Tel: 3-0766)

Deep-sea fishing boats can be chartered at any marina. Sailfish and dolphin are caught March–July; bluefin tuna in May; blue and white marlin in April and May; and kingfish and wahoo May–September.

CANCUN CITY

Cancún City is no longer the rough-and-ready town it was in the early 1970s, when only 200 people—most of them construction workers—lived here. Today its resident population is closer to 50,000, and it offers all the amenities of a city twice that size.

Paseo Kukulcán becomes Avenida Cobá at the Plaza José Martí. Cobá then crosses Avenida Tulum, Cancún City's north-south main street. Two of the town's favorite restaurants are off Cobá to the right just past the plaza and the gas station, where the road turns off to Avenida Nader. **Du Mexique**, one of the newer restaurants in town, dares to be different. Nouvelle Mexican cuisine with a French flavor is served in an art-gallery setting (in fact, the art-work on the walls is for sale) as classical music plays in the background. Some residents consider this to be the best restaurant in town; the price, happily, does not reflect it. Reservations are a must; Tel: 4-1077. **La Dolce Vita**, almost next door at Avenida Cobá 87, looks like a green-and-white soda fountain and serves up hearty portions of Italian dishes. Bright and well-lit at all hours of the day, it's a perfect place for people watching.

Bucanero, a dark "pirate's lair" nearby, was one of the first restaurants in Cancún City, and it still has a loyal following of repeat customers who like its prices and the friendly staff.

Gifri's, up a set of narrow stairs just past Du Mexique, is something of a secret. Modern, comfortable, and cozy, this piano bar is like a small, private club—and anything small in Cancún is a treat. Guests sit in plush gray ban-quettes and listen to the music as they chat. More people want to get in than can fit in, however, so you may have to wait at the door until someone leaves. The bar is related to **L'Alternative**, a sleek, ultra-modern French restaurant at the corner of Kukulcán and Avenida Bonampak that caters to sophisticated high rollers.

The hustle and bustle of Cancún City begins around the corner. Ki-huic, the market, on Avenida Tulum near Avenida Cobá, has every souvenir you'd expect to find, at slightly higher prices than you'd normally pay for them (everything has to travel a little farther to get here). *Huipiles,* hammocks, and sisal bags are among the locally produced items sold.

The city is expanding to the south and west. Several shopping malls have already opened, along with a number of hotels (the Hotel America is one) that Canadian budget travellers like. (Their rates reflect the fact that they're not on the beach, which is a few minutes away by car.) But then, everything seems to be more economical downtown.

At the San Francisco de Assis Supermarket you can find anything you might need and exchange money, too. **Coco's**, across the four-lane Avenida Tulum, is a crazy place where everyone talks to everyone as they enjoy their delicious taco plates. **Pop's**, in the neighborhood around the bus station, sells toiletries and sundries imported from the United States for exorbitant prices and is the closest thing to an American-style cafeteria in greater Cancún, with a menu that includes hamburgers and milkshakes as well as enchiladas and huevos rancheros. Local businessmen like the place for breakfasts and light lunches.

La Habichuela ("The Stringbean"), one block behind the movie theater at Margarita 25, next to the Parque Las Palapas, opened for business when Cancún did and remains popular. You can dine under a tree in a cozy garden here and feel far away from tourists.

Plaza Bonita, a two-story pastel-colored maze of good shops and boutiques in an uncrowded colonial-style setting, is located downtown near Mercado 28 (a public market) and is a well-kept secret that few visitors know about.

EXCURSIONS FROM CANCUN

Although it would take several vacations to see and do everything available in Cancún, some travellers nonetheless feel the need for a change of pace. Excursions offer plenty of such opportunities, none more so than a trip to one of the nearby ancient Mayan sites.

There are over 2,000 archaeological sites in the state of Quintana Roo alone—almost one-fifth the country's total. Tulum is one of the most visited of all.

Tulum

Tulum was one of the few walled Mayan cities. According to legend, Mayan kings came here to vacation. One look at the beautiful beach below this striking site and you'll understand why.

To get there from Cancún, head south on Avenida Tulum, which becomes Highway 307 south of town. Tulum is about 128 km (80 miles) down the coast over the latter, a smooth two-lane road. Be sure to fill up if you're driving, however; there are no gas stations en route.

Many outfits run daytrips to Tulum; most stop at Xel-há (see below). Still, this is one excursion where renting a car and going on your own is advisable. Several new resorts are being developed along this stretch of coastline, with its wide, sloping beaches and offshore reef, and in some places the palm trees grow almost to the water's edge, providing welcome shade. Just look for the signs and follow the dirt roads off to the left (going down) through the jungle. **Chemuyil** and **Xacaret** beaches are particularly primitive and pretty, and **Puerto Aventuras** promises to be a major resort when it is completed. **Akumal**, about 100 km (60 miles) south of Cancún, is already up and running.

Xel-há National Park, one of the best places in the country to see marine life without getting wet, has a lagoon set aside for observation only (diving is prohibited). Food to bring the fish to the surface as you walk through the park can be purchased at the entrance but is usually unnecessary. Those who like to snorkel can explore a special area behind the entrance building on their own. Conditions are ideal on bright sunny days, but never go on a weekend (too crowded). Snorkel equipment can be rented at the park; two restaurants serve snacks.

Tulum itself is about half a mile off the main highway. The parking lot, usually filled with tour buses, is right in front of the entrance to the site. Admission tickets can be purchased in a booth to the left of the site, where the restrooms are as well.

The rather shoddy parking lot is surrounded by lean-to shops—it's better to bring your own picnic and buy only the soda or beer here. Then head over to one of the beaches off the highway to have your picnic.

Tulum dates from the sixth century (one stela found at the site was dated to A.D. 564). It is an unusually compact site, with some 60 buildings, over 20 of which are within the walls of the city. The site has not been completely excavated, and the partially buried rocks strewn around can make walking difficult, so be sure to wear sneakers or comfortable shoes that will not slip on hard surfaces.

Archaeology buffs who have seen other Mayan sites like Chichén Itzá may be a bit disappointed, and you'll have to use your imagination to form a picture of how the city must have looked in its heyday. Still, its proximity to Cancún, the short distances between buildings (which make it easy to explore the site), and the beautiful beach outside compensate for the lack of reconstruction and the relatively small size of the site.

El Castillo, the most impressive structure at Tulum, stands on a bluff overlooking some of the most beautiful turquoise-colored water in the entire Caribbean. (And the white-sand beach below invites visitors in for a dip after they explore the site.) Steep steps lead to the top of El Castillo, but the climb is worth it, both for the panoramic view of the ocean and the overview of the site. There's also a temple with two rooms on top.

The Temple of the Descending God, to the left and behind El Castillo, and the Temple of the Frescoes, to the west, are also interesting, their murals well preserved. And the House of Columns nearby is one of the most photogenic structures at the site.

Cobá

Truly dedicated archaeology buffs can continue on from Tulum to Cobá, about 40 km (25 miles) north and west of Tulum. Spread out over 80 square miles (though most of its excavated buildings are clustered in a much smaller area dotted with lakes), Cobá is one of the largest Mayan cities discovered to date, as well as one of the least-known Mayan sites, and could eventually prove to be as important as Chichén Itzá. (Experts say that it will take at least 50 years to excavate it completely.)

You'll really need to stay at least one night to explore this site fully (as well as to see the sound-and-light show in the evening). A modern hotel—the **Villa Arqueológica**, which is run by Club Med—is three minutes away from the entrance to the site on the shore of one of the lakes. Bikes can be rented to help you get around; an ancient road connects many of the structures at the site.

The Nohoch Mul pyramid, with its 120-step ascent, is the highest pyramid in the northern Yucatán; the Grupa de Cobá, with its corbeled Mayan arches, lies in the middle of a sprawling patio; the Macanxoc group stands on a lake shore (and includes well-preserved stelae that scholars have found relatively easy to decipher); and the remnants of colored friezes can be seen on the interior and exterior walls of the Pinturas group.

Though the jungle reclaims many structures almost as fast as they are cleared, Cobá gives you an almost palpable sense that you are surrounded by ancient history. You will find yourself marveling at the fact that you are indeed walking on roads that the Mayans walked, and the thick vegetation surrounding the structures will sometimes make you feel as if their Mayan architects disappeared into the jungle just a few minutes ago.

Other Excursions from Cancún

There are many more excursions to choose from in and around Cancún. One of the most popular is the "air bridge" to Cozumel. The Aero Caribe flight, leaving from Cancún airport, takes about 15 minutes. For those in no hurry, the ferry to Cozumel leaves from the marina next to the Calinda Quality Inn.

El Tropical leaves from the Playa Langosta dock (between the Hotel Casa Maya and the Villas Tacul) for Isla Mujeres every day at 3:30 P.M. The boat follows the Cancún coastline east and takes you to El Garrafón on the southern tip of Isla Mujeres, where guests can snorkel and swim. An open bar, use of snorkel equipment, and snorkeling instructions are included. *El Tropical* returns to the Playa Langosta dock around 8:00 P.M.

Or try a trip on the glass-bottomed trimaran *Manta*. Lunch, live entertainment, and an open bar are part of the fun before the boat reaches Isla Mujeres. The *Manta* leaves from the Caribmar pier every morning at 11:00 A.M. Tel: 3-0348.

The Columbus, a 62-foot motorized replica of the *Nina,* takes guests on a sunset cruise complete with three-course dinner (steak or lobster) and an open bar. The boat sails at 4:30 from the Royal Mayan Yacht Club and returns around 7:30.

Fun lovers should try the Pirates' Night adventure, a trip that was invented for party people. The fun begins when you dress up like a pirate, and there are plenty of surprises in store on the way to Treasure Island and back. Boats leave from the Playa Langosta dock at 6:00 P.M. and return by 11:00.

Intermar Caribe can arrange all of these cruises; Tel: 4-4266. Or contact the travel agent at your hotel. Intermar also runs trips to Tulum, Chichén Itzá, and Cozumel, as well as scuba diving excursions. With nine offices scattered throughout the Cancún area, they're easy to find, and their pickup point is the marina next door to the Club Lagoon.

The road heading south out of town isn't the only one that leads to adventure. Following Avenida Tulum north will take you to Highway 180, which heads south and west, and eventually will bring you to Chichén Itzá, the most famous Mayan site, as well as to Mérida, the colonial capital of the state of Yucatán and gateway to Mexico's other major Mayan archaeological treasures. Flying is much the better option, however, unless you have plenty of time.

The charming island of Isla Mujeres, on the other hand, is just a short distance north of Cancún via ferry boat; the ferries leave from Puerto Juárez or Punta Sam (see "Getting Around," below, for details).

ISLA MUJERES

Isla Mujeres, a relatively undeveloped island five miles north of Cancún, is not the place for those who want to display their diamonds or show off their haute couture. Instead, it's the kind of place where no one need wear anything more formal than cutoffs and a T-shirt, the perfect resort for those who love the beachcomber's life. You can leave everything but the bare essentials back in Cancún; some purists even leave their shoes behind and just pack sandals.

MAJOR INTEREST

Unhurried island pace
Beautiful beaches on its western side

From the early 1500s, when the Spanish explorer Francisco Hernández de Córdova landed here, until very recently, Isla Mujeres—named for the statues of women that Córdova saw when he came ashore—had remained virtually unknown to everyone except its Mayan inhabitants. After the Spanish left of their own accord, the island remained isolated and was used as a base by the likes of Morgan and Jean Lafitte only occasionally. The United States built a naval base here during the Second World War, but its real popularity came about as a result of the development of Cancún.

The island itself is only five and a half miles long and a mile wide. Its only town is situated at its northern end, and most of its hotels, shops, and restaurants are within easy walking distance of each other. Otherwise, don't expect to find any neon lights, traffic jams, or nightlife here.

According to local legend, a pirate named Mundaca built a hacienda on the island at great expense in order to woo a local beauty known as La Triguena. His plan worked for a while, but La Triguena ultimately spurned him and the hacienda was left to the jungle. The ruins of it, about two-thirds of the way down the island at the edge of the Laguna Makax—taxi drivers know the spot—can be visited after you've had a chance to explore the town.

The remainder of the island is hilly, the vegetation along the side of its main road low and scrubby, with much of it uninhabited. Beaches on the way to El Garrafón, at the southern tip of the island, are pretty and unspoiled, however, and make ideal spots for picnics or swimming. At **Playa Lancheros**, on the southwestern side of the island, you can take a ride on a turtle's back or pet a sleeping shark. (The path to Mundaca's hacienda is across the street from the entrance to the beach.) **Playa Indios**, the next beach to the north, is also a favorite with visitors. Generally speaking, swimming conditions on the eastern side of the island are not as good as on the western side, which fronts the calm, shallow waters of the Bahía de Mujeres.

The tiny town on Isla Mujeres is the kind of place where a visitor could go barefoot right through dinner and nobody would mind. Breakfast and dinner in a

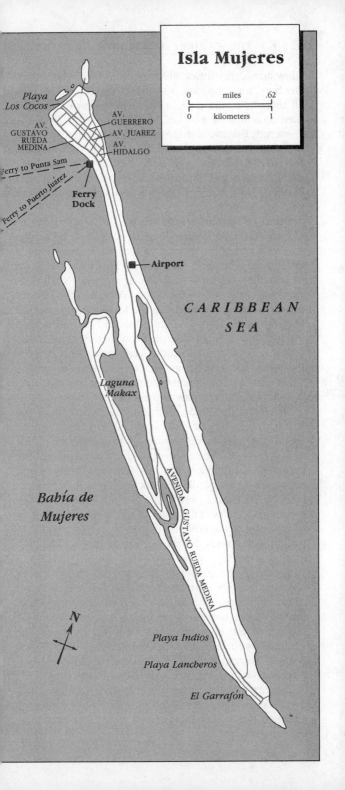

Isla Mujeres

| 0 | miles | .62 |
| 0 | kilometers | 1 |

Playa
Los Cocos

AV.
GUERRERO
AV.
GUSTAVO
RUEDA
MEDINA
AV. JUAREZ
AV.
HIDALGO

Ferry to Punta Sam

Ferry to Puerto Juárez

Ferry
Dock

■ Airport

CARIBBEAN
SEA

Laguna
Makax

Bahía de
Mujeres

AVENIDA GUSTAVO RUEDA MEDINA

N

Playa Indios

Playa Lancheros

El Garrafón

"downtown" restaurant are the social highlights of any day here, and lingering over drinks and a meal is about all there is to do at night (though sometimes there is dancing at **Buho's**, a beachfront disco).

Avenida Gustavo Rueda Medina is the main road on the island. In town, Avenidas Hidalgo, Juárez, and Guerrero run parallel to it. The *zócalo* and city hall are tucked away at the eastern end of town between Juárez and Hidalgo. The ferry dock, farther to the west, is the center of most of what action there is.

Perlas del Caribe, a simple hotel for those who don't like to be totally isolated, stands on a small hill at the southern end of the downtown area within easy walking distance of everything else (guests can walk to the beach in less than ten minutes). The sea crashes under the windows (most rooms have a bay view) and the friendly restaurant/bar is popular with the locals. The **Posada del Mar**, Rueda Medina 15, at the north end of town next to the lighthouse, is likewise plain but has air-conditioned rooms, a restaurant/bar, and a small pool. What you pay for here is the location: good beaches are just across the street and Los Cocos, one of the best beaches anywhere, is only a five-minute walk to the south.

The **Hotel del Prado**, at the northernmost tip of the island, is the biggest and most modern hotel on the island. Although the décor is rather sterile and the rooms a bit spare (reserve one overlooking the ocean, not the entrance), the public areas are attractive. The pool and restaurant are especially pleasant, and the nearby beach is nice. Na Ba Lam, a pretty 12-room place where all the rooms have a view of the water, is on the street leading up to it. Almost all the other hotels are on the main road and various side streets downtown, within easy walking distance of a beach.

Gomar, at the corner of Hidalgo and Madero, is an open-air colonial-style restaurant that seems to have taken a bit more care with its décor than other restaurants on the island. Lobster is the house specialty here, with other seafood dishes giving it a run for its money. In addition, live music strolls in from time to time. **Ciro's**, Avenida Matamoras 11, is a plain, air-conditioned place that tends to be a bit more sedate than Gomar.

The airport, about a third of the way down the island on its eastern side, cannot accommodate big commercial jetliners. Almost everything else of importance here is on its western side.

Maria's, an attractive French restaurant "out on the island," is more elegant than the other restaurants on Isla Mujeres, and is just off the main road about halfway to El Garrafón. The restaurant itself is under a cool *palapa,* and there are also a few rooms to let as well as a marina; Tel: 2-0130.

El Garrafón, a national underwater park at the southern end of the island, was once a snorkelers' paradise. Unfortunately, today there are more people than fish, and the park is usually overcrowded with tourists who arrive in large groups (don't even think of going on Sundays). The combination of people and protruding rocks makes it difficult to enter the water, but for those who want to give it a shot there are dressing rooms and rental equipment available. Nearby is a Mayan temple where women worshipped the goddess of fertility, as well as a lighthouse, but neither is a very impressive sight.

COZUMEL

Cozumel is the kind of place you fall in love with without knowing exactly why. Observant travellers sense its uniqueness immediately, but the *reason* for it takes some figuring out. Eventually, you realize that the Mayan culture is more alive here than elsewhere, and Mayan facial and physical characteristics are more prevalent. At the same time, the island's size brings visitors into closer contact with the resident population, which seems to have a "live-and-let-live" attitude toward visitors. To those who gear down to its own special pace, Cozumel will reveal itself gently and gradually, and once it does you'll want to come back again and again.

MAJOR INTEREST

Unsurpassed scuba diving
Snorkeling at Laguna Chankanab
Strolling the *malecón* and back streets downtown

Isla Cozumel was isolated from the rest of the country until relatively recently. As a result, you'll still hear Mayan spoken here frequently. Likewise, many of the local women still wear *huipiles,* because nothing beats the heat better. At the same time, Cozumel is the only place in Mexico where you're likely to see people wearing full wet suits in the *zócalo,* looking like nothing so much as giant blackbirds against the bright blue summer sky. In fact, every other person here seems to have a diver's bag dangling over a shoulder; there seems to be a dive shop around every corner; and advertisements for the rental of underwater video cameras seem to fill every local newspaper and guidebook.

The strong cultural contrast between the Mayan presence and the emphasis on water sports stems from the island's history. The Maya have inhabited Cozumel since A.D. 300, when the island was used for religious festivals. The Spanish tried to take it in the early 1500s but were held off until 1543, when they finally gained control of the entire Yucatán. In the late 1500s the island's population was decimated by small pox and the few survivors packed up and headed back to the mainland. In fact, it was not until 1848 and the end of the Mexican War that the Maya began to slip back to their former island retreat. Cozumel remained relatively isolated from the outside world, however, until the Second World War, when the United States built an air base here.

After Jacques Cousteau discovered **Palancar Reef** in the early 1960s, scuba divers began to arrive in numbers, and they had the island to themselves until about 15 years ago, when Cancún opened its first hotel. Palancar Reef, off the southwestern coast of Cozumel, is ranked among the top five dive sites in the world. But Palancar isn't the only underwater attraction here. Practically the entire southwestern quarter of Cozumel is surrounded by the kind of underwater reefs that divers dream about, and visibility often exceeds 200 feet. Best of all, there seems to be a reef for every level of diving expertise. Beginners, for example, can head out to inspect a sunken plane in the "front yard" of the Hotel La Ceiba. Elsewhere, coral spires rise 60–70 feet from the ocean floor. It's no wonder that over 20 dive shops are listed in the Cozumel phone book—an enormous concentration for such a small place.

The face of Cozumel has also changed as it has become a popular port of call for ships cruising the Caribbean. Most fishermen in the island's main town, San Miguel de Cozumel, who used to own homes along Avenida Rafael Melgar, the town's main street—and also its *malecón—*

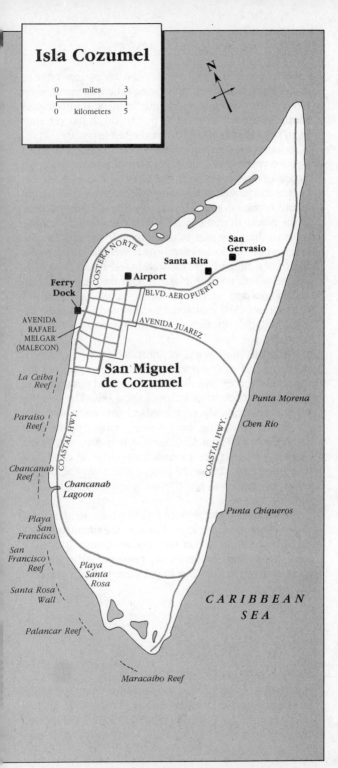

Isla Cozumel

0 miles 3
0 kilometers 5

N

COSTERA NORTE

Ferry Dock

AVENIDA RAFAEL MELGAR (MALECON)

Airport

Santa Rita

San Gervasio

BLVD. AEROPUERTO

AVENIDA JUAREZ

San Miguel de Cozumel

La Ceiba Reef

Paraiso Reef

Chancanab Reef

Chancanab Lagoon

Playa San Francisco

San Francisco Reef

Santa Rosa Wall

Palancar Reef

COASTAL HWY.

Playa Santa Rosa

COASTAL HWY.

Punta Morena

Chen Rio

Punta Chiqueros

CARIBBEAN SEA

Maracaibo Reef

have sold out to make way for the shops that cater to cruise-ship passengers. And though the merchandise offered here does not match the level of sophistication shoppers are accustomed to in Cancún, it has certainly been upgraded noticeably over the last few years.

In light of increasing competition from Cancún, about a dozen years ago Cozumel decided to improve its appeal to non-divers. Hotels were gradually upgraded and refurbished and new facilities were installed as well. Today, the greatest concentration of hotels is at the northwest corner of the island, from the Hotel Mayan Plaza south along the coast to the ferry pier in the center of San Miguel. The latter, where the cross-island road, Avenida Juárez, meets the coastal highway, is the undisputed center of activity on the island, and the major restaurants, stores, discos, and offices are all nearby. Other hotels, a handful of restaurants, some excellent beaches, and Chankanab Lagoon National Park are to the south (the coastal road links them all).

Only half the island is inhabited; the pancake-flat northern half of Cozumel is (with the exception of the northwest corner) given over to jungle and scrub growth, with half a dozen small archaeological sites. The beaches on the eastern side of the island are too rocky and rough for swimming, but picnics (bring your own) at spots such as Punta Chiqueros, Chen Rio, and Punta Morena—where there's a restaurant—offer an unspoiled and refreshing change of pace. Otherwise, the biggest event on the cross-island road is when an iguana or butterfly crosses.

Adventurous travellers can either bike to the small archaeological sites scattered around the island, or hire a taxi to take them to **San Gervasio** and **Santa Rita**, both post-Classic sites that have been restored. Make sure that the taxi driver knows how to get there before setting off, however.

NORTH OF TOWN

The **Mayan Plaza Hotel and Beach Club** is one of Cozumel's deluxe properties. This massive complex, which is situated on the coast at the end of the road leading north from town, is a haven for the kind of well-heeled traveller who wants to relax and doesn't care if he ever leaves the premises. All the rooms have balconies and ocean views, and the giant pool area and restaurants are tastefully done. The Mayan Plaza is a place where many of the island's pleasures "come to you." It stages great Mexican Fiesta nights, for example, and a number of excursion boats leave from the pier right off the beach. There is also a small shopping arcade on the lobby level.

Other, less elaborate properties, favorites of the island's visitors in the early days of its popularity, line the road—the Costera Norte—from the Mayan Plaza south into town. Most feature the kind of friendly ambience that only family-owned properties offer. Guests are usually divers (or friends of divers who have tagged along with the group) that have been coming to Cozumel for years. **El Cozumeleño**, next door to the Mayan Plaza, is one such hotel. The rooms here are old-fashioned and quite spacious, and those guests who aren't out on a dive or snorkeling usually spend the day lazing around the hotel's pool.

Puerto de Abrigo, the small marina south of the Hotel Mara, less than five minutes from town, is where fishermen weigh and show off their catches at the end of the day, and is the place to go to arrange deep-sea fishing expeditions.

SAN MIGUEL DE COZUMEL
North in Town

San Miguel looks as if it belongs under a tropical Christmas tree: Everything is mini-size, including the short, stocky residents, who look as if they had stepped out of a Mayan frieze.

The town that visitors see is laid out in square blocks. Avenida Juárez, the road that begins at the ferry pier and goes east across the island, divides the town into northern and southern halves. Streets to the north of Juárez are even-numbered and ascend by twos. Those to the south are odd-numbered and also ascend by twos. Most of the major shops and restaurants are located along Avenida Rafael Melgar, the seaside drive.

San Miguel is the kind of place that requires shoppers to *shop*. If you want to make a purchase, window shopping won't help you decide; displays here will give you only a vague idea of what's to be found inside. Instead, shoppers have to enter a store and really look around (many dedicated shoppers go to Cancún for the day). The entire island is a duty-free area, but tobacco and liquor are not included as duty-free items.

Resort wear and jewelry are the most popular purchases in San Miguel. Jewelry and small sculptures made from black coral are the real prizes, however. Cousteau discovered this coral at Palancar Reef, and it's extremely valuable because divers have to go to great depths to bring it up (it also takes 50 years to grow just one centimeter). **Roberto's** on Avenida Rafael Melgar is one of the best places to find it.

Cinco Soles, "uptown" at the corner of Calle 8 Norte and Avenida Melgar, is the place to begin your shopping spree; from there you can work your way south. Behind the usual stacks of T-shirts at Cinco Soles you will find folk art and clothes by Mexican designers that can't be found elsewhere.

One of Cozumel's most pleasant surprises is nearby on Avenida Melgar. The new **Cozumel Museum** is enchanting. Installed on two floors of a pink-and-white colonial-style building, it mixes culture and cuisine in a setting overlooking the ocean. Exhibits include diving memorabilia and archaeological relics, and breakfast and lunch are served on the upstairs balcony.

Galerías Galoba, farther down Avenida Melgar in the direction of the ferry pier, also has a good collection of handicrafts. Its selection of silver jewelry, on the other hand, is hidden away like a pirate's treasure in a separate section in the back; don't leave the premises until you've found it. **Aca Joe**, the all-time unisex favorite, is two blocks up from the ferry pier on Melgar.

Carlos 'n' Charlie's & Jimmy's Kitchen is the place for when you're in a party mood. The restaurant is situated on the second floor at the top of a staircase that leads up from a narrow doorway on Avenida Melgar, but you'll probably hear the racket before you find the door. The later the hour, the greater the pandemonium—the young beer-drinking crowd here comes revved up and ready to have a good time.

El Portal, on Melgar right across from the ferry terminal, is open on one side so that customers can watch the passing parade. Three meals a day are served in this informal place, and local businessmen wearing *guayabera* shirts drop in for breakfasts and quick snacks throughout the day.

South in Town

Las Palmeras, which also faces the ferry terminal, is popular as well, but for the moment El Portal is the better choice if you're planning to have anything more than a drink.

Las Campañas, one of Cozumel's first shops, is next door to Las Palmeras. This is the place for typical Mexican souvenirs and embroidered San Antonio dresses. **Los Balcones**, a few blocks south on Melgar, is one of the shops that caters to cruise-ship passengers, its top-of-the-line selection of decorative items well displayed behind its colonial-style façade.

Pepe's Centro, one block east of Melgar on Avenida 5 Sur, was one of the first restaurants in town. Although it remains a winner, **Pepe's Grill** on Melgar has taken over the number-one spot in local popularity polls. The latter manages to be both informal and romantic at the same time. It has a certain elegance that most places in San Miguel lack and attracts people who want to have a special evening in a special place downtown.

Soberanis, at the southern end of Melgar in town, is a steak and seafood restaurant where those in the know have been going for years. It's an oldie but still goodie that serves up live music along with fresh meat and seafood dishes—and there's no need to dress up.

Anyone who doesn't stroll the streets parallel to Avenida Melgar is missing something. Although Avenida 5 Norte/Sur—the first street east of Melgar—is also built up, the streets to the east of it will give you some idea of what San Miguel was like before the crowds came. Pastel concrete-and-wood houses line these streets, and juice stands, a bakery, and tiny restaurants operate out of small frame houses.

The **Sports Page**, at the corner of Calle 2 Norte and Avenida 5 Norte, is for those who hate to miss the Big Game and like hamburgers and beer. This is a home-away-from-home kind of place: If a letter were sent to you here, you'd receive it.

Morgan's, a few doors down, is Cozumel's most romantic restaurant. It's in the old wood-frame Customs House, the interior of which has been polished to a polyurethane sheen that reflects the candlelight, brass fittings, and shimmering table settings. This is a place to linger over dinner and concentrate on your dinner partner, rather than the passing crowd, while the live music plays in the background. Nearby is a small open-air market selling souvenirs. Take the time to chat with the characters that own the stalls here, too.

Casa Denis, a plain pipe-rack place for adventurous palates on the southern side of the Plaza del Sol, is a typical Yucatecan restaurant in a typical Yucatecan house. Oil cloth covers the tables and the tableware doesn't match. You can dine in the dining room, which has a cement floor, or out on the patio under a tree. And they'll explain the menu to you if you ask.

Sooner or later everyone will end up at **El Foco**, Avenida 5 Sur 13, for tacos. They even taste good standing up if you devour them—which is how you might have to eat here.

La Concha, Avenida 5 Sur 141, is one of the prettiest stores in San Miguel. Housed in an old colonial-style building, it has a good selection of folk art, tastefully displayed. That's the good news. The bad news is that the store seems to open and close at the owner's will, so it's best to call ahead and see if the place is open before you go. Tel: 2-1270.

El Acuario, Avenida Melgar at Calle 11 Sur, is the nearest thing to a "citified" restaurant in town, and is the place to go if you want to get dressed up. It's built in the old aquarium and decorated like a corporate boardroom with nautical touches, so it's no surprise that seafood stars on the menu. The town's two top discos are across the street (see below).

SOUTH OF TOWN

La Ceiba, a hotel designed for divers (and run by one until a short time ago) south of town on the beach next to the cruise-ship terminal, is a pleasant, friendly, no-nonsense kind of place with two charming restaurants (the seaside dining room is particularly good) and a small pool. Its small rooms reflect the fact that their occupants spend most of their time underwater anyway. You can dive right off the beach here, or snorkel out (the whole site is superb for snorkeling) to see a plane wreck 50 feet offshore. The hotel's formula pays off: Guests come back year after year.

The **Villa Blanca**, a smaller hotel across the street from La Ceiba, is a talk-to-everybody kind of place for those who like their digs to be small and cozy. Set back from the road, with nicely gardened grounds, the Villa Blanca, like La Cieba, is popular with affluent divers (divers on a budget stay in smaller hotels or crash pads in town). You'll have to cross the road to get to the beach, however.

The **Fiesta Americana Sol Caribe** is one of Cozumel's largest hotels, the bar, pool, and restaurant gigantic by island standards. Be sure to request a room on the higher floors—and by no means accept one below lobby level. The tiny crescent-shaped beach across the road is a perfect place to learn to snorkel.

El Presidente, south of the Sol Caribe, is one of the old Cozumel favorites and the first of the large hotels on the island to fill up. The seaside bar/restaurant is tops—even eating at the bar is fun—and the pretty pool is shaded by palm trees. Travel and car-rental agencies at the hotel make arranging things easy, and there is usually some kind of live entertainment in the evenings. The affluent Mexicans and Americans here know that you never have to leave the premises to have a good time.

El Presidente is the last major hotel on the road going south. From here to the lighthouse at the southern end of the island only Playa San Francisco and Chankanab Lagoon National Park are of major interest.

Chankanab Lagoon, between El Presidente and Playa San Francisco, is a beautiful national park in an unspoiled area, well worth the entry fee. The swimming and snorkeling here are great. If you feed the fish crackers you'll be the most popular person in the water—and you'll even be able to hear them crunching the crackers. Snorkel equipment can be rented on the beach; a restaurant serves light lunches and drinks. In addition, amateur botanists love the botanical garden at the lagoon because its plants are clearly labelled. A replica of a Mayan house stands in the middle of it and is the perfect place to get out of the sun—and there's also a small boutique in the back of it.

Playa San Francisco is a place to make a day of it. Inner tubes and snorkel equipment can be rented on the beach, and you can eat in a beachside restaurant a few steps up from the sand or right on the sand under a private *palapa*. The swimming here is also excellent. Chances are you'll want to stay as long as you can.

Nightlife on Cozumel

Divers like to dance, too. Life after dark, like everything else at Cozumel, exists—but on a smaller scale. There are two discos, neither as elaborate as those found in Cancún, but the energy needed to keep the beat going until dawn (on weekends) is there. **Scaramouche**, the smaller of the two, attracts a younger crowd. If you go for the music this is your place. **Neptuno** is high tech and more sophisticated, with videos, lights, and the disco works. Both are on Avenida Melgar near the southern edge of town.

Mexican Fiesta nights are held at the Mayan Plaza, the Sol Caribe, and El Presidente hotels.

Sports on Cozumel

The underwater scenery in the clear Cozumel waters is exquisite. The waters on the western side of the island teem with colorful marine life and boast a wide variety of coral in sunken gardens. In fact, the reefs are world renowned for their beauty.

La Ceiba Reef is 120 yards long and 30 to 50 feet deep. An underwater trail has been laid out from the Hotel La Ceiba.

Paraiso Reef, off the beach in front of the Hotel El Presidente and 45 feet deep, is one of the best sites for night diving.

Chankanab Reef, 25 to 55 feet deep, is just south of the lagoon of the same name. It has beautiful coral formations and marine life, and is also a good site for night dives.

San Francisco Reef, a quarter mile long and 40 to 55 feet deep, is directly off of Playa San Francisco.

The **Santa Rosa Wall**, a drop-off that begins at 70 feet, is due south of San Francisco Reef. The beach in front of it is uninhabited.

Palancar Reef, off the southwestern coast of the island, is Cozumel's pride and joy. Rated as one of the top five dive sites in the world, it's about a mile offshore and about three miles long. The northern end is about 50 feet deep. Visibility ranges from 150 to 250 feet. Divers say there's nothing quite like it anywhere in the world.

Maracaibo Reef, off the southern tip of the island, begins at 120 feet and has numerous crevices and caves. This is the most challenging of all the dive sites off Cozumel.

The entire underwater area from the cruise-ship dock to Punta Celerain at the southern tip of the island has been designated a marine sanctuary, and dives can be arranged through one of the more than 15 operators scattered around the island. Some give lessons. Underwater still or video cameras can also be rented. Flash Camera Shop will drop off the cameras and also develop and deliver your film; Tel: 2-0280. Here are a few of the better dive shops:

- *Fantasia Divers:* Sol Caribe and La Ceiba hotels.
- *Aqua Safari:* Daily trips to Palancar Reef from
- Sol Caribe, El Presidente, and La Ceiba hotels.
- *Caribbean Divers:* Snorkeling excursions, scuba lessons, night divers. Avenida Melgar 38-B.
- *Dive Paradise:* Day trips and half-day trips for novice, intermediate, and expert divers. Calle 2a Sur behind Orbi.
- *Discover Cozumel:* Lessons and full- and half-day diving excursions. Avenida Melgar in town.

Most dive shops run snorkeling excursions. Don't go anywhere near the water without a mask, because Cozumel is one of the world's best snorkeling areas. Bringing your own equipment from home, however, is your best bet; shops sometimes run out of equipment, and the masks often don't fit as well as they should.

Water-skiing boats can be rented at the Presidente. Hobie Cats and jet skiis are available at the Mayan Plaza. Windsurfers can be rented at the Presidente, Villa Blanca, Cabañas del Caribe, Mayan Plaza, and Divers' Inn hotels. The Mayan Plaza, La Ceiba, and Cabañas del Caribe hotels have schools.

Deep-sea fishing boats and sailboats can be rented at Puerto de Abrigo, the marina on the coast road about five minutes north of town. No golf course has been built on Cozumel as yet, but there is a miniature course next to the Hotel Barracuda. Some hotels have tennis courts, but the same stiff breeze that keeps Cozumel temperatures pleasant prevents the island from being a tennis haven. **Pez Maya**, a beautiful camp for bone fishermen and bird watchers 80 km (50 miles) to the south at Boca Paila, can only accommodate 16 guests at a time. Guides will take you bone fishing or out to see the pelicans, spoonbills, and other species of waterfowl that flock to this natural aviary. For more information, contact the Mayan Plaza Hotel (see the "Accommodations Reference" below for their address).

Excursions from Cozumel

Travel agents anywhere in town will be happy to arrange the following excursions.

The usual tour of the island includes stops at Chankanab Lagoon for swimming (don't forget your bathing suit), and the 10-acre archaeological site of San Gervasio in the middle of the northern half of the island; make sure that any such tour you sign up for includes both.

The *Bonanza* offers snorkeling trips to Paraiso and Palancar reefs, with a stop for lunch at Playa Santa Rosa. Tel: 2-0563 or 2-0699 to make reservations.

The *Robinson Crusoe* takes you to a deserted beach on Isla de Pasión, at the northern end of Cozumel, for swimming and a picnic. Lunch is sometimes caught along the way and prepared on the beach. Tel: Fiesta Cozumel Holidays (2-0522) or Viajes y Deportes del Caribe (2-0322) to make reservations.

You can also fly to Chichén Itzá, the greatest Mayan archaeological site, for the day. Another excursion for archaeology buffs goes to Tulum, with lunch at Akumal. Both trips depart at 8:30 A.M. (pick-up at your hotel). The Tulum trip returns by 2:00 P.M., the Chichén Itzá trip by 6:00 P.M. Tel: Fiesta Cozumel Holidays (2-0522) or Turismo Avio Mar (2-0477) for further information.

GETTING AROUND

Cancún

American, Continental, United, Mexicana, and Aeroméx-ico are among the major international air carriers that offer "direct" service to Cancún. American offers daily service out of its Dallas-Ft. Worth and Raleigh hubs; Continental offers daily service from its Houston hub; United flies three times a week from Chicago (Friday, Saturday, and Sunday) and plans to begin daily service from Washington, D.C. in December; Mexicana flies direct from over half a dozen cities, including Philadelphia, Miami, Chicago, Dallas-Ft. Worth, and Los Angeles; and Aeroméxico offers direct service from New York (five times a week) and Houston (also five times a week). It's a 3½ hour flight from Chicago, Washington, and New York; 3 hours from Raleigh; 2½ hours from Dallas-Ft. Worth; and 1½ from Miami. If Cancún is only one stop on your Mexican itinerary, arrange for it as part of your overall ticketing before you leave; individual domestic fares within Mexico can be costly.

Once you arrive in Cancún, minibuses take passengers from the airport to the Hotel Zone (the length of the trip will depend on the number of stops it has to make). Tickets, which you buy at the airport, cost about U.S. $8.00.

In Cancún, buses run through the Hotel Zone along Paseo Kukulcán to town. The downtown stop to get back to the Hotel Zone is across Avenida Tulum from wherever you got off. (A good bet is to stand across the street from the church of San Francisco de Assis and flag a bus down when it comes.) If you see a bus coming, jump on. Otherwise, be prepared for a long wait; no apparent schedule is kept.

Taxis are the best way to get around in Cancún (unless you are planning a trip to Tulum, for which you should rent a car). Fares are more expensive here than in other Mexican resorts but are still far less than those in the United States and Canada. However, you may have to keep your eyes shut; many drivers here are new behind the wheel and view Paseo Kukulcán as the course at Le Mans. Saying *"Mas despacio, por favor"* will get them to slow down. Drivers also tend to be more surly and expect bigger tips here than in other resorts. If you're going anywhere other than downtown, check the price before getting into the cab.

Cabs can be scarce at lunch and dinnertime. If you don't see one in front of your hotel door, walk down to Paseo Kukulcán and flag one down. Have your restaurant call a cab to take you home after your meal, unless the restaurant is in the Hotel Zone.

The most difficult place to get a taxi is at the passenger ferry terminal upon your return from Isla Mujeres. The law of the jungle applies here. Push to the front of the boat before the dock and prepare to disembark like a sprinter coming out of the blocks. When the gate opens run—don't walk—to the road and flag down the first taxi you can, then jump in to hold your place. This is a situation where you can't afford to be shy. Ask *anybody* if you can share their cab if you don't get one right away.

Isla Mujeres

Aero Cozumel flies to Isla Mujeres from Cozumel. *Passenger* ferries operate out of Puerto Juárez in Cancún, about 15 minutes north of Cancún City by taxi. *Car* ferries leave from Punta Sam, about 15 minutes north of Puerto Juárez. The trip from either to Isla Mujeres takes about 45 minutes. Schedules are rather informal, but ferries leave every hour or so. The fare is minimal. Don't carry anything heavy if you don't have to. There is no place to store luggage and this is a strictly carry-it-yourself operation.

To explore Isla Mujeres, take a taxi or rent a moped. Mopeds can be rented at Kan Kin on Calle Abasolo 15 or at Kin Ha, Avenida Carlos Lazo 1.

You can get around town on foot. To get out to El Garrafón or any of the beaches, however, spring for the moped. Don't try to get there on a regular bicycle unless you're in shape. The hills on Isla Mujeres are not high, but there are several and the trip is tiring.

Cozumel

American, Continental, and Mexicana are the major international carriers that offer direct service to Cozumel. American offers daily service from its Dallas-Ft. Worth hub; Continental offers daily service from its Houston hub; and Mexicana flies "direct" from Miami (daily), Tampa (three times a week), and Dallas-Ft. Worth (four times a week).

Aero Caribe shuttle planes link Cancún and Cozumel with 15-minute flights that depart every other hour. Ferries from Playa del Carmen, a half-hour's drive south from Cancún, take approximately an hour and a half to get to Cozumel's San Miguel pier and cost pennies. There is a "water jet" that makes the trip more quickly, but it seems to be broken down more often than not, so don't count on it.

Private taxis are the way to get from the airport to your hotel on Cozumel. If you're staying on the north end of the island, the trip takes about ten minutes. Trips to the southern part of the island take longer but rarely exceed 15 minutes.

Taxis are also the best way to get around the island, but you have to be armed with patience. It's a seller's market because there aren't enough cabs to go around. Drivers can be surly and the car might look as if it won't make the trip, but the price will be right. Taxi schedules seem to center around the drivers' appetites, however. In other words, taxis tend to get scarce at lunch/siesta time, between 2:00–4:00 P.M., and at night after 9:00 P.M.

Cars, Jeeps, and mopeds can be rented in San Miguel, but be sure to inspect the vehicle to make sure that it's in working order before you sign the contract. You might also want to take your moped for a test drive to make sure you can handle it; loose sand or gravel on roadsides can cause serious accidents. Renting a Jeep or a Safari is sometimes the better part of valor.

Bus service links the hotels. Signs on the front of the rickety vehicles read "Hoteles." They are inexpensive but schedules are sporadic.

ACCOMMODATIONS REFERENCE

The rate ranges given here are projections for December 1989 through Easter 1990. Unless otherwise indicated, rates are for double rooms, double occupancy. Cancún, Isla Mujeres, and Cozumel are in the Central Standard time zone; the telephone area code is 988 for Cancún, 992 for Isla Mujeres, and 987 for Cozumel.

Cancún

▶ **Calinda Cancún Quality Inn.** Paseo Kukulcán, Cancún, Quintana Roo, Mexico 77500. U.S. $65–$84. Tel: 3-1600; in the United States and Canada: 800-228-5151.

▶ **Camino Real.** P.O. Box 14, Paseo Kukulcán, Cancún, Quintana Roo, Mexico 77500. U.S. $185–$340. Tel: 3-0100; in the United States and Canada: 800-228-3000.

▶ **Cancún Sheraton.** Paseo Kukulcán, Cancún, Quintana Roo, Mexico 77500. U.S. $150–$160. Tel: 5-2988; in the United States and Canada: 800-325-3535.

▶ **Club Lagoon Marina & Beach Club.** P.O. Box 1036, Paseo Kukulcán, Cancún, Quintana Roo, Mexico 77500. U.S. $100–$120 (weekend-to-weekend booking policy only during high season). Tel: 3-1111; in the United States and Canada: 800-431-2822.

▶ **Fiesta Americana.** Paseo Kukulcán, Cancún, Quintana Roo, Mexico 77500. U.S. $190–$290. Tel: 3-1400; in the United States and Canada: 800-223-2332.

▶ **Hyatt Regency Cancún.** Paseo Kukulcán, Cancún, Quintana Roo, Mexico 77500. U.S. $150–$215. Tel: 3-0966; in the United States and Canada: 800-228-9000.

▶ **Krystal Cancún.** Paseo Kukulcán, Cancún, Quintana Roo, Mexico 77500. U.S. $140–$160. Tel: 3-1133; in the United States and Canada: 800-231-8484.

▶ **Oasis Cancún.** Paseo Kukulcán, Cancún, Quintana Roo, Mexico 77500. U.S. $110–$130. Tel: 5-0867; in the United States and Canada: 800-44-OASIS.

▶ **Las Velas.** P.O. Box 267, Paseo Kukulcán, Cancún, Quintana Roo, Mexico 77500. U.S. $200; full American plan. Tel: 3-2150.

Isla Mujeres

▶ **Del Prado.** Islote del Yunque, Isla Mujeres, Quintana Roo, Mexico 77400. U.S. $85. Tel: 2-0069; in the United States: 800-782-9639; in Canada: (713) 840-1616.

▶ **Posada del Caribe.** Avenidas Madero y Guerrero, Isla Mujeres, Quintana Roo, Mexico 77400. U.S. $72. Tel: 2-0444.

▶ **Posada del Mar.** Rueda Medina 15, c/o Myrna Montes, Calle 20, Isla Mujeres, Quintana Roo, Mexico 77400. U.S. $42. Tel: 6-0422.

▶ **Roca Mar.** Nicolás Bravo y Zona Maritima, Isla Mujeres, Quintana Roo, Mexico 77400. U.S. $16. Tel: 2-0101.

Cozumel

▶ **La Ceiba.** P.O. Box 284, Punta Paradise, Cozumel, Quintana Roo, Mexico 77600. U.S. $100. Tel: 2-0815; in the United States and Canada: 800-777-5873.

▶ **El Cozumeleño.** P.O. Box 53, Playa Santa Pilar, Cozumel, Quintana Roo, Mexico 77600. U.S. $105. Tel: 2-0149.

▶ **Fiesta Americana Sol Caribe.** Playa Paraiso, Cozumel, Quintana Roo, Mexico 77600. U.S. $80–$90. Tel: 2-0700; in the United States and Canada: 800-223-2332.

▶ **Mayan Plaza.** P.O. Box 9, Playa Santa Pilar, Cozumel, Quintana Roo, Mexico 77600. U.S. $120–$180. Tel: 2-0072.

▶ **El Presidente.** Carretera a Chankanab km 6.5, Cozumel, Quintana Roo, Mexico 77600. U.S. $96. Tel: 2-0322; in the United States and Canada: 800-GRACIAS.

▶ **Villa Blanca.** P.O. Box 230, Playa Paraiso, Cozumel, Quintana Roo, Mexico 77600. U.S. $50–$100. Tel: 2-0730.

CHRONOLOGY OF THE HISTORY OF MEXICO

The Beginnings

- **50,000 B.C.:** Wandering hunters and food gatherers cross into the Americas from present-day Siberia over a land bridge, long since submerged, anthropologists have dubbed "the Bering Isthmus." Little is known of these Stone Age peoples, but over the course of tens of thousands of years various racial types arrive and become diffused over both the northern and southern continents of the Americas.

  At Tepexpán, near Mexico City, the skeletal remains of a man have been discovered near those of a mammoth that was killed with flint-tipped weapons. "Tepexpán Man" has been dated to about 12,000 B.C.
- **9000 B.C.:** Domestication of maize begins.
- **7000 B.C.:** Agriculture is established. After maize, squash, chile peppers, and beans become staples of the Mesoamerican diet—much as they are today.
- **2300–1800 B.C.:** Pottery is introduced; clay figurines begin to be fashioned.

The Pre-Classic Era

- **1800 B.C.:** Small villages are established in the Valley of Mexico, among them Ticomán, Copilco, Tlatilco, and Zacatenco. Many figurines are produced, especially fertility images of women.
- **1500 to 1000 B.C.:** The Olmecs, an advanced people of mysterious origins, establish their first great ceremonial center, San Lorenzo, in the Gulf region. Subsequently, their influence spreads over much of Mesoamerica, and becomes especially

evident at Monte Albán, near present-day Oaxaca City. Jade carving, giant stone heads, and other major stone sculpture are produced.

- **800 B.C.:** The first structures that can be called architecture rise at Cuicuilco and Cerro de Tlapacoya, in the Valley of Mexico. The Maya establish themselves throughout the Yucatán peninsula and the highlands of Chiapas—an area they occupy to this day.
- **700 B.C.:** The Maya, influenced by the Olmecs, build an elaborate ceremonial center at Uaxactún, in present-day Guatemala.
- **600 B.C.:** Olmec civilization reaches its apex at La Venta. Hieroglyphs, numerals, and a calendar are developed.
- **500 B.C.:** In western Mexico, artisans create remarkable clay figurines.
- **300 B.C.:** America's first true urban civilization, Teotihuacán, begins to develop in the Valley of Mexico (the area around present-day Mexico City).

The Classic Era

- **200 B.C.–A.D. 900:** Cities and ceremonial centers are established throughout Mesoamerica, in conjunction with a complex theology.
- **200–350:** The urban center of Teotihuacán covers six square miles and boasts more than 80,000 inhabitants—what is perhaps the largest pre-industrial city anywhere in the world. Centers in the Mayan region, on the Gulf coast, and in Oaxaca continue to expand.
- **650–850:** Teotihuacán experiences irreversible decline. Eventually, internal dissension and, possibly, other factors help nomadic invaders destroy the city. Farther south and east, however, other great Mesoamerican civilizations continue to flourish.
- **750–900:** The great Mesoamerican centers experience decline, collapse, and, most often, abandonment.

The Post-Classic Era

- **900–1300:** Semi-barbaric Toltecs migrate southward, supplanting older cultures while becoming civilized themselves. Their influence extends south as far as the Yucatán, where they build temples, and they develop the cult of the serpent-god and priest-king Quetzalcóatl, supposed to have been born among them in 947.

Another warrior people, the Mixtecs, move into the valleys near the ancient ceremonial centers of Cholula and Monte Albán. Their knowledge of metalworking—first gold, and then copper and silver—improves and spreads, and, as forms of writing are refined, they begin to record their history.

- **c. 999:** Quetzalcóatl flees, promising to return. Warrior kings succeed him at Tula, the Toltec capital.
- **1325:** Aztecs, newly arrived in the central highlands of present-day Mexico, establish their capital, Tenochtitlán, on islands in Lake Texcoco. The settlement will evolve into what is today Mexico City.
- **c. 1400:** So-called "floating gardens," which improve agricultural efficiency, facilitate the Aztec domination of the central highlands.
- **1440–1500:** Aztec domination is extended throughout what is now Mexico.
- **1502:** Móctezuma II is crowned god-emperor of the Aztecs. Disturbing omens punctuate his reign, seeming to foretell the return of the serpent-god Quetzalcóatl.
- **1517:** The expedition of Hernández de Córdova sails along the Yucatán coast.
- **1518:** Juan de Grijalva explores much of the Atlantic coast of Mesoamerica and reports back to his king on its vast size. Its population at the time—a figure unknown to de Grijalva—is put at 25 million by modern scholars.
- **1519:** Hernán Cortés, a Spanish adventurer, lands on a Veracruz beach with 555 soldiers and 16 horses—animals unknown and terrifying to the inhabitants. After a grueling march over the Sierra Madre Oriental, Cortés and his men enter the island city of Tenochtitlán. Although hailed as the returning serpent-god Quetzalcóatl, Cortés soon has Móctezuma seized and makes him a hostage.
- **1520:** The ineffectual Móctezuma is slain by his own people, and the Spaniards are driven from the city.

- **1521**: Cortés, with an army of Indian allies, returns and besieges the Aztec capital. Eventually, Tenochtitlán falls to the invaders.
- **1524**: Cortés kneels to welcome 12 Franciscan friars, who immediately set out to Christianize the country—a task they accomplish with astonishing speed.
- **1525**: Cuauhtémoc, Móctezuma's successor, is executed by the Spanish; he will be the last Aztec emperor. Vast amounts of Aztec treasure are shipped off to Spain.

New Spain

The Spanish crown moves quickly to exploit and evangelize its new colony. A caste system is established, with Spaniards born in Spain at the top; pure-blood Spaniards born outside the motherland, called *criollos,* next; people of mixed race, or *mestizos,* below that; and pure-blooded Indians, or *indios,* at the bottom.

Native art, which is viewed as diabolical, is ruthlessly destroyed. Indian resistance, weakened by plagues, collapses. The few surviving native painted books, called codices, are taken back to Europe; not a single pre-Columbian codex remains in its country of origin.

- **1530**: Construction of the National Cathedral in Mexico City begins.
- **1531**: Juan Diego, a humble Aztec convert, sees a vision of the Virgin on a hill north of Mexico City—a miracle that promotes the conversion of, and gives solace to, dark-skinned people throughout New Spain, because this Virgin is herself dark skinned.
- **1535**: Antonio de Mendoza is named the first viceroy of New Spain; he will establish the pattern for Spain's administration of its New World colony.
- **1542**: Enslavement of Indians is outlawed, only to be replaced by other ways of obtaining their forced labor.
- **1554**: A new mining process increases silver output. Silver will pour into Spain's coffers for the next two and a half centuries, doubling the Western world's supply in the process.
- **1565**: A plot to establish an independent Mexican

kingdom, to be ruled by Cortés's son, is nipped in the bud.

- **1571**: The Inquisition begins its work in Mexico City.
- **1651**: Sor Juana Inés de la Cruz, destined to become New Spain's greatest poet, is born.
- **1700–1800**: Baroque art and architecture are fostered by the Church. Ornate, fanciful architectural decoration—the *Churrigueresque* style—flowers, only to be supplanted by the Neoclassical style at the end of century.
- **1767**: The Jesuits are expelled from the colony by royal order.
- **1808**: In Europe, France invades Spain, precipitating a crisis in Spain's New World colonies.

The Struggle for Independence and Liberty

- **1810**: The Querétaro Conspiracy. Patriots in the Bajío region discuss and partly plan an uprising designed to overthrow Spanish rule. At the same time, Miguel Hidalgo y Costilla, a priest from the obscure town of Dolores, raises the cry of independence and leads a ragtag army against the Crown. The struggle will continue for 11 years.
- **1811**: Hidalgo and other rebels are defeated and executed. José María Morelos, Hidalgo's student and successor, continues the war but is also captured and executed.
- **1821**: Independence for Mexico is proclaimed by Agustín de Iturbide and Vicente Guerrero (Spain will withhold its recognition until 1836).
- **1822**: Iturbide establishes himself as "emperor," but is deposed the following year.
- **1824**: Mexico drafts a democratic constitution, and Guadalupe Victoria is proclaimed president.
- **1833**: General Santa Anna is elected president. Over the course of the next two decades this mountebank, who styles himself "His Serene Highness," will be in and out of power—to Mexico's great detriment.
- **1835**: Texas declares, and then wins, its independence from Mexico.

- **1838**: France blockades and bombards Veracruz to collect outstanding debts owed it by the fledgling Mexican government.
- **1846**: The United States invades Mexico.
- **1848**: The Treaty of Guadalupe Hidalgo results in Mexico ceding almost half its territory to the United States.
- **1854**: Santa Anna sells part of what are now the states of Arizona and New Mexico to the United States in order to raise money for the suppression of liberal democracy in Mexico.
- **1855**: The bitter War of Reform, pitting liberals against the old establishment, breaks out. The Church battles against liberal reform.

Democracy vs. Dictatorship

- **1857**: A new constitution separating church and state is adopted. Civil war continues and Church landholdings are seized. Pope Pius IX nullifies the Mexican constitution.
- **1859**: Benito Juárez, a full-blooded Zapotec Indian and liberal politician from Oaxaca, helps to draft the Reform Laws, which call for the nationalization of Church property, the closing of convents, and religious freedom.
- **1861**: Juárez is elected president.
- **1862**: England, Spain, and France seize Veracruz to collect debts. Spain and England soon withdraw, but France invades and is defeated at the Battle of Puebla—a military victory that is commemorated every year in Mexico on May 5.
- **1863**: A second French invasion results in the capture of Puebla and Mexico City. Juárez flees north, while the Church and Mexican conservatives welcome the French.
- **1864**: The French and Mexican conservatives proclaim Austrian Archduke Maximilian Emperor of Mexico. War continues.
- **1867**: Royalist troops are defeated at Querétaro, and Maximilian is executed. Juárez is reconfirmed as president and enters the capital in triumph. He will lead a liberal government until his death in 1872.
- **1876**: General Porfirio Díaz is elected president.

- **1884**: Díaz, out of office four years, returns to the presidency and will govern as a virtual dictator until 1911. Dubbed the "Porfiriate," it is an era of foreign investment in Mexico, economic progress for the ruling class, and political repression.

Revolution and the Emergence of Modern Mexico

- **1910**: Francisco I. Madero, the son of a wealthy northern family, campaigns against Díaz for the presidency—aided militarily by Emiliano Zapata—but is soon arrested. Díaz begins his eighth term in office.
- **1911**: Díaz, under pressure, resigns.
- **1912**: Madero is elected president. Invasion is feared as U.S. troops mass at the border.
- **1913**: General Victoriano Huerta stages a coup, and Madero is assassinated. Civil war breaks out and Huerta flees. In the south, Zapata leads an armed struggle for land reform.
- **1914**: U.S. troops seize Veracruz, killing nearly 200 Mexican defenders. In the north, Venustiano Carranza, an elderly landowner, forms a constitutionalist army. A power struggle ensues among Carranza, Zapata, and Pancho Villa, a peon turned general and warlord.
- **1915**: At the Battle of Celaya, troops of Carranza and General Alvaro Obregón defeat the forces of Villa and Zapata.
- **1916**: The United States recognizes the Carranza government. In retaliation, Villa raids Columbus, N.M. U.S. troops cross the border into Mexico.
- **1917**: Carranza is elected president under a new reform constitution.
- **1921**: Gen. Alvaro Obregón, revolutionary hero, becomes president. He will later be assassinated by a religious fanatic.
- **1924–1928**: Labor unions become a strong institutional force during the presidency of Plutarco Calles. During the same period, the Church is more sharply restricted, and the old anti-clerical laws are once again enforced. *Cristeros,* religious militants, in armed rebellion against this trend, are gradually suppressed. The *Partido Revolucionario*

Institucional, or PRI, destined to become the dominant political force in Mexican life, emerges.

- **1934:** Lázaro Cárdenas is elected president. During his six-year term he will nationalize the railroads and the petroleum industry (among other sweeping social and political reforms)—to the consternation of the international business community.
- **1940:** Avila Camacho wins an orderly election. Reform in the postwar period will continue at a slower pace.
- **1968.** The hosting of the Summer Olympic Games brings new prestige to Mexico—but the effect is marred by the violent suppression of student demonstrations.
- **1973–78:** Mexico rides a wave of prosperity, thanks to soaring oil prices in the wake of the Arab oil embargo.
- **1982:** President Lopez Portillo nationalizes the banking system, but Mexico is thrown into economic crisis as oil prices worldwide plunge.
- **1985:** Mexico City is devastated by earthquakes.
- **1988:** Carlos Salinas de Gortari is elected president in the first hotly contested national election in modern Mexican history. Amidst charges of widespread fraud, opposition parties on both the right and left make inroads into PRI political dominance.

—Robert Somerlott

INDEX

547